THE WITCH WAR CYCLE

The Dray Prescot Series

The Delian Cycle:
1. *Transit to Scorpio*
2. *The Suns of Scorpio*
3. *Warrior of Scorpio*
4. *Swordships of Scorpio*
5. *Prince of Scorpio*

The Havilfar Cycle:
6. *Manhounds of Antares*
7. *Arena of Antares*
8. *Fliers of Antares*
9. *Bladesman of Antares*
10. *Avenger of Antares*
11. *Armada of Antares*

The Krozair Cycle:
12. *The Tides of Kregen*
13. *Renegade of Kregen*
14. *Krozair of Kregen*

The Vallian Cycle:
15. *Secret Scorpio*
16. *Savage Scorpio*
17. *Captive Scorpio*
18. *Golden Scorpio*

The Jikaida Cycle:
19. *A Life for Kregen*
20. *A Sword for Kregen*
21. *A Fortune for Kregen*
22. *A Victory for Kregen*

The Spikatur Cycle:
23. *Beasts of Antares*
24. *Rebel of Antares*
25. *Legions of Antares*
26. *Allies of Antares*

The Pandahem Cycle:
27. *Mazes of Scorpio*
28. *Delia of Vallia*
29. *Fires of Scorpio*
30. *Talons of Scorpio*
31. *Masks of Scorpio*
32. *Seg the Bowman*

The Witch War Cycle:
33. *Werewolves of Kregen*
34. *Witches of Kregen*
35. *Storm over Vallia*
36. *Omens of Kregen*
37. *Warlord of Antares*

The Lohvian Cycle:
38. *Scorpio Reborn*
39. *Scorpio Assassin*
40. *Scorpio Invasion*
41. *Scorpio Ablaze*
42. *Scorpio Drums*
43. *Scorpio Triumph*

The Balintol Cycle:
44. *Intrigue of Antares*
45. *Gangs of Antares*
46. *Demons of Antares*
47. *Scourge of Antares*
48. *Challenge of Antares*
49. *Wrath of Antares*
50. *Shadows over Kregen*

The Phantom Cycle:
51. *Murder on Kregen*
52. *Turmoil on Kregen*

THE WITCH WAR CYCLE

Kenneth Bulmer

writing as
Alan Burt Akers

Published by
Bladud Books

First published in hardback edition in 2011 by Bladud Books

Originally published separately by Daw Books, Inc., as:
Werewolves of Kregen (1985)
Witches of Kregen (1985)
Storm Over Vallia (1985)
Omens of Kregen (1985)
Warlord of Antares (1988)

This omnibus paperback edition published in 2011 by
Bladud Books, an imprint of Mushroom Publishing,
Bath, BA1 4EB, United Kingdom

www.bladudbooks.com

ISBN 978-1-84319-876-5

Contents

WEREWOLVES OF KREGEN 1

WITCHES OF KREGEN 129

STORM OVER VALLIA 257

OMENS OF KREGEN 389

WARLORD OF ANTARES 513

Glossary 633

WEREWOLVES OF KREGEN

For Simon de Wolfe and the Hundred Henchfolk.

The Witch War Cycle

Dray Prescot tells the story of his adventures on Kregen on cassettes which he sends me from time to time during his visits to Earth. He has had a remarkable and varied career on that remarkable and varied world, four hundred light-years away, eventually being elected Emperor of Vallia. Each of the volumes of his story is arranged to be read as an individual book, so although *Werewolves of Kregen* is #33 in the Saga, it can be picked up and read with enjoyment by a reader unfamiliar with the preceding volumes. Of course, familiarity with the fascinating ins and outs of Dray Prescot's story must give greater enjoyment; but, then, a reader coming to the Saga for the first time has that pleasurable satisfaction in store.

The island Empire of Vallia, sundered by internal dissension and invasion, is gradually reestablishing itself. Prescot returns from the island of Pandahem to the south to help in that struggle. *Werewolves of Kregen* is the first book in a new cycle of adventures chronicling that struggle and the beginning of the Nine Unspeakable Curses Against Vallia. Under the streaming mingled lights of the Suns of Scorpio, Dray Prescot must go on to whatever fate destiny holds for him.

Alan Burt Akers

One

The first deaths

Gray mist parted before the prow of the narrow boat, clung damply to our faces, dewed our evening cloaks with diamonds. Gaunt fingers of mist reached across the canal to the opposite bank where the blank stone rear of a villa patched a mass of darkness against the night.

We were a silent company with only the soft ripple of water as an accompaniment. Then Seg said: "A damned spooky night, this, my old dom."

Seg Segutorio is one of the fey ones of two worlds, and at his words his wife Milsi put her arm through his more securely and pressed closer. Delia responded with one of her silvery-golden laughs and was about to pass a scathing comment on the gullibility of some folk over ghouls and spookies and the Kregen equivalent of things that go bump in the night, when young Fortin, standing in the prow with his boathook, called out.

"Look! On the bank—there!"

We all looked. A man wrapped in a cloak walked unsteadily along the towpath and I was about to inquire with a touch of sarcasm of young Fortin what we were supposed to be staring at when a humped gray mass launched itself through the air.

The man had no chance. Screaming, writhing, he went down into the mud.

A monstrous shaggy shape hunched above him. The impression of crimson eyes, of yellow fangs, of a thick and coarsely tangled pelt, of a beast-form bunched with demonic energy, was followed by the clearly heard crunch of bones breaking through.

The people in the narrow boat set up a yelling. The beast reared his head. He stared out full at us. Smoky ruby eyes glared malevolently. The yellow fangs and black jaws glistened thickly with blood that darkened ominously in that uncertain light.

Seg reached around to his back for the great Lohvian longbow that was not there. We were all dressed for the evening's entertainment, with rapiers and left-hand daggers. A lady and gentleman do not normally need longbows and war-swords and shields along the streets and canals of Vondium, the capital of the Empire of Vallia.

Kregen's first Moon, the Maiden with the Many Smiles, cast down her fuzzy pink light upon the slatey waters, and tendrils of mist coiled up to engulf the light. The air darkened.

"Steer for the bank!" I bellowed.

Old Naghan the Tiller put his helm over at once and we glided into the bank. Fortin fended us off and Seg and I leaped ashore.

The poor fellow was dead, his throat torn clean out.

Delia said, "Call the Watch."

"Can you see the damn beast?" Seg glared about.

In the shifting shards of pinkish illumination, with the mist bafflingly obscuring details, we could see no sign of that monstrous shaggy beast.

Dormvelt, the bo'sun, hauled out his silver whistle—it was a whistle and not a pipe—and blew. The City Fathers, instituted by the Presidio to run many of the day-to-day functions of Vondium, had suggested that a City Watch would be in keeping with the requirements of law and order. The Pallans, the ministers or secretaries, responsible for their various departments of Vallia, had agreed. I was pleased now to see how rapidly the Watch tumbled up, summoned by Dormvelt's call.

These were not the happy, rapscallion, lethargic Watch of Sanurkazz, who invariably turned up too late at a fracas, with swords rusted into their scabbards. These men were old soldiers, with stout polearms, and lanterns, and a couple of werstings on leather leashes reinforced with brass.

"What's to do, koters?" called their leader who wore yellow and white feathers in his hat.

Then he saw me.

He knew better than to go into the extravagant full incline, all slavish indignity in a free man.

"Majister!"

"Lahal, Tom the Toes," I said, for I recognized him for an old churgur of the army. As a churgur he still carried sword and shield. His men shone their lanterns on the corpse.

"A bad business. Did you see a monstrous great animal running off?"

"No majister." Tom the Toes rattled his sword against his shield. "Larko! If you can't keep those dratted werstings quiet in the presence of the emperor, then—"

"I dunno, Tom—look at 'em! They're going crazy..."

Werstings, those vicious black and white striped hunting dogs, are popularly supposed to be tamed into serving humanity as watchdogs and hunting dogs. But most folk eye them askance, knowing with that sixth sense of humans that the dogs are only pretending to be tamed and that they will break out into their savage ways at the first opportunity. Now the two werstings were drawing back their lips, exposing their fangs. They were snarling deep in their throats, guttural and menacing sounds. The hair around their necks stood up and their backs bristled.

Larko held onto the leashes, hanging back, and I'd swear that at any moment he'd be towed along with his heels slipping in the mud.

"The beast's scent upsets them," said Delia. "So we follow."

Trust Delia to get to the heart of anything faster than anyone else.

Tom the Toes, holding himself very erect, huffed and puffed, and got out: "Majestrix! My lady! You are not dressed or weaponed for danger—majestrix—"

Delia, who is the Empress of Vallia as well as the lady of many other realms of Kregen, knew exactly the right answer to this tough old soldier.

"You have the right of it, Tom. Therefore you brave lads can go on ahead into the danger, and I will skulk along at the back. Does that please you?"

"Delia!" I said, and looked at Tom, who bit his lip, and then swung about and yelled with great ill-temper upon his men. He was, of course, a Deldar in command of this patrol, and, like all Deldars, he could bellow.

We all set off after the werstings who now that the backward pressure was released from their leashes seemed mightily reluctant to follow the scent that so disturbed them. They started off, and then they stopped, making horrid little noises low down in the scale.

"They won't have it," announced Larko. Now he was trying to pull them along, and they dragged back. "This ain't like my werstings at all—come on, Polly, come on, Fancy. Don't make a fool of me in front o' the emperor and the empress."

But the werstings, it was quite clear, were prepared to make a fool of anybody rather than follow that scent.

We were getting nowhere so I made the obvious decision.

The City Fathers had allocated houses in each precinct to be turned into guardhouses where the patrols of the Watch were based. Since the Time of Troubles, which had torn Vallia into shreds, peoples' lives were vastly different from what they had been in the old prosperous days of peace and plenty. The times bred restless spirits, men and women hardened by suffering who demanded back from anyone available what they considered their due. A Watch even in Vondium was necessary. We had not worn war-gear; the times, wrong though they were, were not as bad as that.

I said, "Tom, better get back to your guardhouse and report. It is clear the werstings will not track that beast. Tell the Hikdar that I want an immediate check on all known menageries, zoos, arenas—we have to discover where that beast escaped from. And, by Vox, his owner will have a deal of explaining to do, believe me!"

"Quidang!"

"Tell all patrols to be on the alert—well, you don't need me to tell you your duty. Just look at this poor devil's throat. We have to find that animal, and fast."

Delia put a hand on my arm.

"I suppose you will go off—"

"Only until the prefect is alerted and we have men searching—"

"And I suppose Marion will wait?"

This was, indeed, a problem of etiquette.

As I pondered the implications, Seg broke in to say: "Did anyone recognize that beast? I did not."

"No—nor me." No one, it seemed, had any clear idea of just what kind of animal it was who had ripped out a poor fellow's throat.

A cloak was thrown over the corpse and the Watch lifted it up and prepared to carry it back to the guardhouse. The werstings were only too happy to leave.

I held Delia, and said, "Only as long as it takes, my heart. Marion will understand."

"Yes. She will."

"H'mm—that means she won't like it. Well, of course not. But by the same token that she does not want to start the evening until the emperor and empress arrive, I am the emperor and have my duties."

Seg said, "Milsi, my love, if you go with Delia, Dray and I'll be along as soon as we can."

"Oh?" I said, as Milsi nodded immediate understanding acceptance.

"Too right, my old dom."

Sometimes there is no arguing with Seg Segutorio, with the wild mane of black hair and those fey blue eyes. If I was going off into what might appear a mundane business of reporting this killing and seeing that the hunt was up, he intended to be there too, just in case...

With a beautifully controlled touch of temper, Delia pointed out the obvious.

"The prefect will do all you can do, Dray."

"I expect nothing less. All the same—"

"Very well. Off you go. And don't be long!"

The mist swirled about us, clammy and concealing, as the ladies and their escorts reentered the narrow boat.

The smell of the water lifted to us, tangy and tinged with that strange scent of the canal waters of Vallia. Some of the Watch did not venture within six paces of the edge and were without the slightest interest in those slatey waters. Others walked near and did not mind. The first were not canalmen, and while the second might not be vens, either, they could drink of the water and not die.

The narrow boat vanished into the mist.

Seg and I and the others started off to the guardhouse.

"That monstrous brute worries me, Dray." Seg shook his head. "You know me, my old dom, and a hulking great monster scares me sometimes. But this one, this is different."

"We'll find out what idiot let him loose. You know the new laws prohibit wild-beast entertainments. Well, if I find some lout has been enjoying himself torturing animals and killing them in the name of sport—no wonder the thing attacked. It's probably hungry and thirsty, scared out of its wits, and ready to turn on anyone."

"True. And it's dangerous, Erthyr knows."

We did not spend long at the guardhouse. The Hikdar in command there jumped into action when we appeared. Mounted messengers were sent off galloping to warn the other precincts, search parties were organized, and a man was dispatched to haul the prefect out to take overall command. When all that was done Seg suggested we ought at last to take ourselves off to the party.

"Yes. And I own I am looking forward to it."

"I need a wet, and that is sooth."

"I'm with you there. Also, I'm interested in meeting this Strom Nango ham Hofnar."

Seg grimaced.

"The very sound of the name, here in Vondium, rings strange."

"Aye."

"Well, if Marion is set on marrying him, there's an end to it. These women, once they've made up their minds, are never deflected."

"You do not, of course, Seg, include the Lady Milsi in this wild and extravagant generalization?"

He had the grace to throw his handsome head back and roar with laughter.

"You may think you have me there, my old dom, but I tell you—I cannot say which one of us was the more eager."

The truth was, I was overjoyed that my blade comrade had at last found a lady. The Lady Milsi, who was Queen Mab of Croxdrin and who thusly had made Seg into King Mabo, I knew to be right for him, a wonderful lady, a great queen, and a girl any man would joy in. She'd had the sense to pick on Seg and go to very great lengths to make sure she won him. Very soon we would have to make arrangements to take her to the Sacred Pool of Baptism in the River Zelph in far Aphrasöe, the Swinging City. There the immersion in that magical milky fluid would confer on her not only a thousand years of life but the ability to throw off sickness and to recover from wounds in incredibly short times.

The narrow boat returned for us and we boarded at the spot where this mysterious beast had killed his poor victim. We pushed off and floated near silently along the canal.

On duty tonight as escort were twelve men of the Second Regiment of the Emperor's Sword Watch. They made an interesting contrast among themselves. The 2ESW system provided training for young officers who would eventually go to places in the line as well as a corps of seasoned fighting men to take their place in the Guard Corps. So it was that among these twelve were to be found the hard-faced veterans of a hundred fights, and the beardless cheeks of lads just beginning their careers as soldiers.

Their crimson and yellow uniforms showed bravely in the lamplight, their weapons glittered brightly. The rest of the duty squadron would be waiting at Marion's villa where the party for her affianced groom was to be held.

As the craft glided along the canal I still felt a fretfulness at the back of my stupid old vosk skull of a head that by rights I ought to be out there in the streets and avenues of the city, a sword in my fist, leading the hunt for that monstrous and uncanny beast.

Echoing my thoughts, Seg grumped out: "Had I my bow with me..." He heaved up his shoulders, and finished: "I felt so confoundedly useless."

Lights bloomed ahead flooding down a warm yellow radiance. The mist wisped away. The narrow boat glided expertly into the space of water penned between two other boats and her way came off.

Nath Corvuus, the Jiktar in command of the duty squadron, tut-tutted and let out a: "By Vox! Someone will have a red face!"

Seg cocked an eye at me, and I own I smiled back.

The lads of the Guard Corps were mighty proud of their duties, and quick to resent any implied slight of the emperor or empress. It was clear that in Jiktar Nath's opinion, a space alongside the jetty should have been reserved for the emperor's boat and kept clear of all other craft. Well, this is all petty nonsense to me, but I had to maintain the gravitas and mien of your full-blooded emperor from time to time. Now was not the time.

"Let us not worry about that on a night like this, Nath. This is a prenuptial party. And remind your new lads again what will happen if they get drunk."

"Oh, aye, majister. I'll remind 'em."

Drunkenness, either on duty or off, was not a crime in the Vallian Imperial Guard Corps. The first offence would see the culprit run up in front of his Jiktar where he would be solemnly warned. The second offence was the last. The idiot would be discharged, not with ignominy, just sent off, and transferred to another unit of the line. There was much good-natured drinking in the Guard; there was practically never any drunkenness.

We hopped nimbly across the intervening boats and stepped onto the stone jetty. Here the duty squadron lined up, forming an alleyway bounded by crimson and yellow, by steel and bronze. The brave flutter of their feathers caught the torchlights. They were all at pike-stiff attention.

With that suitable gravitas Seg and I marched up between them to the porticoed entrance to Marion's villa. Here she stood forth to welcome us, as was proper. A crowd of guests clustered to one side. Delia and Milsi, looking absolutely marvelous, stood a little ahead of the rest. In the case of Delia, and Milsi, too, this was also perfectly proper. I am the last person in two worlds ever to forget that my gorgeous Delia, my Delia of Delphond, my Delia of the Blue Mountains, is an empress.

"Lahal, majister! Lahal and Lahal!"

"Lahal, my lady Marion. Lahal all."

The greetings were called, the people welcomed us, and very soon we were able to enter the villa and see about that wet.

But before that, the lady Marion came over and looking up said, "Majister. May I present Strom Nango ham Hofnar."

"Lahal, Strom," I said, very formal, not smiling, but trying to be easy. "Lahal. You are very welcome to Vallia and to Vondium."

"Lahal, majister. I thank you. I bear a message from the emperor for you."

"Good! Nedfar and I are old comrades. I trust he is well and enjoying life to the full."

"Indeed yes, majister. To the full."

Studying this Nango ham Hofnar I was struck by his air of competence. He was not overly tall, yet he stood a head higher than the lady Marion. His hair, dark, was cut low over his forehead. There was about the squareness of his lips and jaw a reassurance. This man, I saw, was useful...

He wore gray trousers, a blue shirt, and over his shoulders was slung a short bright green cape, heavily embellished with gold lace. This was smart evening wear in Hamal. Among the folk of Vallia he looked highly foreign and exotic.

Also, I noticed he wore a rapier and main gauche.

A great deal of the rigorous security maintained by my guards had been relaxed in recent seasons, and they now allowed people they didn't know to wear weapons in my presence, although they were still mighty jumpy about it, by Krun.

The Vallians here wore evening attire. Now your normal Vallian will wear soothing pastel colors in the evening, gowns most comfortable to lounge about in. This was a pre-nuptial party and the folk wore startling colors. This was all part of the fun and freedom of the occasion, of course. My Delia astounded me, at least, by wearing a brilliant scarlet robe, smothered in gold. This was a far cry from her usual laypom or lavender gown. Milsi's gown was a virulent orange. She and Delia had struck up a firm friendship, thank Zair, and Milsi was happy to be guided by the empress in matters of dress and protocol in this new land.

Yet, inevitably, there were very very few blue robes among that throng. Green, yes, Vallians have no objection to green. So, sizing up this Strom Nango, I guessed Marion had tactfully suggested he wear a differently colored shirt, and he'd simply smiled and said that he usually wore a blue one because it suited him.

After a few more words the strom was hauled off to meet other folk and Delia could corner me. We stood by a linen-draped table loaded with comestibles.

"Well? What happened?"

"Nothing. Seg and I just got things started and then left."

"I have not mentioned it here. Milsi and I thought it best. No need to spoil the party."

"Quite right."

"And your impressions of this Hamalese strom?"

"A tough character. Hidden depths. He's a pal of Nedfar's now, it seems, although he fought against us in the war."

Delia wrinkled up her nose. She knows full well how dangerous a thing for her to do in public that is. I managed to control myself.

"We beat the Hamalese in fair fight, the war is over, and now we're friends. You put Prince Nedfar on the throne of Hamal and made him emperor. And his son Tyfar and our daughter Lela are—"

"Zair knows where."

"So Marion presumably knows what she is doing."

I gave Delia a look I hoped was shrewd. "She is not a Sister of the Rose."

"Of the Sword."

"Ah."

"And we cannot stand talking together like this at Marion's party for her husband-to-be. It is not seemly. There is old Nath Twinglor who promised me a three-hundred-season-old copy of "The Canticles of the Nine Golden Heavens" and if his price is right I shall forgo a great deal of other fripperies. Now do you go and try to be pleasant to Sushi Vannerlan who is all by herself over there."

"Oh, no—" I began.

Very seriously, Delia said, "Sushi's husband, Ortyg, was recently killed. He fell in a battle Drak only narrowly won. It would be seemly."

Our eldest son Drak was still hammering away down there in the southwest of Vallia trying to regain the losses we had sustained when that rast of a fellow, Vodun Alloran, who had been the Kov of Kaldi, treacherously turned against us and proclaimed himself king of Southwest Vallia. As I walked slowly across to speak to Sushi Vannerlan, with the noise of the party in my ears and the scents of good food and wine coiling invitingly in the air, I reflected that I was not at all ashamed that I had not known Jiktar Ortyg Vannerlan had been slain in battle.

I'd been away in Pandahem until recently and was still in process of catching up with all that had gone on during my enforced absence.

Sushi was a slightly built woman, vivid and dark, and she'd painted on redness in lips and cheeks. Her eyes sparkled indicating the drops nestling there. Her dress was a shining carmine. Her hair fluffed a little, but it was threaded with gold and pearls. I feel I spoke the few necessary words with dignity and sincerity. Ortyg, her husband, had been a damned fine cavalry commander and I was sorry for all our sakes he was gone.

"Sushi!"

The voice, heavy and most masculine, sounded over my shoulder. Sushi jumped and genuine color flushed into her cheeks making the paint appear flaked and gaudy. She looked past me.

"Ortyg! Shush—this is the—"

"No matter who it is, they shall not steal you away from me!"

At the sound of the name Ortyg I felt for a moment, and I own it! that her husband had returned from the dead. Somehow this night with its mists and shifting moonlight had created an uneasy feeling in me. The swiftness and lethality of that shaggy beast seemed out of the world. And now Sushi was calling to her dead husband...

I turned sharply.

The man was like his voice, heavy and masculine. He wore the undress uniform of a cavalry regiment; he was a Hikdar, with two bobs, a bristly moustache, hard dark eyes, and a mouth full and ripe. His smile was a marvel.

"Ortyg! Please—"

"Now now, Sushi! I know I am late; but there had been a furor in the city and I was almost called out." He was not looking at me. "But my Jiktar let me off, may Vox shine his boots and spurs for evermore!"

As he spoke he advanced, still looking at Sushi, and made to pass me. I stood back. I was highly amused. Also, this tearaway cavalryman was doing all the right things for Sushi she needed and that I, despite being the emperor, could not do.

He put his left arm about her waist and then swung about, holding her, to face me. He was flushed and triumphant.

"I claim Sushi, my lad, and don't you forget it!"

Now I was wearing a rather stupid evening lounging robe of the selfsame brilliant scarlet as that worn by Delia. This was her idea. So I looked a popinjay beside this cavalryman in his trim undress. The two bobs on his chest testified to two acts of gallantry in battle.

He saw me.

He didn't know who I was, that was clear, yet my face, despite that I was making heroic attempts to smile, caused him to flinch back.

"By Vox! Sushi—who—"

"I'm trying to tell you, you great fambly! Stand to attention, my dear." She looked at me, and she picked up her voice and it did not quiver, as she said:

"Majister, allow me to present to you Ortyg Voman, Hikdar in the Fifteenth Lancers. Ortyg, you stand in the presence of your emperor."

"Ouch!" said Hikdar Ortyg Voman, of the Fifteenth Lancers.

And I laughed.

Then I stuck out my hand. "Shake hands, Hikdar Ortyg. I know of the Fifteenth. Mind you take care of Sushi."

"Quidang, majister!"

Leaving these two to their cooing and billing I went off to see about a refill. The party really was a splendid affair. Marion, who was a stromni, had spared no expense. There must have been four or five hundred people circulating through the halls and galleries of her villa. Wine flowed in vast lakes and wine-falls. Food weighed down the tables. Orchestras positioned at strategic points warbled tunes into the heated air without clashing one with the other.

Now Marion, the Stromni Marion Frastel of Huvadu, had quite clearly in my eyes not been able to pay for all this luxury herself. In these latter days Vondium and Vallia, it is true, had recovered considerably from the pitiless wars that had ravaged the country. We could throw a good shindig when we had to. But Marion's stromnate of Huvadu lay right up in the north, north of Hawkwa country in the northeast. It was barely south of Evir, the most northerly province of Vallia. All the land up there above the Mountains of the North was lost to we Vallians and was now ruled by some upstart calling himself the King of North Vallia. He raided constantly down into Hawkwa country, and we maintained a strong army up there to resist his encroaches.

This meant Marion's estates were lost to her, and therefore her wealth. It seemed to me that the Hamalese, Strom Nango, must have paid for this night's entertainment.

His stromnate, I gathered from Delia, lay in the Black Hills of Hamal, the most powerful empire in the continent of Havilfar south of the equator. He must either be wealthy himself or be spending lavishly now with an eye to the future. Marion's husband the late strom had only just inherited himself through a collateral relative. If Nango eventually lived up in Huvadu once we had regained the stromnate he'd find it damned cold after the warmth of Hamal.

If Marion decided to go to live in Hamal then she'd cope with the heat. She was a fine woman, not too tall, and full of figure, a strong and forceful personality who did not take kindly to fools. She had a way with her that could at times be misconstrued and sometimes turned people unable to see her good points against her. I wished her and this Nango well, and strolled off to catch a breath of air.

People nodded and smiled as I passed; but I did not stop to talk. A group of girls, laughing and clearly playing pranks on one another, rushed past. I raised my glass to them and they all replied most handsomely. They were all Jikai Vuvushis, I knew, Sisters of the Sword, most probably, in Marion's regiment. They fled off, shrieking with laughter, as far as one could imagine from the tough fighting women they were on the field of battle.

Out under a portico where the fuzzy pink light of the Maiden with the

Many Smiles fell athwart the paving stones I spotted the serene face of Thantar the Harper. He was blind. He was not blind in the way that many a harpist was blinded on our Earth but as the result of an accident in youth. He wore a long yellow robe, and his acolyte walked a few paces astern carrying the harp. He would delight us later on in the evening with his songs and stories. He grasped a staff in his right hand and his left rested on the fair hair of a boy child who led him and was his eyes.

"Lahal, Thantar."

"Lahal, majister."

He knew my voice, then.

"I am most pleased to know you are here. You have a new song for us among all the old favorites?"

"As many as you please, majister." His voice rang like a gong, full and round. A splendid fellow, Thantar the Harper, renowned in Vondium.

A hubbub started beyond the edge of the terrace where the Moonblooms opened to the pink radiance and gave of their heady perfume. I looked across.

A group of roisterers with their backs turned to me staggered away to the sides. Their yells turned to screams. A man stepped through the gap between them, walking in from the terraced garden beyond. He carried a young lad in his arms.

The hard, tough, experienced face of Jiktar Nath Corvuus was crumpled in with grief and rage. No tears trickled down his leathery cheeks; but the brightness of his eyes, the flare of his nostrils, his ferociously protective attitude, told that he suffered.

In his arms he carried one of his young lads, the brilliant crimson and yellow uniform hideously bedraggled in blood and mud. The boy's helmet was lost and his brown hair shone in the lanternlight, swaying as Nath brought him in.

"Look!" choked out Nath Corvuus.

The boy's throat was a single red mass, a glistening bubble of horror.

Two

The Ganchark of Therminsax

We searched. Oh, yes, we searched.

Marion's villa yielded weapons enough to give us some confidence we might meet and face up to a gigantic beast. We shone lanternlight into the shrubberies and arcades, we thrashed the bushes. We shouted and banged kettles and pans.

We found not a sign of that feral horror.

The Watch of this precinct carried on the search farther into the streets and alleys. Seg and I felt firmly convinced the beast must be lurking low, sated by now on a victim he seized and killed without being disturbed.

"I don't want the whole city sent into a panic," I said to the prefect, who attended me at Marion's villa.

"Quite so, majister. We will prosecute the search with the utmost diligence; but I think we shall find nothing until the beast strikes again."

The prefect was a Pachak, Joldo Nat-Su, who had only two arms. He had been long employed by Naghan Vanki, the emperor's chief spymaster, and had lost his lower left in some fracas or other. Giving the post of city prefect in charge of the Watch to a man of Naghan Vanki's had seemed at the time sensible. He ran a tidy force and carried the honorary rank of Chuktar.

"I think you are right, Joldo, bad cess to it. Sink me!" I burst out. "We cannot have wild animals roaming the streets of Vondium! It is not to be borne!"

"If we are ready when it is seen," said Delia in her soothing and practical voice, "then we can catch it and cage it up again."

"Ah," said Prefect Joldo. "You say again, majestrix. So far my men have found no one who owns to having lost a caged animal."

"Too scared what'll happen to 'em," said Seg.

He held Milsi close and I fancied that no man or woman would willingly let their spouse out of their sight until this wild beast was safely caged—or killed.

Marion's party had incontinently wound up. Most of the guests had departed. There were just a few of us left, gathered in a small withdrawing room to talk over the events of the night.

Strom Nango kept to himself and made no effort to push forward or impose his views, and this pleased us. Everyone, including himself, realized he was on approval.

The Lord Farris leaned forward in his chair and said: "I'll put every soldier we have at your disposal, Joldo. I agree with the emperor. We cannot allow this kind of happening in the city."

Farris, the Kov of Vomansoir, was the emperor's justicar-crebent, or crebent-justicar; I could never worry over which way around the title went. He ran Vallia when Drak and I were away. He was a man with an intense loyalty to Delia, a man I trusted, the kind of man Vallia sorely needed.

The conversation became general then as we talked the thing inside out.

And, then, Thantar the Harper struck a chord and we all fell silent.

He sat sideways on his chair so that a samphron oil lamp's glow brought out the hollows of his blind eyes. His harp was quite small, resting between his knees, cunningly fashioned and probably two or three hundred years old. He used it to emphasize what he said, underlining the starker passages with grim chords, using ripples of sound to highlight a passage of action or love.

"You will delight us, Thantar?" said Delia. "We are in your debt that you accepted Stromni Marion's invitation. She is, I think, to be congratulated as well."

Marion looked pleased at this little piece of Delia's tomfoolery; but Delia was deadly serious about Thantar. Great artists are not bidden to perform in the politer courts of Kregen, whatever they get up to in the barbarian lands.

Thantar just said: "It is your presence, majestrix, that does us all the honor."

Well, so it was fulsome; he was dead right, too, by Vox!

In the rich and golden voice that appeared so incongruous issuing from so gaunt and desiccated a frame, Thantar began the story of The Ganchark of Therminsax.

Therminsax was the capital city of the Imperial province of Thermin, to the west of Hawkwa Country. From there a fine canal system extended southward. I recalled the iceboats that flew down from the Mountains of the North. Rough country around there, in places, and rich lands, too. With all the other romantic connections associated with Therminsax, I confess my own most important thought about the city was that it witnessed the creation of the Phalanx, the core of the army which had done so much to reunite and pacify Vallia.

Of course, by Zair, there was still a great deal to do. But then, that is the way of life...

No one spoke as the blind harpist delivered his lines.

The story was of the olden time; but not too long ago, when savage beasts still roamed wild and free in many of the provinces of Vallia. The chark was one such wild animal, untamed, ferocious, cunning, pitiless in a special way that set it apart from your usual run of creatures of the wild. The charks normally hunted in packs and men said they possessed a primitive language of their own. Sometimes a single chark, either female or male, would go rogue, go lonely, wander off as a solitary. These became a menace to the surrounding territory. They were not to be classed, I understood as Thantar spoke on, with the man-eating tigers of India on our own Earth which are too old and slow to catch much other game than humans.

These solitary charks were among the most powerful of the packs.

As he described the beast in glowing words, the Kregish rolling and fierce, subtle and cunningly hinting, I saw in my mind's eye a picture of the beast I had seen on the towpath. That had been a chark. I felt sure of it.

Charks, said Thantar, were considered to be extinct. None had been reliably reported in Vallia for many years, although some men boasted they had seen the gray shaggy forms slinking through the back hills of Hawkwa country.

Then a rash of bloodthirsty killings set all Therminsax on edge. No one was safe. A mother taking her child to school wearing her best dress was set on and slain. Blood splashed the pretty dress, and the hunters followed the trail until they came upon the grisly remains. Men out in the woods burning charcoal were ripped to shreds. The city itself was not safe, for the great beast seemed able to steal in as and when he pleased, to take a life in blood-welling horror.

Traps were set. All were unsuccessful.

Listening intently, I admired the masterful way in which Thantar included blood and death and horror in describing each incident, and yet did not overburden his narrative with so much blood and death and horror as to offend the susceptibilities of the ordinary person. Only the ghoulish and perverted would complain at the lack. Only the sadist would demand more agony.

A change overtook the story. Now Thantar spoke with hindsight, telling us things that were afterwards discovered and deduced, facts unknown at the time of the events.

Even with all the hindsight, the wise men had been unable to tell how the young man, Rodo Thangkar, had first become a werewolf.

He had been a happy, carefree young fellow, training to be a stylor, reasonably well-connected. He had hoped to marry his childhood sweetheart, Losha of the Curled Braids. She was one of the earliest victims of the terror, her face slashed to ribbons, her throat torn out by the fangs of the werewolf.

As the City Elders discussed what to do, and set their traps, young Rodo Thangkar stood by, learning his trade as a stylor and under his master's tuition taking down notes of all that was said and decided.

No wonder the werewolf evaded all the traps with such contemptuous ease!

The reign of terror continued and the ganchark continued to exact a hideous toll of the folk of Therminsax and the surrounding countryside.

Many brave fighting men, champions, came to the city to strike blows with their swords and spears against the ganchark. None survived. Their mangled bodies were reverently buried, and the folk sighed, and stayed close to home.

The City Elders pleaded with anyone to come and help them in their time of trial. Sorcerers and wizards did, indeed, journey to Therminsax. One of them, a Sorcerer of the Cult of Almuensis, boasted that no ganchark could stand against the awful powers locked in his great book chained to his waist.

He was a glittering figure in his robes and jewels, girded with gold, the hyrlif itself a book exuding the aura of thaumaturgy. They found him with his head detached from his body, lying in the roadside ditch. His forefinger was still in place in the half-opened book. It was clear to all that the werewolf had leaped long before the sorcerer had had time to read out the curse to free the land of this terror.

From his island came Goordor the Murvish, of the Brotherhood of the Sorcerers of Murcroinim. He stank. He wore wild animal pelts, belts of skulls, and carried a morntarch, the heavy staff crowned with rast skulls and dangling with objectionable portions of decayed organic matter. Yet he wore swords.

He said he would relieve the city of Therminsax of its werewolf for one thousand gold talens.

The City Fathers collected the money in a single hour.

So young Rodo Thangkar listened to this transaction, and he smiled, and perhaps he raised a hand to his mouth to polish up a tooth.

He, himself, said the story, could not explain why he did what he did, why he transformed himself into a werewolf.

The following night when all the good folk of the city lay fast, the confrontation took place. No man or woman witnessed that sight. Nothing was heard.

In the morning they were found, the sorcerer and the young man, lying near to each other. The ganchark had resumed his form as a man in the moment of death, the sorcerer's dudinter sword through him. And the sorcerer lay crumpled with no face, no throat, no breast. Blood spattered everywhere.

Thantar the Harper finished with a thrumming chord, and said: "So Therminsax was rid of the evil, and the thousand gold talens were never given to the sorcerer Goordor the Murvish but were used to provide a great feast in thanksgiving."

When the last vibrating note dwindled to silence no one spoke, no one stirred. There was no applause. We all sat like dummies, the words spinning in our heads.

Then, bursting out like a thunderclap, the Lord Farris snapped: "No! Impossible. I do not believe it!"

Strom Nango began: "The story, or the—?"

"The story is a story, well calculated to frighten children, and exciting too, I daresay. But as for the conclusion you all seem to wish to draw—no!"

"Tsleetha-tsleethi," said Seg. "Softly-softly. These tales are known. Werewolves are known also."

Delia remained silent.

Milsi looked troubled, and I noticed the way she gripped Seg's hand, her nails biting into his palm.

Marion said: "I'm not sure. Oh, I used to love all these ghostie and ghoulie stories when I was young. They have a treasury of them in the north—but, this—it is so horrible—can one believe? Is it possible? A werewolf at large, here in Vondium?"

Various of the other people in this small select gathering expressed similar views. How could a legend of the past spring into vivid life in this day and age?

Thantar the Harper, having sowed this seed, remained silent. One could not help wondering what was going on in his mind. He had told this story with meaning, with a purpose. A blind man, could he see more than we sighted ones?

Strom Nango bent and whispered in Marion's ear.

She turned her head up, smiling at him, and I saw there was love there.

"You are right, my dear." She turned to face us, and prefacing her remarks with flattering references to the emperor and empress in our midst, she said: "This is too gloomy and horrendous a subject. My party for dear Nango I will not have completely ruined. He has suggested we move on to more salubrious subjects—"

"Oh, indeed, yes!" exclaimed Milsi.

"Very well." Here Marion glowed with inner pleasure. "Thantar and I have devised a new story, one that is supremely worth the telling. I hope, soon, that Thantar will set it to suitable music. But, at the moment..."

"At the moment," rang the golden voice of the harpist, "the story is worthy in its own right, a story of high courage and selfless devotion."

We all called out, demanding that Thantar delight us with this new and wonderful story.

Three

Of a hillside in Hamal

Among the harsh rocks of the Hamalian Mountains of the West a small party of warriors huddled behind boulders or in scrapes painfully dug from the barren and stony soil. There were perhaps twenty of them, twenty soldiers left from the eighty that had formed their pastang. They were tired, thirsty, hungry, bloodshot of eye, striped with wounds, and each one knew that the end could not be far off.

Penning them in, ringing them in a hoop of steel, a horde of the wildmen from the vasty unknown lands beyond the mountains were content for the moment to shoot into the pitiful stronghold, to rush closer in a swirl of noise and action to draw return shots, to drop down—and to wait. Soon the soldiers would have no more shafts to stem the final attack.

This scene, painful though it was, held no originality.

So long as the civilized lands patrolled the borders and contested the notion that the wildmen might raid with impunity, then just so long would parties be cut off and surrounded and exterminated. This was the savage and pitiless species of warfare practiced along the Mountains of the West now that the Empire of Hamal had retracted from its westward march of triumph.

There was no question that the bloodthirsty moorkrim from the wild lands of the west could overwhelm and destroy these last few soldiers. But the wildmen taunted their victims, showed themselves to draw a shaft, and dropped flat again. They did not pour in in a last lethal tide of death. No doubt the chief concern in the primevally savage and cunning head of the moorkrim chieftain was that the trapped soldiers would all commit suicide before his men could lay hands on them.

For the soldiers forming the remnant of the pastang trapped on that desolate hillside were Jikai Vuvushis, Warrior Maidens, every one.

Some distance to the east in the foothills of the ragged mountain chain stood the tumbledown frontier town of Hygonsax. Dust lay thickly everywhere, the suns scorched, hardy semi-desert vegetation drooped in the heat. The adobe fort from which floated the flags of two regiments appeared sunk in lethargy.

One flag displayed the number and devices of the One Hundred Twenty-Sixth Regiment of Aerial Cavalry of Hamal. The other, less obvious, more cryptic, told those who understood that this standard was of the Seventh Regiment, SOS, of Vallia.

Both treshes hung limply against the flagstaffs.

The only sounds were of a calsany moodily kicking a mudbrick wall, and the scrape, scrape, scrape of a little gyp scratching himself for fleas.

In a sudden rush of leathery wings, an aerial patrol whistled over the town. The mirvols extended their claws to seize the perching poles and folded their wings. The riders, stiffly, walking like men who have been too long aloft in the saddle, moved thankfully to their quarters where they might try to wash away the dust inside and out. Their commander fairly ran into the fort and through to the wide, cool room past an abruptly galvanized sentry.

The woman striding uncertainly about the commander's room turned expectantly.

"You have found them?"

Jiktar Nango ham Hofnar halted, embarrassed at his news, depressed, cross, feeling the heat and the strain as though an iron helmet crushed down about his brows.

"I am sorry, Jiktar Marion."

"Then it must be all over with them—"

"I cannot believe that."

"But you have searched everywhere. Your patrols have flown day and night. How could they still be alive without your finding them?"

"I do not know, but I do know that I shall not rest until we have found the answer, one way or another."

Jiktar Nango swayed as he spoke, and put a quick hand to the back of a chair. He gripped the wood harshly, supporting himself.

Instantly, Marion darted forward. She took his arm and made him sit down, and then fetched a pitcher and glass. She poured parclear, and the bright fizzy drink sparkled in the mingled radiance of the suns falling between the columns of the adobe house's open walls. She looked at him critically, and frowned.

"You have not slept for three days and nights. You cannot go on like this, Jiktar Nango."

"I must. You know that."

"But my girls—"

"Your girls are my responsibility out here. I marched with King Telmont against your emperor, and then with him we fought the damned Shanks at the Battle of the Incendiary Vosks. I hated all Vallians. But now—" He drank again, feeling the fizzy liquid cleaving a path down his throat, tingling his toes. "Now we are allies. I shall not rest, Jiktar Marion, never, until we know!"

She understood enough to know that this man spoke with honest conviction. He had hated Vallians; now he was allied to them. But it was not just that causing him to labor so strenuously. He was concerned for her Warrior Maidens, anxious for them, feeling this a matter of honor. He was a man of high chivalry determined to do all and more that could be done. If he killed himself doing it, he'd have only mundane regrets, none for the style of the thing.

Nango lay back in the chair and his eyelids drooped. Watching him, Marion felt an emotion to which she could not, she would not, put a name.

He jerked as a tremor contracted his muscles and then, like a man breasting a swift and treacherous current, he opened his eyes and struggled up onto his feet.

"What am I thinking of!" His left hand raked down to his sword hilt and gripped. "By Krun! Those rascals of mine had better be ready."

"But you've only just returned—"

"The mirvols brought us back. They are exhausted. And I expected good news..."

He glanced at the sand clock on its shelf and made a face. "I gave instructions the patrol could wash, eat and drink and be out on parade again in a single bur. We have enough mirvols to provide second string mounts for us all. So, I must bratch."

Bratching, as Marion could see, meant in Jiktar Nango's book jumping very hard and very fast indeed.

Heavy-winged, the mirvols took off in scurries and flurries of dust. The yellow drifted in the air, and settled, and added another fine coating to roofs and walls. She watched the flying animals wing away aloft, shading her eyes against the bright dazzlement of Zim and Genodras, which here in Havilfar are called Far and Havil, and the sensation of helplessness made her dizzy, so sick and powerful it fell upon her.

In order to retain any semblance of normality she had to convince herself that the pastang lost in the hills was not destroyed. The girls had had food and water for a number of days, plenty of shafts, a local guide, and unbounded confidence. The Seventh Regiment, SOS, had recently been assigned this duty out here along the Mountains of the West. Vallia and Hamal, allied, shared a common interest in preventing the raiding incursions of the wildmen, for the moorkrim had recently destroyed one of the famous flying islands. That had seen the loss of much-needed production for the airboats' silver boxes that lifted and propelled them through thin air.

The scattered detachments of the regiments were being called in. But, right here and now, Nango and she had only their small patrols to call on to prosecute the search.

Even when Nango returned, more haggard, more exhausted, she still clung doggedly to her belief that although it seemed inevitable that it must be all over for her girls, Nango's persistence must find them in the end.

"I shall fly with you, Nango—"

"But—!"

"I shall."

"Very well."

He gave instructions that flying leathers should be found for the Jiktar Marion, and a good strong clerketer. He inspected this harness personally. With this an aerial rider was fastened to the saddle; if it broke in the air—splat!

"I have the strongest conviction, Marion, it is strange, very strange. I know—it is in my bones, my blood—that we shall find your girls. And, even stranger, I know we shall find them alive. Not all, perhaps, but there have been odd portents reported—"

"Surely you don't believe mumbo-jumbo!"

"No. Nothing like two-headed ordels, or Havil drenched in the blood of Far. It is in me. We fly in half a bur, Marion. Are you ready?"

His change of tone jolted her. She nodded. "I am ready, Nango."

How Nango mounted his flying animal, how he had the strength to buckle himself in, grasp the reins, how he summoned the dregs of energy to kick in his heels, all astounded Marion. By Vox! She was tired. But Nango had flown continuously since the pastang had not reported in when it should have, and although his men had flown by rotation, Nango had flown on every patrol.

The man was clearly past the end of his resources; yet his sense of honor, his desire to uphold his own esteem of his regiment and his nation, drove him on.

Also, suspecting her own feelings, Marion guessed there were other similar forces at work in this Hamalese.

The leathery wings of the mirvols beat heavily against the warm air. They flew low over the rounded hills, cutting corners, edging higher into the jagged valley gashes between peaks. Everywhere the contused landscape of desolation met the eye.

Gripping on tightly, feeling the rush of wind blustering past, swaying with the floating, soaring and sinking sensations of the flying animal, Marion found she could cope perfectly well with flying. Given time, she might quite come to like it. She narrowed her gaze against the windrush and peered ahead.

The patrol skirted a jagged cliff edge where a few small birds of prey were quite content to let these large flyers sail past. Flying beasts of that size would find nothing to live on here, where the prey consisted of insects, lizards, animals constituted to live on practically nothing. Around that edge the valley opened out, peaks on either hand lofting against the dazzlement. Ahead of the patrol the eroded valley dozed in the heat.

The four-man advance echelon wheeled up into the sky, and one came hammering back.

He handled his mirvol with consummate, unthinking skill, swirling to fly wing-beat to wing-beat with Nango.

"Jiktar! Many dead bodies ahead!"

Marion's heart went thump in her breast.

Nango thwacked his beast and the flyer surged ahead. Marion copied him and only the leather straps of the clerketer saved her from falling back over the animal's tail.

In a vast swishing of wings the mirvols circled the site of the tragedy.

There were many dead bodies. Many of them. The moorkrim littered the stony ground. They lay abandoned in the attitudes of death, ringing the central area where a semblance of a fortress had been constructed from sangars and scrapes.

Within that central space lay the girls of the Seventh Regiment of the Sisters of the Sword.

As Marion gazed down, the whole scene wavered in the heat waves, and she could feel the blood bursting in her head, the fiery sting behind her eyes, the sense of desolation and panic and misery—and anger.

A tanned arm lifted. A brown-haired head turned to look up. Another arm waved.

Marion swallowed.

Nango shouted: "They live!"

Somehow, in an uproar of wings and fountains of dust, the patrol was down, landing in any cleared space among the bodies. Marion's fingers wrestled with the stubborn buckle of the harness, and the fool thing would not come undone, and Nango was there, his hard tired face smiling, to free the buckle and assist her to alight. They ran across to the nearest Sangar, stumbling in among the piled boulders, ignoring the sprawled wreckage of the wildmen on the way.

It was all a wonder and a salvation.

Hikdar Noni Thostan managed to stand up and salute as her regimental commander ran up. She was dirty, disheveled, wounded, her uniform and armor tattered and dangling; yet she smiled as Jiktar Marion approached.

"Noni—Thank Opaz!"

"Marion—Thank Opaz you came... I've lost good girls—too many—they are gone—"

There were nineteen living survivors and one about to die.

Nango saw to everything that had to be done, moving with quickness, speaking with authority, and his men jumped to obey. The shambles was clear and hideous. The girls had fought a good fight. Yet...

Arrangements were put in hand to transport the living and the dead back to Hygonsax. The Hamalese swods, simple fighting men of the air, spoke in low tones. Nango kept himself on his feet and moving only by a final effort of willpower. He did say: "I could swear we flew up this valley two days ago." But his mind worked sluggishly now. When he had slept and refreshed himself would be the time to rejoice at this marvelous deliverance.

The moorkrim were left where they lay. Their flying saddle animals, tyryvols mostly, had all flown off long since. Marion bent to study one dead wildman. She shuddered. The viciousness in those harsh browned features, the tribal markings, the decorations, all spoke eloquently of a life far removed from that of civilization.

The man bore no mark of wounds; yet he was dead and all his viciousness would slough and decompose as the body rotted and he joined the food chain of the mountains.

The elation that nineteen of her girls had survived could not alter the sorrow that the rest of the pastang had died. So many fine young girls from Vallia, trained up by the Sisters of the Sword, smart and skilled, courageous, eager, and now all lying dead in their neat rows and ready for burial. Marion went through the funeral ceremony numbly.

She could taste the ceremonial wine they had drunk before the regiment left Vallia, still see in the eye of memory the long refectory tables, the candles, smell the flowers so tenderly cared for. As though less than a single heartbeat separated that farewell dinner, she was here, in Hamal, among the dust and heat and flies, the smells of so different a nature. The effort of opening her eyes to look at Nango as he spoke the words he felt necessary consumed her.

Her own emotions were forcing her on, and she could foresee in part what the future might hold.

Less than a heartbeat...

The regiment had marched out with the bands and the banners. Duty called them to a hard life here in the Mountains of the West of Hamal. She had met this hard, competent Jiktar of Aerial Cavalry, this Strom Nango ham Hofnar. It seemed to her less than a heartbeat ago she had left Vallia to serve overseas, and now here she was overseas and in Hamal and far too many of her fine young girls were dead...

Such misery she did not think she could bear alone. As the ceremony concluded with the proprieties reverently fulfilled, and she walked slowly away, she looked across at Nango. At the same moment he turned to look at her.

In that moment, in the enervating heat and the dust tasting of schoolroom chalk in her mouth, her gaze met Nango's. Oblivious of heat, of dust, of flies, negating everything else, they stared one at the other, and their futures were settled.

Four

We disagree over the Werewolf of Vondium

Delia hurled her slipper at me. Catching the silky scrap in my left hand I instantly hurled it back. She ducked, laughing at me, whipped off the other slipper and chucked that one at my head. When I raked out a hand to grab it she leaped the bed and was on me, bearing me down, ramming my back hard into the rug.

"D'you cry quarter, you fambly? Do you bare the throat?"

"Aye, aye, my love, I bare the throat. And my back's digging in most uncomfortably."

She kissed me lightly and then let me up. I wriggled around and sat up and put an exploratory hand down.

"More like digging into *you*!" she said, and laughed. I hauled out the big black riding boot and did not throw it at her. She sat up, flushed, radiant, divine. Well, there are no words too great or grand or divine in themselves for Delia of the Blue Mountains.

"What irks you, then, my heart?" I spoke philosophically, starting to rummage around for my clothes. The hour was still early, but we had a lot to do today.

"I am trying to prevent myself from feeling amusement instead of annoyance that Marion's party was spoiled—well—" Here she reached for the laypom-colored slip trailed across the bed-end. "Well, not exactly spoiled. But the werewolf story, and that poor guard of yours, and the rest of it. I do not think Thantar the Harper's great new story about Marion and Nango was as well received as it otherwise would have been."

"Amusement?"

"You know what I mean. Anyway, I am positive I am preventing that feeling. Marion is a dear. And she has ambitions. She—"

"She is, of course, of the Sisters of the Sword and not of the Sisters of the Rose."

"The SOS put more regiments of Jikai Vuvushis into the field than the SOR. But they do not use the Claw or the Whip, as we do. Now I am not going to talk any more about that. I think I will pay her a call today. That will please her. And her Nango looks—h'mm? Useful?"

"A sound fellow."

"So I deemed him."

"Although, mind you, I own I was a little disappointed in Thantar's story. I have told you of the time Jaezila—"

She interrupted not sharply but firmly.

"Yes, my dear. I still think of our daughter Lela as Lela, and not as Jaezila. I am sure you think of her as Jaezila."

"Yes."

Well, there was no mystery in that. After all, I'd adventured and fought with Jaezila long before I knew she was my daughter Lela. I went on:

"That time Jaezila and Seg and me went off to rescue Prince Tyfar and his father from the wildmen in the Mountains of the West—it must have been a very similar scene."

Delia has had to suffer greatly in her life since she first met me. I own I ache for her, and feel guilt and remorse. But, she is a princess, an empress, and hollow though the titles may be to some, she is a very great lady. She is, also, cunning, shrewd, subtle, tough and altogether enchanting—and damned infuriating. She had come to terms with her extraordinary life long before I'd told her I'd never been born on Kregen, but came from a small planet orbiting a yellow sun that was, by the standards of Zim and Genodras, very small and insignificant. And it had only one silver moon, to boot, and possessed no splendid array of human beings not built in the same mold as apims, as Homo sapiens sapiens, like Delia and me.

"We saw the wildmen off that time, thanks to a very brave Hamalese officer and his men. But, all the same, I own I was a trifle disappointed with the story—"

"We were all tired by then. And the werewolf did not help—"

"You mean the story of the werewolf?"

"Yes."

The breeches I pulled on were sober Vallian buff. The tunic on its stand was of buff. This day I was to begin by officiating at the opening ceremony for a whole new complex of houses and shops. Slowly we were rebuilding Vondium, trying to make the once proud city vital and alive again.

"The story of the werewolf did not cheer us up, true. All the same," and here I tightened up the lesten-hide belt and rummaged around for the boots that had so sorely assaulted me. I felt—to use the imagery of another age—that the snapper was lacking in Thantar's story of Marion and Nango. There was no punch line. I said as much to Delia as I buttoned up the tunic.

"You could say, could you not, my dyspeptic Dray, that the fact we heard the story at all was its suitable finale. Marion and Nango are happy. Surely, one might think, that is a quittable ending?"

I eyed her cautiously.

"One might."

Delia's first task this day was to open a new hospital and rest home for invalid soldiers. The usual customs of earlier times on our own Earth and to a great degree on Kregen, of employing soldiers when needed and when the war was over of discharging them to starve and die in the gutter, could not be allowed to continue in the new Vallia we were building.

The problems did not arise where mercenaries were hired. This had been one of the sticks my opponents had beaten me with when we'd been creating a true Army of Vallia to replace the mercenary forces heretofore used. My reasons for the decision were plain and commonsense. Now we had to pay the reckoning.

Delia, instead of drawing on tall black riding boots, put on softer, lower boots. For the proper atmosphere to be created when she attended the hospital opening she would ride in her palanquin. The gherimcal, carried by her corps of Womoxes, would give just that necessary extra feeling of the presence of the empress without the harsh reminder that trampling hooves would have brought. At least, that was the theory...

"With you, Dray Prescot," she said with some considerable mock-tartness, "one might anything!"

"True, true—and I still think the story lacking."

"Maybe Thantar should have ended it earlier, at the moment of rescue."

"Marion wanted to show the results. The girls have been brought home, and she is on a furlough, although—"

"That, my dear, will be the business of the Sisters of the Sword."

My early feelings of abhorrence that women should fight as soldiers, bequeathed to me from my upbringing on Earth at the end of the eighteenth century, persisted only in certain cases here on Kregen. Folk regarded me as a loon when I stumblingly tried to explain my reactions. If women demand equality with men in all things, as well as their already achieved superiority in others, then they can damn well shoulder a weapon and go off and fight. That was *that* theory...

So when in some mysterious way I found that I was to have another bodyguard force to add to those already created, the fact that this corps was to be composed of Jikai Vuvushis did not discompose me as it would have done before. It seemed that all the women were agreed. If the Empress Delia could have regiments of men in her bodyguard, then the emperor could have a regiment of women—surely?

Two splendid numim girls, lion-maidens, Mich and Wendy, had taken the initial steps—when my back was turned, I might add—and an emperor's regiment of Jikai Vuvushis was recruiting.

With that eerie but wonderfully warming meeting of thoughts, Delia effortlessly picked up on the subject in my mind from what she had been saying.

"Marion's duties, as you must guess, concern your new guard regiment. How much she wishes to tell you about the SOS must remain for her to decide."

"If she tells me twice as much as you tell me about the Sisters of the Rose, that will still be nothing."

"Which is as it must be," said Delia, primly infuriating.

Just as we were leaving the bedchamber to go down to the first breakfast, Delia put her hand on my shoulder.

"Dray—suppose there is a werewolf running loose in Vondium?"

Her tone pushed aside any inane reply of denying the possibility. Delia was penetrating through to the eventuality that a ganchark might really exist, and if so, what were we to do about it. On Kregen they do not take so lightly the stories of the undead, the kaotim, stories of lycanthropy, as we do on Earth. Delia was being highly practical. If a ganchark intended to terrorize Vondium, we ought at least to have thought seriously about the problem and the measures we could take in self-defense.

My reply was therefore considered.

"We must summon all the sorcerers and wizards who may give us answers. Thantar's story suggested there is an answer. We must find, if it is necessary, the appropriate answer now."

"Yes. I do not wish to think of it; but if it is necessary then we must."

"After you have seen to your hospital and I to my complex, we must meet with Nath na Kochwold. He is clamorous regarding the Fifth Phalanx—"

"You worry too much, my dear. The Phalanxes have proved their worth in battle—"

"Surely. They triumph. But I do still worry over the numbers of men tied up in the brumbyte files."

We had four Phalanxes with a fifth building. One was up in the northeast, one was with Turko in the midlands, one and a half were with Drak in the southwest. So we needed a fifth. Yet for every soldier trailing his pike as a brumbyte in the phalanx files, we might have trained up an archer, a kreutzin, a churgur. Oh, yes, it takes a special kind of fellow to be a brumbyte and maneuver pike and shield close packed with his comrades, but, all the same...

Going into the first breakfast we were met with luscious odors and the incessant rattle of animated conversation. Most folk of Kregen like to sit down for one of the breakfasts, usually the first, and then take the second standing up, filled with the doings of the morning and aware of what remains to be done before the hour of mid.

More often than not I took both breakfasts—when I was fortunate enough to eat two—standing up.

The room lay awash in the early rays of the twin suns. Folk were eating and chattering away nineteen to the dozen. Schemes were hatched, plans laid, news reported at this time. Helping Delia and myself to a considerable quantity of breakfast we went over to a group centered on Farris, who looked as calm, competent and in complete command as he always did.

The subject of conversation was, inevitably, the werewolf of Vondium.

Perforce I had to let the talk run on. Any attempt to block off speculation would only arouse more. Balancing a plate and a cup and eating is all very well for folk with three or four arms, or a tail hand; for apims like me with only two hands the process is highly demanding. I listened, chewing, weighing up what was said and what were different people's reactions.

Some just pooh-poohed the whole idea.

Others would believe if there was sufficient proof.

A goodly number were perfectly convinced that a werewolf was running loose in the streets of the capital.

Pallan Myer, stooped over as ever from hours of reading, coughed his dry little tickler of a cough. He was the Pallan of Learning, responsible for education, and now he gave evidence of the way he regarded these stories.

"Utter balderdash. Quite unconvincing. The smallest child in my schools would laugh at this nonsense, for it defies credibility by its lack of logic."

"But logic," pointed out Nath na Kochwold, "is not necessary when one is dealing with the supernatural."

One or two interrupted at this; but Nath went on: "At least, not logic as it is understood by pedants. Internal logic, of course, is essential, otherwise the world would come to an end. We need far more evidence yet before any sound judgments may be made."

"I agree," said Farris, and put a paline into his mouth and chewed. For many people there that was the end of the argument.

One of these fine days, when Nath na Kochwold could be weaned away from his only true love—the Phalanx—he might well find himself standing where Farris now stood.

"My father," he said, "is Nazab Nalgre na Therminsax, who is the emperor's Justicar governing all the province of Thermin. In Thermin you will find many folk who devoutly believe in the existence of gancharks."

Senator Naghan Strandar, a member of the Presidio, glanced across at the Lord Farris before replying, as though to say that Farris had ended the conversation but there was just this little codicil.

"If the proof is forthcoming we must be prepared to meet it."

Delia looked at me and I knew what she was thinking. By meeting the proof, Naghan Strandar openly accepted that that proof would be positive, that werewolves did exist and that one was terrorizing Vondium.

Five

Concerning the phalanx

The day passed, as days do pass with work accomplished, but not enough—by Zair! never enough—to make me feel I'd earned my daily crust.

Truth to tell, with the Lord Farris and the Presidio we had set up perfectly capable of dealing with the problems of empire and the woes of Vallia, there was for me really only left the showy, emperor-type of function. Farris ran the place when I was not here, for which I gave thanks to Opaz, and I had no intention of making any attempt to usurp his functions.

When Drak at last threw out Vodun Alloran from the southwest and returned to Vondium in triumph, then Farris would gracefully retire from his position as Justicar Crebent and let Drak get on with it. Farris's heart was with the Vallian Air Service.

So it was that I opened the complex of houses and shops, then, after the second breakfast, went on to officiate at other functions. Much of Vondium at this time still lay in ruins. We concentrated on rebuilding the most essential structures first. When it was time to see Nath na Kochwold about his new Fifth Phalanx I brightened considerably.

With those thoughts occasioned by the kind of day I'd had I said to Nath as we stood in the anteroom leading from the barracks out to the square: "Well, Nath, there is only so much money and only so many resources. If we spend a thousand gold pieces to build a new school and what-have-you, there are a thousand talens less topside to pay the army and equip the lads."

"A school will not stop those rasts who raid us."

I pulled my ear. "Yet it may teach the youngsters what they will need to know for our future."

"They need to know how to shoulder a pike, to handle a shield, to wield a sword."

"Inter alia, inter alia."

Using the Kregish, the meaning was plain, and Nath smiled.

"You are, of course, majis, quite right. But, all the same—"

"All the same, my fiery kampeon, somehow we will build the schools and hospitals and find the wherewithal to fund the troops—even if the brumbytes in the files, being good soldiers, wear the old vosk-skull helmets still."

Seg walked in at that point and, overhearing, laughed.

"Vosks have skulls as thick through as Mount Hlabro. And, you know what has been said about our skulls."

"Aye," I said. Many and many a time I'd been told I had a skull as thick as a vosk's. Being an emperor made no difference there...

"Now, Nath," said Seg, very briskly. "I do not pretend to the pikes in the Phalanx. I've come to see about you archers. Dustrectium* is, after all, the secret of success."

"They come along, Seg," said Nath. "They come along. But, of course, they will never satisfy your standards."

He spoke only half mockingly.

Seg nodded, still sharp.

"True. But we must do what we can."

Trumpets pealed outside.

"Time to go."

So, out we went, all dressed resplendently for the occasion, and saw the Fifth Phalanx go through its paces.

"Commendable," I said. I did not commit myself further.

Seg puffed a little air between pursed lips, and said nothing.

The Fifth Phalanx contained the Ninth and Tenth Kerchuris, each totaling 5,184 brumbytes, 864 Hakkodin and a chodku of 864 archers.

"The ranks are well-filled," observed Seg.

"Aye." Here Nath stuck a fist onto his sword hilt and stared at Seg. "We had to use the old Fifth Phalanx to replace men leaving. The Tenth Kerchuri—the old Tenth—fought brilliantly at the Battle of Ovalia. The Ninth had a bad time down in the southwest, along with the Eighth from the Fourth Phalanx, when that cramph Vodun Alloran betrayed his trust and traitorously turned against us."

"I heard."

---

* Dustrectium. Firepower as applied to the effects from archery, slings and engines.

31

"There are enough men in this new Tenth to warrant the battle standards, and the honors. I have attempted to build a tradition into the phalanx force."

"And you have succeeded, Nath," I said, speaking with some force.

"I think, if you will permit, Nath," and Seg spoke seriously, "I would like to spend a little time with your chodku. The bowmen can be smartened up."

We knew Seg was not speaking of drill or uniform but of the controlled discharges of flights of arrows, of the rhythm and speed. Seg Segutorio is the finest bowman of two worlds, for my money, and he would work wonders with these lads, even though they were not Bowmen of Loh.

"You will have my gratitude, Seg."

As the Phalanx, neatly divided into its various component parts, marched, my attention left Nath and Seg discussing just what Seg would do. Well, and, of course, the Phalanx looked superb! The lads could, at least, march in rank and file and keep their pikes all aligned. The red flags flew. The uniforms, plain and sensible with much hard leather and bronze, gave plenty of room for strenuous activity. The shields—what the swods in the ranks call the crimson flowers, among other less flattering names—all at the same angle, just then caught gleams of light from the two suns and all together flashed in combined reflections like a bolt of lightning.

I make no apology for mentioning the Phalanx. To have lived and to have seen the Phalanx in motion is to have lived twice over. Yes, the brumbytes in their files were superb. And, staring out with my emotions all stirred higgledy-piggledy by the realities of comradeship and war and peace and repugnance I have often spoken of, I refused to be struck by a self-indulgent and maudlin thought—"What is all this for?"

At my back the duty squadron of 2ESW sat their zorcas in what of patience they could summon. This was not the same squadron as the one on duty yesterday. I had an unpleasant task before me there, for the young lad whose throat had been torn out, Jurukker Larghos Vontner, had a father and mother and they had been informed and an appointment arranged at the earliest possible moment.

They would be traveling up from their small estate in the country now, shattered by this evil news.

This black thought made me turn my head away from the glittering and gorgeous pageant of the Phalanx to stare balefully at the duty squadron. They, of course, looked the splendid bunch of rapscallions they were, hardened old kampeons and fuzz-faced youngsters. I sighed.

Then I stared harder.

By Vox!

Along at the end of the line, tagged on, a group of Zorcanders sat as silently and as still as the rest of the juruk. These riders did not have fuzz-faces. Their faces were smooth. Their eyes in the shadow of each helmet sometimes flashed a liquid gleam; their armor was of a different shape. I looked at them, these Jikai Vuvushis, and I realized that so far I'd been lucky—supremely fortunate—not to have to worry my head personally over the fate of a bunch of hare-brained girls in the day-to-day problems of running an empire. Now, if assassins struck, I'd be more concerned over these warrior ladies—

I halted my runaway thoughts.

Idiot! Onker! These girls were perfectly capable of taking care of themselves. They were soldier women, fighting ladies, Jikai Vuvushis, and now I had them in my juruk—for the guard had taken them in for good.

With the Fifth Phalanx seen safely off to barracks and with the guard trotting at our backs, we set off for the next function of the declining day.

"I could do with a wet, my old dom," said Seg.

"Aye. Even inspecting troops is thirsty work," said Nath.

"The disease is catching," I remarked, and felt no little surprise when they laughed at my comment.

So, laughing, we reined in before a neat little tavern we knew pretty well, The Frog and Jut, and dismounted. Thinking of the juruk jikai—which is one fancy name Kregans have for a guard corps—I was aware that I'd have to make the decision about the kind and number of animals they rode. The guard regiments kept up nikvoves and zorcas. The nikvove, heavy, powerful, is one of the better animals to ride in a thumping, rib-jolting charge, knee to knee. The zorca with his spiral horn is altogether more dainty, short-coupled, exceptionally fast and beautiful. The commanders of ESW and EYJ considered both animals essential. But Vallia was short of riding beasts, juts were difficult to come by in any war, Zair knows, and I had, therefore, to make the decision pretty soon.

The guardsmen dismounted and each jurukker was hell bent on slaking his thirst to the greater glory of Beng Dikkane, the patron saint of all the ale drinkers of Paz.

About to walk up the few steps leading under a brick archway where purple and yellow flowers blossomed exotically under the low rays of the suns, we were halted by the sound of galloping hooves from the street. A rider bolted up to the gate, half fell off and half dismounted, didn't bother with the reins, and came flying across the small courtyard toward us.

As a matter of course half a dozen burly lads of the guard magically appeared before me.

We could all see the man's uniform, a smart affair of crimson and yellow, with tasteful silver lace here and there. We all recognized him as a messenger sent by my chief stylor, Enevon Ob-Eye. In his left fist he clutched a fold of paper. Clearly, therefore, Enevon, who ran the office with meticulous accuracy, had sent me a message. Equally clearly, the lads of the duty squadron were going to keep a very close eye on proceedings.

Well, that is the way of it if an emperor has to have all these fancy body-guards.

"Let Farren through, Deldar Naghan, if you please."

Although I spoke quite pleasantly, Deldar Naghan, exceedingly large, exceedingly scarlet of face, and exceedingly conscious of his position, bellowed in his exceedingly enormous voice: "Quidang, majister!"

The guards stepped aside and young Farren ti Wovoing walked through. He was still breathless from his gallop through the streets of Vondium to find us.

Now I had in my mind's eye a picture of what had happened. Enevon had probably said: "Take this message to the emperor, young Farren. And—bratch!"

The message was quite possibly of world-shaking importance; far more probably it was just routine. That made no difference. If a message he had to deliver had to go to the emperor, then young Farren, like every other bright spark of the messenger service, would break all the speed records getting it to its destination.

I managed a quirk of the lips which passed for a smile and took the paper.

Majister—
Nath Naformo, a messenger from Natyzha Famphreon—not the
Racters—brings a message he will confide to no one but yourself.
Enevon K.S. *

I crumpled the paper.

"Thank you, young Farren. Do you tell Master Enevon Ob-Eye I will return directly."

With a snapped out acknowledgment, Farren turned himself about and ran off to his zorca. He was a young fellow desperate to make a mark for himself, like so many of them in Vallia, so many...

I showed Seg and Nath na Kochwold the paper, and then crumpled it again and stuck it down into a pouch on my belt.

"Say nothing of this, of course."

"All the same," said Seg as we went into the snug of The Frog and Jut, "it rings oddly."

The Racters with their black and white favors had once been the most powerful political party in Vallia. Their insurrection had failed and now what was left of them held the far northwest where they warred against the self-created King of North Vallia northward of them and against Layco Jhansi to the south.

They had previously offered an alliance against Layco Jhansi, as he

---

* K.S.: Krell Stylor. Krell is one Kregish word for Chief.

had offered one against them. I did not think this mysterious messenger was Strom Luthien, who did the dirty work for the Racters in this department.

As we downed the refreshing ale served here by a sweet little Fristle fifi in a yellow apron and her fur brushed to a polish of perfection, Seg went on: "And from old Natyzha Famphreon, herself, personally. Not from the Racter party. I suppose she's still a leading light? Maybe they've thrown her out and she asks your help."

"Would to Opaz someone would slit her throat," was Nath's comment just before he buried his nose into his jug.

"You have to give this Nath Naformo full marks for courage." Seg slugged back a gulp of ale. "Any Racter walking into Vondium is likely to have his throat slit, by the Veiled Froyvil!"

We drank up and then remounted to canter off to the palace where a meal awaited us. Still resplendently dressed, and therefore feeling foolish, I decided to see the messenger from Natyzha Famphreon first. Seg and Nath went with me into Enevon's office where we were shown into a small anteroom. The walls were painted beige, the ceiling was white, there were two desks and four chairs, and the carpet was quite ordinary, with a flower pattern of intertwined Moonblooms. Nath Naformo rose from a chair as we entered.

"Majister." He started to go into the full incline where he'd scrape his idiot nose on the carpet and stick his rump waggling into the air.

I stopped all that nonsense and said: "Sit down, Koter Naformo, and spit it out."

He looked at me frankly. He was in the Kregan way hard, of a middle age, I judged, given that Kregans live better than two hundred years, and wore decent Vallian buff. His weapons had been taken from him.

"Majister. I am not a Racter. I am employed merely as an agent, between you and the person who wishes to speak to you."

"More mumbo-jumbo!" said Seg, blowing out his cheeks.

"Surely you recognize the necessity for a Racter to show circumspection here, kov?"

Seg nodded his handsome head in agreement.

"Well?" I said, and I own my voice made the poor fellow sitting opposite jump. Naformo swallowed down.

"If you will attend the upstairs room at the sign of The Piebald Zorca this evening, the person I represent will await you—alone and unarmed."

Enevon screwed up his one eye at me, and pursed his lips. Despite his seniority, he still managed to get ink on himself. "The Piebald Zorca? H'mm, majis, that was well-known as a haunt of the Racters when they held power in Vondium."

"And in a highly insalubrious part, too," said Nath. As a citizen of

Thermin, up in the north midlands, he'd assiduously acquainted himself with Vondium.

This Nath Naformo certainly did have courage.

"Am I to understand you fear to go through fear of treachery—"

"Fear?" yelped out Nath.

"Oh, I'll go," I told Naformo. "And I'll have a couple of squadrons of my lads ready if your principal attempts treachery."

Uncharacteristically it was left to Seg to say what lay in our minds.

"Treachery? *That* we can deal with. It's this dratted werewolf we've got to look out for."

Six

Natyzha Famphreon sends a request

The Piebald Zorca had been rebuilt since the earlier structure had been burned down in the Times of Troubles, but the upstairs room was furnished with a faded glory that reminded one of bygone days. There were even black and white decorations to the cornices. They could, of course, have been merely an artist's fancy...

Nath snorted when he saw the decorations, and chucked his wide-brimmed hat down onto the table. Then he sprawled out in a chair and stuck his black boots out.

"Drinks all round, landlord, and sharpish!"

"At once, my lord."

Seg and I stared at the person in the black cloak and wearing a black iron mask who rose at our entrance. He wore no weapons. We were fully armed.

"Would I know you, then, koter?" I made the inquiry in a flat voice.

"You might, majister. When the landlord has served us I will remove the mask."

"Make it so."

The room was illuminated by mineral oil lamps, and their slight tang rankled unpleasantly when compared with the sweet aroma of the samphron oil lamps those with more money could afford. When the landlord, a bulldog-faced Brukaj in an almost clean yellow and green striped apron had retired, we broached the bottles and settled about the table.

With a firm gesture the stranger unhooked the clasps and removed the iron mask.

Well, I knew him. But only slightly.

"Lahal, Strom Volgo."

"Lahal, majister."

He was apim, like me, with stern and austere features, bearing the marks of experience. His nose was full and his lips of the thin variety, yet he was not unhandsome. His eyebrows drew down.

"I serve the kovneva, and hold my lands at her hands. She commands, and I obey."

A strom, which is something like the rank of count here on Earth, may hold estates direct from the emperor or king, and also from a kov, or duke. The dowager kovneva Natyzha Famphreon of Falkerdrin owned vast lands. There were many nobles beholden to her.

"Well, jen," I said, which is the correct way to address a lord in Vallia, "you'd better spit it out."

He was not discomposed. He'd heard of me, right enough, since the days when the Racters believed I was merely a propaganda prince, a puffed-up bladder of nothing.

"I have to inform you that the kovneva believes she will soon die—"

"Ha!" exclaimed Nath. "Then you do bring good news!"

Strom Volgo took no notice outwardly; but I noticed his forehead crinkled just a trifle. This man served old Natyzha, and was well aware of the upheavals that would follow the death of a noble.

"She is aware of the enmity shown you by the Racters. She calls to your remembrance her enclosed garden, and the chavonths that escaped and would have killed her and her friends. She grieved, then, that you and she stood in enmity, one against the other."

I said, "I did what was necessary. But I, also, remind her that her son, Nath Famphreon, stood shoulder to shoulder with me. And he was armed only with a rapier."

That had been a blood-stirring little scene, the escaped chavonths, ferocious hunting cats, leaping out ravenous to kill and eat us. Yes, I'd always felt that Natyzha's son, Nath, was not the ninny everyone thought him. His mother was so powerful, so overriding, so intemperate in her demands, that young Kov Nath vanished in her shadows.

As Strom Volgo went on speaking I realized we were handling high politics, secret understandings, the stuff of which empires are made.

He unhooked the black cloak and tossed it over the back of a chair. He wore Vallian buff, and his long black riding boots were still splashed with mud. He'd come a goodly way southward from Falkerdrin, which lies north of the Black Mountains and north of Vennar, over the River of Rippling Catspaws. My blade comrade Inch was still fighting to regain control of his Black Mountains, and my comrade—never a blade comrade!—Turko was struggling to hold onto his new kovnate of Falinur and to hook left into

Vennar whose borders marched westward of him. And, of course, Vennar was the kovnate of Layco Jhansi, the old emperor's chief pallan, traitor, forsworn murderer.

"You still fight Layco Jhansi, then, Strom Volgo."

"Of course, to all outward seeming."

I didn't like the sound of this. Neither did Seg. He sat up.

"Oh?"

Volgo spread his hands. He wore the colored favors and symbol—known as a schturval—of Falkerdrin. Black and gold the colors, a chavonth the symbol. The schturval glittered in the oil lamps' glow.

"I have been commanded by the kovneva to tell you whatever you wish to know, majister. She feels she is near death—"

"And is this sooth? Is Natyzha really dying?"

"Yes."

"From all accounts," put in Nath na Kochwold, "her son Nath Famphreon is no man to be a kov. He'll have his head off before he leaves the graveside."

"Yes," said Strom Volgo.

Seg fidgeted away at what had been said earlier.

"What d'you mean, strom, about to all outward seeming you still fight that bastard Layco Jhansi?"

"I have been commanded to tell the emperor all. The Racters have come to an understanding with Layco Jhansi—"

"The devil they have!"

"Aye. The Racters will turn their main efforts against this maniacal King of North Vallia, and Jhansi will in likewise smash this new Kov Turko of Falinur."

"By the Black Chunkrah!" I flamed out. "This is ill news!"

"And it explains why Turko has been having such a bad time recently." Seg gripped his square brown fist onto the smooth shaft of his bowstave. "I'll have to go up there, my old dom, and—"

"Too right! And I'll be with you, and with reinforcements for Turko. The whole front could collapse and then—by Krun! It doesn't bear thinking of!"

Strom Volgo rubbed salt into our wounds.

"Now that Layco Jhansi has access to the sea through Racter territory he has been hiring many mercenaries."

"That does it," declared Seg. He stood up, big, handsome, his dark hair wild, and prowled about the room like a veritable leem.

"My thanks to you, Strom Volgo, and to Natyzha. She has done us a good service with this intelligence. Although—" and here I confess I stroked my chin, "I am at a loss as to why she should so inform us."

"That is why I am here. When the kovneva dies she is confident that the lords of the Racter lands will descend like warvols upon her kovnate. Her son Nath, whom she loves in her own hard fashion, will be swept aside. He will likely be slain. Certainly, she believes, Kov Nath will never inherit Falkerdrin."

"That seems reasonable," said Nath na Kochwold.

But, having had a glimpse of the purpose and steely determination in Natyzha Famphreon, I thought I could see what she wanted. And I stood aghast. I had to let Volgo spell it out, for it was a request I did not wish to hear.

"The Kovneva Natyzha Famphreon of Falkerdrin begs and demands of you, Dray Prescot, Emperor of Vallia, that you guarantee the legal and actual inheritance of her son, the Kov Nath Famphreon of Falkerdrin."

"Do what?" Seg's voice as he stopped pacing and swung about, head jutting, was a snarl. "Is the woman insane?"

"She has, Kov Seg, taken the measure of the emperor. This request cannot be dealt with by anyone else."

Quite mildly, I said: "If I accede to this astonishing request, and I send—or, rather, ask—Kov Seg Segutorio, to go up to Falkerdrin and sort it all out, then, believe you me, Volgo, Kov Seg will sort it all out—and in a most handsome way, by Vox!"

Volgo blinked his eyes twice, rapidly.

"I'll go like a shot, of course, Dray. But I own I'm a damned sight more worried over Turko."

"So am I. Turko's problems with this Imp of Sicce Jhansi are far more pressing than Natyzha's presentiments of death."

"Your pardon, majister—but the kovneva really is dying. The needlemen and puncture ladies are helpless."

"Well, Volgo, I'll think about it. You have to admire the old biddy, though. She was always the toughest nut of all the Racters. When—"

"Majister!" He interrupted with full knowledge of what often used to happen to folk who interrupted emperors when they were talking. "I crave your pardon. But the kovneva is dying, and she must have your positive answer to comfort her on her deathbed. I am sure you can see that—majister."

"I see you are devoted to her, Volgo, and that I admire. Very well. Take back this word. I have a good memory of Kov Nath—no, by Krun!—I have an affection for that young man. I shall do all I can do to see he is not defrauded of his estates, and that he is not slain. But if all this happens when I am not there, or my armies have not broken through, why, then..."

"You will contrive it, majister. That is why my mistress sent this request."

Knowing Seg of old I tried not to catch his eye. Some hope! His gaze appeared to hook and hold me, to hypnotize me. He laughed that Seg Segutorio laugh.

"There, my old dom! I've told you before." He used Kregish words. But what he was saying was: "You're too much the perfect knight for your own good."

I had to react.

"Perfect knight! By Zim-Zair! After all the strokes we've pulled!"

Nath na Kochwold, good comrade though he was, could only look at us two, lost.

Strom Volgo was most punctilious.

"I shall be happy to carry back your word to my mistress. The dowager kovneva has not had a happy life since the Times of Troubles—"

"Well, by Vox!" exploded Nath. "Who has?"

The ugly meanings of the words hung on the air. The curtains to the tall windows had been drawn, and they were, I recall, of a thick weave from the eastern provinces of Vallia, in a pale gray with silver curlicues. As Nath's intemperate and valid words still echoed in the chamber, a shrill and heartbreakingly terrified scream shrieked outside the windows.

Seg and I were shoulder to shoulder at the window. He ripped the drapes aside. We stared out into the moons-drenched night.

The small courtyard lay directly beneath us. Men of the guard were running out, drawing their swords. The wall confining the courtyard from the street hid their view. But we could see—we could see over the wall and into the narrow alleyway where between overhanging balconies and frowning facades, the cobbles glistened in a narrow streak where the moonslight reached down.

"There!" shouted Seg.

Nath stood at our shoulders, peering out. He yelled, angrily, incensed, violently: "The damned ganchark!"

A lean loping form of shaggy gray fur leaped along the street and in the evil thing's mouth the limp form of a girl showed horridly that he had found and killed his prey.

Now the werewolf was carrying his victim off to devour her at his leisure.

Seven

Of the absence of blood and fur

No other man in two worlds could have done it. Of that I am perfectly sure.

Seg's bow snugged in his hand, where he had been polishing up the shaft as we talked. Now the bow snapped up, the arrow slashed from the quiver, the shaft was nocked, the bow bent, all in so smooth and wondrous a fashion as to amaze any young coy newly recruited into an archer regiment—as to amaze me, by Vox!

Seg loosed.

The werewolf, clearly visible by the fuzzy pink moonlight of The Maiden with the Many Smiles, leaped for the corner. The girl dangling from his jaws flopped about as the ganchark bounded on. The lethal gray form, spikey with menace, angular in motion and yet flowing with evil grace, rounded the corner and vanished.

Seg said: "I don't believe it."

Nath started to say something, stopped, cleared his throat, and then turned back. He went over to the table and poured himself a glass of red wine. His hand did not shake; I had the feeling that had it done so I would not have been surprised.

Seg shook his head.

"I hit him."

He turned to me, and his handsome face was cast in as serious a mold as I'd ever seen it. "Dray—you know I do not boast over shooting, for that is folly. But when I hit, I know I hit. I hit that beast."

"I believe you, Seg. Let us go down and find out."

"The shaft should have taken him just below his forequarters, straight through. It would have pierced his heart."

Nath said: "There is no reliable evidence to prove that gancharks have hearts."

"Then he would have been hit sore. He would not have bounded on so fleetly—"

"Let's go down," I said, again.

The thing was unnerving. Seg knew when he hit. When a mortal being was struck by a clothyard shaft, fetched with the rosy feathers of the Zim-Korf of Valka, tipped by hardened steel, that being was struck through. And if Seg said he'd hit so as to pierce the heart, that mortal being was dead.

Dead.

The other answer to that equation rang evilly in my old vosk-skull of a head.

The jurukkers of the guard knew what they were about and the guardsmen fanned out past the gateway, covering the cross street as well as the one along which we now hurried. The Twins, eternally orbiting each other and throwing down their mingled light, joined the Maiden with the Many Smiles to drown the alleyway in pink radiance.

Two guards sprinted back toward us, and because they were of the Emperor's Sword Watch their equipment did not jingle and jangle. The leader, a kampeon, saw me and yelled.

"Majister! The shaft!"

He reached us, slapped to a halt and held out Seg's arrow. I took it.

"Thank you, Diarmin. There was no blood?"

"Not a drop, as Vikatu is my witness."

I handed the shaft to its owner.

"Well?"

Seg Segutorio is a man of parts. He took the shaft between his powerful fingers, twirled it, checked the flights, and then he lifted the bright steel head to his nose and sniffed.

"Oiled steel," he said. "Nothing else."

The youngster paired off with the old sweat Diarmin and being instructed by him in soldierly virtues, had that clean-cut, pink, shining face that is so heartbreakingly vulnerable beneath the harsh iron brim of the helmet.

Now he swallowed down with a gulp, and said: "I think—majister—I thought—"

Diarmin had served with me for a long time and knew my ways, and what he could get away with. He bellowed: "Spit it out, jurukker! Do not keep the emperor waiting!"

"It was me who found the arrow, majister. When I picked it up I thought—that is—"

"Untangle your tongue, jurukker!" fairly foamed Diarmin, crimson that he was thus being shown up in front of his emperor.

"Yes, Deldar Diarmin—There was a tiny scrap of gray fur on the arrowhead—"

"Fur! Fur! Well, young Nairvon, where is it now?"

"I—I don't know—"

"Dropped it, did you! Lost valuable evidence! That's a charge for you, my lad. You'll jump in the morning when the Hikdar sinks his teeth into you!"

"Yes, Deldar."

"Now just a minute," put in Seg. He waggled his arrow. "You're positive there was a scrap of fur, Nairvon?"

"Yes, Kov Seg—well, almost certain."

Deldar Diarmin opened his mouth and Seg got in first—just—

"But you didn't drop it, did you?"

"No, jen, no. It was evidence."

I said, "Deldar Diarmin, why don't you and the jurukker go back up the alleyway with torches and look?"

"Quidang!" Diarmin's voice boomed and rattled against the gray walls. "Jurukker Nairvon—bratch!"

The two guardsmen started off and Seg shouted after them: "Get some more of your comrades on the job."

Nath na Kochwold had remained silent during this interchange. Now he drew a breath.

"I do not like to disbelieve in the word of young Nairvon. If Seg shot a wolf, and there was fur clipped off, then Nairvon dropped the evidence."

Seg said, "But?"

"Ah, yes. If it was a werewolf then you might have clipped a considerable quantity of fur. But it would not be found."

"And no blood."

"Quite."

The incongruousness of this military protocol, the Deldar bellowing, the youngster stammering, the feel of routine and orders and a settled way of life, when viewed against the eerie happenings, the breath of occult horror, struck me shrewdly. I did not think this damned werewolf was going to be dealt with in Standing Orders.

With that old intemperate rasp in my voice, I said, "Let's get back and finish this business with Strom Volgo."

My comrades agreed, and Nath said quietly: "I don't think they'll find any fur."

"And I hit the beast, of that I am sure."

"So that, Seg, as you hit what you shoot at, and the beast was not slain and did not drop blood..."

Nath shook his head. "This is going to be a bad business."

"We must find out who that poor girl was." I could still see that pathetic figure with dangling arms and legs, the white dress like a moth's wing, clamped in the jaws of the wolf.

"And," said Seg with a most ugly note in his voice, "what the hell she was doing out alone."

When we returned to the upstairs room of The Piebald Zorca, Strom Volgo had donned his black iron mask.

No doubt, I thought, and my comrades must also have reasoned, he had decided this was none of his business.

The order of importance, as I saw it, of what lay ahead of us was: Firstly, to reinforce Turko and hold the front, and conjointly with this to ascertain the situation of Inch. Secondly, to deal with this werewolf; and, thirdly, to do what could be done for Natyzha Famphreon and her son Nath.

This I explained to Strom Volgo.

"I must accept the needle in this, majister. For I see your position. I rest content that you have given your word."

Seg pulled his chin at this, but the deed had been done and there was no gainsaying it.

"Strom Volgo," I said, halting him as he took his leave. "Allow me to send a half-squadron to see you safely out of Vondium."

He hesitated. Then—"As you wish, majister. And my thanks."

A sensible fellow, then...

In pursuance of the decision on precedence I had a perfect instrument to carry out the first task with me now in the shape of Nath na Kochwold. We went off back to the palace with the guard trotting along after, and I was half-amused to see they rode with bared weapons. If Seg shot the damn thing and it didn't drop dead, then these fine lads wouldn't do much better...

"Nath," I said. "About Turko—"

"Ha! You want me to—"

"I want you to finish off training the Fifth Phalanx."

He glowered at me.

"Very well. As you know, there is only one thing I like better than training a phalanx, and that is leading it in battle."

"You're a bloodthirsty villain, all right, Nath."

"Oh, aye, sometimes."

We'd rearranged the distribution of the various Phalanxes—or, rather, they had been rearranged when I'd been away from Vallia. The half-phalanx, or wing, we seldom thought of in those terms, that is, of being a half— rather, we thought of the wing as the Kerchuri, a unit in its own right, two of which formed a single Phalanx. The whole phalanx corps was thus organized.

I told Nath na Kochwold what I intended.

"I shall take the Sixth Kerchuri with me up to Turko. Vondium will be safe with the Ninth and Tenth."

The Third Phalanx had a special place in our affections. The Sixth Kerchuri of the Third had been the unit to move into line and plug the gap when the savage clansmen astride their voves had almost broken through at the Battle of Kochwold. From that battle Nath took his name.

"Very well. After all, the Fifth is not really a green outfit. Plenty of the men served in the old Fifth."

"Good."

"And when you call on us I'll bash a little more knowledge into 'em when we march up to join you."

"As to that, Nath, I would hope to clear this problem without calling on you. Drak down in the southwest might call. And up in the northeast past Hawkwa country—"

Seg said gruffly, "We do well up there, Dray."

"Aye," confirmed Nath. "It's mostly light troops to ride to counter raids. There is a case to be made for withdrawal of a Kerchuri."

I said, "Talk it over with Farris."

Truth to tell, it was these confounded girls who worried me. No matter how many times I told myself that I was just being plain stupid, I still felt that uncomfortable itch when I saw a Warrior Maiden in action. They looked splendid striding about in their tall black boots, with their long legs limber and lithe, their faces glowing with health, their eyes bright. That was all the facade, the parade, the fancy uniforms, the trumpets pealing, drums hammering and the flags flying.

The reality of action, of blood and death were far removed from the fairy-tale romance of the Jikai Vuvushis.

The palace was alive with lights when we returned. No one intended to be caught by a werewolf in the uncanny shifting shadows.

Garfon the Staff, our respectable and highly efficient majordomo, told me that Deb-Lu-Quienyin was waiting in the reception room outside my private quarters. Delia was not there, and she had left me a note, and Deb-Lu-Quienyin, answering the urgent request to return to Vondium, had had a tiring flight.

We went straight through shouting for wine and throwing off our capes. Deb-Lu smiled when he saw us and ceased from his pacing about the Walfargweave rugs.

"Lahal, Deb-Lu. You've heard all about this werewolf?"

"Lahal, majis—aye. A bad business. But there are ways and means."

"Too right," said Seg, seizing up a glass and looking around for the nearest bottle.

You will notice the way Deb-Lu and we spoke—no tiresome formalities, no swaths of lahals and majisters and polite inquiries after health. None of that at this fraught moment in Vondium's history. Yet Deb-Lu and I had not seen each other for a long time—a damn long time, by Krun!

"Now that is what I expected to hear," I exclaimed, taking the glass from Seg. "Although, San, there is still a chance that this beast is not a werewolf."

Almost every time I see Deb-Lu-Quienyin in my mind's eye and recall him with affection and awe, I seem inclined to say that he looked just the same. Well, of course he did, and yet looked changed at certain times. As a famed and feared Wizard of Loh, addressed as San, he was a member of the small band of brothers and sisters clustered about the emperor and empress. I was about to say a respected and valued member; but all the folk in that fellow and sistership were respected and valued.

No. There is still no doubt in my mind that of all the sorcerers on Kregen, the Wizards of Loh rank very very high. As you may be aware, I had only slowly been growing aware of their true powers. Looking at Deb-Lu now and feeling that familiar surge of affection for him, I saw he had taken off his enormous turban. His red Lohvian hair looked disheveled. He was your very figure of a powerful mage, and yet there were no runes embroidered upon his robes, no massive array of skulls and feathers and books. The Wizards of Loh were long past the need for material artifacts to assist in casting a spell.

He did have a staff. It stood propped against a chair. Deb-Lu used to say to me that he really had the staff to assist his weary old bones to hobble about—as you will see he liked to put on the pretense of advancing years in a most unKreganlike way. He must have picked up a deal of his complaining routine from old Hunch...

And that reminds me that there are a whole lot of folk living and working in Vondium who deserve a mention at this time, and yet whom I must for the moment abandon as the unfolding story of the Werewolf of Vondium takes precedence.

What Deb-Lu said was short, succinct—and pretty damn obvious, by Zair, had we listened and used our heads for something else than hanging pretty-feathered hats on.

"Dudinter," said Deb-Lu-Quienyin. "Dudinter."

Eight

The four smiths

Emder, sober-faced, lifted the statue. Emder, sober-minded, meticulous, supremely efficient, is the friend who looks after me when I happen to be in a palace or a civilized place, as Deft-Fingered Minch, my crusty old kampeon comrade, is the friend who looks after me in camp. Now Emder shook his head.

"It is a great pity. The piece has merit."

"Aye," Seg said with some emphasis, and gave Emder no chance of holding onto the statue by tweaking it out of his grasp.

"What the empress will say..." started Emder. Then he halted. "No. I am being foolish. The empress would command instantly that her girls remove what is necessary from her own boudoir and anywhere else."

"You are right, Emder," I said, and reached out for a candlestick, one of a pair, and Seg, hurling the statue into the sack, went over and fetched the other candlestick. Both went clink into the sack.

"Although," said Nath na Kochwold, "if you asked the citizens of Vondium to contribute, they would do so willingly and to the best of their ability."

"They've suffered enough, what with all the wars and destruction. If the palace here cannot find enough then I'll loot some other damned place I'm supposed to own."

On this Earth a couple of thousand years or so ago Pliny described electrum as consisting of one part of silver to four of gold. Native gold dug up with something approaching a half admixture of silver, not less than a fifth, was also reasonably common on Kregen; but we did not have time to go prospecting. To find the quantities of electrum we needed we simply grabbed all the statues and pretty little objects fabricated from dudinter and used them.

Garfon the Staff came in, belted his golden-banded balass staff down and said in what was for him a very soft whisper: "The four smiths are here, majister!"

"Right. I'll see 'em now. Get all this stuff down to the forges right away." Briskly, I strode off and as I went I tweaked a neat little dudinter trinket from a side table. This was a miniature of those enormous statues that come from Balintol, of an eight-armed person, a Talu, dancing with fingers outstretched like an abandoned cartwheel.

The attractive pale yellow color of electrum, named for amber in the old Greek, glimmered in my hand as I went off to the reception room. The four smiths stood a trifle uneasily, summoned by the emperor to the palace. I hoped not a one of them was uneasily running through his mind the list of his latest crimes!

Well, the job was simple enough.

"We have to rid ourselves of this ganchark, my friends. And to do that we have to stick him with a weapon forged from dudinter. Arrow piles— and the broad fleshcutters particularly. Swords and spears. You'll have to get an edge the best way you can."

"We will forge an edge, majister," said Naghan the Bellows, the armorer.

Ortyg Ortyghan, the goldsmith, nodded eagerly. Logan Loptyg chipped in to say that he would work night and day. He was the silversmith.

The foxey Khibil face of Param Ortygno expressed confidence, and also caution.

"I am the dudinter smith you have summoned, majister. Maybe the chief place should be given to me, for, after all, we are to work in my specialty and I am a Khibil." At that he brushed up his arrogant whiskers, a true-blue haughty fox-faced Khibil to the life.

I did not laugh.

"I am grateful to you for your willing offer of help, Koter Ortygno. The fate of Vondium is at stake in more ways than perhaps you may imagine. I think it best if you four work in harmony, as a team, like a quadriga. There should be no need for any professional secrets to be revealed. Those parts of the work may be conducted as each one of you sees fit." I fixed them with an eye that has often, most unkindly, been described as a damned baleful Dray Prescot eye. "Am I understood?"

"Understood, majister!" they sang out in a chorus.

"*Queyd arn tung!*"*

---

* Queyd-arn-tung! No more need be said.

They each gave a respectful little nod of the head and turned to leave. If sometimes I overreact to all this bowing and scraping and condemn it too harshly, I hope the reason is not some deep psychological flaw in me that demands and rejects an attention I cannot bring into the open lights of day. Those four little nods of the head I reasoned showed proper respect not for me as a man but for my position. It was to the emperor the respect was due, who represented Vallia. These men had been among those clamorous crowds who had called me and elected me emperor to sort out their troubles. If a fellow or a girl cannot feel respect for their own country, then the world may not roll around.

Of course, that brings up the knotty problem of what happens when your country falls below the standards you consider to be proper and decent in the world...

I became aware of the little dudinter statue in my hand. I called after the four smiths.

"Wait, my friends."

They turned at once and I threw the Talu toward them. Interestingly enough, it was not the haughty Khibil, Param Ortygno, who caught the thing. He might be the dudinter smith; but it was Naghan the Bellows who took the eight-armed idol out of the air and without a scratch.

"Remberee," I said.

"Remberee, majister."

Delia's note merely said she'd been called away to the bedside of a dying friend. She did not name the friend.

I thought I knew.

The sorority to which Delia belonged, the Sisters of the Rose, was in any terms a powerful Order. Much of their work was carried on in the open; a very great deal remained secret. Through the surprising favor of the Star Lords, I had been afforded the privilege of vicariously sharing in some of Delia's adventures, discovering thereby many secrets Delia would never reveal to a man, and, also thereby, feeling honor-bound to keep them totally concealed. In fact, I never thought about them if I could manage that trick.

One fact, however, I did know. The mistress of the Order, who had once been known as Elomi the Shining, from Valka, was dying. Delia had been chosen to be the next mistress, and had refused. The Sisters of the Rose were in every sense important; for Delia being Empress of Vallia was also important in an entirely different fashion, a fashion in which the idea of obligation and service figured in just as dramatic a way as it did in the Sisters of the Rose.

So, I knew Delia had gone to Lancival. The location of this place, so secret and unknown, remained a secret as far as I was concerned, even although I could laugh with glee along with the SOR at the impudence of the place's disguise in Vallia. There Delia would confer with her peers, politic with some, cajole others, argue, plead, seldom order—although that she could do supremely well, by Vox!—and eventually they would elect the new mistress.

If by some mischance some feminine chicanery landed Delia with the job, I fancied she'd make a different kind of mistress of the SOR from any hitherto in the Order's long history.

All our daughters had been educated and trained by the SOR, as our sons by the Krozairs of Zy. I devoutly believe there is no better education or training anywhere in two worlds.

Because something of that kind had been flowing through my mind when the outlying islands of Vallia had been attacked by the reiving fish-headed Shanks from over the curve of the world, we'd formed an Order, originally in Vallia, based on the Krozairs of Zy. The mystical and superhuman woman we knew as Zena Iztar had been instrumental in aiding us to get the new Order, the Kroveres of Iztar, formed and aware of the fact that it was in the process of creating a tradition for the future.

Seg Segutorio was the Grand Master of the KRVI.

Where there was injustice, where tyranny, where we were attacked by the Shanks, there—in theory—the brothers of the KRVI would be found assisting the oppressed and resisting the Shanks.

A new and what was, I suppose, a daring idea had recently been giving me some interesting prospects for future action.

Why not, I'd said to myself, why shouldn't both men and women join the same order and fight injustice, succor the weak and helpless, fight the damned fish-headed Shanks?

Well, it was a thought...

At this point it is proper for me to mention that I knew very little of the other female Orders of Paz. The Sisters of the Sword, the Sisters of Samphron, the Grand Ladies, the Little Sisters of Opaz, and many others were secret still.

I did know that a new Order, the Sisters of the Whip, had collapsed.

So when Seg joined me the first thing I said was: "It seems to me that this damned werewolf is a suitable job for the kroveres."

"By the Veiled Froyvil, my old dom! You are right!"

"We have lost touch a little lately, of course."

"Well, we've been off in Pandahem. But—let me see—" and although Seg's fey blue eyes did not actually cross in thought, his face took on a most menacing expression as he mentally began sorting out the brothers available to undertake this mission.

In this my narrative of my life on Kregen there are many people who appear illuminated, as it were, in the forefront of the action, only to subside into the background as fresh events overtake us. But these folk were not forgotten. They formed the living breathing fabric of life and friendship. Many of them met and talked with me almost every day. Others I saw at banquets, dinners, rowdy parties or within the harsher environs of business, the church, the law and the army.

Unmok the Nets, for instance, was—still—undecided what business to undertake next. The Pachak twins still cared for Deb-Lu-Quienyin. Our Khibil wrestlers had found ready employment, going eventually with Turko. Tilly and Oby were a permanent part of life. And—Naghan the Gnat. As I said to Seg: "We didn't hoick our friends out of the Arena in Huringa for nothing. Naghan can start fashioning dudinter weapons right away."

Seg said: "Do wha—? Oh, yes, surely. I can put my finger on a score of brothers within a day. And, as for Naghan the Gnat, I am more than happy to wield any weapon made by him."

"Good."

"Although it is a pity Vomanus is still poorly."

"He is taking more time to recover than I like. But he will. He has, like us, bathed in the Sacred Pool of Aphrasöe."

"Don't remind me. I am still totally confused by all the implications—"

"You are not alone!"

"That's as may be. His daughter, Valona, turned up pretty sharpish, so I heard, after Delia sorted out the trouble up in Vindelka."

"Sister of the Rose, business conducted by these formidable women to our confusion. There was a time when I sincerely believed that Valona was my daughter Lela—"

"If I made some humorous remark about that's what you get for chasing off to the ends of Kregen, then I'd be a dolt. Now I know about your comical little Earth with only a yellow sun and only one moon and no diffs, I can understand a lot more that you've never spoken of."

"You can? Maybe, Seg my Bowman comrade, it is time for us to try a few falls on the mat."

"You can take on Korero the Shield. I'm off to find Balass the Hawk and start this werewolf thing moving."

"Korero?"

"Drak has sent the First Regiment of the Emperor's Sword Watch back to Vondium. Well—" and here Seg laughed in his rip-roaring raffish way "—he couldn't hold on to them for a single heartbeat when they learned you were back in Vondium!"

"No," I said. "No, that rascally bunch will insist on putting their bodies between me and danger."

Although I spoke flippantly, I felt the leap of spirits at this news. 1ESW might be a rascally bunch, the regiment was also a smashingly powerful fighting instrument, devoted, very much a law unto itself in matters of regimental honor and pride, and still a unit of the army, standing shoulder to shoulder with their comrades in the defense of Vallia.

Seg moved off and called back: "They'll want to go with us up to Turko, Dray."

"Yes. I shudder to think what 2ESW will say..."

Nine

Werewolf at the party

I draw a merciful veil over the uproarious happenings when my lads of 1ESW flew into Vondium.

By Vox! Carouse! They did not quite tear the place to bits, but they beat up the city sorely.

They were all there, thanks to the mercy of Opaz, and while some had taken wounds, all were recovered. There were new members of the regiment, of course, and it was my task to get to know them all as quickly as possible. No one entered the ranks of the premier guard regiment unless he was a proven kampeon, a swod of merit, a superb fighting man.

They decided they'd better have some kind of formal parade, and march through the streets to the Temple of Opaz Militant, and there render up thanks. The bands played, the flags fluttered, the suns glinted off massed ranks of armor and weapons. The spectacle delighted the crowds who turned out in their thousands to cheer. The rogues had even organized a bevy of pretty young girls, half-naked sprites in silken draperies all a-swirling, to dance ahead and scatter flower petals. That made me give a grotesque tweak of the lips which my friends recognized as a smile.

Not one of them, nobody, not a single swod, got drunk. I have explained how that kind of idiotic anti-social behavior was not tolerated in the guard corps.

Targon the Tapster, Cleitar the Smith who was now Cleitar the Standard, Ortyg the Tresh, Volodu the Lungs, all of them were there. Korero the Shield, a magnificent sight as always, a golden Kildoi with four arms and a tail hand, uplifting his shields in protection, Dorgo the Clis, saturnine and with his facial scar a livid blaze, and Naghan ti Lodkwara together with all our other comrades from the original Choice Band joined by our new fellows, marched in the streaming mingled lights of the Suns of Scorpio.

Vondium, the proud city, as the capital of Vallia is a civilized metropolis of a civilized country. Yet, as I watched the parade and marveled afresh at the panache and bearing, the spirit and devilment of the jurukkers of 1ESW, I could not fail to be aware of the barbaric appearances everywhere, the feeling of passions bursting through regimentation, the savage warrior spirits chafing at and yet understandingly accepting discipline. Mazingle, the swods call that on occasions, and sometimes they call unfair and too harsh a discipline mazingle, with darker and far more ugly meanings.

For a brief moment a vision of the zazzers of the Eye of the World, the inner sea of the continent of Turismond, took my inner attention. Drunkenness was more common among both Grodnims and Zairians there, although still generally regarded as the pastime of the feeble-minded. The zazzers were those folk—men and women, apim and diff alike—who quaffed until they reached a fighting frenzy before battle. Unlike the old Norse berserkers, who either wore bear skins or stripped naked, according to your sources, they smashed into action fully accoutred and armed, ragingly high seas over, roaringly sloshed, and fought until they won or were cut down. The zazzers' philosophy may appeal to many; as a shortcut to personal extinction it repelled more.

A tremendous shindig was held that night; the torches flared their orange and golden hair, the sweet scents of moonblooms mingled with that of exotic foods and enormous quantities of wines. While we might not have shaken the stars, we surely shook all Vondium.

As I say, I draw a decent and merciful veil over the proceedings.

After the orchestra in their platform-shell at one side of the flower garden had played the Imperial Waltz of Vallia, which as you know was the best rendering I could contrive of the Blue Danube, and the folk had danced the whole sequence three times over, I spotted young Oby.

Well, I should not refer to him as young Oby, of course, for he was a grown and limber man. Two girls clung to his arms, another rode his shoulders and waved a bottle aloft, and a fourth in some mysterious way held on with her naked legs wrapped around his waist from the front, and was busily kissing him in between laughing and drinking. He saw me and, disengaging his mouth from its amorous combat, grimaced and called across.

"I cannot help it!"

Oby ran the Aerial Squadron attached to the palace, and always seemed to be in peril of sudden and immediate marriage, which with a sleight of hand much admired among the raffish bloods and despaired of by the maidens, never was—in his words—trapped.

"I would feel envy, Oby, but for good reasons!"

"Aye, Dray, aye! Would that I could find—" and then he was devoured again.

I yelled: "Where's Naghan?"

Oby twisted his head and the girl's lips sizzled down his cheek. She started to bite his ear—of course.

"In the armory—he's finishing up the first of the arrowheads."

"Then," declared Seg briskly, "that's where I'm off."

"I'll join you."

The palace jumped. Lights festooned the alleyways between hedgerows of sweet-smelling shrubs, lamps twinkled in the trees as a tiny zephyr trembled the branches. It was a glorious night, with She of the Veils flooding down her roseately golden radiance.

"I could wish Milsi was here," said Seg. "But she has gone off with Delia."

"Ah! That means, I would guess, your Milsi is about to be inducted into the Sisters of the Rose." I shot my comrade a hard glance. "I don't know if you should be congratulated or consoled, by Krun!"

"Young Silda never had any doubts."

"Your daughter, and my son, ought really to sort things out—Silda is down in the southwest, I suppose?"

"Aye."

We strode through the various gardens and arbors until we'd skirted this side of the palace and so crossing a graveled drive walked up to Naghan's armory.

Naghan the Gnat had once been all gristle and bone; now he had filled out a trifle and his thin and wiry form filled his tunic to greater effect. Amazingly cheerful, quick and lively, he could bash his hammer on his anvil with consummate skill. He is among the finest of the armorers I have known on Kregen. Now he turned as we entered, feeling the heat from the furnace, and he held up between iron tongs a palely yellow arrowhead.

"The edge is the art of it," he said. "Seg—there are a full score over there for you."

"Well done, Naghan," I said. "And a sword?"

Naghan had worked damned hard, that was clear. He had taken the pattern of sword called a drexer which we had developed in Valka and knocked out three of them. His assistants were hard at it, bellows pumping, heat pulsing, hammers ringing, and the hissing turbulence and aromas of quenching going on neatly within the armory. Picking up a dudinter drexer I swung it about experimentally.

"Nolro!" yelped Naghan. "Fetch the quiver."

A young lad, streaming sweat to the waist, jumped to a peg and fetched down the quiver. This was a simple, plain quiver as issued to the archers of the army. Nolro handed it to Seg. It contained a score of arrows, fletched with the rose-red feathers of the zim korf of Valka.

"I had Lykon the Fletcher do these up for you, Seg," explained Naghan. "Speed is the watchword now."

Seg drew out an arrow. It lacked a point. "Thank you, Oh Gnat. I trust Lykon's handiwork. But—"

We all knew Seg liked to build his arrows himself. He now meant that he'd accept another's work in fletching the shafts, but was pleased to bind on the heads himself. This he at once started to do, there and then, at a side bench where the necessary equipment had been prepared.

The party still racketed away among the gardens of the palace. There were Jikai Vuvushis there, out of uniform, dressed exquisitely, laughing, dancing. I own I felt an ache that Delia was not here.

Still, she was removed from the lurking menace of the werewolf. That thought made me speak out, and somewhat bombastically, I confess, saying, "Now let the damned werewolf show his ugly snout." I shook the dudinter drexer. "We'll have his tripes!"

"Aye," confirmed Seg, looking up, holding the first completed arrow. "Aye, my old dom, we'll puncture him like a pincushion."

A shape skulking past the doorway by a clump of pale blue flowers in the torchlights caught the corner of my eye. I swung about. Seg was hard at it pointing up his shafts, but Naghan caught my movement and squinted out into the torchlights across the yard. He wheezed his infectious laugh and swung back to his work, saying; "Well, Dray, you must expect all that, being an emperor and no longer a kaidur!"

"Aye, Naghan, by the Glass Eye and Brass Sword of Beng Thrax himself! But it irks at times..."

The skulking shape flicked a red cape back and, seeing he was discovered, walked forward sturdily. Oh, yes, the lads of ESW and EYJ were on duty when the emperor wandered abroad.

"Hai, Erclan!" I called, and I own my voice sounded mocking even in my own ears. "You'd have been shafted for a certainty then, my lad, and well you know it!"

He looked downcast, a young, strong, eager jurukker from 2ESW, knowing he shouldn't have been spotted as he stood watch. I felt for him, for—and if this be boasting then take it as it is meant—there are very few folk, of Kregen or Earth, who can keep an unobserved watch when I do not desire that condition. I did not take pity on him; but I thought to make a small gesture to cheer him up and brace him for the next turn of this kind of duty.

"Look at this, Jurukker Erclan—a fine new blade fashioned from dudinter with which to spill the tripes of the werewolf. Here, try it."

He took the drexer and swung it about. He was from Valka and he addressed me as majister, because he was a youngster and had grown up with that form of address naturally; his father, Emin ti Vinfafn, called me strom—and no messing.

Now Fate plays us all scurvy tricks from time to time and on this occasion I thought I was particularly hard done by—wrongly, as you will hear.

When Naghan first set up his armory for the palace, he, Tilly and Delia felt it would be nice to have shrubs and flower beds not too far away, and to lessen the effect of raw power at work. So the shrubs by which Erclan had lurked and the graveled walks and the flowerbeds led naturally to other areas of the gardens. A young couple, hands and arms about waists, walked dreamily along, lost to the world in each other. Erclan, swinging the blade, looked across.

"Fodor," he exclaimed in great disgust. "Some people get all the luck and can split the wand, and others have to stand guard duty."

Because of his words I reasoned that the young lady was a bone of contention between the two guardsmen.

About to say something which no doubt would have been highly foolish, I checked. The lethal gray form that flashed into view by the path was no figment of a dream. The foam upon its jaws gleamed in the torchlight. Its eyes reflected the torchlights and speared like two scarlet bolts. Its fur bristled. Undulating with muscle, lethal with fang and claw, the werewolf pounced upon its prey.

"*Fodor!*" screamed Erclan. He flung himself forward.

A single mighty blow from a paw sent Fodor reeling into the bushes. The werewolf hunched above the shrinking form of the girl. Her shriek was lost in the horrid guttural snarls. Erclan, blade high, raced in.

Everything began, happened, and was over.

In a flurry of cape and cords and skidding boots Erclan flung himself bodily at the werewolf. The dudinter blade slashed down.

His body and the flare of the cape obscured the result of his blow. The werewolf shrieked in a hideous screaming whine. It made no further attempt to attack the girl. Erclan lifted the blade again.

The thought scorched into my brain.

"*Now we shall see!*"

The blade flashed, the werewolf snarled and bounded off, Erclan missed and swirled forward. In a few gigantic bounds the werewolf vanished beyond the shrubbery.

Seg stood at my side. He breathed hard.

"What the hell! Erclan hit the beast, I am sure of it—why—?"

I was short, abrupt, haltingly furious.

"The dudinter failed."

Ten

Kyr Emder cooks Deb-Lu-Quienyin's recipe

"The electrum blade failed!"

People were running in now and torches illuminated the scene. Erclan bent to the girl, whose long white dress tangled around her legs. We were running across, shouting. The fury that gripped me I know possessed Seg also. We had put store by dudinter to combat this menace, we had believed it would enable us to fight back at the ganchark. And now—this failure, this disaster...

Naghan the Gnat came running out clutching his three other dudinter blades. Seg snatched one, I another, and we ran along the path following the trail of the werewolf. We could see blood spots upon the gravel, black coins in the light of the moons.

Guardsmen with torches ran with us. In a mob we raced on.

From up ahead the sound of snarling, whining violence blasted the night air. The horrid sounds ceased, to be followed by a single scream, abruptly choked off. Everyone knew the werewolf had found another victim.

Full of apprehension at what we would find we roared along the path and headed past a graceful circle of lissom trees, past a dell, to burst through bushes onto the path beyond.

A guardsman lay on the path, disheveled, sprawled out, his sword uselessly by his side. Blood streamed from his shoulder, glinting black and red as the torches flared high. He tried to lift his other arm, pointing.

"That way—horrible—horrible—"

"Rest easy," I said, finding the words full of ugly uselessness.

"Fetch a needleman," someone shouted.

Some of the guards started to run on to follow the path; the bloodspots had vanished, disappearing in that magical fashion that had evanished the scrap of fur.

"Hold!" I bellowed. "It is no use chasing farther. The beast is gone. See to Wenerl the Lightfoot here. And all of you, stick close."

"Aye," they said, and looked about uneasily.

The doctors could patch up Wenerl the Lightfoot's body; I wondered what this horrendous experience had done to his mind, his courage, his resolution.

"The girl is safe, majister," said Erclan, panting up. "And Fodor has a cracked rib or two. But—" He saw Wenerl the Lightfoot. "By Vox! The beast struck again!"

I felt it incumbent upon me to attempt to take charge of fears that might slide us all into even greater disaster. What to say? Dudinter had proved false—what else was there we could oppose to this evil that stalked among us, unseen until the moment of death?

"Listen, comrades," I said in a voice only slightly raised. As usual that voice issued forth like an old rusty bucket filled with gravel being dragged up a rocky slope. They all fell silent on the instant. "This evil annoying us in Vondium is merely an evil thing. There will be ways found to destroy it. The wise men, the wizards, they will know. The priests will give us strength. I do not call upon you to have courage; for this you already have, as I well know, for have we not stood shoulder to shoulder on many a battlefield? Keep together, and do not wander off alone. I tell you this, there are no greater sorcerers than the Wizards of Loh, and we have their utmost assistance and advice. Death to the ganchark!"

"Aye," they roared. "Death to the ganchark!"

With that, and feeling mighty small, I can tell you, I went off to have a few words with Deb-Lu-Quienyin. Wenerl the Lightfoot cried out as we went off: "Hai, majister! Hai, jikai, Dray Prescot!"

As I say, I felt pretty small.

Wenerl was a kampeon, an old hand from 1ESW. On his chest he wore three bobs, and each one of these three medals represented an act of valor. He was a shiv-Deldar and knew his business. His celebrations this night had been unpleasantly interrupted, and I wondered again if the werewolf attack would shake him. I devoutly hoped not. But facing the thundering onslaught of the enemy when they are flesh and blood like you is one thing; facing the ghastly evil of the werewolf was quite another.

Speculation and gossip must now be raging throughout the folk congregated here to have a good time. Rumor would wear a hundred different guises. Hard news would have to be spread, and quickly.

Until I'd learned the meaning of what had transpired from Deb-Lu, the news would remain not hard but soft—damned soft, by Krun.

Walking rapidly at my side along the alleyways between shrubs with torchlights flaring from the trees and the hubbub of the party all about, Seg twisted the shaft between his fingers. His powerful, handsome face looked troubled.

"If the dudinter is of no use, my old dom—then what?"

"Deb-Lu will know. He would not have told us that dudinter was the answer if it was not."

"I agree. Then there is more."

"Evidently."

The Wizard of Loh was not to be found in his own quarters in his own Wizard's Tower. He'd recently accepted the services of two apprentices. These were never going to become Wizards of Loh, of course; but with the level of training afforded by Deb-Lu they could if they studied diligently turn into remarkably qualified and powerful sorcerers. For the moment they fetched and carried, prepared mixtures, hewed wood and drew water, in the old way gophering for Deb-Lu. One of them, a thin-faced lad with a wart by his nose, which was of the runny kind, looked up as we entered.

"Majister—"

"Where is your master, Phindan?"

"He took Harveng with him, instead of me, and I am to—"

"Where, Phindan, is your master? I have asked you twice."

"Yes, majister, yes. He is with Kyr Emder—"

"The devil he is!"

Seg started off at once, without bothering to lollygag about making footling remarks. I followed. Now what would a puissant Wizard of Loh want with good old Emder?

We found them both in the small kitchen to the side of Emder's quarters where he could supervise personally the preparations of the meals of which he was an expert culinary artist. Everything was spotless. The copper pans glittered in the lamplights. The scrubbed surfaces of the tables gleamed like finest linen. The fires banked to just the right temperature flickered an occasional beam from the grates. The smells were just simply delicious.

Deb-Lu's lopsided turban stood in grand isolation upon a table. He had removed his outer robe and it hung upon a hook behind the door. He and Emder were staring into a copper pot upon the stove, and they were stirring the pot's contents with a long wooden spoon. I sniffed.

"That does not smell like anything I recognize."

Both men turned sharply.

Emder smiled. Deb-Lu, busy, called out: "Jak! Excellent. You have brought the first weapons. You are just in time. Kyr Emder is invaluable in matters of this nature."

I breathed in and breathed out. I thought I understood.

Seg laughed. "So that's the way of it! I am mightily relieved, I can tell you!"

No one else was in the kitchen. I said, "You did not think to put a guard on the door?"

Carefully, Emder said: "We felt that would arouse interest and cause speculation we can do without."

"Yes, you are right."

"Is it ready, San?" Seg walked across and looked into the pot.

"The potion has but now reached the Required Proportions of Evaporation." When Deb-Lu spoke in these clearly heard Capital Letters, matters of import were in the wind.

Seg looked up.

"Potion?"

Deb-Lu sniffed. "Well, yes, Seg, you are quite right. I do not think we will convince the ganchark to open his jaws so that we may pour the liquid down. It will be more in the nature of an injection, by the Seven Arcades, yes!"

He looked around the kitchen, and, quite automatically, put up a hand to push his turban straight, only to discover the absence of that article of headgear.

"I but wait for the return of Harveng. I fear he is almost as idle as his comrade, Phindan; but they must learn hardly if they are to amount to anything in the occult world of thaumaturgy."

Deb-Lu nodded toward a ragged clump of twigs and leaves lying on the floor, striking an incongruous note of untidiness in Emder's immaculate kitchen.

"The lad sorely mistook these plants, when I gave him explicit instructions. Well, well, we were all young once."

Emder gave the mixture a prodding kind of stir.

"If Harveng doesn't return soon, San, I feel—speaking not as a wizard but as a cook—the broth will spoil."

What dire fate would have befallen Harveng we were not to discover, for he pushed the door open and trotted in. He was plump, scarlet-faced, pop of eye and prominent of ear; but he carried a branch ripped from a shrub that made Deb-Lu nod in satisfaction.

"I see I do not have to lose all faith in you, young Harveng. Right, strip the leaves off, and work fast."

This Harveng proceeded to do. With his miraculous aptitude with sharp knife and chopping board, Emder reduced the rolled leaves. His fingertips were tucked in, his knuckles out, and the knife went chop-chop-chop in a radius, first one way then at ninety degrees. Green juice oozed.

Deb-Lu used an ivory spatula to lift the chopped leaves. He weighed them on his own balance, a spindly construction of balass and ivory, silken-suspended, exact. The required amount went into the pot, and Emder took the wooden spoon and stirred with a nonchalant expert cook's twirl.

Deb-Lu heaved up a sigh.

"This must be kept close, Jak. You know the story of the Ganchark of Therminsax..."

"Everyone has heard that dudinter will deal with the werewolf, Deb-Lu. Even the werewolf must have heard—and the vile beast must have laughed, before he struck."

"Oh?"

These two had not heard the uproar, involved as they'd been with the preparation of this potion. We told them what had happened.

"And the girl is safe? And the two lads? By Hlo-Hli—what a moil! I would feel personal guilt had they been killed, for they would have died believing I had betrayed them—"

"Never, Deb-Lu, never. And Wenerl the Lightfoot is no young lad, no green coy, but a kampeon. When he grips a dudinter sword anointed with your potion he will feel very differently, believe me."

"Aye," said Seg. "And that brings up the problem, of course. It's a knotty one."

"How much of this potion is necessary?" I sniffed at the pot. The smell was not unpleasant, with an under flavor of vegetable oil and a tang of bittersweet herbs.

"A single drop is sufficient, given time. But for a more rapid success the more the better up to a reasonable limit—say a six-inch coating upon a sword—before any extra becomes unnecessary."

"Then a shaft can do it?"

"Of course, Seg, of course."

Seg lifted his arrow, looked at the Wizard of Loh, received a confirmatory nod, and so dipped the arrowhead into the pot. He stirred it about, then withdrew, flicking off a few drops. The head looked no different from before.

"That's all very well. But—how do we do it?"

I said, "I had thought, with Deb-Lu's permission, to involve the various temples in this."

"Ha!" exclaimed Deb-Lu.

"I see that." Seg laid his arrow down and drew the dudinter sword. "We must keep this secret so that the werewolf cannot learn it. If the churches bless the weapons, and anoint them, and folk know they must have an anointed weapon—yes. It would work!"

"It will work." Deb-Lu turned and glared balefully upon plump young Harveng. "This is a high secret, of thaumaturgy and of empire. You will not breathe a word of what has passed here. If you do I shall know. Then, I think, you may become—what? A little green toad? A small brown frog? A slinky shiny slimy worm?"

"No, master, no!" Harveng, plump, scarlet, near-bursting, sweating, mightily discomposed, stammered out his protestations. "Never, San, never!"

"So be it!"

Seg, Emder and I remained discreetly silent during this exercise of arcane power.

Then Seg coughed and said: "One thing, San. Steel did not harm the werewolf, for my shaft just clipped a little fur, which vanished away. And now we have this potion to turn dudinter into a proper weapon. But— what of the dudinter sword with which Erclan struck the werewolf?"

"You are right, Dudinter has power, of itself, to wound a ganchark. It will not really kill the thing, as you say you saw. It will make the beast aware that it can be hurt, drive it off."

Again Deb-Lu put up a hand to push the absent turban straight. He glanced across at me, and then away, and heaved up a sigh, and said: "Mind you, Jak. All this is In Theory Only."

"Oh?"

"Aye, aye. Dudinter—well, that is easy enough. And the potion, too, that is from my childhood. But in fact, in action. No, no, Jak. One Must Wait on Events."

"I see. You've never actually dealt with a werewolf before?"

"Precisely."

"If that blade of Erclan's made the thing run off," I said, "then a wound may be inflicted. A shrewd blow across the neck, say, might lop the beasts head, and—"

"Not quite, Jak. The werewolf by the very nature of the change must involve thaumaturgy of some kind, magic on some level. Steel bounces, as we have seen. Dudinter wounds; but it is generally held that the steel does not bounce, it—"

"How can that be?" said Emder.

"The werewolf possesses regenerative capacity of a very high order. The steel passes through fur, skin, flesh and blood, and instantly the wound heals itself. The moment the steel has passed and the cleavage made, the flesh knits together, the blood circulates."

"Would a severed neck and a lopped head have time to regenerate?"

"Indubitably."

"If the theory is correct..." put in Seg. He spoke quietly. I guessed he was wondering what effect an arrow would have, and hating to have to ask.

"Correct or not, we must act on the assumption that San Quienyin's potion will work. There is a lot told in legend and story; we must hold this close."

Deb-Lu got out quite quickly: "Oh, no, Jak. The potion is not mine. I will not tell you its history; but it is named ganjid."

Drawing the dudinter sword I said to Emder: "Have you a pastry brush? You'll get to work to produce more of this ganjid?"

"All day and night, if necessary." He brought across a pastry brush.

"And a vial, a well-stoppered one. A spice phial would do."

Seg and I took turns to paste the ganjid potion onto our sword blades. We laid it on liberally, never mind the six inches that might—or might not—be enough. The liquid sparkled for a moment on the metal and vanished. It did not seem to dry up. It was as though the potion seeped into the metal and was absorbed.

Emder brought a small bottle and this was filled and I popped it into one of my belt pouches. Seg did the same.

"You'll have to contact the four smiths, and Naghan. All the new dudinter weapons will have to be consecrated. I'll get Farris to talk to the chief priests."

"The potion will be ready," promised Deb-Lu.

We four, with Harveng, pop-eyed, looking on, must have presented an odd spectacle. A frighteningly powerful sorcerer, a valet-helpmeet, a formidable Bowman of Loh, and an emperor, standing in a kitchen clustered about a pot on the stove. And I did not forget that that famous Bowman of Loh was a king. We were like a caucus, a cabal, plotting secret doings in dead of night. If anyone had looked in, we'd have appeared downright furtive. We combated a dark and secret evil, and we were employing dark and secret remedies.

"I'll tell Targon the Tapster and Naghan ti Lodkwara to set an inconspicuous watch. We do not want anyone spying in here." I stretched, scabbarded the sword, took a hitch to my belt. "Now there's an Opaz-forsaken werewolf skulking about out there. I think I'll take a little stroll and see what dudinter and ganjid will do."

As I spoke I felt—and I admit this with no shame, no sense of falling-away—a twinge of doubt.

Would electrum coated with werebane work? Would anything work against the foul pestilence that had fallen on us in Vondium?

I saw Seg looking at me, his head a little on one side. Well, he could guess what I was thinking. Good old Seg! I roused myself.

"I want to have a go at the dratted beast myself first. I believe in your theories, your work, what you have accomplished, Deb-Lu. But—just in case—I don't want some young guardsman, some lad, having his head bitten off and me nowhere around."

Seg let rip a guffaw.

"What! Things happening and Dray Prescot not around! Never..."

The others found smiles at this, and I grumped. What I didn't know then was the truth—the awful, horrible truth—behind Seg's chaffing words.

Eleven

How two jurukkers stood guard

Nothing more was seen or heard of the werewolf that eventful night, and for the next few days I and my comrades were plunged into hectic activity. There was so much to do. The forces to be taken up to reinforce Turko had to be selected and organized. There were innumerable delegations from all over our part of Vallia to be received and treated honorably, their grievances dealt with as best as possible. Justice had to be delivered. The budget was a constant thorn. Taxes—well, I spare you that blasphemy, for, although as an emperor I needed taxes from the people to pay for everything necessary to run an empire—rickety though that was—I can wince as well as the next fellow when it comes to paying out taxes. Mind you, by Zair, there are taxes and taxes. A just tax to run your country in a proper and decent way—fine. An unjust tax to fatten up the lords—oh, no...

Still, I was the emperor and no longer a kind of Robin Hood figure. I used the taxes as wisely as I could, with the Presidio, agonizing over allocations. I refused to have any new building undertaken in the imperial palace and merely maintained what of the fabric was useful. A great deal of the old magnificence was falling into ruin.

We had to put a new wooden roof on one of the outer halls and apartments to house the Jikai Vuvushis Marion was so busily organizing for me.

I know Delia had spoken a soft word, for she did not restrict the recruitment of the new regiment to Sisters of the Sword. For this I was grateful.

"I am mightily intolerant in my choice of girls," Marion told me one fine blustery morning as we set out to check the first consignments of electrum weaponry forged by the four smiths in the city.

Among the glittering throng of riders with us, her affianced man, Strom Nango ham Hofnar, stood out splendidly.

"I am glad to hear it, Marion. Although from what little I know of these ladies, every single one is worth a regiment of mere men."

Her chin went up at this. Well, by Zair! I might not have trembled inwardly for the temerity of my remark, jocular though it was intended to be. I spoke a semi-truth, at the very least. Marion chose to change the subject and comment acidly upon the wind and the raindrops which every now and again spattered upon us.

The four smiths had worked hard and diligently. Guards stood about the stacked weapons. As is the way of these occasions, a crowd gathered to gawp.

"Well done, Smiths all," I said. I shook a thraxter high, trying to get the glimmer of Zim and Genodras to flash along the blade, and finding the dappled clouds too clustered, the rain beginning to spitter down in earnest. "See the weapons are all carefully taken to the temple. Orders will be received from the Lord Farris."

"Yes, majister."

The little scene, damp and cloudy, did nothing to cheer me up. By the disgusting diseased intestines and foul stinking armpit of Makki Grodno! Oh, I was in a right state, fretting over the safety of Vallia, itching to get off to Turko and having a bash at Layco Jhansi, cogitating how poor old Natyzha Famphreon's problems could be turned to the advantage of Vallia, feeling the pressure of many another thorny problem I have not mentioned to you. And Delia was away somewhere. Yes, as they say on Kregen, I had to accept the needle in all this.

One thing intriguing me I wished to ask Delia.

"Why," I would say after sufficient time had passed for the very necessary greetings to be suitably dealt with, "why is the new imperial guard regiment being formed from a cadre of Sisters of the Sword? Why did you not specify Sisters of the Rose? It is a mystery to me."

Well, the sooner I got the answer the better. Not, as you will readily perceive, because I'd get the answer sooner—oh no!—but because it would mean I'd be with Delia.

The day chosen for the consecration of the weapons was The Day of Opaz Sublime in Glory. Every single day, of course, has its own name. When different religions are involved then a single day may sag heavily under a burden of names.

Other religions were involved, and anxious to give their benedictions. I will spare you the listings of their names and the names of their days.

Suffice it to say, the populace crowded around to see the new dudinter weapons blessed. The priests performed their parts well. Trumpets pealed. Flags fluttered and cracked, for the day continued the blustery weather. Clouds massed and blotted out the light of the suns. Rain dropped down, and strengthened, and the gusts blew the rain into long lancing streamers into the faces of the crowds.

Someone I couldn't see in the crowd at my back and whose voice I did not know mumbled something about this being a day of ill omen.

I remained fast.

In any great enterprise one has to contend with the faint-hearted. Not by dragging him down, but by reassuring his comrades he would one day achieve success.

All the same; this did in very truth seem to me to be a day of ill-omen.

What chilled me at the very thought of it was simple.

Somewhere out there, among those crowds taking part in the ceremonies of consecration, stood a man who was not a man, was more than a man, was a werewolf.

He would be standing there in a pious attitude, head bowed at appropriate moments, genuflecting, looking up at the open-air altars and the priests, taking part in the chanting and the prayers. What would he be thinking?

Contempt for us poor mortal fools?

Cunning plans to circumvent all our own plans?

Ravenous lust and hot desire at the prospect of his next girl-victim?

Or, just perhaps, a tinge of fear?

A tiny zephyr of apprehension when he looked about at the vast crowds, and saw the dudinter weapons?

No, no. Somehow I did not believe that our Ganchark of Vondium was frightened by all our fancy weapons and our chanting and mumbo-jumbo.

He remained locked into his belief in his own supernatural prowess.

That seemed certain to me as I stood and the rain belted down and we all got soaked.

That night after we'd all taken the Baths of the Nine and eaten hugely, we heard stories coming in from the countryside of all manner of evil portents. Horrid signs had been seen. The usual scad of two-headed animals was reported. Any stupid accident was magnified into a certain pointer to disaster.

Even the Headless Zorcamen had been seen.

Now this one annoyed me, for we'd already punctured that silly superstition. Yet, folk still believed, still thought that evil times brought out the Headless Zorcamen to ride across Vallia in dire warning...

Carrying a goblet of fine Gremivoh I wandered out onto the terrace. The stars were obscured. At my back through the pillared windows the sounds of the people enjoying themselves floated out onto the night air. At the moment I craved solitude; yet if good old Seg had walked out after me I'd have been pleased to see him. He saw me go out and without a smile turned back to talk to those in the group about him. He knew my ways a little by now, did Seg Segutorio, King of Croxdrin, Hyr-Kov elect.

A single thickish figure by the head of the flight of steps intrigued me. The figure seemed to writhe about and then parted. It split into two. I sauntered over.

Well, now!

If this kind of thing was going to carry on when the regiment of Jikai Vuvushis stood guard...!

I knew the guardsman, young Nafto the Hair. He was hairy, at that. He stood tall and straight, rigid. He licked his lip as I approached, and swallowed.

I did not know the girl, of course. She was just such a Battle Maiden as those I'd seen in fights, in skirmishes and ambushes. She wore the kit of a Sister of the Sword, her rapier at her side, and, also, she carried a light halberd. This was her sign of office, stating that she was a jurukker on guard duty.

Handling this trifling but pertinent incident could be tricky. A light touch seemed to me to be essential. A heavy-handed approach might work; I doubted it.

Anyway, when a fellow and a girl catch a monotonous night guard-duty together, well, nature is nature, propinquity will strike, a man is just a man and a woman is just a woman, and well...

I said, "Lahal, Nafto. How is the lady Nomee?"

In the lights of the torches his cheeks flared up. He looked furtive. He had every damn right to be furtive. I happened to know that he was betrothed to the lady Nomee.

"Lahal, majister. She is well, I thank you."

"Good." I turned to the Warrior Maiden. "Lahal, and your name is?"

"Lahal, majister." As she spoke I thought I caught an odd random gleam of the torches from her eyes. They sparkled brilliantly. Most odd. "I am Jinia ti Follendorf, and it please you. I am but recently returned from Hamal."

"You were with Stromni Marion?"

"Yes, majister. We were rescued just in time by the Jiktar and Strom Nango."

"I have heard the story. It was a brave deed, if sad."

"Yes, majister."

"Well, now, Jurukker Nafto. You are from 2ESW, and Jurukker Jinia ti Follendorf from the new detachment of Jikai Vuvushis has no doubt been entrusted to your care."

"That is so, majister. But my tour of duty is ended and I but wait for Larghos the Dome to relieve me." As he spoke we heard the quick step upon the flagstones. "And here he is now, majister."

I stepped back and let the guards get on with it. The Deldar changed guards very smartly when he saw me in the shadows. Yet that is an injustice. Deldar Fresk Ffanglion would do his duty smartly no matter when and where. Larghos the Dome took post. Nafto stepped across to fall in beside the Deldar. Just before he gave the order to march off, Fresk Ffanglion cocked a wary eye at me.

I nodded.

Vastly relieved, he marched off to the next guard post with his detail. Slowly, after a polite word to the new guard and to his companion, Jinia ti Follendorf, I sauntered down from the terrace and wandered off into the gardens.

Once the girls were in sufficient strength to form a full-size regiment, they would stand guard by themselves. All the same, there would be times in the future when men and women stood guard duty together.

Oh, well, nature was nature. If one interfered only worse complications could ensue, tragedy might follow.

The rain had ceased, washing the air to allow the sweet night scents to permeate everything. The moon blooms were particularly strong on a cloudless night, so that with the cloud cover above all the other scents so often overlooked could be savored on this night.

Again I gave no particular thought to the way of it.

A footfall on the gravel at my back was not the quiet tread of the guards. It was, also, not Seg's usual light hunting step. I turned easily, to see Seg walking up and deliberately making all this noise for my benefit.

"Hai, Seg!" I said at once, letting him know he was welcome. Well, hell's bells and buckets of blood! There are precious few times when Seg is not welcome.

"You prosper, my old dom?"

"Hardly." I told him about two jurukkers kissing each other on guard duty.

He guffawed.

"These youngsters don't know how good they've got it, by the Veiled Froyvil!"

"When we get up to Turko and start knocking seven kinds of brickdust out of Layco Jhansi they'll have no time for amorous combat. Believe me."

"Oh, aye!"

We saw the white flitting figure of a girl running between the flower-beds, a moth in that erratic light.

As I say, again I gave no particular thought to the way of it.

Seg started forward.

"The foolish girl..."

What she was about we could only conjecture. We started at a run after her.

The hoarse snarling growls, the desperate screams, the horrid guttural sounds of bestial triumph drove us on in a lung-bursting run.

Twelve

"The dratted thing's dead all right."

Together we burst out beyond the edge of the shrubbery and stared across an open flowerbed area. The blood thumped around my body and I could feel my heart going nineteen to the dozen. The feel of the sword in my fist gave me some reassurance—some, by Krun, only some!

The werewolf appeared huge, menacing. The girl lay upon the path, sprawled, her white dress glimmering in that mothlike appearance in the random illumination.

As we raced up, the ganchark lifted his head. The muzzle gaped, sharp fangs yellow within the darkness. His eyes in that wolfish fashion burned red.

Seg skidded to a halt. His bow was in his fist.

Seg Segutorio, least of any Bowman of Loh, was not going to walk around in our present position without his famed Lohvian longbow. He drew, lifted, loosed in that lightning fast reflex that dazzles the eye.

Bending, I hurled myself forward under the shaft and to the side, keeping out of Seg's line of sight.

Before I reached the werewolf and the girl three arrows sprouted from the thing's breast.

It screeched hideously, pawing unavailingly at the shafts.

Then I was on it.

The dudinter blade smeared with ganjid slid into his belly. The blade ripped up, twisting brutally, tearing, bursting the thing's heart.

It screamed and fell.

It fell on the girl.

I gave it a vicious kick, toppling it over on its side. The girl's eyes were closed, there was blood on her skin through a long rent in the dress; but she still breathed.

Seg was with me.

We were both panting as though we'd run an enormous distance instead of the less than a hundred paces from the point where we'd first spotted the werewolf. Seg kicked the gray carcass. The hair hung lank and twisted, the vicious head lolled, the muzzle gaping, the tongue curled between those yellow fangs.

"We've done it!" said Seg. He whooped a breath. "May Erthyr be praised!"

"Aye," I said. "By Zim-Zair, I really believe the thing is dead."

"Oh, aye, my old dom. The dratted thing's dead all right."

In a hollering rush we were surrounded by guards. High-held torch-lights illuminated the scene. The pooled blood shone crimson. I ripped out an intemperate order.

"Run for the needleman! Run for a puncture lady! The girl is sore hurt."

More than one person ran off, and this pleased me.

We all stood in a ring with the torches streaming their orange hair above us. The light showed up every detail.

Some of us gasped. One or two screamed. Others cursed deep in their throats. Most of us, I was glad to see, stood looking stonily on.

The werewolf changed.

The evil metamorphosis that had gripped him slackened its hold now he was dead, loosening the bonds that chained him to the wolf form. The lank gray hair rippled and curled away. The hideous fanged muzzle shimmered as it changed, turning back into a man's mouth and chin. The ears rounded and flattened. The whole form flowed and melted as a child's chocolate doll melts in the sunshine upon the windowsill.

But, instead of sloughing away into a puddled mess, the ganchark took on another form—its true form.

We stood looking down upon the body of a young man.

Now the people gasped again, and this time there were more oaths, more curses in that crowd.

We stood looking down upon the dead body of Jurukker Nafto the Hair.

Oddly enough, in that moment, the clouds directly above us parted in a waft of an unfelt breeze. The light of the Maiden with the Many Smiles broke through, shedding a pink radiance down. In that moment the petals of the moon-blooms opened. On a sudden the air was filled with the scents of moonblooms, strikingly pungent in the night.

A stout, high-colored, buxom woman pushed through the throng, swinging her bag so that it struck shrewdly against shins in an impartial way as she cleared a path for herself. She wore a tromp-colored dress with a high collar. She glanced at poor dead Nafto the Hair, sniffed, and bent to the girl.

This formidable puncture lady was Prishilla the Otlora—Otlora being translated means something like No-nonsense.

"She'll live," she said, her voice oddly and affectionately gruff. "Now give me some room to work."

That seemed to break the spell.

Garfon the Staff could take charge. He'd handle all the ugly necessaries that, for a dizzy moment, seemed quite beyond me, emperor or no damned emperor.

Seg gave me a nudge.

"Brassud, my old dom. It's all over. Let's go and find a wet."

"Aye, You're right. Although—there will have to be an inquiry."

"Of course. Let's get out of this."

The people already on the scene hung about, and more folk running up crowded in. The place was congested, excitement rippled in the night air like lightning. I made no attempt to halt any of this. Let the people see. Let it be known that the famed and feared Ganchark of Vondium had been trapped and slain.

Bad cess to the dratted thing!

A guard appeared holding high bits of a jurukker's kit. They had been found bundled behind a bush. No doubt Nafto would have returned for them later. Well, he'd never don the kit of an imperial jurukker, never again proudly wear the emperor's insignia. He was no longer of 2ESW.

He had been a werewolf.

And now he was dead.

"D'you think they'll have him down in the Ice Floes of Sicce?"

I considered the thought as Seg led off toward the terrace.

"I don't see why not. He is, after all, a human being now, and he's dead. No doubt he'll trot around the Ice Floes for a space, meet the Gray Ones, before he—"

"Oh, I don't know about that," said Seg. "D'you think he'll ever get up to the sunny uplands beyond?"

"I really don't know. I can't find it in my heart to hate the poor devil. We've got to find out *why* he turned into a ganchark."

"I don't believe anyone ever has."

"A great load has been lifted. A black cloud has passed away from Von-dium. We'll have to have a tremendous celebration and thanksgiving service. The priests will do us proud. And there's Deb-Lu."

"Thank Opaz."

An old, a very old little ditty, popped into my mind as we went across the terrace and through the corridors to our private snug.

"March winds and April showers, Bring forth May flowers."

Well, Zair knew, the seasons on Kregen are markedly different from those on Earth. The idea was that we'd gone through the rain and the winds, now we could look forward to a time of blooming. That was the hope.

Ha!

Kregen—ah, Kregen! The world is wild and terrifying, and beautiful and enjoyable. Much goes on there that is just simply unbelievable by Earthly standards. And, also, because men are men and women are women, much goes on there that anyone on this Earth would instantly recognize. Beauty and terror go hand in hand, it seems...

In the way of things on Kregen, the little meeting of Seg, and Nath na Kochwold, and Farris and me broadened and grew, and we moved to a larger chamber where the tables were well provisioned with wine and deli-cacies. We might be up all night talking and arguing, going over and over what had occurred, pondering, wondering, planning for the future. These night-time gatherings were among the more important of periods for me, as you know, wherein much was decided that would directly affect the fate of Vallia, of Paz, and of Kregen itself. Not, of course, to mention the effect those decisions would have upon Delia and me...

The upshot of one of those decisions was that directly after the thanks-giving service the force destined for Turko would fly off. Seg and I would go. Now that the werewolf was slain, there was nothing detaining us in the capital. Farris could handle everything with the Presidio, as he and they had been doing so splendidly.

As well as being the emperor's Justicar Crebent, Farris was also the Lord Supremo of the Vallian Air Service.

"I can spare you ample vollers and vorlcas for the whole force, Dray. But let me have 'em back as soon as you can."

He didn't have to tell me why he wanted the airboats and the flying sail-ing ships of the sky back so promptly. We in Vondium had to be prepared to send forces anywhere at a moment's notice to resist invasion. We were that blind man at the center, striking out at invisible foes who attacked him from all sides.

"Thank you, Farris. Done."

Nath na Kochwold eased over. He looked just a little flushed and this was not from wine but from a nervous effort he was making. I guessed instantly what was afoot.

"Now, majis, the position is this. You are taking the Sixth Kerchuri with you to strengthen Kov Turko, who has the whole of the Fourth Phalanx. That will give him three full Kerchuris. Now, then—"

Mildly, I cut in to say, "Did you not say that this new green Fifth Phalanx you have formed needs your personal ministrations, Nath?"

"Well, I may have made that statement at one time." He gestured widely. "Of course, that might have been true. But they are not really green troops, as you well know. And they have first-class instructors. No, no. They will improve without me. But, the position of three full Kerchuris in the field, I submit, majis, does demand the personal attention of—"

"Of a Kapt of the Phalanx?"

He coughed. "You have done me the honor to name me Krell-Kapt of the Phalanx. I really do think—"

"Well, let me think on it."

Then Seg butted in, in his shrewd yet fey way.

"Three Kerchuris demand a Krell-Kapt, Dray. I think Turko, and his general, Kapt Erndor, have been controlling the Ninth Army up there excellently. But with these reinforcements..."

I said, "Any high-ranking chuktar can take command of an army and be named its Kapt. When the army's campaigns are over, the chuktar relinquishes his title of Kapt. That is simple."

"But the Phalanx is different. Nath is the Krell-Kapt of the entire Phalanx Force. They will hardly ever serve together. So the Brumbytevaxes take command of each individual phalanx, and, as we all know, the Kerchurivaxes with their kerchuris do the work. So—"

"I think, Seg, you have put your boot into your own argument. If the Kervaxes do all the work, and the Brumbytevaxes are an unnecessary luxury, there is even less need for a superior over them."

Nath took a cautious sip of his wine, did not look at me, did not look at Seg. I could see he was suffering.

The name of Brumbytevax had been given as a kind of nickname, a totem-name, to the commanders of each phalanx. It was true the Kerchurivaxes handled most of the work. And the very name of the pikemen in the files, the brumbytes, given to the commander of the whole phalanx, was in very truth a form of affectionate recognition of their position. On the other hand, the phalanx commanders had been in tough fights, when the phalanx fought as a whole—some pretty fraught encounters, too...

I said, "Brytevax Dekor might very well expect to command the Sixth Kerchuri when it arrives up with his Fourth Phalanx."

"Aye, majis, aye," groaned Nath. "That's the rub."

Fixing Nath na Kochwold—who is a man very strict on discipline—with a stern eye, I ground out: "Can you personally assure me that the Fifth Phalanx will be trained up properly in your absence?"

He stiffened. The wine-goblet drooped at his side. It was empty. He rapped out his words as though on parade.

"Aye, majister! I so assure you, as Opaz is my witness."

"Right. That's good enough for me. Thank Seg. In his cunning way of Erthyrdrin he's twisted all logic inside out. Nath, you'll come with us."

"Thank you, majister."

I turned away to find a refill, thinking what a lot of rigmarole went on when grown men wanted to go marching off to war. Give me half a chance and I'd stay at home and let some other idiot get on with the fighting and the killing. But, then, I had been landed with this job of being Emperor of Vallia, and so I had a duty to go and do what I could for the place...

The foolishness of a girl's heart was discussed, and its near-tragic end marveled at. Nafto the Hair had been something of a romancer. Well, kissing a girl whilst on guard duty was heinous enough. He had been betrothed to the lady Nomee. Yet he'd made an assignation with a young girl from the palace household—a newcomer I didn't recognize—and must have been persuasive enough to cause her to forget the werewolf. She had been warned not to go out alone at night. Yet she'd flitted off to keep her assignation, no doubt trembling with fears that had nothing to do with gancharks.

Poor Filti the Sheets was now abed, nastily cut-up by claws but otherwise physically unharmed. As I had conjectured concerning Wenerl the Lightfoot, so I wondered if Filti's mind would fully recover from her ordeal.

Deb-Lu-Quienyin looked in briefly on his way to bed. He appeared tired; but his indomitable will overcame effects of age without sorcerous aids.

We discussed what had occurred for a time, and then Deb-Lu said:

"Jak, I must comment on peculiar phenomena recently observed by me in the environs of the palace."

"Phenomena?"

"Precisely. Not, I need scarcely add, on the physical plane."

"Scarcely."

This renowned Wizard of Loh and I had passed through some harum-scarum and some frightening experiences together. He had known me as Jak. Now and again he could bring himself to call me Dray, and in general company would use the familiar term majis. But, as with a number of other people, I remained Jak for him.

"The necessity to delve back into my childhood and recall methods of dealing with werewolves, and of the formula—Emder, the dear fellow, called it my magical recipe—for the ganjid potion, distracted me considerably. Some occult force has been up to something, yet I cannot tell what that may be, for the visitations are brief."

"It's not another wizard gone into lupu and spying on us?"

"I think not. There is probably an element of spying involved. Vallia has enemies abroad. But after the death of Phu-Si-Yantong, well, one could hope we had seen the last of evil wizards."

I essayed a smile at my comrade wizard.

"On Kregen, Deb-Lu? Not to be troubled by any more evil wizards or witches? Come now, old friend, you have more faith in the inevitable than that!"

Thirteen

We fly to Turko's Falinur

My decision to fly north to Falinur aboard a vorlca, one of Vallia's sailing ships of the clouds, caused a deal of quiddities, I know, and must have seemed odd. Also, I suspect, there were a few folk who felt quite put out by that decision.

To fly aboard a voller, one of the airboats that had the ability not only to lift themselves into the air but to speed along at a good clip, was a much sought after treat. Vollers were still scarce. The two silver boxes, one containing a mix of minerals, the other cayferm, which lifted airboats, remained difficult to manufacture after the depredations in Hamal where most of them still originated. We in Vallia could make silver boxes that would lift a ship into the air and cling onto the lines of ethero-magnetic force. Thus the ship could put a keel, as it were, out and, hoisting sail, tack and make boards against the wind.

You can easily, therefore, see why I chose to go aboard a sailing flier. For a salty old sea-dog like me, although the scent of the sea might be absent, there was the breeze in the canvas, the creak of timber, the feel of a ship alive and vibrant all about me.

One day—and soon we all hoped—we would produce our own silver boxes to power vollers. I heaved up a sigh.

"What ails you, then, my old dom?" called a familiar voice.

"I was thinking of Jaezila and Tyfar."

Seg turned to look forward. We stood right in the eyes of the ship. Massy clouds soared above us as we soared over the green landscape below. Every shred of canvas was set and pulling, stiff as boards. This vessel, *Logan's Fancy*, might not be the largest sailer of the skies we had built; she was truly among the fastest.

"That Prince Tyfar needs to have his head careened and his brains scraped." Seg spoke seriously, and I did not miss the almost savage note behind his words. He had been *in loco parentis* to Jaezila during my enforced imprisonment on Earth. "By Vox! I wonder what mischief they're up to over in the Mountains of the West."

"If they can keep the wildmen at bay and ensure supplies for the silver boxes, then whatever else they get up to is their own business."

"Well, the quicker they decide, the better. Milsi wants to meet them, for a start."

"Your Milsi, Seg, is a jewel."

"Oh, aye."

"And I could wish she and Delia were with us."

"We'll just have to bash Layco Jhansi and see Turko right, then we can get back to Vondium. No doubt by that time their business with the Sisters of the Rose will be over."

"One can only live in pious hope. Ah, here comes Deb-Lu. There are things you and he must know."

"Lahal, Jak—what are these things, then?"

The breeze whispered past as we were carried along in its warm embrace. Zim and Genodras flooded down the streaming mingled lights of the Suns of Scorpio. The day was good. Yet I had information to tell these two that would cast a dark blot upon their appreciation of that bright scene.

A flurried commotion aft did not make us turn our heads. Back there a series of stout poles protruded from the side of the ship. These were the perching poles for the squadron of flutduins we carried, and these birds are, as I have often said and will no doubt say again, the best saddle birds of all Paz—in my estimation. Their flyers were lads and girls trained up by my Djangs, for Vallia had been lagging far behind other countries when it came to the use of aerial forces of animal and bird flyers.

The birds would swoop in splendidly from either side, give a neat little flick of their broad wings, do a sideslip and so land on their selected perching pole. Strong curved claws would grasp the timber. The riders would unstrap their clerketers and use the nets strung beneath to reach the bulwarks. When I looked at these perching poles bearing their aerial freight I was reminded of an abacus.

"Turko will be pleased to see those," remarked Seg.

"And these things, Jak?"

"Well now, Deb-Lu. I told you we were unlikely to be left unmolested by wizards and witches on Kregen. I've told Seg a little of what we met in the Coup Blag in the Snarly Hills away down south in Pandahem. Our ways parted then, Milsi and Seg sorted out her realm, I did what I could against the perverted followers of Lem the Silver Leem, and also against the armies being formed in North Pandahem to attack us in southwest Vallia."

"I suspect You Bear No Good Tidings."

"Yes. Phu-Si-Yantong might be dead; his shadow still hovers over us."

"Ah! I had heard rumors of a child..." There was no need for Deb-Lu to elaborate on the ways in which wizards circulated their news. He wouldn't tell me, anyway. But they kept up with what went on in their uncanny fashions.

"The Child is an uhu. A hermaphrodite, called Phunik. He has great powers already, although not yet grown into his strength. He is very much an unknown factor."

Deb-Lu looked surprised. He gave that ridiculous turban a shove. "You mean the danger comes from the child's mother?"

"Yes."

Seg said: "She'll be a Witch of Loh, for sure."

"Of course." Deb-Lu rubbed his nose. "This is amazing news. I was firmly under the apprehension that Ling-Li-Lwingling was dead."

Now it was my turn to be surprised. Surprised! By Krun, I felt the shock go through me.

"Ling-Li-Lwingling!" I yelped. "Oh, no, San, not her. The witch is Csitra—"

Seg put out a hand and caught Deb-Lu as he stumbled. If he would have fallen I do not know. If the news had shaken him into an incautious movement, if he felt dazed, I did not know. But he looked up at me with eyes that reflected a greater shadow than that which I thought I was telling him about...

"Csitra," he whispered.

"She queens it over her maze in the Coup Blag and terrorizes the whole district. I was extremely fortunate to escape from her clutches."

The Star Lords may or may not have assisted me in that fraught escape. Powerful though a wizard or witch might be, and supremely powerful though the Witches and Wizards of Loh truly are, yet their arcane knowledge pales to insignificance beside the awesome powers of the Star Lords.

For some weird reason the memory of one of the stories circulating in Vondium added significance to what we were saying. Covell of the Golden Tongue, young still and virile, a master poet, had spent months composing a stunning verse epic. This was duly staged, presented, put on, in Ramon's Club theater, which, belying its name, held seating for upwards of a thousand people on one level alone.

Covell of the Golden Tongue was shattered.

Ramon had emasculated the epic, shortened it, left out the ending, rendered the whole grotesque. I had only heard this story and could not vouch for its truth. What I did realize was that Deb-Lu's reactions at the name of the Witch of Loh, Csitra, indicated that we might plan out how events were to shape, and someone else—the Witch Csitra—would devise a new and horrible ending...

Around us in thin air the flying ships and the airboats of this little force sailed majestically on. Against the forces of sorcery we, ourselves, were puny indeed.

Seg half-turned.

"A glass of strong red for the San!" he bellowed. One of the youngsters, smart in his new uniform, sprang up and bolted aft. In only moments the glass of wine was to hand. Deb-Lu took it and drank gratefully.

"Ling-Li-Lwingling," I said. "She *was* mixed up with that devil Phu-Si-Yantong, then, after all." And, I confess it, I didn't much care for the note of uneasiness in my voice, didn't care one little bit, by Vox!

"Only insofar, from your news about Csitra, Jak, that she was able to elude him. Perhaps, she is not dead. I sincerely hope so, for there was much good in her."

I'd first made the acquaintance, passing, with scant ceremony, of the Witch of Loh Ling-Li-Lwingling down south in Jikaida City in the Dawn Lands of Havilfar. That was no long time after Deb-Lu-Quienyin and I had first met. At that time he'd no idea of the schemes dominating the crazed mind of Phu-Si-Yantong. Now I said:

"She blames us for the death of her wizard. Her uhu, Phunik, hates us all. There is no doubt that between them they mean to continue with Phu-Si-Yantong's insane plans."

A silence fell between us filled with the creak of timber and the whisper of the breeze, the flutterings of the flutduins and the busy work of the ship about us. Gray and white clouds ahead indicated we might have to think about a course change soon. All that fascinating aerial navigation and ship-handling could be left to the captains and their officers. More and more I found these good folk who knew their tasks a trifle reticent when I wandered in to lend a hand. This was understandable; but I regretted the passing of that phase of my career as an emperor.

Seg at last said: "When we were escaping from the Coup Blag and making our way through that dratted jungle in Pandahem, we had a visitation. A phantom in a golden throne appeared in midair. We took that to be Csitra spying on us."

Sharply, I said: "And Deb-Lu, you are confident she has not been spying on us here?"

In answer the wizard began with circumlocution.

"We Wizards and Witches of Loh keep our secrets close, as we must. I can tell you a little, for I know that there has seldom, if ever, been a relationship between Lohvian Sorcerers and non-Lohvian Sorcerers as exists between us." He did not push his turban straight, although it toppled dangerously over his ear. "Phu-Si-Yantong and I studied together. We were not too close. There were others we held in greater esteem. But he and I were on a par."

A shout from the foretop took my attention over the bows. A tiny black dot showed ahead skipping between the clouds. As Deb-Lu continued to speak I watched that distant speck.

"I do know that Yantong desperately desired Ling-Li-Lwingling, and that she, considerably younger, wanted nothing of him. Our codes—well, I can say that he could not force her with thaumaturgy for the punishment that would fall on him. The witch, Csitra, desired Yantong and remained faithful to him throughout—and her powers were mirrored in his."

I said: "I believe her to be a woman who remains faithful to one man."

Deb-Lu nodded. The turban swayed. "That is true."

"Then I breathe a little easier."

Seg's voice reached me over my shoulder, for he stood a little to the rear and side and he, too, I guessed, was watching that approaching dot in the distance.

"Oh, my old dom? That sounds highly mysterious."

I did not laugh lightly, although, in all truth, the situation could have called for an affected reaction of that kind.

"In all the horror and the maze of the Coup Blag, Csitra pretended to be Queen Mab—"

"She what!" exploded Seg.

"I was taken in for a space. Then, when she made perfectly plain that her advances were strengthened by witchcraft, and I came to my senses, and escaped—"

Seg did not quite guffaw; but infectious amusement bubbled in his words. "She took a shine to you! She fancies you! Oh, oh, my old dom, you've a lot to answer for when certain people gather around..."

Well, I still believed passionately that I'd done enough to escape the clutches of Csitra through my own belief in Delia. The Star Lords had given me a breathing space in which to make good my escape. But Seg was right. Csitra had prevented her child, Phunik, from torturing me to death. I still believed she would not allow that. So we had a time in which to fight back.

Yantong had thought to use me, and so had ordered his human tools not to have me assassinated; now Csitra gave the same orders through her misguided passion.

It was, as you will readily perceive, ironic. All I was concerned with was staying alive until my work in Vallia and Paz was completed.

The speck flitting between the clouds broadened and grew, sprouted wings, glittered with harness, turned into a wide-pinioned flutduin breasting the air in a long slanting descent to our leading ship.

"That'll be a messenger from Turko welcoming us in."

"Aye," I said. "And I hope he brings news of better weather. We'll have to circle around those clouds, I think."

Deb-Lu at last lifted a hand and pushed his turban straight. "I shall continue to make observations to discover what these swift flashes of thaumaturgical art may be. I'll have a word with Khe-Hi. He may be experiencing the same effects with Prince Drak in the southwest."

The incoming flyer made a straight line for *Logan's Fancy*. Superb birds, flutduins, masters of the air. The rider sat hunched and I caught no glimpse of weaponry jutting arrogantly upwards, streaming his colors.

With a single half-circle to bring him around and match speeds, the flutduin rippled those powerful wings, his claws extended and he was down, gripping to a perching pole. Seg and I walked aft to greet the messenger. When we reached the cleared space of deck paralleling the line of perching poles, we could see that all was not as it should be.

Four crewmen were out on the nets, balancing, bringing the flyer in. His arms and legs dangled. Those arms under the flying leathers would be banded with sleeves of ocher and umber checks, lined-out in red. Those were the colors of Falinur, the schturval of Kov Turko.

The Ship-Deldar, Bolto the Knot, looked up from the bulwarks where he'd been yelling at his men. As the Bosun, he had, perforce, to possess a pair of lungs. His hard and lumpy face reminded me of the time he'd taken those lumps fighting at my side.

"He's sore hurt, majister. I've sent for the needleman; but there seems little chance for the poor fambly."

We watched as the men brought the messenger inboard and placed him down on hastily piled cloaks. He looked ghastly, and an arrow stood between his ribs. The feathers of that shaft were a hard bright blue.

At this, Seg's face tautened.

The messenger was a Brokelsh, his hair coarse and his ways, no doubt, uncouth; yet he was a man and he was dying. He tried to speak, and blood frothed his lips.

"Kov Turko sends... urgent... meeting place... hurry—"

His head lolled, his eyelids closed, and he was dead.

Dolan the Pills, the needleman, stood back and shook his head.

"There is nothing I can do for him, poor fellow."

We stood there grouped about the dead man. He had given his life to serve Vallia, yet we did not know in what fraught action he had died. There was no need for me to do or say anything regarding the proprieties. The sailors of Vallia know how to respect their dead.

Presently, when we'd gone into the cabin to drink a small private toast, Captain Nath Hardolf came in to say that in his opinion the change of course would have to be made within the next glass. The clouds ahead looked more ugly by the moment...

"Well, now, Captain Nath," I said, lowering the glass. "Let us have the charts out."

He gave me a puzzled look; but the charts of the land ahead were brought in. We bent over them spread upon the table, the glasses and bottles pushed to the side.

"Here," I said, and stabbed a forefinger down, "is where we agreed to meet Kov Turko."

Captain Nath Hardolf could see, all right.

He was representative of those master sailing captains of Vallia, seasoned, experienced, long in the tooth. He had had his share of tragedies and triumphs in life, and command of *Logan's Fancy* was perhaps not with him the pinnacle of his career it would have been to a less-experienced master mariner.

The point where we had agreed to meet up with Turko's wing of the army he commanded here lay directly beyond the storm. The gale could broom us all away, could blow us to Hell and Kingdom Come. If we tacked around the gale we would take so much longer that whatever the urgency that had given that poor dead messenger his quietus would never receive any help from us. By the time we arrived up, Turko and his army could have been destroyed.

"Very good, majister," said Captain Hardolf. "I'll see everything is battened down."

"Excellent. Pass on the message to the rest of the fleet. We are going straight through that damned storm up ahead, and gale or no gale, it won't stop us from reaching Kov Turko in time."

Fourteen

The Battle of Marndor

An armada of sails coursing through thin air... The streaming mingled lights of the Suns of Scorpio sheening from straining canvas... The sparkling glitter striking back from gilding and gingerbread, from ornate high-flung sterns and towers, from shooting galleries and menacing boarding platforms... Oh, yes, the sailing ships of the skies of Kregen provide a spectacle dazzling and inspiring. Silently above the land they soar, the wind of their passage lost and blown away in the breeze.

And I, Dray Prescot, Lord of Strombor and Krozair of Zy, calmly gave orders that would hurl all that mighty armada between the jaws of destruction ahead.

For, make no mistake about it, just because I said the gale would not prevent us from joining up with Turko's army did not mean we would. Oh, no! My bravado could toss all away in ruination...

There is a saying common in the seas of Paz that a smart vessel is 'All shipshape and Vallian fashion.'

In the moments before we plunged into black danger those aerial sailors of Vallia proved the saying true.

The vollers with their command of forward motion took the vorlcas in tow, for the latter's sails would be of no help, would be a positive hindrance in the fight ahead. Tow ropes were passed, the wires made fast. In a sighing flutter of multi-colored collapse, all the canvas came in. There was time for some of the vessels who possessed them to strike their topmasts. We battened down.

The flutduins were brought in off their perching poles. The magnificent birds sensed the foul weather ahead, and made only a few formal protests at being cooped up. A wing beat, the wide gape of a beak, and then they settled down. The poles were run in and lashed down.

All this was repeated in all the vessels, signals flickering like summer lightning from mast to mast.

"We're ready, majister." Captain Nath Hardolf stumped up to make his report.

"Excellent, Cap'n Nath. Now, by Vox, we shall see!"

"By Corg, majister! I think I shall enjoy this day. It will be something to make the blood run more freely in my veins."

I eyed him. Yes, his professionalism and experience were of such an order that little excited him in these latter days of command. Well, now, he was being handed a little excitement. One is never too old to learn, never too old to love, never too old to taste of life...

In his daily life and with his usual professional caution, Captain Hardolf had probably never been anywhere near a storm for years...

The gale would refresh him, test him, and play havoc with the fleet. Battened down, all made fast, we coursed on through the air toward those frowning pinnacles of cloud. The blackness rose up before us and the lights of day faded and muted to a wan ghostly underwater luminosity, which rapidly sloughed away into blackness.

The gale took us in its jaws and shook us. The wind shrieked and howled and scourged us. We forged on.

Well, well... There are gales in life, and we weather them or we do not. Like a broken quarry in the fangs of a leem, we struggled feebly and resisted as best we could. This gale did what it had to do to us, and we took our punishment, and we did not give up the fight, and at last, we broke through into the streaming lights of Zim and Genodras beyond...

A goodly proportion of the folk aboard wore green faces...

Only two tows parted. The shipwrights of Vallia build well and only one vessel was shattered and broken into pieces and so fell all that awful distance to the ground with her people spilling out like dust shaken from a broom.

Not everyone had been issued with a belt containing its two small silver boxes which would keep a person drifting gently to the ground. Not all. We in Vallia built what we could with the resources we had. These horrors are the price of empire. Once more I knew that I was racing past the point at which I could no longer face the spiritual agony of paying that price.

"We have done well, majister." Captain Hardolf's face held a flush along the cheekbones. He looked sprightly. "Now I believe Corg does sometimes smile on us."

The ship that had foundered, *Naghan's Reply*, had been one of the older vessels of the force, containing spearmen. The loss was regrettable, but I felt thanks that we had not lost any brumbytes, or archers, or heavy infantry. Of cavalry we were short—as usual. The flutduin aerial force was going to have to perform prodigiously.

Seg had taken the blue-fletched arrow embedded in the body of Turko's messenger and he studied it intently. I understood his unease and shared it. At least, we did have a splendid regiment of my own Valkan Archers with us.

Marion's Jikai Vuvushis kept in good heart—nor was there any reason to suspect they would not. My own crusty kampeons in the guard corps took everything in their stride, phlegmatically, cursingly, explosively, according to their natures.

So we soared out into the radiance of the twin suns, spewed out like pips from an orange. We were still battened down. We were battered. Some malignant fringes of the gale threw a last cavort of wind at us, tumbling us about. Spread out below us across the plain lay the tents and encampments of an army.

This army had been harassed by the storm, for many tents had been blown down, animal lines broken and we could almost muster smiles at the antics of the folk down there, chasing over the plain after the stampeding animals.

"Plenty of space to let down," observed Captain Hardolf. "We shall not be troubled by trees, I fancy."

"The quicker we are down and can set ourselves to rights, the better." Seg's voice, as sure and calm as ever, reassured me in an odd way. I felt edgy. Well, by Zim-Zair, didn't a fellow have every right to feel off-color and snappy when through his own orders other good men and women went in peril of their lives?

Our appearance caused an immediate stir in the camp below. As we lowered through the air the pale blobs of faces turned up, we could see people running, and many of those off chasing runaway animals started back for the camp.

"Turko has a sizable force here," observed Nath na Kochwold. He leant over the rail, shading his eyes.

"What the hell was his hurry?" demanded Seg.

The first ships touched the ground. Crewmen sprang out to make all secure. When I went over the side I knew there would be a great gang of hulking lads to surround me. And, now, there would be the lithe forms of Jikai Vuvushis among that formidable guard...

The breeze in the aftermath of the gale still blew briskly; the air held that fresh minty tang and the grass glittered with millions of spearpoints of light. One after the other the vessels touched down. We took up a neat and prescribed pattern for landing. A damned great voller came down in front of *Logon's Fancy* and obscured my view of the camp.

"Well, Turko'll be rushing across here as fast as he can," I said. "We'd better go down to meet him."

"I'm looking forward to seeing that man again," said Seg, and he rubbed his hands.

"If you want to try a fall or three with him, Seg—"

"What!" He laughed. "I'd as lief try to wrestle a mountain out of the ground, or a river from its bed."

"Very poetic." A very great Khamorro, a master of the martial arts, Turko. His bare hands were far more lethal than many a weapon in other less-skilled hands.

Afterwards, we tried to work out who had yelled first. No one could say who it was who first raised the alarm. All we did know was that in one moment we were thankful to be down and out of the gale, disembarking to greet friends, and in the next we were facing foemen viciously determined to destroy us all.

"The colors!" The yells racketed up. "Those are not the colors of Falinur! That's Vennar!"

And so it was.

Instead of Turko's banners of ocher and umber checks lined out in red, with the dragon as a dramatic symbol overhead, we could make out the colors of Vennar, ocher and silver, with the strigicaw as the symbol.

"Layco Jhansi!" I said. I felt like spitting. "Now we know what Turko's messenger died trying to tell us!"

Yes, we were caught by surprise. The ranks of Jhansi's men formed as they ran up from their camp. They were smart. The man who had been the old emperor's chief pallan, who had run his empire for him, who had conspired and tried to murder the emperor, whose treason had borne bitter fruit, was no man to employ mercenaries who were not top class.

In all the hullabaloo and rushing about, the lads of the guard corps showed that they, too, were not men to be flurried over falling into a trap. Even if, as evidently was the case, this was an unpremeditated trap.

In the nature of the composition of the guard corps the natural rivalry between the Emperor's Sword Watch and the Emperor's Yellow Jackets impelled mutual speed; by Bongolin! To see the lads whipping on their armor, latching all fast, clapping on their helmets, grabbing their weapons! They were rough, tough, hairy fellows, and I echoed Old Beaky himself when I say that they might not impress the enemy, but, by Zair, they impressed me.

While all this went on I leaped for the ratlines of the mainmast and went up as though I was back in a seventy-four in Nelson's Navy. Up and up to the cross-trees and there I could swivel and take a good look at the wasps' nest we had stirred up by falling into it.

There were a lot of them. This was a sizable force, twice ours, I estimated. I looked for the archers. That blue-fletched arrow through Turko's messenger told me what I would see, and I did.

Bowmen of Loh.

There they were, running to form their shooting blocks. Tall, redheaded men, and each with a great Lohvian longbow and a quiver of the shafts fletched with the feathers of the king korf, they were the most renowned of the archers of Paz. Layco Jhansi's pact with the Racters served him well, for hiring mercenaries of this quality took more than mere money. They demanded certain guarantees before they hired on. Jhansi had clearly given those guarantees; the right to plunder after the victories was only one.

A rapid survey of the situation convinced me that we could win the coming fight if we acted decisively and rapidly. I shinned down to the deck and yelled for Captain Hardolf.

"Majister?"

"Signal the fleet. We are taking off."

"Do what?" yelped Seg.

"Majister!" bellowed Nath na Kochwold. "My lads are disembarking now, ready for the fight—"

"Your Kerchuri will be shot to pieces, Nath."

"My chodku and your Valkan Archers will afford cover—"

"We can't run away," said Seg. "Turko—"

"Turko arranged to meet us here, on the Plain of Marndor, and sent a messenger to tell us to hurry somewhere else. Clearly, he has been driven back."

"In that case we blatter this lot and so relieve him."

The devil of it was, Seg was right. I was growing faint-hearted in these latter days, me, Dray Prescot. Yet the thought of sending this force of fine lads and girls to fight and die repelled me.

In any event, our hands were forced; for Jhansi's men simply put in a thundering great cavalry charge straight at us. Clearly, they hoped to topple us in this first onslaught and so win outright.

Rushing out from the ships and forming up as we were, Jhansi could do it. He could hit us before we were formed.

"Get some vollers aloft!" I bellowed. "Attack from the air. Break out the flutduins! *Bratch!*"

I grabbed Nath na Kochwold. I actually gripped his arm.

"Nath! Keep your Kerchuri close. Shields well up. We'll put you in when their first onslaught is blunted."

"But—"

"Do it!"

"Quidang!"

Targon the Tapster and Naghan ti Lodkwara came up to report 1ESW formed and ready to go and get stuck in—as they phrased it.

I said, "Good. You may have to bear the brunt at the beginning."

"As will we, majister!" roared Clardo the Clis, scarred, plug-ugly, his yellow uniform brilliant.

"Aye, majister," agreed Drill the Eye in his fiery way, squat and with a bowman's shoulders, his yellow uniform a match for Clardo's.

Clardo the Clis commanded the churgurs and Drill the Eye the archers of the First Regiment of the Emperor's Yellow Jackets. They were not to be outdone by their comradely rivals of 1ESW.

Fakal the Oivon, swarthy, was with them, a little in the background as ever. Larghos the Sko-handed, that long-featured hyrpaktun from Gremivoh, was not with us, having gone to command the staff-slingers of 3EYJ.

Marion stepped up, scarlet, ready to burst out with Zair knew what kinds of rhetorical promises.

Quickly, I said, "Marion, I want your girls near me in this fight. See to it."

She jumped, lost some of her color, said: "Quidang!"

Targon leered a laugh. "I'm not too happy about leaving you with a bunch of lassies—"

Marion, again, started to speak, and Seg butted in.

"I'll take the Valkan Archers and play on 'em a bit, warm 'em up. Mind you hit 'em good!"

"Oh, aye!"

The way everyone wanted to interpose their bodies between me and the incoming shafts, the charging lance!

"This should prove interesting, Seg. I trust you'll show these Bowmen of Loh what shafts fletched with the feathers of the Valkan zim korf can do."

"As Erthyr is my witness."

Trumpets pealed. Everyone ran off to their posts. Korero closed up at my back and nothing was going to shift him from there. Volodu the Lungs spat and wiped the mouthpiece of his battered lump of a trumpet.

Cleitar the Standard shook out my battle flag, the flag fighting men call Old Superb. Ortyg the Tresh lifted the Union Flag of Vallia. Well, we were ready as we would be...

Flutduins lifted away. Their riders glittered in the shafts of light from Zim and Genodras. Vollers swept up into the air. We might be outnumbered two to one; we had air support and that would tip the balance.

If it did not—an exit and a quietus for us all.

What came to be known as the Battle of Marndor thus began in a most messy and ill-disciplined fashion.

Jhansi, too, had an air component. He had hired mercenaries riding fluttrells, those awkward birds with the ridiculous headvane that can so unsettle a flyer upon their backs. These swept up in a cloud to meet our own flyers.

Our soldiers tumbled out of our ships, formed their ranks, slanted their weapons. The vollers swept aloft and turned, keeping formation, lining out to rain fire and destruction down upon the heads of the enemy.

Our aerial cavalry might be airborne and surging forward into action; our ground cavalry was in an altogether different state. We had employed properly equipped vessels to transport the saddle animals, ships with stalls and pens and as much comfort as we could contrive. The gale had thoroughly upset the animals. They were refractory, unwilling to leave their pens, kicking and squealing. Only a few burs' time in which to quiet down would have made the difference. As it was, we were going to have to fight this battle with precious little ground cavalry.

I was almost in a mind to order the cage-ships aloft again and get them out of the way. But Jiktar Mophrey, commanding the totrix heavies, pleaded for a chance, and so I relented and he went back to his ships cursing and yelling and waving his riding crop in a veritable fury of determination to get into action.

Here, again, even in this fraught moment, I could review the anomalous situation that here in our army, which was so short of animals, my guards possessed two animals each man—and yet that seemed necessary. The guards performed work astride their zorcas which they could not riding nikvoves.

The commanders of the guards had sized up the situation and seen that this day they'd have to fight as infantry. This they could do supremely well. I stood to watch them form and march out, rank on rank, gleaming, magnificent, marching as one.

"That's where I should be," I said, fretfully, to Korero.

"Maybe. And maybe a commander should be where he can direct the battle."

Sharp, Korero, the golden Kildoi. His two massive shields slanted over me, borne indifferently in any of his four hands or his hand tail. If a shaft winged in past that defense, it was more likely to hit Korero than me, and chafe though I might, this was decreed—by Korero the Shield.

"When I blow," said Volodu, "they'll hear me better here."

Grumpily, I agreed. But I made a compact with myself that when the time came, I'd be up there with the lads, charging home. When I did, my small retinue would be in there with me, hollering and whooping with the best.

The first headlong onslaught of Jhansi's cavalry was checked, as it should have been checked, by our own dustrectium. Then I saw his Bowmen of Loh moving up. They marched solidly, compact, rank on rank. I estimated he had close to five hundred archers there, a full regiment.

Seg had to reduce them to give us the chance to strike back. His Valkan Archers, elated at their success over the charging cavalry, licked their lips and settled down to serious shooting.

The contest was not to be decided by archery alone. From the air our vollers swooped down. Archers shot. Varters twanged and rocks hurtled down. Fire pots spat and sizzled.

Well, as you know I have fought on battlefields that were lost. I have been routed from the field. But, to the honor of Vallia, we had been in the habit of winning our battles recently. This one was going to be closely run.

The massed blocks of Bowmen of Loh did not relish the aerial attack. Many of them shot upwards. Superb archers though they truly are, even Bowmen of Loh have difficulty giving a true account of their prowess against swiftly darting targets swirling bewilderingly above them. When Seg's Valkan Archers loosed into the blocks, we could all see the gruesome results.

The massed ranks of Bowmen swayed. In only moments they were broken. In a rush, they routed off.

We all cheered, unrecking of the horror going on as men fled in blind panic from that field of blood.

Dismayed though Jhansi must have been at the sight of the flower of his infantry thus summarily dismissed, he did not waver. A second great cavalry charge roared in.

This was treated as harshly as the first.

His aerial cavalry had all been seen off, the fluttrells stumbling against the sky to escape. Now our flutduins came winging back, sharp bright points to inflict more grievous wounds on the forces below.

"He still has his infantry," said Korero.

"Aye. He must pay well. They stand firmly enough."

"Not masichieri, I'll warrant."

"No. Volodu, do you blow 'Phalanx Advance'?"

All Volodu did in answer was to put his battered trumpet to his lips and fairly blow a call that pierced shrillingly through all the hubbub.

Instantly the trumpets of the Kerchuri took up the call. Each of the six Jodhris forming the Kerchuri blew the advance, and each of the six Relianches forming a Jodhri echoed that thrilling impulse forward. The phalanx moved. It was not a full Phalanx, a Kerchuri only, yet it shook the ground. The helmets all came down, the shields slanted at the regulation angle. The pikes snouted forward in a bristle of death. The phalanx moved.

On the flanks the Hakkodin with their halberds and two-handed swords guarded any attempt to penetrate the formation. The chodku of archers covered the brumbytes with a sleeting umbrella of shafts.

Alongside the phalanx the heavy infantry, the churgurs, sword and shield men, advanced in their ponderous and yet deceptively swift gait. The whole force advanced.

It was not over yet.

Jhansi had more men than did we. He fought them well, but he could not handle the air.

When the phalanx hit his infantry it was as though a maddened bull burst through a flimsy garden fence.

Splinters of his infantry spun away. The plain was covered with running men throwing away sword and shield, spear and bow. The phalanx stormed after them.

Over the solid files waved the battle flags, and the pike heads gleamed and glittered in the radiance of the suns.

We had lost our spearmen in the gale. We followed up the wreck of Jhansi's army for a space, and then the recall blew. We had no light infantry, kreutzin, to chase and harry the rout, no cavalry to make sure no further stand was made.

We scarcely needed them.

From the air, from voller and flutduin, the ruin below was harassed, pursued, given no rest.

We could let them get on with that until the Suns of Scorpio sank beneath the horizon.

Now we could get our breath back and take stock. Now would come the grim reckoning.

Deflated, drained, I turned away from that dying scene.

Thus ended the Battle of Marndor.

Fifteen

In the Fletcher's Tower of the Falnagur

Turko the Khamorro picked me up, twirled me around, and slammed me down on the mat.

He stood back, hands on hips, and laughed hugely.

"You're getting soft, Dray Prescot! Your muscles are turning to water! Your resolution leaks away like the snows in spring!"

I pushed up, breathing hard, and glared.

"You are right, Turko, damned right. I am grown soft in these latter days. But, my friend—"

And I started after him.

A supreme example of perfection in musculature, Turko. He had a damned handsome face, too, bright and merry, knowing with a way that mocked and cut me down to size. The Khamorros, from the land of Herrell way down south in Havilfar, are famed and feared. It is whispered that they know secrets by which they may break and crush a man's bones. They so do.

No Khamorro is frightened to go up against a man wielding a weapon. In matters of the martial arts they reign supreme, alongside the Martial Monks of Djanduin and one or two other coteries of people who understand the Disciplines and the way of the hand's edge. They are supreme in all of Havilfar, with the Martial Monks. I remain convinced from my own personal knowledge that the Disciplines of the Krozairs of Zy give the Krozairs the edge. But very very few folk of Havilfar or of the other eastward lands of the grouping called Paz visit or know of the existence of the inner sea of Turismond, the Eye of the World.

So in the salle of the palace Turko and I tried a few falls. And it was as it usually was—in the end Turko was flat and, glaring up with that mocking laughter in his face, cried out: "Very well, Dray. I bare the throat. Perhaps you are not so decrepit, after all."

There was no answer to that. So I said, "Let us go up to your Fletcher's Tower and have a wet. Seg will be waiting."

We toweled down after standing for long enough under the showers. With robes slung casually about us we left the salle and crossed to the Fletcher's Tower. This had once been called the Jade Tower before Seg, when he was kov here, renamed it. We were in what Turko called his palace. This was, in truth, the castle-fortress of the Falnagur, which dominated the capital city of Falanriel.

"I own I'm surprised you didn't give the Fletcher's Tower a new name, Turko."

"Names outside Herrelldrin mean little, Dray. And, you will no doubt take the first opportunity to mock me, I sometimes wear a sword—"

I was truly astounded.

"You do what?"

"Oh, aye, I do."

I shook my head.

"Ice should freeze in a Herrelldrin Hell."

"Things have changed for me since you made me the Kov of Falinur."

"For the better, I am convinced, once we've got Jhansi off our necks."

"I wish I'd been with you at that little dust-up. Are you really going to call it the Battle of Marndor?"

"For myself, I wouldn't bother. But it was a fight. Men were killed. There was bravery. The men deserve it."

"Medals, you mean?"

"Why not? It was worth a bob to be worn with pride upon the chest."

"Agreed."

Turko had, as we suspected, been driven in with his army wing, and had sent to change the meeting place. The results of that were lying in hospital. The trouble was that now that Jhansi, with his confounded pact with the Racters to his north, could hire mercenaries from overseas, he could bring much greater forces to bear. The frontier between Vennar to the west and Falinur to the east ran north and south in a virtually indefensible line. Jhansi could pick his place to hit, hit and run. Turko had been doing very well in clearing out Falinur. Now all that work looked as though it had gone for nothing.

The battlemented fortress of the Falnagur had been taken in a furious onslaught, a coup de main, and now Turko could lord it in his own provincial capital. As we went through into the inner ward and up through narrow winding stairs, I recalled visiting Seg here. Times change, times change. Then Seg's wife Thelda could do nothing but prate about Queen Lushfymi of Lome. Now Thelda was happily married to Lol Polisto, the old emperor was dead, and Queen Lush was actively trying to marry my son Drak.

As to where Thelda might be now—well, tsleetha-tsleethi, as they say, softly-softly. That information might unsettle Seg. But, no! Of course not. Seg had thought Thelda dead and gone to the Ice Floes of Sicce. That she was alive and happy with Lol Polisto had brought him a kind of peace, for in Milsi Seg had found the perfect partner.

Kapt Erndor joined us as we went into the private snug.

"Hai, Erndor!" I said, shaking hands. "I am right glad to see you."

"Lahal, strom. We are in a pickle here, as you can see. But, now that you are here—"

"Kov Seg and I bring few regiments."

"I was not, strom, referring to regiments."

I'd guessed he wasn't. But these old Freedom Fighters of Valka, who take such pride in calling me strom instead of majister, they take a lot of beating. They are so hard, so gritty. Kapt Erndor, now, who had fought shoulder to shoulder with me when we cleared out Valka, he could roll between two millstones and grind them to powder.

For all that, Valkans are a lighthearted lot of rascals, ever ready to sing a song and drown a sorrow, to take their jug and wave it in the air as they yodel, as to brandish their swords...

Seg called out: "I've poured. It's a real Jholaix."

"By Morro the Muscle!" exclaimed Turko. "What it is to be married to a lady of a wine family of Jholaix."

Seg looked up as we went in. He was just finishing pouring the wine. Milsi and he had brought cases of the superb vintage after their second marriage in Jholaix. That had all gone off well, and Milsi's family had welcomed Seg. That there might be other reasons for that could be gone into later. Right now, Seg's and Milsi's bounty waited to be tasted.

"Superb!" pronounced Erndor, and his grim face cracked into a broad smile.

"And the news is bad," said Seg. He'd just returned from a private reconnaissance of the lands of which he had once been kov. What he told us made us frown.

"You are only confirming what I already know, Seg." Turko sipped carefully. "But I am glad you can verify what I say. I know I must sound depressing."

"Not depressing, Turko," I said, sharply. "Realistic. You've done extraordinarily well up here in Falinur. But for that damned pact—"

"Well, can't we sabotage that?"

Seg was looking around this room. Once he had lived here with Thelda. I said nothing, could say nothing; I just trusted he was himself.

Turko's ideas of decoration had changed the room. There was a single bow upon the wall, a single sword, a single spear. Pelts covered much of the masonry. Of pictures, Turko possessed a collection of action poses of people throwing each other about. Of statues he had a few silver ones, most of bronze, and these, too, were of men and women wrestling.

The tables were well provided with food and wines. The chairs were deep and comfortable. We could talk and argue and plan here all night.

A flick-flick plant upon the windowsill curled its tendrils, seeking flies to pop down its orange cone. Turko had imported some pleasant-smelling blooms which stood about in pots of Pandahem ware. I sat down, stretched out my naked feet, and took up Seg's Jholaix.

"Here's to Milsi," I said.

We all solemnly drank. By Krun! It was good!

"Now let's find a way of bashing Jhansi."

Erndor rolled out the map upon a cleared space on the table. We all sat looking at it, and, I own, not a little glumly.

"I," I said, "have not a single idea in my stupid vosk-skull of a head."

"One thing," said Seg. "The Ninth Army is in good heart despite the setbacks."

"Oh, aye," confirmed Erndor. "They keep up, they keep up. But I wonder how much longer they can go on being pushed back from territory so hardly won."

"What information do you get from your spies, Turko?" I eyed him alertly. "If we could receive timely news just where that cramph Jhansi intends to attack—"

"Many men and women have been sent. We get scrappy information back. The last two pieces of news were false."

"He's penetrated your apparat there, and misleads you."

"Yes. We marched out to where we expected to find his army, and he crept in behind our backs and sacked two towns."

"A bad business."

A silver bowl of squishes stood on the table. I picked out one of the little fruits, looked at it, then deposited it where it filled my mouth with taste.

"Aye," said Turko. "I'd like to see Inch again. We communicate and he fights like a demon for his Black Hills."

"With Inch and you, Turko," said Seg, fretfully, "we ought to crush Jhansi like a rotten nut."

"It seems to me," I said, "that the days when we were all wandering adventurers, seeking our fortunes in the wide world, are all over. Now you're kovs, with lands and responsibilities—" I stopped. Then I said, "At least, Inch is a Kov with a fight on his hands; you, Turko, are here with your back against the wall—"

"And I am without lands," said Seg. "Well, that does not worry me."

Quite casually, I said, "You are marked to be the Hyr Kov of Balkan when the present incumbent dies off, for he has no heirs."

Turko and Erndor had the sense to remain silent.

Seg fetched up a breath. "I am supposed to be the King of Croxdrin. That means only that if it makes Milsi happy, so be it. We shall go back there from time to time. But Balkan? They always keep out of trouble."

"Precisely. They serve only themselves up there. It's a rich province. You'll do nicely up there, Seg, and if, like me, you're a permanent absentee landlord, then they'll keep the place going and the cash rolling into your coffers."

"It is generous—hell, no, that's not what I mean."

"Well, drink up this splendid Jholaix your wife has kindly provided, and let us get back to thinking of ways of bashing Jhansi."

"I'll speak to you later about this, my old dom, by the Veiled Froyvil, yes!"

So we talked more about Turko's problems. I should mention here that Balkan is pronounced with both a's flat, rhyming with ashcan. It was no ashcan of a province, though; Balkan was an immensely rich Hyr Kovnate. Its schturval was brown and red, its symbol an eagle.

As I sipped the splendid wine and the talk drifted on I found myself reflecting on just how funny a lot it was to be an emperor. The powers of such a one may appear enormous to the uninitiated. The truth is, as I have pointed out, the powers vary with strength and character, with the influence of other governing bodies, with factions, with the goodwill of the populace, with business and banking interests. Many an emperor takes the estates of deceased nobles who have no heirs into his own hands. He may then, if he pleases, bestow them upon loyal friends. How easy, it may seem, just to say to dear old Seg: "You are the Hyr Kov of Balkan!"

Well, in the ferocious and pragmatic ways of Kregen, Seg might have to fight for his new kovnate.

The talk turned then and drew me back.

"With the new accretion of flyers," Kapt Erndor was saying just as the knock came on the door, "I can set up a reasonably efficient system of aerial patrols."

The door opened to admit Nath na Kochwold, looking dusty. He made a gesture with his fingers, pointing to his mouth. Laughing, Seg hoisted a jug and Nath took it, swallowed, wiped his mouth, said: "By Vox! It's like a night of Notor Zan out there!"

"All to rights?"

"Aye. The lads are all tucked in. And, I can tell you, there were only four fights among the different Kerchuris. Remarkable." He drank again and glanced at Erndor. "These aerial patrols. To cover the entire border they'll have to be spread very thinly."

"Very."

"Still," said Seg cheerfully. "There must be well-known routes. I recall reconnoitering over there and thinking it was open land. But there must be well-trodden ways we can omit."

"True."

"If you'll release the flutduins to me, strom, I'll set up a system first thing."

"Excellent, Erndor, excellent."

Nath said: "It is a great pity the fleet has had to return to Vondium. We do not really have enough aerial transports to get a large enough force into action quickly enough."

"That," pointed out Turko, "caused my retreat and you your Battle of Marndor."

"H'm," I said. "Maybe we can persuade Farris to spare us a voller or two. I am sorry that Deb-Lu-Quienyin had to return to Vondium. He is a comfort."

They did not reply; but drank. They all knew exactly what I meant.

"If you'll pardon me, strom, I'll turn in. I have a heavy day tomorrow."

"And us all, I think."

Erndor left, saying his good nights, and Seg, standing tall and powerful in the room, downed the last of his wine. Nath na Kochwold poured the last of the bottle.

"I'll just finish this. There are details I wish to talk over with Turko."

So Seg and I left together. We'd been quartered in a fine accommodation block across the courtyard. The stone entrance was guarded by one of Turko's men and also by a kampeon from 1ESW. They saluted as we bid them good night. The entrance hall was carpeted, and featured jars of Pandahem ware, an over-life-size statue of a dancing talu, heavy sturm-wood chairs and a wide table where visitors might deposit their cloaks. The carpet felt thick underfoot.

Seg yawned.

"I shan't be sorry to get to sleep, my old dom. See you in the morning." With that he ran fleetly up the stairs. He almost collided with a girl coming down. She wore a yellow apron and carried a brass tray whereon reposed a half-flagon and two jugs, besides a dish of palines.

With his habitual gallantry, Seg apologized, made sure the girl was all right, and then went leaping on up.

She passed me with eyes she intended to be downcast, but she could not resist a single liquid glance up. I managed a grimace that might pass for a smile, and said, "The guards are grateful that you look after them, believe me."

She colored up, managed a mouselike: "Yes, majister," and skipped outside. Her slippers were red with pretty white bows.

I'd reached the top of the stairs when I heard the crash from outside. Stopping, one hand on the balustrade, I turned to look down into the entrance hall.

The lamps threw scattered illumination across the carpet, picked out the fantastic decoration on one rotund jar. The blooms filled the air with a perfume at once heady and sharp.

Through the open door two sounds reached me, mingled together in horrid counterpoint.

One—the terrified screaming of a girl. The other—the snarling growl of a beast.

I started down the stairs like a madman.

Halfway down, I saw the gray feral form leaping after the girl who struggled to run and who fell asprawl across that luxurious carpet.

In the next second the werewolf would sink those long yellow fangs into that soft body.

93

There was only one thing I could do.

With a ferocious yell I plunged down the stairs, ripping out my sword, that useless sword of steel.

Sixteen

A corpse speaks

Steel! *Steel!* Useless...

That beautiful drexer fashioned in the armories of Valka, designed to take all the best of the Havilfarese thraxter, the Vallian clanxer and what we could contrive of the Savanti Sword—all that skill and cunning, that knowledge and craft—all wasted, impotent, useless...

I went down the stairs so fast I almost pitched onto my nose. The were-wolf saw me. His eyes, reddened in the lamps' glare, seemed to shoot sparks. The saliva that dripped between his fangs hung thick and clotted. He panted. He looked what he was, vicious and deadly and utterly without understanding of human mercy.

He leaped the girl to get at me. He snarled up the stairs, lips drawn back blackly to bare those curved sharp fangs. His hair spiked in a thick bristle about his neck. Oh, yes, as I went hurtling down I could see he was a very devil of a werewolf.

The penultimate step before I'd be on him—or he on me—I took off. I jumped. I soared clean over his back and landed cat-footed on the carpet beyond. With a growl from some blasphemous bowel-region he swiveled about. In the heartbeat before he turned I slashed the sword at him, sliced deeply into his hind leg.

He screeched—who wouldn't?—and swung away. My second blow siz-zled past his nose as he went back.

The wound in his hind leg affected his agility in no way at all. He seemed not to have been touched.

With a guttural explosion of sound he leaped again.

This time I contrived to roll under and to the side and as I went I gave him the old leem-hunter's trick.

Had he been a leem, even, one of the fiercest of all Kregen's preda-tors, his guts would have spilled out through that long slicing slash along his belly. I saw blood ooze. I saw it, I swear. But he landed on the carpet, screeching, and cocked that lean body around to get at me once more.

In this oddly one-sided combat, weird and uncanny, there was no raw stink of spilled blood. I've fought many a wild beast, as you know, and have developed techniques for dealing with the different species—to my shame, I add, for a number of them merely fight so savagely because that is their nature—and by this time any four-legged animal of this wolfish mold, large though he be, would have been done for.

When the ganchark charged again I caught the distinct impression that he was as speedy as an ordinary wolf, a fast one, admittedly. I did not think I'd slowed him at all by my blows.

This time I tried a new ploy and smashed him full across the muzzle. He yelped and catapulted past to the right as I slid to the left. Again no wound appeared.

Only a moment or two had elapsed since I'd rushed so recklessly down the stairs. The girl lay in a swoon, and we antagonists circled her to get at each other. He came on, I struck and slid, and once more he charged. This could go on all night...

In a few moments more Seg would come roaring down and that prospect alarmed me and nerved me to make an end quickly—but how?

He came at me headlong, muzzle agape, and I struck more to fend him off than to try to hurt him. Where the guards at the door were was probably down wandering among the Ice Floes of Sicce.

The next attack saw me crash sideways into a gorgeous jar of Pandahem ware. It went over with a smash. Bits of ceramic sprayed. I dodged sideways and nearly did myself a serious injury on the outspread fingers of the dancing talu.

My left hand gripped the bicep of one of the statue's eight arms. I held myself straight to face the next attack—and then I realized.

Fool! Onker! Get onker! Of course!

Now it had to be arranged. The stoppered vial in my pouch remained intact. I reached in, fumbled about, and drew it forth. If I dropped it now, when the ganchark, slavering, leaped again...

I dodged away, swiveling, fending the thing off and yet not allowing myself to remain in the path of his leap. His teeth looked mightily unpleasant. Again I circled to the statue of the dancing talu. The eight arms, extended in that familiar wagon wheel of abandonment, were fashioned, like the trunk and legs, of bronze. The head, all artful secret smiles, was of gold.

But the fingernails...

I smeared the ganjid on as many fingernails as I could reach on that pass, slashed nastily at the werewolf and saw a chunk of gray fur fly. That was about as much as I could hurt him—yet. More ganjid smeared over other fingernails. I drew out, dropped the vial, poised.

Seg's yell reached me from the stairs.

"Dray!"

"Stand back, Seg!"

The werewolf leaped. I waited, flashed the sword as I had flashed it so many times before in his reddened eyes, and then skipped sideways. But, this time, I drove the sword full at his face and let go. It slid into an eye. I felt it go in as I went sideways.

He paused, shrieking, and then...!

The sword began to ease out of his eye. Bodily, it moved back. He stood trembling, his tongue hanging, as the sword was pushed out of his eye by supernatural forces and dropped with a thud upon the carpet.

He snarled now as though admitting that the thrust would have killed a lesser beast, a savage animal who was not were...

He leaped.

I took the over-life-size statue of the dancing talu by two of his lower arms and I lifted him and turned him. I held him angled forward. The ganchark leaped at me and hurtled straight onto a hedge fashioned from the dudinter fingers of the statue.

Later we counted the number of fingernails that pierced him.

Five.

Five electrum fingernails coated with wolfsbane, five of them, they did for him, all right.

Seg raced down into the hall, yelling. Other people appeared and if they'd been watching then I did not fault them. They'd had the courage in that case not to run away. We stood in a ring looking at the werewolf, and two of the girls bent over the limp form of the serving girl.

"The puncture lady's coming," said a Pachak wearing his badge of office.

We watched.

Who would lie revealed when the evil occult force leached away from that fearsome gray form?

The gray fur shimmered, the fierce head rounded, the form softened until the body of the guard who had stood at the entrance and bid us good night lay on the carpet.

"Larghos m'Mondifer," I said. He was a doughty kampeon who had recently been enrolled as a jurukker in 1ESW.

Then something happened for which we were totally unprepared.

The corpse opened its eyes.

Before anyone could scream or faint, the mouth opened. A sighing of air, as of the opening of a long-disused tomb, and then the corpse of Larghos m'Mondifer spoke.

"This, Dray Prescot, was not my doing."

Now the screams rang out, now the fainting ones slid to the carpet.

The body of Larghos m'Mondifer turned black. The skin shone like enamel, then dulled to ash. Cracks appeared running all over in a spider-web. The guardsman collapsed. He fell in on himself, and then only an outline in black dust showed on that thick carpet, and then that whisked away and there was nothing left of a fine fighting man of Vallia who had been changed into a werewolf.

Seventeen

The Emperor of Vallia's werewolves

The Werewolf of Vondium, then, had not been alone...

Stringent inquiries revealed nothing to distinguish poor Larghos m'Mondifer from any other of the guard corps. He'd done his duty, stood his guard, fought well in the Battle of Marndor. I just didn't like the way the two werewolves had been members of my own bodyguard.

And just what was a corpse doing, spouting mysteries?

Seg said, "We were told, Milsi and me, that there were werewolves up along the plains of Northern Croxdrin. Werewerstings, they were supposed to be."

Marion cocked her head at him at this. Nath na Kochwold looked grim. We were taking our usual second breakfast standing up and nobody was feeling at all cheerful.

"What the hell did that poor fellow mean?" demanded Turko.

"He spoke my name. A dead man. All right, I am at a loss. If Deb-Lu is engaged on his own weighty affairs we must send for Khe-Hi-Bjanching right away."

Khe-Hi was down in the southwest with Drak. I'd not argue about calling him, for this mystery deepened and we needed a Wizard of Loh.

In the days that followed we went about our business in a dour, almost sullen way. There were two more werewolf attacks that left the victims with torn-out throats.

We sent for the dudinter weapons from Vondium.

Khe-Hi-Bjanching, red-haired, his austerely handsome face a trifle plumper in these latter days, arrived by fast voller. He was abreast of the situation. Wizards of Loh have their means of communication.

In his chiseled-steel voice he said, "I have the ganjid recipe and will begin at once, majister. This is a bad business. Rumors fly wildly all over Vallia."

"Rumors won't sink supernatural fangs into you, Khe-Hi."

"There are facets to this business that intrigue me. Deb-Lu has a great deal on at the moment."

I wasn't going to pry into what was going on between these two puissant wizards. They were friends. I was convinced about that, and they had both served Vallia and me well in the past. Khe-Hi went off to the kitchens and his acolytes began the collection of the necessaries.

There would be no fumbling in the gathering of ingredients required by Khe-Hi. Oh, no! A deal younger than Deb-Lu, his powers grew every season, or so it seemed. I had known him longer than Deb-Lu, and because Delia had told me to pull him out of a hole, he fancied he owed me a debt. We had talked around this, and I think both had come to the understanding that our friendship and mutual loyalty reached a much higher level than mere gratitude.

Looking back at those infuriating days spent in Falinur trying to hold the border, to repel Layco Jhansi and to deal with the damned werewolves, I recall an oppressive feeling of bafflement. I was frustrated at every turn. We put out aerial patrols and we caught a number of raids. Everyone did their work well. The soldiers flew or marched and got stuck in. We held Jhansi, and even put in a few raids on our own account.

But—everywhere the Emperor of Vallia went, there went also the werewolves.

This became patently obvious.

We caught three more of the poor fellows. All three were from my own guard corps.

I began seriously to consider sending 1ESW and 1EYJ back to Vondium or to Drak.

Then a particularly nasty outbreak occurred when we were up north chasing a retreating raid. We'd surprised the devils as they burned a farm. Afterwards, when we rested around the ruins of the farm, no fewer than four of the local girls were killed in that nauseatingly familiar way. Their throats were uniformly ripped out.

We laid a trap. We caught the unholy ganchark.

And he turned out to be Nalgre the Rear, a member of Turko's select body of personal guards.

Andrinos, the Khibil wrestler who was now on very good terms with Turko, shook his head, pursing up his lips as we stood looking down on the body.

"This bodes no good—" he began.

"Wait, Andrinos. Let us see if he speaks."

But no other corpse than that of Larghos m'Mondifer opened his eyes and mouth and spoke to me—so far...

In those evil days much of the old Dray Prescot returned. I saw more than one man flinch away when I looked quite reasonably at him. The atmosphere grew strained. We were overstretched, true; but that was no new thing, that was almost always the norm.

By chance one rainy evening I overheard a conversation through a tent flap. Eavesdroppers never hear good, as they say.

Two soldiers out of one of Turko's regiments were talking in that low-voiced rumble that indicates they are old friends, and have no fear of being overheard.

"I tell you, Nath, the land is accursed."

"That's true, by Vox. And all since this Kov Seg returned. He was thrown out before—"

"Aye. But Kov Turko is harsher against the slavemasters."

"That may be, Mondo. But it is certain sure this Seg was infected by werewolves in his own kingdom, wherever in some foreign devil-land that may be. He said so himself."

I rounded the corner of the tent-flap, stepped over the guy-rope, and said, "Stand up. Attention."

They saw who I was. They scrambled up. They tried to stand to attention, and made a poor hash of it for the trembling fits that seized them.

"I shall not have you flogged, or beaten, or tortured, nor even have you neatly put to death. I will tell you this. Kov Seg Segutorio is not the cause of this plague of werewolves. He is not a sorcerer. Had he been, perhaps you would have been turned into little green toads for your stupidity."

They stood there. They looked ghastly. No thought of trying to make a run for it entered their heads, and certainly no thought of trying to tackle me would even reach them—they knew what the Krozair longsword across my back could do.

That I would have used that superb brand was certain sure. These were the rumors that were doing so much to destroy the credibility of myself and my friends.

The two, Nath and Mondo, I dismissed with a few final words of caution. Then I added an admonition to cheer up, for we were bound in the end to triumph over the gancharks. They trailed off looking as though they'd fallen off a cliff onto the rocks beneath.

I hadn't touched them physically, but that old face that transforms me, the face men call the devil face of Dray Prescot, must have flamed out in all its evil power.

The decision not to tell Seg what I had overheard could easily be made; implementing it was quite different.

As we flew back to Falanriel, Seg remarked in his deceptively casual way: "These rumors are flying thicker than flies around a corpse."

"So it seems."

The breeze blew in our faces, the suns shone, the air smelled sweet with that particular sweetness only found on Kregen, yet I felt the chill of unease.

"Yes, my old dom. Seems people are blaming you directly. I've had a few words with 'em."

That I could imagine.

So I told Seg what Nath and Mondo had said.

"Oh, yes, sure. I've heard that, too. But they lay the blame on your shoulders, Dray, because everywhere you go the werewolves appear."

"Just a coincidence."

Seg squinted off at the horizon.

"Maybe, Dray, and maybe not."

I remained silent. Seg, I knew, had had a thought.

He went on: "We may not know if this is true or not, but let us assume for a moment that it is. We may never know just why it is. But, if it should be so then surely it will give us a lead, a chance, a lever to use against the dratted werewolves. Yes?"

"If it be so, if this unholy thing you're suggesting is true, then how do we use it?"

"I'll have a few words on that score with Khe-Hi."

I faced him. "Yes, Seg. Yes. Do that. I own the whole evil business is getting me down."

A sad incident occurred shortly after we touched down.

One of the girls who had been so gruesomely slain by a werewolf—and, of course, we could not tell if the werewolves we caught were the ones who had committed the crimes—had been just such a young, carefree lass as to warm the heart of the crustiest old curmudgeon. Pansi the Song, that was her name. She'd worked in a tavern of good repute in Falanriel, and she'd been found torn to pieces in a back alley.

Her father, Nolro the Abrupt, a thickly built man with a luxuriant mop of brown Vallian hair and an abdomen rotund yet solid, took his daughter's death ill. He must have heard the stories and rumors circulating so wildly. He must have brooded. His wife was long since dead. After Sasfri had been taken from him, all his hopes and affections centered on Pansi the Song.

And now she was dead, dreadfully killed by a werewolf brought to Falanriel by the emperor.

We walked from the voller and Nolro the Abrupt, crazed by grief, desperate, hurled himself through the ranks and bore down on me brandishing a thick iron bar.

Thank Zair there was nothing physical and immediate I had to do, save shout: "Do not harm him!"

My lads closed up and took the iron bar away.

Nolro was screaming hysterically, all his bulk shaking.

"Werewolf lover! Murderer! Death to the emperor!"

I said to Jiktar Vandur: "See to him, Vandur. Fetch a needleman. Try to treat him gently. When he is calm I shall visit him."

"Quidang!" Vandur, as tough as they come, with a chestful of bobs, pulled his moustache. "Although I give you odds, majister, against his full recovery."

100

"I hope you are wrong. But I fear you may be right."

"If I catch these rumor mongers I'll string 'em up and have their tripes out, by the Blade of Kurin!"

So, as you may easily imagine, I was not a happy man as we went up into the Fletcher's Tower. It seemed to me that the werewolves and the rumors were alienating me from the populace. The very people who had cried for me as Jak the Drang and then as Dray Prescot to become their emperor and get them out of their troubles were now baying for my blood.

Later on Jiktar Vandur sent word that Nolro the Abrupt was quieted down. The doctors had stuck him all over with acupuncture needles, and he could hear and speak coherently. I went down to the little medical room where he lay in bed. His wrists and ankles were tied to the bed. At this I felt a leaden thump of my spirits.

"Majister," he said. "As you can see, I cannot give you the full incline."

As sarcasm it was lost on me. But it gave me an opening. I said in what I hoped was a cool yet friendly voice: "You should know, Nolro, that I do not care for the full incline, and detest all this bowing and scraping. It seems you are deceived in your understanding of me."

"I do not misunderstand that my Pansi is dead or that where you go the werewolves go—"

I did not so much argue with him as cajole as though he were a fever patient. I pointed out the obvious; that as the confounded emperor I was hardly likely to cause this kind of suffering to the people when it harmed us all. His face clouded at this, and I could see he was chewing this simple-minded piece of logic over in his mind.

Then: "But the werewolves appear wherever you go."

"That I do not deny, Nolro. I deny I cause them."

He shook his head fretfully. "But it is one and the same."

I said, "You have the grief of a lost daughter upon your shoulders. I know how you feel." And, by Zair, I did...

He pulled at his bound wrists, but I went on quickly, thrusting those old ugly thoughts away: "I have the grief of all the daughters, all the sons, upon my shoulders, Nolro."

We talked for a little more. The doctors were there, hovering in the background, and the guard, and an old cleaning lady stood by the door, her hands folded into her yellow apron. I thought Nolro was still in a state of shock at the death of Pansi the Song; but that he now understood that the reasons were not as simple as he imagined.

"I promise you, Nolro, as Opaz is my witness, we shall discover the evil secret of the gancharks. We shall make sure they cannot harm anyone else. I pledge you this, Nolro, and all the people of Falanriel, all the people of Vallia."

"I believe you, majister—"

I took out my knife, my old sailor knife I keep snugged over my right hip. I slashed his bonds. He looked startled and I was aware of a quick movement from the doctors, the guards, the old cleaning lady.

"Stand fast," I snapped without turning around.

I extended the knife hilt first to Nolro.

"If you condemn me, Nolro the Abrupt, then use this knife. Strike home and deliver justice!"

Well, by the Black Chunkrah! That was a dangerous gesture...

Nolro took the knife. I was interested to notice it did not quiver in his broad red hand. He looked at it. He looked up at me. With a great gulp of indrawn breath he hurled the knife down onto the bedclothes. His face was so twisted that I felt my own spirit twist in response.

There was no need for anything further. Retrieving the knife, I sheathed it. I went out without another word.

There was no need to tell anyone to spread this story. The witnesses would rush out to tell everyone they met what had passed between the Emperor of Vallia and Nolro the Abrupt.

And, for all that, nothing would bring back the smiles and the music of Pansi the Song...

Eighteen

Of a volunteer from the Jikai Vuvushis

The ugly truth was that I must be to blame. Somehow wherever I went the damned werewolves appeared.

This could not be mere coincidence.

And the corpse of Larghos m'Mondifer speaking to me. I trembled to think just who might have been using his cadaver to communicate with me. If the idea I did not wish to allow into my head proved true, then, indeed, Vallia was in deep water.

During this period, as we attempted to prosecute the campaign against Layco Jhansi, I decided it would be best if I did not frequent Falanriel, or any town at all. Spending days in camp or on the march I hoped would deprive any potential werewolves from preying on simple young girls. In this I was proved right. But the atrocities continued, and soldiers were ripped to shreds on guard duty. We caught the werewolves. Useless to place two men or a girl and a man on duty. One so often became a werewolf and destroyed the other. We mounted guard by audo, by a section of eight or ten men, and still, as is the awkward nature of humankind, the werewolves appeared and caught men on their own. Despite the strictest orders there were still those foolish enough to go off alone.

One example showed us the way of it.

Three men detached were all good comrades, men who had fought together in the files and trusted one another with their lives. One went to fetch the wine, keeping in full view of the tent, under observation at all times. When this man, Fonrien the Latch, returned to the tent he found one of his comrades, Nath Furman, dead with dreadful wounds, and the werewolf just running wildly off. When the pursuit eventually gave up, the third comrade, Nugos the Unwary, trailed in covered in blood with some story of chasing after the ganchark.

The case seemed open and shut.

"Suppose," said Nath na Kochwold—for the men were brumbytes, "Suppose Nugos the Unwary is not the ganchark? How can we slay him in cold blood?"

"The proof seems very clear," said Dekor. He stood imposingly in his pikeman's uniform, massive and bulging with muscle, his face hard as the edge of the kax covering his chest. Dekor, as the Brumbytevax, shared Nath's concern for the phalanx. "It is cruel. But it must be done."

The marquee-like tent in which we gathered resounded in that dully flapping way of tents with the voices of the arguers. It seemed perfectly plain that the moment Fonrien the Latch, who was a brumbyte, had gone off to fetch the wine allowance, Nugos the Unwary, who was a Faxul, a leader of the file, had transmogrified himself into a werewolf. Then he had ripped out the throat of Nath Furman, who was the laik-faxul, and had sought to escape.

"This is a matter for the Phalanx," declared Brytevax Dekor. "Acting under the orders of the emperor direct."

This was a typical hard-nosed attitude by a commander to keep his own affairs to himself. It implied the absence from the deliberations of Kov Turko and of Kapt Erndor. I fancied Turko would chafe at this, and then welcome the chance to distance himself from a nasty business. He was hard, was our Turko; but he was a man with a human heart, as I well knew.

The swiftly grown tradition of the Phalanx, inspired, guided, given impetus by me at a time when the fate of Vallia hung on the performance of untried troops using new-fangled weapons, had, indeed, blossomed into a marvelous growth. The Phalanx might not quite be a law unto itself, but it cherished its own ways, and fiercely defended its conduct, on the field and off. This is, I suppose, one of the prices one pays for creating an elite.

If one of the Phalanx was a damned unholy werewolf, then the Phalanx would deal with him. Queyd-arn-tung.

All the same—suppose Nugos the Unwary was not a werewolf?

Upon being asked simple leading questions, Nugos just shook his head. He replied openly enough; he remembered nothing from the moment Fonrien the Latch had gone to bring the wine to the moment he discovered himself, covered in blood, crawling along the ground. He supposed he must have chased after the werewolf, injured himself and lost all memory.

"That is a probability," said Nath na Kochwold.

They all knew, these tough men in the marquee, that the Emperor of Vallia did not countenance torture as a method of extracting information. The temptation to use that disgusting system did not tempt me even now.

I said, when Nugos had been carted off to the guardtent: "We must try to use this to our own advantage. Set up a hut—not a tent—with two compartments. Let there be a spyhole. We will set Nugos in one half and keep an observation on him from the other. A strong guard at all times, of course."

"And who will be the bait?" Seg in his fey way knew how to put his finger on the nub of the question.

"An audo of your lads with dudinter-tipped shafts should stop him. The guard ready to rush in. Yes, I think you might ask for volunteers from the Jikai Vuvushis."

Well, distasteful though this was, it was done.

Poor Nugos the Unwary! Well-named, indeed!

A girl, lithe, splendidly formed, swinging along in her battle-leathers, stepped forward. Minci Farndion, a Deldar in the new guard regiment, unhesitatingly volunteered. She was by a half a heartbeat only quicker than her companions in the ranks

I expressed no wish to see the result of this nauseating experiment. The Phalanx, jealous of its position and privileges, handled all. Minci stepped in alone, carrying a tray with food. Poor Nugos transformed himself and was instantly pierced by shafts and slashed to ribbons by the dudinter blades of the guard who rushed in from their hidden vantage points.

Well, as I say, if I was the cause of all this horror and misery I'd reck little to the cost of clearing it all up—but I could do without scenes like these, by Krun.

Flinging ourselves into the task of dealing with Layco Jhansi, we kept up the aerial patrols, and caught two of his columns in ambushes. We felt a distinct sense that he was growing cautious. We planned for a bolder advance into the territory of Vennar.

At this time, too, news came that Natyzha Famphreon, the Dowager Kovneva of Falkerdrin, rallied against her illness. She still clung to life with the same stubbornness she had always shown. A tough and stringy old bird, Natyzha. Despite that she, as an avowed Racter, had stood against me, I owned to a feeling of loss in the world when she eventually passed on to wherever she was bound.

Khe-Hi reported that he, too, like Deb-Lu, was aware of these quick stabs of occult power from time to time.

"They come at random, San?"

"Yes, Dray. I think they must be connected with the ganchark phenomenon."

"So do I. But who—"

"If he was not dead, I'd have no hesitation in knowing just who, by Hlo-Hli."

"There is his wife and child."

"So it must be them."

"I fear so."

Khe-Hi pulled at the crimson cord cincturing his waist. His clean-shaven face looked both sad and grim. He said, "Deb-Lu and I have fashioned over the seasons a powerful defense for Vallia—and for yourself, as you know. But any defense, I suppose, may be pierced if the thrust is hard and concentrated enough."

"As for myself, I fancy the lady has taken to me. This is her misfortune. The child, the uhu Phunik, is the truly malignant power."

"You know of the love Csitra had for Phu-Si-Yantong? Yes. Ling-Li-Lwingling came along and turned his head. Deb-Lu has apprized you of these facts. If Csitra does truly imagine herself to be infatuated with you, Dray—and pardon me for putting it quite like that—she is a woman who will adhere rigidly to her own obsession."

"I suppose I ought to feel thankful."

"Oh, indeed, yes." The wizard's metallic voice held no levity. "If this is the handiwork of Phunik, Deb-Lu and I can handle him and his powers. It will take many seasons before he approaches anywhere near our combined kharrna."

"And Csitra?"

"We felt her assisting Yantong when we blew him away in the Quern of Gramarye. She has power. I think even with her uhu she cannot master us."

"Then," I said, and I spoke with more acerbity than I intended, "Then by the disgusting diseased left eyeball of Makki Grodno! Why do you not stop them?"

"I will reply to your perfectly reasonable question when I have consulted further with Deb-Lu."

The rebuke was merited.

I nodded perfunctorily, and Khe-Hi took himself off.

I, Dray Prescot, Lord of Strombor and Krozair of Zy, did not wish to turn into a veritable ogre. But, by Krun, these diabolical occult events were forcing me down that ugly path.

Mind you, as I went off to find Seg and Nath and have a wet and discuss plans for the forthcoming offensive, I reflected that there'd been something distinctly odd about Khe-Hi during this conversation. Now, just when was that? I found Seg and Nath in the mess tent, and I snatched up a glass at random, my mind working back on that conversation.

"Hai, Dray! You look as though you've lost a zorca and found a calsany."

"Something like that," I said, and then I had it.

The Wizard of Loh had looked decidedly shifty when he'd talked of Ling-Li-Lwingling, the Witch of Loh I'd met in Jikaida City in the center of Havilfar.

Now, why was that?

Nath resumed the conversation my entrance had interrupted. Strangely enough, this concerned Khe-Hi.

"We do not know the locus of infection, Khe-Hi was telling me. It might be anything. If a victim can be kissed by dudinter very soon afterwards, there is a chance he may be cured."

"It is safe?"

"Not at all. The transformation, I was told by those who witnessed it in Nugos, was exceedingly swift."

I said, "But he had been a werewolf before—for how long we do not know."

"The devil of it is," said Seg, "there could be a dozen of the dratted things prowling about out there right now."

That thought could unsettle anyone, could waft an icy draft of unease down any spine

We deliberately pushed those unwelcome thoughts aside and got down to serious planning. Seg, Turko, Nath, Kapt Erndor—any one of them alone could have planned out the forthcoming actions. I was not needed. As the emperor, it could be said, my place was at the center, at the fulcrum, in Vondium.

By Zair! I wasn't going anywhere near Vondium while my every footstep was dogged by these blasphemous werewolves, these ghastly visitations from malignant sorcerers. Not a chance, by Krun!

By chance I was aware of some work done on this Earth in connection with werewolves and the disease of lycanthropy. The myths and legends insisted that silver was the metal to dispose of the weremonsters. A test had been made of Nugos, a simple thing, when a dudinter ring had been slipped on his finger. He had not appeared disconcerted.

So we did not have that handy way of detecting the gancharks amongst us in human form. Mind you, any intelligent bloke who knows he's going to turn into a werewolf come full moon can always smear shellac or some similar coating onto his hands to pick up the silver candlestick.

We were all mightily heartened when Tom Tomor sent a regiment of Valkan Archers to join us, and two crack regiments of Pachaks from Zamra.

Our strength grew slowly. As ever, we were short of saddle animals. Now if what I considered the unlikely schemes of my kregoinye comrade, Pompino the Iarvin, came to fruition, he ought to be sailing back to Vondium in his fine new galleon. He'd gone faring forth to Pandahem to bring hersanys, heavy, six-legged, chalk-white-haired beasts, from Seg and Milsi's kingdom of Croxdrin. I wondered if he'd run into any of the werewerstings up there that Seg had mentioned.

Incidentally, I confess that although I had the comfort of Makki Grodno, I did miss the Divine Lady of Belschutz...

Well, all that rascally crew had sailed with Pompino. When he sailed back, if he ever did, and he had managed to procure saddle animals, no doubt shamelessly using the specialist merchant in saddle animals, Obolya Metromin, he would be mightily welcomed. Pompino, I fancied, would be pretty sharp with Obolya, calling himself the Zorcanim. Also, if I knew my Khibil comrade Pompino, he'd earn his nickname of the Iarvin by letting it be known that he was a personal friend of Jak Leemsjid, who just happened to be a personal friend of the King and Queen of Croxdrin.

These thoughts made me break in to ask Seg how his friends from Croxdrin fared in Vallia, to which he replied that the two pygmies, Diomb and Bamba, had been taken off by Milsi, and that the rest of his cutthroat bunch were either organizing themselves or being organized into the regiment I'd told him he ought to raise.

"They'll come in handy, Seg, when Balkan comes along. News is scant out of that hyr kovnate. I hope it all goes smoothly when the time comes."

Even as I spoke I knew that, this being Kregen, it would not go smoothly...

Letters came in and went out. I heard from Drak who said that Dayra had been through like a windstorm. His sister, he said, was desirous of visiting his other sister, Lela, out in Havilfar. This astonished me.

Still no reasonable results were obtained with the werewolf business and we were, on that problem, as Seg said, like a pickpocket with no fingers.

We were pushing Layco Jhansi's forces back. In more than one conversation on the eve of battle it was suggested that after the coming victory we should push on to the town he had made his provincial capital, Vendalume.

"We catch the rast there, string him up, and the rest will fall into line," promised Turko. He had no need to swell his chest and bulge his muscles, as so many Khamorros did. He was grown in stature in quite unphysical ways, was Turko, in these latter days.

"Your spy network is working better now," I said.

We stood watching the twin suns set, Zim and Genodras flooding down their mingled light upon the stricken field where the medics worked devotedly. The battle had been arduous, for we'd caught a sizable Jhansi force, and destroyed them. That was the Battle of Farnrien's Edge. The new regiments had fought magnificently, lost few casualties, and now our lines resounded with victory celebrations. "I could wish I had a certain barrel of a fellow to spy for us—"

"Naghan Raerdu?" Turko laughed. "Aye, I remember him, and the way he cried hot tears when he laughed."

"An acute, brilliant and invaluable man, Turko."

"Well, we've done pretty well. And the news from Inch is good."

"Yes. I rather thought—and I'll let you and Inch sort it out—that we could split Vennar down the middle. Half to you, half to Inch."

"That is not only fair, it is generous to both—"

"You'll both have to agree—"

"Of course. I see no problem at all, by Morro the Muscle! With Inch on my western borders I'll sleep well."

How quickly Turko had picked up the affectations of nobility, of thinking like a kov!

The uproar from the lines continued. We'd left the main camp a few miles to the rear with the tents and impedimenta and the camp followers. We'd rest up and then march back. The twin suns sank and the Maiden with the Many Smiles, already aloft, poured down her fuzzy pink radiance upon the land. As we stood drinking in the cool night air shadows moved out across the plain beyond the battlefield.

"What—?" said Turko.

Nath na Kochwold cantered across astride a zorca. He pointed out.

"The lurfings of the plain try to scavenge the dead—" He stopped himself and raised in the stirrups. He stared.

"Well?" snapped Turko.

"I think—by Vox! It is so! Many and many of them—"

I was jumping up onto a varter, climbing to balance on the ballista. I looked out across that moon-drenched landscape. Rosy light flooded down and the shadows lay long and undulating. And in that wash of fuzzy pink radiance there was no mistaking the nature of those hideous forms that leaped along in a baying pack.

Howling, a monstrous pack of them, their gray backs like a tidal rip, the werewolves poured past in a torrent, hell-bent on our undefended camp and all the camp-followers there.

Nineteen

Howling under the Moons

There was nothing else to do but race like a madman for the zorca lines and fling myself across the first animal I laid hands on. She was a fine chestnut and she quieted instantly as I grasped her mane. Bareback, head low, feet tucked in, I roared off after that blasphemous rout.

Nath rode with me. Magically, Seg and Turko were there. Others joined us. Volodu was blowing his lungs out, shrilling the alarm over the entire camp.

In a straggling bunch, heads low, we raced after that streaming howling pack of werewolves.

Every man jack of us, I was sure, wore among the usual Kregan arsenal of weaponry a dudinter blade.

Nothing was going to outrun a zorca, on four, six or eight feet, or on two. Among the bunch of riders following me were men and women riding sleeths, two-legged dinosaurs, swarths, four-legged dinosaurs, totrixes, six-legged lumbering saddle animals of great stubbornness, zorcas with their four nimble feet and single upflung spiral horn, and there were even a few souls aboard nikvoves.

Roaring with the fury to get at the gancharks, we raced across that mysterious moon-drenched landscape.

If that howling pack of unholy beasts got in among our camp... There were women there, men who were representative of the gentle races of Kregen who wouldn't know which was the naughty end of a spear or a sword. They could all be destroyed, their throats ripped out, their guts torn and ripped bleeding from them... No. Oh, no. I couldn't allow that.

As the fleet zorca, a beautiful animal, bounded beneath me, I wondered anew over the problem of just how these werewolves kept making their appearance—and, always in my vicinity.

This was the malefic work of Csitra and her uhu, Phunik. Well, our two Wizards of Loh were hard at work trying to prevent this diabolical interference in the affairs of Vallia. Csitra might have taken a fancy to me; Phunik hated me, hated us all, both for the destruction of his father and for the wrecking of his insane ambitions to dominate all of Paz. If Phunik went the same road as his father Yantong, we were in for another period of great distress, another horrendous Time of Troubles.

As that howling tide of gray horrors leaped on it seemed likely that the Battle of Farnrien's Edge would be followed by the Massacre of Farnrien's Edge.

The women and camp followers, the servants and batmen, the grooms and cooks, would stand no chance at all when that ravening horde leaped upon them.

There are races on the bizarre world of Kregen who are not warriors, do not produce fighting men and women. The Relts, gentle-cousins of the Rapas; Xaffers, mysterious and distant; Dunders with their flat heads; ahl-nims who are a race who produce mystics and wise men, all these and many more go about their daily lives while the world's stage resounds with the deeds of Chuliks and Khibils, with Rapas and Fristles. These people, then, were more than deserving of every effort to save them.

Fleetly the zorca galloped. She proved her quality on that night when the werewolves swarmed to attack the camp. Other zorcas stayed with us in the van. We were able to head the howling pack, to bear inwards, and then to ride alongside. Seg, legs clamped, was shooting already.

I used the ganjid-smeared dudinter blade. It was like slapping at a river in torrential flood. Grimly along the backtrail the corpses dotted the plain. We rode on, swords rising and falling, and the rout lessened.

At the last a few gancharks turned on us in a desperation that, I judged, came from their own natures and not the occult power impelling them. These we dispatched. Only a scant three or four ran off, howling mournfully.

Seg shafted two, and a bunch of the lads rode after the others.

Our camp was in a frightful commotion; but men rode off to reassure the people. A deed had been done this night. Then began the grisly business of collecting the corpses. Well, there were men there I did not know, and others I did. This screeching pack of werewolves had been composed of men from many regiments. Some of them had blood on their lips; we suspected there was yet further horror to be discovered.

"There's just one good thing to come out of this night's work." Seg stood with me watching as the corpses were brought in. All of us bore faces like death masks.

"Oh?"

"Aye, my old dom. I've been expecting trouble among the troops. Mutiny. A lot of regiments were growing restive serving alongside the guard."

This I had suspected and dreaded.

Turko—wearing a dudinter sword—said, "Then whoever is doing these unholy things miscalculated tonight."

"We're all in this mess together, the guard, the regiments from Vondium, those of yours, Turko, those from Valka. If we fall apart now..."

"This fight has given us a real edge." Seg's fey blue eyes in the torchlight drove at me like twin lightning bolts, a stupid fancy; but exactly conveying the sensation. "Farnrien's Edge has given us an edge over Jhansi. I vote for an immediate forward movement of our whole force."

Our general growl of agreement was interrupted by the noisy arrival of a gang of soldiers dragging along two poor wights covered in mud and blood, their uniforms in tatters. When order was restored we understood that these two unfortunates had been discovered by the party who'd ridden after the escaping werewolves. The story was the same as that of Nugos the Unwary.

"You know what must be done." I spoke in that cold and hateful voice. By Zair! I was not a happy man in those dismal days. I took myself off and let other folk get on with the nasty business.

Passing a campfire I saw two of the Jikai Vuvushis clasping each other, sobbing their hearts out. I felt this was no business of mine. Whatever it was that was causing their distress—well, perhaps a quiet word with Marion...

She told me that, in the nature of things, liaisons had grown up between her girls and the men of their choice; strong affections—love, even—and that marriages were in prospect.

"But?"

"But, majister, many of the men they chose have been slain, some in battle, some turned into werewolves, some as victims of werewolves. I find it distressing—"

"Why have you not reported this before?"

"It is a feminine matter. I did not wish to burden you with unnecessary problems, seeing the many you already have."

She was quite right, of course. My Delia would have very quickly put me in order on that one. I bid Marion good night and went off to my tent.

A considerable quantity of bodies stood about my tent.

I sighed.

Each one of these fine lads and fair lassies was there personally to interpose their bodies between me and the enemy. Even if, as could easily be the case, the enemy was a horrendous ganchark. The thought that any one of those superb people could turn into a werewolf and rend the person nearby filled me with a hollow, aching passionate anger that was completely useless.

The habit of addressing a superior with "jis" for a man and "jes" for a woman was, as you know, increasing, paralleling the words "sir" and "madam" on Earth. These folk would call me majister if they were formal, majis if they knew me a little better. By the Black Chunkrah! My fine guard corps was being eroded, eaten away, destroyed by this occult and evil menace of the werewolves. It occurred to me that an expedition into the Snarly Hills of South Pandahem and a quick extermination of the horrors within the Maze of the Coup Blag might be an option I could not afford to ignore...

Just as I was about to flop down onto the spread furs, absolutely fagged out, a girl glided into the inner compartment of the tent. She was a Jikai

Vuvushi I was more accustomed to see wearing her war harness, girded with steel weapons. Tonight she was half-dressed in a flowing rose-colored gown and bearing even more lethal weapons, not of steel. She carried a small hip-harp of eight strings and a pressel.

"May I sing to you, majis, for a short time before you sleep?"

I was too damned tired to argue.

"Very well, Floring. I am afraid I shall be a poor audience."

So Floring Mecrilli, a Jikai Vuvushi, a Sister of the Sword, struck the strings of her harp and played. She had a fine voice. I haven't the foggiest idea what she played and sang. The whole incident was unusual.

Presently she put her harp upon the rugs and, with a movement undulating and voluptuous, crossed to me and sank upon her knees. Her hair fell forward half-obscuring her face. Her dress was loose.

"If there is anything else I might do—"

"No, and I thank you, Floring. Now just let me sleep."

"If that is your command." She pouted. At once I felt alarm. "At least, for the love I bear thee, let me kiss you on the lips—"

I sat up, moved back and in a voice that might have blown out the gate of a fortress, said, "That is not for you, Floring Mecrilli. Now leave this tent—now!"

She flinched back. Her breast heaved with the suddenness of released passion. The single eye I could see past her downfall of hair looked glazed and staring. She licked her lips.

"Please, my love—"

I jumped up, grabbed her by the shoulders, spun her about and carted her off to the tent flap.

There I placed her on her feet. I did not wish to shame her before her comrades.

"Now go out, Floring, and I shall forget this. If not, you are a soldier and are subject to the mazingle and strict regulations for all soldiers of Vallia."

With a final look, a look I swear was a startled look of self-revealed astonishment, she ran off. I went back to bed and gave her harp a kick on the way.

Just before I dropped off and thought of Delia, as I do on every single night of my life, I remembered my puzzlement over Khe-Hi's attitude when he talked of Ling-Li-Lwingling. Maybe romance was the cause of that, too?

Wizards and Witches of Loh spell their names as they please, and sometimes capitalize all three parts, sometimes not. There was no set rule. Capital letters at the beginning of words are highly erratic on Kregen. But, then, that mysterious and terrible world four hundred light-years from Earth is an erratic enigma at the best of times...

Perhaps only in the great word jikai are Capital Initial Letters of exact meaning.

Catching Khe-Hi at breakfast I tackled him directly.

"When I was down in LionardDen, known as Jikaida City, and fought in Kazz Jikaida, the game was controlled by Ling-Li-Lwingling as the Jikaidasta."

"Yes, Dray. She is very good at Jikaida. The game has not, however, become an obsession."

I stared him in the eye, sternly. "She knew that I was from Vallia, and although I was called Jak I feel sure she knew who I was. Now I understand why."

He started to say something; but I went on, still fixing him with that baleful eye. "I believe you know that I bear you considerable good will, Khe-Hi. If there is anything I can do to further your—ah—relationship? romance? with Ling-Li—then for the sweet sake of Honeyed Soothe Herself, tell me!"

He did not exactly go cross-eyed; but he colored up—and he a renowned Wizard of Loh!

"I will tell you. Ling-Li traveled to escape the unwelcome attentions of Phu-Si-Yantong. One port of call was Jikaida City where you met her. She was, I can tell you, far more surprised to see you than you can imagine. She detested Yantong, and was happy to help circumvent his evil plans."

"So you knew I was there and just about alive?"

"More or less. We lost you for a space after that. Ling-Li went off to Balintol."

"And you? Look, Khe-Hi, I do not wish to interfere. But if you Wizards and Witches wish to remain a force in the world, it follows you must have families. So?"

"All right, Dray. Yes. I wish to marry Ling-Li, and I have high hopes she reciprocates."

"Well—go into lupu and see her and tell her to come to Vallia! By Krun! You know how welcome we'll make her."

"She has told me you were as hard as the granite of the mountains. That you did not bow the neck to her as any quivering frightened mortal man must before a Witch of Loh."

A sound that might have been a laugh burst from me. "By the suppurating armpits and vermin-riddled hair of Makki-Grodno!" I was very amused. "So your lady was offended by my uncouth ways. Well, I was in a fight—" I refused to think of the fight and of Mefto the Kazzur. "If she travels to Vallia she will be received with all the honor and respect due her. But, as you know, Khe-Hi, we do not keep slaves any more in Vallia."

"I will see what she says, Dray. And—I thank you."

Andrinos wrinkled up his foxy Khibil face. "My adorable wife, Saenci, has just presented me, as they say, with twins. Werewolves or no werewolves, San, I am glad to leave the horrific scenes of the night when feeding is due."

Turko finished swallowing a slice of roast bosk and remarked feelingly: "You may rail against the married state, Andrinos, my wrestling dom; but in me you see a pitiful object. A kov without a kovneva. A man without a helpmeet, a wifely companion, a warm snuggle at night. Well, then?"

Andrinos in the Khibil's superior way handled that with great aplomb.

"There are so many maidens, Turko, you cannot keep count. And now we have these Jikai Vuvushis, even on the battlefield you're at it, I know."

At Turko's astounded face we all broke into roars of laughter that, I fancied, were triggered as much by the desperateness of our situation as by true humor at Turko's amorous proclivities.

I said, "I had a visit last night from Floring Mecrilli who plays the harp and sings. I fear, pour soul, she is in great need, as dry as the Ocher Limits."

Turko quizzed up at this. "Plays the harp? Floring Mecrilli?" He reached for the first of the after-breakfast palines. "I wonder if the Sisters of the Sword have taught her aught of the martial arts? H'mm—I wonder, does she wrestle?"

Twenty

An Occult Romance

Turko's Ninth Army of Vallia poised to strike directly at our foemen's capital city, Vendalume.

We were not a particularly strong army; but our formations were hardened, seared by the fire, still invigorated by victory. Layco Jhansi, renegade, would-be imperacide, murderer, traitor, was growing increasingly nervous and apprehensive at our attacks. No longer could he send with impunity columns to burn and sack the towns and villages of Turko's Falinur. He lost men in numbers to hurt him. He must have suffered desertions.

For our part when we captured a town or village, we did not burn it. Of course not. The place was Vallian.

Of the people who came into our protection, those who were out-and-out mercenaries, paktuns who made a living hiring out as fighting men, were shepherded off to the coast and passages out and away from Vallia arranged for them. We kept no slaves; we hired no mercenaries. The code was harsh in Vallia on those subjects.

Of those who were civilians, we told them that they were first and foremost Vallians. They had mistakenly sided with Layco Jhansi because he was their lord. He was no longer the Kov of Vennar. He was outcast, leemshead. As Vallians, we must create the island of Vallia whole once again. In view of my decision of the fate of Vennar, they would swear allegiance to Kov Turko as their new lord. Well, human nature is human nature; there were very few folk who felt that they ought still to cling to Layco Jhansi.

The knowledge that he had conspired against the old emperor, had willfully slain Ashti Melekhi, was a proven traitor, moved many of these folk. And, too, Turko's name bruited abroad as a kov at once firm but just gave them confidence in the future.

Good old Tom Tomor at home in Valka contrived to send to me another splendid regiment of Valkan Archers. He also said that he'd like to fly across and join me, whereat I had to be cruel and forbid him, saying that he ran Valka and that was his most important post.

Nath na Kochwold again raised the concept of bringing a Kerchuri down from the Second Phalanx in Hawkwa country. We were discussing this in a desultory way when the sky filled with wingbeats. We all looked up, standing outside the tents, shading our eyes, exclaiming in wonder and delight.

The two commanding officers of the two Valkan Archer regiments, Jiktars Fangar Emiltur and Nalgre Ephanion, laughed with the release of their hoarded secret.

"Tom Tomor bid us not to tell you, strom, for it was to be a wonderful surprise."

"It is," I shouted, elated. "It is."

Tom had sent across no less than five beautiful squadrons of flutduins, ridden by Valkans, highly trained, fiery of spirit, kings of the air. With these priceless reinforcements we could look forward to secure flanks as we advanced on Vendalume.

Khe-Hi cornered me later on that morning. Everywhere the camp resounded with the tinkering noises of men preparing for the great advance. The air misted with the campfires. The smells of cooking wafted on the breeze. And, over all, the Suns of Scorpio threw down their mingled streaming lights.

"Well, Khe-Hi?"

"Well, Dray. I have spoken to Ling-Li. I cannot repeat how it happened—"

I interrupted. "I assume she said something to the effect that she accepted my apology for my boorish behavior?"

"You know us too well, Dray!"

"Not quite. Not a Wizard or a Witch of Loh. Go on."

"She will come to Vallia." He looked down and while he did not shuffle his feet, for he was, after all, a very great sorcerer, he did wear the appearance of a wight in love. "And I hope, I have every hope, that she will, she will come to—that is—"

"Khe-Hi. You have my blessing and that of the Empress Delia. All that we can do, we will do."

"Thank you."

"How fared Ling-Li-Lwingling in Balintol?"

"Not well. They are indeed a strange people, all of them in that vast subcontinent. She has been in Pandahem."

I was not more or less just making polite conversation, for the welfare of all my people, including the Wizards of Loh, ranks high on my list and one is polite. In all our troubles the happiness of two people, a man and a woman, is and remains of supreme importance.

"Interesting, for I was there recently, as you know. North or South?"

"South."

I stared at Khe-Hi.

"You are working up to saying something, San. Spit it out."

"It is something you will not like to hear."

"Yes, well, I've heard a lot of that in my time."

"Ling-Li was not aware of it all; she warns me that she could be totally inaccurate. But she feels—"

"My dear San. If a Witch of Loh feels something, then, by Krun, that something usually is!"

"By Hlo-Hli, you are right."

"So?"

His red hair gleamed in the grateful lights of Zim and Genodras, his white gown, cinctured by the crimson cord, was spotless. His metallic voice took on a harsher ring as he spoke.

"What I propose must be done in secrecy. We must gather the Jikai Vuvushis, the Sisters of the Sword, who came back from Hamal with Marion and Strom Nango—"

I held up a hand. I felt a distinct pang.

"If what you are saying is sooth—and I see no reason to disbelieve you—we are, indeed, in evil waters."

"The Witch Csitra has planned well and cunningly."

"By Zair!" I felt awful. "I can only guess at what she has wrought. But she is in good case to destroy us."

"With the help of Ling-Li, of Deb-Lu, and of my own small powers, we can unravel the mystery. Then we may take steps to defeat her and her hermaphrodite child."

"Do what you have to do, Khe-Hi. I'll tell Targon the Tapster and Naghan ti Lodkwara to afford you every assistance. Who else must know—apart from Turko and Seg?"

116

"It matters not who knows apart from Marion and her girls. It is sad, but—"

"Sad! It's heinous, diabolical, outrageous!"

"Yes."

"And this Hamalese, this Strom Nango ham Hofnar?"

"It remains to be seen how he will come out of this affair."

"You of all men, Khe-Hi, know how disastrous it is to attempt to fight thaumaturgy with a sword!"

"You can cut off a Wizard of Loh's head as easily as any man's if you catch the right moment." Khe-Hi lifted his upper lip. "I say this only because you already know it and because most people disbelieve it."

It would have been mawkish to have remarked on the other reason Khe-Hi could mention the fact.

Looking back at these events across one of the great watersheds of my life on Kregen, I must endeavor to place the alarums and excursions in their correct running order. These events formed links in a chain. If one was removed or misplaced the causality of the whole would fail. Already, from what Khe-Hi had told me, from my own observations here, my knowledge of Csitra and her hermaphrodite offspring, and the unpleasant results of all this occult scheming, I was partially able to grasp at the grand evil design.

That design was grand and it was evil; it was also simple. I didn't know it all yet; with the help of the sorcerers we would unravel all the twisted strands...

Of the survivors of the pastang from Marion's regiment cut-off in Hamal there remained only fifteen.

The others had fallen in battle, to our grief. One, Wincie ti Fhronheim, had returned to Vondium to have her baby in peace and quiet. The girls gathered in the tent put aside for that purpose. The canvas was surrounded at a discreet distance by a strong guard of 1ESW, 1EYJ, and by Sisters of the Rose, the Grand Ladies and other sororities in the Jikai Vuvushi regiment which, as yet, had no name.

"Where is Floring Mecrilli?" demanded Marion, who had—rightly—insisted on being present.

No one knew.

Khe-Hi pursed up his lips.

"No matter. We may proceed with those gathered here. Jurukker Mecrilli will be found when necessary."

So that meant there were thirteen Sisters of the Sword gathered to bear the scrutiny of a Wizard of Loh.

There was no doubt at all about it. Khe-Hi-Bjanching looked imposing, awe-inspiring, dominating the proceedings. About him clung that mystical aura of thaumaturgy that can shrivel the heart in the breast of the bravest.

He placed us in the positions he required us to take up.

The girls sat on folding camp stools in a semicircle. At the center Khe-Hi stood facing them. Each Jikai Vuvushi could see his face and look into his eyes. I stood at the back of the semicircle so that I, too, could look into his eyes. I knew what might follow if a mortal man looked into the eyes of a Wizard of Loh...

Slowly, Khe-Hi raised his arms. There was no mumbo-jumbo about a Wizard of Loh. He needed no arcane objects, no skulls, no morntarchs, no rattle of bones. He needed no fire stinking with incense. He had no requirement for Books of Power. Totally from within his own sorcerous resources, using the arcane knowledge painfully learned over the seasons and stored in his brain, he could draw forth the Powers he required and use them to awful effect.

Close at my elbow I could hear Seg breathing. This was unusual, hearing the hunter betray his presence. Seg was just as powerfully affected as I. Turko had flown off to inspect a churgur regiment, and on my other side Nath na Kochwold and Kapt Erndor stood, gripped like us all by the import of the moment.

Looking over the heads of the seated girls I became aware of a movement beside Khe-Hi. It was as though the air shimmered with heat. A second narrow column of disturbance grew into life at his other side.

I knew what this portended. The phantom shapes coalesced, thickened into the semblances of real live human beings. They were, indeed, real live human beings; but they were not physically present in the tent. They were miles away and by use of their kharrna they had gone into lupu and projected phantasms of themselves to join us in this weird interrogation.

At Khe-Hi's right appeared the familiar form of Deb-Lu-Quienyin. He could have been there in person, half-smiling at me, pushing his turban straight. I felt a great comfort at sight of his projected image.

At Khe-Hi's left shone the shape of a woman I had not seen since Jikaida City. She seemed to look the same, but her lupal projection was not as strong or as firm as that of Deb-Lu. Her red hair burned in the light from some source not confined within the tent. Her small face still looked as though it had been carved from finest ivory of Chem, unlined, smooth, with a firm compactness of flesh and distinct delineation of the lines of lip and jaw. Her blue eyes regarded me for a single glance only, still with that direct and challenging look. Then she devoted herself, as did the two Wizards of Loh, to the reasons she had projected her image here.

And yet—and yet in those fraught moments of high tension when everyone present knew that catastrophic events were to be unfolded, I caught the tiny interplay between Khe-Hi and Ling-Li. They were aware of each other. I saw that. Truly, this was an amazing circumstance for a plain sailorman like me! These two had carried out the rituals of courtship, they had plunged into romance separated by mile after mile of nothingness and yet still sundered by the truly vast distances of the world that separated them. They were involved in an Occult Romance—and I wished them joy of it.

Slowly, Khe-Hi brought his extended arms down. His hands passed through the phantom presences at his side. Now I could only look at his eyes. I was aware of nothing else.

From the eyes and brains of the Jikai Vuvushis, into the conjoined eyes and brains of the three thaumaturges, the pictures flowed, and so out again and into my eyes.

I saw.

The preliminaries had been done away with. We began *in medias res.* A party of warriors huddled behind boulders, crouched low to the dusty ground. Spearing into the sky about them the jagged peaks of the Mountains of the West of Hamal leered down upon that desolate scene.

The wildmen crept closer, and shot and laughed, and dropped flat, taunting the Jikai Vuvushis.

The end was not far off.

The girls were hungry, thirsty, bloodshot of eye, and many bore wounds. Yet their spirit did not falter. They were Sisters of the Sword, and they would fight to the death.

Weirdly, to me, I recognized their faces. I knew them all, for in the present time they served as jurukkers within the guard corps. Jinia ti Follendorf stared around a boulder, her bow gripped, the last shaft notched. Hikdar Noni Thostan, the pastang commander, positioned at the center of that pathetic ring of defense, held herself ready to plunge to any threatened point, her sword clenched in a brown and dirty fist. Minci Farndion, not yet a Deldar, crouched low, ready to degut the first moorkrim to leap over her boulder. Floring Mecrilli was there, with two arrows left, and as I watched that scene she handed one of them to a companion whose quiver was empty.

Noni was the first to react to the eerie phenomenon. The viewpoint swiveled sickeningly and I was looking out across the scattered boulders, away over the evil slinking forms of the wildmen, up to a buttress of rock jagging from a sheer mountainside.

On that rocky shelf a light grew and blossomed.

I heard—or thought I heard—Seg gasp at my side.

The light expanded. The radiance soared from the cliff edge and sailed out over the rocks below. Now I could see a throne-like chair moving through thin air shimmering with uncanny power. Silks trailed from that throne and did not flutter in the wind of passage. Chavonth pelts and ling furs smothered the throne and steps in luxury. Rearing above the throne the jeweled canopy fashioned into the likeness of a dinosaur's wedge-shaped head seemed to glare down in demonic fury. The jaws gaped, the fangs glittered silver, and each eye was a vivid ruby furnace. Overpowering in effect, the throne and the risslaca canopy, sailing silently through the air.

Yet, all this was a mere frame for the woman who lolled in the throne.

Dressed in green and black with lavish gold ornamentation, she lolled with one white hand to her chin. Her pallor was intense. Her dark hair descended into a widow's peak over her forehead and swept in voluptuous tresses to her shoulders. Her green eyes regarded the scene beneath her, luminous slits of jade. Around her forehead a jeweled band held at its center a wedge-shaped reptilian head, jaws agape, scaled, ruby eyes malevolent.

Seg's hiss of indrawn breath was unmistakable.

"Csitra!"

The throne soared above the moorkrim. Two or three of those more brave or foolhardy than their companions chanced a shot. The shafts passed through the apparition. The woman's eyelids, coated in gold leaf, partially closed. Her mouth, a purple-red bud-shape, pouted.

The wildmen collapsed. They fell and lay in their windrows, unmarked, unwounded; but dead, all dead.

The Jikai Vuvushis stared up. No sound, no smell, nothing apart from the ghostly advance of the phantom throne and the Witch of Loh disturbed the mountains.

The whole scene fluctuated and wavered. I blinked. Black and red flashes of light and darkness slashed across like lightning upon a night of Notor Zan. The rocks, the mountains, the abandoned corpses of the moorkrim, the very throne itself, all shimmered as though seen through smoke or deep beneath the sea.

Csitra—if this manifestation was of the Witch of Loh of the Coup Blag—was putting forth occult energy. She had destroyed the wildmen for her own purposes; now she influenced the Jikai Vuvushis so that one by one they dropped upon the harsh ground, sprawling into the dust.

The vision faded, flickered—and was gone.

I came to my senses with the sounds of men and women coming alive about me, the smell of the tent and of oiled leather, the feel of sweat upon the air.

What we had witnessed was of immense importance. That would be investigated. I had the utmost faith in Khe-Hi and Deb-Lu. But there was a certain thing I must do...

Deb-Lu's image wavered as though he prepared to begone. Ling-Li-Lwingling's projection remained, and she half-turned toward Khe-Hi. I called out, harshly.

"Sana! A moment. We have met, as you will recall. I must tell you that you are heartily welcome in Vallia. I—"

"You have changed your tune, tiks—" she began to say, and then halted herself. Perhaps she had realized that as no one likes being addressed as tikshim—worse than our Earthly my man—thus to address an emperor in whose lands she might wish to live was little short of impolitic.

"Come to Vallia, Ling-Li-Lwingling. I hold Khe-Hi in the highest possible esteem. As for this Csitra—I can feel sorry for her, for she was enamored of an evil man."

"I will think on it, Dray Prescot."

Then, suddenly, like a smashed lamp, she vanished.

The Jikai Vuvushis sat on their seats like mice, hushed, shattered by what had been revealed to them, secrets locked into their unremembering memories.

Khe-Hi did not waste time on his own affairs. He said: "I believe I have the way of it now, Dray. I do not yet know the details of *how* it was done; but it is enough to know that it *was* done."

"Csitra bewitched the girls through her occult magic." I took a breath, feeling through all the evil horror the first hopes that now we could conquer the plague of werewolves. "They did not know—do not know. But it is they, the Jikai Vuvushis who survived in the Mountains of the West, who have been creating the werewolves."

"Yes. Without doubt."

"By the Veiled Froyvil!" burst out Seg. "*Turko!* I had an idea he wasn't inspecting that churgur regiment—and Jurukker Floring Mecrilli is not here! I'll wager—"

"That's Turko—and that girl tried hard to entrap me..."

We all rushed out of the tent. Turko! If we were right, and we knew we were right, then our comrade Kov Turko, Turko the Shield, was being transmogrified into a werewolf!

Twenty-one

Csitra's Pronouncement

"Kov Turko! Turko the Shield!" People rushed about the camp, shouting, yelling. "Jurukker Mecrilli! Floring Mecrilli! Kov Turko!" Everywhere men and women were running, ripping open tents, upturning carts, burrowing into piles of stores. The noise soared up to the suns. I was in a terrible state. Old Turko—turning into a ganchark! It didn't bear thinking of.

After I'd raced up and down yelling uselessly, I forced myself to calm down. This had to be thought out. A flutduin patrol was sent winging off to the churgur regiment out on the plain just in case Turko had really gone there.

Khe-Hi came panting up. "Dray, Dray! There is still a chance nothing has happened yet."

"What?"

"The stabs of occult energy. They must be the signals by which Csitra triggers a girl into action. I believe she bewitched the girls so that she could use her kharrna to spy through their eyes—"

"My Val!"

"—and when a victim and situation were ripe, she would order the girl to—"

"Do what, bite a chunk out of him—?"

"No, but—"

"Perhaps..."

I thought of what had happened. Of guards on duty kissing. Of the way Floring Mecrilli simply wanted to kiss me. Of the spots of blood on the mouths of men, caught as werewolves, who had not killed a victim. I thought I saw.

"Csitra peers through the eyes of a girl, sees a man, and then stabs her power. The girl and the man kiss."

"I will have all their teeth examined. It is known that teeth may be hollowed out and poison secreted. This will be no ordinary poison..."

"By Vox, no!"

"A bitten lip, a drop of blood, is that so unusual?"

Seg rushed by, yelling. "They think he took a voller! Come on, Dray!"

"Khe-Hi!" I fairly yelled. "Go into lupu and find him, and then tell us!"

"At once."

Even as Seg and I sprinted for the voller lines a ghostly figure materialized by the voller's chains, its turban toppling over one ear.

"He has gone to Gliderholme with the Jikai Vuvushi. There is a tavern there, The Sweet Gregarian."

"Warn him, Deb-Lu! Warn him!"

Deb-Lu's lupal projection wavered and vanished. Seg and I vaulted into the voller and the handlers cast off the chains. As we rose a frantic figure fairly hurled itself at the airboat. We looked over the side. Nath na Kochwold hung there, gripping onto a dangling chain, yelling blue bloody murder up at us. We hauled him inboard, and you may judge of our feelings when we made no uncouth jokes.

On that swift desperate flight to the little market town of Gliderholme which we had recently liberated from Jhansi's clutches, we tried to talk coherently about this affair and not to jabber mindlessly in anticipatory dread of defeat and Turko's ghastly death.

For, make no mistake, we knew what would have to be done...

"Hollowed-out teeth," said Nath. He shivered. "Well, how many teeth, then, per girl?"

We started to figure the computations.

"A damned lot," growled Seg. "Look at that howling pack after Farnrien's Edge."

"A lot of kissing went on then, that's for sure."

Other airboats fleeted after us. There was no further apparition either of Deb-Lu or of Khe-Hi. The air rushed past. We smashed the speed lever over to the stop. We roared on through the sweet air of Kregen under the twin suns, and we prayed to all the gods and spirits.

Although the ancients on our Earth speculated and the wise men of Kregen, also, had scientific and medical knowledge well beyond comparable levels on the Earth of that time, I was not fully aware of what a virus was or could do. Now I understand that Csitra employed the virus that caused the change in a man and turned him into a werewolf. The disease of lycanthropy, in which a person imagines himself to be a werewolf, must have played a part. The girl smiled and beckoned, and the foolish man succumbed, and Csitra watched all through the girl's eyes. A sweet kiss, succulent and juicy, and then the quick nip, the love bite, the token of passion. And, later, the awful change when Csitra willed, and the howling pursuit and the screaming and terrified victim... Yes, the Witch Csitra had done great damage...

And those poor damned Jikai Vuvushis did not know a single iota of it all...

How Csitra must have laughed when they were incorporated into my guard corps. She could never have anticipated such a tremendous boost to her plans. And her plans had been working. She was quite clearly trying to alienate me. If wherever I went I was trailed by gancharks, the people would fall away, the fingers would point, there would be muttering, and dark looks, and then rebellion. She did not want to kill me, just to make sure I had no home in Vallia.

Her uhu, fruit of her unhappy liaison with Yantong, had quite other motives. Now I understood what Csitra meant when she spoke to me through the corpse of Larghos m'Mondifer. As a werewolf, Larghos had been impelled to attack me by Phunik. That could be the only explanation.

His mother still held power over him. While that situation lasted, I could feel a little freer. But, what when the uhu Phunik came into his own powers?

I had to look to Deb-Lu-Quienyin and to Khe-Hi-Bjanching. Also, with luck there would be Ling-Li-Lwingling to help. I trusted so.

"There it is!" yelped Seg. "There's the town. Now where's this dratted tavern?"

The thought of all that would be lost if we could not save Turko caused me to quiver as though straining against a dead weight. I thought of the times when Turko and I had escaped from the Manhounds, when we'd ventured down into Mungul Sidrath, of a score of adventures together, when we'd escaped from the wrestler's booths in Mahendrasmot. No! I wouldn't lose Turko! I couldn't!

Seg spotted the tavern by the sign. He simply slapped the voller down into the courtyard, thus smashing up one of Farris's fleet, and we leaped out, not stopping for the shouts, and roared into the tavern.

Now Seg is a fine large fellow and the great lump of belly and chins that got in his way simply somersaulted out of it. Nath straddled the fallen man and we crashed up the blackwood stairs. Four doors at the top of the stairs, one half-open and so could be ignored. Three doors...

We each kicked one open.

The noise from below must be reaching up to the occupants of the rooms by now. Someone was going to go to investigate. The fates that run our lives, if such things as fates exist, sometimes smile and more often frown upon me.

A furred and feline Fristle swung open Nath's door even as he kicked. Then my boot crashed against my door and I went barging through. The fates, then, had selected me...

Turko, wearing a most fetching robe, was in the act of pouring a goblet of wine. The room was a simple tavern room with curtains, lamps, tables and chairs and a bed in the alcove. Upon the bed lay Floring Mecrilli wearing not very much but enough to maintain her estimation of herself and her decency. Turko looked up and the wine shot across the table.

"What the zigging hell!"

A scream of so rich and fearsome a quality burst from Floring that both Turko and I jumped to stare at her. She flung herself up from the bed, shedding draperies, her face ghastly, her eyes enormous, her forefinger pointing...

She pointed at the ghostly form of Deb-Lu who waveringly materialized at the foot of the bed.

"Khe-Hi!" came the faint voice of Deb-Lu. "Muster yourself, San, and quickly—"

Deb-Lu vanished.

Turko yelled: "What the hell's going on?"

I shouted: "Stand away from that girl, Turko, as you value your immortal ib."

Csitra, schemingly watching the scene through Floring's eyes, made her last cast. She knew there was but one chance. Her stab of occult power penetrated the defenses woven by our two Wizards of Loh; but they were far stronger than she and would quickly annul her ascendancy.

Floring Mecrilli, a Jikai Vuvushi very quick and lithe, impelled by sorcerous powers, simply leaped on Turko.

He staggered back and yet, being Turko, one hand supported both himself and the girl around her waist.

"Throw her off, Turko!"

She did not kiss him. Like a snake she struck. Her mouth opened and a star splintered whitely from her teeth. She bit into his lips. Her head snaked back and blood glistened on Turko's mouth.

"By Erthyr!" yelled Seg at my back. I saw the point of a dudinter arrow appear at my shoulder, aimed at the girl, and as Seg loosed I struck the shaft up. It caromed away and smacked into the ceiling.

"What the—?"

"Look at Turko. The girl's part is over."

There was—as usual—the one slender chance.

By the kiss of dudinter...

Turko's transformation began to take place as Csitra's planning bore this evil fruit. Hair began to sprout on his hands, on his cheeks. He started up, and his eyes showed the horror dragging at him. I leaped.

The dudinter blade, smeared with ganjid, cut into his mouth. He tried to evade me, and I held him, I held a famed and feared Khamorro, and I cut into that bleeding lip.

Seg was there, gripping Turko, and Nath, too. We held him, and I cut his lip deeply, and dragged the flesh away, and then sucked and spat, sucked and spat, and shuddered deep into my vitals...

All this cutting and sucking and spitting is usually of little value; for the poison runs deeply and quickly. But the ganjid and the dudinter swayed the contest. Turko looked terrible. His eyelids closed and they were like overripe plums. He sagged in our arms. We carried him to the bed, stepping over the unconscious body of Floring on the way. We put him down and there was no need to send for the needleman, for Dolan the Pills who'd followed us in a voller, appeared, knowing he would be needed.

Critically we watched the hair on Turko's hands and face. Slowly, the hair vanished and he was our old Turko again. Dolan gave him one of his pills, as famed and feared as a very Khamorro himself, and Turko slept.

"By the Veiled Froyvil, my old dom. I'd not like to go through that again!"

"Nor, by Vox, would I!" quoth Nath na Kochwold.

"It would be best not to move the kov until he has rested," said Dolan. "But the girl had better be removed."

"It's not her fault," I said, somewhat harshly. "She must go back to her friends until we find a way to rid them of this curse."

A strong guard was posted on Turko's room, on the Sweet Gregarian, on the town of Gliderholme. When we reached the courtyard Oby stood contemplating the wreck of the voller, clicking his teeth against his tongue and fingering his chin.

"Some people," he said to no one in particular as we appeared, "should go back to learning to fly."

But he knew the score and simply expressed his feelings elliptically.

"See what you can do, Oby. Turko is asleep and is our own Turko."

"Thank Opaz!"

During the next sennight as we finalized our preparations for what we hoped would be the final advance, news came in that the sorcerously duped people of Vennar were massing to resist us. Jhansi employed a certain Sorcerer of Murcroinim, one Rovard the Murvish. In his skins and bones, his leem-skull upon his head, shaking his morntarch, he conveyed the impression of a fearsome power. Also, he stank. The effluvium of rasts and sewers clung to him and preceded him by a goodly length of smelling range. He it was who overbore ordinary folk, turned them into screaming fanatics ready to fight until they were slain.

With Jhansi's regular paktuns leaving him, he had once again called on Rovard the Murvish for ungodly assistance.

Recovered, Turko had rejoined, and at this news he said, "I've had my belly full of sorcery. Let us go forward and blatter them. The Wizards, to whom I owe much, will do what they can. I do not think the issue will be in doubt."

"I agree," said Seg.

The coming campaign would not be easy, would not be a walkover. But we felt uplifted that we had removed the plague of the werewolves. The girls' teeth had been examined. They were not hollowed out. The virus, as I now know it to have been, had been precipitated by thaumaturgical art ready for use when the girl bit into the soft flesh of her lover's lip. The Wizards of Loh assured us the girls could be cured, completely, and could take up normal lives. At this we rejoiced.

Just before we were due to march and fly out, a voller winged in over the camp. We looked up and did not recognize her, although both Korero and Oby were confident she had been built in Balintol.

Khe-Hi started forward eagerly.

Well, yes... She looked as she had looked when she'd spoken so abruptly to me from the gherimcal upon the field of blue and yellows, just before that tremendous fight with Prince Mefto the Kazzur. Her ivory-smooth face, the level blue eyes, the piled masses of her auburn hair; all were as I remembered them. But, now, she stepped from the voller, inclined her head in greeting, and then walked swayingly towards Khe-Hi.

He looked radiant.

The Lahals were made, and everyone considered this a good omen for the coming campaign.

Khe-Hi said: "Dray. Ling-Li wants a private word as soon as possible."

"Of course. Oh, and when are you being married?"

"When you have heard what Ling-Li has to say, and decisions have been made, we will then set a date."

"Bad as that, is it?"

"Worse."

I refused to feel premature alarm. Seg, Turko, Nath and I went with Khe-Hi to this meeting with the Witch of Loh. Her tent was furnished luxuriously with her own belongings brought in her flier. She had a small retinue.

"Lahal, Sana. Tell us this dire news."

"Sit down, Dray Prescot. And the rest. Wine. Listen. I bear you no ill-will; I deprecate what I have to say. But if I am to live in Vallia with Khe-Hi, then I must do what I can to make my new home agreeable."

"A most sensible attitude," I said gravely.

She shot me a hard blue look that seemed to inquire if I mocked her. Taking up a goblet of wine, she said: "That is sooth. I have had a hard life. I was a pawn in the affairs of Phu-Si-Yantong and Csitra. But I learned. Khe-Hi and I have come to an agreement—oh, not in the flesh but through our own arts—and I feel confident I shall be happy in Vallia—if..."

I did not, and neither did my comrades, give her the satisfaction of idiotically mouthing: "If?"

She sipped. "You have penetrated to the core of Csitra's designs with the werewolves. You are just beginning."

Again we sat silently.

"Yes, Deb-Lu," she said on a sudden, dipping her head in a quick bird-like motion. "You may enter." Then, softening that haughty tone, she added, "You are very welcome."

The lupal projection of Deb-Lu glowed into phantasmal life within the tent.

Khe-Hi said: "Tell us what you learned of Csitra's plans."

"Willingly. She has made a Pronouncement."

At this, I saw Deb-Lu's hand go to his turban, and halt, transfixed. He stared anxiously at the Witch of Loh.

"With all due ceremony, with many human sacrifices, much shedding of blood, great agony of body and spirit, she has Pronounced the Curses."

We four mere men, not sorcerers out of Loh, listened to the Witch's words as she spoke on, and we listened numbed and drained and desperately concerned for the future.

"Occult forces have been stirred. Beings undisturbed for thousands of seasons have been roused. The reek of the ash pits, the screams of the dying, the long moaning wails of those in torment who may not die—all have been raised up against you. For the Witch of Loh, Csitra, has Pronounced the Nine Unspeakable Curses Against Vallia."

A silence followed. The tent's atmosphere cloyed. The two Wizards of Loh were overcome. Seg and Turko and Nath were unsure. Well, by Krun, so was I. But it was no good shying at shadows. I cleared my throat.

"Well, and, Sana. What does that mean?"

"Who can say what form the Curses will take? Werewolves—but of course! Vampires, and not the Vampires of Sabal, I can assure you. Plagues, famine, fires and pestilence. Infestation and Zombies and the Undead. Vallia has been cursed nine times. You may expect what you will receive."

I said: "On the morrow we march out to fight a great battle. After we have won that battle I will think what best to do about Csitra and the Nine Unspeakable Curses Against Vallia." That is what I said. What I thought was: "this sounds like it, Dray Prescot. I know what I'm going to do. I don't know what my Delia will say. I must take my chances and, perhaps for the first time in my life, go against Delia's wishes. But I know what I must do."

So we marched out to do battle with the traitor Layco Jhansi and his army of ensorcelled people, and, after that, as you will hear, I made my plans and proposed what I, Dray Prescot, would do. But, by the putrescent eyeballs and decomposing nose of Makki Grodno! What I proposed, what Delia proposed, and what happened, bore no relationship at all to one another. Not a single little bit, by Zair!

WITCHES OF KREGEN

Witches of Kregen

The story of Dray Prescot on the fascinating world of Kregen four hundred light-years from Earth is arranged to be read in individual volumes. Taken to Kregen first by the Savanti, the mortal but superhuman people of the Swinging City of Aphrasöe, he was rejected by them as too unruly and rebellious a spirit. The Star Lords—the Everoinye—selected him to carry out their mysterious projects for Kregen and, in between these exploits, Prescot hurtled headlong into adventures on his own account. The people of the Empire of Vallia called him to be their emperor and bring them out of the Times of Troubles, and one of his tasks is to rebuild the empire and clean out the slavers, the reiving flutsmen and those who batten on misery.

The plan to re-unite all Vallia is now under threat from the obstructions caused by Csitra, a Witch of Loh, who has Pronounced the Nine Unspeakable Curses Against Vallia. A plague of werewolves has left many of the people who shouted for Dray Prescot as emperor suspicious and fearful for the future.

There are many foes still to be overcome on Kregen; but Prescot has many good comrades and his never-failing source of strength, the Empress Delia, to stand at his side. Now in the streaming mingled lights of the Suns of Scorpio, the jade and ruby fires of Antares, Dray Prescot must go forward to whatever of peril and headlong adventure his future may bring.

Alan Burt Akers

One

Frogs

The first frogs fell from the sky on the morning of the day selected for the decisive battle against Layco Jhansi's army of crazed fanatics. Kov Turko's Ninth Army, busy preparing the first breakfast, stopped as the sky filled with the tumbling bodies. Frogs fell everywhere, into cooking pots, sizzling in the fires, impaling themselves on spears, stampeding the riding animals, bearing down tents by the sheer weight of their numbers.

Frogs, roklos, toads and lizards blackened the brightness of Zim and Genodras, the twin Suns of Scorpio.

Some squashed as they hit the hard-packed earth here on the border between Vennar and Falinur. Most hopped about, their ribbing filling the air with clamor. Everywhere the ground appeared an undulating sea of shining green backs.

"That dratted witch!" Seg's black hair swirled as he batted at the descending swarms.

Nath na Kochwold hoisted his red pikeman's shield aloft and the crimson flower rang and bucked with the rain of bodies buffeting it.

Turko ran to join me under the hard projecting edge of a fighting gallery of a ship of the air. His powerfully muscled body, that of a master of the arcane wrestler's arts, as much as his lofty rank of kov, eased him through the press of men sheltering under the gallery. He looked mad clean through.

"That Witch of Loh! That Csitra! This must be another of her Curses."

"Indubitably."

He glared at me, for a tiny moment unsure of my tone, and then: "Yes! And she's successfully spoiled our plans for today."

"It seems to me," I said, and I spoke mildly, "she has made a grave mistake."

"By Morro the Muscle! How?"

"Why, if she'd waited until we were about to come to handstrokes with Layco Jhansi's poor deluded—"

"I see that. Those screaming idiots would have believed it was the doing of their own sorcerer, and—"

132

"Precisely," said Seg, storming up, looking ugly. "But she's done enough damage as it is. Look at them!"

The Ninth Army had turned into a mob. Frantically the soldiers ran and yelled and flailed away at the falling frogs. The succulent early-morning odors of breakfast were replaced by the stink of roasting and charring amphibians. The uproar was prodigious. Any resemblance to a disciplined army was entirely lost.

"It'll take all day today and tomorrow just to get the animals back."

"And," I said, "if Layco Jhansi attacks we'll be mincemeat."

I spoke with deliberate emphasis, expecting to be instantly contradicted.

I was not disappointed.

"If Jhansi dares to attack," rapped out Turko. "By Vox! We'll have him. Have him whole and spit out the pips."

"He'll certainly break his rotten teeth on my lads," promised Nath na Kochwold, as hard and intolerant of imperfection as ever, a true fighting leader of the Phalanx.

The uproar overturning the camp racketed on unabated. There seemed no end to the supply of falling toads and roklos. Frogs hopped everywhere, clambering over one another, tumbling off the heaped piles of squirming bodies, and their ribbiting croaked on and on.

"Where's Khe-Hi?" Seg buffeted a luckless toad who tried to hop into our refuge under the fighting gallery. The men with us pressed close to the wooden curve of the ship's lower hull. A few feet away the packed bodies were piling up breast high. We'd be drowned under frogs soon if the rain did not cease in a very short time.

"Like any sensible man, he's with his lady love." Turko held a sensible respect for Wizards of Loh; but he was still Turko the Shield and therefore his respect was inevitably tinged with a quizzical amusement. "And even though she may be a Witch of Loh, Ling-Li-Lwingling is a remarkably attractive woman."

No one of my comrades offered to make some cuttingly amusing remark about Turko's qualifications for making that judgment. The situation here for all its unlikely bizarreness was damned serious. The piles of bodies continued to rise higher out there on the plain and most of the campfires had been unpleasantly extinguished.

"So," said Seg, "he's likely to be occupied and not realize what's going on."

"Then," I said, and in that familiar yet empty gesture that indicates determination, I hitched up my sword. "Then we'll have to bust our way through to him."

"Through that lot?" yelped Turko.

"Any other ideas?"

"No. But we'll have to move sharpish."

"Right. Wenda!"

"Wenda!" said Seg with enormous sarcasm. Wenda means "let's go!" "We'll be like men sludging through treacle."

Seg was right. There was another way, though its employment would give me little pleasure. But when it is a matter of your life versus a trifle of valuable property, there is no conflict of interests. None at all, by Krun!

A creak overhead snatched our attention.

The wooden fighting gallery projecting from the side of the sailing flier of the air groaned again, and a little spurt of wood-dust spouted from a joint. The gallery had been designed to carry archers in aerial combat, with spearmen to back then if boarding was in the offing. It was a slender construction; but it had been built to carry the weight of men in combat.

A plank of the flooring abruptly snapped and snagged downwards, disgorging a flood of green bodies upon our heads. The flopping green hoppers leaped about croaking.

"They must be piled up mast high!" yelled Turko.

"That lot'll collapse any second," said Nath na Kochwold.

"It'll hold for a bit yet," said Seg. "All the same, that gallery shouldn't break under the weight of a bunch of frogs—"

"So the confounded witch has increased their weight."

Seg's fey blue eyes regarded the gallery above us. Sometimes my blade comrade's powers startled even him. He said, repeating himself: "It'll hold for a bit yet," and we all knew he spoke sooth.

The frogs were now coming down hammering like roundshot. Anyone hit on the head would be killed outright and probably decapitated into the bargain.

Now, on Kregen when you go to breakfast you naturally use cutlery, and some of the men had theirs still with them. But, as this was Kregen, you also take with you what you take just about everywhere you go—your weaponry.

Thus it was I was able to bellow at a couple of Hakkodin to use their axes and halberds on the hull of the ship. I will agree that the pikemen do not usually take their pikes to breakfast, for the brumbytes stack their pikes in a most neat and orderly prescribed fashion; they will have their swords with them. On Kregen you never know when the next emergency will spring on you.

The axemen soon bashed a way through the hull of the ship. This destruction displeased me, as I say; but needs must in this situation. We ripped the planks apart and dodged roklos and frogs toppling from the sagging gallery.

"Hurry! Get inside, all of you!"

We only just made it.

As I felt Seg and Turko grab my arms and haul me in through the hole, the gallery at last collapsed. It broke up with the sound of a twenty-one-gun salute. The lot smashed down onto the ground where we'd been standing scant moments before.

Nath na Kochwold was furiously angry.

"That's like him," Seg said. "Stupid clean through."

"Aye," amplified Turko. "Daft as they come."

"But—but—" Nath had known me in good times and bad, as had Seg and Turko. But Nath genuinely felt that things had changed. "You're the emperor!" he got out. "You should not have been the last man—"

The gloom of the tween decks before our eyes adjusted made it difficult to see the expressions on the hard faces of my comrades. But I knew for a certainty that Seg and Turko were enjoying themselves. Oh, yes, we were a mighty high-up lot these days, kings and kovs, emperors and nobles, yet my blade comrades still remembered the old days, days when we'd been slave, when we'd adventured over the hostile if beautiful face of Kregen, days when we'd not known where the next crust was coming from, although we were damned sure we knew where the next lot of grief was due to arrive.

Comrades in a fellow's life are precious—precious!—and worth all the tomfoolery of gold and jewels in the fabled Gardens of Hoi Parndole. Nath na Kochwold was a good comrade and had proved it on a score of occasions; yet still he was used to me as the emperor, as the man who had forged the Phalanx that was his pride, as the man to whom he looked as the savior of Vallia. He had not been slave with me.

So I bashed the dust from my face and clothes and bellowed out: "Get this ship aloft, famblys! *Bratch!*"

Seg and Turko took my meaning.

Men ran to the controls. A couple of Jikai Vuvushis ran past, the girls determined that they should stand at the controls and send the skyship into the air, and damn all onkerish men who got in their way.

The timbers of the ship groaned. The hull heaved beneath us. With the power conferred by the two silver boxes buried deep in her hull, the ship lifted into the air. She was not a voller. She did not have the power, conferred by the two silver boxes, of propelling herself through thin air. She could rise with that mystical power, derived from the mix of minerals in one box and the cayferm in the other; for forward propulsion she must use her magneto-etheric keel and the force of the wind in her sails.

If anyone was foolish enough to venture out on deck to try to set the canvas he'd have his skull driven in by a frog as hard as a cannonball.

The flying ship lifted. The vorlca drifted with the breeze, as we could tell by her movements. Oh, yes, I was the emperor all right. I spoke and men and women acted. But I was growing sick and tired of all the pomp and circumstance surrounding this emperor nonsense. The quicker my lad Drak took over the reins of empire the better I'd like it. I had given my word to be the emperor, and had sworn to liberate the people—my people—of Vallia from the slavers and aragorn, the flutsmen and all those who oppressed them. Once the island was reunited, why, then, you wouldn't see me for dust.

As for Delia, my Delia of Delphond, my Delia of the Blue Mountains, who was the Empress of Vallia, I knew she shared my thoughts, I knew she wished to be free of the burdens of empire and go with me once more aroaming the broad and beckoning lands of Kregen.

The vorlca lifted and moved and the breeze drove her downwind. From a porthole we could see the incredible sight of the frogs and their kindred dropping from heaven.

If Delia and I did take off for a life of adventuring, I was certain that Seg Segutorio would come with us. I had a shrewd suspicion that his new wife, Milsi, who was Queen Mab of Croxdrin, would not be averse to the picaresque life of adventure. And what a life that would be! By Zair, we'd live life to the full, then—although, by all the devils in a Herrelldrin Hell, didn't we live life to the full right now?

In this tiny breathing space as we waited for the vorlca to drift downwind and clear the rain of frogs, I had time for reflections of different kinds. Yes, we lived life to the full—but whose full? Yes, I wanted to see Vallia once more united and peaceful. Yes, I most certainly wanted to see all the lands of Paz unite in a great league, a grand alliance, against the reiving Shanks who raided our coasts and slew without mercy. Yes, this was true. But, also, sometimes the burdens crowded too close and too heavy. Sometimes I understood with horror that I might yet grow callous and uncaring of anyone else save myself and my friends and family. If the disease of empire took me, I was big-headed enough to guess that not only all Vallia and Paz would suffer; all of Kregen would suffer.

"Almost clear, Dray," called Seg, peering out through the gash in the hull. "What a sight."

"That malignant witch." Turko looked out at Seg's side. "My Ninth Army—"

I did not think of the frogs and Turko's fine Ninth Army; I thought that perhaps I might really and truly only care about Delia and my family and my comrades, and to hell with the rest of Kregen. That was how I had behaved and believed in my reckless past on this planet. I had changed. Now I tried to be the enlightened emperor.

Could I change? Could Dray Prescot, the Lord of Strombor and Krozair of Zy, really stop being the reiving tearaway rascally fellow he was?

Seg bellowed in a too-loud voice: "Cheer up, my old dom! You look as though you've lost a zorca and found a calsany."

"Aye, Seg, aye."

The overhead abruptly split, the wood shattering away in scything splinters, and a couple of frogs belted down. They hit the deck under our feet with almighty crashes and instantly were up and hopping about. Turko caught them easily enough. He whistled.

"You're right. They weigh like stone."

"The whole picture is different," I said, forcing myself to return to the present and what was going on. "When Csitra dumped cartfuls of frogs onto our heads it was all a bit of an occult lark. She was plaguing us. But now, one of these damned frogs can knock down a fine soldier, between 'em they'll destroy this ship if we don't drift clear in time. She can destroy the whole Ninth Army at this rate."

"Khe-Hi just has to wake up!" Seg, like the prudent man he is—sometimes—positioned himself under a thick beam. We all did likewise, crowding shoulder to shoulder. The frogs began to batter their heavy way through the upper decks and shred the planking away. Soon they were hopping and croaking about our feet.

No one was going to venture out from the thick beam's protection to shovel them outside. No, by Vox!

My comrades are, by and large, a harum-scarum lot. Clearly, and despite the eeriness of it, they'd been taking this infestation of frogs and roklos and toads in an off-hand manner, seeing the ludicrousness of the situation. A whole piling-up of frogs from the sky would inconvenience us, make the beginning of the battle delayed, perhaps cause one or two hearts to tremble a little more than they had. But it was an infuriating delay, that was all.

Now, with what amounted to stones from catapults hurtling down around our heads, the whole picture became potentially disastrous.

"I suppose the possibility exists," said Nath with a casualness that totally failed in its object, "that Khe-Hi is unable to halt the infestation, that countering the thaumaturgy is beyond his art and strength."

"It exists but is unlikely—" Turko began.

Seg said brutally: "The better chance is that poor Khe-Hi has had his head bashed in."

So now it was in the open, the fact Nath had danced around, sounding querulous, which was a state very far from the fiery yet disciplined Krell Kapt of the Phalanx. If Khe-Hi had been killed, or even incapacitated, when would these damn frogs stop? Ever?

"Where's the woman getting 'em all from?"

"If," I said in that weirdly mild tone of mine, "they are real."

Seg shot me such a look of suspicion as to tell me I was overdoing the mildness bit. Seg had dragged the chief fear in our minds into the open. I just had to go back to being rough tough Dray Prescot again, hard corners and all.

We were able to speak in easy tones, and for just a queasy moment I couldn't grasp why that was strange. Then I realized that the incessant banging and crashing of frogs' bodies against the decks had dwindled away so that now only the last outriders of the descending column struck us.

"Praise Opaz for that!" exclaimed Nath na Kochwold.

We climbed up past the splinters and the wreckage to the deck and found ourselves perches. Truly, the scene was fantastic. It was awesome too, in a shivery way, for the solid column of frogs falling from the blue sky spread a considerable area and thus by their very bulk oppressed the imagination. Individual bodies were impossible to see in the shining flanks of the mass; colors shifted and reflected, the bright green of a lizard, the orange of a roklo, the brown of a toad, and over all the liquid green glinting of the frogs.

I was just saying: "I don't care for all this sorcerous stuff," when I felt a distinct thump, as it were, in the very air itself.

"What—?" said Turko, and, instinctively, the muscles along his arms rippled ready for instant action.

"Odd," said Seg, and turned himself around and stared out over the land.

The flying sailer drifted with the breeze and we saw a few other ships that had broken free. But, always, we turned back to stare at that infernal, impressive, diabolical torrent of frogs falling from a clear sky.

But...

Seg, with that feyness of his race, was obviously the first to see and recognize what had happened.

He let out a yelp, and then: "By the Veiled Froyvil, my old dom! Khe-Hi's done it!"

"What—?"

"*Look!*"

We all stared narrowly at the shining frogfall.

"Yes—Khe-Hi's done it."

"I like it," said Seg, cheerfully. "I like it!"

The column of frogs remained, as solid, as torrential, as impressively diabolical as it had been before. But now the frogs rained upwards.

Khe-Hi-Bjanching was sorcerously sending the damned frogs back whence they'd come, we hoped to fall out of the clear sky onto the head of the witch Csitra.

"Good old Khe-Hi!"

"And his lady love," pointed out Turko. "Ling-Li will have had a hand in this."

"I do like it," said Seg.

We stood to watch those damned frogs whirling back up into the sky and the relief was enormous, by Zair, I can tell you!

The experience through which we had just gone had been mind numbing. It had blunted out senses. At least, I felt that inner dizziness as though I had difficulty merely in keeping balance, in finding the right words, in carrying out even the simplest action. Sorcery sometimes plays a great part in the lives of people on Kregen; mostly it is just there, heard of but peripheral to busy lives.

There was little we could do until the frogs had all been returned from whence they came. A jury-rigged mast and a scrap of sail gave us control; but I felt it essential to return to the camp as fast as possible, so I bellowed out orders to land the ship. We'd go back on foot. There would be a tremendous amount of work to do back there sorting out the damage, caring for the wounded, preparing defenses, putting what regiments we could into shape for any possible attack from Layco Jhansi and his screaming fanatics.

The tall roof of the village barn glistened into view as the upward torrent of frogs continued. The cottages buried in the squiggling mass began to show a gable here, a twisted chimney there. This tiny village of Gordoholme, although within the area occupied by the Ninth Army, was generally out of bounds, off limits, to the swods in the ranks, and the officers, too, unless on duty. We had liberated the place from the clutches of Jhansi's offensive people; we did not wish to continue the crimes of which they were guilty.

This village of Gordoholme represented the farthest point we'd reached in our march into Vennar so far. Jhansi had refused the great and decisive battle we'd expected outside Gliderholme. We knew he was in trouble finding fresh mercenaries, for many of his paktuns had renounced their service and either returned home or joined the usurping King of North Vallia. This puzzled us, for the journey entailed shipping in order to circumvent the activities of the Racters who were at war with the King of North Vallia.

Whatever obscure motives prompted Jhansi and his sorcerous adviser, Rovard the Murvish, a highly aromatic Sorcerer of Murcroinim, into the various courses of action they had undertaken against us, one fact remained more than most probable—Jhansi would hurry to hire on more mercenaries, and his agents would be overseas now scouring the markets and barracks for tazll paktuns.

In the meantime he had the mobs of ordinary people driven into a state of fanatical frenzy by the thaumaturgical arts of Rovard to hurl against us in waves of screaming humanity. This disgusted us. As I watched the stream of ascending frogs I seriously considered the usefulness of sorcery to any world among the millions of worlds in space.

The people who had taken refuge with us in the ship—the vorlca was named *Wincie Smolek II*—gathered at the rails to watch. Among them I spotted a group of cavalrymen wearing pale-green uniforms, the dolmans well-frogged and the pelisses smothered in fur and gold wire. This habit of carrying a spare coat slung over the shoulder to put on when the weather turns chilly is well-known on this Earth, and is sensible enough for many fighting men of Kregen to adopt as a matter of course. These jutmen were from the Forty-Second Regiment of Zorcabows, raised and led by Strom Larghos Favana. The irony in the situation, which I savored as a man with toothache might savor a poultice, lay in their regimental name—Favana's Frogs.

"The damned things are nearly all gone," I said. "If we're going, we'd better make a start."

Seg and Turko did not reply but just climbed down the shattered remnants of the ladder to the ground. Nath clipped out a command to the men clustered along the rails, and they began to go over the side. They were not all chattering away among themselves as one might have expected. They were very quiet. The enormity of what had happened affected them, affected all of us, deeply.

Soon we were marching off toward Gordoholme and the ruined camp of the Ninth Army.

Other vessels had lifted clear and no doubt the people aboard them would be doing just what we were doing. The flying saddle birds had mostly, fortunately for them and us, been dispersed on patrol duties.

"What a hell of a mess!" said Turko, highly disgusted.

"We'll soon have your army back in shape, Turko," said Seg, striding on, his bow slanting up over his back.

I didn't say anything. The catastrophe might yet prove decisive. Certainly, it had put back our plans for this part of Vallia to what might be a disastrous degree.

In his decisive way, Nath na Kochwold said, "The discipline of the army will hold up, Turko. I'll see to that, by Vox."

Well, that was Nath for you, tough and uncompromising, dedicated to the ideals of order and discipline.

He glared upon the men trooping along from the stranded sailer. His fierce eyebrows drew down.

"Look at 'em!" he exclaimed. "By the Blade of Kurin! A bunch of washerfolk with the laundry would look smarter."

With that, off he went, rounding up the soldiers, bellowing orders, cutting into them. He did not wave his arms about frantically. He did not even draw his sword and brandish that. He got in among the mob and his incisive personality and reputation very quickly sorted them out.

It made no matter who or what they were. Whether pikemen without pikes, cavalry without mounts, heavy infantry without shields, they jumped to his cracked-out commands.

Very soon they were in a column of march, three abreast, and striding along, heads up, chests out, swinging their arms. It wouldn't be beyond Nath na Kochwold to have them singing in a moment or two.

"You've got to admire—" began Turko.

"Aye," said Seg. "What's that?"

His keen bowman's eye picked up the tiny black cloud in the distance before any of the others. We all swiveled to look.

Seg, Turko and a small group of the lads from my bodyguard, standing a little to the side of the marching column, watched that small cloud as Nath strode up to join us.

"That's got 'em..." He stopped himself, swung about, shaded his eyes against the Suns.

Seg said: "Flyers."

"A returning patrol?" But Turko spoke the question without conviction as to the answer.

Glints of light speared off the aerial riders, armor and weapons flashing in the suns-light.

"Damned flutsmen," I said.

"Aye," someone at my back ground out. "May they rot in a Herrelldrin Hell."

We'd all had experience of flutsmen, unpleasant experiences, tending to result in sudden death if you were not the quicker.

Flutsmen, reiving bandits of the air, had preyed on Vallia during and after the Times of Troubles. They owed allegiance to no one apart from their own bands. They would hire out, serving as mercenaries, if the prospect of loot was good. They fought hard and viciously. They were not nice people, to use a phrase once coughed out concerning them. Loric the Wings had died after making that pronouncement. But he was right.

"Whatever they are," Turko said, "they are enemies to us."

"And if they've been newly hired by Layco Jhansi," amplified Seg, carefully taking his bow off his shoulder, "they've caught us at a remarkably inconvenient moment."

At this distance it was still only possible to make an estimate of the numbers of flutsmen. From the apparent thickness and extent of the flight, I judged more than a couple of hundred approached. Well, we'd find out their real strength soon enough.

Nath shot off to the marching column not wasting any time and instantly the soldiers began to fan out and take up the best defensive positions they could find.

"So much," said Seg, stringing his longbow with that cunning application of flexing power that betrayed long experience and great strength. "So much for our friend Nath's neat marching orders."

Around us grew little vegetation to afford cover. There was no handy river. The ground puffed dust-hard underfoot. No, we'd have to stand and fight these reivers of the air where we were.

"I make it better than two hundred and fifty," remarked Turko. He had no sword to draw and I noticed the way he flexed his arms, as if instinctively limbering up for a contest in which all his skills in unarmed combat could be negated. Yet that was a foolish thought. I'd rather have Turko the Shield with me, unarmed, than many and many a man lumbering in full armor and with a whole arsenal of edged and pointed weapons.

With a flash of the old quizzically mocking Turko, he turned to me, half-smiling.

"I do not see Korero the Shield, Dray."

"And I don't see a single shield, either."

"So your back—"

"My back will have to be the business of myself, and your back yours, if we are parted."

In that quiet way of his, Seg Segutorio glanced across as he reached out for the first shaft from his quiver, and said: "I'll fight alongside you, Turko."

I nodded. The arrangement was sensible.

Turko contented himself with: "Aye, Seg. It is a pity Nath didn't hang onto that shield."

Just that, a pity. We looked as though we might be entering on the last great fight. If we were, if we were all to die here, well, I couldn't hope to go down to the Ice Floes of Sicce in the company of finer comrades.

The oncoming flutsmen spread out into individual dots. The dots sprouted wings and became fluttrells, and the riders on their backs, brandishing their weapons, became men.

There were more nearly three hundred of them.

We set ourselves and grasped our own swords and spears. Seg lifted his bow.

Streaming their flying silks and furs, their standards fluttering in the breeze, their armor and weapons a blaze of glitter in the radiance of the Suns of Scorpio, the flutsmen swooped upon us.

Two

Concerning feet caught in stirrups

Seg shot. As always, he shot superbly. Four shafts spat from his bow, rose-feathered slivers of death. Four flutsmen screeched and toppled to hang from their harness, the clerketers strapped about them, their weapons falling away beneath.

The birds' wingbeats thrashed the air. Dust spumed. Some flutsmen circled, trying to shoot with their crossbows into the confusion. Some of my lads fell.

The majority of these aerial bandits, seeing the great preponderance of numbers on their side, just landed their fluttrells and jumped off ready to fight.

I, Dray Prescot, was not prepared to let any foeman, particularly not these unhanged rasts of the air, dictate the tactics of a fight. They might land and hop off their birds and prepare themselves to chop us up. Nath might very well have placed our lads in defensive positions, the proper course at the beginning when we expected to be shafted. Now, though, the situation was different...

There is something revolting about the easy, leisurely way some people prepare to kill others. This is nothing to do with the careful preparations that must be made, for killing is an arduous task, and not one to be undertaken lightly. No, I mean in these flutsmen you could almost see them licking their lips as they dismounted and drew their weapons for ground work and so, settling themselves, decided at last to advance and finish toying with us, ending their pleasurable anticipation for the real thing.

Well, they'd get no time allowed by me, no, by the stinking eyeballs and suppurating nostrils of Makki Grodno!

"Form!" I screeched it out, hard and high. Nath jerked as though I'd goosed him. "Form line, two ranks deep. *Bratch!*"

The lads here, many of my bodyguard corps, many from the Phalanx, were what one could call elite quality.

They bratched. They formed a two-deep line. I had no time to think of the panache of it, of the show-off I must appear. I leaped to front and center, yelling words like "Vallia! Charge! Get stuck into 'em!"

With a whooping yell we simply rushed pell-mell on the bunch of flutsmen as they were in the process of dismounting and thinking pleasant thoughts about carving us up.

They had not expected this reaction.

They were not panicked. Oh, no, flutsmen were not riff-raff. They partitioned off the sky to their own nefarious ends, and whenever we came across them we put them down. But they would not run away just because we charged them.

They usually had the pickings of fine weapons. Their crossbows could have been deadly; but I had had long experience of flutsmen and knew that once the crossbow was discharged the fighting fever of the fellow astride his fluttrell wouldn't allow him time or patience to reload. This was a common tactic with them, as I knew. And here and now most of them had just landed to fight.

Their weaponry would be the usual mix of sword and spear. Some would have shields. As you know, the shield was still, at this date, an innovation in Vallia. These flutsmen might hail from Havilfar—almost certainly—and so would know and use the shield, although many an aerial bandit couldn't be bothered with the flying discipline required to handle a shield aloft.

As for us, well, the new sword we had designed and built in Valka, called the drexer, had proved itself in battle. The drexer now equipped most of our regiments. As for me, well, it is true to say that almost anyone of Vallia who walks abroad without a rapier and main gauche feels naked. In this coming dust-up I'd use my drexer, like the lads.

And—the lack of shields would serve to remind them of earlier days, before a maniac called Dray Prescot had turned up in Vallia—to marry their princess!—and inter alia to foist upon them the coward's weapon— the shield.

The Suns of Scorpio shone upon the scene, a little breeze blew, the dust spumed up under the stomp of impatient feet, the smell of sweat and oiled leather, the sting of dust in eye, the slick of it along tongue and lip—well, well... A fight is a fight...

"Don't bother about dressing!" I screeched the words back over my shoulder. "Fast! Get into 'em!" And then, because I felt the occasion warranted the use of the great words, I bellowed out: "Hai Jikai!"

The lads responded. They rushed on, the beat of their boots loud upon the earth. They yelled.

"Hai Jikai! Vallia! The emperor! Dray Prescot! Hai Jikai!"

It was all a bedlam and rush and tumult. And then, the evil flicker and tinker-hammering of swords...

No, the flutsmen didn't run away when we so unexpectedly charged slap-bang into them as they dismounted. But they were caught, as it were, with one foot in the stirrup.

In that first mad rush I swear each one of our lads dispatched at least one of the thieving bastards to the Ice Floes of Sicce.

The fight spread out, for saddle birds take up a lot of space when they flutter their wings and land. This was where trouble could hit us. If some of us were caught out of formation, straggling, chasing after the foemen, they could be cut down before we could come up with them again. The birds did not like the uproar going on about them. Some incontinently flapped up into the air again. Those that had been quickly staked down slashed their wings about and struck here and there with their beaks, so that we gave them all very wide berths. The fight settled down to a slogging match in which, I fancied, my lads would have the upper hand.

In a tiny segment in that scarlet rush of madness, Seg, hardly panting, his handsome face hard-set, brought his man down and then turned, panther-swift, for the next. Him, I dispatched. Seg nodded.

"They didn't know what hit 'em. Dray."

We glared about between the birds, seeing the clumping as the fighting raged.

"They picked the wrong target today, that's for sure."

A flutsman flew through the air toward us.

Nothing unusual in that? Wrong. He was flying without his saddle bird. He turned over twice and came down on his back with such a thump as must have broken his spine into smithereens. Turko smiled.

"They are not enjoying themselves."

The implications were obvious.

Seg laughed and then started off, sword poised, to where two flutsmen were chasing one of our lads around a bird. Seg was brief and to the point. The soldier—he was a brumbyte—didn't bother to gasp out thanks but went charging off to where a group of his comrades battled equal numbers. Seg let him go and strolled back to Turko and me.

"Seen Nath?"

"No."

The area was now a maelstrom of dust, wings, the flicker of steel, and the phantom shapes of running bodies. Just how the day was going was, for the moment, impossible to tell. Seg and Turko were sublimely confident that the flutsmen would soon have had enough and would fly off.

"They don't like taking casualties," I said.

"That is true. They like easy pickings."

"May a green-fanged demon from Ledrik's Nether Hell take 'em all." Turko swung his arms and glared balefully about. Dust swirled about us and the fluttrell's noise and confusion gave the whole fight an unreal air, as though we fought in a nether bird-hell of our own.

Three more flutsmen ran at us and were summarily dispatched where they belonged. Although, to be honest, there are some flutsmen who aspire above the generality of their calling, some I have known I have even called friend. Sometimes a fellow is swept up by fate into a life not of his choosing. Well, by Zair, hadn't I been dragged up by the scruff of the neck from Earth, four hundred light years away, to be dumped down all naked and unarmed on Kregen to make my own way?

"That's interesting," observed Seg.

Half a dozen of our men who by their neat and tightly fitting uniforms were flyers from Valka were busily at work. As it were, with one hand they fended off flutsmen and with the other made sure the fluttrells were securely chained down to their stakes.

"My lads of Valka," I said, with what I admit to being a comfortable feeling, "are indeed great scallywags and rogues and terribly fierce fighting men; they also, thanks be, have an eye to turning an honest profit."

Mind you, no flyer of Valka, trained up by my Djangs to fly a flutduin, would change that superb saddle flyer for a fluttrell. Not in a million months of the Maiden with the Many Smiles!

Just how much longer the fight would have gone on must remain conjectural. Certainly, in the dust and confusion the flutsmen had lost all idea of thrashing us and taking the spoils. Our resistance—indeed, our sudden and overwhelming attack—had knocked them back on their heels with a surprise from which they did not recover. They fought; but increasingly they sought to escape.

Then our flutduins descended on them.

After that it was a mere matter of rounding up those who would be rounded up and seeing off those who would not. When that was going on strong, parties of my lads of 1ESW and 1EYJ ran up, more in anger than sorrow that they had missed most of the fight.

The men of the Emperor's Sword Watch and of the Emperor's Yellow Jackets, sworn to protect the life of the Emperor of Vallia and his family, do not take lightly the discharge of their duties. They were very thorough in their rounding up of flutsmen, severe in their chastisement.

One flutsman, green in the face and with an arm and a leg missing, from which he was dying, stared up with eyes that would soon glaze over. He saw us pass by.

"By Barflut the Razor Feathered," he got out. "I wish I'd never taken the gold from Layco Jhansi."

I bent to him.

"Think of Layco Jhansi when the Grey Ones meet you and you wander through the mists of the Ice Floes of Sicce, dom."

"I'll remember, Hanitcha the Harrower take him. I'll remember and curse his name."

Seg glanced at me as I straightened up.

"A dratted Hamalese."

"A renegade, evidently."

Turko said, "There's more to this. I wonder if they were out on a scavenging expedition on their own account?"

"Or are they scouting for the main force?" Seg looked up at the sky at this, instinctively, and his sinewy fingers curved around his bowstave.

Then, of course, the lads of my bodyguard corps arrived, as I have said, highly incensed. Korero the Shield, magnificent and golden, a Kildoi with four arms and a tail hand, swung his two enormous shields about as though they were saucers. I wondered if he and Turko might exchange a few words.

In the event Turko, who was, after all, now the Kov of Falinur, contented himself with a very politely-spoken: "You are welcome, Korero the Shield."

And Korero contented himself with: "I am glad to see you, Kov Turko." He put no heavy emphasis on the word kov. Of course, they could have been so fearfully polite just because I was there and in earshot. These two who had carried shields at my back in battle epitomized the way in which men and women strove to put their heroic bodies between men and the incoming shaft, the slashing blade. I sighed. I knew damn well I didn't deserve such devotion. But, also, I fancied these two had come to an arrangement, one with the other, and each saw his duty ahead.

"Secure all here," Nath went past, shouting. He saw me.

"Time we returned to the camp, I think."

"You're right. And what we'll find does not amuse me."

"By the Veiled Froyvil, my old dom, we'll soon have the army to rights."

"Aye," said Nath na Kochwold in his grimmest voice. I was not so sure.

If these confounded flutsmen *were* the advance patrol of an army, that army would find ours in parlous case, that seemed certain. We had no time to shilly-shally about.

Layco Jhansi, who had once been the old emperor's chief pallan, virtually in charge of Vallia, had turned traitor. His schemes had backfired and he had been forced to flee to his estates in the northwest where he had set out on the road of conquest. He was ruthless. He'd had no hesitation in striking down Ashti Melekhi, one of his tools who had failed him.

Recently he had concluded a treaty of non-aggression with the Racters to the north of him so that he could concentrate all his efforts against Turko's Falinur. If he was recruiting fresh mercenaries, even low-grade ones, to give a hard core to his army of crazies, we'd need every man and animal, every bird, every engine, to hold him and beat him back.

So, as we returned to the shattered camp of the Ninth Army, I began to seek out ways in my mind to draw fresh forces into the field to counter Jhansi's schemes. The Empire of Vallia, of which I was hauled into being the emperor, was a rickety and ramshackle old construction these days. We ran on a knife edge. One mistake, one error of judgment, one lapse in our spirit of high resolve could let in the ravening monsters of destruction to tear down into ruin all that we strove for.

Three

Of a few words to Kov Turko

The main beam of the catapult lay on the ground, the massive arm of laminated wood smashed through in two separate places. The rest of the engine looked as though a maddened giant had jumped up and down on it with hobnailed boots.

Seg brought across a bronze helmet. The crown was dented into a recurve in the shape of a frog. If any poor devil had been wearing that at the time...

Swords were shattered, spears splintered, shields torn to shreds.

Annoying though this destruction of equipment might be—annoying! It was downright infuriating!—it meant nothing beside the distress caused by the casualties.

Many of the men had saved themselves by simply running flat out. The swods near the circumference of the frog storm had raced away to safety. Many men fortunate enough to be close to their saddle animals had been able to gallop off. The vollers had all taken to the air and some of the vorlcas had drifted downwind as we had. The flutduins had not been touched, for which we gave thanks to Opaz.

There remained many men injured, maimed, many dead. The lads had used their shields cannily, sheltering under whatever of cover there was and slanting the shields to take the blows glancingly. As we walked about the camp amid these scenes of desolation, we saw many pitiful examples of the horror that had blackened the Suns, many men crouched and smashed presenting bizarre and ghastly tableaux of death.

If a frog falling from the sky could smash the great beam of a catapult, it would not be stopped by the flatbed of a cart, the angle of a shield.

No, I will not elaborate on what had happened to the Ninth Army or the scenes I saw.

Suffice it to say that we devoted all our resources to caring for the injured and burying the dead.

All Turko's usual quizzical mockery fled. As we carried out the necessary tasks he grew silent and cold. His mood remained somber. He was not dejected; both Nath and Seg were able to reassure him that his Ninth Army, although grievously wounded, was not irrevocably destroyed.

"Yes, we will rebuild the army." Turko got the words out as though they ground between granite mills.

Seg looked over my shoulder just as I was about to make a remark I had pondered on and had, at last, decided to speak out.

"Here come Khe-Hi and Ling-Li-Lwingling."

Turning about slowly at Seg's words, I saw the Wizard and the Witch of Loh approaching, stepping carefully over debris and corpses. Men were hard at work clearing up; they could not be everywhere at once and I was helping in a particularly bad patch where the frogs had rained down like stone hail and the ground was windrowed with men and women.

Ling-Li wore a bandage around her head, the yellow cloth making the pallor of her face look sickly. She did not seem to notice the ghastly moil about her; I fancied she did and marked all.

"Majister," said Khe-Hi.

I looked at him, seeing him as he usually appeared, wearing his white robe, his red hair neatly arranged, the handsomeness of his face a little, just a little, plumper than it had been in earlier days. His voice was the same metallic meticulous instrument of his will. But I felt a tiny tremor of anxiety. Khe-Hi in these days usually called me Dray. Very few people aspire or are granted that method of address. Now he used the full formal majister, not even the familiar majis of those close to me, and so I knew he wished to put this on a politico-formal basis. Well...

"Khe-Hi," I said, refusing this opening gambit. I half-inclined my head to the Witch of Loh. "Ling-Li. I trust you are not seriously injured."

"A scratch."

She did not use majister; I did not think she had as yet earned any right to call me Dray although she had materially assisted us in the matter of the werewolves. I have likened her small face with its piled mass of auburn hair to a superbly carved mask in the ivory of Chem, the smoothest and mellowest of ivories. Her skin clung tightly to her bone structure without hint of a sag; yet she was not gaunt, for her beauty, aided by the startling blue of her eyes and the scarlet of her mouth above a firmly rounded chin, seemed to me to be a trifle more than skin deep and was self-evident. All the same, it also seemed to me a deal of her force was absent, that the sickly pallor of that perfect skin was not all created by the yellow bandage.

"I trust you will soon be recovered." I turned back to the Wizard of Loh. "Tell me, Khe-Hi."

Now Wizards and Witches of Loh enjoy deserved reputations upon Kregen. Their powers are immense and unknown and simple men believe anything of them. But I have known Wizards and Witches of Loh who were mediocre in their control of the thaumaturgical arts. Of course, they would be more powerful than most sorcerers of other disciplines; most, not all. These Wizards of Loh who are somewhat less than their fellows unashamedly use the reputation of any Wizard of Loh. They trade on the fear their fellows engender. In this wise they make a living.

Khe-Hi-Bjanching and Ling-Li-Lwingling were both very highly powered mages. Khe-Hi, I fancied, would one day when he reached the prime of life, become perhaps more powerful than almost any other Wizard of Loh. Certainly, he had at the least caught up with Deb-Lu-Quienyin, who was many seasons older, if he had not surpassed him.

Csitra the Witch of Loh was also extraordinarily powerful, and the kharrna of the child, the uhu Phunik, would grow to match and surpass hers. I wondered—with horror—if Phunik would outgrow the kharrna of his father, Phu-Si-Yantong, who was dead and gone, the bastard.

As I, a layman, saw the situation, then, here we had a very powerful sorceress aided by her child of lesser mastery of the arts, versus two very powerful mages. There should in theory therefore have been a clear-cut advantage to our side.

There was not.

Naturally there was not, given the mazy, chancy mystery of thaumaturgy and its applications to the problems of life.

When Deb-Lu joined in, then we did have an advantage. But Deb-Lu at the moment was off on business of his own. That business, I shrewdly suspected, knowing Deb-Lu, had to do with the welfare of Vallia and, not least of all, of Delia and myself.

Khe-Hi motioned slowly with his right hand, for his left was held by Ling-Li's hand. "I grieve for the dead soldiers..."

In this I knew Khe-Hi spoke the truth. I do not care to associate with people who have no respect for human life. This too marks me as being an ordinary fellow without certain special qualifications for being an emperor, a ruler of men, a person whose will to the grand design discards lives without thought.

At my nod, Khe-Hi went on with his explanation.

"You are aware that Csitra can stab a pulse of great power through the defenses we have arranged, simply by virtue of the old military saw that concentrated force will smash through attenuated defenses." Khe-Hi looked up at me, and added: "Some of our defenses are not attenuated."

What he was saying in this roundabout way was that a great deal of magical art had been put out by the Wizards of Loh in the past to safeguard certain people thought necessary to the well-being of the emperor. I had had to push aside all notions of guilt that I, and Delia, and my family and blade comrades were thus protected. If we went down, Vallia would go down with us. We had seen what that would entail during the Times of Troubles. No sane person wanted those times to recur.

This was not just a question of who would be master in the empire. Those flutsmen we had just seen off were a tiny representation of what the whole island had groaned under, would suffer from, if the evil days returned.

"Also, majister, you will understand that I had to fabricate a caul for Ling-Li and myself, for had a frog knocked our brains out, well, I need not go on."

"In this you judged right."

The two mages, Seg, Turko and Nath stood in a semicircle with me, removed from other folk. That suited the other folk. Wizards of any kind, and Wizards of Loh in particular, were held to be unpredictable to any casual wandering person chancing by. The swods got on with clearing up, and very few even raised their eyes to glance curiously at us.

Because of this isolation, I was able to say, "Now, Khe-Hi, we have been friends a long time. Why are you addressing me as majister all of a sudden?"

Ling-Li said: "I feared you would be displeased we had taken so long, would judge and condemn us—"

I almost said that she'd changed her tune remarkably since she'd called me tikshim and told me to clear off to the benches beside the Jikaida board where they were playing Death Jikaida. I did not smile.

"If you believe yourself to be guilty of some crime, perhaps you would care to name it?"

Very quickly Khe-Hi shot out: "No, Dray, we are not guilty of any crime, and we know we are not. We did what we had to do as quickly as we could. It took time. Ling-Li believed that you—"

"You, Khe-Hi, ought to have known better."

"I do. But I could not convince—"

"Next time, Ling-Li," I said in that old gravel-shifting voice, and I know my face must have held some of the old devil look, for the Witch of Loh flinched back. "Next time believe and trust in Khe-Hi's word."

She said nothing in reply; but those tell-tale mottlings of color seeped up across her cheekbones.

Seg with his laugh and apparently brash words cloaking subtle schemings, said, "I'll tell you, Khe-Hi, when those dratted frogs were tumbling out and bashing us about it seemed two seasons long."

"Yet," added Nath na Kochwold with his military instincts at work: "The time was remarkably short. That it appeared long was natural."

That summed up this little minor crisis within the greater.

There was a great deal to do, most of it unpleasant, and so I will pass over the next few days with but one final word. Repugnance.

The crazed army of Layco Jhansi did not attack, and Kapt Erndor, the army commander who thankfully had survived, was positive this was because his advance patrol of flutsmen had not reported back. Every last one had been brought down by our flyers.

"All the same," said Kapt Erndor as we sat around the campfire on the last evening. "All the same, he will attack, now. I feel confident he will have had news of our disaster."

I said: "I do not usually call councils of war. In this case I would be interested to know what you think should be our next course of action."

Erndor, one of my old Freedom Fighters of Valka, hard and gritty, lifted his goblet. He stared at me over the rim.

"Normally, strom, I'd counsel a swift attack on our part. Stick him before he sticks us."

"But."

Kapt Erndor heaved up a sigh, swallowed a mouthful, wiped his mouth.

"The army has taken a few hard knocks lately. We had the werewolves. Now the frogs. They've suffered casualties in a way that is foreign to a fighting man. I hate this, I hate myself for saying it; but I think a great deal of the heart has gone out of the army."

Nath na Kochwold burst out: "It is a terrible thing to have to say; but it is true. I have watched the lads. They are bewildered, fearful, not knowing when a fresh disaster out of their experience will fall on them."

"Dratted sorcery," rumbled Seg.

In his latter mood of somberness, Turko said nothing.

"The Ninth Army," I said. "A fine fighting force. Sorcery has ruined it."

"All we need is time—" began Erndor.

"Give us a month of She of the Veils," said Nath.

"Will Layco Jhansi allow us that?" I stared at them, and I saw the answer in their faces.

The wine passed around. Above us the stars glittered. The night lay cool upon the land, and the scents wafted in fresh and clean, cleansed of the raw horror of the shambles of a few days ago. We talked around the question, and the problems remained. We were, in truth, a mightily despondent group.

At last I said: "Erndor."

At the tone of decision in my voice Erndor rapped out: "Strom?"

"You will have to go to Valka. Tell Tom Tomor the truth. Bring as many regiments as he can let you have. I won't ask for any specific number; I know he will do his utmost. Valka, after all, should be secure now."

"Quidang, strom!"

"Seg, if you'd like to fly down to Vondium and dig up what you can—"

"First thing, Dray. I'll wring some regiments out of Farris, somehow."

"Good. Now, Turko—"

Turko looked up. His eyes were heavy, his face gaunt.

"Turko, this is your province, this half of Vennar earmarked to go to your Falinur."

Now I said what I had determined to say earlier.

"In statecraft you have proved yourself. You are the kov of this province, of all Falinur. You'll have to stay here, with the lads, get their morale back. You'll have to start with—"

"Aye, Dray, aye. I know. I'll have to start with myself."

"Make it so."

Seg quaffed a good-sized slug. I've no idea what wine we were drinking that night. "And you, Dray?"

"Khe-Hi and Ling-Li will stay with you, Turko. They'll want to be married as soon as it's practicable. As for me—I'll nip across to Inch."

Instantly, Seg objected.

"A messenger will tell Farris. We can dredge up the regiments. I'm coming with you, my old dom, to see Inch."

Turko opened his mouth to protest in his turn.

Nath said: "You can't go alone, Dray!"

"And you're not coming with me, Nath, so get that idea out of your head. You're needed here, to help get the army to rights."

"But, Dray—!"

"But nothing. Of course I'll go alone. We can't spare anyone. I'll have to sneak off so my lads of the bodyguard corps don't know. By Vox! It'll be good to stretch my wings again."

"I don't know—"

"Well, I do!"

"One lone man, to fly across hostile territory, no, Dray, it won't do, by the Veiled Froyvil, my old dom, it won't do at all!"

"All the same, each one of you has a more important job to do than nursemaid me. If I'm the emperor then I'll be the bloody emperor and dish out orders! Sink me!" I burst out at last. "I'm going across to see Inch on my own, so Queyd-Arn-Tung!"

Four

A sick bird brings a task

Down south in the continent of Havilfar where saddle birds and animals are much more in evidence than here in Vallia or in Pandahem, they say that if the velvety green feathers of your fluttrell show a lemonish-yellow tinge around the edges—beware!

The beigey-white feathers of the fluttrell I had chosen glistened healthily. His eyes were bright. His talons sharp. That stupid head vane fluttrells have been cursed with—or blessed with, perhaps, if it materially assists their flying—was undamaged. His harness shone with saddle soap and leather polish, ministrations of his late dead owner.

I suppose, to be perfectly truthful, there *was* a faint tinge of yellow around his green feathers. I ought to have taken more care about that; but, then, I was saddling him and cutting him out from the rest by the light only of She of the Veils, dwindling into the west. Also, there was a tinge of apprehension in me that one of my hulking great lads would patrol along here and get stuck into this sneaking thief before I could yell.

The Emperor of Vallia, sneaking off so that his bodyguard corps should not fly with him!

This had happened before and would happen again. My guards understood that sometimes I had to go off by myself. They'd do their damnedest to go with me, and it had turned into a species of game between us. If they suspected I intended to go off alone they'd be on the *qui vive* and I'd be at shift to take great pains to outwit them.

This time they were not expecting me to fly off, as our night conference remained secret.

The fluttrell—I, of course, did not know his name—bore on through thin air as She of the Veils finally sank. The night pressed in, for the moment a pseudo night of Notor Zan, when no moons float in the sky and the star glitter cannot make up for the lost illumination.

Flutsmen habitually decorate their mounts and themselves with multitudes of feathers and silks and trailing cords and sashes. These are things I abhor. Oh, they look fine enough; I do not care to have a foeman grab a pretty shoulder cord or waist sash and reel me in to be spitted.

In addition, these decorations announce the allegiance of the flutsman. One band may tell another in the air. The protocol of aerial meeting is strict by virtue of the need to know if the flyers approaching are friend or enemy. I did not know if the flying silks I had with me would proclaim me a friend or an enemy to other bands of flutsmen. Certainly, there were no survivors of the band from whom this fluttrell and these silks had come.

By morning when Zim and Genodras rose to flood down their mingled streaming lights, the fluttrell had flown me a goodly distance on the journey. Now was time, I felt, to rest him, feed and water him, and, perhaps, myself catch forty winks.

We slanted down over open country, the fields large and quite unlike the intensive cultivations farther south. In fact, very little of the land looked as though it was being worked. A town—a straggling place of stone houses looking as though it humped itself out of the very ground—showed up ahead.

Now I was not intending to hide on this flight. I looked what in very truth I was—a paktun, a fighting man ready to hire out as a mercenary. This cover had stood me in good stead in the past. With Deb-Lu-Quienyin's skill, taught to me, of subtly altering the planes and lines of my face so that I could pass unrecognized through a crowd of friends, I should not be molested on the score of being that arch devil, Dray Prescot, the Emperor of Vallia.

So I circled the fluttrell and slanted down to the town. There were no regular perching poles for the birds; but a makeshift one had been erected outside a tavern.

The flight across Vennar to Inch's Black Mountains appeared to me at that time as a hiatus in my plans. I wanted the journey over as soon as possible; yet fluttrells are flesh and blood birds, they are not machines.

I decided to call this saddle bird Salvation because he had been brought out of bad company.

He went up onto the perching pole gladly enough, and flickered his wings proudly enough, for there were two other birds perching there. It was then I noticed how strong that betraying yellowish cast was to the fringes of his velvety green feathers.

"Poor old Salvation," I said to him. "Looks as though you are in for a bad time."

There might be a vet in the town, which from its placing and my knowledge of the geography of Vallia, I knew to be Snarkter, an oddly un-Vallian name. There were mines nearby, from which was extracted the ore that yielded cryspals, so precious that I might have to rule harshly on who owned the mines when Inch and Turko took over. Maybe there would have to be a border line right through the middle, dividing up the cryspal mines fairly. If there was a vet he might be able to doctor calsanys and plains asses and mytzers and quoffas, and the occasional zorca, but what would he know of fluttrells?

A few people were shuffling about, and, I admit without shame, they struck me as dull and lethargic. From people like this, then, was Layco Jhansi's Sorcerer of Murcroinim, Rovard the Murvish, creating the crazed mob of fanatics who opposed us?

Then I frowned.

Among the citizens of Snarkter, other people crept along, wearing gray slave breechclouts, bearing burdens, getting out of the way as the citizens passed.

If for no other reason—and there were plenty of others—this alone was cause enough for us to liberate all of Vallia.

The Quork Nightly looked to be typical of taverns in this part of the island, being built of stone from the local quarries, slate roofed, low pitched and with a washed-out peach-colored munstal growing over the door which, however, exuded a sweetly pleasant scent. I ducked my head and went inside, carefully observing the fantamyrrh as I did so. I courted no trouble here.

The innkeeper was apim, a member of Homo sapiens sapiens, like me, wearing a blue-striped apron, and with rounded red forearms bristling with brown hair. His nose, I recall, looked like a red cabbage.

He was prepared to serve a lone mercenary. Over in the corner sat a couple of hefty lads, with cudgels down by their chairs. No, the innkeeper, Loban the Nose, had no good reason to refuse to serve me.

I spread a silver stiver on the counter along with a couple of copper obs. Flashing gold here would not be prudent.

The ale was thin watery stuff; but it was wet and it went down along with a couple of rashers of bosk, a heel of bread and, afterwards, a pottery dish of palines. I savored the yellow berries, sovereign cures for hangovers and sundry other ills. It is extremely difficult to find palines that are not good anywhere on Kregen, although I have been to some places where the palines were a disgrace. That is rare, thankfully.

"Come far?" was the usual opening gambit.

I chewed.

"Nope."

"Going far?"

"Yep."

"Hiring out to the kov, are you?"

"Yep."

Wondering how long I could keep up this tight-lipped pose amused me. Overdoing it would make these local yokels hostile. So I said, "Have a drink with me, doms. Times are hard."

"Aye, dom, times are hard, we thank you."

There were no other patrons in The Quork Nightly at this time of the morning. I stood the landlord and his two bully boys a drink of their own weak ale, and we talked desultorily. I asked for a vet, and was directed to a house with a black front door over on the other side of town.

As I took my leave I said: "Thank you, Koter Loban. Do you do a good meal here at the hour of mid?"

"Aye, koter, that we do. Roast ponsho, ponsho pie, ponsho puddings— we do a very fine meal."

"Good. Remberee."

I took Salvation walking alongside me, the reins in my fist, as I crossed to the house with the black door. The sign read:

MASTER URBAN THE UNGUENT

The paint was cracked black, the lettering a wobbly attempt at the severe formal Kregish. Underneath in smaller letters was:

ALL ANIMALS TREATED LIKE LORDS

I went in.

Salvation had to wait outside, tied up to a post. No doubt there would be a treatment yard round at the back of the house.

One breath inside the house and, instantly, I was back in the house where I'd been born, long ago and far away on Earth. My father had been a horse doctor, and the house constantly witnessed a struggle between the smells of liniments and oils and those of freshly-baked bread and cabbage and furniture polish. I shook my head and went into the room where a crude picture of a human hand pointed the way.

"Yes, koter?"

Master Urban the Unguent was small, untidy, his hair a mop, and his clothes stained by the marks of his trade. He was in the act of dropping oils into a mixture in a brass pot upon a tiny brazier, and by his movements I saw that he knew, at least in this, what he was doing.

I told him the problem, and he pursed up his lips and shook his head, and looked serious.

"Since these troublous times I have had to learn about these marvelous birds that carry men through the sky. I have heard of this disease. It is called the Yellow Rot, or Strugmin's Rot, from the veterinary who first diagnosed it."

"Can you cure it?"

"I will try. My unguents are renowned throughout Vennar, and beyond, to Falinur and even to the Black Hills. I will do my best." He glanced up quickly. "It will cost you—"

I showed him a golden talen.

He nodded, and took the coin.

"That will do nicely, koter."

"The bird is called Salvation and is outside. How long—"

He waved a hand. "Who can tell?"

This was infuriating.

The peaceful appearance and laziness of this town of Snarkter struck me. Here I was in the heartland of the enemies of my people. I had to get on to Inch in the Black Hills. Seg would raise regiments from the Lord Farris in Vondium; Kapt Erndor would bring regiments from Valka provided by Tom Tomor, Turko and Nath na Kochwold would build up the morale of the Ninth Army; all this was so. Yet the help that Inch might be able to provide could prove decisive. He might not be able to offer any help at all, for he fought Jhansi on this front and the damned Racters to his north. Up there they had a habit of changing the names of places and rivers to mark a special occasion. I wanted the names to reflect our success, not our defeat.

So my hurry was of my own making. All the same, if poor old Salvation was going to take time to mend I'd have to try something else. There'd been two other saddle birds perching outside The Quork Nightly...

My guess was they did not belong to Loban the Nose's two henchmen. Rather, they'd be the mounts of two paktuns who were still, at this early hour, snoring away in one of Loban's upstairs bedchambers.

The patter of bare feet heralded the entrance of a short, plump woman wearing a dingy black dress. Her face, round and shining, with a snub nose; her brown hair once neatly caught up in a bun now straggling over her shoulders; her eyes, all told of tragedy.

She was sobbing and crying, and trying to speak all at the same time. She staggered, and I put out a hand and caught her and so eased her to a chair.

Urban the Unguents looked alarmed.

"What is it, Kotera Minvila?"

Through her caterwauling she got out: "My Maisie! Have you seen her? I've been everywhere, all over, no one's seen her! My Maisie—"

"She has not been here." Urban glanced up at me. "A mere child, but pretty. She likes to help with the animals—but she has not come here today."

"Where is she? She was not in her bed when I called her—Maisie! Maisie!"

"A little cordial, I think, Master Urban."

He reacted at once and went to a cabinet, returning with a glass containing colored liquid which Kotera Minvila spilled half over her dress, a third over her face, and managed to gulp down the remainder. She was in a distressing state over the disappearance of her daughter.

In a low voice, bending close, Urban said: "I do not like the sound of this, Koter Kadar." That was the name I'd given him. "There have been a number of disappearances of young girls just recently."

In a slow and heavy voice, I said: "They were all young, about two to four, say, pretty, and from families of the poorer—"

"Yes. Mostly they are slaves, which is bad enough, Opaz knows. But three or four have been from the families of respectable citizens, like Kotera Minvila. Her husband was killed in the war."

Poor devil, no doubt he'd been swept up by Layco Jhansi's Deldars, thrust into the ranks with a spear, and then sorcerously inflamed by Rovard the Murvish. He'd been just one in that army of crazies.

I could feel the chill in me.

There was no certainty about what had happened. Salvation could have had the Yellow Rot for no other reason beyond the normal.

But I harbored the deepest conviction that no accident had caused me to choose a fluttrell that would delay me here.

No, oh no, by Zair!

Once more, in this fashion, I was convinced the Star Lords had set a task to my hands.

Five

Two Paktuns

A theory formed itself in my head.

Now theories are tricky beasts and can land a fellow in all kinds of trouble if he's not careful.

Still, the probability of this particular theory being valid struck me as quite high. I wouldn't pitch it any stronger than that.

Among the flim-flammery of gaudy silks and sashes brought along from the flutsman's kit I drew out a scarf of green and blue eye-watering silkiness, with silver edgings. None of this stuff was being worn, for obvious reasons. I wanted these people to take me for a simple paktun and not a reiving flutsman.

The silver came away as the point of my dagger probed it free. I twisted up some of the strands into a special spiral arrangement, one I knew and loathed. Together with the snip of feather I'd taken from Salvation's darker parts, the brown and silver insignia would have to serve.

I pinned it to the reverse flap of the khiganer I'd selected to wear. This khiganer, shaped in the usual fashion with a wide flap caught up over the left side with a row of bronze buttons from belt to shoulder and from point of shoulder to collar, was tailored from a heavy brown material. The collar was not as stiff and high as usual. I valued comfort more than ostentation. Naturally I wore the old scarlet breechclout; but this was decently covered by bronze-studded pteruges. When I'd finished and pinned on the evil badge, I walked back to The Quork Nightly.

My assumption proved correct, for two hard characters were seated at table wolfing the second breakfast. They were dressed as soldiers of fortune, their weapons were scabbarded to them, and while one bore a scar from forehead to ear, the other bore a scar from nose to lip.

"Llahal, doms," I said, cheerfully, as I went in.

One spat a bit of gristle onto the floor and grunted something. The other slugged back a mouthful of weak ale, belched, and said: "And what's so all-cheerful about it, then, rast?"

These greetings, you will perceive, were not those conducive to friendly relations.

I sat down.

"You called me rast, dom," I said, still in that overly cheerful voice.

"Aye, cramph, yetch, rast you are."

I stared at them. Big, hard, muscled, hairy. Their iron helmets rested on the floor by their chairs. Their booted feet stuck out at arrogant angles. They made a mess when they ate. They wore thraxters, the cut and thrust sword of Havilfar. I wore a drexer, and if anyone questioned why I carried a Valkan sword, I'd simply say I'd won it in battle and taken it from a dead Vallian.

Also, I wore my rapier and main gauche. They did not have scabbarded to their belts the rapier and left hand dagger, the Jiktar and the Hikdar.

They did have axes, small and nimble, rather like tomahawks. Those, I'd have to watch.

I said, "I wonder why I have not thrust your teeth down your throats. By Hanitcha the Harrower, I marvel at my reticence!"

They jerked up at this and swiveled to stare more closely at me.

"Hamalese?"

"Are you? You speak and act like clums, like guls. Are you all that Hamal can find to dredge up out of the gutters and send forth as fighting men?"

They reared up, their hands groping for the hilts of their thraxters.

I waved them away as though I waved a fly away.

"I've no time to waste on you, by Lem, no!"

As I used that hateful word I watched them narrowly.

Their whole appearance changed.

They sat back, and their hands left their sword hilts and reached for the ale.

"Well, dom," one said, and belched. "You could have said."

"Aye, we but tried your mettle," said the other.

That was probably quite true. Fighting men like this became bored with frightening speed. Some excitement stirred up the blood. I could never stomach them or their like, for my idea of a fighting man is vastly different. Still, it takes all sorts to make the wonderful and terrible world of Kregen revolve about the twin star of Antares.

After that the necessary secret words of the initiate in the cult of Lem the Silver Leem were spoken. They were swods within the cult; I pitched myself a little higher, giving myself the ridiculous rank of Hikdar-majisponti. At least, they'd be polite from now on.

They told me much of what I already knew or suspected and a deal that was new.

Mercenaries were flooding into this northwestern part of Vallia again, coming via Racterland to the north, guaranteed passage by the Racters and payment by Princess Mira.

I nodded as they spoke as though I understood. But I'd no idea who this Princess Mira was, apart from the fact that as an enemy of Vallia she would have to be dealt with.

"There is much gold, dom," said the one called Helvcin the Kaktu. "I saw the ships unloading. The string of calsanys stretched from ship out of sight through the port gate. By Kuerden the Merciless, if one of those beasts had stumbled and spilt his load...!"

"By Krun!" amplified his comrade, one hight Movang the Splitter. "In the riot I'd have made my fortune. Hanitcha take me else."

"Now Malahak is my witness you speak it aright, Movang!" And Helvcin put a gnarly finger into his mouth to free a scrap of food caught in his teeth.

"These great ones of the world," I said. "If only Kaerlan the Merciful smiled on me..."

"Oh, we'll never smell any more of the gold than our pay. And that's fair, I grant you."

They completely took me for a Hamalese, for I had spent a long time there, and was able to tell them more than they knew about Ruathytu, the capital of Hamal. By chance I also knew Dovad, from which town hailed Helvcin the Kaktu. I'd spent a few days there with Avec Brand and Ilter Monicep before taking the boat down the River Mak. I'd never visited Mardinglee, where Movang the Splitter had been born.

I expect you can share some of my feelings at this resurrection of memories long ago, of times and places in Hamal. Then the empire had been ruled by poor mad Queen Thyllis, before she became the Empress, and Hamal was a deadly enemy to other nations beside Vallia. Now, with Prince Nedfar placed on the throne by me to become the new emperor, we were allies.

By their lack of rapiers and left hand daggers, these two betrayed the fact they'd never been Bladesmen, never ruffled it in the Sacred Quarter of Ruathytu.

Carefully letting drop tidbits of information, I casually built up the image of me I required them to have. When we got onto the topic of Lem the Silver Leem, I did feel relief that neither belonged to the temple to which I'd been taken by Nath Tolfeyr, himself a man of mystery, and been inducted into the vile cult to save my life. They had heard of that temple, though, by the aqueduct in Ruathytu, and accorded me even more respect. Apparently that particular temple held a big reputation among these decadent and torturing murderers of the Brown and Silvers.

In due time they told me all they knew about Princess Mira. This was pathetically little. She was merely the name by which the paymasters knew who was providing the gold to pay the army against Vallia.

I ventured a shaft.

"It seems to me that perhaps Princess Mira will take what you win in Vallia for herself."

"If she does," said Helvcin, spitting, "I shall not care, no by Krun, so long as I get my pay and a share of the loot."

Inch would have to wait.

Even as I dredged their shallow minds for more information, I found myself thinking how grand it would be if Pompino the Iarvin were here. By Vox! He was a tool of the Everoinye, the Star Lords, as was I. He and I had burned a few temples to Lem the Silver Leem. As Kregoinye we both felt that we would burn more, although I desperately sought another solution to this monstrous disease calling itself a religion.

They left to see to their fluttrells and we parted on the understanding that we'd meet in the evening. There was to be a ceremony this night. They'd be there to enjoy the sacrifice, the torture, the blood and the horror and the orgy that followed.

I'd be there, too, but I'd be there for a vastly different set of reasons...

They expected a good turnout for the ceremony. A camp lay only a few dwaburs off, containing a goodly number of adherents. The cult was being brought into my Vallia by mercenaries from Hamal.

This was a situation so intolerable that it could not be allowed to continue past this night...

Of course, once I'd got over that initial burst of anger, I saw that just burning the temple—as ever—wouldn't stop them. We must smash up this conspiracy, defeat Layco Jhansi and the Racters, unite all true Vallians. Then we could completely expunge all traces of Lem the Silver Leem.

For a weak moment I contemplated taking one of their fluttrells and continuing my flight to Inch. The war could be helped along if I did that, and that was my first concern.

Then I recalled the anguish of Kotera Minvila over her daughter Maisie.

That settled that, then.

Six

The Chief Priest

Waiting for the night to arrive turned out to be a cruel business.

Numerous schemes flitted through my mind. The evil of Lem the Silver Leem was self-evident, at least to those who had witnessed its diabolical practices. If I worked myself into a feverish state, dwelling on the problems we faced and the hardness of the road that led to eventual success, I believe you will understand.

At last Zim and Genodras sank beneath the horizon and the Maiden with the Many Smiles shone among the stars, with the Twins, eternally orbiting each other as they orbit Kregen.

The dubious scheme I settled on at last did not call for me to walk out with either the two paktuns or the other people walking in from the camp. Back home in Vallia there were plenty of silver masks fashioned in the shape of the ugly faces of leems, trophies from successes of the past. There were also golden zhantil masks there...

So it was necessary for me to creep out alone and unobserved and waylay one of the people walking in from the camp. I'd have a look at that camp as well, on the morrow, I promised myself. If I was still in the land of the living by then, that was.

The fellow collapsed and I took his silver mask, his long brown cloak, and also his badge of brown and silver feathers. Mine had served its purpose, convincing Movang and Helvcin, but was clearly not as authentic as an original. Donning the cloak, arranging the longsword comfortably within the capacious brown folds, I strapped on the mask and set off for the temple.

This, I saw, was merely the entrance tunnel to an abandoned mine.

No chance, then, to set the place on fire. I might smoke a few of the rasts out.

The cloak, the mask, the badge, gained me entrance without question or trouble. The foul stink of incense affronted my nostrils. Many tapers burned, and torches, and the glinting tunnel walls and roof loomed semi-circularly above, a blasphemous temple indeed.

There stood the altar, a solid block of stone. They'd not carted that around with them but, most likely, had found it conveniently within the mine. The image of Lem, gleaming silver above, would be carried about, and I judged it to be fashioned from lightweight wood with a silver-gilt finish.

To one side rested the cage, of split timbers, and within the cage, clad in a white dress and decked with flowers—Maisie.

She was quite happy.

Oh, yes, they knew how to handle their sacrifices, the damned Brown and Silvers.

The new white dress. The flowers. The doll, the sweets and candies. She would burble happily to herself until the sacrificial knife descended. Her heart would still beat after it had been wrenched from her body; but before that she would have suffered tortures that could only make her death a release.

Well, the bastards were going to be disappointed on that score, at least, this night.

If this fragile scheme I had concocted was going to work I'd have to make my way through the throng gathering before the altar and the image, ease along to the rear, and then sort out whatever and whoever lay beyond.

The tunnel held a dank, stale smell which the incense worsened. The place struck me as eerie and unhealthy. The altar had been set up where a side passage led off into darkness. The opening, half blocked by a rotting wooden gate, held no interest for me, and I eased around the other side where the opposite tunnel, forming a cross, showed lights. Voices came from beyond hanging curtains. Three guards stood there, clad in brown and white, bearing spears, and they looked at me keenly.

I used the formula words on them, letting them understand I was a visiting adherent of high rank. I wished to speak with the chief priest on a matter of the utmost urgency, and if they wished to retain their privates they'd better let me through at once. *Bratch!*

They bratched and saluted, and I passed through the opening in the curtain into the antechamber beyond.

More curtains concealed what lay to the left hand side; but the sound of voices and the clink of equipment told me the acolytes and the butchers were in there preparing themselves for the night's tortures. To the right the curtain was half drawn and I caught a glimpse of men and women with the grander masks of the under-priests. Straight ahead lay my goal.

The two guards here, both apims, did not wish to let me pass, so I had to put them to sleep standing up. I caught them left and right handed and eased them to the ground, which here was covered by a silver-patterned carpet. I did this not to break their falls but to prevent their noise alarming the occupant within.

When I pushed through he looked up, the mask in his fingers, his robes already flowing about him.

"What—?"

His face was fleshy from good living, veinous, vinous, too, I daresay. He wore many rings, a habit I detest. He was firmly built and around my height, and I cut him down without a word. I caught the mask as it toppled from his nerveless fingers, and he fell on his face onto the carpet and his blood stained out across the bright silver threads.

His robes fitted well enough. The rings were a nuisance; but they had to be slid on as part of the full regalia. His own sacrificial knife, sharp, curved, I picked up with great distaste and slid into the sheath ready for it. Then I strapped on his mask in place of the one I'd worn. When I was ready I took a breath, picked up his staff with its head fashioned like a leaping silver leem, all wedge-shaped head and eight legs, snarling and vicious and well-designed to impress the gullible.

I shoved the curtains aside and hauled the two guards in by their ankles. I hit 'em again, just to keep 'em quiet a little longer, and then stalked out to stand at the far curtains. In only a few moments the acolytes and under-priests trooped out and the procession was formed and ready to go.

The closeness of the stink from incense, the heat of tapers and torches, the brazier fire burning with its ghastly implements heating up, all this discomfort had to be pushed away. There was a job to be done. I'd chosen this harebrained way of going about it, so there was just the thing to do.

I, Dray Prescot, the Lord of Strombor, Krozair of Zy, dressed as a chief priest in the debased Cult of Lem the Silver Leem, led out the procession of abominations.

Marching out front and center I raised both arms. Imposing, these debauched chief priests, no doubt about that... The noise of the congregation quieted. I addressed them. Oh, yes, I knew their stupid fancy rigmarole ranks and titles, and could work them up as I'd seen high priests do before, until they were ready for the Great Word. But, this time, and, too, of course because I probably was not performing in exactly the way a chief priest would go about conducting the ceremony, the Great Word was understood by the congregation to be different.

It would be different, too, by Krun!

After the introduction I hurried the next part, although speaking with the sonorous and, if the truth be told, deadly dull intonations of some of the priests.

"Your own chief priest has been stricken down by Lem!" Well, it was obvious that by now many of the people out there clustered listening to me would have recognized I was not the man they knew. I went on: "He has blasphemed. He is stricken in his own quarters and lies in his own blood. The Name that Must Not Be Spoken has wrought this justice, and has sent me to reveal unto you the truth."

The ensuing hubbub died away as, still with my arms raised to create that very necessary aura of power, I towered over them.

Then: "Listen, devotees! We serve Lem, the Silver Wonder. We have been betrayed by evil influences. We do not do well in this land of Vallia. Our deaths are written in the blood of Lem if we continue."

The whole atmosphere was conducive to making a person believe. The incense, the brazier, the tall unwavering flames of the torches, even the unspoken menace of the torturer's implements, the altar, and the sacrifice herself, all exerted a powerful mesmeric spell. I claim no credit for the deed. What skill at oratory I have—apart from hailing the foretop in a gale—has been used, and I do grasp at the essentials of the art. I bore down on them.

"I come to you at the first temple in this strange land of Vallia, to reveal the thinking of the Name that Must Not Be Spoken. We shall be destroyed here. We shall be betrayed. This is written. Return to your homelands. Return to the warm embrace of your friends, your lovers."

Thus I harangued them, building up a picture of disloyalty, of greed and of vengeance, seeding their minds with the belief that they had been betrayed into hiring on here in Vallia.

Slowly, I lowered my arms.

They stood, silent, attentive, yet half-hypnotized.

With a firm and steady tread I crossed to the cage. The door was unlocked, ready for the ceremony. I opened the cage door, bent and, in a low voice, said: "Lahal, Maisie. Your mother has a special treat for you, and nicer sweets than these," and with that I took her up into my arms.

If I fouled it up now, we'd both be chopped...

The sea of silver masks below moved, glinting in the torchlight. If Helvcin the Kaktu or Movang the Splitter stood there, as, indeed, they must, they might recognize in me the person they had spoken to in The Quork Nightly. But they would be held by the attitude of reverence for authority ingrained in them in Hamal, in Hamal of the Laws. They would reason that I had simply told them I was a Hikdar-majis-ponti so as not to reveal the true altitude of my lofty rank. For, I must be an important chief priest within the hierarchy to be doing what I was doing. Anything else was impossible, was beyond belief.

Sheer bluff carried me through. Slowly and with enormous dignity I walked through the throng, carrying Maisie, and she just put her head on my shoulder and sucked a sticky sweet on a stick. One false move, one question, one slip… I walked on and I felt the sweat trickling down under that infernal silver mask. On I strode, calm, giving the impression of a figure full of authority. On to the exit from the mine tunnel. On and out into the sweet night air away from the stinks of that blasphemous place.

When to start to run like hell?

I had to hold on, to continue that calm and steady progress. Then a thought occurred to me. I stopped.

I turned about. I lifted my free arm, and the silver-masked throng who'd followed me out halted, silent and waiting.

In a strong clear voice, I shouted back: "Do not be deceived, fellow adherents. Lem is not deceived. The gold—the gold is false. The Princess Mira gives gold freely with one hand, and her sorcery will take it away with the other when you have done her work for her and she has no further use for you. Be warned! Vallia is no place for you."

With that, about I turned and walked off. And this time, by Zair, I walked a trifle faster.

They did not follow. Some way down the back trail I could still hear their voices raised in argument. Once I was well away I just picked up the hem of the brown robe and ran—ran like a zorca pursued by a leem.

Seven

Inch—and squishes…

When I walked into the great hall of the palace of Makolo, situated on a cliff overlooking Makanriel, the capital city of the kovnate province of the Black Mountains, they had just finished the evening meal. I was followed by a great crowd of retainers and guards and servants, all amazed and agog that the Emperor of Vallia had arrived.

The sweet and luscious smell of squishes hung in the hall.

I sighed.

I knew what to expect when I walked into the small room at the back of the hall where folk would retire after the meal to drink wine and talk and relax after the day's exertions.

I was not disappointed.

Squishes are, indeed, flavorsome morsels on the tongue, tiny fruits that melt and create incredible delights on their way. The dish had probably been squish pie, I guessed, and I felt the old juices starting up in my mouth. I'd flown hard and long on the stolen fluttrell, and poor old Salvation had perforce been left with master Urban the Unguent. The new fluttrell was a fine flyer, with a wicked eye, so I'd called him Salvation the Second.

Maisie had been restored to her mother Minvila amid many tears and protestations of gratitude. I'd been able to press a little gold into her unwilling hand. Good folk, cruelly brought down by the evil times that had fallen on their province, they would, I felt sure, welcome a return to more settled and prosperous days when at last the Emperor of Vallia liberated the whole island.

So, now, here I was, in the palace of Makolo in Makanriel in the Black Mountains.

The colors of the Black Mountains, Black and Purple, shone from tapestry and streamer. The schturval, the emblem of the province, emblazoned in panoply about the hall and the retiring room, was an axe. At one time this axe had been of a common variety, double-bitted and not particularly well-crafted as to haft. Now that axe was of the Saxon pattern, small of head, long of haft and with that cunning curve and recurve to the wood that transferred such power and accuracy into the blow.

I noticed, too, in the banded sleeves of the men and the draperies of the walls, that the black and purple did not meet but were separated by two narrow lines of yellow enclosing a narrow line of red. I smiled. That was also new.

The sweet smell of squishes remained strong as I entered the room. There was even a scrap of pie crust on the floor and a pretty young serving girl was in the act of sweeping it up with a brush and dustpan. She was neatly dressed in a yellow tunic, her sleeves bearing the schturval, and in her combed hair a glitter showed where she wore a vimshu, a kind of small tiara set with brilliants much favored even by girls who were not considered vain.

She missed her sweep with the brush, for her head was cocked up and to the side and she was looking over at the far corner of the room. She might have seen that sight many and many a time, and yet I could well understand her bright interest and amusement.

In the corner—where I spotted another scrap of squish piecrust—I could see a man. He was inordinately tall and thin. He wore a scarlet tunic and a golden belt. His long yellow hair was tightly wound into a red bandage-cap somewhat like a turban. He was a strange and powerful figure, well, enough.

The trouble was, he was standing on his head.

I could feel my harsh old lips stretching into the broadest of smiles.

He saw me.

Now I give him his due. He did not fall over.

To one side stood another fellow almost as tall wearing a proper decent Vallian evening robe of midnight blue. To him I said:

"Tell me, Brince, how long?"

"Majister!" This tall streak recovered himself. "But a couple of murs more, majister. And lahal, I am overjoyed to see you. As is my cousin—"

With that the tall man standing on his head flung himself in an amazing contortion around so that he landed on those spider-long legs. He towered in the room. He advanced on me, hand outstretched, beaming away like a searchlight.

I grasped his hand as he grasped mine.

"Dray!"

"Inch!"

Seven foot he stood in his socks, and not an inch shorter. I looked up and I laughed, and I gripped his hand as he gripped mine.

Good old Inch!

As he had said on an occasion before, so, now, he said, "As a rascally comrade of ours would say, Dray—Lahal, my old dom!"

"Aye," I said, "and he is well and I've sent him back to Vondium for reinforcements. And that is why I'm here."

"You do not surprise me." He lifted his voice, as gangling and bubbling with life as ever, and yet with the marks of his responsibilities upon him in the line of lip and jaw, the crinkle around the eyes. "Wine! Wine for the emperor! The best we have—Jholaix! By Ngrozyan the Axe! Break out that crate of Jholaix hidden behind the racks of Stuvan! And hurry!"

Men ran off to do the kov's bidding, and he rubbed his hands at the ends of those long thin arms where the bunched muscles showed strongly. "I've waited a long time for something worthwhile to celebrate."

"Maybe celebrations are a trifle premature, particularly when I wish to deprive you of some fine fellows of your best regiments."

"We have had a turn of fortune up here, recently, Dray. The Racters are quiet. Brince says they're so quiet they're up to something fiendish. Isn't that so, Brince, you lathe of stubborn willpower?"

Inch's second cousin, who'd come over from their native Ng'groga to help out with five hundred axemen, nodded.

"I've grown to love Vallia. When all these troubles are over, majister, we'd like to settle down here, if that falls within your will and permission—"

"Falls within my gratitude, Brince. You are all most welcome."

"I thank you, majister. But what my long streak of a cousin says is true. I believe the Racters merely withdraw a little to regroup and so strike us with full force."

"That is a sensible reading of the situation. I think, however, that the true picture is even more dire."

Then I told them, as the Jholaix hoarded against a special day was brought in and opened and we drank, savoring the superb vintage, told them of the schemes of Layco Jhansi and the Racters. Jhansi concentrated against Turko in Falinur. The Racters turned their attentions to the King of North Vallia, upstart and usurper though he was. When, if not before, they had accomplished those tasks, they would crush Inch in the Black Mountains between them.

Inch quaffed the wine.

"Very well. We strike first. It can be done."

"Agreed. But I still need regiments to assist Turko." Then I spoke of the disaster that had sorcerously overtaken the Ninth Army.

The moment I had finished speaking Inch burst out: "Anything Turko requires from me he can have, and at once. We'll get started first thing. By Ngrangi! I can't abandon Turko—and, anyway, we can keep the Racters in play and then, when we've won, *we'll* be the ones to crush them in a vise!"

Many and many a time I thank Zair for good comrades. And, more, I thank all the gods and spirits that my blade comrades are blade comrades one with another. Not for me the system which sets subordinates at one another's throats, filled with petty jealousies, unwilling to act together, trying always to steal a march. That this system does work, after a fashion, has been proved. But its inefficiency puts it out of court to anyone with a heart and an eye to the main chance. If all my blade comrades ganged up together on me—well, then, by the disgusting diseased liver and lights of Makki Grodno, perhaps I would deserve that fate.

That I had not a single qualm that that could happen does not indicate I was a blind fool. I give trust seldom. When I do, I judge fairly that it is given in full.

Then Inch raised a point I had known he would, and had rather wished he wouldn't. Still, the ridicule would have to be faced.

"Tell me, Dray, the army with Turko that is so badly shaken. Did you say—Ninth Army?"

"Aye."

He looked down on me with a comical expression and said: "Well? You'd better tell me what's been going on."

"Yes, I suppose so. The Presidio have been doing very well running the country, and their council has been invaluable. Also, they handle the day-to-day affairs that are so time-consuming."

"That I well believe. But—"

"They decided that for the glory of Vallia and the better management of the army as a whole, each Kapt commanding an army should be given an army with a number. Turko's happened to be the Ninth."

"And the other eight?"

I made a face.

"Drak has the First down in the southwest. The Second was serving up in the northeast. The Eighth I had, and although that army no longer exists, its brigades being distributed among the others, I still hang onto the number. As for the others, they served in Hamal."

"I have heard somewhat of what went on down there. You must tell me of it over supper."

"I will. Also I will tell you about Tilda and Pando—"

"You have seen them again? Spoken to them?" He bent down, eager, concerned for our old friends who had turned out so different from what we had expected.

"Aye, I've seen 'em and spoken to them. I'll tell you."

He frowned at my tone, and so I promised to tell him all over supper. At that, he had been very decent over this grandiloquent business of numbering the armies, and had not mocked the notion at all. He would, though, he would, when the time was ripe.

To scotch that plan, I said, "I think I shall ask the Presidio to allocate your forces an army number, Inch. How does that seize you?"

"My lads will laugh."

"So well they may. They'll still fight."

"Oh, aye, that is sooth."

Then we sat down at the tables to concentrate upon the wine, upon miscils and palines, and upon the forces Inch could spare to march to the east to assist our blade comrade Turko—who was never a blade comrade in the sense of wearing edged weapons. I found that Inch had, as I suspected, been waging his struggle to free the Black Mountains with very slender resources.

His own Black Mountain Men, bonny fighters all, were in truth fearsome irregulars. His main disciplined strength resided in the regiments sent over from Valka, and a handful from the Vallian forces who had been flown in from time to time. For a good few seasons no direct land link had existed between our sections of Vallia and the Black Mountains.

So we fomented our plans. I was sorry to have missed Sasha, for she had proved tremendously popular in Vondium and had worked damned hard at being a good kovneva alongside her husband the kov. The twins—and there was another boy child as well now—had gone with their mother back to Ng'groga. Inch said, "Don't ask me what my Sasha did to break that particular taboo. It meant she had to go to Ng'groga, and so we felt it good that the children should see the place. I hated losing one of my fliers, though."

Always, around Inch of Ng'groga, one had to watch for his own infringement of his taboos. Wonderful and fearful they were, too, and never understandable to anyone who wasn't seven foot tall and as muscular-thin as a tentacle. The way he exorcised his taboos was even more remarkable. Well, we talked and in the end agreed that Inch could spare two regiments of Valkan archers, a regiment of Vallian spearmen and a mixed regiment of totrix cavalry, lances and bows.

"There is no point in taking any of your Black Mountain Men," I said. "They do best where they know the ground."

"Aye."

"Although soon you'll be breaking beyond the river to the north and attacking the Racters in their own lands."

Then I told him of the astonishing request received from Natyzha Famphreon, the dowager kovneva of Falkerdrin, that, owing to the unfortunate but inescapable fact that she was dying—or considered herself to be dying—she wanted me to ensure the legal inheritance of her son Nath, who was regarded as a weakling.

"But she's the chief biddy of the Racters!" exclaimed Inch.

"Certainly. But she seems to think I'll make sure Nath gets his dues."

"As a Racter," put in Brince, "his dues come at the sharp end of a sword, or the edge of an axe."

"But," said Inch, and he put his head on one side in a most comical-wise fashion, "if the Emperor of Vallia ensures his safe succession, he might renounce the Racters and join us. That would be a stroke!"

"My thoughts exactly."

"When—?"

"When Natyzha shuffles off to the Ice Floes of Sicce. By Krun! The gray ones had better look sharp when she gets there."

The laugh came easily. The future did hold a gleam of brightness through the gloom. I told Inch I'd make arrangements to transport his troops. He said he was sorry to see them go, for they were veteran fighting men.

"You'll get 'em back the moment we've finished Jhansi. Then we hit north."

"Look after 'em, Dray. And those two archer regiments, splendid, splendid. Endrass's Avengers, and Ernelltar's Neemus, they're dubbed. Fine fellows."

"We'll hit Jhansi from the east, you'll carve him up from the west, and when we meet in the middle, you'll have your regiments rejoin."

Making it sound casual, as though it had already happened instead of only being in the offing, I said, "I'm going to split Vennar down the middle, north to south. Turko will take his half into Falinur, and you your half into the Black Mountains."

Inch just said, after a pause: "I give you thanks, Dray."

"Now," and I spoke briskly. "Where's Salvation the Second?"

"Do what?"

"My fluttrell. Is he ready?"

"He's been fed and watered, and no doubt perched for the night—"

"Then he'll have to be dug out."

"You mean you're off—"

"Of course! By the Black Chunkrah! An emperor can't spend his time lollygagging about when the empire is falling into wrack and ruin! You have to be up and about. I'm off to the Blue Mountains."

Inch opened his mouth, shut it, said: "Give the lahal to Korf Aighos for me." Then he bellowed for his lads to ready the fluttrell.

Very soon, under the Moons of Kregen, I shouted down the remberees and took off, flying south.

"Remberee, Inch!"

"Remberee, Dray!"

The wind blustered into my face and the fuzzy pink moons light fell about me as Salvation the Second bore me on to the next stage in this venture.

Eight

A flying visit to High Zorcady

Korf Aighos was pleased to see me. I flew into High Zorcady with the pangs of memory tingling, and made damned sure my portable possessions were firmly chained down.

Great rogues and bandits are the Blue Mountain Boys. The province of the Blue Mountains owes the utmost devotion and loyalty to Delia. They knew my mettle from of old. They worshipped Delia's children. Apart from those few, anybody else was fair game.

High Zorcady remains always for me a place apart, lofting high on its crags above the pass, eerie and awesome, cupped by mountains, shielded by clouds. High Zorcady frowns down from the mists. Yet it is a place of color and liveliness, where Delia and I have spent many happy times.

Korf Aighos, his eyes still that brilliant blue so unusual in a Vallian, still strutting with a swagger, and yet half cautious as well as half arrogant, not a tall man but possessing a massive chest and arms corded with muscle, made me welcome. I will not detail our transactions, for essentially they followed the pattern I had established with Inch.

The Blue Mountain Boys had cleared the mountains of our foemen, as their compatriots had cleared the Zorca Plains extending out to the south.

Filbarrka was still away in Balintol. Now they planned an excursion to the large island of Womox, off their west coast.

"We merely hold the ring against Jhansi," the Korf told me as we supped in the great hall of High Zorcady with the trophies upon the wall and the hunting dogs lolling upon the rugs. "Womox is our target. They are a full lot there; but we hear there is much treasure."

An itchy-fingered lot, Delia's Blue Mountain Boys.

I nodded. "That is probably best. We can take Jhansi out with what we have. I sent a mob of his paktuns packing by a stratagem." Then, telling him of what had passed at the temple of Lem the Silver Leem, I solemnly warned him again of the danger of the cult.

"We have seen no sign of the rasts. If we do..."

The sign he made eloquently conveyed his intentions.

The time I spent with Korf Aighos was even less than the time with Inch.

Delia had long ago sent over from Djanduin, of which country in the far southwest of Havilfar she was queen, a stud stock of flutduins. These magnificent flyers, the best in all Havilfar for my money, had taken to the Blue Mountains and they throve. There had inevitably been a hiccup in the ecology of the region; but the flutduins were saddle flyers and partially domesticated, so that the wild life, after the first shattering alarm, survived albeit in somewhat altered food chains. Now the Blue Mountains boasted a formidable flutduin force of aerial cavalry.

The Korf insisted I exchange Salvation the Second for the finest flutduin he could provide, a saddle bird called Lightning. He was a marvel. I accepted.

So, ascending strapped to Lightning, I bellowed down the remberees and set course for Vondium.

My hopes of meeting up with Seg were dashed, for he'd shot in aboard a voller, brow-beaten everyone into instant action, and shot off again spurring the reinforcements, as it were, before him. Farris had responded with all the vollers and vorlcas he could spare. As ever, our resources were spread thin as butter over the crusts in the poor quarters of Ruathytu.

Delia was not in Vondium, so my side trip was entirely wasted.

Anxious though I was to get back north and finish off Layco Jhansi, I knew well enough the lads up there were in good hands. I indulged myself. I admit it.

The Half Moon, an old theater, now boasted a brand new roof. The seats had been freshly painted and their fleece-stuffed cushions were of high-quality ponsho. There were even a few gilded cornices to add a little glitter. The vision and acoustics remained first class.

Thither I took myself with a few of the pallans and high officials, a few of the officers of the garrison, for a new play was being offered and this night would see the first performance.

Master Belzur the Aphorist, renowned as a playwright in all Vallia, had produced another masterpiece. He'd called it *The Thread of Life*, and a deeply probing piece it was, making the audience take a fresh look at some of their actions, and the motives, and the results that were never the expected ones. The play was rapturously applauded.

During the interval, as usual, a frothy piece was staged, with much buffoonery and half-naked girls prancing about the stage, and a deal of four-armed tomfoolery.

Afterwards, not feeling in the least tired, I told Farris and the other nobles and pallans that I intended to fly now, right away, and leave for the front.

They set up such a clacking at this that I was persuaded at least to drop by a favorite tavern where we would not be disturbed.

"A flagon or two, majister! By Vox! Do we not deserve that?" So called Naghan Strandar, a trusted pallan.

"You and your colleagues most certainly do, Naghan," I told him. "As for me, I am not so sure. I remain always itchy and irritable when there is work to be done and I cannot get on with it."

"Aye, majister!"

They wanted to troop off to The Risslaca Transfix'd but I bellowed out: "Oh, no! Oho no! If you insist on my company then I insist on the tavern."

They whooped at this, sensing my change of mood.

"Where, majis? Where?"

"Why, what better place is there than The Rose of Valka?"

That tavern and posting house was very dear to me. Situated on the eastern bank of the Great Northern Cut, the inn had witnessed important events in my life upon Kregen. The owner was Young Bargom, still, and he was overjoyed to see us. Not overwhelmed. As a Valkan making a good living in Vondium and running a respectable house, he was now himself an important member of the community.

We rollicked in and the wine came up and we sat and stretched our legs and talked, and, inevitably, we sang.

I forbade the great song "The Fetching of Drak na Valka" for that would take too long. There were plenty of Valkans there, naturally, and they all called me strom, much to the disapproval of the Vallians of Vondium. So we sang "Naghan the Wily", a Valkan ditty, and "King Naghan his Fall and Rise."

We sang relatively few soldiers' songs, and this, too, was understandable given the company. We did, though, have a bash at "Have a care with my Poppy" and "The Brumbyte's Love Potion."

In an interlude I leaned over to Farris and spoke quietly. "I really must leave soon, Farris. I'll just ease out unobtrusively. You can calm 'em down when I'm gone."

He knew me by now.

"If you must, Dray. Opaz knows the work never ceases."

"We must all come to the fluttrell's vane," I said, and at the next opportunity to excuse myself did so and went outside. The night breathed sweet and still, and She of the Veils sailed golden above. In those moon-drenched shadows I started off, swinging my arms, feeling the lightness of freedom once again.

A shape at my side, a small hand clutching my arm, a girl's voice, whispering in alarm in my ear—

"Dray! Dray! Your face! What are you thinking of, you great fambly! Here—in here, bratch!"

With that she hauled me into a narrow slot of shadowed rose-colored radiance in which we were hidden from all sight from the inn windows.

The shadows fell across me, the shifting illumination across her face.

I did not know her.

She was clad, as best I could make out, in trim-fitting russet leathers, rapier and dagger scabbarded to a narrow waist. Her face was not beautiful. Rather, in its round perkiness it held a cheekiness that would infuriate and enchant. Her eyes—I thought—were Vallian brown. Her large floppy hat drooped about her ears.

I just managed to bite off an instinctive: "Who the hell are you?" No one I do not know and cherish calls me Dray. No one. But she had.

She stared at me anxiously. She made no move to draw her dagger to spit me.

"It seems you believe you know me, Kotera," I said, and my growly old voice came out alarmingly small.

"Oh, you clown! What d'you think you're doing, parading around with your face?"

"It's mine—"

Now it happened that I'd swung a plum-colored flying cloak about me as I'd stepped out of The Rose of Valka. A furtive movement from the end of the little alley into which this remarkable lady had dragged me drew my instant attention.

My right hand crossed to fasten upon the hilt of my rapier.

A man enveloped in a cloak moved across the alley mouth. I could not see his face, turned away from me and shadowed. But he looked a nasty customer. Big and ugly, no doubt, strong and powerful, and ready to knock some poor innocent down and rob them as to quaff a stoup of ale. He moved not at a crouch but as though coiled and ready to spring savagely upon any who stood in his path. I must say he'd give anyone a queasy turn.

The girl saw him.

She turned that round cheeky face up to me and I saw it was transfixed with horror.

She choked out words, shattered.

"By Zim-Zair! It's—My Val!"

With that she fairly flew along the alley, burst out, grabbed this ugly customer by an arm as she'd grabbed me, and the last I saw of this unlikely and highly suspicious couple was their twinned shadows fleeting over the cobbles. Then they vanished.

I shook my head, "Now what in a Herrelldrin Hell was all that about?"

I did not shrug my shoulders; but I kept my fist wrapped about my rapier hilt as I went off to find Lightning.

There was, of course, no sign of either of them beyond the alley, not the lissom saucy girl or the big ugly fellow who looked as though he ate a whole chunkrah for breakfast.

At the last there, as she'd grasped his arm, he'd turned to her. I'd seen his face. As I say, he was a ferocious plug-ugly brute, with a strong nose and arrogant jut to his chin. He was a fellow I'd think twice about before dealing with. He forced me to think the unwelcome thought, the memory I sidestepped. He held in him something of Mefto the Kazzur, and that was a puzzlement indeed.

Lightning flapped his wings twice and then we were airborne. I shoved the silly incident from my mind and concentrated on what lay ahead.

As they say: "No man or woman born of Opaz knows all the Secrets of Imrien."

The flight under the Moons proved uneventful.

When, after the regulation number of halts along the way to refresh Lightning, he slanted down to the new camp of Turko's Ninth Army, I was feverish with the desire to get things moving.

This time we'd defeat Layco Jhansi, defeat the Racters, deal with the upstart King of North Vallia, and finish up with all this section of Vallia happily re-united.

The Ninth Army was well back to being once again a formidable fighting force. The reinforcements brought the strength up, Seg and Kapt Erndor had brought in regiments of fine fellows, the Phalanx was up to strength, and as soon as Farris brought in Inch's people from the west, we'd have as fine a fighting army under our hands as you could wish for.

On the morning of the next day, the very next morning after I'd joined the army, the air filled with millions of buzzing insects.

Wasps, bees, hornets, all stinging and buzzing, drove the camp into instant confusion, and sent the men of this fine fighting army running madly in every direction.

The Witch of Loh, Csitra, had struck again.

Nine

Stung

Pandemonium! Utter confusion! Men ran and swiped and flapped and swatted everywhere I looked. The river fringing the camp splashed and spouted as men leaped bodily in. Soon the water was dotted with human heads, ducking and surfacing, like berries washed in a basin.

The wasps and bees and hornets—and other typically Kregish stinger horrors—swarmed so thickly in the air they appeared solid clouds, black and yellow, red and orange, bottle green.

Our poor saddle animals, of course, both of the ground and the air, went mad. They galloped or flew off and with a sinking heart I knew we'd not see them again for some good long time. Or, to be more accurate, some evil long time.

I was not stung once.

Everywhere I looked the swarms pirouetted and swooped. They were maddened and had no hesitation in stinging. They'd been goaded before being unleashed on us. Men with faces like pincushions ran past, screaming. I saw a couple of Jikai Vuvushis slapping and beating at each other, their slim bodies and pretty faces swelling grotesquely.

Still I was not stung.

As abruptly as they had appeared, the swarms vanished.

One moment the ground was darkened by their shadows, as if at the heart of a thundercloud, the next the morning lights of Zim and Genodras streamed apple green and rosy pink across the plain.

Once more I will pass over the scenes that followed.

Enough to say that we had injuries to throw back our calculations, men and women shaken by this fresh show of sorcerous power.

Khe-Hi and Ling-Li told me that while they had had no real problem in dispersing the swarms, and, indeed, their reactions had been swift, still it had taken time. Also, and this was far more serious, Khe-Hi said: "We felt the power of the twinned kharrnas against us distinctly. The mastery of the arts of the uhu, Phunik, has grown alarmingly."

"Someone once speculated that Csitra and Phunik could never achieve the power of Phu-Si-Yantong or constitute a serious threat."

Khe-Hi's wry grimace told me what he thought of that theory.

"Who can say that? What knowledge do they have of the arts? Oh, no. Any Wizard of Loh may grow into the mastery his powers confer. Phunik could easily surpass his father. There is no one in the whole wide world who can guarantee he cannot or will not."

"Drawing a knife across his throat," put in Nath na Kochwold, speaking through bloated lips, "might settle the issue."

No one commented on the pun, for it didn't exist in quite that form in Kregish. We did agree with Nath. All the same, although Csitra and Phunik quite evidently were a serious threat to us, I clung onto my feeling of confidence that our three mages would achieve the mastery.

As we broke up this small conference to see about the immediate tasks, a voice at the back piped up.

What that voice said—and I didn't recognize the speaker—was: "All these catastrophes fall on us when the emperor is here."

There was the sound of a scuffle and then people were moving off. I made no attempt to follow up an inquiry for there were still people here, loyal to me, who expected emperors to have off the heads of all those who spoke against them.

What that comment did make me do was understand that, indeed it was true, Csitra only struck when I was around.

She had left me alone when I'd been in the Black Mountains and in the Blue Mountains and in Vondium. Why? What was different? Surely a blow there would be even more damaging?

Only Seg and Turko commented on the fact that I'd not been stung, everyone else apparently conceiving it the divine right of rulers not to be stung when the swods were.

"I told you, Dray," said Turko. "She really does fancy you."

"Right, my old dom. She doesn't want to spoil your pretty face."

I glared at them, comrades both. I didn't laugh; but they did, despite the gravity of it all. Then we went to work to bring the army back to its senses. The needlemen and puncture ladies ran out of ointment and unguents and we sent fast vollers for fresh supplies.

We were delayed; that was all.

Our two mages now kept a continuous vigil, turn by turn; but they reported no further sorcerous attacks.

My bodyguard corps had been stung more severely than most for the simple and warming reason that they conceived their duty lay in standing between me and danger. Targon the Tapster, hardly able to speak, his face a molten red lump, reported in, for he it was who commanded by rote 1ESW this day.

"I am very sorry to see you in this case, Targon. And the lads, too. Particularly when I am the only one who escaped."

Useless to attempt to reproduce the sounds Targon made when he spoke. What he said was: "We all volunteered to serve you, majis, and of what worth a man if he cannot stand by his word? And, anyway, you are wrong."

"Oh?"

"Aye. Wenerl the Lightfoot also was not stung."

I saw at once. My face must have registered the shock, for Targon croaked out: "Majis! You—"

"Call the lads," I said, my words harsh and grating. "First Emperor's Sword Watch only. Somewhere off a little way across the plain where we can be alone and unobserved. I'll meet you all there in a single bur."

"Quidang!"

When I found Khe-Hi and Ling-Li—who were also not marked, but one did not expect wizards and witches to fail to protect themselves—with our small group we walked out to the plain where 1ESW formed impeccable lines. They all understood.

The jurukkers of the guards, splendid fighting men every one, many of them kampeons, stood in impeccable ranks; but they were fidgeting and trying not to scratch at themselves, and their faces and exposed portions of their bodies wafted the pungent fumes of unguents and liniments.

"One mur for scratching!" I bellowed. "Then attention."

Scabbarded at my waist and in addition to my usual armory, I wore a particular blade. That sword was forged from dudinter. The electrum did not gleam sharply, for the blade had been smeared with ganjid, the wizard's preparation that, in conjunction with the dudinter weapon, could drink the transformed life from a werewolf. I knew that many soldiers carried their dudinter blades in their kit—just in case.

The ranks quieted down as much as I could reasonably expect.

During that werewolf period, Csitra had controlled some of the warrior maidens in our army from her distant lair. When the girls kissed a man, they bit—and the man, at Csitra's pleasure, staring through his eyes, turned into a ganchark, a ravening werewolf.

Wenerl the Lightfoot had been on guard duty in the palace gardens in Vondium and he had been attacked by a werewolf which escaped. I remember how I'd wondered if his mind would recover as easily as his body. Now he wore four medals on his chest, when at the time of the werewolf attack he had worn three bobs. He stood there in the front rank, trim, hard, a fighting man from helmet to boots, his weapons sharp and clean. I felt the pain in my breast.

But he had not been stung.

Csitra, then, had made a mistake.

I shouted: "Wenerl the Lightfoot. Front and center."

He marched up with a clang and stood to attention. I guessed he'd been crowing over his comrades about his good luck in not being stung. Poor Wenerl! He didn't know, of course.

"Jurukker Wenerl! Tell me what you remember of the night you were attacked by the ganchark."

"Quidang, majister—but, majister, I recall nothing. I must have run after the beast—for I only remember waking up with a full clang of the Bells of Beng Kishi in my head, and a wounded shoulder—"

Although to read the expressions on the faces of those assembled here was well-nigh impossible, I guessed from the deep hush that fell upon the regiment and those gathered with me, that many grasped the hideous truth, as in all Opaz's truth, that truth was hideous.

I unlimbered the ganjid-smeared dudinter blade and held the point at Wenerl's throat. He did not flinch. Was I not the emperor whom he served loyally?

I looked deeply into his brown Vallian eyes. I could see the veins, and the little lights, and, in truth, just brown eyes.

I said, "Csitra. With this man you have failed. Is there need to claim his life?"

Wenerl said, "This man means nothing to me."

"But he does to me, Csitra."

"And you mean much to me, Dray Prescot, and yet you scorn me—"

"Wrong, witch. I do not scorn you. I feel sorrow for you—"

That was a mistake.

"You pity me! You dare to pity me!"

In my ear Khe-Hi whispered: "I have it now, Dray, if you wish to see..."

"Thank you, Khe-Hi; but no. My concern is with Wenerl and I will not be distracted—"

Wenerl's voice broke in, saying: "Who is it that stands at your shoulder, Dray Prescot, for there are shadows there—"

Casually, I said, "Just a shadow or two, Csitra, they are nothing." Khe-hi had obviously wrought a little stroke of his own to avoid Csitra's observation of him through Wenerl's eyes. I went on: "This man is held in thrall to you, the poison in his veins will turn him into a werewolf when you desire. But instead of that you have used him to spy on us. If you do not agree to spare him, then I shall surely kill him—and with my own hand, not entrusting the task to another—so that, in either case, you will have no eyes in my camp."

"Why do you not travel to the Coup Blag and see me, Dray Prescot? You know I can offer you much—"

"Give me an answer, woman!"

"You swear to me that—"

"I promise you nothing, witch."

"I have Pronounced the Nine Unspeakable Curses against Vallia, and they cost me much pain and blood and life energy. They may not be drawn back so easily. Yet this I would do—"

"You know my answer. Spare me this man—"

"So much effort, so much concern, for one stupid tikshim, worth perhaps a few coins in the bagnios?"

Will against will. Stubbornness against Obstinacy.

Then, surprising me, she said: "You do not ask to see me, Dray Prescot. I am a woman not without attractions. Why do you not look upon me, instead of this worthless man? Or is it that you are afraid?"

"One last time, Csitra the Witch. Spare this man's life. There can be no other dealings between us."

"You would think well of me if I did?"

My face must have ricked up in some devilish way, for I swear I heard the voice in Wenerl's throat emit a noise very much like a gasp.

"Think well of you? How can I, after the damage you have wrought?" Then, and thinking primarily of poor old Wenerl the kampeon standing there like a straw dummy, I added with cunning: "But I should certainly think better of you."

So we stood, locked through the eyes of a man whose life trembled in the balance of greed and lust and cunning and contempt. Wenerl gave a great shudder.

His voice said: "Take him, Dray Prescot."

And Wenerl half-stumbled, snapped to immediate attention, and bellowed out: "Quidang, majister!"

I did not relax, and the dudinter blade did not tremble. It had brought a small spot of blood out on Wenerl's neck when he stumbled. Khe-Hi exclaimed at this.

"She has kept her word. Wenerl would be dead else."

"All the same, best keep him under observation for a time. Wenerl," I barked at him. "You are excused normal duties for three days. Attend to your comrades."

So that was done, and the regiment marched off in good order, and each man there understood a little more of what being a dratted commander entailed.

At least, a commander on the magical and mysterious world of Kregen!

Before news circulated that the emperor had in some mysterious way prevented any further plagues from descending upon us, Nath reported in a way that was, in the circumstances, entirely inevitable.

We stood in under the flap of the HQ tent, a rather ornate affair used for the business of running the army, and Nath rubbed his chin, saying gloomily: "The rate is up to a marked degree. One in fifty and—"

"Not to be wondered at. The rate should go down once the men get to know they won't be plagued again." Then I added in as somber a tone as Nath na Kochwold's: "Until that she-leem worms another pair of eyes into the camp."

"The worst is that one of Turko's Falinurese regiments has deserted entire."

"That is bad. Whose?"

"Jiktar Robahan Vending's Snarling Strigicaws, the Fifth of Spears."

The Fifth Spears were called Snarling Strigicaws for their shields, which were red and brown and striped above and double-spotted below. In the center they carried the schturval of Falinur. They had not been, in my estimation, a top-line outfit; but they were four hundred and eighty men less to us.

"A bad business. I'll only repeat the old saw; we're better off having the desertions now than later on when we're committed."

"That will not be long now—"

"Thank Opaz!"

So, the next day we broke camp and set off. We were a tidy bunch. One cannot, on Kregen, say we marched off Horse, Foot and Guns. One says we marched off Air and Ground Cavalry, Foot and Varters.

The swods in the ranks sang the moment their swollen lips allowed them that surcease.

We marched west, toward the perfidious Layco Jhansi's capital of Vendalume, and we marched looking for a fight.

Ten

The Battle of Vendalume

The Battle inevitably came to be called the Battle of Vendalume.

Most, not all, battles are interesting. In an academic way they hold great fascination for the student not only of tactics but of human nature. The actuality of battles is disgusting.

I had grown in my seasons upon Kregen to dislike fighting and battles and violence exceedingly, as I am sure you will have perceived. Yet I was still the old intemperate Dray Prescot underneath all the acquired veneer of calm and rationality.

When your countrymen and women—as the peoples of Vallia certainly were by now—are enslaved and treated vilely, then if you are able to liberate them it seems a chivalrous notion to go out and do what you can to restore them to their former freedoms and dignity. I am very wary about this idea of chivalry, and although being called a chivalrous knight, much to my chagrin and inward amusement, I do subscribe to the idea that tasks to be done in this life must be done. If I can get out of the more awkward particulars, then I'll get out sharpish. I am an old paktun, an old leem-hunter, and I value my hide as dearly as the next fellow.

The folk of Vallia had demanded that I become their emperor and lead them out of the Times of Troubles. To be honest, not every citizen of Vallia had demanded this; the dissenters were universally to be found in the ranks of those who profited by the country's misery and who battened and fattened on slavery, confusion and strife.

As usual in my battles when he was present, Seg Segutorio would take the vaward.

These mainly consisted of those lithe and limber young lads, half-naked, armed with javelin, sling and bow, who formed the light infantry, the voltigeurs, the skirmishers. In general they were an unruly bunch. They were formed in regiments, bearing grandiose and pugnacious titles, and they served as a cloud before the storm.

The main of Seg's effort lay with the bowmen. Here his painstaking labors saw fruit in the perfection of our army's shooting. Our dustrectium could paralyze an opposing army.

Now I am aware that accounts of battles are not to everyone's taste. But they do form part of human history, and one can learn much of human nature from their mystery, their patterns, even, if you will, their mystique.

To clear away once and for all any misconceptions, as we marched out onto the wide and dusty plain where we saw the opposing masses forming against us, it would be appropriate to settle finally the business of nomenclature. The pikemen in the Phalanx were called brumbytes, this from the mythical animal, the brumby, all thrusting horn and massive onslaught, that furnished the symbol at the center of their crimson shields. The heavy infantry, equipped with metal armor, with sword and shield and often with a short-range throwing weapon, were called churgurs. The skirmishers, as I have said, were called kreutzin. These Kregish names do not seem to me to be too hard to recall even in the heat and dust of battle.

Any man who rides a ground saddle animal is known as a jutman, or, in the case of a lady, a jutwoman. A rider is a vakka. On Kregen they are not horsemen.

The shrill and tumultuous screeches of Jhansi's trumpets filled the air before us. His banners waved. The word for flag in Kregish is tresh. Our treshes waved back in defiance.

My people had advised me to wear the Mask of Recognition. This oversized mask of a thin gold plating over iron concealed my face, was damned hot and uncomfortable, gave some protection to my ugly old beakhead, I suppose, and marked me instantly to our men.

Our aerial reconnaissance told us the layout of Jhansi's host. Its composition was more conjectural. He had his hordes of sorcerously inflamed crazies, and I felt a pang at thought of the revolting necessity of fighting them. He still had many paktuns, for I'd seen off successfully only a relative few by my ruse in the temple of Lem the Silver Leem. They'd fight and earn their hire this day. I could hope that when, as was damned-well going to happen, the day went against them, they'd have the sense to slope off even if they didn't attempt to change sides.

I said to Seg and Kapt Erndor, standing by Turko and Nath na Kochwold: "The old barn door."

"Right you are," said Seg. "I'll tickle 'em up, by the Veiled Froyvil."

"The Phalanx," said Nath, "will fight this day under its proper commander." He indicated the Brumbytevax of the Fourth Phalanx, Brytevax Dekor.

I nodded, not speaking, waiting for my comrade to come out with what was clearly his own cunning scheme. Nath na Kochwold, the Krell-Kapt* of the entire Phalanx Force, all five Phalanxes of it, in theory had no real field command. Each half of a Phalanx, each Kerchuri, was commanded in action by its Kerchurivax, the men who did the work in battle. We already had the Sixth Kerchuri with the Ninth Army, and the losses from those damned frogs had been made up by Seg's reinforcements. Also, he had flown up the Tenth Kerchuri, half of the newly raised Fifth Phalanx. So we had four Kerchuris.

Nath na Kochwold gazed at me with rather the expression a young man might bestow upon a flagon of the best ale of Vondium suddenly chanced upon in the Ochre Limits.

"This is the position," I said. I spoke largely, for, Zair forgive me, I relished the serious and disciplined Nath's anxious hanging-upon every word. This was a grievous sin on my part, and I own it, for I paid for it in the end, by Zair I paid, as you shall hear...

"We have the Seventh and Eighth Kerchuris of the Fourth Phalanx. These will be commanded by Brytevax Dekor. So well and good. We also have the veteran Sixth Kerchuri of the Third Phalanx, and they are superior lads in all senses." I glanced at Nath and went on: "I'd rather thought I'd hold them in reserve."

Nath managed to croak out: "I see, majis."

I didn't miss that use of majis, either...

"As for the newly arrived Tenth Kerchuri, of the Fifth Phalanx, they are not as green as they may seem. They inherit not only the glory but also many of the lads of the old Tenth who fought so valiantly at the Battle of Ovalia."

"Also they inherit the insignia of the old Tenth," pointed out Turko, "the Prychan grasping Thunderbolts. I was there. That was the Eighth Army. Oh, yes, we sprang the thorn ivy trap on them all right. Layco Jhansi ran off then with his tail between his legs, and he had some of the iron legions of Hamal to fight for him."

"We've come a long way since then." I spoke in a way that conveyed

---

* Krell: chief. Kapt: general. *A.B.A.*

184

more to listeners than idle boasting. "We've driven Jhansi back, Turko has secured his kovnate of Falinur, and now we have driven into Vennar and have him forced to turn and fight for his capital. Slow we may be; but we are re-uniting Vallia, even if to the outside world who knows little of what goes on in the islands we seem to be doing nothing."

Nath's face was a wonder to behold; I hoped he wouldn't blow up before he was put out of his misery.

To that charitable end, I said: "We have a few regiments of swarths, chief among them Jiktar Nath Roltran's unruly mob, who I am told call themselves the Trampling Green Scaled Regiment." Swarths, reptile mounts with four legs and wedge-heads all, as it were, designed to lumber forward in a straight line, do have strength and power but their turn of speed leaves much to be desired. I went on: "Jhansi has received a sizeable reinforcement of swarthmen. It is probable that he has stopped running and turned to fight us because they do add considerably to his strength."

"There's Vendalume," pointed out Turko. "That's making him fight, too, I expect." He was as well aware as I what went forward with the suffering Nath.

Seg said: "Or he didn't relish running on and going slap-bang into old Inch. But, these swarthmen, now..." Seg, like Turko, had poor old Nath na Kochwold to rights.

Sharply, I said: "Nath! You will command the Sixth Kerchuri. In reserve. They are under your hand. You will have a flutduin reconnaissance flight. Those enemy swarths are yours. The moment you see their direction get the lads moving and chop 'em up." Almost, I finished with a cracked out: "Dernun?" which means savvy, do you understand, and is not particularly polite.

Nath braced himself. He looked so relieved as to make Seg and Turko look out across the open plain toward the distant city.

"We will hit those swarthmen, Dray," he said, and his voice was level and sure.

No doubt with all these high-flown commanders and officers in their correct positions, he'd actually contemplated not having a command this day...

Then Turko put his oar in.

"Ah, Dray—Seg brought up from Vondium the Fifth Churgurs. They were with us at Ovalia. I'd rather like—"

"Certainly. What do they call themselves now?"

"The Prickly Thorns."

"Yes, well one or two regiments can play on that variety of name..."

So we sorted out what went where and who commanded whom. The regiments looked splendid under the suns, for not a cloud darkened the sky. The war had not so far ruined this part of Vennar and the grass sparkled, sweet-smelling and fresh. In the distance the walls and towers of Vendalume beckoned us on.

Already as the columns moved into position the swods were singing hymns, chants, paeans. The religious observances had been scrupulously performed with due solemnity and ceremony.

Now I have said that it was usual in *my* battles for Seg to take the vaward. But this battle rightfully belonged to Turko and Kapt Erndor.

Turko had matured into a first-class commander, and Kapt Erndor became more and more the Chief of Staff. I made a decision.

"I'll drift across to my lads," I told Turko. "I rather fancy a little arm-swinging will be good for all of us. You and Kapt Erndor can run the battle."

"Well, now, Dray—"

"Good," I said, briskly. "That's settled."

The standards of the Phalanx fluttered splendidly. Each Jodhri, six of which formed a Kerchuri, carried its own colors. The original Prescot flag, a plain yellow cross upon a scarlet field, specially presented to the Phalanx Force, was now variously identified by symbols for each formation. Also the colors carried battle honors. Bullion and golden threads weighted those colors... A wreath of thorn ivy decorated each color within the Tenth Kerchuri. A similar wreath gleamed from the standards of the Fifth Churgurs. Other regiments carried that proud battle honor—not many, for the Eighth Army had been a force remarkably few in numbers.

When I joined 1ESW, no thorn ivy wreaths decorated their standards, for 2ESW had fought at Ovalia. The battle honor gleamed above the treshes of 1EYJ. My lads set up a racketing yell when I trotted up aboard a borrowed zorca, Tuftears. They flashed their swords aloft and yelled, and the Hai Jikai roared to the heavens.

Just across from us the Twenty-first Brigade of Zorcabows waited, fidgeting a trifle, proud zorca heads tossing so that the spiral horns glittered in the light. This brigade, commanded by Chuktar Travok Ramplon, was part of Seg's vaward, assigned the task of clearing away the enemy's forward forces. To beef up the brigade somewhat, a regiment of Zorca Lances had been assigned to Chuktar Ramplon as an extra unit.

Seg, with his personal bodyguard, trotted past, standards fluttering, suns light glinting from armor and weapons. By Vox! But he looked an impressive sight!

The units gave responding cheers, and then Seg was gone, gone out to his post of command in the vaward to face the perils and dangers of being first into action.

Well, not quite first, for the aerial squadrons were already aloft and snuffing about ready to throw back any aerial advance made by Jhansi. Once that necessary preliminary had been accomplished the fliers and the flyers would swarm over to the attack. The torments they were likely to inflict on Jhansi's forces could sway the course of the battle.

The Second Regiment of the Emperor's Sword Watch, not a little cocky with their thorn ivy wreaths of honor in presence of the First Regiment, with that very same 1ESW and First and Second EYJ, formed the guard brigade here today. They were not often thus collected together with the emperor. And, still, Drak had regiments of ESW and EYJ with him in the southwest. I anticipated using the brigade of jurukkers as the final all-out battle-winning hammer stroke.

With steady pace and as impeccable a drill as one could legitimately expect on such an occasion, the swods formed the battle line.

Over there, between us and the ramparts of Vendalume, the dark masses of the enemy could be seen forming their battle line. Aerial scouts reported every movement, and attempted to deny the enemy air any observation of our own maneuvers.

Over there, Layco Jhansi and his cronies, chief among whom I suspected was still Malervo Norgoth, if he wasn't already dead and gone down to the Ice Floes of you know where, would be anxiously preparing their people. The stinking sorcerer, Rovard the Murvish, would be inflaming the poor deluded dupes in the ranks. I'd spoken to Khe-Hi about this.

The Wizard of Loh had replied: "There is a limit to all things. Rovard will probably have drugged the wines, as well as using his brand of sorcerer's art upon the people. We have been fully tied up combating Csitra and Phunik." He spoke with his usual metallic precision. "Rovard will operate on an individual basis. We would have to take far too much time to rectify his mischief."

"I understand." Then I passed on to a more cheerful subject. "I suppose the moment the battle is won you and Ling-Li will wish to be married."

He smiled. "We shall marry here in Vallia, for we wish to make this our home. But, of course, we shall have to travel to Loh at some time to ratify the contracts."

"Oh, of course." I knew there was a lot more sorcerous proceedings to be gone through in Loh to take them back there, and nothing much to do with ratifying contracts.

There is little I can tell you about the battle itself, for, as I have remarked, it is impossible for a single man to grasp at all that goes on during these absences of sanity from the world. Even the commander in chief can seize on only the salient points. To build up a picture of a battle one must patiently seek out many sources.

The aerial combats could be seen easily enough and our flutduins overmastered the enemy's fluttrells and mirvols. Our force of vollers smashed his. Seg did his usual competent job and cleared the front so that we had the main of it from the beginning. Then he went off to make sure his archers—I will not say beloved archers, for Seg was as intolerant of his bowmen's shooting as Nath was of his brumbytes in the files—added to the carnage.

Charges went in and were successful or were repulsed. The old barn door stratagem, by which one end of the line is firmly anchored and the whole then pivots about this fulcrum, smashing everything in the way, once again proved itself. Jhansi, at any rate, was caught by it. He no longer had the advantage of being counseled by experienced Hamalese Kapts.

Nath na Kochwold judged his particular moment to perfection and when the enemy swarths charged the Sixth Kerchuri received them and broke them as a wave is broken upon rocks.

When it came time for the guard brigade to charge, we went in with a whoop and a holler and slashed into the fleeing flanks of the mobs who were attempting to run away from the charge of the Fourth Phalanx.

Oh, well, the battle went our way and the poor crazed idiots fought well, and died, and then, suddenly they were all running. The paktuns employed by Jhansi fought redoubtably for some time and then, being professionals, and seeing the way of the day, they sought to make good their escape.

We let them go.

After it was all over and the gates of Vendalume shut in our faces, we imagined that a siege must follow.

"Look!" Seg pointed, tall in the stirrups.

The gates of the city opened. A party appeared with flags of truce. Among the flags were three tall poles with bundles at their tips.

Nath said: "I think we can judge what this portends."

"Aye."

All over the stricken field the wounded were being collected and cared for. Fundal the Pestle-Breaker, an experienced doctor, reported that the crazies were crazed no more. They had returned to their senses and were bewildered by their situation and what they could not remember doing. There was a deal of wailing and yelling, I can tell you, and not all from the wounded.

"There's your reason." Turko indicated the bundles at the tips of the poles.

I suppose that of treacheries like these, empires are made.

Rovard the Murvish's head still stank, even stuck on top of a pole. Alongside him the head of an extremely ugly woman even in death half-turned away. She had been called, I believe, the obi-stromni Dafeena Norgoth. These two heads dribbled blood down the shafts of the poles. Alongside them the sightless eyes of Layco Jhansi showed pits of reddened black horror. Little blood dripped down his pole.

The fellow who had torn his clothes and smeared mud upon himself yet wore a silver and gilt chain about his neck. He was the mobiumim, the chief representative of the civil power, equivalent in many ways to the mayor. He went into the full incline, nose in the dirt, rump in the air.

I let him.

The three heads moved against the sky, their bearers trembling beneath, faces pinched, hardly daring to look at the emperor. The other dignitaries all flopped down, following the example of the mobiumim, so that I was presented with a sea of rumps.

This was too ridiculous.

"Get up, famblys! Stand on your own feet!"

They scrambled up as though red hot irons had tickled them up.

I said: "Where is Ralton Dwa-Erentor?"

He was the son of a minor noble, a great sleeth racer, and I knew he had been forced against his will to follow Layco Jhansi. With him, I would deal.

"He has been gone from Vennar for many seasons, majister," spluttered out the mobiumim. "Gone overseas to be a paktun."

"Your name?" I was disappointed; but there would be god-fearing and good men to be found here.

"Larghos Nevanter the Lace merchant, majister, an it please you."

"I do not know this name of Vennar you use. Half of the city of Vendalume stands in Kov Turko's province of Falinur, and the other half in Kov Inch's province of the Black Mountains. I am sure you know that."

"Oh, yes, indeed, majister, oh, yes, I know!"

"Good. Now report to my people and do as you are told." I urged Tuftears around and then turned to bellow over my shoulder: "And give those disgusting objects a decent burial, for the sweet sake of Opaz!"

Cantering off I wondered if Tarek Malervo Norgoth had already been dead or if he had escaped. Well, we'd soon find out. Khe-Hi and Ling-Li were just riding across to me, and as I saw them I felt a distinct glow of pleasure.

"Vondium!" I shouted to them. "We're off to Vondium first thing to see you two safely married!"

That activity was far more preferable than battles!

In this wise ended the Battle of Vendalume and the death of the traitor, Layco Jhansi.

Eleven

An Occult Wedding

The first rats ran swarming between the legs of the people just as the wedding procession left the Temple of Opaz Unknown.

The edifice had not been damaged during the recent Times of Troubles, and folk whispered that this was because the temple was dedicated to the manifestation of Opaz in his guise as arbiter of all things magical and arcane—Unknown and therefore awful—and no sane man or woman brought *that* kind of trouble on themselves.

The temple glittered with gold and ornamentation beneath its jet-black dome, music soared, and the flagstoned square pent between canals flanking the temple's entrance stairway was carpeted with thousands of yelling citizens of Vondium cheering for the wedding of Khe-Hi-Bjanching and Ling-Li-Lwingling.

The day, also, was the Day of Opaz Unknown.

Everybody was pleased for the wedding and that Khe-Hi and Ling-Li had found happiness together in their magical way. For, to be honest, no one was going to chance not cheering for them or wishing them well.

This lavish wedding ceremony should be the culmination in Vallia of the Occult Romance between these two mages. They both looked magnificent, gorgeously dressed, and no expense had been spared. Well, again, who was going to chance sparing an expense when a Witch and a Wizard of Loh got married...?

Between the hordes of rats ran leepitixes, wriggling on their twelve legs and unhappy at being out of water. Thousands of schrafters, millions of these creatures who infest dungeons and sharpen their teeth on the bones there, ran and chirruped through the throngs. And rasts—the six-legged animals dragged from their dung-heaps—ran crazily over the flagstones, leaping upon people's backs, clawing at them, fastening their claws into flesh and blood.

Rasts—running in their millions along the avenues and boulevards of Vondium!

For the wedding ceremony, Deb-Lu-Quienyin had put in an appearance. He'd been working his magics to defend Vallia. Now, standing in the position occupied by what on Earth would be called the Best Man, he looked furiously angry. He wore a brand new turban, and I'd insisted that it should be properly festooned with pearls and precious gems and gold bullion. Also, we had fixed it so that it wouldn't keep slipping off—or so we imagined.

"Just give me a mur, Khe-Hi," he said. "I do not think you should be troubled on your wedding day."

Ling-Li stood there, calmly, very lovely in her wedding gown, and seemed to soar above the problems. She simply waited for Deb-Lu to fix the problem, as though he was looking for a dropped glove.

She had surprised me vastly by asking me to take the position which, again on the Earth, can best be described as Father of the Bride. I had given her away.

Delia had laughed fit to bust at this, and, the most perfectly beautiful and most perfectly devious woman in two worlds, had helped wholeheartedly.

Now Delia said: "This is disgraceful. Poor Ling-Li—oh, Deb-Lu, dear, do hurry!"

"Of course, majestrix!"

Delia's rapier flashed into her hand and she twitched away a rat that tried to climb Ling-Li's wedding gown.

I was wearing a whole wardrobe of popinjay finery, and somewhere in there I had a rapier. I groped among all the folderols for the hilt. Come the day when Dray Prescot couldn't grip his rapier and draw in a twinkling!

The blade came free in time to slash a schrafter from Seg's shoulder where the thing was about to try to gnaw on Seg's skull. His own blade flickered in return and I felt the body on my shoulder flicked off. The tall collars we wore, highly ornate, called mazillas, gave us some protection; but if the rats started climbing up inside all our gorgeous clothing...!

Khe-Hi held Ling-Li's arm. But his eyeballs swiveled to regard Deb-Lu with great concern.

"Yes, yes," said Deb-Lu. "I can manage, thank you."

Shortly thereafter the swarms of sewer-rats and schrafters and leepitixes and rasts vanished.

The square, a moment before a torrential mass of people running and slapping and shouting, slowly began to quiet down.

Contrary to popular opinion there had been no greatly unpleasant lot of stinks from this infestation.

By dint of a great deal of exertion we got the wedding procession formed and moving again. The happy couple proceeded to their waiting narrow boat, hugely freighted with flowers, and the volunteer crew sent the boat smoothly along the canal. The cheers were far more muted than I cared for; but they picked up as the boat glided along between the throngs clustered on balconies and jetties, throwing petals, singing, and generally realizing that the excitement of an unpleasant variety was over and the excitements far more to their taste could now begin.

The reception—to give an Earthly name to the wild party it truly was—was held in one of the better-preserved chambers of the palace. Some of the windows were still boarded up; but the carpets were new and the tapestries had been collected from here and there to hide the burn marks on the walls.

We seldom used this chamber—the Hall of Drak Exalted—because it was pretty big and draughty, preferring the more cozy rooms where we ate and worked. Still, on this wedding day it served admirably.

As for foods and wines—we fed all Vondium this day and never recked the cost. I, for one, and there were many like me, was glad to see the happiness in the faces of Khe-Hi and Ling-Li.

And that had nothing to do with the fact that they were mages, a Wizard and a Witch of Loh.

During a moment when the dancers were changing places and people were buzzing with joy at the way we had managed to extricate ourselves from a nasty situation, Khe-Hi came over to me. He was carrying a wine goblet. His bride was dancing away with Nath na Kochwold. Everyone had come to Vondium for the wedding.

Khe-Hi lifted the glass.

"To you, Dray. In thanks."

I smiled and replied in proper form, and then he went on: "If we have a child, or children, they will have to be born and raised in Loh if they are to be Wizards or Witches of Loh. There are certain arcane matters to be attended to."

"I can well believe."

"I would ask your permission and that of the empress to call our eldest son Dray and our eldest daughter Delia."

Seg laughed.

"I didn't ask permission. But, then, I thought my old dom was dead."

Inch, towering above us, and being the subject of the sternest admonitions from Sasha not to eat squish pie, said: "My eldest is Dray, too. I think there will be a plethora of Drays in Vallia before long."

Delia was out on the floor dancing with the Lord Farris.

I said: "I know I am delighted, Khe-Hi, and it is to me you do the honor. As for Delia, I am sure she will feel the same. Still, you'd better ask her."

As I spoke I saw Nath na Kochwold and the Lord Farris, in their dancing, glide closely alongside each other. The two women dancing with them, for a moment in the whirling gyrations to the beat of the music, paused.

Khe-Hi smiled and said: "Ling-Li is pleased, too, for there is no more gracious lady than the empress."

My Val! Here in the dilapidated although decked out Hall of Drak Exalted, in the palace in Vondium!

Sorcery at work, clearly, for Delia had given her acquiescence to the request.

I suppose we'd be the Earthly equivalent of God parents, too...

The music and the laughter and animated chatter enveloped everyone then and so, for a space, I was able to lean up against a curtain-shrouded pillar, in a trifle of shadows, and look out on the spectacle. Scents and perfumes were discreetly in evidence, for all the ladies were well aware of the empress's views on scents. Many and many a face I saw there, in that throng, I knew, and of them you have been introduced in my narrative to, what, ten percent? If that. A planet is a large place, inhabited by millions, and a thousand years is a long time.

Often at functions like this I had seen, perhaps, a scuttling red-brown scorpion, or a scarlet and golden raptor flying above my head, and I'd been whirled up by that enormous phantom blue Scorpion of the Everoinye to do their bidding. I now experienced a most weird sensation.

For I was seriously worrying over the lack of communications from the Star Lords. I had things on my mind, problems of which I was aware through what the Star Lords had revealed to me. I wanted to know more. When you have been snatched up by a phantom Scorpion, or indulged in slanging matches with a speaking bird, you tend to think of the immediate items first, you do stand in awe. My questions, wrong though they might be, were for quieter moments. And so, the weird sensation? Why I, Dray Prescot, seriously considered how I could get in touch with the Star Lords, how I could originate that fearful communication between us.

I actually, really and truly, wanted to see a scorpion, or the Gdoinye. I wanted to be snatched up by the phantom blue Scorpion of the Star Lords.

Thinking these surprising and, if the truth be known, fractious thoughts, I saw Marion walking up to me, half-smiling, with Strom Nango in tow. They were both, as befitted the occasion, resplendently dressed.

I roused myself.

"Not long now, Marion, before you and Strom Nango give us all this same pleasure."

"We look forward to the day, majister. I trust no unfortunate happening will upset *our* day."

"Marion!" said Nango, in that kind of whispering, half-chiding voice that denotes unease at what a lovedove says.

I brushed that away, seeing beyond these two the hall gyrating, as it were, around the dancers, the orchestras playing by rote, the scents of good wines and foods in the air. Marion—the Stromni Marion Frastel of Huvadu—and Strom Nango ham Hofnar were not just paying the required polite moment of conversation here. Marion got it out smartly enough—well, she would, seeing she was a Jiktar in the Jikai Vuvushis raised by the Sisters of the Sword.

"Majister! After this period of time, do you not think my unfortunate girls can return to the imperial bodyguard? I mean—" she gestured with a beringed hand, "—they were not to blame that they created werewolves. And that is all over. We missed the Battle of Vendalume. Many of the girls were most cross about that."

"Anybody who can show good reason to miss a battle should congratulate herself."

She looked uncertain at this; was this, it was clear both she and Nango were thinking, was this the way an emperor should speak?

Letting the conversation wander on a little after that without directing its course, I realized that Marion felt deeply that her new regiment of warrior maidens had not been in the fight. But more worrying was the way she kept inadvertently referring to "unfortunate" incidents, and "regrettable" occurrences. If she reflected the general feelings in Vondium—and she was representative enough to persuade me she did—then the folk here were damned uneasy about all these sorcerous goings on. As they would be, of course, and understandably so, to be sure. But it was the way in which these fears were expressed that depressed me.

What Marion seemed to be implying was that: "It's all your fault, majister, that we suffer so; but we don't really blame you for our misfortunes."

Was I to be an emperor on sufferance, then?

"As to your girls, Marion, Wendy and Mich are handling affairs commendably. The regiment comes along, I am told. I feel it correct that it should be composed of Jikai Vuvushis from various sororities."

"Yes, majister. Also, the regiment is called The Beckoning Leems. Everyone agreed on the name, and—"

She saw my face.

"Majister!" Her voice quavered. Strom Nango put a hand down onto her shoulder, and I wondered who was supporting whom.

This name was just another example of that weird warped Kregan sense of humor, that the girls would beckon their foes and then like leems devour them. The leem was very often the symbol for savage power, untamed and destructive, and in the normal course of events one saw leem-symbols along with chavonths and strigicaws and mortils and all the other wonderful varieties of Kregan wildlife. Marion did not know, I believed, of Lem the Silver Leem.

"As well call your girls a regiment of churmods, Marion. Malignant, malevolent, not to be trusted. You must think of another name."

"Yes, majister."

They went away after that, very subdued.

Regiments liked to give themselves high-flown and resounding names. For the lads of my guard corps the number and the initials could not be bettered. That thought made me call over Chuktar Emder Volanch. He was a much-decorated kampeon, a Freedom Fighter of Valka, and an old comrade whom I do not believe I have mentioned before although we had served together enough times, by Vox.

"Strom—the regiment prospers, thank Opaz."

He knew exactly why I'd beckoned him over. His face, hard as a nut, contrasted sharply with his casual evening robes. He told me that the new guard regiment had been superbly trained up and he was greatly desirous of seeing it in action. The regiment was the First Emperor's Foot Bows. As Chuktar Volanch said: "Even Kov Seg Segutorio has given 1EFB the accolade for their shooting."

"Excellent work, Emder," I congratulated him. "You have done well. And, believe me, there will be work for you and your lads when we hit the Racters, Opaz rot 'em."

"We are ready, strom."

"Chuk Loxan is not to be seen?"

Chuktar Emder smiled. "Balass the Hawk took his regiment off into the wilds for rigorous training. Loxan welcomed this. He and I, strom, well, there is a rivalry between his 1ELC and my 1EFB to become the first into action."

I could well believe it.

If my blade comrade Balass the Hawk was knocking sword and shield work into the First Regiment of the Emperor's Life Churgurs, then, by the Brass Sword and Glass Eye of Beng Thrax! they'd find out what rigorous training meant!

I said to Chuktar Emder, "This is a bet that will never be collected. 1EFB and 1ELC are likely to go into action together."

"As Opaz will, strom."

A tremendous racket burst up just then and everyone turned as the happy couple prepared to make their exit.

Khe-Hi and Ling-Li really did look happy, and this gladdened me. We needed all the happiness we could scrape up in Vallia. Many and scurrilous were the shouted remarks as they were sent royally off, remarks that in other circumstances no one in his right mind would shout at a Witch or Wizard of Loh. They were showered with flower petals. When, at last, their narrow boat glided off into the moons light, we all trooped back for a final round of dancing and drinking, of talking and singing.

I said to Delia: "One dance, my girl, and then I'm off."

Her gaze did marvelous things to my spine.

Later that night I said, "I really am going. Up to Falkerdrin—I'm not waiting for Natyzha Famphreon to die and then be called in."

"Dray!"

"Oh, yes, I know. I shan't slip a knife between her ribs or drop poison into her wine—although there are many and many who would say she deserves that quietus."

"So you're rushing off like a chunkrah—"

I kissed her and later said: "I'm going to have a little spying on my own account. We have to beat the Racters fast, because of this oaf the so-called King of North Vallia."

She turned over and stretched. "I wish I could come with you. It would prove interesting. But I am committed to—"

"The Sisters of the Rose."

I dearly wanted to know if she had been maneuvered into becoming the mistress of that secret Order. She would not tell, naturally. This, then, was another reason why I wanted so badly to contact the Star Lords. They'd know.

She made no direct answer, as I expected, but said, "If you are gone from Vondium that she-leem Csitra will search for you."

"Without dupes she will not find me. And I have perfect confidence in Deb-Lu."

"As have I, thank Opaz."

So, after due preparations and fully kitted out I slipped quietly out of Vondium, heading north, flying in the mingled radiance of Zim and Genodras, and set course for Falkerdrin.

Twelve

Nalgre the Point

Oby, Dwaby and Sosie Fintle set me down safely into a small woodland some way inside the borders of Falkerdrin. Triplets are not all that common on Kregen, twins being far more common than they are on Earth, and the Fintle triplets provided an interesting study for the student of genetics. They were alike as three peas in a pod, except for the fact that Sosie was a girl.

They belonged to my secret group of agents, and they'd been trained by Naghan Raerdu, who was a spy par excellence. His attitude was either to go invisible, or to go big.

He, himself, habitually went big, and yet could become inconspicuous on the spot if needs be—when he laughed. These triplets were of the invisible variety; once seen never remembered. They handled the flier I'd prised out of Farris very well, and I was confident we had not been observed.

"If only you'd let us go with you, majis," grumbled Oby.

Dwaby added, "We wouldn't get in your way, majis."

And Sosie finished: "Majis, please say yes."

I said, "Nope, and that's final. Get my gear off and then you can shove off. Farris needs this voller."

They didn't enjoy this; they obeyed and soon my zorca, preysany and piles of kit were overside and under the trees. I bid them the remberees in a most cheerful fashion; they replied in a way that suggested that they'd seen the last of me. The voller rose beyond the trees, turned and fled hugging the contours.

I said to Snagglejaws, my zorca: "Well, my lad, you and Swivelears here are in for it now."

He tossed his single spiral horn in reply, and stamped a hoof. That spiral horn was not particularly long. His hide was of a mangey grayish color, rather more hairy and tufty than smooth and sleek. He had a damned wicked eye. He looked a mess. Yet Snagglejaws was among the strongest, sturdiest, most willing of all the zorcas; he wasn't in Shadow's class; but then, what zorca was?

This reminded me of the time in Djanduin when I'd made the acquaintance of just such a zorca, Dust Pounder—although, to be fair, Snagglejaws looked a mess while Dust Pounder was a blood zorca.

The preysany, Swivelears, showed the whites of his eyes as I loaded the kit onto his back. It was perfectly clear he was saying in preysanish: "Why by all the gods do I carry the kit and Snagglejaws doesn't?"

Still, that was the way of it on Kregen, and when I swung up into the saddle on Snagglejaws' back I fancied Swivelears gave a whinny of satisfied amusement.

So we set off along a trail toward Fakransmot, a town where, so our intelligence said, Natyzha Famphreon recruited paktuns.

For, of course, despite the zorca between my knees, following Naghan the Barrel's advice I'd chosen to go big. I'd be a hyrpaktun, one of the most renowned of all mercenaries. I'd wear the pakzhan at my throat, the silken cords looped up over my shoulder, and the golden dazzle of the Zhantil's head device would tell any onlooker that here was a free lance of formidable reputation.

Naturally, I'd shifted my features around a trifle and allowed my whiskers to grow so that they helped disguise me, and the multitude of bee stings on my face that was the price of too drastic changes could be substantially muted.

The small golden or silver rings that secure the golden or silver devices to the silk at a paktun's neck serve another purpose. If one paktun slays another in fair combat he takes the ring and threads it up on a trophy string called a pakai. I'd put on a whole hefty chingle of rings on my pakai. If I got into a fight I could secure it firmly so that no foeman could grab it and so catch me at a disadvantage. All the same, I didn't like the thing.

Very briefly, then, I will say that I was equipped as a Kregan would like to be equipped—a stout zorca between my knees, a tough preysany loaded with kit, and armed with a Lohvian longbow, a drexer, a rapier and main gauche, a few odd knives and terchicks about my person, and the great Krozair longsword scabbarded down my back under the plain black cape.

In addition, a tough shield of an oval shape and with a snarling neemu on its face lay athwart Swivelears' rump. I had no lance. There was a reason for this. When I was employed by Natyzha Famphreon's officers, I intended to go for a swod as a bowman, not a lancer. The shield I would explain away. It was black, and the neemu of bright brass.

The forests up here in Falkerdrin extended for considerable areas over the kovnate. Some of them were infested with wild hatchevarus; but they were fierce enough to drag down a charcoal burner and not powerful enough seriously to challenge a soldier with a sword. I trotted on, easily, guiding Snagglejaws with my knees, although he followed the track and did not need guidance. Swivelears trotted along behind on the leading rope.

He was carrying the bits and pieces of armor I'd thought suitable. Reluctantly I'd discarded any idea of taking some of the superb supple mesh from the Dawn Lands. I had a kax, shoulder pieces, pauldrons, pteruges and greaves. Even then it was doubtful if I'd use the lot all at once. Wearing armor is a funny old business; you most devoutly need it in the heat of battle, yet you chafe under it and wish for the freedom of movement you'd have if you chucked the lot down.

Still, there it was if I needed it. Easing the zorca to a walk I let him amble along. The edge of the woods was soon reached and I debouched out into a long slanting valley, well-watered and lush with flowers, and with the sea distant and blue on the horizon.

We'd chosen to land here because the port of Roombidge on the north coast of the kovnate received the argosies from overseas bringing in the mercenaries hired by Natyzha Famphreon. The paktuns were streaming ashore at many ports along the coast, and at ports on the coasts of the Belains to the southwest and of Vekby to the west. The plan was for me unobtrusively to join up with a caravan journeying to Fakransmot.

To this end I reined in when a village showed up ahead. The suns were declining and I was lucky. A string of riders wended along the trail clearly intending to put up for the night in the village of Rernal, and as they dismounted by the single inn I eased in among them, as though seeking for a good position. I did not make a fuss over it. I was gambling that in the short distance from the coast everyone might not have come to know everyone else. From the conversations as the mercenaries spread out I realized they had traveled aboard ships different from their countries of origin. There were plenty of diffs among them.

I stayed with that bunch all the way to Fakransmot. The state of the kovnate impressed me. Natyzha was a damned hard overseer of labor; there were many slaves and the fields were in good heart. We had done as well down south; I doubt if we'd done better.

During the ride I spoke when spoken to, kept to myself and stayed out of trouble. This was the attitude of most of the paktuns; some of the youngsters—untried, green, coys—starting out on their first mercenary job skylarked around a little; the old hands kept clear of them.

Every day I rode for a considerable period with my eyeballs, as it were, out on stalks and scouring the skies. There was no sign of the Gdoinye, the scarlet and golden-feathered bird sent by the Everoinye to spy on me. Typical! Just when you wanted the flaming onkerish thing, it didn't show up!

"Duck your fool head, dom!" The voice purred level and habituated to command.

Without thought I ducked.

The tree branch went past over head and the leaves snatched off my fancy wide-brimmed hat with the maroon feather. Hauling up Snagglejaws I looked around. We'd been riding slowly through a field moments before, when I'd been apostrophizing the Star Lords; feeling down, I'd put my head down for a space, and an angle of the woods had nearly kinked it off.

"I thank you, dom." I hopped off the zorca and fetched my hat. "My head is of little value; I wouldn't like to damage this hat."

"Ha!" he said. "A joker."

By the dripping mucous and yellow puss of Makki Grodno's left eyeball! What would folk say to that? A joker?

"One has to live," I said, and climbed back into the saddle. He reined alongside and gave the lahal.

"I am Nalgre the Point—not, I hasten to add, a name of my own choosing and one of which lately I grow tired." He was not apim like me. He was an olumai, and he looked like a panda; he wore a white tunic with a golden hem and he did not carry a rapier, instead he had a lynxter strapped to his waist. The lynxter instead of a rapier and main gauche, which many of the paktuns wore for travel, indicated Nalgre the Point's origin. He was from Loh. Also, like me, he concealed his pakzhan at his throat.

I said my name was Kadar the Silent. Kadar was a name used by me aforetime and happened to be the name inscribed on the reverse of the golden image of the zhantil on its silken cords at my throat. By Zair! That had all happened a long time ago! Now, I was a properly accredited and legal hyrpaktun—I was no fake.

We talked occasionally and I gathered Nalgre the Point hankered after something he kept secret. He did say: "I find myself feeling a strange emotion for the people of Vallia. I almost feel sorry for them. Yet troublous times give us our livelihood, brother. Who are we to complain?"

A trifle incautiously, I said: "When all Vallia is pacified we paktuns will find employment elsewhere."

"For one dubbed Silent, Kadar, when you speak you enlarge grandly upon the course of events."

Acting my part, I did not reply.

When we reached Fakransmot we discovered that mercenaries were being hired on there; but the dowager kovneva had shifted her headquarters northwards, almost to the Mountains of the North, often called the Snowy Mountains.

Nalgre the Point looked out from the tavern windows where they were signing men on to the yard, where the red and green suns smoked dusty ruby and jade across the waiting men, the saddle animals, the hurrying slaves. He put a powerful paw to his chin.

"I have been told that in Vallia it is not cold weather until you cross the Snowy Mountains."

"That is right, zhan*," said the Hikdar at the table. "Now just sign on with us and—"

"My heart was set on joining the dowager kovneva."

Instantly, standing at Nalgre's side, I got out: "Mine too."

"That is, of course, your privilege." The Hikdar, flamboyantly attired and smothered with the black and white favors, Racter colors, gave a grimace which indicated he was conveying a private confidence. "We fare better down here against the forces of the so-called Emperor of Vallia than they do up in the north against the King of North Vallia."

He made a further attempt to induce us to join his regiment, and when we refused, waved us pettishly away.

Outside, Nalgre said: "So we ride north?"

"Aye."

"Let us, for the sake of Beng Dikkane, find another tavern to refresh ourselves first."

Without wearying you with details of our ride north, I will content myself with saying that Nalgre the Point proved an agreeable companion. He nursed this secret hurt, something troubling him he wrestled with constantly; but he remained cheerful and alert. I made what inquiries I could and discovered that everyone believed the two wars, north and south, were being won handsomely. The dowager kovneva shuttled from front to front. There was not the slightest whisper that she considered herself to be dying. As for her son, Kov Nath, he was universally condemned as a weakling and of no account in statecraft.

If the old biddy really wasn't at death's door I could be wasting my time up here. There was comfort in the fact that Csitra couldn't spot me and therefore should not be bringing further plagues and curses upon my people.

In the end I decided to have a good look around, find out everything I could, and then get back home sharpish.

Ha!

Natyzha Famphreon could really be dying, could even already be dead, and for obvious reasons of state no one at her court would admit to that. This was the possibility that caused me to travel north with Nalgre the Point. I'd given a promise to Natyzha, enemy though she was, and I intended to keep it as best I could.

---

* Hyrpaktuns, wearing the pakzhan, are known as zhanpaktuns. Hence the form of address as zhan. Paktuns, wearing the pakmort, are known as mortpaktuns, and the form of address is mort. Ordinary mercenaries, although often called paktuns, a title to which they have no real right, are called whatever comes to the tongue. *A.B.A.*

Nalgre came from Whonban in Loh and he told me somewhat of that mysterious place. I told him I came from Hamal, which seemed reasonable at the time.

Once he'd commanded his own group of mercenaries. Zhanpaktuns can attract followers with the promises of employment and loot. Lone zhanpaktuns usually have a colorful history. His band had been chopped in a disastrous battle and, from his demeanor and what he didn't say, I gathered he hadn't had the heart to create a fresh band of followers.

I simply said I'd been fighting in Hamal and preferred to be a loner.

Most wealthy fighting men when they travel and go by road ride one animal and have a few in the string to carry their belongings. I had Swivelears. Nalgre had three preysanys and a totrix. Naturally, being a sensible fellow, he rode a zorca. The very ride itself, wending through the country, proved delightful. Neither of us was in a hurry. The war would still be there when we arrived.

The Snowy Mountains appeared on the horizon ahead. The weather remained good, for Kregen's enormous temperate zone assures sensible weather from the equator north and south over a much wider series of parallels than on Earth. We put up at inns, ate and drank well, and got on famously.

The absence of bandits was welcome. Natyzha policed her kovnate with a hand not so much of iron as of carbon steel. We suffered only two assaults, and of these the first fracas was over in a twinkling with a few lopped heads and limbs, a few writhing bodies and the rest running on bandy legs as fast as they could get away.

The second fracas was of a more serious nature.

As Nalgre said, carefully wiping his sword on the tunic of a fellow with no face: "I do wish these fellows would think before they acted."

Casually, returning my sword to the scabbard, I said: "Oh, they mistook us for a couple of idiots, easy prey, I suppose."

The bandits had chosen a narrow trail between overhanging vegetation-clothed banks from which to make their attack, and these drikingers consisted of fellows to make your hair curl, all dripping furs and golden-ornaments and fierce eyes and bad breath.

"They might have profited from the wasted year I spent at school learning of the philosophic theories of Olaseph the Nik." Nalgre mounted up, chik-chikking to his zorca, Goldenhooves. "I cleared out as soon as I could and went for a mercenary. That was a long time ago, by Hlo-Hli!"

We trotted on out of the shadowy trail into the twinned sunshine. There had been little of value to be liberated from the dead drikingers, although Nalgre found a nice ring, which I indicated I wanted nothing of.

He went on, as though ruminating: "I remember that fool teacher hammering at me that appearances are all. What one sees on the surface is all there is. Nothing of what lies beneath can be revealed by insight or self-analysis because there is nothing beneath the surface."

"Umm?" I said, letting Snagglejaws take me along, and thinking what a powerfully intellectual comment that Umm was. It takes all kinds to make a world, and all kinds of philosophies and theories to furnish that world with concepts to play with and, perhaps, to extend understanding.

"Those drikingers looked down and saw your execrable zorca, the string of pack animals, my Goldenhooves, who no doubt brought the light of avarice into their eyes, and they failed to observe the glitter of gold at our throats. They saw two men lumpily riding and talking, taking no notice of the world about them. They went by appearances, sensing nothing below the surface."

"You stretch the analogy a trifle, I feel. The surface did include the pak-zhans at our throats. It was faulty observation, surely—"

"I grant you that." His panda face showed intense pleasure, as a panda's face, diff or not, quite clearly could reveal an emotion understandable by an apim. "But my argument encompasses their reading of the gold as a mere ornament. They saw an appearance of a couple of ponshos ripe for the shearing, and they fell upon a couple of leems."

"They fell right enough. I grant you that."

"But you agree, also, that one cannot judge all there is to be judged by surface appearances alone? A person is more than his outward shell, more than his words?"

"Sometimes."

"Well, if you grant only one sometimes, the philosophy of Olaseph the Nik must fail."

"You have me there, Nalgre. Hip and thigh."

"Although the philosopher marshals vituperative arguments, suggesting for example that people prone to self-analysis have not grown to adulthood, he finally does not convince me. And, through your admission, you either."

Nalgre used Kregish words and language concepts, naturally, encompassing what I have rendered here, including "self-analysis." It struck me that I was not, in this context, yet adult because I continually questioned what I did. Did this mean, therefore, that anyone who simply knew that they were always right was fully adult? The theory would seem to imply this.

Back in the real world, of Kregen or of Earth, anyone who always knew they were right usually trailed a whole string of catastrophes in their wake. Also, did I patter on too much about my problems? I could simply bash straight on, as I used to do, and hell take anyone else. That, to me in those days, seemed the immature approach to life. What I felt about Vallia, about all of Paz, about our coming confrontation with the Shanks who appeared to want only to raid and kill us, nerved me into taking decisions the enormity of which would appall me if I felt those decisions to be—not so much wrong as ineptly directed.

The real world impinged again as Nalgre lifted in the stirrups, pointing ahead: "There's the tower we were to look out for. And I can see the walls of Tali. Good! I'm for the very first tavern and a stoup of ale."

"And a dish of palines." *Now* we were talking of the important things of life, by Krun!

There was no doubt that the philosophic theories of Olaseph the Nik were supremely correct about this city of Tali. The walls were tall and thick, the towers many and strong, the twinkle of weapons along the ramparts clear evidence of a powerful garrison. Stringing blue-white along the far horizon the Snowy Mountains floated against the sky. From there descended the perils Tali guarded against.

Up here past the northern boundary of Natyzha Famphreon's Falkerdrin we rode through the vadvarate province of Kavinstock. Kavinstock's ruler, its vad, had been Nalgre Sultant. He and I had had our run-ins before; he was a fanatic Racter, and a mad-dog in many people's eyes, certainly a man who hated my guts. I did not much care for him myself. He could easily be reported dead, and his heirs could now rule here in Kavinstock for all I knew.

As one of the inner circle who controlled the actions and plans of the Racters, Nalgre Sultant did what Natyzha bid him. If I ran into him the ending might be six inches of steel through his guts.

As Nalgre the Point and I rode toward the massive gate in those frowning walls I tried to imagine just what Natyzha wanted up here if she thought she was at death's door. That she held the most powerful voice in the councils of the Racters was without question. Equally the Racters, people like this Nalgre Sultant, and Ered Imlien, whose estates of Thengel were long since lost to him, fought to gain an ascendancy over her and one another.

We rode unmolested through the Thoth Gate of Tali.

Most of the walls surrounding the cities of Vallia are old, built in the long ago when the country was divided up into petty kingdoms. Some are kept up. The walls of Tali were thick through, for I measured off in my mind the paces and there were a full sixty of them. Against the predators from the Mountains of the North those walls had been reared. Now they served as a bulwark against raids from this King of North Vallia.

Thick walls and many regiments guarded against the perils from the north. Was it too arrogant of me to wonder how much peril I posed to this fortress city of the Racters?

Thirteen

On the Day of Nojaz the Shriven

Thwack! slammed the rudis against the soldier's chest and then quite quickly Smash! against his head. The girl doing the smiting, naked save for a breechclout, panted with effort, her body shining, her hair bound into a fillet. The soldier was carapaced with straw-stuffed wooden armor. He jerked about like a marionette and the girl hit him cleanly about one in four.

Wearing a highly ornate uniform, a confection of ribbons and streamers, slashes and sashes, in a virulent greenish-yellow, Nalgre the Point stepped forward.

He thrust his sword against the girl's wooden sword and turned the rudis away.

"Not quite right yet, my lady. Look—"

Nalgre showed the girl the trick of turning the hand over between blows. His panda face expressed no impatience. He spoke normally. He taught this high-flown girl the rudiments of swordplay—or the art of the sword, as I prefer—matter of factly. The exercise yard smoked a little dust from the tramp of feet; but a cooling shadowed tree overhung the south wall and this far north in the temperate zone violent exercise could be indulged in without discomfort.

I stood in the shadows of the little porch by the entrance gateway and waited for Nalgre to finish up.

When at last he let her go, streaming sweat and panting as she was, he said: "Tell your father, my lady, I am only half-pleased with you."

"Oh, Nalgre! You'll spoil it all!"

She looked a willful thing, long of brown hair and finely formed, with a twisting pout to her lips a little suffering would help—not that I advocate suffering for anyone. More often than not it drags down rather than enno-bling the ordinary sort of person.

"All the same, my lady, that is my word."

Nalgre said to the swod: "Thank you, Garnath. You performed well. Same time tomorrow."

"Quidang!" rapped the swod, and took himself off.

He was earning an extra silver piece or two. He dumped the wooden armor neatly onto its pole hanger as the girl threw her rudis at the two slave girls who hurried into the yard. She was a most hoity-toity young lady.

The scent of freshly baked bread wafted over the other wall from the bakeries. Nalgre Sultant—or, rather, his son Ornol—lived well on his estates of Kavinstock. Raids from the north might harry the folk here; their food and drink could be brought up from farther south, and in the good old Kregan way they liked their six or eight meals a day.

The slave girls wrapped the young mistress in a cloak and she hustled out without a backward glance for Nalgre, who looked across at me, gave his panda smile, and collected his kit. He walked across.

"Do you have time for a throat-moistener, Kadar?"

"I do, Nalgre, I most certainly do. Trouble, is she, that one?"

"For the fool who weds her, yes. She does what her father Ornol tells her to. I give thanks for that."

"The Open Hand?"

"I rather thought The Feathered Ponsho."

"As you wish."

The narrow streets of Tali thronged with folk come in from the country specially for the Day's celebrations. If you looked down on the Kyro of Asses, you had to imagine you looked upon a slice of bread running with ants. The people jammed in solidly, dressed in their best, causing a continuous bee-buzzing of excitement. The smells are best left unmentioned.

The followers of Nojas the Shriven, a decent religion of these parts, took full advantage of the license allowed them. That the day happened to be the Day of Opaz the Meek was not overlooked, and the priests of Opaz kept quietly to themselves on this day of Nojas the Shriven.

Nalgre and I squeezed along and eventually popped into the narrow door of The Feathered Ponsho. We were let in by the hefty guards stationed there because we were known, if new, patrons, soldiers, and not a couple of gawp-faced bumpkins from the country.

We were where we were owing to my insistence that I wished to join up with a regiment as close to the person of Natyzha Famphreon as possible. The closest I could manage, given the circumstances, was the bodyguard of Nalgre Sultant. He appeared seldom, and his son Ornol ran all.

No one had seen the dowager kovneva in a month of the Maiden with the Many Smiles; but her edicts came down with their usual frequency. Ornol, it was generally recognized, took more and more power into his young hands.

"When this Ornol hired us on as bodyguards, he was overjoyed to attach two upstanding zhanpaktuns to him," said Nalgre, and sipped the first soothing slug. He wiped his mouth. "The opportunities are rare enough, Lingloh knows. But to employ me to teach his daughter the sword...!"

"A wise fellow, then. Who better than you?"

"You miss the point, my apim friend."

"I hadn't; I merely forebore to mention it."

Clearly, Ornol Sultant did not want any bright apim blades hanging around his daughter. As an olumai, Nalgre the Point was unlikely to fashion any sexual relationships with the lady Fanti Sultant.

The street outside resounded with brazen gongs, with plunklinglings, with trumpets. The masses swayed to and fro, surging as the tide surges between rocks into a cove. When the processions passed by they remained as still as the rocks themselves, making the secret signs, spraying stinking incense everywhere, and throwing petals with swift, almost furtive movements of their hands and arms only.

A sensible ruler lets people worship what gods or goddesses they prefer, and tries to see that the sects don't knock their skulls in instead of breaking one another's arguments with counter debating skills.

The stupidly fanciful uniform worn by Nalgre was of the same issue as the idiocy of feathers, bows and streamers I wore myself. We wore a trifle of armor beneath, to be sure. I'd made certain alterations to the confection so that if I got into a fight a couple of quick tugs at loose threads would enable me to discard the lot in a trice.

This uniform did confer some degree of respect for us. The vad's personal bodyguard would not be trifled with. And although a vad was the rank below a kov, it was still exceedingly exalted among the nobility.

We had another stoup, and then Nalgre sighed, finished his drink and stood up.

"We are on duty in a bur, Kadar."

Thinking I'd been running off at the mouth too much lately, and thus belying my sobriquet of the Silent, I said nothing but stood up, downed the last of the drink and started for the door.

Because of the congestion of the streets we only just made the palace in time.

Our Jiktar, Lomon the Jaws, was a Chulik. His yellow skin glistened. His pigtail hung down his back, plaited and threaded with gold and dyed a bright green. His jaw was exceedingly square and heavy, and the two four-inch tusks jutting upward from the corners of his mouth were banded in gold and gold tipped. His eyes regarded us intolerantly. As a hyrpaktun himself he ran the guard impeccably and was the guard captain, the cadade, and let everyone know it.

Nalgre and I had been given the provisional ranks of Deldar, and we each had four men under command. We had our areas to patrol, corridors and stairs and hallways. We had considerable authority.

Now I have stood guard before in palaces not too dissimilar to Nalgre Sultant's palace of Tali's Crown, and the duty is boring, dull, and unless livened up in some way, brain-rotting.

Nalgre used to play over in his head games of Jikaida. This does pass the time. I kept thinking of ways to get higher into the palace and seek out Natyzha. Nothing made sense and so I fumed away seeing my four paktuns stood their watch properly.

Tali's Crown was an imposing place, ancient, and built atop a crag that dominated the north face of the city.

If you stood on the ramparts of the north wall and looked back and up you could see the towers and walls and terraces of the palace crowning that crag. The cliff face lay in the shadows of the suns rays falling across the southern sections. The rock looked gray and sullen, striated, deeply fissured, a swine to climb.

The ornate buildings atop showed windows and terraces glowing with light in the evening, and many lights remained shining all night.

Well, the inner guards of Natyzha's personal juruk changed by rote and if I didn't catch that duty soon I'd have to essay the climb from outside.

During this period I was not unaware that I was taking time off from the problems besetting me. Natyzha had requested my help, and I'd given my promise. She might be an old biddy, the chief antagonist in the Racter Party; she could also prove the fulcrum by which my lever could topple the Racters' power. This time was not wasted.

There was no hope of stealing an airboat.

For one thing, almost all the tiny aerial fleet here were on constant patrol duty against the Snowy Mountains, and for another the handful in the city were guarded as a maiden is guarded in some countries of Loh. Those guards were not provided by the juruk which Nalgre and I had joined.

I saw no sign of saddle birds or animals.

Ornol Sultant looked not unlike his father, Nalgre Sultant. They had the thin lips and arrogant eyes of your true noble. They knew their position in the world. Ornol, true, showed unmistakable signs of too good living, and he tended to rub his stomach with an irritating gesture which indicated there might be trouble brewing up in his intestinal tracts.

Now during this period there occurred a number of incidents which even to me, accustomed to the cunning interlocking designs of Kregen, seemed totally unconnected.

I should have known better. Experience has taught me that on Kregen events can vary wildly, appear to have not a shred of connection, be totally dissimilar; yet all the time there is a devious brain plotting in the background.

The very next time I assume causes and results are not fully integrated might very well be the last time I make such an elementary mistake. Effects appear to be at random, and often one cannot tease out the pattern. My dealings with the Star Lords and their apparent indifference to my personal plight blinded me to reason.

When we got off duty, Nalgre and I went down to a reserved space on a balcony to the side of the great Kyro of Kavin. The plaza, floored in octagonals of umber, ocher and green, the colors of Kavinstock, lies beneath the south face of the palace of Tali's Crown. The declining suns set deep shadows from column and tower against the brightness of the stonework. Toward the center of the building a long and wide balcony projected.

Here Natyzha Famphreon showed herself to the populace.

She had chosen well, for the city was crowded on this day when the devotees of Nojas the Shriven flooded in.

She did not speak, for her voice would not have carried. Instead a giant-voiced Stentor bellowed out her words. They were rote stuff, fustian, calculated to please the mobs. They added up to promises to see their futures secured, to prosecute the war against North Vallia and what they called South Vallia. The speech went down well. I noticed, however, that no donations of wine or food or money were on offer.

She made a point of emphasizing how the good citizens of Kavinstock and Falkerdrin, and the other Racter provinces, enjoyed the services of slaves.

"This privilege the foresworn so-called Emperor of Vallia would remove from you!" The massive voice bounced and echoed from the buildings, reverberating across the plaza. A few gawky birds fluttered about, startled at the volume of noise. The crowds shuffled their feet, and cheered, and perfumed the evening atmosphere.

I had no spyglass handy, which was a pity; but I'd see Natyzha soon, I promised myself. If she was the same, then her face was still like a nutcracker, walnut-brown and inscribed with a lifetime of intrigue, and her pampered body was still lush and voluptuous. What an old biddy she was!

She was all a glitter of gold, with black patches to set off the gleam, for black and gold are the colors of Falkerdrin's schturval, the symbol a chavonth.

She was carried back into the palace in her chair, hooded in brilliants, and the suns flicked a liquid gleam of flame reflecting from the gems as she vanished into the purple shadows within.

That night the city of Tali ran riot. Everyone, followers of Nojas the Shriven or not, celebrated. Torches illuminated the night and the raucous sounds vibrated up to the stars. So—this seemed my opportunity.

The necessity of wearing the stupid green uniform of ribbons and furbelows annoyed me; but that might give me a slender chance of sudden action if things went wrong. I bound up most of the dangling bits. Beneath I wore the old scarlet breechclout. I carried no bow; but I did take the Krozair longsword, suitably lashed across my back, to provide the ultimate argument if the drexer and rapier and main gauche at my belt failed. I could climb well enough in all this kit, being accustomed to such activity.

A goodly length of rope from the totrix stables was filched with ludicrous ease, the hostlers all being paralytic, and I went carefully around to that dark and hostile north face of the crag.

In all probability Nalgre the Point had given up looking for me to go on a debauch, thinking I'd found myself a sweet little shishi. Well, he was out of my hair.

The first section of the ascent proved easy enough, fallen rocks giving me the most trouble. The fissures were usable. I went up like a grundal of the rocks, and soon started on the more severe section of the climb.

The way I'd mapped out ahead of time turned out to be negotiable. I had one or two nasty turns as splinters broke under my fingers; but always I held on with at least two points of contact. Above my head lights bloomed into the night, and below the noise of the roisterers boomed up like surf.

Deepest shadows lay on the face of the crag.

Against a string of lighted windows above I could make out a frieze set against them. If that was a section of grating it would have to be avoided or broken in. Up I went, hauling steadily, testing each handhold and foothold. The angle of the cliff face steepened.

As far as I'd been able to make out there was no question of an overhang. Some of the terraces projected; that would be a bonus rather than otherwise.

Higher still and that puzzling frieze above began to look more ominous by the minute. There had been no sign of it during the day, of that I felt sure.

Closer still and I saw the truth.

By the disgusting diseased liver and lights of Makki Grodno! The situation was perfectly and horribly plain. During the night the guards slid out thick iron bars from slots in the rock. They were set close enough to one another to prevent a normal man from squeezing through. I have shoulders that are broader than most peoples'. Even on my side against the face I'd have a problem.

The shock of this discovery must have nerved my fool foot, for a chunk of rock broke away and clattered off.

For an instant I clung on, swinging, and then found a fresh purchase. I was plastered against the crag like a poultice on a chest.

A voice spoke from the black wall above my head.

"D'you hear that, Fardo?"

"A stupid bird. Roll your dice."

The second voice sounded tipsy.

I hung on, seeing blackness, sweating, trying to press myself into the living rock.

The first voice: "Better take a look."

"Do we have to? I'm winning and your silver is—"

"I'm the Deldar here, Fardo! Take a look!"

"Very well, Nath the Obdurate, by Vox, you hew to rules and regulations."

There followed the scraping sound of a stool on a stone floor. A metal clang resounded in the night.

Then a shaft of light sprang into being above my head, began to swing down to where I clung on with fingers and toes to that naked crag.

Fourteen

The pakzhan opens a few doors

"By the Black Chunkrah!" I said to myself. "This is an infernally unhealthy spot to be in."

There was not much of a breeze that night up in the city of Tali in Kavinstock, not even across the face of the crag; but I can promise you I felt a distinct draught across the back of my neck!

And then, to make my night, my left foot began to slip. There was no time at all to think. I acted at once and in the next instant found myself rearing up one-handed for the hard round spike jutting from the socket. My right fist clenched around the iron like the skeletal hand of Death.

Inevitably, I let rip a gasp of effort. That, together with the breaking tumble of the shard from under my foot, brought another growl from the opening above.

"Hear that, you fambly! Shine the light down."

An unhelmeted head poked out from the sheer wall above the spikes and a hand thrust forth at the end of a rigid arm. The lantern in that hand cast its light in a reflector-shaped beam and it swung down toward me.

My left hand grabbed for the spike. My right fist let go—and my right foot at the same time slipped. Dangling by my left arm I looked up as the lantern swiveled to shine downward.

The chances were that the fellow's eyes would not yet have adjusted to the gloom outside his lantern-lit guard chamber. I had perhaps half a dozen heartbeats. Then he'd poke a damn great spear down and twitch me off into space as he might dislodge an inconvenient bird's nest.

The rope coiled up into my fist. The crack of my muscles as I hurled I was convinced could be heard clear to the Snowy Mountains.

The rope snapped around his neck, looped down and around.

I hauled.

His terrified scream clanging in my ears, I held on like a limpet as his flailing body hurled past. He didn't stop yelling all the way down.

The rope unwound, swung free. I hauled it in, staring upward, and all the time my feet scrabbled around for a purchase.

Another head appeared.

The darkness smashed back with the fall of the lantern.

"Fardo?"

Fardo's dwindling yell was abruptly chopped off.

"Fardo, you intestinal disease of calsanys!"

The rope looped into my hand. It flew up again, coiled around that head outlined against the stars. I hauled and limpet-like clung on. Deldar Nath the Obdurate did not belie his sobriquet. He didn't come out cleanly. He was holding on with might and main and I heard an odd gargling sound. That was Nath the Obdurate trying to yell with a coil of rope around his neck and throat.

Impatiently, I yanked again.

This time he popped out like a cork from a bottle and, true to his nickname he took the rope with him. I had to let go, otherwise he'd have taken me too. Obdurate fellow indeed!

I whooped up a breath, felt sorrow for those two who had gone all unprepared down to the Ice Floes of Sicce, and then hauled myself up to sit astride the spike. I couldn't squeeze through; but by a neat trick of acrobatics an agile topman might have used in a frigate thrashing into a stiff northwesterly, I angled myself over. At that I took a triangular rip of cloth from the fancy green uniform.

After that and with no time wasted to get my breath back, a few moments more saw me jumping lightly down into the tiny guardroom. It had been hewn from the rock, and provided with the mechanism to run out the frieze of spikes. The place was gloomy and stank of dried fish fried up in oil. I padded to the door, listened, and then opened wide. If anyone was going to be standing there, he'd be more surprised than I.

The corridor stretched to right and left. No doubt there were more doors opening onto other spy holes in the cliff. Well, I have served my time traipsing up and down corridors in palaces on Kregen. I did not intend to shilly-shally about in this particular specimen.

There are techniques for finding your way around in a Kregan palace, and I knew and had employed a fair old number. But I am always willing to learn new tricks.

This time I marched briskly along to the end and turned inward toward the spiral stairway leading up. I wasn't going down to ground level just yet.

The next floor I assumed to be the basement of the palace sections built at the very apex. My guarding had all been at the lower levels. If I'd been assigned to guard duty up here, things might have been easier. Perhaps not. Climbing that cliff had been an experience; it still could have been easier than bluffing my way here. Now that I was up here, the bluff would be of a different order, for most of the hard work was done.

At any rate, as I penetrated upward people passed who took no notice of me. Most were slaves. That covered that. The palace flunkeys did not seem put out to pass a guardsman here. One jurukker with a uniform just like mine but wearing a flaunting favor in black and gold with a badge of a chavonth pinned to it stopped me.

"What are you doing up here—?"

He went to sleep standing up, far too quickly for him to feel surprise, and I dragged him into a closet and bound and gagged him with his own fancy folderols. I pinned up his gold and black schturval of Falkerdrin, and prowled on.

If any of the tame slaves witnessed this—and none did—I would not have been too perturbed. Slaves tend to enjoy fights between their so-called betters if the action does not discommode them.

I chose a charming little Fristle fifi, all pale gold fur and enticing shape, who glided along the carpeted corridor with a linen-covered tray in her hands. She wore the slave gray breechclout. She wore no ornaments.

"Where away, please, is the bedroom of the dowager kovneva?—for I am newly appointed to guard her."

I shouldn't have said please.

She did not drop the tray; but the linen quivered like canvas of a ship caught in irons.

"Master—"

"Just direct me to the dowager kovneva."

"She always sleeps in the Chamber of Solars Gratitude, master..."

I tried to smile and she flinched back; but she gave me coherent directions in the end. I did not say thank you. That single please had nearly scuppered me.

What a society it is that uses and abuses slaves!

A parcel of guards marching all in step along a cross corridor made me hide in the lee of a pillar. I did not think the Deldar in command would easily be bluffed.

When they'd swung off, I emerged and continued on through halls very sumptuous toward the Chamber of Solars Gratitude. I'd climbed up on the north side and it was quite clear that the Solars Gratitude apartments must lie on the southern side.

In one hall of considerable extent with the usual mix of night-duty slaves and guards about, a guard said to me as I passed his door: "Hai, zhan, what's afoot?"

I stared at him with the arrogance of a zhan-paktun addressing an inferior.

"Special duty, dom. Best keep your black-fanged winespout shut."

"Quidang!"

I marched on, and I put a fist onto my rapier hilt, and I gave it a little of a tilt, and swaggered more than a trifle.

Now completely without the shadow of a doubt there were secret passages by which ingress might have been made. I didn't know the architecture of them and had no time to discover their secret entrances. So, this bold and arrogant bluff would have to suffice.

It lasted until I reached a bronze-bound door of balass black as a night of Notor Zan. Here four Rapas stood guard, their vulturine heads beaked and fearsome, their feathers variously colored. I marched straight up and made as though to pass between them and so open the door. The handles were entwined risslacas.

"Llanitch!" cracked out the Hikdar in command.

Obediently, I halted. That militarily formal demand to "Halt!", that snapped out "Llanitch!", is not lightly to be disregarded. Their spears lined up.

"Your business, zhan, if you please."

Although a Hikdar, a rank usually to be found in people who command a company-sized group, he was polite addressing a hyrpaktun. I returned the compliment, and added to it.

"Why, Hik, you may well ask me. I was summoned from a nice little supper party to proceed at once—at once, mind!—to the Chamber of Solars Gratitude to wait upon the dowager kovneva." I heaved up a soulful sigh. "I've served well since I joined. I pray Havil I have not offended in any way I wot not of."

"They are hard taskmasters here," said the Hikdar. He eyed me with his beaky face on one side. His feathers were a tasteful shade of green, and he wore extra feathers in a lighter color. "But I have not been passed the word."

I put the butter thick and heavy upon the slice.

"That is indeed strange, Hik, for a man in your important position. Maybe the word went before you came on duty? I cannot understand it else."

"Yes, you must be right. There is no other explanation. I shall speak to Hikdar Morango about this, for he should have written it upon the slate."

"Indeed, Hik. Well, I dare not keep the dowager kovneva waiting..."

He waved his men aside and a couple actually opened the door for me. I gave a few last polite words and marched through. The stratagem would never have worked for a mere mercenary, possibly for a mortpaktun. Wearing the golden glitter of the pakzhan at your throat can work miracles—can open doors!

Once into the labyrinth of the Solar Gratitude apartments the bluff continued to work smoothly. No one walking about these luxurious halls could be other than he seemed, for no one was allowed in here by the guards unless he was entitled to be here, and since I was here, ergo, I was entitled to be. This would last just as long as it took me to reach the final bedchamber. After that...

Five Jikai Vuvushis stood before the last door. That door was all of beaten gold plate. These were the apartments reserved by the vad, Nalgre Sultant, for his most important guests. The old emperor would have stayed here during his tours of the northwest of his empire.

"Well?" demanded the Hikdar. She was a fine strapping wench, well-endowed, and with creaking armor. She held her spear in a grip that showed that she not only knew how to use it; but would do so if given the opportunity. I caught the impression in the thick lines of her jaw and the frown between her eyebrows that she'd been longing for the opportunity to stick someone for some time.

I tried the same story.

These girls would have none of it.

"That cannot be so. I have not heard." She glared at her Deldar, ramrod stiff, almost as bulky. "Have you heard of this, Deldar?"

"No, Hikdar Saenci."

"Well, tikshim. Speak up!"

The story had to be adhered to now...

"Have you checked your order slate?"

"You insolent cramph! I know my duties better than you do, you apology for a hyrpaktun! I've had more than you for breakfast, aye, and spat out the pips."

I said, "I happen to know the dowager kovneva. If you do not immediately open this door and let me through, your pips will never be spat out, not even into the Ice Floes of Sicce."

She blanched up at this. But, give her her due; she stuck by her duties and her responsibilities. And, of course, she was absolutely right.

She said, "You may very well know the dowager kovneva; but you are a mere man and will not be allowed into her private chambers. You may not know her, as I believe. Therefore I shall hold you and make inquiries."

There were five of them, of an Order I could not know. They were not Sisters of the Rose or the Sword; that I could tell. I could not fight and slay them.

Once I saw Natyzha and she understood the position it would be all right. I might be a foeman, but she and I understood each other. She'd arrange a pass for me, and the Emperor of Vallia had never even visited Tali's Crown. Her concern for her son, Kov Nath, would dominate her actions.

So I took another tack.

"Very well, Hik Saenci. I respect your devotion to duty. I shall find the proper authority. And, believe me, I shall request Natyzha not to punish you too harshly."

With that I turned briskly, hitched up the rapier, and marched off along the side of the hall. The girls stared after me—I could sense that. But they did not follow. I guessed the Hikdar was only too glad to have me off her patch. All the same, being the officious girl she was, she'd put in a report. I had to finalize this escapade before that happened, get the thing done with sharpish.

The door at the end of the hall gave ingress onto a small connecting passageway. Here I was on the south of the palace and a faint luminosity through the windows told that the night was still dark, with only one of the smaller moons frantically flying past above. I took a breath, made sure the coast was clear, and then climbed out of the window onto the ledge. It was broad; but the stonework was treacherous. I inched along gingerly.

Just how many windows I would have to pass before I reached one opening onto Natyzha's inner rooms I didn't know. I found a line of three small windows, then a larger one, a round one with a fancy set of panes inset, and then came to the first of a group of three ornate casements.

This had to be the right set of windows...

Useless trying to see in, for thick drapes obscured all beyond. The window was closed and locked. I offered a few choice observations, and tried the next. This center window of the three was open on a latch to let the bedroom beyond breathe fresh air. Kregans are not too superstitious, at least in Vallia, about the bad effects of night air. I was able to turn sideways, adjust the Krozair brand, and so slide through. My feet hit thick carpet without a sound. I stood perfectly still, silent, listening.

A voice I was confident belonged to Nalgre Sultant was saying: "...should have arrested him! I'll come. Alert the palace. Search everywhere. And *Bratch!*"

"At once, jen!" in the voice of Hikdar Saenci.

The sound of a heavy door closing... Silence...

This was it, then...

I eased the drapes aside and looked in. Samphron-oil lamps burned here and there in the bedchamber. An enormous canopied bed occupied one wall, tables and loungers were scattered about, you'd need a periscope to negotiate the thickness of the carpet. The scent of Moonblooms hung upon the air.

Just inside the door stood the carrying chair in which Natyzha had made her appearance this afternoon. That was odd. The solid mass of diamonds covering the hood of the gherimcal glittered hard and bright in the lamplight. The legs of the chair were fashioned like chavonths.

I stepped onto the carpet clear of the window.

A girl's voice, clear and hard, snapped out: "You rast! Die, then!"

She came at me from the side, very quick, very lithe. She had little skill. Well, Nalgre the Point had been kind with her. I parried her blow and the sword whispered past my ribs. I caught her as she fell and eased her to the carpet. She'd slumber peacefully for a time yet.

I crossed to the shadowed bed, immense among its hangings and looked down. The bed was empty.

The chair?

Softly I padded to the gherimcal, rounding the long and thick poles, leather-wrapped, padded, which might be carried by men or animals, and looked into the interior.

"Well, Natyzha, so I've found you at last!"

She sat there, upright, her wizened face as intent and cunning as ever, the lushness of her pampered body clear through the silks and sensils. She was smothered in gems, and the gold and black of her attire glittered. Her eyes glittered also, like glass.

She said nothing and her expression did not change.

"Well, Natyzha—have you no greeting for an adversary? And, anyway, what in a Herrelldrin Hell are you still sitting uncomfortably in your gherimcal for when..."

My voice trailed off.

With a movement like that of a striking risslaca I bent down and peered closely at her.

She was dead.

Dead as a doorbell. And, what is more, she'd been flayed and stuffed, her eyes of glass glaring fixedly and unseeingly at me, all that gorgeous body a mere covering of skin over straw.

Fifteen

Of the Lady Fanti and Nath the Onker

If the giant blue Scorpion of the Star Lords had whisked me up right there and then I'd have been profoundly grateful—believe me.

Here I was, at the apex of a hostile palace where guards and dogs searched for me, and the one woman who could have saved my bacon was dead—dead and stuffed and on display as though she were still alive.

It was enough to make a fellow snatch off his hat and jump on it, by Vox!

The lady Fanti let a sigh ripple from her lips. She'd wake up in a moment or two, for I'd dealt gently with her, so that it became vitally necessary for me to put on a change of face, suffering as I did so, in the way taught me by Deb-Lu-Quienyin. With my craggy old physiognomy feeling as though a million bees swarmed all over it, I was able to snatch up a glass of water from beside the bed—an artful touch in the deception, that!—and cross to the girl. Putting my arm under her shoulders, I lifted her up to a sitting posture and then held the water under her nose.

"My lady!" I said in as high-pitched a voice as I could reasonably manage. "They have apprehended the monster who did this. Here, my lady, drink and give thanks you are unharmed!"

I rattled on and shoved the water at her and she, vicious, in the way of young nobility, smacked it out of my hand. The glass went smash and the water sprayed the priceless rugs.

"You clown! What—"

"Hush, my lady, please! You must rest—your handmaidens will be here very soon—"

"What is going on! I was attacked—"

"Yes, my lady. But that is over. And no one knows the kovneva is dead."

"Who the hell are you? What are you doing in this bedchamber—?"

"I helped apprehend that monster, my lady. I was left to care for you after the others went back and sent for your handmaidens. Please do not over-excite yourself."

"Why did not they leave a Jikai Vuvushi—oh, I expect I know why."

I didn't. But I hazarded a guess that the fighting maidens did not get on with this hoity-toity missy who was not one of them, who attempted with little success to emulate their martial prowess, and who was the vad's granddaughter. She was a handful, that was certain.

Through all this nonsensical chatter I still could not see a clear escape route for myself. I didn't want to put her to sleep again; but if the lady Fanti insisted on being her obnoxious self—despite the apparent situation and my explanations—then I'd have to keep her quiet long enough for me to climb out of the window and start the escape.

She glared up at me. She wore an evening lounge dress of a pale green color, with too many jewels, and her hair was caught up into looped pearls.

"Did anyone besides you see the kovneva was dead?"

"I do not know, my lady."

"If they did, then they must be killed, too."

I didn't miss, nor did I like, that little "too."

"Oh, my lady," I said, putting braggadocio and confidence into the words. "I am quite confident the secret is safe. No one outside can possibly know the dowager kovneva is dead. Least of all her son Nath."

"Mind your tongue, rast! These matters are not yours!" She moved her hand pettishly, for I still supported her. "Where are my stupid girls? And you, cramph, what is your name?"

Her manners were deplorable.

"Nath the Onker, my lady."

And she laughed.

When she'd had her spiteful little laugh out, she said: "When Kov Nath and I are married I think I shall have you in my guard. You will amuse me."

"Yes, my lady."

"And I won't have my court with Nath in Falkerium. My father will bring Nath here, whether he wants to or not."

"Yes, my lady."

"And do you show no gratitude, you rast?"

"Certainly, my lady, I thank you."

"The Onker! I shall enjoy you!"

This was no damn good at all. I'd learned a very great deal, reached into the heart of the conspiracy. Now I had to get away. Sober common sense told me I'd not now make my way through the palace the way I'd come. No, it was the window for me.

I sat up so quickly that she fell back and I caught her just in time.

"You stupid onker—what—?"

"The window, my lady!" I whispered very dramatically. "A noise. Lie still, I beg you—I will investigate..."

Like a spider I scuttled across those priceless carpets and hoisted myself up to the windowsill. With a quick sideways movement I was through the opening of the central casement and so dropped to the ledge. Without waiting I shuffled as fast as I could along the way I'd been going, away from the corridor where I'd first taken to the outside wall. A deep column buttressed here and I only just made it to its shelter before that intolerant young voice was screaming into the night.

"Nath the Onker! Where are you?"

I made no reply but hurried along as fast as fingertips and toes would take me.

"Onker! Nath the Onker! Oh, when I have you in my guard you will see! You will see!"

Eventually that youthful, silly, hateful voice faded and I found a way down in the shadows. Even then it was nip and tuck; but by playing the old trick of joining the hunters I got clear. Being a hunter was easy. Was I not dressed and equipped like the hunters? Was I not one of them?

Nalgre the Point brushed up his whiskers and said: "A fine night for a shbilliding, and what happens? Some tomfoolery about an intruder. It spoiled my night."

"And mine. And it was all probably a scare, anyway. They found no one, so there probably was no one."

"Aye, by Lingloh. A great waste of time."

But I, Dray Prescot, had not wasted my time this night. By Zair! What a scheme! And what prizes for the winners!

Once you'd seen the scheme, of course, it was obvious, simple. But then, that is the nature of hindsight. You had to hand the palm to the Sultants, father and son. If they could only hang on long enough, without discovery, why—the prizes were fabulous!

They faced problems. Well, of course, they would in so parlous a gamble. From my previous experiences with the Racters I believed that Sultant did not get on with and hated his fellow Racter nobles, particularly Ered Imlien. I had a hunch that Imlien was involved in this.

Then I spent a moment mentally saluting the ib of Natyzha Famphreon. Her shade was on the long way down to the Ice Floes of Sicce. The Gray Ones would stalk through the mist to meet her. Would she find her way through to the sunny uplands beyond? Well, for all her enmity and deplorable way of life, I could not find it in my heart to wish her ill.

What now concerned me was my pledge to her.

I had to prevent the death of her son Nath and to ensure he came into his rightful inheritance.

A flashing memory of myself with feet dangling over emptiness, hanging onto that damned spike with one hand, and a fellow with a spear about to push me off for the long drop overwhelmed me. By Zair! I hadn't enjoyed that, and I gave a little shiver.

Nalgre the Point said: "What's up, Kadar?" Then he burbled on in his confident way: "You need a little stiffener, that's clear."

So we went to see what we could retrieve of his shbilliding, which is by way of being a riotous assembly of devotees of liquid refreshment, and spent a sizeable portion of our wages. Later we were sitting at a wine-stained table with the bottles mostly lying on their sides.

I said to Nalgre: "I am buying back my hire."

"Oh? What ails you, dom?"

"Naught ails me, dom. Look, I'm for an enterprise. I could do worse than have a fine fellow like you with me—"

"Is there loot in it?"

"Loot? Well—cash, certainly."

"I'm bored with guard duty. If you promise me loot and action, I'm your man."

"As to action, there may be a quantity of skull-bashing to be accomplished."

I did not add that I wanted to do the next part of my promise to Natyzha as quickly and cleanly as possible.

Nalgre looked at his empty glass.

"I swore off fighting—once. Like I swore off drinking—once. I'll go with you, Kadar the Silent. And if there is skull-bashing to be accomplished, then I shall do the same with alacrity."

Maybe that was the secret that ate at him, that he had grown tired of being a mercenary and wished to try something else, and was not fitted. Maybe that was why he'd accepted the tame job of being a guard to a noble. And he'd had his fill of that...

Next day and without explanation we bought back our hire, discharged ourselves from the service of the vad, and rode southwards.

There was no reason to suppose that Nalgre or Orlon Sultant would put two and two together. We had no connection with the intruder of the previous night. We were clearly bent on finding action down south against the hateful puppets of the Emperor of Vallia who were moving once more from the Black Mountains and from Falinur.

"First stop, Nalgre," I said. "Falkerium."

"The capital is rich, I've heard. When you tell me the task ahead, I shall take more interest. Now, as to the philosophy of Naghan Deslayer the Fifth—"

Well, he talked and I listened and we jogged along. We took passage aboard a narrow boat with all our animals and kit and so sailed neatly into the basin of Falkerium on the day when news had broken that hordes of foes were marching north from the emperor's lands to invade Falkerdrin.

"If that is your task, to fight these fellows, then—" and he rubbed his hands "—let me get in among 'em!"

"No, Nalgre. The dowager kovneva's son, Kov Nath, is here in Falkerium."

"I've heard the stories about him. A ninny."

"Maybe not."

"Oh?"

"Aye. There may yet be found somewhat to amaze the people about that young man."

"And your task—?"

"Is to free him, if he be prisoner. And to put him aright if he is free."

Nalgre the Point quizzed up that panda face.

"You speak of high matters here, dom. Hanging matters. Also, you speak in riddles."

"Not so. You and I are going to take young Kov Nath into our custody."

Sixteen

In Falkerium

The efforts of Seg, Inch and Turko after our successes in Vennar—a province no longer—had clearly been rewarded by a rejuvenation of the armies. The work they had put in must have been prodigious. To mount a fresh offensive so soon after the conclusion of a victorious campaign indicated a sustained effort of will and determination.

For those whose understanding of the military extends to picturesque uniforms, or rightly bewailing the casualties, or merely blanket condemnations, the difficulties of putting armies into the field are probably unknown.

Once you have reluctantly decided that fighting is a lesser evil—sometimes it is not, of course—and you must provide for men and women actually to go out and do the fighting, the realities of armies strikes home cruelly. Armies are organisms. Organic, they have a life of their own, and a death, too, not infrequently. The sheer scope of organizing, running, supplying, is enough to run people ragged; the intense need to boost morale saps even more of the strengths of those in command.

Yes, it might appear to the onlooker, as I have said, that the reunification of Vallia dragged on and on; the truth was that with our limited resources we had done wonders. Most of the credit lay with people like Seg and Turko and the Kapts and logistics people of the army. If we were on what we hoped was the last leg of the course, no one would be more pleased than they.

Except myself.

I wanted the whole messy business over and done with, the slaves liberated and everyone knuckling down to the tasks ahead which we could not avoid.

There would be no evasion of the onslaught from the Shanks. That was very clear.

Nalgre the Point and I put up in a modest inn, The Queng and Scriver, and we kept our ears open.

I explained enough and no more. If I could do this thing quickly and cleanly, well and good. If I could not—well, that problem would be faced when it occurred.

The situation was crystal clear. I might not have all the pieces of information; I had enough to make a just reading.

Natyzha was dead. Her son, Kov Nath, a reputed weakling, was expected to be putty in the hands of whatever strong noble or group of ambitious people controlled him. The Sultants knew that Natyzha was dead. Ered Imlien, if it really was he who had Nath, did not know. So that gave rise to the interesting situation that each side had one piece, and neither could deal with the other. Clearly, if that hoity-toity young miss, the lady Fanti, wanted to marry Nath on the orders of her grandfather, Nath had to be got out of Imlien's hands. But the Sultants could not tell Imlien Natyzha was dead. And Imlien would never let Nath go. So Nalgre the Point and I, as it were, stood in the center of the web.

We made no attempt to join any of the regiments forming in the city. The capital of Falkerium was just such a proud provincial capital as may be found over the length and breadth of Vallia. Strong-walled, tall of tower, wide and deep of moat, powerful in artillery, the place with its population of citizens and much swollen military presence, could hold off a siege for a good long time.

If we brought Nath onto our side... There would be no need for a long and costly war, a terrible siege. We could conclude the treaties and go home to our firesides.

Surely, that was a victory worth attempting?

Falkerium, then, would be the site of this final battle in this particular campaign. Nalgre told me somewhat of his history, and I made up a rigmarole that satisfied him as to mine. He'd left Loh and traveled extensively in the other countries of Paz. He'd fought some arduous campaigns in the ever-squabbling Dawn Lands of Havilfar, and had then migrated northwards to seek employment with Hamal.

"But the confounded war was over by the time I arrived. So I came on here. I met a fellow who told me what was afoot." Here Nalgre's panda face expressed absolute distaste. "He wore the golden pakzhan at his throat and pretended he was a hyrpaktun. Only a few moments' conversation unmasked him."

"You can always tell the fakes."

"Aye! By Hlo-Hli, but I berated him! I never did discover where he'd stolen the pakzhan from, but the name was never his, the nulsh."

When your peers in the mercenary trade confirm you as a hyrpaktun and you wear the pakzhan, there are certain secret words you learn, also. No, some rash young fellow who might by chance have the golden insignia fall into his hands would never pass off the deception.

We put up at the sign of The Hen Downwind and went out to look at the sights.

The front line forces down south on the provincial border were, we were told, holding the line. But everywhere in the city regiments marched, bugles blew, hooves trampled as Falkerdrin gathered its resources to strike back and this time bring the Racters to total victory against the emperor.

We were idly watching a group of coys growing weary trying to march in step and align their spears. Nalgre said: "Y'know, Kadar. From what I've heard of this new Emperor of Vallia, I'd sooner be fighting for him than against him. But, the strange fellow, he does not employ mercenaries." Nalgre rubbed his squat nose. "Most odd."

"Aye."

Whether Nalgre the Point knew it or not, he was indeed going to be employed by the Emperor of Vallia!

That gave me pause. I'd had more than a few qualms lately, particularly over the casualty figures, about my avowed policy of having Vallians free, and be seen to free, their own country. If I employed men who fought for a living, would not that release from what could be a frightening bondage those young men of Vallia who had no wish to chance the battle, the outcome of war? I was not growing weak in my resolution; I was looking at the problem from a different angle.

Maybe, if I chose wisely, it might be possible once more for Vallia to pay gold for fighting men instead of paying with the blood of her sons...

I just hoped to Zair I had not been arrogantly blind in my so lofty pronouncements.

All during this time with Nalgre the Point in Falkerium as I listened and looked, made inquiries and put together a plan, I constantly watched for a sight of the messenger and spy of the Star Lords. But the Gdoinye made no appearance. That superb golden and scarlet bird of prey did not come flying down out of the suns, sent by the Everoinye, to squawk insultingly at me.

I missed the onker. By Krun! I missed him!

Came the day when I heard positive news of the whereabouts of the young Kov Nath.

A guardsman in his cups told us with many sniggers that the young Kov really thought he was running the war. This ran so strongly with the tide of general opinion about Kov Nath that it was easily believable. I harbored doubts. I knew Kov Nath possessed a quick courage. Of his mental attainments I had no readily accessible first-hand knowledge; but I supposed it was feasible that devious and cunning Kapts could persuade a not-too-bright noble that he was in command and running the war effort.

Nalgre, having agreed to abide by our contract that he would be told all that was necessary when the time for action came, busied himself finding out all he could of the Barange Fairshum, the central fortress palace from which Nath and his officers ran affairs of state. As befitted a proud provincial capital, Natyzha Famphreon's palace was, indeed, a marvel. I detected a fanciful resemblance to her in the building, for it possessed a hard granite carapace of towers and battlements and an architectural lushness of feature in the walls and buttresses.

"We could join this young kov's guard, Kadar," suggested Nalgre.

"He's not so young these days; but the impression he gives makes people refer to him like that. As to joining the guard, well, I've had my fill of standing like a statue at the heads of staircases or against walls. There will be another way, you'll see."

So we ferreted about and snuffed into unlikely corners and slid surreptitious gold into dirty and clutching palms.

"It will not be easy, by Hlo-Hli! But we can take him. The ransom will make up for all our trouble."

"You've entirely glossed over your philosophical qualms."

"Not entirely. I'd sooner earn a dishonest crust this way than an honest one killing people."

I couldn't allow this to pass. I said, "I am not taking up the kov for ransom, Nalgre. I have said I will explain it all when the time comes." I gave him a hard look. His panda face couldn't really flush up. "But I abhor kidnapping—"

"If, in our short acquaintance, Kadar the Silent, I had not formed a certain opinion of you, I would not be here with you on a harebrained escapade. Logical dialectic would indicate my own madness. I do admit I doubted your motives, and the talk of ransom was to test your reaction—d'you mind?" The last, Nalgre shot out like a bolt from a crossbow.

"Nope."

"Ha! There is the Kadar the Silent we all know and love!"

These olumai folk from mysterious Loh—there may not be many of them upon the gorgeous and terrifying world of Kregen, but they are a people to be reckoned with. The toppling towers and slaked walls of his own country of K'koza in Whonban in the continent of Loh might have been the cause of Nalgre the Point's traveler's itch; but they exerted a strong and mesmeric force upon him, that I knew.

The exotic names of faraway places attract with magnetic force the dreams and desires of the ordinary mortal man and woman. Zair knew I'd like to go off exploring into Loh, and Balintol and many many other strange countries of Kregen, yet my whole life was spent working away in the place where I found myself. There just had been no time that I could see in which I could just have upped sticks and departed for a little exploration without a reason for going. Every time I'd flown off into adventure I'd gone with something to be accomplished, and this was true of those occasions when the Star Lords dumped me down naked and unarmed to sort out a problem for them.

Now if I heard that a comrade was in trouble in far Balintol, or slaved in chains in Loh... But, then, I'd brought back my comrades to Vallia, or Drak had done so, or they'd found their own way back. Vallia, the unity of Paz, and the fight against the reiving fish-headed Shanks took precedence, *must* take precedence, in my life.

On the following day, the cups of our guardsman friend being filled to overflowing, he told us between hiccups that Kov Nath was to inspect the Second Frant of Foot Spears. Nalgre sociably poured more wine.

"So the kov is to leave the palace. Mayhap the Suns will burn his pallid cheeks."

"You have the right of it, dom!" The guardsman, Orban the Stick, laughed. He delighted, as we could see, that he, a simple jurukker, was able to address two ferocious hyrpaktuns as dom. Of such petty prides are great treacheries made. "And they'll have a baby's leash tied to him as well, by Vox, I don't wonder!"

We laughed companionably at his jest.

His head slumped onto the wine-stained table when we left the tavern. His hair, of a paler than usual brown in Vallia, stained a deep vinous ruby around its curly edges.

"You'll never snatch him off a parade ground! It is madness, Kadar!" Nalgre twitched himself around in our upstairs room to stare at me over his shoulder. He threw his lynxter on his bed and repeated: "Utter madness!"

"Perhaps."

Well, it was a madness, in all truth. But Nath was being allowed out of the Barange Fairshum. He would dress in his pomp and finery and ride out to the parade ground outside the city walls. This had to be our chance, surely?

"We need two stratagems," I said. I spoke firmly. But the plan was as shaky as a two-hundred-and-fifty-year-old's legs. "One: we must block the Avenue of Grace. Two: we must enlist a gang of rascally cutthroats."

"And then?"

"Oh, it'll be a desperate affray. No doubt of that."

Nalgre the Point unlatched his tunic and then paused, the points between his fingers. "I'll undertake to block the Avenue of Grace. I can see that the escort with Nath will then have to pass through the Souk of Weavers to reach the palace by the quickest route."

"Exactly so."

"You may enlist your cutthroats. I have noticed that in Vallia you apims do not take altogether kindly to folk who are not apims. I think of the people of the world as divided up between olumai and diffs. It makes no difference to me. But in Vallia, apims and diffs are regarded in vastly different lights."

Useless for me to protest. What Nalgre said was depressingly true. This, as well as slavery, was a blot that would have to be removed.

"Done."

Then we refined the plan until we felt we had it as well-oiled as we could make it. On the morrow we would each do what was necessary, and in the afternoon see if the ramshackle plan would work.

Natyzha Famphreon's carbon-steel grip on the country had put down the bandits and so opened up the communications; the paradoxical effect had been to drive the drikingers into the cities where they festered. To recruit a gang of cutthroats was not easy; it was not difficult, either. These were men accustomed to robbery and murder as a way of life. Every day they ran the risk of apprehension. My plan struck some as too bold.

In one ill-favored tavern a black-bearded rascal with a gold ring in his only ear spat out: "We're with you! And you, Ortyg! Catch that stinking Lart before he runs out!"

The fellow Lart, whose effluvium did pervade the atmosphere, was hauled back by a dangling strap and sat on.

"He'd have warned the watch, as sure as my name's Mangarl the Mangler!" This Mangarl twisted the ring in his ear. "Don't you worry, Koter Nath, we'll see to him." They knew Nath wasn't my name; but they accepted it readily enough.

Their weapons were mostly cudgels, or stout sticks, some had short swords, and all had knives. There were also five slingers, whose stones I fancied would materially assist in the plan.

I let them see the rapier and left-hand dagger, and, as well as knowing my name was not Koter Nath, they knew I'd use the rapier and spit them if they started anything untoward. I left them with:

"Three glasses after the hour of mid. As they go through the Souk of Weavers."

"Aye," said Mangarl the Mangler. "I've a score or three to settle with the soldiers! They'll pay for what they did to my sister's sons."

These drikingers did not seem dismayed that with their cudgels they planned to go up against soldiers armed with spears and swords. If I read the picture right, they'd do all their fighting from hiding places. This was exactly what I wanted. It would take only a handful of the braver or more vicious among them to jump into the affray for the scheme to work as planned.

Nalgre the Point reported he had arranged a most beautiful furor concerning four quoffa carts. Once a quoffa—huge, shaggy, lumbering, patient—sits down, a great deal of encouragement is required to get him up again. When Nalgre added that he'd put in a string of calsanys also, I smiled.

"I shall give them a wide berth if they become upset, by Vox!"

Almost all the gold I'd brought from Vondium in the waist belt was now exhausted. Despite the unholy character of the ruffians the gold had brought into our employment, the money was spent in a good cause. And I'd stressed that I wanted no wanton killing, we were just out to make the biggest disturbance we could.

This, again, suited these desperadoes, for they also wished not to disturb overmuch or enrage the soldiers who administered the law in Falkerium.

Saddle animals, whether of the air or ground, are scarce and valuable in wartime. I had to pay out just about all the balance of the gold to secure a zorca. He was a lop-eared animal, whose horn was rather too thin and rather too long and not quite spirally coiled enough. But he was a zorca, and he'd run as best he could until he could run no longer. The zorca handler from whom I bought him in a disreputable market assured me his name was Greatheart; but Greatheart seemed never to have heard of his own name.

A patch of hide on his rump bore a nasty scar.

I asked no questions. I just hoped his real owner would not spot him before my use for him finished.

So, then, see me astride Snagglejaws and with Greatheart—or whatever his name was—following along on a leading rein, riding out to the parade ground beyond the walls of Falkerium. The day bloomed with color and scents and noise. Many folk had come to see a new regiment on parade. Out of professional curiosity I gave them a keen appraisement.

They were from Frant, a middle-sized island in the northwest, between the larger island of Ava to their northeast and the narrow strip of island of

Yuhkvor to their southwest. Odd folk up there, of course—well, all folk are odd from one village to the next. They stood in their ranks well enough, wearing bronze helmets and leather jacks. Their spears slanted at more or less the same angle. They did not carry shields. Each one had a flamboyant favor of ribbons and bows pinned to his left shoulder, all black and white. Black and white were the Racter colors.

The mobs set up a caterwauling when the nobles rode onto the parade ground. They glittered in the lights of the Suns and looked splendid and important and they went through the inspection with sufficient enthusiasm as to fool one into believing they enjoyed it. All except Nath. He looked as I remembered him, for people age incredibly slowly upon Kregen over their better than two hundred years life spans. I looked closer. On each side of the slim, upright figure of Kov Nath rode two men I recognized.

One was short and squat in the saddle, beet-red of square face with deeply set eyes of Vallian brown. He wore a fancy uniform and armor, yet he still carried his riding crop, with which he belabored any and sundry impartially. Trylon Ered Imlien. Yes, I remembered his abrupt ways and consciousness of personal power and of the way he had spoken of Dayra. So the rast was in the conspiracy! At the heart of it, too, if you asked me.

The other man, the Trylon Vektor Ulanor, of Frant, was to be expected to be here when his Second regiment of Foot Spears marched on parade. Crimson-cheeked, pouchy eyed, impatient and intolerant of all—yes, he was a fit companion to Imlien, a pair of high-flown Racter nobles indeed. I'd met Vektor Ulanor far away when he was the ambassador to Xuntal. I'd treated him with a high hand myself, at the time. But, then, I'd just returned from a twenty-one-year exile on Earth, had been lost at sea in Kregen, and was in no mood for a petty official to stand in my way.*

The band played, the people shouted, the dust puffed up, the swods marched and, at last, the parade was over and the two Racters, one each side of Kov Nath, led off to return to the city.

Unhurrying, I nudged Snagglejaws along to follow among the crowds.

I overheard a chance conversation between two upright citizens—stout, solid Vallian merchants.

"The people shout for them now, Markman. But I wonder if they will shout when the emperor arrives?"

"The Racters have always had my allegiance, Naghan; but now—" A tiny resigned grimace. "All this war is bad for business. The nobles grow too puffed up. The dowager kovneva should return and take command."

"By Beng Llamin! I grow weary of this continual struggle for power between the nobles—"

"Caution, my friend." A frightened glance from slanting eyes. "There are ears everywhere these evil days."

---

* See Dray Prescot, Volume #12, *The Tides of Kregen.*—A.B.A.

I rode on, taking no notice.

If only my plan encompassing the lever and fulcrum worked! Then these two solid merchants, Markman and Naghan, should have cause to rejoice.

The soldiers of the Second Frant of Foot spears marched off to their barracks, the procession of the nobles and their escorts trotted along through the city gate and began their ride to the palace. I spared a single glance for the graveyard away across the parade ground. In the natural course of life and death on Kregen, no less than on this Earth, burial customs varied from place to place. Here the dead were reverently placed to rest in graveyards outside the city walls. The markers showed gaunt limbs against the dusty ground, or marble slabs, or fabrications of branches bright with flowers and ribbons, or gray and hollow shells of gourds, gonging sonorously through the night.

With these unwelcome reflections on man's mortality, and woman's too, for although they may outlive men they too, in the end, must die, as witness Natyzha Famphreon, I chick-chicked Snagglejaws and with Greatheart following trotted after the procession of the nobles.

A cluttered side road paralleling the Avenue of Grace led me into the Souk of Weavers at a right angle some distance down from its junction with the avenue. If the plan was working, Nalgre was up there now organizing his catastrophe.

Here the weavers not only sold their products; they wove them. The Souk, originally a broad thoroughfare with shops and booths along the sides, had over the seasons been encroached upon, so that most of the space was covered by little awnings and shelters, crammed with people, and the noise battered away aloft. There was no communal roof as in many of the Souks of other parts. Congestion and turmoil, constant comings and goings as people forced their way along, marked the market. Flies upon a honey pot... Well, humans have to earn a living somehow.

In the surf roar the added noise of the confusion at the mouth of the Souk passed practically unnoticed. The numbers in the crowds watching the soldiers parade made no appreciable difference in the numbers continuing their daily work here. Whatever mischief Nalgre had accomplished with his four quoffa carts and the added complication and undeniable panic the calsanys would cause when they did what calsanys always do when they are upset proved enough. No doubt Ered Imlien, bluffly impatient as ever, had bellowed angrily and turned his zorca and Nath's away from the muddle, seeing the mouth of the Souk so conveniently to hand. They'd just ride down there, knocking people out of their way in the comely fashion of that kind of noble, and make the journey back to the palace by a slightly more roundabout route.

As I expected, Trylon Ered Imlien came into sight first, striking out with his riding crop. His face was a black mask of anger, and while I couldn't hear what he was bellowing over the hubbub, it did not take a clever guess to sense that, by Vox!

His left hand dragged along Nath's zorca. Vektor Ulanor urged his mount along on the other side. The cadade of their guard followed on in the rear, and the soldiers of the escort followed him. People staggered out of the way of this proud group, and those laggards not quick enough to jump were clouted for their tardiness.

In any contest between nobles, as had been spoken of so bitterly by the merchants out on the parade ground, the ascendancy here of Imlien over Ulanor was undeniable.

A ferocious whiskery face peered down from a wickerbasket-hung balcony opposite. A stout pole protruded at an angle supporting an awning, and its mate supported the other end some ten paces along. Those poles were whole cedar trunks. The awning, I recall, was green and yellow. A second rascally face showed perched alongside the second awning support.

Mangarl the Mangler timed it perfectly.

This part of the scheme was mainly his in inspiration, and I guessed they'd done this kind of thing before. They detested the soldiers. They had no fear of being caught here in the seething squalor of their home ground. Also, these bandits knew that if they didn't kill a soldier the hunt for them would be entirely superficial. This, I had learned, was just another result of the absence of the kovneva.

The drikingers were doing this as much to revenge themselves on the soldiers as for my red gold. They'd bash a few heads, steal everything they could, and vanish.

The first cedar trunk fell just abaft Ulanor. He incontinently fell off his zorca. The second trunk and the swathing mass of the awning fell slap bang over the escort, swaddling them in green and yellow stripes. Bulges rose and sloughed away under the canvas. With fiendish whoops the rascals dropped from their vantage points, bludgeons raised.

My concern was with Kov Nath.

Now this might be the home of the weavers, and plentiful evidence of their handiwork everywhere decorated the Souk, but the folk of Kregen like their food and drink and were not stupid enough to fail to provide these necessary requisites conveniently to hand. Many little stalls selling food and drink were scattered among the other booths.

I kicked over the charcoal, all glowing red and splendid with fire, of the roasting nuts stall. The gold I'd given its owner cleaned me out. The flames sizzled under the hooves of the zorcas.

Absolute utter and glorious pandemonium!

Without a second's delay I urged Snagglejaws forward. Imlien's riding crop sliced down over the butter-golden skull of a Gon, who shrieked and tumbled over. Other people were running away and running in. I reached Nath's zorca. A fellow twisted under the hooves. The fire was taking hold of a booth filled with straw bundles, and the owners were screaming and carrying off their stock in trade.

In all this hullabaloo I reached for Nath.

My arm around his waist simply hauled him from the saddle. Imlien let his riding crop dangle by its loop. He snatched out his rapier. He still held Nath's zorca and he dragged the reins in cruelly. He saw Nath in my clutch as I turned.

"You rast! You are a dead man!"

"Come easily, Nath," I said, hard and even.

Then that inconsiderate, ungrateful, selfish beast called Greatheart simply broke away, kicked over a fat man with a red nose, and bolted away down the alley. I was left with Nath dangling in my clutch and beginning to try to hit me.

Imlien gave a huge cry of triumph and urged his mount close. Nath caught me a glancing blow on the forehead. Ered Imlien poised his rapier, aimed for my ribs, and thrust.

Seventeen

Nath Famphreon, Kov of Falkerdrin

With a frantic heave to swing Kov Nath out of line, I twitched desperately sideways on the saddle. The rapier ripped through my buff tunic and the damned skewer scored a bloody weal all along my ribs. This upset me.

Useless to hang so stupidly onto the leading rein so disgracefully chewed through by Greatheart. I dropped it. That left me one free hand, for being an apim I do not have the luxury and convenience of three or four arms like some of the folk of Kregen. I used that free arm to jab a rocky fist into Imlien's face as he bent forward with the ferocity of his thrust.

"Let me go! Let me go!" Nath was babbling away.

"Shut up," I told him, with a growl.

He quieted a little. Imlien sprayed blood everywhere from a squashed nose. Some of the people who a moment or two before had been desperate to escape from the noble's riding crop had stopped and were turning back and taking an interest in what went forward.

For the second and last time I put out that arm and fist, and, this time, Ered Imlien fell off his zorca.

With that other half of my ration of arms I laid Nath flat on his stomach before me. Zorcas are extremely close-coupled so that riding two-up is uncomfortable. Nath flopped along belly down, face over one side, legs over the other, yelling blue bloody murder.

"Oh, do shut up, Nath," I said, again, bending a little to bellow in his ear.

Snagglejaws was only too anxious to get away from all this riot. He moved smoothly enough along under the double weight and, with only one poor fellow shouldered out of the way—he'd been gawping so hard he appeared stapled to the spot like a poor damned levy—we started off along the parallel alley.

I heard Nath spraying words like: "You'll be sorry!" and: "I am the kov, you poor fambly!" and: "Take me back at once!"

Back there the soldiers might be sprawled insensible under the green and yellow awning, their portable possessions just about to pass from their ownership. Ulanor was probably also among the list of those rendered *hors de combat*. As for Ered Imlien—I cast a quick look back.

He was not following.

He was, in all probability, tenderly rubbing his nose.

I reflected that there would probably have been time to have snaffled one of the zorcas. The plan had envisaged what had happened, that Imlien would be holding Nath's zorca reins. Still, perhaps I ought to have attempted to grab a zorca in those fleeting moments. That was smoke blown with the wind, now...

The most important item on the agenda now was to quiet down the squirming, kicking, yelling Kov Nath.

I said in a harsh voice: "If you do not keep quiet I shall have to strike you. I do not wish to do this, Nath, but, by Vox, I shall if you don't shut up."

We were almost through the parallel alley—I believe they called it Splitter's Alley—and the open parade ground lay beyond the gate. I'd have to risk that small end section of the Avenue of Grace.

Nath spat up at me: "Strike, you rast! I shall cry out the more strongly, for my people will recognize me and rescue me—Help! Help!"

I hit him.

This grieved me.

Oh, yes, indeed, in a sinful work in a sinful world, Dray Prescot is right up there among the chief sinners.

The flap of a cloak about his dangling body, a rearrangement of myself in poor old Snagglejaws' saddle so that we rode more easily, and I struck out across the last few paces of the avenue.

The guards lounging in the gate counted but two—the rest had gone hurrying officiously off to sort out the confusion wrought by Nalgre the Point. I put a semi-imbecilic look on my face, and wobbled a trifle, and let go with a bellowing croak of "The Maid with the Single Veil" which I finished on an enormous hiccough.

"Hai, doms!" I called in that bright bucolic voice. "The day is fast going and there are things I must do if I could remember them."

"Beng Dikkane has merited your praise," said the swod, leaning on his spear, laughing. Of course, for all this banter, had he tried to stop me I'd have kicked him in that lean-jawed face of his, for sure.

I walked Snagglejaws out of the gate, and called back: "My comrade worshipped twice as fast as did I. To him the glory and to him the—ah—hic—praise."

Serenely, carefully, not quite as I had planned, I let Snagglejaws carry me away from the city. Past the cemetery with its pathetic reminders lay open fields and orchards, and white dusty roads. On I went, with an itching back. Once we were in among the trees I could relax and find a good spot to rest up.

Kov Nath groaned as I eased him to the grass under the shining green leaves and greenish yellow fruit of a postan tree. I tied him up, tightly enough to let him know he was restrained. I did not gag him. I picked off a postan and pushed it between his lips into his teeth.

His eyes, those Vallian brown eyes, fastened their gaze upon me. In their depths raged passion and fury and, of course, the deep sense of outrage he experienced.

I said: "Listen to me, Nath. I have a comrade due to arrive shortly and there are three things you must know before he comes up with us."

He managed to spit most of the fruit free and started in with a bitter vituperation. I put a hand across his mouth. "Just listen, Nath. One piece of information will surprise you, although it is not particularly important, and I would not have my friend know it. The second, I am sorry to have to tell you, and regret it, for, despite all it saddens me. The third is the future, in which lies your hope, the hope of Falkerdrin, and the hope of Vallia."

I made—and it was easy enough—the necessary rearrangements to my old beakhead and there, before the eyes of Kov Nath Famphreon of Falkerdrin, stood Dray Prescot, the Emperor of Vallia.

I lifted my hand.

He said nothing at first. He panted for air, and then he got out: "What time you have left to live, I do not know. I will do all I can to prevent them making your death unpleasant."

"You remember the chavonths in your mother's garden? I marked you then, Nath. You had my message from Strom Volgo?"

"I did. I failed to understand—"

"You do not ask me what other news I have for you?"

Well, of course I felt sorry for him. I wasn't sure just how he regarded his mother. She had ruled his life with controls that were stronger than bonded steel. But she was still his mother. That old scandal about the marriage of his father and mother had been put forward to explain Nath's apparent weakness and lack of character. I felt differently.

He stared up at me, flushed of face, not understanding what was going on, and yet, I know, remembering that time when he'd stepped forward lightly with his rapier to take on the chavonths who would have ripped off his head in a trice.

"Well, emperor?"

"Your mother, Nath. I am very sorry to have to tell you that she is dead."

He closed his eyes.

After a time of silence, he said an odd thing.

"So I was right. But she would not listen to me. I do grieve for her, although she would not believe it of me. Can you tell me...?"

"No. I know only that she is dead."

"So you cannot confirm who killed her?"

"Old age, I expect."

He looked shaken, now, the fact that he'd said he was right giving me an inkling that he'd been expecting this. He tried to move sideways and toppled over. Seeing no help for it I untied him, and he chafed his wrists slowly, deep in thought.

"I grieve—aye, despite what the world will say. But the Sultants killed her—yet you do not seek to profit by this, emperor—"

"There is no proof that I am aware of. What do you think of their daughter, the lady Fanti?"

"The less I see of that handful the better."

So I spelled out the plot for him, and he managed a tiny smile at its incongruity. One side dare not reveal that the dowager kovneva was dead, for the other side would instantly have proclaimed Nath as the new kov and controlled him even more harshly than had his mother.

Yet the kov and the lady Fanti had to be brought together somehow, and Imlien and his faction would never allow Nath out of their sight or keeping. It was an interesting moil, which, as Nath said in a voice abruptly husky: "You cut in twain, majister."

"You have not asked me about the future."

"Oh, you will seek to control me as they would have done."

"Not quite. I own to having invested in you, Nath. Nath Famphreon, as Kov of Falkerdrin, is a man I value as a friend." Then I told him that his mother had asked me to help him. "I cannot do otherwise. All I wish to do is set you on your own feet, as the true kov. After that, you can go to hell in your own way—except that if you work against Vallia you will be answerable not just to me but to all of Vallia."

Then Nalgre the Point rode up with his string and Swivelears, and I cautioned Nath to circumspection.

After the pappattu was made, Nalgre said: "You may be a kov, jen. I ride Goldenhooves. You may ride my totrix, Slowback, if you wish."

That being settled we set off. Nalgre bubbled with the story of his doings, boasting that never had such a confusion been seen. As for calsanys, well...!

We rode carefully and we kept out of trouble. Nath was read the situation in no uncertain terms. The Racters fought against the Emperor of Vallia. They were proud and intolerant, jealous of their power and privileges. The Sultants in Kavinstock and Ered Imlien in Falkerdrin controlled the party. They would never allow Nath to be free as Kov.

"If you tell the people that as their Kov you will reform hated laws, administer justice, not seek to be too greedy in the matter of taxes, well—" I waved a hand. "Well, they might believe you."

"If they do not?"

"Rather, believe they will. For then we will bring Falkerdrin, at least, back into the empire where the province belongs. The day is now not too far off when all of Vallia will once more be reunited."

"With you as emperor!"

"Me? No. Oh, no—"

Nalgre reined around.

"Do what?"

I said, "By the disgusting diseased left nostril of Makki Grodno! Nath!"

"Why should I concern myself with your charades? Oh, everyone in Vallia knows that Dray Prescot flies around in a scarlet breechclout brandishing a monstrous sword. Schoolchildren lap up the stories. There are plays, and mimes, puppets and book after book. And it is all true, as I believe. After our meeting with the chavonths I studied the plays and books, and their philosophy is—"

"Philosophy?" said Nalgre. "Ha—apprise me!"

And then, to my unbounded astonishment, this pair started in on a long, involved, intellectual discussion about far more than merely the philosophical implications of the stories of Dray Prescot.

That evening when we pitched camp in the lee of a grassy bank, Nalgre the Point, in his panda-like olumai way, had the truth out of me.

He said, "I am a hyrpaktun. So are you. That means more to me than this emperor title. And your face has been knocked lopsided—for it is subtly different now."

"A trick of the light. But as to being the emperor, yes, I am, and will force my son Drak to take over as soon as Vallia is respectable again."

"Drak Prescot?" said Kov Nath Famphreon. He grimaced. "He and I have had words."

"Well, of course! You're a damned Racter."

"I was."

"Ah!"

Later still Nath managed to organize his thoughts well enough to convey the fact that he did feel thanks for my rescue of him. For he saw that it was a rescue in all truth.

"There must have been a difference between the way Ered Imlien imprisoned me and my mother's way. Yet both held me in chains."

I said the easy thing. "You're your own man now, Nath."

But I added, "And you'll get no mercy from me if you foul it up. Being a kov is a tough job."

"I look forward to it. By Vox, I do!"

I told him of my theory of the lever and fulcrum, and added: "I would like to reunite Vallia without bloodshed. I know that to be impossible. But, in Falkerdrin, at least, with the Racters overturned, the task is not impossible for determined men and women."

Simply, he answered: "I will play my part."

"Your borders march on the south with those of Kov Inch and Kov Turko."

"Comrades of yours."

"They have done the equivalent of facing chavonths with me before, yes, many times. You will find them good friends if you are a good friend." And here I gave that small growly laugh that could be called a chuckle if there was aught of amusement in it anyone else could understand. "You will find them bad enemies."

He did not reply.

We rode south again on the next day, taking it gently, not wishing to attract attention. Ered Imlien would have the country roused against us. Now had we had a flier...

As we rode so I counseled Kov Nath. My own estimate of him was more and more proving true. If we could just get the people of Falkerdrin to renounce their Racter allegiance, join with us—I reiterated the immense menace the Shanks from over the curve of the world represented to us all in Paz, not just in Vallia. As the fulcrum supports the lever and the lever can move a world, so my plans must work for the good of us all. Facile— well, of course. But true, damned true.

One penetrating point Nath wanted cleared up echoed unmistakably in his words as he said: "And I suppose you will rule from the center, holding all power in your hands?"

"Fair representation to all regions," I said. "I support the smallholders, the local merchants, the people who know their own area best. On larger matters a wider perspective is necessary. When nobles act responsibly, there is no reason at all why they should not control their own estates as they have always done. The Racters believe they hold the welfare of Vallia at heart; but I believe they are blinded by selfishness and self-pride. They do not see the world of Kregen about them clearly."

"Nevertheless they receive support from the common people."

I stared at him. "Common people. That is it. What makes a kov, a vad, a trylon, a strom, and all the rest, so uncommon? Can they eat two meals at once? Can they flap their wings and fly? Can they do two days' work in one? Common people! Why, my young feller-me-lad, I'm one of the common people and I don't forget it!"

He saw my face and had the sense to change his tack. Eventually, wanting to get my head down for the night, for we'd camped in a pretty little dell by a stream, I said, "Look, when we get to the Black Mountains and you meet Inch and, if he's there, Turko, you'll find they won't stand for this nonsense. Also, you would do well to make your peace with Kov Seg Segutorio. He shares my views on the subject."

"I look forward to meeting them."

For a short time I lay on my back on a blanket spread on the sweet night-scented grass. I was feeling very pleased with myself. Usually I am at odds with myself, aware that what I had set out to accomplish has not been achieved, crossly conscious of my failings, filled with doubts about my actions and what I should be about on Kregen. You may well be amazed that these thoughts should trouble Dray Prescot; believe you me, trouble me they did. In this I feel I am like everybody else. Ups and downs. Sometimes I feel I am a complete failure, at others that, well, perhaps I may have achieved some few deeds in life.

So, like a veritable onker, I lay there with a palmful of palines munching on the appetizing berries and ready for sleep and these oafish thoughts that the future looked far more promising, now the lever and fulcrum were to come into play, filling my fool head with a pink glow.

I was wearing the old scarlet breechclout and, as was usual, the great Krozair longsword rested by my side. The scabbard had been made by Delia. I liked to touch that scabbard just before I dropped off to sleep.

Fuzzy pink moonlight from the Maiden with the Many Smiles turned the leaves into shadowed chips of rose overhead. The night scents wafted cool and refreshing. Against the radiant orb above a silhouette moved, and hovered, and spread wide wings. I lay there, looking up.

The black silhouette against the Moon remained, sharply outlined against all the streaming pink moonlight. The Gdoinye hovered up there, head bent, cruel talons extended, the powerful hunting bird, spy and messenger of the Star Lords, lowering upon me and watching me.

Instead of hurling up some genial insult as would be normal, I waited, hoping...

No voice, no sound, no warning. Quickly, the enormous phantom shape of the Scorpion, vast and blue and all-encompassing, closed off everything about me and snatched me away into the unseen gulfs.

Eighteen

Wine from the Star Lords

Now I must put out all my willpower, all the force of which I was capable. Now I must test the theories that I could in some small measure stand against the superhuman authority of the Everoinye.

If the Star Lords were in the act of swirling me up from my night's sleep and intent on hurling me down all naked and unarmed into some fraught situation on some other part of Kregen, then I must do all I could to stop them. I needed to talk to them as I had, once or twice, done in the past. I was in no mood for more deeds of derring-do to further their mysterious purposes.

"Oh, no, Star Lords!" I bellowed up into the encompassing blueness that was the fantastic giant Scorpion. "Oh no! Not this time! Show yourselves—"

A wedge-shaped streak of viridian sprang into life along the lower edge of my vision. Stark, brilliant, acrid, the violent green color broadened and strengthened and coiled up into the zenith.

The dullness as of a wind from the frozen wastes of Forlorn Zinfross the Lost cut me, enveloped me, gripped me in fangs of ice.

Blueness—the giant Scorpion that whirled me away!

Crimson—the presence of the Everoinye!

And Green—acrid, bilious green—the domineering ambitious and impatient Star Lord known as Ahrinye!

If that unknowable entity seized me up and did as he had promised, my life hitherto on Kregen would appear a bed of roses. He wanted to drive me, to run me harder than any mortal man had been run.

"No!" I bellowed it up, but the bellow was more of a scream of desperate fear. "No. Star Lords! We have a compact! You cannot—"

Head over heels I went flying up—or down, or sideways, I couldn't tell. Stars sizzled like fireflies. I felt that harsh coldness as of the frozen wastes, and I felt the hot lick of flame as though I bathed in the Furnace Fires of Inshurfraz.

Frantically in that chiaroscuro of colors as I swung this way and that in insubstantial emptiness, as the blue and crimson and green coiled and lapped about me, I looked for the welcome gleam of yellow. Yellow—the promise that Zena Iztar still favored me with her patronage.

My feet hit harsh grit. The colors continued to clash in my eyes and resonate soundlessly in my head. If I'd been dumped down into some wild part of Kregen to struggle against odds—who had hurled me there? For whom was I the pawn now?

The grit slicked into cold marble. I lurched forward and, as a fighting man will, ricked up the sword in my fist.

A sword!

With the Star Lords?

I held the scabbarded Krozair longsword. I wore the scarlet breech-clout.

Hitherto in my dealings with the Everoinye, with but a few remarkable exceptions, they threw me down into combat naked and unarmed. I felt I might change my opinion of this practice. I might be less contemptuous than I thought I might be if they left me with a sword...

The marble under my feet felt cool.

They did not set me in a chair which hissed as it bore me along. I did not break through veils of spider silk. There were no chambers of various colors to penetrate until I reached the ebon robed room at the end.

The black walls rose about me instantly. The colors cleared. Millions of luminous motes danced away to my left, receding into infinity. Along the opposite wall three pictures, framed in heavy silver, showed views of Kregen. I had seen those pictures before and guessed that movements had taken place in the world, perhaps movements that would shatter empires.

A spindle-legged table stood in the room. Upon the table rested a costly golden goblet.

I stared and then I laughed. I, Dray Prescot, in those superhuman and awesome surroundings, laughed.

"You do not waste much on hospitality, Star Lords!"

For that goblet belonged to the Emperor Nedfar of Hamal. I had toasted him in best Jholaix and then the Everoinye had brought me here, and I'd drained the cup and placed it on the mushroom-shaped table. And it was still here. I crossed to the table, ready to make some scornful remark, and looked down and—loh! the goblet was filled to the brim with best Jholaix.

The voice whispered in, sounding in my ears and in my head.

"Things are not as they were, Dray Prescot."

First things first...

"The Shanks—?"

"Look!"

The oval silver-framed picture that showed the familiar outlines of the continental grouping known as Paz swirled and appeared to radiate outward. I felt that odd sensation as of falling into the picture. The focus swept up to the northeast, past the enormous continent of Segesthes, up to the large island of Mehzta.

From Mehzta came my comrade Gloag, who was not apim, and who ran Strombor for me in the city of Zenicce. Now his homeland ran with fire and blood.

"The devils..."

The Shanks, fish-headed, quick, tridents gleaming, ravaged the island of Mehzta. Men fought back.

"They will conquer Mehzta; but the task will take them a few seasons yet."

"How—?"

"Questions are not to be answered by us, Dray Prescot, as you know."

"Aye! I know!" I shouted back into the echoing emptiness. "But if things have changed, then why not tell me so that I can aid the fight against the Shanks? Surely—"

"The fight against the Shanks is only one of our concerns. Kregen is not the whole."

Unknowable, the Star Lords, as I thought then; but in the words, through the lethargy and tired despair, could I detect that note of humor, as of the last bubble in a forgotten glass of champagne?

The voice whispered, "Let us ask you a question, Dray Prescot, and will your overweening pride afford you the answer?"

"What pride? I own to no pride—as you damn well know—"

"Why do you think, Emperor of Vallia, that we permitted you for so long to go about your affairs? You will soon reunite Vallia. You will deal with the Witch of Loh, Csitra. You *must* unite all of Paz. Why, Dray Prescot, do you imagine we have chosen you when for so long you were just a stupid onker, a get onker, an onker of onkers? Well, tell us."

I didn't know.

I'd been whisked up to Kregen by the Savanti and by my own intense longings. Then the Star Lords had taken me over to run their errands for them and do their dirty work. I'd resisted as best I could. I suspected the Everoinye were not only growing old, as they'd told me, and tired; I felt they were failing seriously in performing what they wanted to do on Kregen—and elsewhere. I own to being a rogue and a rascal, a paktun, a leem-hunter; that I was also an emperor of this and king of that and kov of somewhere else was beside the point. I was a plain sailorman, a fighting man, a warrior—could I be more to the Everoinye than merely a strong sword arm?

"Well," I said. "Perhaps because I get things done."

"After a fashion."

Again—that champagne bubble of tired amusement?

Then the acrid voice of Ahrinye broke in, fiercely, so far different from the husky whisperings of the other Star Lords.

"The man has the power, the yrium—then let us use him to the full! Why delay—?"

This squabble among the Star Lords affected me deeply. If Ahrinye won this argument I could say good-bye to liberty and more probably than not to life.

"Because he has the charisma," the whispering voice said without hint of impatience. "He can unite Paz."

"Well, you bunch of onkers!" I bellowed up, so scared my throat hurt. "Isn't that what I started off to do long before you ever suggested it?"

Silence.

Then: "So you believe you created the thought yourself?"

"Yes."

Silence.

A voice that perhaps by the thickness of a butterfly's wing was different from the first husked out: "The man believes he speaks the truth. There is merit in his belief." He sounded as though he might be a million years or so younger than the first. Still, what was a mere million years of age to superhuman beings like these?

"I'll unite Paz," I said, "given half a chance. That sounds willfully boastful in my ears. The task is bedeviled by what I sorrowfully imagine is Savanti-inspired animosity by apims toward diffs—"

"They have their beliefs, which we have failed to alter."

By this time I'd found a weird acceptance of the way the aloof and dispassionate Star Lords were prepared to talk with me. Not just to talk to me. We weren't bandying words; but I felt I might open up a few other locked doors while the opportunity presented itself.

"Tell me," I said. "What of Zena Iztar in all this?"

Ahrinye's hateful voice burst out. "She is a mere woman who has everything backwards, as is normal among them, and refuses to understand and learn—"

Despite its apparent weakness, the whispering voice had no difficulty cutting in and blotting out Ahrinye's spiteful tirade.

"Zena Iztar has not grown up, Dray Prescot. She is as once we were. She believes she has a mission and she will do all in her not inconsiderable powers to further her ends."

Well, now!

"What is her mission?"

"Onker!"

Well, I suppose the question was foolish not on the grounds of the Everoinye's refusal to answer questions—they'd been forthright enough now, by Zair!—but on the grounds of Zena Iztar's actions. Yes, her mission was obvious enough in all seeming; I just wondered if that was all there was to it.

I said, "Zena Iztar commands my loyalty—"

"We are aware of that. Where there is no conflict it is of no concern to us."

"The Kroveres of Iztar, I believe, will materially assist in the ideal of uniting the people of Paz."

"That is why it still exists."

I felt the chill.

By Krun! Was there really no limit to the power of the Everoinye? Or were they failing? Either way, I was in for a damned hard time.

Often and often I'd pondered the question of the questions. Wherever I happened to be on Kregen—in the thick of a bustling city, out under the stars at night, prowling through some unhealthy jungle—the tantalizing thoughts would flood in to mock and bedevil me. Why, I'd ask myself the question, why don't I just damn well ask the Everoinye the questions? Then some flashing slice of action would occur and I'd be far too busy swinging a sword, or double-dealing villains in chicanery, or—as recently—climbing up some horrendous crag on a damn-fool errand. All questions outside those demanding immediate answers for survival went out of the window then, and sharpish, too, by Krun.

And, as so often happened before, just as it was now, I'd ask questions of the Star Lords and they'd come back in their aloof way that such concepts were beyond my understanding, competence and business. Except for this time. Except that now they had deigned to give me some direct answers.

Of course, I reasoned, some of my sheer scared witlessness leaving me, I could only be paddling around in the shallows of the secrets they kept.

I licked my lips, and then out of braggadocio or simply because my throat was dry I picked up Nedfar's golden goblet and took a good swig of the superb Jholaix.

I swiped the back of my hand across my mouth.

"By Mother Zinzu the Blessed!" I said. "I needed that!"

Ahrinye's acrid voice lashed in, dripping venom.

"You are a kregoinye and you are in the presence of the Everoinye! Show more respect. You are not in some stinking tavern where you might meet Zena Iztar in Sanurkazz."

Respect! Since when had I ever shown respect for the Star Lords? And I was a kregoinye, one who worked for the Star Lords, willy-nilly. But! But I'd learned a little more about them from that single outburst.

Ahrinye was probably a good few million years younger than the others, and he still hadn't learned the value of deviousness in dealings. The Everoinye could see that Zena Iztar by giving her patronage to the secret Order of Kroveres of Iztar would substantially assist me to do the Star Lords' bidding. Zair preserve me from that unpleasantly impetuous Star Lord!

Further to needle them, I said, "When do we expect the main onslaught from the Shanks to arrive?"

I'd seen that enormous armada of Shank ships sailing across the ocean. That force would demand a very great deal of effort and dedication to defeat.

"Mehzta will detain them for a few seasons yet, Dray Prescot. You still have time to carry out our designs. Vallia must not obsess you." Then, they gave me another little jolt of surprise. "Your dealings in Hamal met with our approval. Continue thus."

I was sensible enough to say nothing in reply.

After a space of what might have been uncomfortable silence, I said: "This will take time."

"If necessary, we will manufacture time."

They could, as I knew.

"But we must insist that this occurs only as a last resort. We have no need of explaining to you; just believe."

"Oh, I believe all right."

And, almost, like the veritable onker I was, I added, "You're growing too old and past it." But I held my tongue.

That they could read another person's thoughts I knew, for I'd had the trick performed for me on my comrades. They passed no comment. They told me again what they required, that Paz unite to stand against the Shanks, which I knew, and I tried them with more pertinent questions which were ignored.

The way I saw it then was that the Star Lords recognized I possessed the yrium, that is the special Kregan form of charisma which blesses or curses its owner with the capacity to lead other people, to influence them, to create bonds of loyalty unbroken by death.

Fretfully, I said: "And Mehzta? Is there nothing to be done?"

The soft voice said, "A kregoinye has been dispatched."

Soho, I said to myself. I just hoped they hadn't sent my comrade Pompino the Iarvin. He was supposed to be bringing us saddle animals from South Pandahem.

When I asked I was brushed aside. Still, with this new rapport between us, I fancied the Star Lords would have given me a better answer had Pompino really been the kregoinye dispatched off to Mehzta to help repel the Shanks.

A new voice which was by a double-thickness of a butterfly's wing different from the others, spoke up. That voice spoke in what were urgent tones for the Star Lords.

"An emergency—end location—running..."

The center picture on the wall, which usually showed the oceans of Kregen between our group of continents and islands of Paz and the other grouping called Schan on the other side of the planet, cleared. Mist formed and coiled, and then in an odd perspective I was looking at an angle at a flight of wide marble steps leading up to an imposing palace.

No sound issued; but one did not need sound to wince at the soggy blows being struck by the knobbly cudgels of the ruffians belaboring a man in a black coat and trousers.

Another man wearing a tall black cylindrical hat and black coat ran up. Moonlight washed the scene. This second man lifted an ebony cane with silver bands. He muffed it.

He tried to hit the ruffians in their nondescript coats and flat hats, and sending the first one reeling back down the steps, he was instantly set on by three others and fell beneath the rain of blows.

One of the Everoinye said something I had no possible way of understanding.

When they operated, these mysterious Star Lords, they operated fast.

Blueness just swelled up around me.

I yelled.

"No! I will not go—"

That moonlight... That was the most important factor in that fracas.

That moonlight gleamed silver upon the marble.

Head over heels, the icy cold washing me, I soared up and away.

A voice followed me, a whispering voice cutting through the lambent blueness.

"A short time only, Dray Prescot. This we promise you."

Headlong, tumbled head over heels, away I flew, hurled back to the planet of my birth four hundred light-years away.

Nineteen

The Everoinye play a jest

Well, of course. I was there. I was the one on the spot. All the Everoinye had to do when their stupid kregoinye fouled up was ship me off, head over heels, to pick up the pieces.

They'd done exactly this trick upon me before, many times.

This time I landed with a thumping great slam upon the icy steps. Moonlight fell about me. Silver moonlight!

Gone was the warm fuzzy pink moonslight of Kregen.

Gone, too, were the scarlet breechclout and the Krozair longsword.

I was not naked.

I wore a black coat and trousers identical to those worn by the poor devil of a kregoinye who lay bleeding on the marble. I could feel a ring pressing down on my head, and guessed I wore a top hat. In my hand, in place of the longsword, I held an ebony cane.

Beneath my fingers I could feel a catch in the wood, a metal latch familiar to me. I pressed. There was no time to dilly-dally with the gentry intent on lulling the gentleman screaming upon the steps.

I came up fast and silently and hit one of the ruffians over his head. He fell down.

His companion swore. I caught a 'Verdammt!' and he caught the cane and dragged it toward him, intent on finishing me with his cudgel.

The wood slithered off the metal with a chingling evil sound.

The poor devil stared sickly at the sword cane.

I did not slay him; just stuck him a little and then instantly slashed at another would-be murderer who came a rush at me from the side. He staggered back, shrieking, an eye hanging out, blood everywhere.

The kregoinye had vanished.

The other ruffians could either stay and die or run.

They ran.

Glaring about and breathing gently and evenly I saw there were no more potential slain in the offing and so bent to the injured man. He was unconscious. I could feel the cold bite of the wind, the ice upon the steps unpleasant, and faintly the sound of a city reached me. I picked the man up and started down the steps.

Properly dressed, the sword pushed back all bloody as it was into the cane and invisible, I was able to attract the attention of a horse-drawn carriage. The driver knew the way to the hospital. Even without my tutor's genetically coded language pill, given me by Maspero in far Aphrasöe, I could have conversed easily enough.

I was in Vienna.

Well, that suited me only in that I wasn't in some outlandish place. And—I had clothes! And—money!

Truly, the Star Lords looked after their regular agents. I'd been so used to being dropped in, all naked and unarmed, at the last minute, any other way of going on smacked of sybaritic luxury!

There is little need to make a meal of my doings on Earth at this time of the turn of the century. I had to believe that the Star Lords meant what they'd said. In view of that, and my doting passion for the music of Johann Strauss the Younger, I went the round of the best places to hear the music. I was Waltz mad, of course. And, at the same time, I caught up with what had been going on on Earth during my recent absence.

My education in matters terrestrial was materially furthered. The man I had rescued, I can now reveal, turned out to be a most important personage later on, and did, in fact, have an impact on world affairs. Still, as ever, it is not my intention to relate my life upon Earth; but to narrate what befell me on that gorgeous and barbaric world of Kregen.

The time went by and it dawned on me that I was keeping myself busy learning about science and philosophy and medicine so that I didn't notice

the passage of the days. I began to grow alarmed. I took the train to Paris—
and a fabulous and luxurious train journey that was, to be sure!—and
checked into a high class hotel. What the hell were the Everoinye doing?
Had they played me false?

Now I have mentioned that last bubble in the forgotten glass of champagne. I suspected the Star Lords did own to a sense of humor.

They proved it, at least to my satisfaction, then.

The Parisian hotel bed was comfortable enough. I'd eaten well, drunk
moderately, smoked a single cigar, and I dropped off to sleep with my
usual fretful thoughts gradually submerging under the most important
thought of all. That thought never left me, and grew strongest as I closed
my eyes in sleep.

Someone touched me on the shoulder.

"*Bonjour*," I mumbled, starting to turn over and open my eyes. "*Je
suis*—"

"What gibberish is that you're spouting, you hairy old graint?"

Delia!

The bedclothes went one way, I went the other, and Delia was in my
arms.

"When—" she managed to gasp out. "When did you get home and why
didn't you tell me?"

I hugged her and then held her off and looked at her.

Divine! Superb! Absolutely stunning!

"Delia," I said, hardly aware of what I was saying. "My heart!"

"Well?"

So I told her.

"One little yellow sun and one little silver moon and no diffs?"

"Right."

"You poor old fellow!"

"And the Star Lords just whisked me back when I was asleep. I think, I
really do think, they've turned over a new leaf. They played a jest on me!"

Then we fell to and told each other the news and joyed in each other
and talked and talked, and we sent for food which we did remember to eat,
and so I was back once more upon Kregen, my adopted home, and where
in all the galaxy I most wanted to be. With my Delia, my Delia of Delphond, my Delia of the Blue Mountains!

There were hundreds of items of news to catch up on.

So many story lines were going on, continuing dramatic threads, and
I've not mentioned one in a thousand in this narrative, hewing to a central
line. As an example: Nulty over in Paline Valley had done a deal to acquire
more land and had taken over the next valley. Hundreds and hundreds of
items that are the life blood of Kregen.

So when I mention here the news conveyed by courier to the capital—for

I was in Vondium—about Seg, Turko and Inch, it is because that was uppermost in my mind, and has formed the substance of this section of my narrative.

There had been not a single plague visited on Vallia in my absence.

During a time when I could not gabble on by reason of a mouthful of palines, Delia said: "I don't know what you did to Kov Nath Famphreon. What a change in that young man!"

"You've seen him?"

"Of course. I think he'll turn out all right. At least, Seg seems to think so."

"Well, minx, go on!"

"Oh, they had a wonderful time up there in Falkerdrin. Most of the people were so tired and resentful of the Racters, particularly of Nalgre Sultant and his son, and of Ered Imlien, that they cheered like mad for Nath."

"No fighting?"

"Hardly any. Not down south. There is a pocket up north against the border of Kavinstock where Imlien marches his army about, creating a mischief—"

"What? Well, what's Turko doing about it?"

"They are, my heart. A battle is imminent, I'm afraid. We ought to win, but—"

"Yes."

Delia had said: "I'm afraid." So was I. I detest battles and fighting and only indulge in them because as I see it the alternative is worse. But, in this...?

"I'll get up there straight away."

She sighed.

"I knew you'd say that, of course—"

"And is the reason you held the news back this late—"

"Well!" she flared up. "And weren't you fascinated by the news of Queen Lush? Tell me true—"

"Yes, yes, I was. And about Dayra and Lela, too. But this is here and now. If there is no more vitally important information I should know, then I'll fly up first thing in the morning." I eyed her. "I suppose I can always find time to spend another night with you."

"Despite this so important affair of state you must manage?"

By Zair! But she was beautiful! And sharp, too, sharp and lovely and altogether the most wonderful girl in two worlds. And devious with it, believe me...

We flew up together the next day.

There was nothing I could say to stop the Empress of Vallia flying where she willed.

The news she had given me of Drak must wait for a small space...

Now quite a few Kregans are interested in gaining recognition and renown for great deeds, what they call absteilung, and fellows or girls with a great deal of absteilung to their credit are called kampeons. Just about all the lads in my guard corps were kampeons. Not all, for we trained up youngsters there, as you know. So, when Delia and I flew into the camp where the Ninth Army waited for the battle everyone hoped would be the last of this campaign, there were vast quantities of absteilung in the camp and many kampeons, with the prospect of more to come.

They were all there. All those gallant comrades whom you have met in this narrative. And great was the rejoicing when we sat down to the serious business of deciding how best to bash the Racters, with a glass or two for counsel as well, I might add...

I said, "You do extremely well without me. So go to it. Your plans are ineluctably fine."

Seg offered to shaft me, Turko wanted to twist my arms off, Inch swore he'd give me a short haircut, and Nath na Kochwold said tart words to the effect that the Phalanx wouldn't take kindly if the emperor was not on parade.

Delia, laughing, said: "You don't think this grizzly old graint could keep his ugly old nose out of it, do you?"

One item of information Delia gave me I considered interesting and then filed away in my mind. That was a mistake, as I was to discover.

She told me that Marion had insisted on the new guard regiment of Jikai Vuvushis being committed to action, and Kapt Erndor, now Chief of Staff to the Kov Turko as well as the Ninth Army, was enthusiastic to have this addition to his strength. Marion had stalwartly refused to marry Strom Nango until the emperor could dance at her wedding. Now that I was back, she declared that as soon as the battle was won she'd finalize the wedding details. Of course, meekly, I agreed.

Among the Vallian military officers attached as aides-de-camp to Strom Nango was Hikdar Ortyg Voman of the Fifteenth Lancers. I was surprised to see him. He'd been with his regiment down in the southwest with Drak. He was paying court to Sushi Vannerlan, and through her friendship with Marion the appointment had been arranged. From what I knew there was no shortage of action with Drak, quite the reverse. Sushi was here also, one of the camp followers we tolerated, as we tolerated very very few, for she played a demanding role in the hospital service, and Hikdar Ortyg Voman had pulled strings to be with her. I couldn't blame him.

The army was in fine fettle, crowing over their relatively unhindered march northward.

"By Bongolin!" declared Nath na Kochwold. "Once Nath Famphreon talked to a few of 'em, they ate out of his hand!"

Perhaps you can make some little attempt to gauge the depths of my feelings of relief that we had won through so far with so little blood spilt? That my plan of the lever and fulcrum had worked?

"Just bash the last of 'em," said Seg, smiling at Delia and me, "and we can all go home."

"Oh, no, Seg!" I said.

"Do what, my old dom?"

"It'll be Balkan for you. The High Kov's time is near."

"Yes, well—" He coughed a dry little cough. "I was contemplating taking an army over the mountains to deal with this so-called King of North Vallia."

"That will be done. It's Balkan for you."

He knew what we were talking about. He knew I wanted to see him established on his own estates, legally and morally, as the Hyr Kov of Balkan.

So far news of the invasion by the Shanks of Mehzta had not reached here. When it did arrive I knew damn well that high-spirited young people would want to take to the air instantly and fly over to help. This question had to be debated most carefully. The Presidio would have to make the final decision. As for myself, I would not leave the work set to my hand here, particularly when the Star Lords had assured me they had one of their agents out there already.

The lads gave me a tremendous welcome when I rode out to inspect the various units of the Ninth Army.

As for my guard corps, now they were back in business. Their business was looking after my hide.

The "Hai Jikais!" rang over the parade grounds.

This last battle looked to be open and shut and I was seriously debating whether or not I should take myself off somewhere else where I might be more useful. Zair knows, there was enough to do.

Delia in her practical no-nonsense way, said: "It will not take long. And you know how they relish having you there—"

"You're right, my heart. But—!"

"But nothing. And, I'm coming with you when—"

"You're doing no such thing!"

"We'll see."

So I knew I'd lost that argument.

We sent out heralds all duly signposted to talk to the chief Racters, and received back only words of spite. The heralds uniformly reported that the army with the Sultants and Imlien thirsted for the forthcoming fight.

I said, "Is this more sorcery?"

"Who can tell, majister. They are confident."

Seg growled out, "I feel sorry for 'em. But, by the Veiled Froyvil! We've tried to accommodate them in the decent way, now we'll accommodate 'em in six feet of earth."

"Seg!" said Milsi, and put her hand on his arm. At once he bent to her, attentive, and she smiled and for a moment they were oblivious of us.

Whetti-Orbium, who as the manifestation of Opaz concerned with the weather, smiled on us from time to time and rained on us at others, decided to smile. The army marched out and in good order, took up positions around the smallish town of Stocrosmot and prepared for the final attack.

To my great joy Nalgre the Point had kept a good hold of Snagglejaws. I could have had the choice of many a fine zorca, blood zorcas all. I chose snuffy, tufty, drab old Snagglejaws, for I knew his mettle. Nalgre, in his olumai way, accepted the position I offered him as an aide de camp. His panda face smiled warmly.

"I'll call you majister, Kadar the Silent, and be respectful. But you cannot wash away some memories."

"Nor would I wish to, Nalgre. Just don't get yourself killed."

"Oh, I won't do that, by Lingloh! And, anyway, I'll be off home to K'koza as soon as we're finished up here."

"I shall be sorry to bid you remberee."

The battle plan worked like a charm. Even though I'd expressly requested that Marion's warrior maidens be held in reserve, they got themselves into a fine old knock-about with a regiment of Brokelsh, and in the end they broke and routed the coarse and hairily uncouth bunch facing them. The whole line advanced. We sounded the view-halloo and the chase was on.

This pursuit was necessary if we were to see and conclude an end to the unpleasant affair.

I wanted none of it and left it to our cavalry to continue. With 1 and 2 ESW and 1EYJ, together with the new guard regiments, 1EFB and 1ELC, I looked across the edge of that battlefield where the dead lay in their wind-rows, and sighed, and ordered camp pitched. The baggage wagons came up and we set to do what we could.

Hikdar Ortyg Voman passed staggering.

"Hik!" I called. "You are wounded?"

The twin suns had set and the stars were out, and the Maiden with the Many Smiles inched above the horizon.

"No, Majis. It is Sushi—she is out there among the wounded and the dead—and I do not like that—"

"It is her wish, Hik."

At that moment the Hamalese, Strom Nango, walked up.

"Marion requests, majister, that you meet her at once by that twisted tree—" Nango pointed. The tree, bent out of shape, leaned against the wind. I nodded.

"Very well, Strom."

Seg and Turko appeared, and Delia walked out of the tent. Inch would be inside securely fastening up his yellow hair.

"What's to do?"

"No idea. Marion wants me over by that tree."

We all walked across, passing campfires where some of the lads were brewing up or roasting slices of meat. Most were flat on their backs, spark out after the battle. A group from the various duty squadrons followed. The night breeze cooled our flushed cheeks. The stars glittered with that particular brightness of Kregen. The silence was acute. There was no long low and dreadful moaning from the scene of battle.

Under the tree, Sushi Vannerlan, her apron stained black-red, stood with Marion. The Jikai Vuvushis were camped nearby, and they were as tired as the men.

"Hai, Marion. What is it?"

She gripped Sushi's arm. I looked at the two women, surprised. Just past the gnarled tree lay an ancient burial ground where for generations the dead of the town of Stocrosmot had been laid to rest. I thought of the cemetery outside Falkerium and other towns and cities.

"Sushi?"

"Majister—" She swallowed and started over. "Majister—the wounded and the dead—they are—strange—"

Turko said, "When you're dead you're dead."

"Not," said Seg, "in some places of Kregen."

Just then the breeze blew chill, colder than it should be on such a night.

A low rippling movement across the ground beyond the tree took all my attention. Could it be? Why not? I had seen the dead walk when I'd been down the Moder. Kao is one of the many Kregish names for death, and the kaotim, the undead, specters, zombies, call them what you will, these are well known over Kregen.

Were the dead walking?

"May Erthyr the Bow keep us now!" said Seg in a hard, tight voice. He unlimbered his great Lohvian longbow.

"By Morro the Muscle!" said Turko. "It is true!"

A voice at our backs, strong, unperturbed: "Ngrangi is with us, for the Maiden with the Many Smiles floats alone in the sky." Inch, not a single strand of his brave yellow hair exposed to the fuzzy pink moonlight of the Maiden with the Many Smiles, joined us. He carried sword and shield and was armored.

I took the Krozair longsword off my back. I said to Delia: "You had best—"

And she said, "At your side, fambly."

So we stood, a little group of comrades, with our kampeons, and watched as the ground rose up before us.

Dead men and women, people just slain in the battle and others long dead, moved toward us. The pink moonlight caught on armor and weapon, glinted fuzzy rose. Skeletons, mummies, men and women apparently full-fleshed and filled with blood, advanced upon us.

"Csitra the Witch of Loh has planned this well! How do we slay men already slain!" The voice was lost in the night.

So we gripped our weapons and arrayed ourselves as the grisly horde bore on.

Abruptly, with a shriek as of sundering metal, the mob of kaotim rushed upon us and we puny mortals were at hand strokes with the crazed hordes of the Undead of Kregen.

Twenty

Undead of Kregen

No nightmares trouble me over that horrid fight with the Undead. The poor creatures were husks only, shells, their spirits already wandering the Ice Floes of Sicce, seeking the sunny uplands beyond. Bundles of bone, swathings of rotten cloth, stained with the dirt of the years, many of them simply rushed in with clawed fingers seeking to rip us to pieces.

These already dead we could deal with. The recently slain posed a tougher problem, for in their ghastly resurrection they snatched up sword or spear, pushed helmet straight, and wearing what armor they had worn in life plunged screeching upon us.

I say we could deal with the dead. At first this did not appear to be the case.

"They are dead!" screamed that same voice at my back. "How can we kill dead men?"

Without looking back, I shouted: "Take that man into custody. Shut his damnfool mouth!"

Then I really shouted, really let my old foretop-hailing voice belt out.

"They are dead therefore half our work is already done! Chop 'em! Cut their legs off! Sunder them into pieces! And, my friends, go with Opaz for this night's work."

Seg said: "You're right, my old dom. But, first—just one..."

A marvel with a bow, Seg Segutorio... He loosed and his aim, unerring, sent the rose-fletched shaft directly into the backbone of a prancing skeleton leading on the grisly mob. Bits of vertebrae sprayed. The skeleton's top half fell, arms scarecrow-wide, bone bright. But the lower half, the pelvis and the legs, continued to run on toward us.

"If," said Seg, "it's like that..." He thrust the longbow away and drew his drexer. "It's leg-chopping time."

Milsi was back at the camp, and for the moment Seg had no fears for her. I had fears for Delia. By Zair! I was terrified for her. Yet she stood at my side, lithe and limber, sword poised, and she had possessed herself of a drexer in place of the rapier. She wore no Claw. The enormous shadow over me that was Korero the Shield would have to be spoken to; but he knew, as Turko the Shield had known before him.

"Aye, Dray, aye. Rest easy."

"To you, then, Korero—"

"Aye."

More shafts flitted from our ranks into the howling shambles running on; they did little damage. We were poised, braced, as the contents of the local graveyard crashed into us.

By Makki Grodno's dangling right eyeball and dripping left armpit! Csitra had gone too far with this latest curse. As we fought I could feel not red roaring anger but cold impatient venom.

The superb Krozair brand sliced around in a whirl of roseate steely light, shattered bones, went on and no stain of blood marred that blade. We chopped the skeletons as we might chop firewood.

Do not ask me how skeletons may be wired up so that they run and fight and their lower jaws clack in a ghastly grin against their upper teeth, let alone how they may be animated. Grotesque angular dancers, limbs flinging about in abandon, bony and thin, they tried to bite and claw even as we chopped them down.

The skeletons were bad enough. The corpses dead long enough to begin decomposing were far worse. For all his macabre dancing parody, a skeleton is clean in a way a rotting corpse is not. Far, far worse to glimpse a row of exposed teeth, a jaw, a naked eyeball, a vine-net of veins, than just a bald skull, a long bony arm! Stinking, the corpses poured down on us. They were falling to pieces even as they charged.

Seg slashed a foul thing of rags and bony fingers away and said, "Even Skort the Clawsang wouldn't give these things the time of day."

"Your back, Seg!"

He dodged, slashed, and a skull toppled. He and I and Turko and Inch fought there in the front rank. Useless for my guard corps to rage and protest and try to shove up. In this horrendous conflict we all must play our part.

Skeletons, rotting corpses—they were bad. But the worst, by far and away the worst, rushed charging at us with wild war cries. Some of my lads cried out in horror.

Through the din, distinctly, I heard one anguished scream: "It is Vango, my brother, Vango!"

The voice of Nath na Kochwold: "Vango seeks the sunny uplands, Deldar

Vangwin! This is not your brother! This is evil from the pits—chop, Deld Vangwin, chop as you value your life!"

So we fought our own dead comrades.

Ghastly, horrible, and pathetic, yes, it was all these things. Also, the fight could have seen us all trooping down to the Ice Floes of Sicce by regiment, all wailing dolorously for the Gray Ones.

Poor Nath na Kochwold had to see his brumbytes fighting dead pikemen. Swords in live hands clashed against shields clutched in dead, and swords in bloodless fists smashed against shields in the grip of the living. Useless to thrust. Useless to try anything except great hewing strokes that swept the dead away into bundles that mewed and tried to scrabble along, drawing legless torsos by bare hands.

And, in all this horror—where were Khe-Hi-Bjanching and Ling-Li-Lwingling?

Others in that great fight shared those fraught doubts, and Delia said: "They will be here soon. They just have to be!"

Fascinating to see how my lads formed their ring about Delia. No skeleton penetrated that devoted circle of bronze and steel. Of course, Delia was mightily put out and kept advancing to take her share, and the ring would move and shift and so encircle her again. I approved. By Zair! If my Delia did not survive—well, the Star Lords could look for another tool, that was for sure.

A churgur from the new regiment, First Emperor's Life Churgurs, staggered back with a stux embedded in his neck. He fell. Immediately a comrade stepped up to take his place and front the gibbering horrors. I saw the dead man sprawled on the ground. I saw his right hand relax to let the sword fall away, I saw that hand turn inward, lift and fasten on the javelin. The fist ripped the stux free in a gush of blood. The man threw the stux down, picked up his sword, stood up, turned, hurled himself full at his comrades of a moment ago!

A long Saxon-pattern axe swirled. The churgur fell in two pieces, still with blood enough to stain across the trampled ground. Targon the Tapster finished him off by chopping his legs away. Inch's great axe flashed in that deadly circle as he cleared the zombies from his front, and I noticed the swathing mass of bandages about his hair fallen away so that strands of his yellow braids showed.

Poor Inch! He would have to expiate this taboo after the battle—if he were still here and not suffocating in some Herrelldrin Hell.

Many the macabre scenes enacted that night. My lads were tired from the day's battle and now they were forced to struggle in another and far more hideous conflict. No. Far better to pass over that ghastly time and record that, on a sudden, all the skeletons and decomposing corpses and bodies of our dead comrades and enemies fell.

They collapsed and the sound of bones clanking down rang like carillons.

"Thank Opaz!"

The Wizard and the Witch of Loh stepped from the small two-place flier. Their faces were strained. They looked grave.

"As quickly as we could, Dray," Khe-Hi told me. "But the power of the uhu Phunik grows remarkably."

"Nine Curses," I said. The piece of cloth in my hand wiped up and down the blade of the Krozair longsword. "Nine. There will be more to come."

Delia started to say something, changed her mind, went on cleaning her sword.

If I interpolate here that we cleaned our own weapons, this was true most of the time. Now it gave us something to cling onto as we digested the latest information in our struggle with Csitra and Phunik.

Counting the cost of that miserable fight was a melancholy affair. We'd lost good men and women. The dead—the pieces of the dead—were duly buried and appropriate ceremonies held and words spoken. But the memories weighed heavily upon us.

When I made inquiries concerning the man who had spoken so ill at the beginning, calling out that we could not slay men already dead, the escort wheeled up Hikdar Ortyg Voman. I was astonished.

He looked in a terrible state. Sushi Vannerlan had been badly wounded and it was feared for her life. This had unnerved him, clearly. Yet...

"Well, Hikdar. What have you to say?"

"Nothing, majister. I know only that Sushi is near death and I am frantic—"

"Yes. You have my sympathy. But you called out when the fight began. You did not act as I expected."

Miserable he was, his uniform torn and bloodied, mud over his knees, all his handsome good looks shrunken away.

"I do not recall—"

"You don't remember?"

"No, majister."

Delia said: "Khe-Hi?"

"Yes, yes, it would fit." Khe-Hi turned to me there in the Headquarters tent with the escort holding onto Voman, more to keep him upright than to restrain him. "I was not in Vondium at the time of the first werewolf outbreaks. But—"

I nodded, sick with the revelation. "Hikdar Ortyg Voman turned up late at Marion's party, after the werewolf struck. And now Csitra spies on us again—"

Hikdar Ortyg Voman said: "Dray Prescot, you are a stubborn man! Is there nothing in all this world or the other world that will move you?"

I said, "You know the answer to that, Csitra."

"My uhu grows impatient."

"What other world do you mean?" I did not think she referred to Earth but to the mystic other dimension in which so much of the traffic of these Witches and Wizards of Loh was carried on.

"A world open to me and not to you. But I would have you share much of what I can offer—will you not visit me in the Coup Blag? Phunik can be—"

Instead of blurting out: "Phunik can be hanged!" I said, "You released Wenerl the Lightfoot from his thralldom to you when his usefulness had gone. Will you now release this man?"

Staring into Voman's eyes and seeing only human eyes regarding me blankly, I wondered for a fleeting moment if he could feel or understand what was going on through his brain. Far away south in Pandahem, in the Coup Blag, this woman, this Witch of Loh, and her malignant brat planned to make over the world in the way they wanted. But so, of course, did I.

Voman stood unseeing, supported by his escort. The others in the tent, comrades all, watched silently. I tried again.

"You know I would think better of you, Csitra, if—"

"Perhaps that is not enough, Dray Prescot!"

"Then you condemn this man to death."

"Which means nothing to me."

"Therein lies the barrier."

What the Star Lords had told me, what Delia and I had discussed, all tended to the same answer. It would not be easy and it would not be pretty, but, by Zair! I could see precious little else to do.

I said: "You are proving an obstacle to my own plans, Csitra. You are an inconvenience. Maybe Phunik will grow into powers greater than yours or his father's. Maybe he will fall down a great pit and impale himself on spikes. Should I care about that?"

"You would not dare to ask me to choose between you!"

"Not dare, Csitra, care."

"Visit me. Come to see me. You know what I can offer you in the Coup Blag."

I knew that all right, by Krun, I knew that!

"Maybe I will visit you. Will you release this man?"

"If I do, do I have your promise?"

Delia touched my arm and I put my fingers on hers. The touch gave me strength.

"Yes."

Hikdar Ortyg Voman closed his eyes. Then, just before he opened them, he said: "And can I rely on your promise?"

My fingers held Delia's and I could feel the warm firmness there without a tremble as Voman's eyes snapped open and he gasped out: "What—? Where—?"

I didn't know if the Witch of Loh could hear me or not but I said, "Oh, yes, Csitra the Witch. Oh, yes. You can rely on my promise to come to visit you."

STORM OVER VALLIA

Drak the Prince

Storm over Vallia is a complete story of the magnificent and mysterious, beautiful and terrible world of Kregen, a planet orbiting Antares four-hundred light-years from Earth. On that world of headlong adventure much may be achieved and much lost. Far more than merely a strong sword arm is required for victory. Far more than a cunning and devious brain is needed to secure success.

For Drak, Prince Majister of Vallia, son of Dray Prescot and Delia, emperor and empress of Vallia, and Queen Lushfymi of Lome, passionate, willful, extraordinarily beautiful, mysterious, and Silda Segutoria, daughter of Seg and Thelda Segutorio, are caught in a web of fate and intrigue, of blood and death, that demands of them all that they are.

But the story begins with Lon the Knees, animal handler, as, dragged from caring for his domestic animals, he marches in the victory parade of Kov Vodun Alloran, traitorous and usurping master of all Southwest Vallia.

Under the streaming mingled lights of the Suns of Scorpio the fates of these people of Kregen twine among the destinies of that exotic world.

Alan Burt Akers

One

Lon the Knees

In Vodun Alloran's victory procession the wild beasts, placed ahead of the lines of carts containing trophies and treasure, followed immediately on the heels of the captives. The wild beasts, carefully and expensively gathered, were of many varieties, different of shape and form, of color and physiognomy. One thing they shared in common. They were all hungry.

At the rear of the sweaty reeking mass of savage beasts penned in the cage-carts, Lon the Knees marched along sturdily, for all his legs in their bandiness might have circumscribed a barrel—whence his sobriquet. He was of Homo sapiens sapiens stock, clad in rough homespun with decent sandals upon his feet. The long ash stick he carried was more sharply pointed than perhaps the authorities might have allowed in a beast handler, had they known.

"They're restless, bad cess to 'em," said Fandy, walking at Lon's side.

She did not wave her stick at the animal in the cage for which she and Lon were responsible. As a Fristle, a cat-woman, Fandy the Tail's whiskers bristled and her gray-marbled white fur slicked sheening where the universal dust did not coat it in a dull ocher.

"They should have fed them." Lon's nostrils filled with the savage beast smell, thick and clogging. The noise hammering into the bright air made conversation impossible beyond a few paces. "The lord saves money where he should least afford it."

Up ahead, squadrons of cavalry rode clearing the way past the mass of onlookers thronging the streets of Rashumsmot, the town having gained greatly in importance since the capital, Rahartium, had been tumbled down into ruin during the wars. Following the wild beasts, bands blared music, and gauzily clad girls, flowers in their hair, flower garlanded, strewed the roadway with petals. Only when all this pomp and pageantry had passed would the high and mighty of the land ride arrogantly along, luxuriating in their wealth and power and prestige.

Fandy the Tail glanced sidelong at Lon, seeing his florid face scowling and paler than usual, the nose still purple but with harsh lines extending downwards to the corners of his mouth, which, uncharacteristically, resembled a snapped rat trap. She was well accustomed to reading facial expressions of other races, as anyone must do who lives on Kregen.

"Lon! You feeling—?"

"Oh, I don't know, Fandy. We're ordinary beast-handlers. I don't care for these monsters. And I suppose I worry over Nol—for a twin brother he's so vastly different from me as to make me wonder at times."

"Twins from different fathers?" Fandy flicked her tail, long and thick and glossy where the dust did not cling. "It's been said. I am not so sure."

The bands played, the people shouted, the soldiers marched, trumpets blew and the beasts penned within their cages paced forward and back, forward and back, bristling.

"Well, Nol went for a mercenary, having the shoulders for a slinger. They took me into the cavalry stables. He fought for our lady the kovneva and when the new kov defeated her—"

"You're here, Lon. He will be all right, you'll see."

"I pray to Opaz that be true. I just feel—by Black Chunguj! I would this damnfool procession was all over!"

The roadway here was ill-paved, cobbles having been ripped out for the catapults, and the wheels of the cage-carts snagged and leaped in the ruts.

Among the gawping crowds Lon was well aware that his friends and acquaintances would be busy. They left the poor folk alone. They dipped the fat and wealthy. It was said Crafty Kando could slide the gold ring off the finger of a woman who'd never taken it off since the day it was placed there. Lon was not a member of the thieves' fraternity. When his work was done and theirs, they'd enjoyed good times in one another's company.

In all the shrieking bedlam of bronze gongs, of brass trumpets, of drums and bells, the screams from ahead and the snarls and deep-throated growlings could not be mistaken.

Into that clogging miasma of smells, the raw rank taste of blood shocked through like red wine spilled onto a yellow tablecloth.

"I knew it!" Lon's face pinched in. He gripped his pointed stick. "I told you so!"

Instantly, Fandy swiveled to glare not up ahead where the bound captives were being slaughtered by the escaped beasts, but at their cage. Everything remained battened tight. The latchings, the bolts and bars, were all in place.

Inside the cage the silver-blue unpatterned hide of the churmod reflected light in a ghostly silky-smooth patina. Her blunt head lifted. Her tail thumped once upon the floor of the cage. Languidly, with all the arrogance of a churmod, she lifted on her four rear legs, so that her head, ferocious and deadly, rested still upon her front legs. Two crimson slits regarded Fandy with all the malevolent enmity of any churmod, surly and sadistic and vicious beasts that they are.

Everywhere people were running. The procession broke up, fragmented. Demented with terror, men and women hurled themselves into doorways, clambered up into windows, tried to shin up the pillars to the safety of the balconies where the bright scarves and the flowers and feathers waved still in mockery of the pandemonium below.

The churmod stood up on her eight legs. Eight sets of claws whicked out like razors. Without a sound, the churmod stood there, swaying with the lurchings of the cagecart. In the last moment before the cart stopped, its off fore wheel dropped into a rut. The whole cage tilted, groaning, and remained canted.

The churmod's enormous hissing sounded like a volcano spitting steam.

She hurled herself at the front bars, splintered them through, catapulted out onto the roadway, a lethal silvery-blue phantom of horror.

Fandy the Tail vanished in the opposite direction, the last tip of that fat tail flicking out of sight past a bundle of bandsmen all struggling to rid themselves of their instruments.

The churmod in those long lazily-leaping bounds soared toward the fracas ahead, toward the screams and toward the luscious scent of blood.

Cursing everyone—and Kov Vodun Alloran most of all—Lon the Knees did not give himself time to stop and think. Had he done so he would have followed Fandy the Tail.

He began to run toward the sounds of death.

Just why he was doing this he didn't know; of course, he was scared stiff, of course he was an Opaz-forsaken fool, but he did owe a responsibility for the safety of the churmod. Churmods are amazingly rare and costly beasts. Larger than leems, more treacherous than chavonths, they are highly coveted prizes in the Arena. And rumor had it that Vodun Alloran, the new kov, was intent on introducing all the spectacle of the Jikhorkdun, the Arena, the training rings, the barracks, all the gambling and the panoply, into this newly conquered island of Rahartdrin.

Lon ran on his bandy legs, and his tongue lolled.

Very quickly he came upon the ghastly work of the untamed animals.

Headless bodies, and disembodied heads, arms and legs, a scattering of inward parts, bestrewed the roadway. Some of the animals had stopped to appease their hunger. Others, the more unremittingly hostile, continued in their orgy of slaughter.

There was no sign of Lon's churmod.

Sense slapped back to him like a shower of ice across his face.

By the sweet name of Opaz!

What had he been thinking of!

At once he scuttled across the littered roadway, thankful not to be encountered by a stray leem, or a strigicaw, or anything with sharp teeth and claws, and dived into the black rectangle of an open doorway.

His feet tangled in a body by the doorstep. He caught his balance and glanced down. He frowned.

The body was that of a young woman, a firm, proud young woman, who had been slashed so grievously by giant claws that she must have died almost instantly. She wore black leathers, tightly fitting along slender legs and around a narrow waist, flared as to hip and breast. Her helmet with the brave feathers lay rolled into the angle of the doorway.

She was, Lon saw readily enough, a Warrior Maiden. Her rapier and left-hand dagger had availed her nothing, although the sword was still gripped into her black-gloved right fist.

Thoughtfully, he bent and picked up her dagger.

As a mere animal-handler, he could never aspire to wearing a rapier. The dagger, awkward though it might be in his right hand, was still of far finer workmanship and temper of metal than anything he was likely to be able to afford to buy down at the Souk of the Armorers.

The street outside looked something like the aftermath of a battle. Bodies lay everywhere. Blood ran to foul bright clothes and dabble in artfully curled hair. Some of the escaped beasts still roamed looking for fresh victims. The sounds of other animals eating crunched sickeningly into the brightness of the day.

Lon stepped over the dead girl and ventured farther inside, anxious to put a strong door between him and the horrors outside.

Along the short passageway from the front entrance to the inner courtyard he padded. A door stood in each wall, that on the right being closed, that on the left open. He looked over his shoulder before moving to the open door and saw a chavonth putting an inquiring head into the entrance. Lon swallowed. The chavonth, his fur in the familiar blue, gray and black hexagonal pattern, spat in sinister fashion. He braced on his six legs. Treacherous, are chavonths, and Lon knew that this specimen would spring in the next heartbeat.

With a yelp of pure terror he dived past the open door and without hesitation flung the solid wooden door shut.

He stood with his head bowed against the door, shuddering. He was just a simple animal-tender, and so the kov had ordered him, along with others in the same trade, to take charge of his new menagerie. These savage beasts had been gathered from far afield across the seas. Lon was used to ordinary sensible animals, used for pulling carts and ploughs, for riding on, for performing the ordinary sensible tasks demanded by ordinary sensible people.

He was not used to these ferocious assemblages of claws and fangs. No, by Beng Debrant, patron saint of animal husbandry!

A low spitting awful growl from the room at his back stiffened his spine as though he'd been shot through by an arrow.

He wriggled himself around, slowly—slowly!—to stare in appalled horror upon the scene in that downstairs chamber of an unknown house.

The girl clad in black leathers like the poor dead girl in the entranceway snapped: "Stand still, dom!"

Lon the Knees had no intention of doing anything else. Long before he could get the door open the chavonth in the room would be on him. And if he did, the thing's mate waited for him outside.

The sweat ran down his nose and into his eyes and he dare not move. The blue and black and gray hexagons upon the hide of the beast pulsed. He lifted his front left paw and Lon saw the blood glimmering upon it. There was more blood upon the beast's hide, fouling that hexagonal pattern.

There was blood, too, upon the sword in the girl's fist...

Lon did not know the name of that sword or of what pattern it might be. It looked something like the common clanxer, the cut and thrust sword of Vallia; but there were differences that even he could see. His brother Nol, now, would probably know. Lon stood and sweated and was thankful he was so bandy his knees could not knock together and so enrage this frightful beast.

Of the details of the room Lon took in absolutely nothing, apart from a vague awareness of a heavy table in the casement window, a few chairs, and the three bodies on the floor. The Warrior Maiden stood with her black-booted feet firmly planted in front of the three corpses.

The twin suns, Zim and Genodras, slanting their mingled streaming light upon the scenes of carnage outside, twinkled in odd refractory reflections of jade and ruby within the shadows of the room. Lon just stood, petrified.

He could feel that both his hands were empty. Now, if he'd kept his long pointed stick... The mere idea of actually trying to push that stick in front of him at the chavonth gave him a dizzy feeling of extreme ill health.

From the time before dawn when the twin suns rose in the sky, Lon had been murkily convinced that this was an evil day. He'd said as much to Nath the Goader, an intemperate and ill-humored fellow at the best of times. Nath, in charge of the wild animals and worried out of his wits by the unwelcome responsibility, had merely growled in his beard and sent Lon off with a flea in his ear, or, as Kregans say, a zorca hoof up the rump. The truth of Lon's premonitions was here, awfully here, in this savage chavonth, and the corpses, and the blood, and the shambles outside...

The girl's downdrawn level gaze did not waver from the chavonth.

When the thing launched itself into its lethal leap, she would be ready. Lon knew that. It was evident in every line of her body, every vibrant inch that, he saw with suddenly uncluttered eyes, was of extraordinary beauty.

Her sword did not waver.

Her left arm was held at her back, the hand hidden.

She was a Jikai Vuvushi, a Battle Maiden, and she had been riding with the cavalry at the head of the procession. No doubt these three poor corpses, all men, with the girl at the entrance-way, had been also with the advance guard. They'd spurred back to find out what the trouble was and had encountered horror.

So now this girl, this Jikai Vuvushi, faced the terror alone.

Lon swallowed again and slowly began to draw his right hand down to the awkward hilt of the main gauche thrust through his belt. Something about this girl attracted him in ways he was too wise to encourage. She was not for him. He tumbled the girls in the taverns when he could, and joyed in that. This girl possessed an aura, a flickering flame of power and allure, and she was tough. No doubt of that. She was battle-hardened.

The blood along the chavonth's flank matching the blood on her blade proved that.

The chavonth sprang.

The girl leaped aside with such grace, such beauty of movement that the breath caught in Lon's throat.

As she leaped and so avoided the long slashing stroke from the beast's front claws, she struck. Her sword scored all along the animal's fore sixth. She span about, sword blurring up for another stroke and the chavonth backed off, spitting.

"By Vox!" she said, viciously disappointed. And still her left hand remained invisibly at her back.

The hunting cat showed no interest in the three bodies on the floor. He glared from hating, slit eyes upon the living breathing form of the girl. And, again, he lifted one front paw, the claws sharp and curved and shining.

A scratching began on the door, and a hideous meowling. The other chavonth, mate to that one penned here, sought entrance. Lon felt his famous knees giving way; but still his right hand dropped cautiously lower and lower to the hilt of the left-hand dagger.

With the sudden and ferocious changes of fortune that overtake any-one who lives on the world of Kregen, the noise outside the door changed. The chavonth's scratching ceased. The mewling screeched into a spitting snarl. Mingled with that noise another noise penetrated, a long ominous hissing.

Whether or not chavonths, or any other of the many and varied life forms represented by Kregen's savage fauna, could communicate with one another, Lon didn't as yet know. But the noise outside the door was easily understood within the room.

That low evil hissing was the churmod—Lon's churmod for which he was responsible to the lord. In the next heartbeat it was all over. The snarl-ing uproar ceased on a long screech of agony. No sound of the chavonth remained. Then, again, low and demonic, the hissing of the churmod.

What happened then Lon could not afterward well remember. His hand reached the dagger hilt and he drew ready to throw. He ranked himself as a man who could throw a knife, even one so clumsy as this left-hand dagger.

The chavonth, distraught at the death of his mate, for he had read those bestial sounds outside the door as accurately as the humans, whicked his tail and leaped.

Lon hurled the dagger.

He saw the point go into a blue patterned hexagon. He was aware of the girl's sword sliding up and then he blinked in the abrupt blinding wink of fire, he caught a blurred impression of steel slashing, of the brilliance of the emerald and ruby suns light glancing off polished metal. The girl swung back and the sword licked again. The chavonth reeled about spouting blood, half its muzzle ripped away. One eye dangled. It screamed. The Jikai Vuvushi, very assured, very calm, stepped forward and drove her sword deeply into the beast's side. That blade, Lon knew, and trembled, had burst through the savage heart and stilled its beating forever.

Strangely, without speaking, the girl turned her back on Lon the Knees. A brown canvas strap and sack thumped against her side. She swung about to face him, the sword dripping red in her fist.

She spoke evenly enough, yet lightly, on a breath, as though the horror of the past moments had not been so easily disposed of in the thrust of a sword.

"I give you my thanks, dom. Your name?"

"Why, my lady—it is Lon the Knees—"

"Yes."

And she smiled. And Lon the Knees was overwhelmed.

He licked his lips and swallowed and got out: "My lady! You have slain a chavonth! It is a great jikai!"

He would not dare, naturally, to ask her name in return.

Her smile did not falter.

"A little jikai, perhaps, Lon the Knees. To gain the great jikai, let alone the High Jikai, one must do far more than this. Far more."

He opened his mouth, and she went on: "Now give me a hand with this young lord. His companions are dead, which is unfortunate for them, although no doubt somewhere in this land of Rahartdrin someone is giving thanks to Opaz for this eventuality."

Lon didn't follow all this; but he stepped across, knees trembling, and helped to raise up one of the corpses.

This body was clad in gorgeous clothes of a nature that, while they filled Lon with envy, filled him also with repugnance.

As though inconsequentially, she said: "You throw a cunning knife, Lon."

"Aye, my lady."

"It did the trick. Gave me time—hold his arm, the idiot keeps on falling over—now, you young lord, open your damned eyes!" She slapped the corpse around the face and, lo!, the corpse's eyes opened.

"Help!" The puffy lips shook as the man screamed.

The girl shook his shoulder. "It is all over! You are safe, Jen* Cedro."

This young lord Cedro in the foppish gaudy clothes took some time to calm down. He was sick. His eyes, of a pale transparency so unlike the normal deep Vallian brown, stared vacantly at the room, the dead chavonth, his two dead companions. He shuddered and vomited again.

Only now, this close to the girl as he helped with this petulant young lord, was Lon aware of the blood scored along the rip in her black leathers. The slash from razor-sharp claws bloodied her left shoulder. That, Lon surmised, was why she'd held her left hand at her back.

"My lady! You are hurt—"

"A scratch. As soon as I've handed Jen Cedro over I'll have the needle lady attend to it."

"At least let me bind it up—"

"Don't fuss, Lon the Knees."

He felt chastened, and so said no more.

"That damned churmod is still prowling about outside." She sounded fretful and just as savage as the damned churmod. "I don't fancy having to go up against her with—"

"My lady! That would be madness!"

"Oh, aye, by Vox, absolute madness. So I won't."

"Thank the good Opaz!"

"We'll sit tight in here and wait until Kov Vodun sorts out the whole stupid mess. You can tell me about yourself."

So he told her, not that there was much to tell. Orphaned at an early age and sent to work on a farm, been looking after animals all his life. His twin brother, Nol, gone for a mercenary slinger and who might have any sobriquet now, a source of ever-present foreboding.

"Why, Lon?"

"Soldiers get themselves killed, my lady."

"Oh, aye, they do that. But then, so do beast-handlers who don't know their job."

"My lady!" Lon was aware of deep disappointment that he should not have felt. The great ones of the land would always blame someone other than themselves. "I am not trained to handle wild beasts—give me a Quoffa, or a mytzer, a zorca or—"

"I know, Lon. I am not blaming you. Far from it."

"They should not have put the captives so near the wild beasts, and—"

---

* Jen: Vallian for lord. Notor is Havilfarese. Pantor is Pandahemic. *A.B.A.*

"And the cages were ludicrous. Yes, I guessed that. But, Lon the Knees, do you not think it strange that so many wild animals escaped—all at once?"

"I saw the churmod break the bars. It was frightening."

"Assuredly. Yet I suspect that a hand loosened the bars of the cages—not yours, Lon, believe me, I did not intend to mean that."

Oddly enough, given his usual attitude to the high and mighty of the world, Lon believed her, believed she spoke the truth. She was, he could see, a most remarkable young lady.

"You do not ask my name, Lon."

"That is beyond my reach, my lady, as you know."

"Oh—I see. Yes. I am a Jikai Vuvushi and am used to rough ways. Well then, Lon the Knees, I am Lyss the Lone—well, that is one name by which I am known."

Very gravely, Lon said: "Llahal and Lahal, Lyss the Lone. Now we have made pappattu properly."

"Lahal, Lon."

So the introductions were made.

Lord Cedro groaned and started to roll over so Lyss the Lone pushed him away to avoid his own vomit.

Added to the rank smell of blood in the chamber the sour stink of Cedro's sick gave Lon a queasy sensation, he who was used to the stenches of a farmyard!

Lyss walked to the window and looked out. She shook her head.

"The beasts still stalk arrogantly. There is no sign of a human being—alive, that is."

"Oh," said Lon.

"The kov will be rounding up his people now. Pretty soon they'll come back and try to round up the beasts—"

"I should be there to help them."

"You will stay here and help me."

"Quidang, my lady."

"So you never wanted to go for a mercenary, then?"

"Oh, I went off with my brother Nol. They took him for a slinger; me they sent home, laughing. But I was in one army for a time, looking after the totrixes."

"Someone has to, otherwise the army would not ride."

Nervously, trading on this amazing friendship he sensed between them, Lon ventured: "And you, my lady. You have been in many famous battles?"

"Some."

"A—I see..."

"A battle is a battle, Lon. A messy business."

"Yes, my lady."

The idea that a battlefield was not exactly the right place for a young lady could only occur to Lon the Knees, or any of his contemporaries, as it might apply to one particular girl, one prized loved one. Girls had always fought in battles, and the Jikai Vuvushi regiments were justly feared.

Lon was perfectly content, now, to sit tight in this chamber and wait for Kov Vodun to come for them. That the kov would come, Lon felt no doubt. Now he knew this young and unpleasant lord was Jen Cedro, he knew him to be one of Kov Vodun's nephews. If the foppish idiot was valued by his uncle, then rescue would not be long delayed. Thus reasoned Lon the Knees.

Also, and in this Lon felt unsure, he would meet the kov, face to face. Vodun Alloran might lord it over wide lands; the common folk could hope to see him barely more than a handful of times during their lives. The great ones of the earth rode past in a glitter of gold amid the trumpets and banners; the common herd cheered from the crowds and saw only what the dazzlement in their eyes allowed.

Assured that Cedro was still alive, Lyss the Lone did not seem bothered that he relapsed into unconsciousness. She sat on one of the chairs twisted to face the windows. She sat still and trim in her black leathers, and Lon felt the pang strike through him. If only...!

Well, jolly fat Sendra down at The Leather Bottle had been kind to him in the past, and he could always shut his eyes and dream.

Noise and fresh uproar in the street told that at last rescue had arrived. The clatter of hooves, the screeching fury of wild beasts skewered and feathered, the high yells of men and women drunk on slaying, filtered in through the window. Lyss stood up. She hitched her rapier and main gauche around, picked up her other sword, solid and powerful, and started for the door.

"My lady!" Lon was alarmed to such an extent he scared himself at the intensity of his own feelings.

"Well?"

"You cannot—I mean—why go out now?"

"I am a Jikai Vuvushi."

Lon stiffened his spine.

"Aye! And like to be a dead one if you go outside that door now—my lady."

Thankfully, she did not say: "And you would care?" Such banality, they both recognized, had long since vanished between them. She smiled that dazzling smile.

"I believe your justified concern no longer applies—listen!"

From outside the door the sounds of the churmod's death hissed in, and Lon had no difficulty visualizing the hail of bolts from the crossbows, sleeting in to shred and bloody that ghostly silvery-blue hide.

Lyss opened the door.

"Hai! The lord Cedro is here, unharmed. Hurry, famblys, and take him up carefully, for he is beloved of the lord kov."

Men and women wearing a variety of colorful uniforms entered the room, and at once began to attend to Cedro. Lon stared at the open doorway.

Vodun Alloran, Kov of Kaldi, conqueror of this island of Rahartdrin, entered. Lon stared, fascinated, quite unaware of his own peril in thus staring so openly at a great lord.

Alloran looked the part. His clothes were sumptuous, for he no longer wore the normal Vallian buff tunic and breeches; golden wire, lace, feathers and folderols smothered him in magnificence. His shrewd, weather-beaten face contained harshness engraved as a habit, and the bright brown Vallian eyes, partially hidden by down-drooping lids, revealed a little of the fury of ambition seething within him.

He wore an aigrette, the feathers of maroon and gray, the colors of Kaldi, and the golden device, that of a leaping sea-barynth, a long and sinuous monster of Kregen's seas. His own personal retainers wore sleeves banded in maroon and gray in the old style of Vallia. He stared about from under those drooping eyelids, and Lon abruptly switched his gaze to Lyss.

She stood, upright and slim in her black leathers.

"My nephew," said the kov. "He is unharmed?"

"He is well, my lord kov, praise be to Opaz—"

"Yes. He would escape from a pack of leems without a rent in his coat."

Lyss said nothing. Lon stood with his tongue cleaving to the roof of his mouth.

Alloran stared about with that aloof, disdainful look of the great ones of the world.

"There has been a mischief done here," he said. He spoke through his teeth. "And I will have the guilty ones hung by their heels over the battlements until they are shredded to bone."

Watching Lyss the Lone, Lon saw the way she held herself, the tautness of her, the poise. Was that a fine trembling along her limbs, the ghost of a twitch of muscle in her cheek? He'd conceived the instant idea that this glorious girl feared nothing. She had faced and overcome a savage wild beast, not even claiming a jikai for the deed. Now she stood watchful, like a falcon poised ready to take flight, alert and wary.

Naturally Lon stood in awe and fear of Kov Vodun Alloran.

But did this Battle Maiden, this superb Jikai Vuvushi, stand in fear of the kov?

No. No, Lon the Knees could not believe that this girl feared anything in Kregen.

Two

Of the concerns of Drak, Prince Majister of Vallia

The battle was lost a half an hour after it began with the totally unexpected appearance of a second hostile army swarming up from the sand dunes on the left flank. The Vallians broke and fled.

The First Army, commanded by Drak, Prince Majister of Vallia, trudged dispiritedly back from that disastrous field. Then the rain fell.

Jumbled regiments on foot slogged through mud that thickened and stuck like glue. A few artillery pieces saved from the ruin, ballistae and catapults swathed in coarse sacking against the rain, struggled on drawn by a motley collection of animals, and by men. The cavalry, who had suffered grievously, walked their animals, and everywhere heads hung down.

The wounded, those who could be collected, were transported in improvised fashion, for the supply of ambulance carts proved woefully insufficient.

Sliding, slipping, dragging themselves through the mud, the First Army staggered on eastwards across the imperial province of Venavito in southwest Vallia.

Jiktar Endru Vintang led his zorca through the mud, holding the bridle so that he walked to the side, for the zorca's single spiral horn jutting from his forehead could inflict a nasty nudge if anyone was foolish enough to walk directly in front of so superb an animal. His saddle dripped water, and his orderly would spit brickdust cleaning up the weaponry strapped both to zorca and Endru.

The long lines of men and animals kept doggedly on in the rattle of the rain and the gruesome footing.

Jiktar Endru commanded one of the prince's personal bodyguard regiments.*

He was three-quarters of the way up the ladder of promotions within the Jiktar rank, and hoped soon to make Chuktar. With this disastrous Battle of Swanton's Bay to ruin their plans, Endru morosely felt that promotions for anyone were a long way away. You'd have to take the place of a dead superior and soldier on in your own grade for a bit yet. That was his surmise.

Nobody talked. They all went sloshing on in a profound and gloomy silence, broken by the slash of the rain, the creaking of axle wheels, the

---

* The four main ranks in most Kregan armies are: Deldar, commander of ten. Hikdar, pastang or company, or squadron commander. Jiktar, regimental commander. Chuktar, general. A Chuktar is selected as Kapt, commander in chief. *A.B.A.*

suck and splash of feet in mud, and the groans of the wounded. All these distressing sounds faded within the bitterness of the silence engulfing the army.

Endru Vintang ti Vandayha*, tough as old boots, efficient, a superb zorcaman, a warrior who understood discipline and let his regiment know he understood, had fought as a Freedom Fighter in Valka, and counted himself supremely lucky to be selected by the Prince Majister to command the bodyguard regiment called the Prince Majister's Sword Watch. The best part was that, feeling a real and powerful affection for the prince, Endru knew that Prince Drak liked and trusted him and treated him as a friend.

He knew he felt as many and many a poor wight in this defeated army felt. He felt they'd let Prince Drak down badly, very badly indeed.

But, still and all! That second army, suddenly appearing over the sand dunes where scouts had reported nothing apart from shellfish and crabs! That had been the stunner.

Those Opaz-forsaken Kataki twins had been the cause of this defeat. That seemed certain.

Glimmering spectrally through the slanting rain, a light appeared ahead. Wearily, Endru flapped back the cloth over his saddle and with a soft word to Dapplears, his zorca, stuck a leg over and mounted up. Even then, quick as he was, he sat in wetness and felt the discomfort through his breeches. One thing was for sure in all the surrounding desolation; this uniform was ruined beyond repair.

He nudged Dapplears, for no true zorcaman put spurs to so fiery and spirited a saddle animal, and walked him up alongside his regiment.

"Deldar Fresk! Ten men with me. *Bratch!*"

Eleven of them, they rode out ahead of that bedraggled rout toward the light which Endru knew to be shining in a window of a house in the little village of Molon. He said nothing, did not turn his head, as he passed the powerful figure walking sturdily beside his zorca at the head of the column. The prince would be in no mood for polite conversation now, by Vox!

The inhabitants of the village, apprised by that seemingly magical dissemination of country news, had fled.

There were beds for the wounded, and roofs for a fair number of those fortunate enough to cram into the little houses. There was even a little food. Fires were lit and clothing began to steam, filling the close confined atmosphere with that particular charring, moist, fibrous smell of drying clothes. When he had seen to his duties, Endru reported to the prince.

"They'll get some rest for the night, jis," he said, using the "jis" as the shortened form of majister, for Prince Drak did not care to be addressed as

---

* ti: "of" indicating the holder as a person of some substance in the locality or town. Of as "na" or "nal" indicated persons of higher rank and greater estates. A.B.A.

majister. He was not too keen on the slightly more formal 'majis', although that was how most of those not in his immediate circle addressed him.

"And those we have left on the field will sleep even more profoundly." Drak sounded depressed.

"The odds were more than two to one, nearer three to one. Had we not—"

"Run off?"

"Aye, jis! Had we not done so, many more of us would sleep on the field this night. And then, what of the morrow?"

"You are right, Endru. We must look to tomorrow."

Endru was of an age with the prince. He felt perfectly confident in his ability to be allowed to say: "Bitterness over this defeat, jis, will avail us nothing. Those damned Kataki twins wrought the mischief, I'll be bound."

"I did not see them in the fight. Did you?"

"No."

Drak sat himself down on a rough wooden seat and put his forearms on the scrubbed tabletop. The fire threw harsh shadows into his face. Yet Endru could see the power there, the arrogant beak of a nose, the jut of chin, all the charisma he possessed, shared and inherited from his father the emperor. They were much alike, yet Prince Drak for all his austere ways, his uprightness, his dedication to his duty, possessed a streak of more gentle character from his mother, the divine Empress Delia.

The small cottage room contained other men and women: Kapt Enwood nal Venticar, the prince's right-hand man and his chief of staff, crusty old Jiktar Naghan the Bow, commanding the prince's bodyguard regiment, the Prince Majister's Devoted Archers, his personal servants, one or two of the sutlers come to report the damage, various people who had business with the prince, and Chuktar Leone Starhammer, commanding Queen Lushfymi's regiment of Jikai Vuvushis. Now Kapt Enwood resumed the conversation Endru's entrance had interrupted.

"Jiktar Endru confirms my view, then, jis. I am confident the Kataki twins commanded. It is certain that Vodun Alloran was not there."

"The quicker he is put down, the better it will be for Vallia."

"Yet he is clever and resourceful. He commands many men. And he's getting his gold from somewhere—"

"Aye!" burst out Drak. "But where?"

"It is my view," put in Leone Starhammer, "there is sorcery involved here."

No one cared to answer that. This Leone, a full-bodied woman, plain of face, dark of hair, with biceps that could smash a sword through oak, kept herself and her girls up to a very high fighting pitch. Fortunately, in Drak's mind as in the others', the Jikai Vuvushis had not been heavily engaged during the short fray.

"Let's have the maps out and see what we can cobble together and call a plan."

Again Endru felt that stab of dismay at the depths of the prince's despondency.

The maps were brought and spread upon the table and the people gathered about them in the light of a lamp, a cheap mineral oil lamp.

Drak began by stating the obvious.

"We are fighting for Vallia. The whole island empire has been broken into pieces, and slavers and slave masters, villains who batten on our misery, have swarmed in to ravage and despoil. We will not allow slavery in Vallia. We will not allow honest folk to be crushed into the mud. So we fight for them. And, this day, we have been defeated."

"Tomorrow, jis," said Kapt Enwood, "or the day after or the day after that, we will be victorious."

"And how many days must the downtrodden wait for us?"

"As many as the Invisible Twins made manifest in the glory of Opaz decide, my prince."

Drak took that well enough. He stabbed a finger at the map.

"At least, they did not pursue their victory."

"I lost the better part of a fine totrix brigade," said Kapt Enwood, grimly. "Then the rains came." He drew a breath. "No. They did not pursue."

Where Drak had stabbed his so savage finger the little bay, known as Swanton's Bay, gouged a piece out of the Venavito coastline. To the east lay the province of Delphond, the Garden of Vallia. Delphond was the province of the Empress Delia. The people were languid and easygoing, joying in the good things of life which they produced so profusely from their lovely land, not easily aroused. During the Time of Troubles they had changed. From slitting the throats of stragglers in ditches, they now sent many strapping sons and daughters to swell the ranks of the regular Vallian army. Delphond was cut off from many direct routes and canal trunk systems, and invasions usually passed the province by. Drak did not wish to contemplate what his mother would say if he allowed invading hordes once more to ravage her lands.

Northward lay the vadvarate of Thadelm, mostly occupied by Vodun Alloran's mercenaries. There was some resistance to his schemes there, though, and a small force watched the borders.

To the west the kovnate of Ovvend was now once more solidly in Alloran's grip. Ovvend was on the small size for a kovnate province; it was undeniably rich.

West of Ovvend lay the diamond-shaped kovnate of Kaldi, Vodun Alloran's own province. The westerly point of land was the last on the mainland of Vallia. Beyond that extended many islands, chief of which was Rahartdrin, with Tezpor to the north. No word had been received from these islands, or those further west, for many seasons, and spies sent in did not return.

Two divisional commanders had been killed in the battle, so the council was thin on the ground. Brigadiers would have to be appointed to take over the divisions; as Endru had suspected, they would not advance a grade within the Chuktar rank.

"I am determined to hold them on this line," said Drak, indicating a river some miles to the east. "We must draw them north."

He was aware that these people, all well-meaning, gathered here to help and advise, would know why he wanted to do that. The thought of Delphond once more put to the torch and the sword made him limp with anger. He had spent some of his childhood there and he loved Delphond's lazy ways, her soft rivers, the winding dusty lanes, the fields of fruit and hop gardens, the fat ponshos with fleeces as white as the clouds above. Oh, no, he must draw Alloran's army, commanded by the Kataki twins, toward the north where they could be entrapped in mountains.

Kapt Enwood said: "We shall have to send to Vondium to ask for reinforcements. I see no alternative."

"They are short of troops in the capital."

"If you appeal to the emperor—"

Drak's head snapped up. Almost, almost, he burst out: "Ask my father? Oh, yes, we'll ask him. But he won't be there. He never is. He'll be off gallivanting around the world doing derring deeds, hurtling under the Suns in his scarlet breechclout and swinging his Krozair longsword. Oh, yes, ask the emperor, an' you please. Much good will it do you."

Instead, he said: "Send and ask, Kapt."

"Quidang!"

Their faces harshly highlighted by lamp and the fire, they thrashed out some kind of plan. They would draw the enemy on, try to chivvy him northwards, get him in unfriendly country, continuously ambush him, run him ragged. They could not stand up to a face to face set-piece battle. Not while they were now, having sustained casualties, at a worse ratio than one to three. When the reinforcements marched and flew in, why, then, with the blessing of Opaz and the strength and cunning of Vox, they'd knock Vodun Alloran's teeth down his throat.

And his two whip-tailed Katakis with him, too...

"We must preserve the Phalanx intact," said Drak, stating the essential and the obvious. "Without them at Swanton's Bay we would have been destroyed."

"Aye, jis."

"Get the kervaxes moving at first light and withdraw the entire Phalanx force to the east. We will need light infantry for ambush work, and light cavalry."

They talked on for a space, settling details, then at Drak's suggestion, they retired to try to sleep for what was left of the night. The rain continued. The sky was a mere black platter pressing down on the land. Leone Starhammer lingered.

"Jis?"

"Yes, Leone?"

"The queen—I fear she will take this news ill."

"She will have to be told, I suppose..."

"Jiktar Shirl the Elegant fell today—"

"I am desolated! I did not know."

"A stray varter bolt pierced her through the throat, above the corselet rim. She died in my arms." Leone's hard plain face revealed no outward emotion; Drak was not deceived.

"She was handmaid to the queen; but she kept on pestering to go with the army and be a Jikai Vuvushi. In the end the queen relented and gave her assent. Shirl the Elegant was very dear to the queen."

"I see. Then she will have to know. I give thanks to Opaz that the queen stays in Vondium."

Leone stared at him, and the slight movement of her right eyebrow was of enormous significance.

"I believe the queen would dearly love to be with the army, to march with her regiment of Jikai Vuvushis, to be with the man she—the prince she—"

"All right, Leone. I know, you know, the whole damned world of Kregen knows Queen Lushfymi of Lome wants to marry me. Well, I am not so sure."

"May I say, prince, that it would be a splendid match? Lome is a very rich country, and Pandahem is allied to us now, after the wars, and—"

"Allied to us! By Vox, Leone! You saw that fresh damned army come shrieking off the beaches! They were from Pandahem. They were Pandaheem. I wouldn't be surprised if there weren't more than a few men from Lome among 'em!"

"Majister!"

"Aye, and a few girls, too!"

"Jis—you do me dishonor—I cannot—"

Before Drak had time to spit out that he didn't really mean what he said in the heat of angry resentment, Leone fled from the room. Drak swore. He swept the maps off the table, then he kicked the table leg, then he swore some more.

Women!

The trouble was, ever since Queen Lush—at once he mentally corrected himself. He ought to refer to her as Queen Lushfymi, although she was generally known as Queen Lush. She'd come to Vallia to marry the old emperor, Drak's grandfather, and when he had been killed, Queen Lush, after some fraught experiences with sorcery, had decided her best bet would be to marry the Prince Majister. One day Prince Drak would be the emperor.

Well, and so he would, if his father had his way. Drak refused even to think about all that. He had a campaign to run and Vodun Alloran, the damned traitor, to whack. Time enough later to think of marrying.

And then—of course!—he could not stop himself thinking of Silda.

Daughter of his father's boon companion, Seg Segutorio, the finest Bowman of Loh in the world of Kregen, Silda Segutoria troubled Drak in ways he just couldn't fathom. He knew she loved him. She had risked her life, willingly offering it up, to save him from death. She was marvelous, wonderful, impetuous, quicksilver, and damned devious, too, like all the women who were members of the famous if secret sorority the Sisters of the Rose.

Into the bargain he knew that Seg Segutorio, who was like an uncle to Drak, and his father the emperor and his mother the empress, all wanted Drak and Silda to marry. That seemed in their eyes to be inevitable and wonderfully apt.

And here was Queen Lush, sophisticated, alluring, a woman of the world, sensual and clever and reputed possessed of some sorcerous powers, setting her cap at him.

It was all a muddle.

He glanced at his own great Krozair longsword standing in the corner by the fireplace. The coals were mostly burned through now and he'd better turn in before the room became too cold. He was a Krozair of Zy, a member of that martial and mystical Order. Yes, life was a lot simpler out there in the Eye of the World, the inner sea of Kregen. Out there, where his brother Zeg was King of Zandikar, life was simple. If anything wore green you killed it. If anything wore red you fought for it with your life.

As for Silda Segutoria—where in a Herrelldrin Hell had the girl got herself? Where the blazes could she be? She might be in Vondium, where Queen Lush was no doubt living a life of luxury. She might be off on a wild adventure for the Sisters of the Rose. There was a strong possibility she could be with his sister Dayra, or his mother, the Empress Delia, although recent letters had not mentioned her. She could, even, be haring off into breathtaking adventures with his father, the Emperor of Vallia.

Thoroughly dissatisfied, Drak rolled himself up in his cloak and drifted off to sleep where he dreamed dreams of men with no eyes sloshing about in the bloodied surf of Swanton's Bay.

Three

The kov who would be king

The loss of so many fine specimens was not to be allowed to interfere with the festivities—not if Kov Vodun Alloran na Kaldi had anything to say, no, by Vox!

"There are captives aplenty," he shouted at his chamberlains. "Use them! Do I have to think of everything?"

In preparation for the many ceremonies the streets were garlanded, tapestries and carpets hung down from balconies, ales and wines were brought in by the cartful, trees were decorated with strings of colored lights for the evening entertainments.

Strolling players, whose numbers had declined during the Time of Troubles, were now reappearing. If folk believed that these new troublous times were over, then they could be encouraged in that belief. Troupes of actors and actresses, singers, jugglers, fire-eaters, animal-tricksters, gathered in the town to add their color and sparkle to the festive occasion.

In the natural course of his own estimation of himself, Alloran took his personal tailor on his travels. This functionary shared quarters, meals and salary with the hairdresser, the bootmaker, the perfumer, the mistress of the linen and other men and women whose sole function in life was to care for the person of Vodun Alloran.

"I want clothes more beautiful, more sumptuous, more glorious than any seen before," Alloran instructed his tailor, a snuffily little Och called Opnar the Silk.

"It shall be done, my lord kov," gabbled Opnar.

"After all," said Alloran, looking at himself in the tall mirror in the angle of the room, "after all, this is the first time I have been crowned king." He smiled widely at his own reflection, pleased with the air of authority and regal command he himself sensed emanating from his reflection. "Although I am completely persuaded it will not be the last."

"Assuredly not, my lord kov."

The little Och bid his assistants bring in bales of materials so that a beginning could be made on the choice of fabrics. He was pleased in one way that the kov spoke to him in so familiar a fashion, and in another trembled lest inadvertently a great state secret should slip out and necessitate the removal of his head from his narrow shoulders.

Alloran expressed dissatisfaction with everything he was shown, which was perfectly normal. Opnar did not take out his own fears and ill humor on his assistants. He was in general a gentle man who just wanted to make fine clothes.

"And let there be a great quantity of gold," declared Alloran, forcefully. "Gold lace, gold bullion, gold leaf, gold everywhere. The people must see and know how great a king I am."

That seemed a perfectly logical request and desire to Opnar the Silk. He bobbed and nodded and unrolled more cloth.

A sentry at the double doors bellowed: "Kapt Logan Lakelmi, my lord kov, desires admittance."

Naturally Alloran had installed himself in the finest residence in the town and already plans fomented in his head to increase the size of the place, and build higher walls and more sumptuous chambers. Once he had decided where in his new realms he would build his capital and palace, he would indulge himself in a frenzy of building on a colossal scale.

He gestured negligently with a beringed finger, the sentry vanished to reappear with Kapt Logan Lakelmi.

"My lord kov!" rapped out Lakelmi, saluting.

"Kapt Logan. The news?"

"Is good. The Kataki Strom has gained a great victory over the Prince Majister. A place called Swanton's Bay. The Vallians run in rout, and—"

"Hold, Kapt Logan! Yes, the news is exceedingly good. The Kataki Strom has done well, although I sent him a great reinforcement for his army. But, Kapt Logan, softly. We are all Vallians in Vallia—although you are a mercenary from Loh—do not forget that. When I am king over all, when I am emperor, I shall be the Emperor of Vallia."

"Yes, my lord kov."

"Vallia!" breathed Alloran. There was genuine emotion in him, his eyes bright. "Yes, I shall be Emperor of Vallia, and Vallians will rule in their own country as is proper." He glanced under down-drawn lids at Lakelmi. "But I shall not forget loyal servants, Kapt Logan. You will not be forgotten."

"I thank you. Do you wish to see the lists—?"

"Later."

Kapt Logan Lakelmi, with the red hair of Loh, with his spare, tall, erect figure, looked every inch the fighting man. Now he acted as Alloran's chief of staff, and longed for an independent command. That would come, he felt sure. The kov's plans encompassed many more campaigns and battles, and there would be employment for many mercenaries for seasons to come.

Lakelmi knew something of Alloran's history. The kov, despairing of ever being kov in those peaceful days before the Times of Troubles, when his father was set to live, it seemed, forever, had gone abroad. He had become a mercenary as a very young man. Then he had worked and fought his way up to become a paktun, a mercenary with a reputation. The next step had been to mort-paktun, a warrior elected by his peers, who wore the silver mortil-head on its silk ribbons at his throat. His fame had spread among his own kind. Before he had taken the next step, to become a zhan-paktun, wearing the golden zhantilhead at his throat, tribulations and disaster had fallen upon Vallia.

Alloran, returning home, his father killed by malignant hostiles, had fought for his kovnate, and lost, and fled to the capital of the country, Vondium.

There he had joined the new Vallian army and, given a brigade by the new emperor, had fought well. He had been selected to go to the southwest with an army and to clear out the slavers and all those festering upon the misery of Vallia, and to return all those provinces to the empire.

Just how the corrosive ambition had at last broken through, Lakelmi was not sure. What was certain was that Vodun Alloran had rejected loyalty to the emperor. He had fought for his own kovnate province, had won that back, had taken neighboring provinces, and then declared his own independence.

The next inevitable step was to crown himself King of Southwest Vallia.

With the latest victory against the forces of the Prince Majister of Vallia to crown his efforts, nothing appeared to stand in his way. His ambitions would be rewarded.

Yes, Kapt Logan Lakelmi felt convinced a bright and prosperous future lay ahead.

That was—if he didn't get himself killed in some stupid affray.

The golden glitter of the pakzhan at his throat on its silken cords told everyone that he was a zhanpaktun. That lofty eminence within the mercenary fraternity was to Logan Lakelmi of far greater importance than his present position as Kapt to Kov Vodun.

Now he pushed the rolled lists back under his left arm. Later, the kov said. Well, that suited Lakelmi.

"Jen," he said. "There is a matter of the runaway slaves who have been recaptured—"

"That is a matter for the judiciary, Logan."

"Assuredly. But I would like to offer them the chance to enroll in the ranks. We do need men."

Alloran scowled.

"Men! They cost gold, you pay them, and sometimes they fight and sometimes they run away. And they get killed and where is the gold then?"

Lakelmi remained silent. Opnar held a roll of watered green silk in his hands, unmoving.

"Slaves who show how ungrateful they are by running away must be punished. I hew to the old traditions of Vallia. Slavery is an institution hallowed by age. I could not live in the new Vallia created by the emperor where he has abolished slavery. The man is a fool, there is no denying that."

"Yes, my lord kov."

"After they have been punished, after they have been striped jikaider, you may attempt to recruit them."

"Thank you, my lord kov."

Already schemes jumped into his head. He'd have a private word or three with the Whip-Deldars. They would not stripe the slaves badly, and certainly he'd avoid jikaidering them, a savage punishment in which a left-handed and a right-handed lash crisscrossed their backs with a checkerboard of blood. He'd get himself some prime flint-fodder, by Hlo-Hli!

Then Alloran said with a smile of great craftiness: "But, good Logan, who is to pay the rightful owners of the slaves? Always assuming they do not wish the return of their rightful property."

This emphasis on the rightfulness of it disturbed Lakelmi.

"I will speak to them, my lord kov, and see what may be done."

"Do that, Logan, do that."

"The fact remains, we still need more numbers to fill the ranks of the armies."

"Yes, and I suppose those lists you hold so tightly under your arm tell me of more gold lost with the men of Strom* Rosil's army?"

"Casualties were light—"

"Thank Takar for that!"

"A fresh recruitment should land this afternoon, the argenters have been sighted sailing in without trouble and if each ship carries three hundred men there should be at least six thousand or so."

Lakelmi had deliberately changed the subject of conversation from Strom Rosil. Lakelmi knew that the Kataki Strom had provided most of the gold for the army fighting on the mainland. No one knew where the gold came from; they knew where it went, though, by Lohako the Bold!

"I hope," grunted Alloran in his offensive way, "there are good fighting men amongst them. We have enough of these mewling weaklings you call flint-fodder."

"That is so, my lord kov."

"And I need first-class cavalry. And air!" He glared at the Kapt. "What I would give for some aerial cavalry, and squadrons of fliers, airboats, to give me mastery aloft. As it is, every battle is touch and go in the air."

"This is true of all armies, jen. We shall manage."

After a few more words the audience was finished and Kapt Logan Lakelmi went off about his duties. Alloran threw a bolt of cloth at Opnar and his helpers, swore at them, told them they must find finer stuffs than this shoddy, and went off to eat his customary huge midday meal. After that he went down in panoply to see about the new arrivals whose ships, having anchored or moored up, were discharging their freight, both human and material.

---

* Strom: a rank of nobility equating with count. *A.B.A.*

He was joined on the battlemented walls above the harbor by his nephew, Jen Cedro. The twin suns streamed their magnificence, the air crisped with the tang of openness and the sea and of bracing good health, gulls wheeled and screeched, the breeze blew amicably, and the crowds of folk gathered to watch the new arrivals and speculate upon the treasure brought with them.

The argenters, ships of broad beam and comfortable lines, of plain sail configuration, could hold immense quantities of cargo. Already lines of slaves were shuffling to and fro along the narrow gangplanks, empty-handed outwards and massively burdened on the inward journey. The scent of the sea and the breeze did much to subdue their odors.

The mercenaries came ashore, pretending to lurch about on dry land after their weeks at sea, skylarking, pleased to have arrived safely. Alloran eyed them meanly. Cedro provided the kov with his own telescope, and this Alloran employed to give himself a better idea of the quality of these warriors. He let fall an oath.

"There any many women there—Jikai Vuvushis!"

At the back of the two men, keeping out of the way yet ready instantly to step forward if his advice was sought, Kapt Lakelmi reflected that the Battle Maidens had served the kov well in the past. That view was shared by the entire group of women standing a few paces along the ramparts watching the bright scene spread out below.

All the women's faces turned to the kov, as though a flower-field came alive under the suns.

Standing perfectly still, Lakelmi put his tongue into his cheek so that a bulge jutted above the line of his beard. His lips remained closed. He fancied he was about to enjoy himself.

Chuktar Gilda Failsham, brusque, hard-bitten, her handsome face seasoned by experience, battle, and manipulating men and women, was clearly about to speak her mind. She was a member of the Order of Sisters of the Sword. As a chuktar, Gilda Failsham was in overall command of all the kov's Warrior Maidens and was a well-trained and competent commander. She did not suffer fools gladly, and suffered men even less, although at times acknowledging that they had their uses.

"My lord kov," she called across the small intervening space along the rampart walk. "There are indeed a goodly number of Jikai Vuvushis. For that we should give thanks to the Invisible Twins—do you not agree?"

Intemperate, hot-headed, consumed with self-pride and arrogant he might be: Kov Vodun was not a fool. He had lost much of that gravitas which had once clothed him in the aura of superiority and integrity so comforting to those he commanded. But he was still a man of substance. He could not manage the fulsome smile the situation might call for; he did say: "You are right, Gilda. Completely so. I am sure you are aware of the esteem in which I hold your girls."

Lakelmi sighed inwardly and took his tongue out of his cheek; he felt disappointed, cheated, even, of a spot of amusement.

Among the small group of women, Lyss the Lone also sensed disappointment. How satisfying it would be if only Gilda Failsham—who was a splendid if misguided woman—should fall out with this rascally Kov Vodun! Among any collection of people forming a circle or a court around a great noble there were bound to be jealousies, rivalries, secret hatreds and plots hatching thicker than snow on the Mountains of the North. In her experience, which she would be the first to admit was hardly extensive, she had known precious few courts where intrigue did not flourish.

Around the Emperor of Vallia had assembled people who made up what to her represented all that was best in the new Vallia. Even around the Prince Majister intrigue carried on in whispers and furtive glances. This saddened her. Here she was, risking her life with these Opaz-forsaken blots with Alloran, and for all she knew some loose-lipped bastard could blow away her cover and reveal her to the merciless interrogations of Kov Vodun Alloran and his damned sorcerer and their thrice-damned torturers.

Despite the brilliance of the day, the streaming fires of Zim and Genodras, the cooling breeze, she felt choked up, suffocated.

She favored the lord Cedro with a look that should have melted him where he stood.

Neither he nor his uncle the kov had spoken a single word about what had passed in the room where the dead chavonth and their two dead comrades spoke eloquently of great deeds. Not that she worried over that. It merely pointed out what these people were like.

She'd sent little bandy-legged Lon the Knees off very smartly, swearing him to absolute silence about what he had seen. He had been only too tremblingly anxious to agree. She had a meeting with him later. She didn't want the good Lon running off at the mouth. No, by Vox!

The news of that unhanged villain the Kataki Strom beating Drak in a battle was grim and unpleasant. She knew Drak was safe because had he been killed or captured the news would have gone around like wildfire. That was the obvious common-sense reason she knew Drak was unharmed; the real reason she knew was that had Drak chanced on ill fortune, she would know at once and with the utmost certainty, know it in her heart.

Standing here with these unpleasant people watching more reinforcements for their benighted army streaming ashore, she sighed. She thought of home. Her life had not so far turned out the way she would have wished. She had hoped that Drak's sister, Lela the Princess Majister, known as Jaezila, would have married her brother, Drayseg, named for the emperor. But that had not happened. Lela was off somewhere in Hamal, enamored of a Prince of Hamal called Tyfar, and the pair of them circling around each other without the least clue how to come to grips with what fate had ordained for them.

As for Drayseg, the last she'd heard of him he was a zhanpaktun somewhere in Balintol. All very distressing. And to cap it all this fat luxurious Queen Lush was openly going after Drak! It was unbearable!

Silda Segutoria, known in these unhealthy parts as Lyss the Lone, returned her attention to where it belonged, as a dutiful little Jikai Vuvushi dancing attendance upon a damned traitorous kov—the bastard.

Four

In which Lyss the Lone keeps a straight face

The complex series of ceremonies, rituals and religious observances that would transform Vodun Alloran, Kov of Kaldi, into King Vodun of Southwest Vallia, were planned to run for a whole six days. This, said the know-alls, was pitching it just about right. Any less amount of time would indicate faint-heartedness upon the part of the kov, a lack of certainty, even more probably, a lack of the wherewithal. To run longer than a Kregen week would smack of inflated ambition and ego beyond control, which would—inevitably said the wiseacres—bring down the just vengeance of the gods.

A number of dissatisfactions gnawed at Alloran, among which he felt most resentment that he was not able to crown a queen. Mercenaries seldom marry in the nature of their employment, unless they settle down to a long-term bodyguard occupation. His plans to marry the Kovneva of Rahartdrin, and thus lend color to his claims upon the island, had failed to materialize.

He slid his rapier up and down in its scabbard with his left fist wrapped into the fancy hilt. He scowled. The old biddy! Katrin Rashumin, Kovneva of Rahartdrin, had fought his armies from the hedges, from the ditches, had battled from the mountains, and had at the end escaped somewhere across the sea.

All pursuit had failed to discover her.

Well, one day she'd be found, dead or alive. When that day dawned, Alloran would think afresh how best to act. Possession—that was the key! He held Rahartdrin fast in his grip. Soon his armada would sail north for Tezpor.

The other dissatisfaction lay all around him.

He sat slumped back in a huge winged armchair, his feet in gleaming boots stuck arrogantly upon the polished table. Each time he rammed his rapier down, the chape hit the floor. Well, golden chapes would be no problem now, for the island was potentially enormously rich and he'd sweat everyone here, make 'em work. He'd buy or capture more than enough slaves so as to make every kool of the island give forth its wealth.

But—this was Rahartdrin, this town was Rashumsmot. They were not home. They were not Kaldi and Kalden.

And this town wasn't even the proper capital of the island. That was Rahartium, and that place was in a mess. He'd tried to prevent the fires, and then to extinguish them; the task was beyond the powers even of the fabled Nath of legend and song.

He took the conqueror's grain of comfort in the knowledge that to be seen donning the crown in a foreign and defeated country aggrandized him. He could always arrange further coronations to be held in his own provincial capital of Kalden.

When he was emperor, of course, he'd have to be crowned and enthroned in Vondium.

That was all ordained.

He had no doubts about that outcome whatsoever.

Well—he swung his boots off the table and stood up ready to march out to the waiting crowds—well, so far all had gone as prophesied. Arachna[*] had always been right. In the future his confidence could only increase.

The bedlam of noise of the crowds hit him like a surge of intoxication as he stepped out onto the balcony alone. He waved to the mob. The declining suns showered faces and heads with slanting glories of emerald and ruby, brought blood-red winks of light from the weapons of guards and soldiers, sheened rivulets of viridian down their armor.

Among the crowds and posted at vantage points around the square, somberly clad men and women watched all that went forward. At the first sight of anyone lifting a bow to take a shot at the kov, a far faster trigger finger would contract, loosing a crossbow bolt to snuff out the impious idiot's life without compunction.

Waving, managing a grimace that would pass for a smile at the distance of the balcony from the ground, Alloran showed himself to his people. To his new people. Most of the civilian crowds were native to Rahartdrin. His functionaries worked on transferring their allegiance wholeheartedly to him. That was a skill. He used men and women with skills, and used them skillfully after his own fashion.

---

* Arachna. Prescot says he has translated this name as Arachna because the original in Kregish was of extraordinary length and complexity and inappropriate for normal terrestrial use. *A.B.A.*

Nath the Goader had managed to convince his questioners that he had known nothing of the loosened bars of the cages. He was completely innocent. When this was reported to Alloran, the kov had merely said: "The rast's duty was to know all concerning the wild beasts. He failed. He is of no further use."

Then, he'd paused, and a real smile passed over his face. "Yet he can still be of use—in place of handling the beasts he can feed them—with his own body."

His retainers and functionaries showed they appreciated the jest.

Now he waved one last time, and stepped back from the balcony feeling the solid sound from the mobs as being, if not totally, then convincingly genuine.

Using people as he did, Alloran had no use for a failed tool, no compunction in its disposal.

The folk who served him knew this.

When he went to the newly decorated robing room to change his clothes from the ornate and easily distinguished applause clothes to equally magnificent but far more elegant evening wear, his servants made no mistakes.

Clad in gorgeous silks and dripping with jewelry, Kov Vodun strode into the chamber he already called the banqueting hall.

The late owner of this villa still dangled over the town's battlemented walls, and some portions of his anatomy remained intact.

Food and drink in gargantuan quantities was served. The banquet catered for a hundred diners, and of them all only Naghan the Obese and Glenda the Slender ate more than the kov.

Quite a few among that hundred flushed and gluttonous crowd drank more than the kov...

Afterwards, replete, Alloran was escorted to his private withdrawing room. He waved away a pearl-draped Sylvie who would have waited upon him, and went in alone. The door was closed on his order: "In one bur!"*

He sat on the divan, kicked off his light slippers, hoisted his legs up and so, putting his head upon a silken pillow, nodded off to sleep. If he dreamed, he had no memory of it when the door opened and a flunkey, nervously, said: "One bur, my lord kov."

He roused himself; servants provided golden bowls filled with warm scented water, and softly fluffy towels. Refreshed, he allowed his slippers to be placed upon his feet. He stood up, adjusted his rapier and dagger belts, golden-linked and gem-encrusted, automatically clicked his rapier up and down, and, satisfied, left the withdrawing room.

Along the corridors guards stood at measured intervals. They wore

---

* bur: the Kregan hour, 48 to a day, each of 50 murs. A bur is 40 Earth minutes long. *A.B.A.*

gaudy costume for fighting men; but they were all well-tested by now and Alloran trusted them as far as any prudent ruler trusts his bodyguards.

Full-fleshed, confident, Alloran strode along and the subservient lackeys followed after, as was proper.

He did not have far to walk before he reached the double doors covered in dark green velvet, studded with golden nails and decorated with a border of engraved golden panels. He'd had that door installed. When he built his own palace he would still arrange a series of chambers beyond a door just such as this that would still not be a long walk away.

Farther along in a cross corridor walled in blue marble stood Battle Maidens on sentry duty. Alloran merely flicked a quick glance at them, before lifting his heavily ringed right hand and knocking three deliberate times upon the golden lockplate. A girl appeared in the blue-marbled corridor looking with a fixity of purpose upon each Jikai Vuvushi. She could smell the distant odors of stale cooking, yet Lyss the Lone did not wrinkle up her nostrils in disgust. In this place and at this time that could be misconstrued, could prove a most expensive mistake.

She moved smartly from one girl to the next, and as she did so she looked down the corridor. Sideways on to her, Kov Vodun was knocking upon that mysterious green door.

Lyss the Lone very much wanted to know what could be beyond that ornate door.

Very much indeed.

If Alloran continued his routine tomorrow, as he had for the past few days, then at this precise time he should be knocking on the door. That was the reason Lyss had taken it upon herself to inspect the girls of the guard at this precise time.

Alloran's current light of love, Chemsi the Fair, lived in a plush apartment in the top floor of the west wing of the villa. Lyss felt confident Alloran did not have a woman behind the green door he visited every evening.

Chuktar Gilda Failsham, despite being a member of the powerful Order of the Sisters of the Sword, kept her light of love, Ortyg the Burly, in vast comfort in the upper rooms of The Blindell and Korf.

All over the town there were plenty of men and women being kept as a light o' love by someone of position and wealth. These were facts of life that had to be accepted as perfectly normal for the times.

She had stopped long enough and must cast a most critical eye over Sosie the Slop, who was always the worst turned-out girl in Lyss's pastang. Although a Jiktar, she commanded merely a company-sized pastang of sixty girls, and Gilda, although a Chuktar, commanded the small three-hundred-sixty-strong guard regiment. This was a perfectly normal arrangement for bodyguards and differed from the regular structures of the line.

"Well, Sosie, and what is it tonight—ah!"

"It came off in my hand, Jik—I swear it!"

"Oh, I believe you, Sosie, I do. You will just have to sew your buttons on much more tightly. Won't you?"

"Yes, Jik."

Turning away, Lyss said, not unkindly: "I'm glad I'm not a man with whom you might fall in love, Sosie. He'd go in dire peril, believe you me."

Swinging back, Lyss stared stony-faced at Sosie. The girl's full lips twitched, a barely perceptible tremor. Then her face became as stony as that of Lyss.

Satisfied, Jiktar Lyss the Lone marched briskly off.

"As Dee Sheon is my witness!" she said to herself, crossly, striding along. "If a task is set to your hands, then that task must be performed as well as you possibly can and with all your heart and mind and muscle. I hate a sloppy regiment. So I drill and train and discipline the girls—and for what? So they can go and fight my friends who serve with Drak! It is really monstrous."

She could see the funny side of it, though...

As a Sister of the Rose, she knew she was a member of the very best sorority there was without having to think about it. The Sisters of the Sword, the Grand Ladies, all the other female Orders, secret, martial, mystical, charitable, it mattered not, paled beside the magnificence that was the Order of the Sisters of the Rose.

Among the regiment commanded by Gilda were a bare handful of girls from the SOR, and none knew Silda Segutoria. She had kept away from the new arrivals, and would take enormous care investigating them, unseen, before introducing herself as Lyss the Lone.

She was off duty in half a bur and would then keep her appointment with Lon the Knees. She would far rather be breaking and entering the rooms behind that infuriating green velvet door with its tawdry golden ornaments.

Reaching the left-hand guardroom reserved for the Jikai Vuvushis, she was met by gusts of laughter, a quantity of horseplay, a ferocious squabble over the ownership of a pair of black tights, and a sweeter scent by far than most of the stinks in the villa. She ducked a thrown hairbrush and sidled past two girls indulging in a little arm-wrestling, and so reached the small cubicle-sized space reserved for the Jiktars.

All this was a nonsense, of course. She didn't mind sharing a guardroom with the girls, who equated with the men called swods in the army, the girls having a variety of colorful names. Because the villa was so small for all the people Kov Alloran crammed into the place, everyone had to share. At least, she and the other Jiktars did have a private space, and a personal locker and a peg to hang their duty uniforms.

She shucked off the silly tabard-like garment revealing her black fighting leathers. The tabard was stiff with threaded wire—not gold wire. Kov Vodun was not so enamored of dressing up his bodyguards as to throw gold away like that. Rumor had it that all the colors would change once Alloran crowned himself king. She hung the tabard on the peg and heard the smash and crash of something glasslike and fragile breaking outside. The girls were in riotous mood tonight.

They were a good bunch, really. If only they fought for the Prince Majister, for Drak, instead of his bitter foe!

"Got a man for tonight, then, Lyss?" shouted Jiktar Nandi the Tempestuous, shoving her head into the cubicle.

"No."

"Of course," said Nandi, cheeks aglow, hair falling over her forehead. "I should have known better than to ask. We don't call you Lone for nothing."

"You ready to take over, Nandi?"

"I am. But what's your hurry?"

"No hurry. Nothing special. When you bring my girls in I want to be gone. That's all."

"Been rucking 'em again, have you? You'll be one of the first to get a shaft through your back, come a battle."

Nandi was only half-joking. Everyone in the regiment knew the strictness of Lyss's control over her pastang.

Without replying, Lyss sat on the cramped three-legged stool and took off her villa shoes, started to pull on her tall black boots.

Nandi did not offer to help.

Lyss was too bloody-minded to ask.

In this she recognized that herself, the real person sitting here, Silda Segutoria, was perilously close to being sucked whole into this strict and harsh woman, Lyss the Lone. She thought of herself as Lyss for obvious security reasons. To think of herself as Silda, twin to Valin her brother of whom she had not heard for season after aching season, was to court disaster.

She looked up under her eyelashes, both hands on the straps of her left boot.

"When Sosie the Slop trundles in, she is down for four burs' extra duty in the washroom. I'll tell her Deldar on my way out."

"Washroom? Just as well. If she caught punishment duty in the kitchen she'd crottle* everything she touched."

A thin flicker of a smile touched Lyss's lips. Silda would have laughed out loud in delight.

---

* crottle: A word describing the effects of burning or charring, of over-cooking food so that it becomes tasteless and generally inedible. *A.B.A.*

Nandi took herself off, and Lyss, after a last quick look in the tiny oval mirror and a pat at her hair, followed.

She stamped down to wriggle her boots on comfortably, and gave her weapons belts that familiar hitch that settled them comfortably about the swell of her hips. Never one to let herself be untidy or in discomfort, Silda, in the shape of Lyss the Lone, followed that maxim to the best of her ability.

She headed directly for the nearest exit of the villa. Many of the massive and ornate statues had been removed merely to provide that amount of extra space. The marble floor looked paler and more polished in squares and star-shapes where the statues had stood for so long. Lyss moved with a sure easy pace, not swinging about too much, keeping in a straight line. People passed, going about their business. She felt a pang at the sight of slaves in their gray breechclouts and kept her face set in that stony mask.

Raised voices, as of a group of people all talking at random, reached her from the hall leading to the exit. She walked on and saw the group entering the building, a gaggle of the new arrivals being led to take up whatever duties they had been assigned. If many more bodies were crammed in here the walls would burst.

She stopped abruptly. She did not swear out loud; but the soft curve of her lips tightened.

To herself, she said: "Oh, damn! Just my luck!"

In the approaching group and laughing up at a tall Bowman of Loh, walked Mandi Volanta. Mandi had been through Lancival at the same time as Silda Segutoria, and it was sure that she would recognize her. Lancival, where the Sisters of the Rose trained their girls in many arts and educated them for life on Kregen, bred a very special kind of person. Silda was immediately aware of the stab of sorrow and then of anger that Mandi Volanta had turned against the majority of her school friends and against the emperor.

There was nothing else to do but swing about and go marching off back the way she had come and by a circuitous route reach the next exit along, which lay past the Corridor of Bones.

She looked neither right nor left and, with her nose stuck arrogantly in the air, strode on past the detail of Chuliks on guard. For all her attitude of haughty superiority, she was aware of the Chuliks' yellow skin, of their green-dyed pigtails, their round black eyes, and most particularly of the upthrust tusks set in the corners of their mouths. They wore good quality armor and bright uniforms, and their weapons were clean and sharp. Born to be mercenaries, Chuliks, and highly prized.

When she reached the outside air the suns were nearly gone.

Crowds meandered about the streets waiting to gawp at the illuminations to be provided by the kov in this night's contribution to the festivities of his coronation, and no doubt hoping that free wine would flow in torrents.

A musky odor hung on the air, compounded of sweat and dust and the exhalations of many people. The streets echoed to the surf roar of the crowds, and the occasional shrill yells of laughter piercing through did not sound incongruous. Lyss hated it all.

All these people should be shouting for Drak and the emperor. Still, she could hardly find it in her heart to blame them too harshly. Those ferocious Chuliks back there and all the other warriors under Kov Vodun's command would quickly smash them back to their new obedience.

Already there were drunks lurching disgustingly about the streets.

Taverns were doing, in the liquid jargon of the profession, a Roaring Trade. Dedicated drinkers were not hanging about waiting for job lots of free wine from the kov that might or might not materialize. The worshipers of the circle around Beng Dikkane, patron saint of all ale drinkers in Paz, were not going to soil their lips with wine, free or not. So the liquid refreshment flowed and, inevitably with people of small brain capacity and inferior character, the drunks staggered about.

With the last upflung rays of red and green scoring the darkening sky the twin suns sank, Zim and Genodras settling down for the night. And, to relieve them on their eternal vigil over the face of Kregen, the fourth moon floated into the evening sky, resplendent with light. She of the Veils shone down in fuzzy pinks and golds, lighting the whole world in her own special and mysterious way.

Silda—off duty she was firmly going to be Silda and not Lyss—always felt comforted when She of the Veils drifted serenely in the night sky. She knew that many of her special friends felt that way, too.

Now the four hulking lads, two sets of twins, whose names were Ob, Dwa, So and Ley Dohirti, must have been imbibing very freely very early. Otherwise not a one of them in his right mind would have offered to insult a Jikai Vuvushi. They each carried a heavy wooden cudgel, as was the right of any free man of Vallia.

With the four clumsy farm lads, and undoubtedly the cause of the trouble, Nath the Sly urged them on. He was short, slightly built, squinted, carried a knife and was a very devil in determining to have his own back on the whole world for not providing him with a powerful fighting man's body that would attract the girls. He was a stylor at the farm, and ink smudges stained behind his ears and along his fingers. He squinted up at Silda, leering.

"A prime one this, lads! Ready for the plucking."

Nath the Sly had heard those words used in a mummer's play only three days ago, the actors prancing in a canvas booth, and he considered them apt to the situation and himself as an educated man for quoting poetry.

"A real right beauty," said Ob Dohirti, and hiccoughed.

His twin, Dwa, spluttered out: "I'll fight you for the first—"

"Plenty there for us all," cut in Nath the Sly, anxious to avoid internecine warfare. "Grab her now!"

Silda did not know if these louts had chosen their spot with cunning skill or if the fortune of Coggog the Unmentionable had blessed them. She did know that as she swiveled to face one pair of twins, her hand going for her rapier hilt, the other pair rushed in from the back.

Used to snaring recalcitrant animals on the farm, the Dohirti twins used a twisted rope with great skill. Silda felt the strands lap about her, tangling her arm.

"Keep her quiet!" yelped Nath the Sly.

The spot in question, either chosen by these five cramphs or by the chance of Coggog's favor, gave the opportunity for the twins to drag Silda into the black mouth of an alley penned between sheer brick walls. Burn marks, like distorted clouds, showed in the moon's light on the brickwork. Windows were boarded up. Silda knew the place all right, for it was a structure selected by Alloran to be demolished to make way for his building extension program.

She kicked and got a black boot into a gut, and then thrashed aside with the other, and missed a vital spot, and then she thought it was time to start screaming.

Nath the Sly took out his knife, held it by the blade, and clouted Silda over the head.

At once she slumped, her body went slack, and she fell all asprawl with the rope into the blackness of the alley.

Five

Of Lon's Fine Feathers

Silda toppled forward into blackness and slid herself forward over worn cobbles. A single tap from a knife hilt wielded by a scrawny runt like this specimen wasn't going to knock her out. Her head donged a trifle, as though the famous bells of Beng Kishi tolled muffled.

Her onward movement stripped the tangling rope away from her arm.

This situation was very familiar indeed from her years of training at Lancival. There they taught their girls how to take care of themselves.

The men were already arguing fiercely among themselves.

"Grab her, you great hulu!"

"Git outta the way!"

"Can't see a thing—"

"That's my foot!"

A rough hand raked along the cobbles after Silda's boot.

Obligingly, she rolled over onto her back, peering back to see the silhouettes of the men against the vague luminosity of the moon-drenched street. She felt regret, as she lifted her boot, that as a zorca-rider she did not wear spurs. Still, the boots were solid. The heel crunched down with a nice juicy smack.

One of the louts yelled blue bloody murder.

In the next instant Silda was on her feet and the sound of the rapier as it whipped from the scabbard jolted half an ounce of sense back into the drunken heads.

"She ain't—"

"She's got her sword!"

Nath the Sly felt cheated.

"Get on her, you fools!"

One of the men surged forward, a black batlike shape.

Silda had no wish to slay them. Oh, yes, there were plenty of girls who would joy in sticking a length of tempered steel into their bellies, one after the other. But Silda's emotions were held in check. She was a cool fighting machine, and as such not about to spill blood that could be avoided. Her cover remained more important than simple vengeance.

Delicately, she pinked that outstretched arm.

The fellow yelped as though branded and stumbled back.

"Onkers! Idiots!" Silda poised ready for anything.

"Get her!" screeched Nath. He did not lunge forward, preferring to leave the heavy stuff to his half-drunken companions.

Standing in the darkness she was practically invisible to them, while they stood out as black silhouettes.

"Run off, you unhanged cramphs, or I'll spit you through, one after the other! *Bratch!*"

They did not bratch there and then, although they hung back. Nath whispered ferociously and Silda just glimpsed in time the upraised arm and the flung cudgel.

The common folk of Vallia are adept and swift at throwing cudgels and knives.

She ducked. The wood clipped her across the forehead, bounced, clattered against the cobbles. She felt a wave of dizziness sweep over her, and ground her teeth together and fought the ugly wave of weakness that dragged at her knees. She remained upright, warily watching, and she used her training to push away the pain.

"Right, you rasts. You're done for now. By Vox!" she got out, half-gasping. "I'll have your ears!"

Her head felt light, like a feather, and as she moved forward that silly head seemed to want to go ahead on its own, her body stumbling after. She flicked the rapier into line. The little 'un. He was the bastard to go for...

One of the men husked out: "I'm off. Come on—she's probably got no gold, anyway."

Silda lined up, poised, and lunged.

With a cry of pure horror Nath the Sly leaped like a salmon, just avoided the blade that would have skewered his right arm. He took the point in his elbow and for a breathless heartbeat Silda fancied the rapier would hang up entangled in his bones. She whipped it free and immediately slashed it hard down the arm of the next fellow.

That settled it.

Their clumsy farm shoes clattered on cobbles.

This unpleasant incident, Silda was aware, was one of the ugly results of drink.

Except—except that little 'un, the one the others called Nath, had clearly been intent on dark business.

Well, there were thousands of Naths on Kregen, named for the fabled hero of many an epic legend. Nath was just about the most common and most favored name in Kregen. The precious metal Nathium was reputed to hold magical qualities in its silky texture. She put her left hand to her forehead, and felt stickiness.

She had not drawn her main gauche. The whole stupid incident hardly seemed to merit great concern. She took her hand away from her forehead and lightly touched the brown leather and canvas bag slung at her side.

Poor hulus! If she'd... Well, they'd have either run screaming, or tried to scream without faces...

It was absolutely imperative then for her to lean against the greasy wall and to suck in draughts of the evening air. She did not so much shudder as let the shakes cleanse the feeling of dirt from her.

After wiping her forehead, she cleaned the rapier on the oiled rag all prudent warriors carried against this kind of eventuality, and sauntered out onto the street.

There was, of course, no sign of the four drunks and their evil genius, Nath. What his sobriquet might be, Silda did not know. Probably it was the Cunning, or the Clever, or the Fixer.

Plenty of the girls she knew would piously hope that the little runt's elbow would seize up and would never work properly again.

And, being apim, Homo sapiens, he had only two arms.

The various races of Kregen blessed with four arms, or a tail hand, were, she had often thought, extremely lucky. To have four arms in a fight! Or to have a tail with a dagger strapped to the tip, or, like the Pachaks, a hand with which to grasp a blade... How perfectly splendid that would be!

Walking along, she kept herself more on the qui vive than she would have done before the fracas. Lon the Knees had said that he did not think The Leather Bottle would be the nicest place for a lady to meet him, and had suggested an inn, The Silver Lotus, which he considered suitable. In the ordinary course of his life, Lon would never dream of entering so expensive and so—to him—high class an establishment. But he'd mumbled something to her about a deal he could arrange, and she'd gathered he was going to do something particular to find the silver stivers necessary for admittance.

People like Lon, and those louts back there, habitually worked in copper or bronze coins. Silver was hailed with joy. Gold—wha' that?

Just about the only way they'd get their Diproo-fingers on gold was the way they'd tried in the alley. And, to be sure, during the Times of Troubles many lawless men had snatched more gold than they, their fathers and grandfathers, and sons and grandsons, would ordinarily see in their combined lifetimes.

Lon the Knees, face aflame, nose a purple beacon, eyes brimming, looked splendiferous. He glowed. He waited under the dismounting porch so that he might enter the inn with the lady, and glory in the feeling that all eyes would be fixed upon his companion.

"Lahal, Lon."

"Lahal, my lady."

Silda composed her face. Then she contrived a dazzling smile. She really wanted to bust a gut laughing.

Lon! Lon the Knees! His famous bandy legs were encased in riding breeches that almost fitted, and their color owed more to judiciously applied brown chalk than to natural cloth. He'd borrowed those, that was for sure. Yet they were not too far removed from the usual Vallian buff breeches the gentlefolk wore.

His boots glittered. Silda did not make too close an inspection of them. But that superb polished shine, that had come only from loving ministrations right here under the dismounting porch, for most people's boots were dusty if they walked a pace or two. Her own were a sorry mess compared with Lon's.

And his coat! Now where the hell had he got that from? Originally the garment had been a khiganer, a heavy brown tunic that fastened by a wide flap along the left side of the body and along the left shoulder. The neck came in a variety of styles, and this specimen possessed what appeared to Silda to be the highest, stiffest, most constricting neck she'd ever seen fitted to a khiganer. Lon's chin jutted out like a chick sticking his neck out of the egg.

The arms of the khiganer had been cut off to reveal the loose flowing sleeves of Lon's shirt. The color was ivory, for he did not wear the normal bands of color denoting allegiances. Silda was prepared to take a bet that Lon was wearing sleeves and no shirt at all.

He wore no hat. This was probably, Silda decided, because he had been unable to beg, borrow or steal one of the typical Vallian floppy hats with the brave feathers. His own headgear, a skull cap, a head band, would be quite inappropriate here.

The main gauche was thrust down into his belt and from somewhere he'd cobbled together a quite respectable scabbard for the dagger.

Lon quivered.

"Shall we go in, my lady?"

"By all means, Lon. I am looking forward to a pleasant evening."

"Shall you wish to see the illuminations, my lady?"

He wouldn't normally speak like that. He was trying to suit his language to the importance of the occasion.

She halted.

"Lon—two things. One: speak nicely but normally. Two: Don't keep on my lady all the time. My name is Lyss. Use it when you have to."

Lon swallowed.

"Yes, my la—Yes, Lyss."

So that meant that Silda was back into the persona of Lyss the Lone again. She sighed and went up the steps with Lon into The Silver Lotus. She'd be damned happy when all this present untidiness was over and she could go home and see Drak. That made her think of that awful Queen Lush. The fat scheming bitch! No doubt at this very minute she was fluttering her eyelashes at Drak, and oohing and aahing, and arching her back—the fat cow—and stinking of too much scent and—and—and she was with Drak! It was just about too much.

Still and all, Silda was a Sister of the Rose, and so Silda must be Lyss and soldier on.

The buttons of the khiganer along Lon's left collar bone, fashioned of pewter, had their embossed representation of Beng Debrant almost polished away. The buttons down his left side started out in exactly the same way, the pewter shining nicely. Halfway down, the buttons were made of bone, some with inscribed and worn away pictures, the lower ones plain. Toward the bottom of the tunic the buttons were of wood. Lon kept his right hand casually across his stomach as much as he could, concealing those wooden buttons.

The Sisters of the Rose learning at Lancival were told that if a person made an effort, if they did the very best they could, and tried to their utmost, then, win or lose, they couldn't be faulted. The results of those contests lay with the Invisible Twins made manifest in the light of Opaz.

Lon had made a tremendous effort.

Silda gave him full marks.

She was uncomfortably aware, with a feeling she tried to tell herself was not self-conscious superiority, that in Lon's mind no thought of any sexual approaches existed. He was just pleased to be out, and to be seen out, with a young lady of so different a background from those girls he habitually consorted with. And the very thought made Silda feel conscious of her unworthiness. How her sisters in the SoR would chortle at her now! And—she'd tell 'em all to go hang!

The inn was of the middling quality, clean, and the wine varied from reasonable to good. If some patron felt the rush of blood to his head and ordered a bottle of Jholaix, there was just the chance one might be found. The chance was very slender, for of all the wines of these parts, Jholaix was acknowledged to be the finest. Its cost was astronomical. She turned to Lon as they sat in the seats indicated by the serving girl, and said: "Something very simple, Lon, for me."

He stared at her with a concerned expression.

"Now, my la—Lyss—in the lights, I can see. Your head—there is blood—"

"Oh!" she said crossly. "Didn't I wipe it all off?"

She hauled out the kerchief and spat on it and scrubbed, wondering what the hell her mentors would say if they could see her.

"Each time we meet, Lon, I am bloody. Take heed."

"How? I mean—what—?"

"Louts, drunken, out for a laugh and robbery."

"The Watch is lax, I think." Then Lon let one eyelid droop. "Which is fortunate, at times..."

Silda laughed.

The serving girl was a Fristle, all laypom-colored fur, and a saucy tail, and brushed whiskers, clad in a yellow apron. She was not, therefore, a slave. In her meek obedience Silda sensed much of a slave's mentality.

"I am parched. I would like to start with a glass of parclear. The fizzy sherbet will clear my throat."

"Two," said Lon, importantly. "And, after?"

The Fristle fifi said: "There is quidgling pie, roast chicken, any kind of fish you require, ordel pudding—"

"Ordel pudding for me," said Silda unthinkingly.

"Two," said Lon again.

"Wine?" Silda twiddled her fingers on the table. "As I said, keep it simple."

Lon said, "What would you like?"

Decisively, Silda said, "Kensha, with herbs."

"Two," said Lon.

Was that a slight nervous gesture to the wallet-pouch strapped to his belt? Silda fancied she'd have to be highly tactful if it came to push of pike, as Nath na Kochwold would say.

Kensha wine, a delicate rosé, was best drunk with a sprinkling of herbs into the glass. They gave the wine a lift, a fragrance, and turned it from merely a good cheap wine into what was truly a fine vintage.

So the evening progressed, eating, drinking and talking. The usual subjects of conversation were dealt with gravely by Lon. He was seething and bubbling inside with delirious pleasure. He'd live on this night's dinner for the rest of his life in memory, drawing spiritual nourishment when he drank up his cabbage soup and gnawed a heel of cheese or a crust of bread. This girl was superb!

He told her that Nath the Goader had vanished. He, himself, had been exonerated. All the same, he'd sweated blood for just a little too long...

When he apologized for his coarseness of expression, Silda laughed out loud, hugely amused. She was enjoying this evening as she'd never imagined she would. The day had been fraught enough, Opaz knew.

The Silver Lotus was doing moderate business, people entering and leaving, and folk nipping in for a quick one before the illuminations. A brilliant laugh from the opposite corner of the alcove drew Silda's attention. A woman was in the act of throwing her head back, laughing with open enjoyment at some sally of her partner's. Her black skin sheened with health, her raven's-wing hair shone like an ebony waterfall, and her eyes gleamed with a challenging brilliance. Her ankle length gown of eye-catching emerald green suited her superbly, and the silver adornments were in perfect taste.

On her left shoulder a little furry likl-likl crouched contentedly munching on the scraps of food she passed up, the little pet no doubt proud of his silver-studded green collar. The silver chain attaching him to the woman's left wrist glinted as she moved.

Her companion's teeth shone in his black face as he laughed with her, gallant in decent Vallian buff, with bright bands of color to indicate his loyalties. They made a dazzling couple. Silda warmed to them. She did not know their names, nor was she ever likely to; yet she sensed this unknown woman was relaxing and letting the evening take over, rejoicing in her good fortune, letting life be lived and flow by.

A noisy party entered, all chaffing the old jokes between themselves, and sat down around a table across from the couple who had so aroused Silda's admiration. The water dropped in the clepsydra, and a serving girl turned the glass over, and Silda began to think that she must now see about the possibly unpleasant business of ending this enjoyable evening.

She had ascertained that Lon the Knees really did know nothing about whose hand had loosed the bars of the wild animals' cages. He genuinely had no idea who might have done that hideous deed. He had not shared whatever macabre fate was reserved for Nath the Goader only because it was proved by subsequent inspection that his bars had not been loosed, that the very size and ferocity of the churmod had splintered them through.

Lon swallowed and lifted the last of the herb-fragrant Kensha in his glass.

"Shall I—that is, Lyss—do you wish to see me again?"

The true answer was that Lon had failed her. She had hoped to pursue the lead afforded by that mysterious hand loosening the bars of the cages. With that as a dead end—why, there was no reason to see Lon again, was there?

He drank the last of the wine down, looking at her. She wetted her lips and realized she could not destroy his happiness so callously.

"Of course, Lon!"

His smile in that florid face would have warmed up the Ice Floes of Sicce. He reached down to his wallet on his belt, and Silda saw his face go stiff.

The smile dwindled. The color fled from his cheeks, and his nose lost its purple sheen, and shriveled.

"Lyss! My money—it is gone!"

Six

Tavern brawling—Silda style

No doubt whatsoever entered Silda's mind that Lon was lying, was trying to trick her into paying. She had summed up the animal handler, and she trusted her own judgment.

Lon had gone to a tremendous amount of trouble for tonight. He had obtained his wonderful costume from somewhere. He had silver enough in his wallet to pay for what they had consumed. She was convinced of that.

So—some thieving bastard had stolen Lon's money.

Instantly, she said: "Don't fret over paying, Lon. That presents no problem."

"But! My lady! I cannot—"

"I'll have a word with the landlord. Thieves will do the reputation of his establishment no good at all."

"I'd like to—"

"Quite."

Something light touched Silda's side, a feather-like glancing touch she barely appreciated. She opened her mouth to chide Lon and to tell him to brace up, when a shrill agonized shriek burst up from the seat at her side.

She looked down, shocked.

A round furry bundle rolled onto the seat.

She knew what the little animal was, at once. The spinlikl, with a body of multi-colored fur, and eight long prehensile limbs each equipped with a powerful clutching hand, was one of the favorite methods by which the Thieves of Kregen secured their loot. A spinlikl could move about with amazing speed and deftness, quiet as Death, and open locks and bolts, steal treasure, and return to its master or mistress worth a fortune.

She turned sharply as the spinlikl, screaming, gathered itself on seven of its eight limbs.

The eighth limb glistened brightly with blood.

The animal sprang past Silda. Swiveling her head she saw it clambering up to the shoulder and neck of the man who sat at the next table along. His face was that of a hairy Brokelsh, uncouth yet powerful, and now that lowering visage was black with anger.

"What have you done to my lovely Lord Hofchin?" the Brokelsh bellowed. He grabbed the flailing arm and blood spurted. "You have fairly cut his hand off!" And, indeed, the poor creature's hand dangled limply with the blood pouring out.

Silda knew what the poor creature had done. After he had stolen Lon's money, he'd opened her brown canvas sack and groped inside with that hand that was now half lopped off. Served him right, of course, yet he was not to blame. His master, who trained him in all the arts of thievery, was the true culprit.

Two other hairy Brokelsh sat with the thief. Now they stood up, hands going to their belts where weapons dangled. They were all decently dressed in finery that chimed well with the festivities, bright colors, and sashes, feathers and the wink of imitation gems.

Lon stumbled up onto his feet, passionate with rage.

"You rasts! You stole my money! I'll have you—"

He started around the table and Silda snapped, sharply and impatiently: "Lon! Sit down!"

"But—"

The thief snarled his words, quite as angry as Lon. "Have me, hey? I'll have your hide!"

One of his companions stared down the dining room. "By Diproo the Nimble-fingered, Branka! Keep it down. Here comes the landlord..."

This Branka, white-faced and savage at the damage to his spinlikl Lord

Hofchin, would have none of it. He ripped out his clanxer and started for the table where Silda and Lon still sat.

Silda stood up.

"Landlord!" she called in a voice accustomed to ordering regiments about. "This rast has stolen our money. I intend to have it back off him. You may send for the Watch if you wish."

With that, Silda Segutoria, the daughter of Seg Segutorio, started for the thieves. She drew her rapier.

"Lyss!" Alarmed, Lon dragged himself up, lugging out the main gauche.

This thief, hight Branka, sneered at the rapier.

"That pinprick, missy? I'll show you what real tavern brawling is all about!"

"Like this?" said Silda, and snatched up in her left hand the chair and hurled it full in the fellow's face. Her left arm, hard and muscled from long hours with the Jikvar, powered the chair so that it smashed the fellow's nose, knocked out an eye, and sent him tumbling backwards into his companions.

She didn't stop there.

The screams from the staggering men meant nothing. She snicked the blade through the arm of one of them, withdrew, slashed it across the guts of the next so that his fancy clothes all fell down, and then she was on Branka.

He was shrieking and gobbling on blood. Half his teeth were knocked down his gullet. His eye dangled. His nose spouted blood everywhere.

Silda ignored all that, carefully making sure she did not touch the mess. The spinlikl crouched on the floor, whimpering, sucking his damaged limb.

Silda dived her own fist into Branka's wallet and dragged out a handful of coins.

"Lon!"

He was just standing there, goggle-eyed.

"Yes, Lyss—"

"How much?"

He swallowed. "Uh—seven sinvers. Oh, and four obs."

Again Silda did not doubt Lon's honesty. If he said seven silver sinvers and four copper obs, that was what had been stolen. She sorted the money out and started to put the rest back, then she paused.

"The rest of this is stolen, too, I suppose. Landlord!"

He was standing there with his hands wrapped in his yellow apron and his eyeballs out on stalks.

"Yes, my lady. I am here. The blood—"

"You've seen plenty of that before. Keep the money and let the Watch sort it out. You have a nice place here, but I wouldn't let your clientele know that you allow this kind of thief free access."

"But, my lady—"

"We are leaving now. Tell the Watch. Oh, and what is the reckoning?"

"No, no, my lady," he babbled. "Please, say no more. You have been troubled in The Silver Lotus. I am desolated, please, my lady, with my compliments..."

"That is considerate, under the circumstances. Here, your money, Lon."

Lon wasn't sure if the money could ever make up for the glory of the moment. What a girl this Lyss was!

As they went out, Silda noticed the black couple staring after them eager and alive and thoroughly enjoying the free entertainment.

The lady stroked the furry likl-likl crouched on her shoulder, and the creature's bright eyes regarded with great wisdom the fracas upon the floor and the maimed form of the spinlikl. They were not related much as species, although, obviously, they shared much physiology in common. Also, Silda was reminded there were other reasons for carrying a likl-likl upon the shoulder.

Yes, they were lovely little furry bundles, to be stroked and cuddled and petted, splendid companions. They were friendly little creatures, only resorting to violence if aroused by some extraordinary cruelty. The spinlikl had made no attempt to steal from the black lady in the emerald green dress. Her likl-likl would have known at once and set up an outcry.

The other fact that had not passed unnoticed by Silda was Lon's possession of silver in the form of sinvers, the currency of Hyrklana, among that of other nations. The stiver was the usual Vallian silver coin. This meant, clearly, that the new recruits from Pandahem had already been parted from some of their cash. There'd be dhems as well, silver coins of Pandahem, circulating. Well, as they said on Kregen, gold and onkers are like oil and water.

The ugly side of this was that nations over the seas were sending men and money to assist this rast Alloran in his dreams of conquest.

Outside, as they walked along the street heading for the Urnhart Boulevard, the illuminations were just beginning, brightening the sky. She of the Veils rode behind a wisp of clouds, gilding them with her light.

Lon wasn't concerned with the illuminations. Oh, no, not when he could walk along with this superb girl at his side and be, as he was confident they were, the cynosure of all eyes.

"Well, Lon," said Silda in her fine free way, striding out, lithe and limber, "a free night's dinner can't be bad, can it?"

"By Beng Debrant, no!"

They strolled on, savoring the air, seeing the sky erratic with the illuminations. People hurried past.

"Fish hooks, was it?" said Lon.

"Fish hooks? Ah—er, yes, that's it."

"Just because I borrowed the belt and wallet from one-eyed Garndaf, I didn't have my own, which is nicely defended with fish hooks. The spinlikl is known to defeat the hooks, though. Well-trained animals can."

"So I have heard."

"Yet, yet—Lyss—the thing's hand was nearly off!"

"It looked worse than it was."

"Yes, but—"

"The Watch must have marched up to The Silver Lotus from the other direction, for we have not passed them. I trust they were in time."

"Clumsy, those Brokelsh. Nature has not cut them out to be thieves. Not like Crafty Kando."

"Crafty Kando?" A zephyr of impending delight passed across Silda's mind.

"Why, yes, Lyss. He's the most cunning disciple of Diproo the Nimble-fingered I know. And I've known some in my time, I can tell you. Why, back when I was in the army there was—"

"Yes, yes, Lon. But this Crafty Kando. You know him well? He is trust-worthy in a thief? Can I meet him?"

"Why, Lyss!" Lon was shocked.

"Don't be so po-faced, Lon! Can I meet your friend, Crafty Kando? I may have business with him."

"You won't give him to the Watch? That's not—"

"No, no, that's not it. There is something I must do, and I have been rack-ing my brains to find a way to do it. Now, by Vox, you may have found the way!"

Seven

Secrets around the campfire

This time the battle was more prolonged, swaying to and fro, and finally ending in stalemate. Drak could feel the ache in his bones, the tiredness dragging him down. He could always remember in those long ago days when he was a child his father saying: "Tiredness is a sin, my lad. Brassud! Brace up! If you use your willpower and your spirit you can always find the extra strength to go on."

It was damned hard. But it was true. As a Krozair of Zy Drak had learned the Mystic Way. He could control himself. He was well aware of the way people regarded him.

The upright one, they'd say, dedicated, solemn, filled with niceties and integrities, never willing to admit to defeat. He supposed this was true. As for himself, all he ever wanted was a happy life with his father and mother, at home in Valka. Oh, yes, he loved Delphond, and Desalia, his mother's estates along with the Blue Mountains. He'd not had a lavish private province of his own, only Vellendur, of which he was Amak; but it was a tiny island, for when he was emperor he would come into all the imperial provinces.

He could envision life there doing all the things he liked to do. And here he was, acting as the Captain of a Host, running a war, and not doing very well at it, either.

This fight, which no doubt the scribes would call the Battle of Cowdenholm, ending in a draw, saw both armies haul off and make camp. The fires painted the clouds in lurid oranges and reds. There were no billets or barracks, and it was bivouacs for those lucky enough to find something with which to build them. Drak, Prince Majister of Vallia, sat hunched in his cold cloak before the fire, and felt sick.

The First and Second Kerchuris of the First Phalanx, and the Fifth Kerchuri of the Third Phalanx had done splendidly, as ever. Their massed array of pikes had broken the wild leem-like charges of the foe and hurled them back. The heavy infantry, known as churgurs, had fought like leems themselves. The cavalry had foamed across the field like tidal waves. Yes, all in all everyone had done splendidly; but it had not been enough.

Reinforcements had come in from Vondium, notably those madmen of his father's bodyguards. Everyone had fought to the limits of their strength. And they had not broken the enemy forces commanded, as he now knew, by this evil cramph, Strom Rosil Yasi of Morcray. He was a damned Kataki, one of that low-browed and violent race of diffs who were slavemasters under any circumstances. The Kataki Strom's twin brother, Stromich Ranjal Yasi, was not here. No doubt he was somewhere else stirring up trouble and enslaving innocent people.

He stirred himself as Jiktar Endru Vintang walked up to the fire, shivering and holding his hands out to the blaze.

"The prisoners, jis," began Endru.

"Yes, yes. We took that traitor Chuktar Unstabi, I believe. His damned archers caused us some grief before you charged them."

Endru was far too politic to remind the Prince Majister that when Vodun Alloran was being sent down to the southwest to regain his province, it had been Drak himself who hired on the Undurker archers. And this had been against the wishes of the emperor.

"There are also some Katakis taken—"

"Hang 'em all."

"Oh, yes, never fear, jis."

"If there's one thing the country folk like to see it's a damned Kataki swinging in the breeze by his neck."

"And Chuktar Unstabi?"

About to order the same summary justice, Drak paused.

"Send him to me under guard. I will question him."

"Quidang!"

"We have not taken anyone of so high a rank as a Chuktar in this war. He might sing."

Everyone knew that Drak, like his father, would not tolerate torture as a means of gaining information.

When Chuktar Unstabi wheeled up with a detail of Endru's men, grim-faced, about him, Drak felt the sorrow.

He glanced up, seeing the wreck of the archer's uniform, the wound in his shoulder, the hangdog look of him.

"When last we met, Unstabi, you swore allegiance to me and I hired you on. You went with Alloran to the southwest, and you turned traitor. Tell me why you should not be hanged."

Unstabi was not bound. He fingered the golden pakzhan at his throat.

"What can I say, majister? Hang me, and have done."

The man's long-nosed face, canine, held nothing of the usual supercilious look of an Undurker. He hailed from the Undurkor Islands, a group off southwest Segesthes, west of Balintol. He had sailed a long long way to find his death. But then, was not that the fate of many and many a fine paktun?

"By Vox!" snapped Drak. "You mean that?"

"Yes. I am not a Pachak who gives his nikobi, his gift of honor, and so foolishly fights to the death to earn his hire. I am a zhanpaktun. But, majister, I cannot explain why I left your service so willingly and fought for Kov Vodun Alloran."

"The emperor warned us of the dangers of mercenaries, and will not hire paktuns. He was right, at least in your case. What d'you mean, you can't explain?"

The long canine face turned, as it must have turned many times in battle to loose the Undurkor arrows.

"Just that when the kov said he would take control, make himself king of south west Vallia, and then Emperor of Vallia, it was the most natural—"

"Emperor of Vallia? Is the rast bereft of his senses?"

"I think so, majister. Also, I think sorcery—"

"Ah!"

Endru felt the chill. His men remained fast about the prisoner; but Endru knew they, too, did not relish the way this conversation was going.

"Well, Unstabi. Tell me."

Somewhere off in the night, hard-faced men were hanging Katakis and rejoicing that the opportunity had come their way. Chuktar Unstabi probably knew that, too. He said, "May I beg a sip of water, majister?"

Crossly, Drak said, "Oh, give the Chuktar a mug of wine. Have you eaten, Unstabi?"

"No, majister. But if I am to die—"

"Sit down, you fambly, and eat something. I want to know all you know of this damned sorcery Alloran has. By the Blade of Kurin! Cold steel is one thing. But wizardry..."

"Aye, majister," said Unstabi, unsteadily sitting down. "That is indeed foulness from the Pit of Untlarken."

Drak didn't agree entirely with that, not that he knew what the Pit of Untlarken might be, although it sounded unpleasant. His good friends and comrades, Khe-Hi-Bjanching and dear old Deb-Lu-Quienyin, were Wizards of Loh. They were the most famed and feared wizards in this part of Kregen called Paz. Now they were off somewhere on their own mysterious errands. But they did weave a net of thaumaturgy to protect the family of the emperor. That, Drak knew, was a fact.

Food on a wooden dish was brought and although it was cold and congealed, Unstabi wolfed it down, and then swigged back a jug of wine. He wiped those canine lips.

"All I know, majister, and I give you thanks for the food and drink, is that Kov Vodun vowed vengeance on those who had ruined his province of Kaldi, one day. The next, he was friendly with the two Katakis, and was planning his career as king and emperor."

"Katakis are not renowned as sorcerers."

"Exactly so, majister."

"Well, then?"

"It is said that Katakis, seeing only slaves in the world for their use, make good tools for those who lust after power."

"That is so, as Vallia knows to her cost."

"The kov once spoke to me of Arachna."

"Arachna?"

"Aye, majister. What that might be I do not know."

"Well, what did he say?"

"That he needed a fine strong man from the prisoners we had taken. Arachna, he said, was most demanding. Also, he said that the helpers were called Mantissae. I gathered they were slaves."

"Slaves and Katakis go together, to the shame of the world."

"Aye."

"And that is all you know?"

Tiredly, the Undurker nodded his head.

"If it has served to keep me alive for another bur, and give me food and drink, then it has served me, at least. But, majister, it is true, as I am a zhanpaktun."

Drak hunched his cloak about him.

"And I suppose, Chuktar Unstabi, you imagine I am going to offer you fresh employment with me? As a hyrpaktun you can hire on as and when you please. Is that it?"

"I had hoped so, majister. But after—"

"Precisely!"

"I can, at least, plead sorcery led me astray. And I can offer you information about the Kataki Strom's forces."

Upright, filled with honor, a man of integrity, Drak the Prince Majister might be. He was also not a fool. This kind of information could be invaluable. He saw he would have to bargain for it. And, too, he knew that once he had given his word, Unstabi would know he would not break it.

"Very well." He made up his mind at once. "You have my word. Your information proving of value, you will not dance on air."

"Your word as a prince of Vallia?"

"Yes."

The canine face allowed at last some expression of satisfaction.

"When Kov Vodun set off to reclaim his province, the emperor gave him the Army of the Southwest. Apart from slingers and archers and churgurs, that army contained the Eighth Kerchuri of the Fourth Phalanx, and the Ninth Kerchuri of the Fifth Phalanx."

This was so. The Eighth and Ninth Kerchuris had straggled back to Vondium. Subsequently, the Ninth had been broken up to replace losses elsewhere.

"Go on."

"They refused to join Kov Vodun. The other regiments of the Vallian army, likewise, refused to join, except a single regiment of slingers. They allied themselves to the body of the paktuns who went over to Alloran."

"I see. What caused that?"

"The sorcery I spoke of, majister. But what I am saying is the kov was wroth at the loss of the phalanx. Such a body is unknown. To me, an experienced fighting man, it has been a revelation. So the kov sought to create his own phalanx."

Drak sat back. Someone brought more wood for the fire. Sparks blazed up like fireflies.

"That takes great skill."

A Phalanx was an intricately built-up structure. Many months of training were needed to persuade that structure to perform as a single giant organism. A static Phalanx was of only partial use.

Any body of pikemen in the field could be called a phalanx; a Phalanx was a particular number of men arranged in a particular way.

The basic building block was the Relianch, consisting of 144 pikemen, called brumbytes, and 24 Hakkodin, the men armed with halberds, axes and two-handed swords. Six Relianches formed a Jodhri. Six Jodhris formed a Kerchuri. The Kerchuri was the wing of a Phalanx, one half, so that the total number of brumbytes was 10368 and the Hakkodin 1738. Also in the Phalanx were lads who ran with caltrops and chevaux de frise. The missile component consisted of two Lanchans of 432 bowmen forming a Chodku, attached to the Kerchuri.

"Yes, majister," said Unstabi. "Very great skill so to combine all the arms of the phalanx, the pikes and shields, the archers, to make the men obey the call of bugle and drum and whistle. But Kov Vodun suborned—and now I may use that word freely—enough men of the Vallian Phalanx Force to train up his own version of a phalanx."

A low rumble of anger traveled around the tight circle of men who had gathered as the prince questioned the prisoner. Kapt Enwood ground his sword into the mud. Two or three Chuktars showed their displeasure. Jiktar Naghan swore fiercely. Even Chuktar Leone Starhammer said a few words to express her horror. All knew the seriousness of this calamitous news.

Drak summed it up.

"So be it, then. If Opaz wills. One must accept the needle. No man or woman born of Opaz knows all the secrets of Imrien." He heaved himself to his feet.

Unstabi scrambled quickly up as was proper.

"You promised to tell me of the composition of the Kataki Strom's forces, Unstabi, well knowing we must have a shrewd idea ourselves. Yet I encouraged you to speak."

Unstabi stood still. "You are known as a stern and sober prince, majister. Also, as one able to salt a leem's tail. I knew you would understand my information would go further. The bargain is good, majister?"

"Yes, Unstabi. But I cannot hire you on again, as you must see. Give all the facts and figures you can to my stylors. Then you will be provided with a mount and gold enough to see you home to the Undurkor Islands."

Unstabi bowed.

"I give you my thanks, majister. But I am a zhanpaktun and cannot go home quite yet. I accept your gifts and will travel somewhere where they need fighting men."

"So be it."

Not all the men and women gathered at the fire might grasp the significance of the lower case or upper case for the initial letter of the word phalanx; all understood the seriousness of this intelligence. Capital letters are strange beasts in the Kregish, and a slight inflection in the way the word is pronounced can indicate capitals, although in general Kregans are not too fussed over capital letters. What fussed Drak now was that Unstabi had religiously referred to Alloran's forces as a phalanx, not a Phalanx.

This could mean, at a simple level, that some component of a proper

Phalanx had not been represented in the men who had deserted to Alloran.

He could remember his mother's telling him once that the word phalanx was not really Kregish, that his father had invented it out of the air, or out of space, from somewhere. The lower case phalanx sounded with an "f." The upper case Phalanx sounded with a "v." This had seemed to him perfectly proper, as it should be in an empire run on sensible lines.

The Vallian Valanx sounded supremely apt.

What the hell this bastard Kov Vodun Alloran was going to do about being crowned king and going on a rampage of conquest among the western islands remained a mystery.

Unstabi, sensing he was dismissed, turned to depart, and then swung back. He hesitated.

"We shall," said Kerchurivax Mantig ti Fillan, "wish to know exact details, Chuktar. So far you speak, as I believe, with veiled words."

Hearing this, Drak checked himself. Mantig was a shrewd fellow. Had Unstabi been fooling the prince?

"I swear—" began Unstabi.

"It may be," interrupted Drak, "that the Chuktar is not aware of the knowledge he possesses. After all, he has, as he acknowledges himself, no real comprehension of the Phalanx. If you question him, Kervax Mantig, I feel confident he will tell you a great deal of what you wish to know."

Mantig nodded at once. "My pleasure, jis."

Of the Kerchurivaxes commanding his three Kerchuris, Drak had, by reason of wounds, sickness, death or promotions, contrived to lose eight of them. That was a high loss rate. In these battles, commanders could fall just like the swods in the ranks. Chuktars Nath the Murais and Larghos the Oivon had been provisionally promoted from brigadiers to divisional generals. Drak valued his soldiers, both men and women, and felt the pangs of agony when they died. No. Far better, for all his stern devotion to duty and his desire to rid Vallia of the reiving human predators leaching her life blood away, far better to be at home in Valka, playing music, reading the ancient books, riding in zorca races, practicing the artistry of the sword, and dancing and singing the night away in the good old Vallian tradition. Far better, by Zair!

So Kervax Mantig ti Fillan, as a new commander of his Kerchuri, was anxious to create a good impression. He would find out the truth concerning that rast Alloran's newly created phalanx.

Chuktar Unstabi tilted his long canine nose a trifle higher into the night air now. The relief in him must be enormous, and Drak felt genuine pleasure that there had been no need to hang him as high as the damned Katakis.

"Yes, majister," said the Undurker. "I will answer every question to the best of my ability."

Drak's thoughts, when he dwelled on a sensible life in Valka or Delphond, did not encompass a vision of a woman at his side sharing that life. Queen Lushfymi was a remarkable woman, there could be no doubt of that. She had played a useful part at the very end of his adventure down in Faol when he'd rescued Melow and Kardo, his comrades who were Manhounds. Mother and son, jiklo and jikla, they were. He would value their presence now. He could remember that return to Vondium when all the city danced and sang, and he'd been swept up into the arms of his mother, the Empress Delia. That had been a homecoming! And—his father, the emperor? That man had been nowhere to be found, he'd just upped and disappeared as he so often did, without explanation.

He had no proof, he just felt with odds of nine-to-one certainty, that his father and mother did not share the general view of Queen Lushfymi. Everyone regarded her with respect and awe, dazzled by her beauty and power, her charm of manner, her jewels and clothes, and more than a trifle apprehensive of her sorcerous powers. Yes, it was quite clear she would make a splendid wife. Her country of Lome, in the northwest of the island of Pandahem south of the island empire of Vallia, might be small. It was awash with wealth even after the wars. Yes, she would be a fine match.

She had not, as a certain other young lady had done, thrust her body between him and certain death. She had not fought with her life for his. But, then, she was a queen, not a savagely ferocious female Jikai Vuvushi, a sister of the Order of Sisters of the Rose. She hired other people to fight for her.

Still Unstabi waited on his dismissal now that the conversation had again included the Prince Majister.

Kapt Enwood, bluffly, was saying to the three Kerchurivaxes that he'd want more information from the Undurker zhanpaktun than only intelligence on that rast Alloran's new phalanx.

"We'll have him, aye, and his rascally Kataki Strom. We have more reinforcements coming in. We'll have that Kataki by the short and curlies, and hang him higher than any of the whiptails we've hanged today, by Vox!"

"Amen," said Leone Starhammer.

Drak roused himself.

"After today's standoff," he said, and he put force and dynamism into his words. If he was supposed to be the leader, he'd damn well lead, by Zair! "Today has shown us that we will win. Strom Rosil Yasi must know his strength will dwindle as ours increases. A few days to rest the troops and put fresh heart into them, the reinforcement sent from Vondium joining us—and we shall sweep the Kataki Strom away!"

Growls of savage agreement rolled throatily around that group of people clustered about the Prince Majister of Vallia.

And then Chuktar Unstabi, the Undurker mercenary, said: "It will not work out like that, majister. If you gain any significant victories here and threaten his own province of Kaldi, the kov will gather all his forces from the islands and hurl them against you on the mainland." He stared about the group. "I thought you realized that."

Eight

With the Jikai Vuvushis

The two ladies, stripped stark naked and with bodies heavily oiled so that the mingled lights streaming from the high windows ran liquid runnels over their skin, sized each other up and then grappled with savage ferocity.

"Hai Hikai!" screeched Chuktar Gilda Failsham, and hurled herself on Silda, grasping hands cunningly reaching for holds on that smooth slippery body.

Both ladies had their hair bound up tightly. They gripped fast, chest to chest, squirming to change grips and so throw the other onto the matting floor. That coarsely woven matting might be softer than the hard boards beneath; a heavy fall and a sliding slip across it could scorch up skin woefully. Silda was not prepared to let that happen to her so she slid Gilda's first impetuous attack. She twisted the heavier woman over and instead of depositing her upon the mat held her long enough so that she could flail out an arm and seize Silda by the upper leg. Silda rocked aside and Gilda, a hoarse cry of triumph bursting unstoppably from her, crashed down—underneath.

Silda allowed the Chuktar to do the obvious next step and roll over. The matting stuck to her bottom; but it was nowise as nasty an experience as falling upon it with that portion of her anatomy. She took a professional's pride in thus allowing the Chuktar to win. She felt it politic to win the odd fall or two—and then she'd let poor Gilda Failsham drop down to feel what it was like—but as for emerging the victor in these bouts, why that, she'd decided, might not be clever in a spy.

Gasping and panting, heaving herself up, rosy and oily, Failsham blatted out: "You are improving, Lyss; but you have a long long way to go in the art before you best me."

"Too true, by Vox," said Silda, and stood up in a single fluid motion that would have knocked out the eyes of any mere male spectator. Here, in the private villa given over to the Jikai Vuvushis, any man venturing in might not return with all he brought with him.

The girls sitting on the benches arranged around the salle laughed and cheered. Silda was not convinced that not one of them had the skill to penetrate her deception; probably Mandi Volanta could. She'd chosen her time, pounced, catching Mandi as she was toweling her hair, and said in her most winning and at the same time most compelling voice: "It were better, Mandi, if we pretended not to know each other, and most particularly to keep secret that we are Sisters of the Rose. Do you agree?"

"I am shattered, Silda! You—here—why, I—"

"My name is Lyss the Lone. You do not know me."

"As to that—by Dee Sheon, you gave me a start!" The towel slid down Mandi's neck. Then, recovering herself, for she was, after all, one of the SoR, she went on: "Of course I agree we know nothing of the Rose. But—why should we not acknowledge that we know each other?"

"It is best. Do you agree?"

"Oh, yes, if you wish it, Lyss," said Mandi, crossly. Silda did not heave a sigh of relief. She was well aware that the intolerant yet basically kind and sound training of Lancival produced people perfectly capable of handling this essentially simple circumstance.

"Although," and here Mandi looked studiously away from Silda. "I own I am most surprised to see you in the service of Kov Vodun. Why—I thought you were devoted to the emperor and that ice block of a son."

Silda took the proffered opportunity.

"I thought he was not an ice block."

"Well, he must be with that Queen Lush for all one hears. A dreadful family, all told, don't you agree?"

"Oh, quite dreadful."

So Silda was gratefully aware that one problem was neatly overcome by the process of Mandi's quick wits and native cattiness constructing the theory that Prince Drak, the Prince Majister, had turned his face away from Silda Segutoria. She had, then, Mandi's theory went, taken herself off fuming with anger and frustration and bitterness, and joined up with Kov Vodun. Out of spite.

After a few more cautionary words, Silda added: "Oh, and Mandi, by Dee Sheon, it is good to see a familiar friendly face here."

"Is that why they call you Lyss the Lone?"

"Life sometimes presses down with the weight of all the marble in Pentellharmon's Quarries."

Mandi looked meaningfully at Silda's brown canvas and leather bag hanging at her side.

"I see you carry your—"

"The bag passes muster as an ordinary knapsack that any soldier might have. It contains other items, as well."

"I shall do the same. But, do you use—?"

"Only when forced. We in Vallia know of the Sisters of the Rose, and I sometimes think folk begin to know too much."

"They will never know, not while the mistress lives."

"That is so."

With that problem if not out of the way then temporarily shelved, Silda could concentrate on her upcoming meeting with Crafty Kando. Lon the Knees, when they next met was full of apologies.

"He is not to be found, Lyss. I have searched out all his usual haunts, and I had to stick a weasel of a fellow who tried to rob me. But Crafty Kando has gone to ground."

"I will try to be patient, Lon."

She could guess that Lon was rather pleased. The delay meant he had the excuse to see her again. She had summed up Lon as a man who would not lie too much to gain his ends with her; with those for whom he had contempt, for the slavers whom the poor folk slanged as greeshes, he would pile lie upon lie and joy in it.

So, perforce, Silda had to wait in patience, and drill and discipline her pastang of girls, and stand guard duty, and ride out with the kov on his journeys. He was now King Vodun—at least in his and his cronies' eyes— and she would have to get used to addressing him thus. It stung.

When the girls sitting around the walls on their hard benches cheered Chuktar Gilda Failsham on yet another victory, Silda carefully avoided looking at Mandi Volanta. Flushed, rosy, shining with oils, the women passed through the warmed corridor to the Baths of the Nine. There they wallowed in luxurious steam, hot, warm and ice cold water, and so emerged at the end, spruce, glowing, filled with vigor and ready for what the world of Kregen might bring.

"Mind you, Lyss," said Gilda Failsham in a reflective tone of voice as they walked toward the refectory. "As the kov—the king—keeps us as his personal palace bodyguard and we have not seen a proper fight for a long time, we cannot expect to receive too many of the new girls into the regiment."

"They are to form a new regiment, I believe."

"Yes. By Karina's Steel! Some look likely. But there are far too many I would not trust on the field at my side, let alone at my back."

Thankfully, Silda knew that would not occur for her. She could not face the prospect of actually having to go into a battle and fight against Drak and his soldiers. She'd just up sticks and desert and return to her proper allegiance. She would have failed in her task if that happened; but the thought of fighting against her own friends disgusted her.

"We are to have a few of the new girls, Lyss. And we can send some of ours in replacement." Failsham slid a sidelong look at Silda as they sat at the scrubbed wooden tables and the slaves scurried with food. "I suppose you will send Sosie the Slop into the new regiment. You are to have five more girls to add to your pastang."

This was an eminently sensible arrangement. Any commander would dismiss her worst soldiers, get rid of them to some other unfortunate. The best girls would be taken into Alloran's own private regiment of Jikai Vuvushis.

The delicious aroma of vosk pie wafted to Silda's nostrils. Momolams, yellow and succulent with butter, piled on the side dishes. There were vegetables in abundance. She indicated to the serving wenches what she required, and as her plate filled, she said: "Well, Gilda, no. I would like to keep Sosie. Oh, yes, she is a Slop. She is a mess. But she fights well."

"I cannot pretend to be surprised. Just make sure the king never catches her looking like the wet end of a mop."

Silda smiled, and went on: "I would like to claim one of the new girls for my pastang. Mandi Volanta. She looks useful."

Jiktar Nandi the Tempestuous leaned across the table and waved her knife in Silda's face.

"You have sharp eyes, Lyss. But I will not claim her, for her name and mine—well, confusion is to be avoided in a fight."

"If you cannot remember or disentangle names," said Chuktar Gilda Failsham with prim smugness, "you will soon find yourself cut down and shipped off to the Ice Floes of Sicce."

"Oh, yes, of course!"

"As to this Mandi Volanta, Lyss. Yes, you may take her into your pastang."

"Thank you, Gilda."

Nandi used that dangerous knife to spear a chunk of vosk pie. "She and you, Lyss, are of the Sisters of Renunciation. A strict Order, I hear. I do not see why you don't join us in the Sisters of the Sword."

The name Sisters of Renunciation was often used by members of the Sisters of the Rose as a cover name. It was a well-concealed secret. Now Silda smiled again and chewed her vosk and cabbage without replying.

The deception was not quite meaningless, for the vast majority of the SoR had not gone over to Alloran. They had remained loyal to the empire and the empress. And, that meant they were loyal to the emperor as well. Once a Sister of the Rose went into action as only a girl of the SoR could, why, then, there would be no concealing the secret from anyone who understood. She felt that even had Lon the Knees seen the fight with the chavonth clearly, he still wouldn't really have grasped what he was looking at.

There was no doubt about it, in the special and particular Disciplines of the SoR, Silda Segutoria was quick, was extremely quick, was a most rapid lady...

The brown bag called a knapsack she wore might not be as easy to open and close as a more normal jikvarpam, which besides being designed for the job with specially strengthened corners and sides and a fastening that would not delay nimble fingers by a hairsbreadth, would have a few rows of bright red stitching to distinguish it from the next girl's; but the knapsack looked just as it was supposed to look. Any girl was entitled to a bag to carry her kit in, surely? No one was going to think for an instant the humble canvas bag was a jikvarpam, were they now?

Silda sincerely hoped not.

The refectory began to fill as the officers of the regiment drifted in, sniffing the food, licking their lips at the odors of wines.

"...kicked him where it made his eyes water," said one of the Jiktars, casually, sitting down and reaching for the wine, evidently finishing a story.

One of her Hikdars, sitting at her side, laughed and said: "Apt, Jik."

The Hikdar on the other side said, "Of course, Jik, if you go on like this you'll cause a calamitous population drop—"

"A what drop?"

So they all three laughed.

Bright conversations, laughter, the clink of cutlery and glass, the rich odors of first class foods and wines, the taste of luxury all about, all these sensations crowded in and they made Silda Segutoria hopping mad. Confoundedly angry! These stupid women all enjoying themselves and living high off the vosk were avowedly out to destroy what was left of the responsible and caring part of the structure of management for Vallia. They were going to install a creature like Vodun Alloran. It was outrageous.

Nandi the Tempestuous, gesturing widely, knocked over her glass of wine. She swore and laughed, and flung a taunt at Silda.

"You're looking down-in-the-mouth, Lyss! Drink a little wine—"

"I was just thinking that we are underemployed here."

Now she'd opened the ball, as it were, she'd go on.

"Yes, Lyss?" put in Chuktar Gilda Failsham. She spoke in that tone of voice that brought a waiting silence around the refectory table.

"Why yes, Gilda. Badly so. By Vox! All we do is stand sentry along the corridors."

A nodding of heads confirmed her words.

The Chuktar said: "We are paid by and in the service of the kov—the king—and obey orders."

"That may be so," objected Nandi, speaking only just in time as she swallowed a chunk of juicy fruit. "But what about the king's apartments beyond the green door?"

"Yes, yes," called a number of the women. "We are excluded from duty there." "The king keeps us at arm's length." And: "He reduces our status as a guard regiment."

"This may be so." Gilda Failsham frowned. "But the king employs his own Katakis and Chuliks within his most private apartments. That is his privilege."

"By Janette of the Cunning Dagger!" burst out Nandi the Tempestuous. "I'd like to know what goes on in those secret rooms!"

Gilda Failsham shook her head. "I think not, Nandi. It is sorcery, surely. It must be, thaumaturgy, necromancy, witchcraft. We're much better off having nothing to do with sorcerers, as any right-minded person knows."

Nine

Arachna

Chuktar Gilda Failsham was perfectly correct.

The ordinary folk of Kregen steered well clear of sorcery of any order higher than the corner mage who might find a strayed animal, or cure warts, or make up a potion to entice a negligent loved one.

There were many and various cults and societies and orders of wizards upon Kregen, having different powers. Many a wandering wizard was a fake, gaining his living from the credulous. Everyone knew there were real wizards and witches, people who could shrivel the marrow in your bones.

In the series of confusing chambers and apartments in the private portion of the rambling old villa appropriated by Alloran, the Chuliks stood guard. Their small round eyes surveyed what went on dispassionately; when they fought and killed they did so with extreme efficiency. Even renowned fighting men like Chuliks, though, looked askance when a sorcerer walked past.

The figure swathed all in a dark green cloak with the devices of Kaldi upon its breast had a golden chain girdled around its waist from which swung sword and dagger. The figure's arms were folded upon its breast, hands thrust deeply into capacious sleeves. The enveloping hood allowed no glimpse of the face and only a fugitive gleam of an eye told that a mortal head existed within the hood.

The Chulik sentries, sweating of oily yellow skin, martial and chunky in harness of armor, smothered in weapons, breathed easier when the ominous figure in the green robe had passed by. They would furtively rub a thick thumb along a tusk, polishing it up, taking racial comfort from the action.

The eyes within the hood observed these actions; the agile and cunning brain behind the eyes noted, and sighed, and once again returned to devising ways and means of staying alive in King Vodun's palace villa.

For times had changed for San Fraipur.

Never had he been one for shriveling a person's eyeballs out, or melting the jelly in their bones, or turning them into little green lizards. People might believe he could do these things, and that was no bad thing, and if they did believe and he mumbled a few words and wriggled his fingers in the air, then they might feel symptoms that would prove salutary. But as for little green frogs—no, San Fraipur had no illusions about his power there.

He liked to be called San, the title given to a dominie or master or sage. He'd worked hard enough, Opaz knew, up in the island of Fruningen to gain the arcana to enable him to earn his living as a Wizard of Fruningen. He'd served Vodun Alloran faithfully since his father had been killed in the Times of Troubles, seeking refuge with the kov in the mountains as the mercenaries and the flutsmen sought to destroy them. He'd gone to Vondium and been impressed with the proud city even in her ruined state. All his arts and all his skill had been given to Vodun Alloran.

And this—Fraipur was not quite sure what to call the Opaz-forsaken thing—had subverted everything good, had turned the kov, had made him into this quasi-monster of legend, had even caused him to turn his face away from the divine radiance of Opaz.

Arachna. That was the thing's name. Fraipur had sensed the aura there, had shriveled within himself at the evil he felt, and knew it was evil because it stood blackly against the radiance of Opaz. Arachna, and her servants were the Mantissae.

Arachna was the name by which she was known; but still San Fraipur did not know what she was, of what race she might be.

When he thought of her that agile brain of his pained him.

He did know, with very great certainty, that he stood in mortal terror of her and her assistants.

Beside that continuing horror this summons from the kov who must now be called king meant—almost—nothing. Alloran wanted to see him. That, in itself, made this day different from very many that had been blown with the wind.

These interior corridors were never as busy as those outside the green door. Slaves hurried everywhere, of course; but they were a normal part of life. Fraipur did not incline his head as stupid fat old Naghan the Chains the chamberlain passed with his fancy woman on his arm. Fraipur knew little of women. They had been denied to him in his youth during training and he'd never bothered to open new relationships when all the worlds of thaumaturgy lay awaiting his inspection.

Naghan the Chains trembled so that his chins shook; the woman on his right arm looked quickly away, and made a secret sign. Tosie the Hiffim and Naghan the Chains both devoutly believed in San Fraipur, despite the kov's—the king's—apparent recent slighting of the Wizard of Fruningen.

For Fraipur, the fact that Naghan and Tosie were walking together like this meant the chamberlain was off duty and was going out. Stupid and fat he might be, but he oversaw protocol at audiences. Anxiety grew in Fraipur like an ulcer.

As he walked through the various sentry-guarded rooms and passage-ways he saw the changes made since his last visit. This villa was large; but it was overcrowded in the outer parts where everyone was jammed up together and that was largely caused by the amount of space given over to these secret inner areas. The name of the villa had been banned from everyone's lips by the king, and he was in the process of choosing a new name. He did not wish to give the place a too resounding name, for obvi-ous reasons. He also did not wish to give it a mean-sounding name, for equally valid reasons.

At a green velvet door with golden strigicaws decorating the panels, Fraipur halted. The two Chuliks looked at him, and one used the butt of his spear to hit one of the slaves crouched by the door. The two slaves jumped up and opened the double-doors. Fraipur walked through.

In the old days Alloran, like everyone else, used slaves. He had used them with some consideration. Fraipur had not bothered his head over-much about the new emperor's edict that slavery was to be abolished. He could quite see that the slaves here would welcome that law.

In the anteroom beyond the door he was met by Jiktar Rakkan, who was a Kataki. Fraipur, like any honest citizen, detested Katakis. Now, he kept his face expressionless and followed the Kataki Jiktar, walking as though he trod on eggs.

The next archway, swathed by cloth of gold curtains and guarded by four Katakis, gave ingress to the chamber where Alloran sat in his throne waiting for the wizard.

"Come in, San Fraipur! Advance!"

"Majister," said Fraipur, and he went into the full incline, nose on the car-pet and bottom in the air. He was never one to take unnecessary chances. Alloran showed his pleasure at this slavish display, ordered Fraipur up, and waved a slave forward with a stool. The three-legged wooden stool was provided with a green and red cushion, and Fraipur understood this to be a mark of distinction.

He sat down, thankful to get off his knees, which resembled jellies.

"Majister?"

"You have not served me well lately, San. I forgive you in this, as a mark of my pleasure. Now I am king. That washes away all that is past. Now we look to the future."

"Yes, majister."

"I shall test your powers, San. Tell me what I wish to know, and great rewards shall be yours."

"Majister?"

"Strom Rosil Yasi, the Kataki Strom, does not fare as well as he might upon the mainland. You see I am well-served by the Katakis." He waved a beringed hand around the chamber and Fraipur saw the guards along the walls, harsh in black and green, feathers still in the hothouse atmosphere. Low-browed are Katakis, snaggle-toothed, owing little to humanity. Each has a long flexible whiptail to which is strapped six inches of bladed steel. A whiptail can slip that deadly dagger up between his legs and into your guts in a twinkling.

Fraipur swallowed. "So I see, majister."

"Strom Rosil sends news that he needs more men. He has recently been held by that brat, the Prince Majister, and has conducted a strategic withdrawal across Venavito into Ovvend." Alloran lifted a hand and a Sylvie wearing pearls and tissue placed a golden cup of wine into the outstretched paw. Sylvies are so voluptuous that they appear as though dreamlike, capable of gratifying all the hothouse desires of men. Fraipur did not look at the slave girl as Alloran continued: "You know, San, what province lies to the west of Ovvend."

"Your own Kaldi."

"Quite."

"The question then, is one of the relative powers and strengths of Strom Rosil and the Prince Majister, of the numbers of troops to be sent, if any should be sent, and of the chances of success or failure—"

"There will be no failure."

"Naturally, majister."

"Can you tell me, San Fraipur, what is going to happen? And, then, what I must do?"

"As to the first, majister, I will try. As to the second, the king will decide."

Fraipur sat a little straighter on the stool. Yes, he was just deciding in a congratulatory way, that was a most cunning and crafty answer, when the king frowned and leaned forward spilling the wine onto the carpet.

"I shall decide, Fraipur! But you will tell me the issues on which to base my decision! By Vox! Must I always deal with imbeciles."

Fraipur shrank on the little three-legged stool. He could feel the hardness of the wood through the cushion.

From nowhere, slave girls appeared like ghosts to swab up the spilled wine and to pour more. The tinkle of their ankle bells affected Fraipur oddly, as though the Bells of Beng Kishi, instead of ringing in his skull, came clamoring in from the far distance. He opened his mouth, not quite sure what to say, when King Vodun spoke with the snap of command.

"Clear out, Fraipur. Return in four burs, and then tell me true. Dernun?"*

---

* Dernun: an impolite way of saying: "Do you understand?" Savvy? Capiche? A.B.A.

"Majister!" yelped Fraipur, and scuttled off the stool and out the golden-swathed doorway, trembling.

The sound of those eternally damned ankle bells followed him, mockingly.

Alloran swigged the wine back and threw the cup casually over his shoulder where a slave girl—a Fristle fifi—caught it expertly.

"Sorcerers!" he said. "And to think I once doted on that man and all he told me."

A figure cloaked all in deep blue velvet, silver trimmed, glided toward Alloran's throne from a narrow side opening. The hood extended in a cup shape to enclose the vast mass of dull black hair, springy as wire. Alloran stood up as the blue-cloaked figure halted before him.

"Is all prepared?"

"All is prepared."

With great satisfaction, Alloran took up a fresh goblet of wine and with this in his hand followed the blue-cloaked figure through the side opening into a passageway. The room at the end of the passage, although fitted out as a bedroom, with a broad canopied bed in the center, and dressing tables and mirrors and stools, conveyed the impression of the sanctuary in the inmost recesses of a temple. The walls were draped with blue velvet. The ceiling's blue velvet hangings depended from five central points toward the cornices to create the impression of a blue star. Silver glitter heightened other impressions, and the waft of hidden fans blew pungent scents upon the air.

If this place could be likened to a sanctuary, then the bed represented the high altar.

In the near right-hand corner stood a tall chair facing the bed. Alloran walked steadily to the chair and sat down, resting the wine goblet on his knee. The five other blue-cloaked figures all gave him a slight perfunctory nod of the head, whereat he lifted his goblet to them. He was well aware of the power of these Mantissae. Their wiry hair frizzed into bowls of blackness, their lowering foreheads and snaggle teeth, the ferocity of their natural expressions, gave little clue to the fact they were all female. Their whiptails were curled up into their cloaks; Alloran knew that even here and engaged in these holy rites they would still have six-inches of bladed steel strapped to their whiptails...

When Arachna entered the chamber she formed, as it were, the centerpiece of a small but imposing procession.

The figure of Arachna was entirely covered by a swath of blue silk cloak with a mask drawn across the opening of the hood so that only the two eyeslits gave humanity to that impression of power. Alloran shifted on his chair. Humanity? Well, he trusted so...

The little procession included half-naked boys waving fans, two more of the blue-cloaked Mantissae, a giant and stupid Womox bearing a massive double-headed axe over a shoulder, and a Fristle fifi holding the silver leads of a couple of baby werstings. The bundles of black and white behaved with a docility amazing in spirited puppies.

Arachna was assisted onto the bed by her retainers who then took up positions which did not obstruct Alloran's view.

One of the Mantissae struck a silver gong.

At once another door concealed by the blue hangings opened and a second procession entered.

Fascinated by these slow and deliberate proceedings, Alloran took a sip of his wine. His throat was dry. He looked at the figure of Arachna on its back on the bed, and saw only the two eyeslits. Was she looking at him? What could she be thinking? He dragged his own gaze away to stare at the man selected for this day's investigations.

He stood between four of the Mantissae, naked, his wrists bound at his back. He was a Khibil, with a proud foxy face, with reddish whiskers that now were not brushed up arrogantly but drooped in dejection. A supercilious, superior race of diffs, Khibils, and this pleased Alloran, for the best results could only come from the best material.

A thread of red wine dribbled down the Khibil's chin.

Arachna's voice rustled like bats' wings.

"You have your question ready to ask at the right time, Vodun?"

"I have, Arachna."

"Do you continue to deny Opaz?"

"I do."

"Do you continue in steadfast loyalty to Takar?"

"I do."

"Are you content that Arachna and her Mantissae serve you so well?"

"I am."

With a single sweeping movement as of a bird opening its wings, Arachna threw the cloak wide.

On the bed lay a Khibil girl. Artful strings of jewels enhanced her beauty and the lushness of her body glowed into the overheated air.

The Khibil jumped, staggered, was caught and held upright. He could see nothing else in all of Kregen but the most beautiful and desirable girl in that terrible and beautiful world.

"Your question, Vodun!"

Rapidly yet carefully, Alloran asked of Arachna what he had demanded of Fraipur.

Groaning, spitting, fighting with his bonds, the Khibil struggled to break free.

One of the Mantissae slashed his bonds loose.

Instantly, without hesitation, he flung himself forward.

Alloran knew that had the girl on the bed been apim he would himself have been demonically impelled forward by passions bursting into flame all over his body. The Khibil had been given to drink, and had no control over himself of any sort.

Watching with a fascination that grew on him each time he witnessed this sacrifice, Alloran saw the climax approaching. A Mantissa moved to the side of the bed. She carried a heavy-hilted dagger. The blade was not a Vallian dagger, being snake-curved; Alloran blinked involuntarily, and took another sip of wine.

From under the figures on the bed a hand showed, a left hand. It moved between their legs with deliberate speed down the bed. The hand opened at the end of a long and flexible tail, stringily muscled, ridged, glinting in a shade far removed from the reddish skin tint of the Khibils' bodies.

Into that tail hand the Mantissa placed the snake-curved dagger.

Alloran sucked in his breath and the wine slopped from the goblet.

The tail hand struck. Viciously it sliced the dagger upwards, upwards and in, deeply in. The Khibil's scream compounded of agony and ecstasy shrieked into that blue-draped room. He collapsed. With a gesture finicky yet savage, Arachna pushed him off and he fell limply to the carpet. The Mantissae did not move. No one moved. Blood smothered the breast of the Khibil girl.

The voice from Arachna was entirely different from that with which she had spoken to Alloran. It husked as though reaching in past cobweb veils of mystery and distance, remote yet penetrating, the voice past reason.

"Strom Rosil will continue to retreat. His powers are limited and grow weaker. You must seize the leem by the throat, not by the tail. Water will not always wash away blood."

The voice swelled so that undercurrents of passion shook the husky words.

"You must choose to drink water or drink blood!"

The voice ceased.

Arachna lay still, eyes closed, the blood shining upon the glorious Khibil body. The Mantissae closed in and wrapped the blue silk cloak about her, drew the concealing mask across those glowing features.

Slowly, Alloran stood up. He was shaking with the passions of the sacrificial ceremony.

He was King Vodun of Southwest Vallia! That could not be denied. There was no more to be discovered here and he walked purposefully to the exit. If Strom Rosil failed him...

Water or Blood? Would he drink Water or Blood?

Which was more fitting for a king?

Ten

At the Leather Bottle

Lon the Knees said: "If you insist, Lyss..."

"I do damn-well insist, so that's an end to it."

"The Leather Bottle is not the place for—"

"Look, Lon. A poor weak defenseless girl has been known to stick a knife into a hulking great brute of a man insulting her. Well, is that not true?"

"Aye, aye. But—"

"That's an end, Lon! *Queyd-arn-tung!*"*

They were standing in a shadowed doorway of a respectable street, the Lane of Sweetmeats, and the evening drew on in long mingled shadows of emerald and ruby. Already the Maiden with the Many Smiles floated over the rooftops of Rashumsmot casting down her fuzzy pink light to blend oddly with the last trailing remnants of the radiance from Zim and Genodras. The air tanged with spicy odors. Folk moved with purpose, to reach home after the day's labors, to find the first wet of the evening, to see what pickings there might be in any of the thieves' quarters abounding in any town where an army is quartered.

Lon stared at this glorious girl, and shook his head.

She wore a beigey yellowish dress that gave a dusty impression and the patterns of green leaves threaded in the material did not please Lon in an obscure way he couldn't fathom. The dress was halfway thigh length and her legs were bare. She wore sandals tied up with, on the left foot, a leather thong and on the right foot a piece of string. She carried her brown leather and canvas knapsack on her left hip.

Over her right hip a frippery of the dress created a flounce that effectively concealed the long Vallian dagger scabbarded to her belt there. Her hair, lustrous and sweetly clean, was tightly bound up. As a Battle Lady she did not habitually let her hair grow long; but she was too much a woman to allow it to be cropped mercilessly, as so many of the Jikai Vuvushis did. Her face, though, was not sweetly clean. That gorgeous face was decidedly grubby.

Black spots dotted it here and there, her eyes were smudged, and an unwholesome looking sore extended down from the right corner of her mouth. She'd painted that on herself in this quiet doorway, with her back to the Lane of Sweetmeats and with Lon standing vacantly at her back.

In one of her belt pouches reposed a small vial of a secretion from the skunk-like animal called a powcy. It really did, as one of her dear friends would say, pong 'orrible. So far she had not had the courage actually to daub the nauseating gunk over herself.

---

* Queyd-arn-tung: no more need be said. *A.B.A.*

If the going got too rough, though, she would—by Vox, she'd stink the place out!

Lon tried one last time.

"Look, Lyss. Yes, all right, we'll go to The Leather Bottle. But if you wore your black leathers and carried swords—"

"D'you think anyone in there would trust me, talk to me? I'd be more likely to be stuck through than I am now, dressed like this."

"Women!" said Lon to himself. "By Black Chunguj! There's no way past them."

With which piece of sage internal logic he set off with Lyss the Lone toward their rendezvous at The Leather Bottle.

As for Lon the Knees himself, his finery had had to be returned from whence it came, that is, back to those from whom he'd borrowed the attire. He wore his own decent rough homespun, a tunic that was improbably hard wearing and might even see him out. The color was indeterminate but tended to the brown. The main gauche was stuffed down inside in its scabbard. He carried a cudgel. He was a Vallian citizen, not a koter, out for the evening and dressed for the occasion.

At that, he'd never really got on with those danged breeches. Yes, so all right, his legs were on the—curvy—side. But there was nothing like a clean breechclout and bare legs. He felt limber as he walked along beside Lyss, reveling in this aspect of the evening alone.

Even had there not been mineral oil in abundance, folk tended these days not to be so strictly bound by the twin suns in their going to bed and rising. The seven moons of Kregen among them, at different times, cast down light. The Leather Bottle, therefore, at this early hour, had not yet begun to hum.

The place looked snug under its low ceil, with wooden benches aptly situated in nooks and with a rotund barrel-row mounted on trestles behind the bar. The landlord polished up a tankard with his upper hands while his middle pair poured drinks for the two Fristles leaning against the bar. They were giving inconspicuous glances to the six Rapas sitting in the bay window, making a deal of noise and clearly intending that this should be the start of a night to remember.

The Rapas looked out of place here, even to Lyss, for no one else was a soldier in uniform, while these Rapas were churgurs, sword and shield soldiers out of one of the new king's regiments of foot. Their feathers bristled, brick red and dusty black, and their fierce beaked faces showed animation as they toasted one another in turn. They were in undress, wearing the king's colors of maroon and gray with the badge of the sea barynth.

"And, Lon," said Lyss when they were served at a small table in the opposite corner, "you wanted me to come here all dressed up in black leathers."

"Upvil, the landlord, may be an Och, but he knows how to respect a lady." Lon gave her a mean look. "You do not, Lyss, look a lady right now."

"I suppose not."

For this night's adventure, Silda Segutoria had consciously forced herself to think and act as Lyss the Lone. So she did not throw her head back and roar appreciation of the neatness of Lon's remark. She just quaffed her ale and looked about, and her right hand rested easily at her side, not too far from her dagger.

The Rapas were kicking up a din so that Lon shook his head and said: "Pretty soon Upvil will have to call the heavy squad and have them chucked out."

"But if they weren't soldiers?"

"Oh, well, that'd be different."

"Well, I hope your friend Crafty Kando turns up before the fight starts."

Lon started to say something, halted himself, and then spat out: "So do I."

His cudgel propped against his stool would be adequate in the typical tavern brawl; against the straight cut and thrust pallixters of the Rapas it would soon prove lacking.

The tavern began to fill, ale flowed, fruits and biscuits were available, and pretty soon customers began to ask for wine. Lon kept on looking at the door. Crafty Kando might be too crafty for his own good in this business, for while Lon did not know what Lyss wanted the thief for, he felt instinctively that there would be profit in it.

There were girls circulating in the tavern, gauzily dressed, clashing bangles, heavily made up and wafting scents that cloyed in the odors of ale and wine and food. They drew shouts of approval and the occasional coin. They indulged in a few ferocious hair and bodice-pulling fights over the money. And still Crafty Kando did not put in an appearance.

Seeing girls in this condition upset Silda far more than watching them on the battlefield.

The people patronizing Upvil's Leather Bottle were mostly from the rough side of life, folk like Lon who did the unpleasant jobs. The regular patrons grew restive with the high spirits and uproar from the Rapa soldiery.

It made not the slightest difference who started the fight. That there would be a fight was perfectly clear. Lon suddenly half-rose and then sank back on his stool. In a low voice he said, "Thank Opaz the Merciful! Here he is now."

Looking quickly toward the door past the bulky shoulders of a Brokelsh just standing up with a bottle in his hand, Lyss saw the fellow in the doorway. He was dressed inconspicuously in drab browns, with a down-drawn hat obscuring much of his features save for a sharp chin. On his hip rested a goodly sized canvas bag.

Then the Brokelsh threw the bottle, the Rapas bristled up with feathers flying, and the tavern erupted.

Lon sprang up to run to the door after Crafty Kando and was instantly engulfed in a crashing moil of men striking out with joyous abandon. One Rapa was already down with a bent beak. The hairy Brokelsh who'd thrown the bottle ducked just too late to avoid the stool that thwacked solidly into his thick Brokelsh skull. Men were staggering about locked together, others were swinging wild punches, others were flailing with bottles and stools. No one—so far—had drawn a steel weapon, edged and pointed. This was a tavern brawl with unwritten laws.

How long before the Rapa churgurs, massively outnumbered, would draw their swords was in the jovial hands of Beng Brorgal, the patron saint of tavern brawlers.

A big fellow with a purple nose rose up before Lon and hit him over the head with a bottle. Lon yelped, managing to duck most of the force, and stuck the end of his cudgel into the fellow's ribs. He yelped in turn.

A man with the effluvium of the fish market upon him lashed out with his boot at Lon's undefended back.

The boot did not quite reach Lon because a sandal tied up with string stuck itself out sideways and the man's shin smacked into the edge of the sandal-clad foot. The shin came off worst from that encounter.

Lyss didn't stop. Her foot whipped down, planted itself firmly on the tavern floor and her other sandal, with the leather thong, swirled up as she swiveled forward. Her toe investigated most forcefully portions of the man's anatomy that could not bear the scrutiny.

He let out a gargling screech and fell down.

Lyss put her fist into a fellow's mouth and felt teeth break.

She skipped quickly sideways to allow one of the Rapas to go charging past. She let him go and clipped the man following him alongside the ear. The Rapas might be Rapas, fierce vulturine diffs, but they were soldiers and they were outnumbered.

The tavern resembled a chicken coop when the fox breaks in. Men—and some of the women—were tangled up everywhere, lashing out, kicking, biting, scratching. Bottles flew. Upvil the Och landlord put his head down behind his bar and wondered if being a landlord was worth the trouble. The Watch might be along soon; by the time they arrived he'd be well out of pocket.

The original locus of the fight around the Rapas had long been forgotten. Men hit anybody handy. It would not have been surprising if one Rapa had hit another in the confusion.

Lon dragged himself off the floor, whooped a breath, spotted Lyss hitting a Gon beside his ear, and yelled.

"He's run off!"

"Well, run after him!"

Lon's face empurpled to match his nose. He dragged in another breath smelling the dust of the floor mingled with spilled wine and blood, and thought savagely to himself what he wouldn't yell out at Lyss.

"Run—in this lot! Like flies in treacle!"

He climbed up onto his feet and instantly a bulky fellow tangling with two furry Fristles collided with him. He was knocked flying again, skidding across the floor on squashed juicy gregarians, the fruit greasing his swift passage under a table. That fell over on him and the tankards of ale upon it liberally baptised him with libations to Beng Dikkane the patron saint of all the ale drinkers of Paz.

Lon shook with frustrated anger.

He clambered up, his cudgel still gripped in his fist.

His hair fell over his eyes. He glared about. There was red in the eyes of Lon the Knees.

He spotted a Rapa and a Brokelsh, representatives of the diffs who'd started the fracas, locked together, each trying to throttle the other.

Lon marched over, knocking a fellow out of his way.

He used the cudgel twice.

One blow knocked the Brokelsh senseless to the floor.

The other struck the Rapa down so that he collapsed in a flurry of his own feathers.

Someone grabbed Lon's arm.

He swiveled, enraged, swinging the cudgel up for a blow that would brain this new rast troubling him.

Lyss said acidly, "We didn't come here to enjoy ourselves! Your friend's run off and he'll be long gone if we don't—"

"Oh," snapped Lon, swinging the cudgel away from Lyss's head. "He'll be in some sewer by now. Forget him for tonight."

Lyss breathed hard through her nose.

"I suppose you are right. By the foul armpit and lice-ridden hair of Sister Melga the Harpy Herself! This is another day wasted."

Lon was taken aback by her vehemence.

The fight caterwauled on, the noise prodigious, the maids all run off, the air thick with flying stools and bottles.

"Well, Lyss. I suppose we could try The Dancing Flea."

She fixed the animal-handler with an eye of gimlet steel.

"Let us do that."

They moved aside to let a man somersault between them and go thump onto his head on the floor.

"Is there no back way out?" Lyss jerked her head at the doorway. "That's choked up worse than the first bend in a zorca race."

"Yes. Through the kitchens."

"Lead on."

A couple of times Silda had heard the emperor add a word that sounded like "makduff" when he'd said that.

Duff was one of the many Kregish names for spoon, for each size and use had its own nomenclature, and what a black spoon had to do with leading on Silda couldn't fathom. One of these fine days she'd ask the emperor. If Opaz smiled, that was, and she wasn't shipped off to meet the grey ones on the Ice Floes of Sicce...

They whistled through the kitchens without stopping. Upvil's charming Och wife, wringing her hands in her apron, watched them wide-eyed. The serving maids huddled, although some of them were peeking through the half-open door taking a lively interest in the entertainment. The smells of the kitchen faded as Lyss stepped out into the night air.

"This way," said Lon, and started off at a brisk trot.

In the fuzzy pink moonlight they hurried along, watchful, naturally, as any sensible person must be in a town of Kregen where soldiers are quartered and there is counter-deviltry afoot. Not everyone accepted Vodun Alloran as the new kov instead of Katrin Rashumin as the kovneva, let alone as some new puffed-up king.

Lyss the Lone, thinking as Silda Segutoria, intended to make more stringent inquiries concerning this aspect of the new regime in Rahartdrin.

The distance was not far and Lon led her into a side street, the Alley of Washerwomen, where he halted at the front of a tumble-down building. The place next door no longer existed, having been demolished in the battle, and on the other side an even more disreputable construction loomed blackly with no discernible purpose.

"This it?"

"Aye. This is The Dancing Flea."

Lyss wrinkled up her nose.

"Yes, Lyss, well. You are sure?"

"Let's not have all that again, my wild churmod trainer!"

He had to smile at this, and pushed the door open.

By comparison, The Leather Bottle was a veritable top-class establishment. The clientele looked as though they'd far prefer to slit your throat than stand you a drink. Shifty faces, furtive eyes, unshaven chins, hands hovering above weapon hilts—oh, yes, a Sister of the Rose would understand hell holes like this.

Silda had often felt that any self-respecting man would either grow a proper beard or shave himself clean. Two or three days' fuzz on the chin gave a man a dirty look. He couldn't be bothered, he was on the down trail, a trail no doubt littered with empty bottles. Some men, she'd been told with sneering laughter by some of the girls, actually thought they looked romantic unshaven. When they scrubbed that bristle brush down a girl's cheek when they embraced her, surely they didn't think she enjoyed the experience?

Moustaches, of course, were an entirely different and exciting matter...

Lon's quick birdlike gaze took in the familiar scene, spotting quondam friends, people he might rely on in trouble, allies, and also those he would not turn his back on, those indifferent to his welfare, and those who were deadly enemies. Of these latter he could see only one, black-browed Ortyg the Kaktu. He was sitting with his cronies playing the Game of Moons at a side table.

There was no sign of Crafty Kando.

Lon said, "You'd better wait outside, Lyss. I'll ask Ob-eye Mantig if he's seen Kando."

Before Lyss could reply, a girl wearing light draperies and imitation gems, her face plastered with paint, her hair a frizz of blonde in which the tiara-like vimshu glittered artificially, glided up and threw a tankard's contents in Lyss's face.

Lyss licked the suds off her lips and wiped a finger across her eyes. The stuff was very thin beer.

Lon yelped: "Climi! You crazy shishi!"

"We don't want her in here!" Climi swung the pot back. "Clear off!" She threw the tankard.

Lyss stuck up her right hand, took the tankard out of the air and hurled it back. The pewter edge struck Climi on the forehead. For an instant she stood. Then her eyes crossed and she slumped down, her gauzy tawdriness swirling like the canvas of an argenter being handled.

Instantly, with a bull roar, Ortyg the Kaktu reared up. The Game of Moons went flying. He ripped out a knife and charged headlong for Lon.

"Run, Lyss!" yelped Lon.

Silda Segutoria battled with the persona of Lyss the Lone. One said: "Run, you fambly!" The other said: "Run from that scum?"

By that time it was too late.

Ortyg threw himself at Lon. The animal-handler used to fractious beasts twisted aside and swung his cudgel. Ortyg was quick and the blow missed. He roared back, foaming.

Lon ducked and Lyss put one fist into Ortyg's guts, kicked him in the face as he doubled up and smashed a hard edge down on the back of his neck. Only then did Silda take over, grab Lon and fairly bundle the pair of them out through the door.

They ran up the Alley of Washerwomen.

At the corner they halted and looked back. There was no pursuit.

"He wasn't there, anyway, Lyss."

"No. As I said, another day wasted. Next time you get hold of Crafty Kando, Lon, we'll meet in a place where we don't get into a fight the minute we draw breath!"

Eleven

Drak changes plans

The black-beaked yellow-winged flyer soared on through the early morning mists, tinted palest apple-green and soft rose-red by the veiled radiance from Zim and Genodras. The breeze blew past the flyer astride the flutduin's back; but no blazonry of apparel in fluttering scarves and trailing cords, no swirling confusion of feathers, marked the flutduin or his rider out from the half-squadron who flew escort right, left, above and below and to the rear.

Drak, Prince Majister of Vallia, flew this early morning recce patrol in person. His brown Vallian eyes looked down past the curve of his mount's neck. His brain noted, numbered and catalogued all he saw.

The bird's powerful wingbeats carried him on in a long undulating series of perfectly judged strokes. Drak did not have the opportunity to fly a flutduin as often as he would have wished. There was, truly, little to compare with the experience. Riding a zorca, well, that was superb in its own way, a quite different way from this joyous flight through thin air.

Two ulms* off and spread out below like toy soldiers on parade lay the host of Rosil Yasi, Strom of Morcray; Kataki.

Despite the nibbling advances made and local victories gained over him, the Kataki Strom still could field a formidable force. Drak's icy brain went on figuring the numbers, the formations, the qualities and types of the troops spread out below.

The Jiktar who had taken command of this half squadron to escort the prince shrilled a warning cry. He used his long flexible lance to point up and ahead.

Well, by Vox, you couldn't expect to carry out a recce without meeting opposition.

Strom Rosil's aerial component consisted mainly of fluttrells and mirvols, birds and flying animals in general use among the aerial cavalry of many nations. So far as Drak was aware, the flutduin, which he considered the best of all saddle birds, was to be found only in the country of Djanduin. His father, who was the king of that distant land down south in Havilfar, had organized the supply of top-quality flutduins to his island stromnate of Valka, to the east of Vallia's main island.

A goodly force of flutduin aerial cavalry had been built up over the seasons, and a fresh colony had been established in his mother's province of the Blue Mountains. The more hidebound elements of Vallia had resisted this uncanny idea of fighting from the backs of great birds of the air; but

---

* ulm: five sixths of a mile, approximately 1,500 yards. A dwabur equals five miles. *A.B.A.*

the proof of the soundness of the scheme had been seen when the aerial cavalry of Hamal, among other nations, had so plagued Vallia.

Drak would have liked a force of Djangs from Djanduin. Those four-armed warrior Dwadjangs were among the most formidable, powerful and feared fighting men of all Paz.

Still, the Valkan flyers he had with him, trained up by Djangs, were efficient at handling their mounts in the air and consummate in the art of aerial combat.

So he had no real problems over the patrol that flew down toward his own little force. The recce was almost over, in any case, and he had the Kataki Strom's dispositions filed away in his head, so they could swirl their wings and fly home.

One or two of the flutswods astride their birds, tough soldiers of the air, let rip a few pleasantries at thus turning tail. But their job was to escort the Prince Majister, not to tangle with benighted fluttrell-riders.

The recce patrol tamely flew back to camp.

Jumping off his bird and letting him be gathered up in the skilful hands of young Emin the Cheeky who couldn't wait until he was old enough to become a soldier and as a flutswod join the ranks of the aerial cavalry, Drak gave the graceful bird a gentle pat.

"Well done!"

"Aye, jis," quoth young Emin the Cheeky. "When you chose my Bright Feather you could not have chosen better."

Drak favored the lad with a smile and then said: "You keep him well-groomed. Your Bright Feather could sort out a whole squadron of those fluttrells before the second breakfast."

"What!" exclaimed Emin. "No, jis. Before the first breakfast!"

Drak laughed and took himself off to the tent where the chiefs of the army waited. He handed his spyglass to his orderly, Nath the Strict, for telescopes although relatively common and much-used were still valuable property needing care in use, and ducked his head to enter the tent.

He greeted the assembled chiefs and succinctly gave his impression of Yasi's host, the dispositions and his intentions.

Kapt Enwood nal Venticar, as the senior officer present, nodded his head and spoke first.

"The plan is good, jis. Since we have drawn him north our fortunes have changed. This day—well, this day may see a victory we can follow up."

The barrel-bodied man wearing simple pikeman's kit with the addition of a few discreet touches of gold here and there, and a cloak a trifle more scarlet than that generally allowed, cleared his throat. His face might have been constructed from weathered oak, old boots and black iron. His eyes, of good Vallian brown, were deeply sunk and his eyebrows grew like twin thorn-ivy hedges.

"Majister," he said in his gravelly voice. "Did you see anything of their phalanx?"

"I saw no pikemen, Brytevax Thandor. And I would prefer you to remember to address me as jis."

"Your command, jis!"

This man, Thandor Veltan ti Therfuing, this chunky, stubborn, immoveable Phalanx commander, had started out as a brumbyte in the files with the original Phalanx of Therminsax. He had gained recognition and promotion. Now he had been appointed brumbytevax, generally abbreviated to brytevax, to take command of Drak's phalangite force. He was known as Thandor the Rock.

The divisional commanders began to give their views, Drak listened, nodding from time to time. All of them recognized the importance of the intelligence. If that Kataki cramph did not have a phalanx force, the task this day would by that amount be less difficult. It would not be easy. By Vox, no, it would not be easy!

The army already in motion since before dawn would now move into those positions selected to give them the greatest advantage. Initial layout was highly important. With the phalanx force as the central pivot, Drak intended to refuse one wing and sweep the other around in a massive onslaught of everything he could spare. The air would be cleared by the flyers and the few airboats he had under command. Once the first contacts had been made and the light troops, the kreutzin, had done their work, and if Opaz Militant smiled on them this day, they should roll up Strom Yasi like a worn-out carpet.

Jiktar Endru and Jiktar Naghan the Bow, commanding the prince's bodyguard regiments, stood near the doorway, a part of the proceedings inside and a part of the constant watch kept outside.

Because his father's bunch of maniacs, called his juruk jikai, his guard corps, were organized in their own idiosyncratic way, Drak had to bare the throat to seeing different people representing the two regiments. They had some kind of rota system to choose commanders. He had representatives of the Emperor's Sword Watch and the Emperor's Yellow Jackets with him. One thing Drak did know. He'd not just far rather have them on his side than fight against them—he just wouldn't even think of fighting against them.

He looked about, raising his eyebrows.

Of no one in particular, he inquired: "Where is Leone Starhammer?"

An instant silence dropped down like a curtain. Then three or four spoke at once, and stopped. Drak looked puzzled. Now what the hell was going on?

He called across to Endru near the entrance. If anyone ought to know it ought to be commanders of the other two of his bodyguards.

"Endru?"

"Yes, jis. Leone has gone to greet Queen Lushfymi."

To Drak it appeared a volcano had gone off inside his head.

He opened his mouth, couldn't speak, shut his mouth. He swallowed. He looked balefully about. Then he got out a tithe of the words seething in him.

"Queen Lush! By Vox! Why does the woman have to choose the day of a battle to come visiting!"

Diplomatically, Endru rapped out: "It is clear she did not know a battle was due today."

"I don't know," said Drak, almost snarling. "I wouldn't put anything past her—and she is very, very welcome, of course. Always. Except—perhaps today..."

No one in the tent cared to mention that the queen had been referred to by her nickname by the prince. The old emperor, whom Queen Lushfymi had hoped to marry, had said with great meaning that anyone who called her Queen Lush would have his or her head off. And he'd meant it.

For all that, in these latter days Queen Lush was the name by which most folk thought of Queen Lushfymi of Lome.

Drak scowled. He stuck his fist onto his rapier hilt and fiddled, an uncharacteristic gesture.

"Kapt Enwood, you'll have to take the right wing and I'll handle the left. Brytevax Thandor will command the center. By these means if the queen cannot be persuaded to watch the battle from a safe distance she will at least not be in the thick of it."

"With pleasure, jis!" exclaimed Enwood. He rubbed his hands. He'd thought he was in for a dull day. The plan called for the right wing to attack and the left to be refused.

"And not a word to the queen about the battle plan! Is that understood?"

"Understood, prince!" Everyone spoke up as though on parade.

Drak looked about on these people, folk he counted as friends and companions as well as loyal subordinates, all working for the good of Vallia. He could, had he wished, have become emotional. Instead, and without drawing his sword to bless them, he said: "Fight today with Vox to point and sharpen your weapons. May the light of Opaz go with you and your soldiers, every one. Remberee!"

"Remberee, prince!" they said, and then took their leave and went about the business of the day.

Nath the Strict came in with a tray bearing a cup of scalding hot Kregan tea and a silver plate of miscils and palines, all of which Drak tumbled down his gullet, not taking from the delicacies the enjoyment he should. His mind was plagued with doubts, which he knew he would throw off once the trumpets pealed the advance.

Concern for Queen Lush preyed on his mind.

His own small juruk jikai, consisting of Endru's PMSW and Naghan's PMDA, would see he came to no personal harm. Also, he was well aware that his father's bunch of madmen, ESW and EYJ, although much preferring to be with the emperor, would take particular care of his son.

So that left Leone Starhammer's QLJV a free hand to care for the queen.

He had often heard his grandfather complaining about the way his people insisted on looking after him and standing in the way when the old devil wanted to get to handstrokes with the foe. His father, an even greater devil, said the same, even more vehemently. Now Drak understood much of those complaints.

If he told anyone of the bodyguards corps to go off and reinforce the right wing, as had been the original plan, they'd kick up an awful rumpus. They might not refuse; they'd make damn sure they were within striking distance of where he placed himself in the battle line.

Damn Queen Lush!

Then he felt remorse at his own churlishness.

She was a wonderful woman, who worked wholeheartedly for Vallia. Once her own country had been properly cleared of the flutsmen and slavers and aragorn who festered there, as they still did in the unliberated parts of Vallia, she would have to choose where to live. She would always be welcome in Vallia. Drak was sure of that.

Finishing the tea which as ever was the best drink a man could quaff, good honest Kregan tea, he snatched a handful of palines and quit the tent. There'd be strong wine for the swods in the ranks, for the soldiers deserved that, at the least.

Before him the army moved like a multi-colored quilt spread over the ground. He enumerated off the formations, saw the flutter of flags, the treshes brilliant under the growing power of the suns. Armor and weapons glinted. Bands played. Nearer and in the center the three Kerchuris of the phalanx force sent up their paean, a strong solemn hymn to battle. Every now and again they'd change into a sprightly and usually risqué song, simply open-handed joyous ditties they'd sing as they marched forward into hell.

On the right of the line marched the First Vallia. The center was held by the Second Therminsax. Over on the left the Fifth Drak marched like a solid wall.

The Second had received their name from the town where the emperor had first created the phalanx. The Fifth were named for the half-man half-god mythical figure of Vallia's dim and legendary past. He, too, was thusly named.

The other Kerchuri of the Third Phalanx, the Sixth, were called the Sixth Delia. He wished they were with him today.

As for the Second Phalanx, up in the northeast past Hawkwa country, they consisted of the Third Opaz and the Fourth Velia.

He tried to brisk himself up as he mounted aboard his zorca, Happy Calamity. The days after the Battle of Corvamsmot were over. Alloran had won crushingly there. He'd had this blight mysteriously called Zankov with him then. In letters from his father and mother, Drak had been warned against this Zankov. The most disturbing item of news was that his younger sister Dayra might be implicated with the fellow's misdeeds. There was a suspicion that he was acting as the paymaster for Alloran. Whatever the truth of all these rumors, one thing was known.

Zankov had slain the old emperor and blamed Drak's father, the new emperor. This slander was proved by Queen Lush, who knew the truth. At this memory Drak suddenly, overpoweringly, found himself longing for today never to happen.

If only... If only he were back in Valka, or Delphond, riding zorcas in the wide plains below the Blue Mountains! If only he could give up the time necessary to study the old books... If only—well, he had a battle on his hands and a queen to cosset. A fugitive glimpse of Silda Segutoria's face and form passed before him, and he sighed, knowing if she were here they'd never keep her out of the hottest fighting.

His retinue closed up. Trumpeters, standard bearers, messengers, they were all tense, quivering, anticipating the excitements of the day. Also, they should expect the horrors. He rode out ahead, stony-faced, still and erect in the saddle.

The mass of soldiers ahead moving out with purpose, must act like a gigantic organism this day. They must crush Strom Rosil Yasi for good and press on through Ovvend and hurl into Kaldi and so reclaim all the mainland for Vallia.

One of his aides, beside himself with excitement, called out: "Jis! The queen!"

Drak turned his head and looked.

The blaze of color and glitter of gold and gems would fair blind anyone. Queen Lushfymi rode at the head of her regiment, with Leone and the high officers in close attendance. The queen rode a gray, and the zorca was so white as to appear ghostlike. The zorca's single spiral horn jutting from the center of her forehead was completely coated with gold leaf. Every scrap of harness was studded with gems. Drak was not so foolish as to suppose those jewels to be paste.

Queen Lush wore armor, golden armor, encrusted with gems. Enormous clouds of feathers floated over her helmet. She carried the usual arsenal of Kregan weapons, and spare weaponry as well. Drak didn't know if she looked splendid or foolish.

He tended to suspect she was absolutely splendid and only his own ill humor could make him think otherwise.

Her cavalcade halted, pushing his own folk a trifle to make room. Zorca hooves stamped. The suns glinted blindingly off armor and jewels and weapons. The strong sweet perfume of the women wafted across the small intervening space.

"Lahal, majestrix."

"Lahal, my dear Drak. I've come to make sure you poor silly dear that you don't get yourself killed."

Twelve

Of Water and of Blood

The manacles of iron, old and rusty, cut into his wrists cruelly. The fetters were of the same rusty antiquity and bit into his ankles. He was stripped naked. He hung suspended against a dismal brick wall, all running and slimy and green, and considered he was very hard done by. Very hard indeed.

The cell was small enough, in all conscience, and light entered through a barred opening high in a tunnel-like slot indicating ground level was high above his head.

The jailers had, at the least, taken away the skeleton hanging on the opposite wall that had greeted San Fraipur when they'd dragged him down here. By the sacred radiance of Opaz! This was a dolorous place.

The jailers did feed him. One was a Gon, a tallish fellow rather stooped, with the bald shaven head of a Gon smothered in butter. The other was an apim, with half a left ear, a bent and broken nose, no teeth that were visible, and hands like claws. They fed him thin gruel, without honey, and crusts of bread green as grass. On this dreadful fare San Fraipur perforce kept body and ib together.

And why?

In the great and glorious name of Opaz—why?

Because he'd told Vodun Alloran the truth?

Or, perhaps, because that thing Arachna had so willed it?

"Return in four burs," King Vodun Alloran had said, "and give me the answers to my questions."

This Fraipur had done to the best of his ability.

He'd noticed, there in that stifling throne room with the black and green clad Katakis standing guard around the draped walls, that Alloran was flushed so that his face shone with sweat and passion. Since he had dismissed Fraipur he must have gone through some profound experience. So judged the sorcerer.

"Well, Fraipur! Speak out, man!"

No longer, then, the polite address as San...

"I have given the question much thought. The forces with Strom Rosil are known, unless he has suffered another reverse."

Alloran didn't like that. With a sad and ugly feeling, for Fraipur had been devoted to this man, he recognized that he felt pleasure at his shaft.

"Go on, Fraipur. Tsleetha-tsleethi!"

"Yes, majister. The strengths of the Prince Majister are known only as to the last reports. I judge, and with reason, that he will receive reinforcements that will enable him to do more than resist the future advance of Strom Rosil." Fraipur hurried on. "If Kaldi is to be prevented from falling into the hands of Prince Drak, then we must send more troops."

Alloran leaned back. He looked pleased. "Yes?"

"That is the simple-minded reading of the situation, one any school child could arrive at."

"And?"

"Not and, majister, but. You would need to strip forces from their garrisons here in Rahartdrin. You would have to postpone the invasion of Tezpor and the other islands." Here he shot a hard look at the king. "You do remember, majister, what you have promised regarding Fruningen?"

Alloran roused himself in his throne. He leaned forward and his face blackened.

"You are insolent, Fraipur! What I choose to do with Fruningen, with any conquest, is mine alone to decide! Is that clear?"

"But, majister—Fruningen is small, a home for my friends, the teaching academies for the wizards—"

"If they are all as you are—well, never mind that. I will think on it. Go on with your answers."

Fraipur felt a drop of sweat plop off the end of his nose. He closed his eyes, opened them, and said: "What will happen is this, majister, if you decide to reinforce Strom Rosil Yasi against the Vallians—"

"I am the true Vallia!"

"Of course. Against the usurpers. They have greater resources now, they have more regiments. You will be sucked in and overwhelmed—"

"I do not care for this, Fraipur!"

Fraipur struggled on.

"I judge the situation to be one for negotiation. If you hold Rahartdrin, the other islands, you will prove to be extremely hard to attack and dislodge. The sea crossing will be dangerous, and you have a fleet to protect the shores. Rather than lose many men in attempting to oust you, the emperor may come to terms, will recognize you—"

Alloran stood up. His face was a blot of anger.

"And I thought you a great mage! You are contemptible. You see nothing. Don't you understand I have many mercenaries sailing to join me? They come from North Pandahem, thousands of them. Soon I shall be so strong as to overwhelm this brat Prince Drak."

"The people—the usurpers—in Vondium know that. They have a fleet, in the air they are far more powerful than are you. They will take steps to prevent the paktuns from reaching you—"

"Enough! You have failed me yet again, Fraipur."

Alloran sat back on his throne. He put his chin on his right fist, gazing levelly at the sorcerer. His left hand began to run the rapier up and down in the scabbard.

"Tell me, what do you know of Water and of Blood?"

"Water and blood? Why, one you may drink with relish, the other not. One passes in to comfort, the other passes out to end it all. If there is a choice—"

"You prattle like an infant with a rattle in its teeth. I know the answer. I have been shown. Water is thin, not for a warrior. Blood is thick, and will slake a warrior's thirst. I choose blood!"

A conceit took Fraipur then, so that he was able to speak up.

"If you must choose between water and blood, majister, then my advice is to choose water. For the water represents the seas about Rahartdrin and the islands, which will wall you off in safety to come to terms with the emperor. The usurping emperor, to be sure. The blood will flow to everyone's ruin if you try to fight on the mainland."

So, here he was.

A famed Wizard of Fruningen strung up in rusty chains that were like to take his hands off soon. It was intolerable! His powers were real enough and he was confident he had read Alloran's riddle aright. That damned Arachna had told him that about the water and the blood. Well, the she leem, she'd been clever enough, seeing what was ahead, to cloak her answer so that the idiot Alloran brought his doom on his own head.

Oh, yes, Fraipur's powers were real enough; but they did not extend to getting him out of these chains and up that tunnel and through the iron-barred opening and out into the blessed fresh air of Kregen.

He closed his eyes and began to work his mind away from the pain in wrists and ankles, and the pain all over, come to that. He made himself think of the long scrubbed table at the academy on his island home of Fruningen, of the other lads all tussling and laughing and learning. He thought of the books, the lifs and the hyr lifs, of the scrolls. He thought of the mingled suns shine of Zim and Genodras. And he thought of the food the slaves brought out at meal times, which was attacked with such zest by the acolytes learning the arts to become Wizards of Fruningen.

Somehow or other, San Fraipur fabricated defenses against the madness-inducing situation in which he found himself.

Some distance away from Fraipur's miserable dungeon and considerably higher, Silda Segutoria sat polishing up her sword, the drexer glitteringly bright already, and thinking dark thoughts.

By Vox! This time she'd go armed to the teeth!

Still, poor old Lon the Knees. It was not really his fault. He lived in a parlous society, a heaving mass of humanity not far removed from the slaves. He'd have made enemies as well as friends. And, to be sure, she found herself warming to the bandy-legged fellow. He was a real character. Still and all, he had to produce Crafty Kando soon, or Silda Segutoria, if not Lyss the Lone, would blow up like a volcano in full eruption.

She strapped on the drexer on its individual belt alongside the rapier and shifted the various straps and fittings until they felt comfortable. The knapsack nestled on her left hip. She could dive her left hand in there in a jiffy, and she'd not cut herself up as that poor little spinlikl had done.

Her black leathers were soft and supple from skillful ministrations. Over her shoulders she swirled a dark plum-colored half-cloak. On her head, in place of the uniform helmet, or the lady's version of the universal Vallian floppy-brimmed hat, she slapped a charcoal-gray boltsch, a round hat fabricated from a felt-like material, flat and wide which could be pulled down fetchingly on one side. Within and padded to her head was a hard-boiled leather skull.

She'd bought the thing yesterday, it had cost two and a half silver stivers, and she'd ripped out the bright yellow and green feathers. No doubt the hat represented plunder, for the feathers were not local. No doubt, also, that was why she'd been able to haggle down to two and a half. The thing was worth a trifle more than that.

The schturval* of Rahartdrin, now officially extinguished by King Vodun, was yellow and green with two diagonal red slashes, together with a lotus flower.

Making sure everything was shipshape and Vallian fashion, she stomped out in her tall black boots.

Perhaps, this time, she could arrange what amounted to a meeting between two worlds.

High life and low life having failed, she'd fallen back on the sensible person's course of action and gone for religion.

All folk tended to have one chief god in whom they reposed trust and confidence, although some of the horrors called religions in Havilfar created sheer terror in the believers. As well as Opaz, chiefest among the spirits, the light of the Invisible Twins made manifest, Vallians gave their

---

* Schturval: The emblem entire consisting of colors and symbol considered as an entity. A.B.A.

allegiance to a bewildering variety of other gods, godlings, goddesses and spirits.

Vox stood in a category apart; from being the favorite of the warriors Vox had spread into universal use.

Mind you, said Silda to herself as she marched briskly along in the mid-afternoon suns light, all these temples gave openings for a whole slew of priests and priestesses to wax fat on the credulous. Cities claimed precedence very often on economic, military or political grounds. The factor of the number of temples within a city could never be ignored. The city with more temples than its neighbor always made its citizens feel they had scored heavily even before any argument began.

Rashumsmot, as its name indicated, was a town and not a city. If King Vodun decided to stay on here he might well build and enlarge the place and call it Rashumsden. He would have little need of inviting new priests, temples and godlings into his new city, for Rashumsmot was already lavishly provided, as any self-respecting town must be, with a splendiferous array of places of worship.

"The Temple of Applica the Bounteous," she'd told Lon, most firmly. "I don't give a damn if Crafty Kando thinks Applica is a fat old besom. Just get him there. The Day is the Day of Applica Conceived, so there will be crowds."

"But, Lyss—"

"It's hard enough to arrange my off-duty to coincide with the whims of your friend. By Vox, Lon! Time's a-wasting."

"Yes, Lyss..."

So, here she was, a plum-colored cloak swirled about her black leathers concealing her weaponry, a hat pulled over one ear, striding off to the half-ruined temple of a fat old lady goddess who oversaw the production of twins—if you believed that, of course.

The temple had not suffered too badly and had not burned. The roof over the priestess's quarters had been stoved in, no doubt by an airboat falling on it, and they had shifted the acolytes out of their rooms to take them over. The main area lay open, fronting five tall columns and a broad flight of steps whereon the priestesses performed. The congregation was composed of a wide variety of people, three quarters of them women. The most noticeable common denominator was that they were pregnant.

Lon spotted Silda and trotted over and they stood in the shadows of the first interior wall, shoulder high, to watch. Lon quivered.

"There he is. And Lop-eared Tobi's with him, too."

Following Lon's inconspicuous gesture, Silda saw the two men. Crafty Kando appeared much as he had when he'd put his nose into The Leather Bottle. His companion had made some attempt to smarten himself up to visit the temple, and still contrived to look an unhanged ruffian, bad teeth, pocked skin and stringy hair and all.

Two worlds, meeting on neutral territory, said Silda to herself, and sighed, and thrust away weak thoughts of happier days and places where she'd rather be right now.

Incense smoke drifted across, mingling with the choked smells of the mass of people. Many were kneeling. They were being led through the rites of the service by the priestesses and chanted and responded to order. Crafty Kando and Lop-eared Tobi eased across and Lon moved forward by the low wall to speak with them. Silda waited. At last Lon turned, smiling, and Silda walked over to join them.

The pappattu was made quickly, informally, and Silda, about to broach the subject burning uppermost in her mind now she'd actually made contact with the thief, saw over his shoulder a woman in a brown dress beckoning to someone hidden beyond a pillar. Before Silda spoke she saw a bull-necked swaggering fellow step out from beyond the pillar. By his black brows alone she would have recognized him as Ortyg the Kaktu. The last time she'd seen him in The Dancing Flea she'd knocked him down. Well, well, now...

Without more ado, Ortyg hurled his knife and then whipped out his sword and charged. The knife thudded into the wood trim of the corner as Silda shoved Crafty Kando out of the way. Four other men ran in the wake of Ortyg the Kaktu. He knocked over a pregnant woman kneeling in his way. His face was black with passion.

"I'll have you now, rast, cramph, vermin!"

The three men with Silda swung about sharply, and exclamations unfit for utterance in a temple fell from their lips. Silda didn't bother with any of that. Out came her rapier in a twinkling and the main gauche, the Jiktar and the Hikdar. She leaped forward. Ortyg recognized her. His scowling face broke into a dazzling smile, black teeth and all, and he fairly howled down.

Silda had no time to waste. This was not the time for pretty expositions of the art of the sword. Anyway, Ortyg was out to kill them all, that was clear, and she could not afford to take risks, for herself or for Lon.

So she took the clumsy blow along the left-hand dagger, stuck Ortyg through the guts, withdrew, slashed the next fellow down the face, came back into line to stick the third in the eye. The fourth was gasping up blood around the knife in his throat. Lon started forward.

"I'll buy you a new knife, Lon. Run!"

Incontinently, the four of them ran out of the uproar spreading within the Temple of Applica the Bounteous.

They didn't stop running and then walking swiftly until they were past the Street of Krokan the Glorious where they could ease down and catch their breath. Of them all, Lop-eared Tobi whooped in the most gasps and wheezes. Silda's breathing was scarcely troubled.

"By Diproo the Nimble-Fingered!" said Kando. "What she-cat have you found yourself this time, Lon?"

Thirteen

To smash a dragon's egg

King Vodun Alloran found he was most vexed with himself for being troubled over San Fraipur, the Wizard of Fruningen. Fraipur had served Alloran's father and then himself with devotion and expertise, his advice sound and well-judged. What troubled King Vodun was simply that he could not make up his mind if Fraipur should be killed out of hand, left to rot in his dungeon, tortured to death or smothered. And, if torture was decided on, then Alloran would have to make his choice of the various alternatives the torture masters could offer. Yes, it was a vexing question.

"By the Triple-Tails of Targ the Untouchable!" he burst out. "I'll throw the problem to Five-handed Eos Bakchi."

At his outburst the Kataki guards around the walls swiveled their narrow demonic eyes upon him. He was apim, not Kataki, yet he used Kataki oaths. He continued to call upon the name of Opaz in public, for Arachna counseled him it was as yet unwise to move too rapidly. He certainly counted himself the most fortunate of men that he had discovered her and that she had entered his service. The Katakis served him well.

There was a time, he remembered, when he loathed Katakis with their bladed whiptails and their slaving ways, but that was before Arachna had opened his eyes.

He gave his orders to his chamberlain Naghan the Chains and in due time four husky fighting men were wheeled in. Each was naked. All were apim. They stared about, dazzled by the magnificence all around, nervous yet relieved that they had not been thrown to the wild animals or sold off as slaves.

Chin propped on fist, Alloran studied them. Yes, they looked evenly matched; he would not take a certain bet on any one of them. Eos-Bakchi, spirit of chance, would decide.

As the men stood huddled and limp with dawning apprehension, Alloran's serving girls tied colored ribbons about the men's left arms. White for smothering. Red for death. Green for torture. Black for rotting. Each man was handed a Vallian dagger, long, slender and lethal.

"Fight!" commanded Alloran. "All against all in melee. The winner will gain his life." To himself, he added with a sly self-pleasing humor: "And if he is in respectable condition, the honor of Arachna!"

The men fought.

Afterward slaves cleared away the mess and swabbed the floor and the man wearing the black arm band, streaming blood, was carried off in a blanket. He still lived. Him, Alloran made the promise, he would reward by a visit to savor the honor of Arachna.

With that tiresome problem out of the way, he could turn to the question of building this wonderful new phalanx his people had promised him. He knew the Phalanx of Vallia, and understood that Strom Rosil mayhap did not. With the thousands of mercenaries flooding in from North Pandahem, funded by Zankov's gold, he would crush the usurpers and then begin the great march on Vondium.

The phalanx he was building would be a vital component of his army. He sat back and held up his hand and a sprite in silver gauze placed a golden goblet therein. Alloran drank. Life was going to be good and get better, by Takroti!

When everything was prepared he was informed by a Mantissa and went through into the inner chamber. All proceeded as before, except that the man was a Fristle. When Arachna threw back the cloak the golden furry body of a Fristle fifi drove the breath thick and clogging into Alloran's throat. The tail-hand crept out along the bed, took up the snake-curved dagger and thrust the blade deeply into the Fristle's vitals. The mingled shriek of agony and ecstasy, the blood and the limp falling away, and Arachna spoke in those husky cobwebbed tones reaching in through mazy distances.

"If you do not wish to be eaten by the dragon, you must smash the egg in the nest."

Pondering Arachna's words, Alloran walked slowly from the secret chamber, through his throne room without pausing, and so on toward the top floor of the west wing.

Naghan the Chains hovered, and to him Alloran said, "Fetch food and wines for the lady Chemsi and me."

"At once, majister, at once."

Just before Naghan hurried off Alloran snapped out: "And find Scauron the Gaunt and send him to me."

"Your command, majister."

Scauron the Gaunt, decided King Vodun as he strode off to share a pleasant meal and company with his light o' love, was the perfect tool for smashing dragon's eggs.

Three victories having taken the Prince Majister of Vallia across the province of Ovvend to the borders of the kovnate of Kaldi, he paused there to consider the next steps. The first victory, Vongleru, had been hard fought, as expected. The second, Ondorno, gained slightly more readily. The most recent battle had seen the Vallian forces routing their opponents at Naghan the Folly's Ford with convincing ease.

All the same, Drak was under no illusions that the war was won. He could not just march his army across Kaldi without a by your leave. The Kataki Strom was reeling back with a bloody nose; he was a long way from being beaten.

Also, Prince Drak must take careful thought for the other fronts in Vallia. Up in the northeast they were having continual trouble and an army containing the whole of the Second Phalanx swatted this way and that. He could expect, at least for the moment, no reinforcements from there. Up in the central portions of the island Kov Turko fought for his province against Layco Jhansi and also against the Racters. Turko had the Fourth Phalanx consisting of the Seventh Lela and the Eighth Seg, two Kerchuris who were seeing a lot of action. Turko would rather be asking for more men than releasing them to fight elsewhere.

In the capital, the Lord Farris and the Presidio ran the country in the absence of the emperor and the Prince Majister, and loyal and competent they were, too, thank Opaz! They were in the business of raising fresh troops. But soldiers, saddle animals and flyers, artillery, weaponry, did not grow on trees or sprout from the ground.

Pacing restlessly up and down inside his tent, jurukkers on guard outside, abstaining from wine until the hour grew on, Drak pulled at his lower lip and struggled with the decisions he must make. As for Queen Lushfymi—the woman was a treasure and a jewel, no doubt of that. She had behaved herself during the battles, and had come to no harm. Her conversation, easy, educated, witty, turned on topics increasingly concerned with the desirability of Drak, as the putative emperor, finding a wife and thus ensuring the succession. No doubt was left in anyone's mind, least of all in Drak's, that he was expected to choose Queen Lushfymi of Lome. After all, she outshone all other women, did she not?

Well, pondered Drak, cut by guilt and memories, well...

He heard the sentries bellow the ritual challenge: "Llanitch!" Anyone ordered to "Halt!" quite like that halted at once, otherwise they'd be shafted. Then the tent flap was thrown back. Drak half-turned, expecting to see a sentry barging in to announce whoever the visitor was, and he saw a lithe and limber young lady, clad in russet leathers, a rapier and main gauche at her hips, a long evil-looking whip curled up over her shoulder, a plain bag with red stitching slung so that she could dive her left hand into it without thought. Her face glowed at him, mischievous, beautiful with that familiar heartbreaking beauty he knew so well, yet fierce, dominating, and haunted by some inner conflict not yet resolved.

"Drak, you old shaggy sea-leem, you!"

"Dayra! You little monkey! What in a Herrelldrin Hell are you doing here?"

Brother and sister clasped each other, old sores forgotten, joying in seeing each other again. Life in the turbulent world of Kregen drives folk apart and makes reunions all the more joyful.

Presently Drak said, "Now you are here it is appropriately enough the time for wine."

"Assuredly, brother. But a mouthful only for me. I must fly on sharpish."

"Oh?"

They sat side by side on the sprawl of cushions on the floor and Dayra took the goblet of wine.

"Yes. I'm flying to Hamal. It's about time I saw Lela again and I want to size up this bright new prince of hers."

"I hear Prince Tyfar of Hamal is a splendid fellow."

"So I hear. I want to see for myself. And you know he calls her Zila. That's because father and he knew her as Jaezila. Father calls her that nearly all the time instead of Lela. Mother sometimes despairs of him, I tell you."

They talked on, exchanging news, happy that now they could talk thus without the black memories of the past intruding. Dayra just said, almost in passing: "Zankov is dead, or I think he must be, seeing that Cap'n Murkizon broke his backbone across."

Drak took up his wine, drinking to cover the pause for consideration. Whatever the troubles with that bastard Zankov may have been, Dayra possessed a bright spirit that reacted emotionally and which might not be altogether rational still. He was just about to make some noncommittal remark when Dayra went on speaking as though the subject had not been brought up.

"Oh, and Drak, you great fambly, when are you and Silda to be married? I cannot understand why you are leaving it so late."

Because he was so genuinely glad to see this wayward sister who had caused such concern to the family and heartache for his mother, he refused to become stupidly pompous and indignant. He swallowed the wine.

"It is not arranged in any way that I shall marry Silda."

"There, you see!" flamed Dayra, known as Ros the Claw. "Why is it that you shall marry her? Why is it not that Silda hasn't decided to marry you? Because you are a man?"

"No, you fambly—I apologize. I have to remember to think like the Prince Majister who may someday be emperor. Surely you recognize that? As for Silda—I think she would marry me if—"

"Would! If! Why, you insufferable onker! She loves you!"

"Yes."

"Well, then—?"

When Drak did not answer, Dayra burst out: "It's this fat Queen Lush! That's it, isn't it?"

"Well, Dayra, look—"

"Since I've been back with the family—or at least those who've been around—I've learned a few surprising things. Anyway, what about Uncle Seg? What about mother and father? Oh, I know you can't marry someone because your folks think you should, but, Drak, dear—Queen Lush!"

"She is a remarkable woman—"

"Of course."

They both sat silently after that, the air as it were, exhausted between them.

Then Dayra, very much Ros the Claw, snapped out: "Anyway, where is Silda now?"

"I've no idea."

"You've no idea! By Vox! What a brother I have."

Studying this stern, sober, upright brother of hers, Dayra saw that perhaps, just perhaps, he might be overawed by this Queen Lush and her magnificence and undoubted beauty and worldly-wise ways. She wasn't really fat, of course not, just a trifle on the plump side. She might, in Drak's eyes who must think of himself as an emperor one day, far outdo Silda Segutoria in those qualities deemed necessary in an empress. Also, and this thought bore a great deal of truth, Drak might be more than a little offput by what he knew of the Sisters of the Rose. Their father might go off on mysterious jaunts; but so did their mother the Empress Delia. Any woman who was a sister of the SoR could expect to work for the Order, and be absent from the hearth and home.

Equality in Vallia, as was not true in some countries of Paz, cut both ways.

Slowly, unhappy at what he felt he must say, Drak wet his lips and said, "Look, Dayra. I must say that really this is my business—"

"You mean you think it is no concern of mine!" She flared it out, scornful, brilliant of color, her eyes marvels in the soft samphron oil lamps' glow. "I tell you, brother, it is of great consequence to me. Not just because Silda is a dear friend. Not just because you will be emperor one day and must have the very best empress possible. Not just because Queen Lush for all her magnificence is pathetic. No, by Vox, Drak! Because I'm choosy about who is to be my sister-in-law, that's why!"

"I think—"

"Yes! You are right, by Chozputz!" She stood up like a flame in the light, stamped her tall black boots on the carpet, looped her evil whip about her shoulder. "I'm going!"

"Dayra—please—it shouldn't—"

"By Chusto, Drak! D'you take me for a ninny! I can't stay lollygagging about here. I'll be back. I want to see Jilian, among others. Give my remembrances to those here who knew me. Remberee!"

She was gone like a tornado before Drak collected his wits. "Remberee," he called after her, feeling a fool.

Outside the tent checking on the guard, Jiktar Endru Vintang slammed himself up to rigid attention. The swirl of russet leathers, a swift: "Thank you, Jik. Remberee," and the princess was away astride her flutduin. He sighed. He wouldn't relish being wed to that one—and yet, and yet...!

He saw Hikdar Carlotta walking across from the queen's guard detail and decided to hang around for a time. Carlotta was a jolly, red-cheeked girl with a good humor for everyone except a sloppy soldier. He smiled as she approached in the torch's streaming light.

The prince whom Endru guarded snatched up a goblet of wine, drained it, and hurled the thing at the floor. Women! Sisters! Queens! They were enough to drive a man into the claws of Mak Chohguelm the Ib-Cracker!

Anyone observing Prince Drak act like this would have been astounded.

He had to sort out his private life, yet there was never enough time to handle all the affairs pressing him. He was somberly aware that each time he made a mistake men and women died. A carpenter might make a table with one leg shorter than the other and the table wobbled. What a pity. The Prince Majister made the wrong decision and regiments could be cut down. That, to Drak, seemed too monstrous even to be encompassed by pity.

Troubled as all hell he saw a girl with a white shawl wrapped about slender shoulders and hair unbound sidle into the tent. She put a finger to her lips. Endru must have let her pass. He did not know her.

"Majister. The queen craves an immediate and private meeting. You must come at once—"

"Is the queen ill? Has evil befallen her?"

"No, majister. Hurry!"

Alarmed, Drak snatched up his belts where his rapier and dagger swung scabbarded and followed the girl out of the tent.

What jumped demonically into his mind was monstrous and totally unthinkable. Wasn't it?

Fourteen

Deviltry under the Moons

They were a right rapscallion bunch. They met in the damp and tumbledown house of Yolande the Gregarian because Silda was tired of trying to meet where fights kept erupting. She had provided silver to buy wine and food and she wanted to complete her orders before they all fell down paralytic. When the time came, she promised herself, there'd be damn little if any wine, by the broken teeth and oozing eyes of Sister Melga the Harpy Herself!

"Well, I dunno," said Crafty Kando, sounding most cool.

"It's against reason," said Rundle the Flatch, a low-browed, tangle-haired fellow with half an ear missing.

"Since when, Rundle," said Lon the Knees, taking a handful of palines from the red pottery dish, "have you and reason been on speaking terms?"

As Rundle started to bristle up, Long Nath said: "But against the king? It'd be like washing away the Rahart Mountains with one cup of water."

"By Dipsha the Nimble-fingered!" exclaimed Yolande the Gregarian. "What do you know about washing, Long Nath? When was the last time you washed?"

"I'll have you know—"

"There's gold in it," cut in Lon. He continued to wonder what the hell he'd got himself into with this glorious girl; but he was in and wasn't going to back out now. "Lots of gold."

"Well, gold, now..." And: "There's ways and ways..." And: "He's for the chop, that one, anyway, by Black Chunguj!" They argued, as it were, to clear their minds and to gain sustenance one from the other.

Looking at this unlikely gang of cutthroats, Silda understood that a Sister of the Rose used whatever tools came to hand suitable for her purpose.

Lop-eared Tobi could still hear the shuddersome thud of that knife as it struck the wood instead of embedding itself in his back. Or Crafty Kando's back. He owed this girl his life, at the least.

"You call him king," spoke out Lop-eared Tobi. "But he's no more than a thief like us."

"I never stole from Kovneva Rashumin," said Ob-eye Mantig, with a shake of his head and such droll seriousness that the others laughed at him.

"We would be," said Lon carefully, "taking back what rightfully belongs to Rahartdrin."

No one there dreamed that, if they succeeded, they'd return the gold to the kovneva. There were limits, by Diproo the Nimble-fingered!

Useless to try to browbeat these people. They knew what they knew and understood their trade. Silda took a paline from the dish and before speaking held the little yellow berry between her fingers.

"I understood that you were masters of your art. But, of course, if you do not have the skills required—"

They broke out into uproar at this, their professional thieves' competence questioned. Crafty Kando quieted them. He looked at Silda meaningfully.

"You have not told us, my lady, why you wish to burgle the king's gold."

"Why not? It is not his, as we have said. And he is bad for the country. We all know that."

"That is sooth. The kovneva was different. Times were good in those days."

Silda knew enough from what her father had told her about Katrin Rashumin to know that having lost her husband the kov, Katrin had allowed her island to fall into a disreputable state through bad management and incompetent and mercenary managers. The emperor had helped her sort out her problems. Rahartdrin had prospered until the Times of Troubles.

The people of Rahartdrin, the Rahartese, would dearly love to throw King Vodun Alloran off their island, back to his own province of Kaldi. They might do more, given the opportunity. But no one was unaware of the drably clad men and women with their crossbows who seemed to be everywhere. Spies, too, had to be looked out for, and Silda felt thankful that everyone in this gathering had been vouched for.

No one it appeared to Silda was as yet fully convinced. Crafty Kando raised a point of great importance.

"My lady, are there Pachaks among the guards?"

"No."

So that cleared away one obstacle, for Pachaks are notorious for the honor and zealousness with which they discharge their duties when hired on as guards. Pachaks, with their straw yellow hair and two left arms, one right arm and powerful tail hand, give their nikobi and will not desist from the honorable course until they are discharged by their employer or by death.

Silda did not mention that there would almost certainly be Katakis. A way around that problem had to be found.

Yolande the Gregarian stood up. A strong woman plump with muscle, she had buried four husbands and was on the lookout for a fifth. Her face showed signs of her struggles with life. Very deft with a loop of rope, this Yolande. At first she had vehemently if privately detested this new supple stripling of a girl; but when she realized that Lyss the Lone had no designs on the men in Yolande's life, she welcomed Lyss as a female companion among the men.

"My loyalty remains with Kovneva Katrin. I will go up against this new despicable king. Also, I need the gold, for I shall marry again soon."

This latter remark caused more concern among the men present than Yolande's other decision. Silda seized her chance, spoke briefly and eloquently, cast a look at Lon and lapsed into silence.

Now the decision rested with Five-handed Eos-Bakchi.

Drak followed the girl in the white shawl out of his tent. The sentries saluted. He saw Endru talking to one of the queen's guards and called across: "Endru. I am to see the queen. You need not turn out the men."

"Quidang!"

Endru and Carlotta watched the prince and the girl walk toward the queen's tent.

Torchlight pooled around the tents. The ever-present murmurous noise of an army even at night floated in from the camp. Carlotta and Endru resumed their conversation.

The white-shawled girl and Drak vanished into the darkness between the two pools of light.

"I suppose, my famous kampeon," said Carlotta, joking Endru for whom she had a deep respect, "you fancy that chit of a girl instead of a jurukker like me."

"Why, Carlotta!" Endru put on a show of gallantry. "You malign me cruelly. Anyway, who is she? I have never seen her before."

"Nor have I. The queen is highly choosy about the girls who serve her. I saw little of this one in the torchlight; but she looked beautiful, as I'm sure you noticed. The queen does not often have really beautiful young girls about her person."

Carlotta saw no need to give the reason for that.

Looking at the queen's tent in its sheath of light and the Jikai Vuvushis on guard there, Endru waited for the girl and the prince to appear. He'd have a careful look at her. Prospects might be improving... He waited expectantly.

Presently, he said, "Where are they?"

Before Carlotta had time to answer, Endru bellowed at his men. The shock hit him like a thunderclap.

"Turn out the guard! Alarm! Follow me!"

He ran like a maniac for the darkness between the tents.

Carlotta, abruptly aware of the situation, shrilled: "Bring lights!" and took off after Endru.

Past those pools of light the night clamped down with only one of Kregen's lesser moons vaulting past. The starlight did nothing to assist Endru's eyes, still dazzled by the torches. He ran on, blinking, whipping out his sword, trying to see.

The horror he experienced drove him on. The prince, who considered him as a friend, depended on him. And he had failed him! He ran on dementedly.

A vague shape ahead...? The fugitive starlight wink of a blade...? Endru peered ahead. That was the petal shape of an airboat. Figures, dark and ominous, clustered below and then he saw the sudden blob of white rising up against the flank of the flier.

That was the white shawl of that Opaz-forsaken girl!

They had been duped. The prince was in mortal peril. Endru shouted, screaming, and ran on headlong. Carlotta, up with him now, fleetly running, saw what was going on. Her sword snouted. Together, they rushed on as the last figures clambered aboard the airboat. It began to rise.

A lump and then another showed above the bulwarks.

Endru felt nothing. One moment he was running on, the next he was pitching forward, flat on his face, with the crossbow bolt through him. He tried to yell, and froth and blood bubbled. Carlotta fell on top of him. He tried to push her off and she felt like all the Mountains of the North. He stared up as his men reached him, swords and spears brandished, and saw the airboat rise and turn and, as his eyes misted over, she vanished into the shadows.

King Vodun Alloran beamed. He felt the glow of pleasure all through him. Chemsi the Fair had not been treating him just lately as he considered a king should be treated, and she had packed her baggage and been seen off. Just where she'd been sent, Alloran did not inquire. He was too wrapped up in his new light o' love, Thelda the Voluptuous.

And, on top of his new conquest—this!

With deep, delicious delight coursing all through him, King Vodun Alloran stared down upon the bound and unconscious body of Drak, Prince Majister of Vallia.

"You have done well, Scauron the Gaunt. Exceedingly well."

"If I have served you, majister—"

Alloran's wits were quick enough.

"What, fambly, that will requite you? No gold, then?"

Caught out, Scauron bowed. "I am at the command of the king, majister."

"Good. Then get this proud prince sent into the custody of the Mantissae. Tell them that never have they been offered a choicer morsel. No, by Takroti, never!"

Again, Scauron bowed, and started on his duties. He accepted orders and carried them out. He didn't much care for all the Katakis thronging about Alloran. But he did know, as they say on Kregen, to keep his hat on in the rain.

Frightened slaves carried the limp form of the prince through side corridors from the anteroom where Scauron the Gaunt had delivered him to the king. Drak was passed on through a triply guarded doorway into the clutching claws of the Mantissae.

Fifteen

Tells of a wisp of straw

Although the darkness was not that of a night of Notor Zan—when no moons shine in the skies of Kregen—the Maiden with the Many Smiles would be late, and only a lesser moon raced across the starfields. The night breeze whispered along the cobbled alleyways of Rashumsmot. Lights flickered erratically. This was a night for ghosties and ghoulies to prowl the shadowed streets seeking soft throats and warm blood. Silda Segutoria firmly ensconced in the persona of Lyss the Lone, threw off these childish fancies.

She had put in a great deal of hard work on Crafty Kando's nefarious band. They were not drikingers, bandits, but they were a cutthroat crew. At the smell of gold, a number of newcomers had been recruited by Kando, all men and women he certified as safe.

Between them and under Silda's guidance they had scouted the back areas of the villa and Kando had pronounced no difficulty in getting into the grounds. These folk had their ways of avoiding sentries. But, to get into the building itself was an altogether different kettle of fish. Silda had rejected any ideas of introducing this hairy bunch into the normal entrances. They'd not be chucked out on their ears immediately. Oh, no. They'd be rounded up at the points of spears and sold off as slaves.

So she was forced to arrange a break-in. All the ordinary windows would be no use. Many of the men in the gang were accomplished bar breakers or benders, and others specialists in door-opening. If Silda's plan was to work, these folk were of paramount importance. The other important side of this operation nearly caused the whole show to come to grief.

"Swords?" said Lop-eared Tobi. His voice did not so much quaver as shrill in alarm.

"Swords?" yelped Long Nath. "Oh, no!"

"But," said Silda, nonplused. "If we meet up with sentries—"

"Run, or loop 'em, or the knife," quoth Yolande the Gregarian. The meeting, the last before Silda felt herself fully committed, being held at Yolande's crumbling house again, provided remarkable calm after earlier attempts at meetings. "Or," added Yolande, "a short spear, perhaps."

"Very well," snapped Silda. "I will provide short spears. By Vox! I thought you'd have handled swords in your lives."

"Oh, no, my lady. Swords are not for the likes of us."

So, outfitted as a gang of thieves with the addition of short spears purloined from the armory by Lyss the Lone, they'd set off. And the night was dark.

Silda, a Sister of the Rose, needed no assistance in scaling the outer wall. She was as adept as any of the skulkers at skulking. A funny little thought hit her that Dayra, or Jilian, would joy to be with her now. They prowled on toward the wall of the villa, shrouded in darkness, and if there were any sentries in this quarter their presence was not made known.

Crafty Kando said between his teeth: "Wait here."

He slid off with a few of his people to check the last approaches across a greensward. Silda with the others waited in shrubbery. The night pressed down.

Presently, Kando returned. His whisper breathed like a furtive slipper on polished wood.

"The damned windows are all boarded up. Bricked up. You promised us an entrance, my lady."

"Let me have a look." Silda was fed up with handing about. "There are windows all along the wall here."

She and Kando slid ahead, ghostlike through the darkness. Kando had to acknowledge that this fine lady certainly knew how to skulk. They reached the wall and in the dimness Silda saw two windows bricked up.

"They are all like this at the back," said Kando.

"What about those?" Silda indicated windows set in the angle of wall and ground. "They are barred, yes. Does that prevent you?"

"No, But they must lead below ground."

"And a good place to start. I'll get the rest of the people. You start."

Silda, without more ado, started back for the shrubbery.

A voice from out of the darkness said, "Silda."

She stopped as though shot through by a crossbow bolt.

"Silda!"

Her first thought was that this must be Mandi Volanta out on sentry go. But that voice—she knew whose voice that was...

Off to the side and hidden from observation from Kando at the wall and the others in the shrubbery a yellow light bloomed. That glow looked for all the world like the radiance from a samphron-oil lamp. She ran silently straight for the glow, halting, peering, saying, "Deb-Lu!"

"Yes, Silda, my dear, it is me. There is very little time. Drak—"

Silda felt her heart contract. "What of Drak?"

"He needs your help. You defended him against the clansmen and would have given your life. The emperor used his skill with the Krozair long-sword through my arts in gladiomancy. You remember, Silda, up there in Ithieursmot in Northern Jevuldrin?"

"I remember."

Deb-Lu-Quienyin, a magical and mystically powerful Wizard of Loh, did not really stand in the garden of King Vodun's villa in Rashumsmot. Deb-Lu could be anywhere in Vallia. In his plain robes with his funny old turban that was forever falling over one ear, he was bathed in the lamp's glow, here in the darkness of a single-moon night!

Silda was vaguely aware that the two Wizards of Loh exerted their thaumaturgical powers in defense of their comrades. She had never considered the matter over much. Now Deb-Lu-Quienyin rattled on passionately.

"I will try to guide you, Silda. Drak has been taken by the madman Alloran. He is to be sacrificed, and there is sorcery involved. My arts—such as they are—are at you disposal. But I must work through a—well, never mind that. Choose the fifth window from the right end of the villa, and break through. And, Silda—hurry!"

"I will, I will. Drak—"

"By Hlo-Hli, Silda. Run!"

The eeriness of this confrontation, the insubstantial wraith-form of the wizard, projected by the power of his kharrna for miles and miles through thin air, could not be allowed to affect her. She fairly flung herself on, calling in a low penetrating voice. The people from the shrubbery came out, warily, casting glances in every direction. They did not see the Wizard of Loh.

At the wall Silda, impatiently, said, "Break through the fifth window from the right. And hurry."

"Now wait a minute," said Kando, standing up. He'd been working on the first window. "Why—?"

"There's no time to argue. The fifth window."

Crafty Kando saw the girl meant what she said. One window or the next, so what was the difference? He got his people started on breaking a way in. Expert at their tasks, they had the bars out and a rope down and then all eyes turned on Silda. She didn't hesitate. She grabbed the rope, put her booted feet into the chute-like opening and slid down. The darkness and the stench hit her as though she'd plummeted into Cottmer's Caverns.

Deb-Lu's voice whispered, "Tell them to wait."

She called up the slot, "Wait!"

Another voice, faint, husky with soreness, said, "What? Who's there?"

"We have come to save you in return for a favor," said the ghostly apparition of Deb-Lu, now faintly visible. He must have turned down his lamp so that his shrewd friendly features, highlighted, took on that upwardly shadowed aura of omnipotent power. He did not look the cheerful, pottering old buffer Silda knew and loved. Now he looked what he truly was, one of the most powerful mages in all of Kregen.

"I am chained and helpless—"

"You will soon be set free. In return you must use your powers, aided by mine, to guide my friends. We seek a certain person whose value to us is immense. I am sure you understand the nature of our bargain."

"You are a Wizard of Loh?"

"Yes."

"Then, San, I must agree and place my ib under the hand of Opaz into your protection. I will do as you command."

"Thank you, San Fraipur."

A wisp of straw among the dire scatterings on the floor lifted, it seemed of its own accord, and rose into the air. It curved toward Silda and she took it into her hand.

"When San Fraipur is free, give him the talisman. There is power therein. He will know how to use it. I have done what I can for now. There are portents in Vallia, werewolves to be dealt with. Time is running out. Hurry!"

The glow faded and Deb-Lu was gone.

"Come down!" Silda called up the tunnel slot.

Lon the Knees was first down. He made a face at the smell and then started to strike a light. Kando and the others followed, and although they crowded the cell, they made no more noise than the schrafters in their hidden recesses gnawing on dead men's bones.

As they started in on the job of freeing Fraipur, two men appeared at the cell opening, took one look, and tried to flee. One was a butter-head Gon, the other an apim with half a left ear. Both were hit on the head with just sufficient force to put them to sleep. They were bound.

Silda gave Fraipur the wisp of straw. Truth to tell, she could feel no difference in the straw; but Fraipur took it up and in the covered-lantern glow she could see him as it were swell, grow taller. He put on the unconscious apim's rough clothes and without a word immediately led off out of the cell. Silda felt a rush of confidence.

The layout of the villa as it had been in the past was known in the thieves fraternity and Silda was able to indicate the likely places where Alloran had altered walls and made doors to create his secret apartments in the rear. There was no certainty about any of that, of course; but common sense told her that if she went up and remained in the rear she would emerge beyond that mysterious gold-framed green velvet door. She urged the band on with vigor, and San Fraipur, talisman in hand, went in the van.

With shielded lights they went up the stairs, broke quietly through a locked door, and so came into a carpeted corridor. Fraipur unhesitatingly turned right.

He felt gripped in the talons of a power so much greater than his own that it was like being swept away in a tidal wave. He was content to keep his side of the bargain and then, afterwards, he would have to think about his future. As for Alloran, Fraipur now knew he did not care what happened to that evil man.

No one appeared to inhabit this corridor and the rooms at each side were merely bedrooms with little of value. The gang pressed on. Fraipur did pick up a long curved knife.

The passage ended at a green velvet door.

"Open that, and quietly," ordered Silda. "We are bound to find a few guards on the other side. You need not be gentle with them."

When the door had been swiftly and expertly opened, the first through were Silda and Lon, side by side.

They found themselves in a small anteroom with an open door before them and not a sound anywhere. Cautiously, they padded through. They were in a set of chambers of considerable magnificence, strewn with silks and furs, with elegant furniture, sweetly scented, plants in exquisite pots of Pandahem ware. Iron-bound oaken chests, six of them, stood in a line against one wall. Crafty Kando smiled.

"Diproo the Nimble-fingered blesses us now."

The first chest revealed a mass of gems. The brilliance smote upward with the fierceness of the suns in the Ochre Limits.

At once the gang, crowing with delight, began to stuff their bags and sacks. Loot!

Silda said, "You task is only just begun. We must go on beyond the last door. There is—"

"What?" said Kando. "This is the treasure. We will fill our sacks and be gone. We shall be rich for the rest of our lives!"

"But—"

"Oh, no, my lady. You have shown us the treasure as you promised. We go not a step farther."

Sixteen

"Kill me now and have done!"

Vodun Alloran, King of Southwest Vallia, sat on the chair in the corner gazing upon Arachna's bed of offering and of prophecy, and brooded.

The four Katra Curses of his new Kataki friends take it! The Mantissae in the room sensed his mood. They stood silently. Perhaps they couldn't understand why the king was so sullen and enraged when he had taken up into his hand this great prize.

Well, ran the savage thoughts of Alloran, they were just stupid Kataki women, ugly as sin, doing as they were told. What could they know of the greater diplomacy of the outside world? Two items of news, one on the heels of the other, had shaken him far more than he cared for. By Takroti! Things looked black. The great force of mercenaries he'd expected from

North Pandahem was not coming. Their fleet had burned, and they'd got down to knocking hell out of their next-door neighbors. And, on top of that, a messenger brought news from his spies that a tremendous reinforcement fleet had arrived in the battle area along the border of Ovvend and Kaldi. That fleet was commanded by many famous kampeons, and with it flew King Jaidur and Queen Lildra of Hyrklana. At a stroke, Alloran had been deprived of an army and been faced with a fresh one.

No wonder he ground his teeth. Yet—yet! He had this whipper-snapper Prince Drak. Had him! He'd ask Arachna the questions and put Drak to her so that she could not complain that her sacrificial victim was not puissant enough. No, by the Triple Tails of Targ the Untouchable!

His bitter thoughts twined on. This King of Hyrklana, now. He was Drak's youngest brother. Yet he'd been made a king, all right, with all the huzzas. Alloran had had to fight for his kingdom.

He'd set off from Vondium to regain control of his province of Kaldi and he'd been given the Fifth Army by the emperor, and a miserable lot they'd turned out to be. He'd had to recruit himself to make up the desertions. And he'd paid good red gold for the paktuns, so that, in one way, the very worst news he'd received, a deadly body blow, was to learn Zankov was dead.

Just how Zankov got hold of the gold didn't concern Alloran. Bleakly, he stared into the future, and he flinched white-faced from what he saw.

But—but, he'd have the answers when Arachna took her sacrifice and prophesied! Then he would know what to do…

"What are we waiting for?" he rasped out. "Is that bastard Drak proving troublesome?"

"No, majister," said a Mantissa. "He has been kept drugged. Listen! I hear Arachna now."

Moments later the procession entered the room. Alloran, savage, bitter, stared eagerly, desperate for the ceremony to progress so that he would know what to do. He'd have to look away at the moment of revealment; but that made no difference. Arachna—ah! All his hopes now reposed in her and her mystic powers.

One of the baby werstings decided to act as a wersting should act. He leaped forward with his babyish snarl, all yellow teeth and dripping saliva, and was hauled up in an undignified tumble by the silver lead. The giant Womox shouldering his axe moved a little away; he might be stupid, he wasn't silly enough not to know that a wersting like any hunting dog could give him a nasty bite. The Fristle fifi hauled in the dog and decorum was restored.

Clad in her swathing blue silk cloak with the mask drawn across the face, Arachna was assisted onto the bed. The liquid gleam like oil on water within the eyeslits gave Alloran a fresh upsurge of hope. Surely, this powerful sorceress must know the answers to his problems.

The silver gong sent out its trembling notes. The Mantissa replaced the padded hammer before returning to her place beside the bed. The second door opened sweeping the blue hangings aside and four Mantissae brought in the bound and naked form of Drak.

The questions were asked, the answers given, and then, almost gobbling in his eagerness and anxiety verging on panic, Alloran asked what he must do.

Arachna threw the cloak wide.

Alloran turned his head aside.

As though he looked through a glass where milk drained away in streaks of obscuration, Drak tried to see what was going on. His head hurt. By Zair! His head felt like the top of a volcano. He could clearly recall the girl in the white shawl saying the queen wished to see him urgently. Then what had happened? Had he heard a chink of steel? He was sure he could remember the wind in his face, and the feel of an airboat under him. Where in the name of Beng Raindrek was he now?

His vision began to clear. His wrists were bound at his back. He could see a bed. On the bed... He felt lust shoot through him like melting snow in spring. The girl reminded him of someone—Queen Lush? Yes, there was much of the queen in this beauty. And—Silda. Silda whom he had seen half-naked and bloodied and fighting like a zhantilla for his life.

Whoever she was, she was his. He struggled against the bonds at his wrists. He panted, staring, making gobbling sounds, and saliva speckled his lips and ran down his chin.

The Mantissa with the knife stepped forward to slash away the hampering bonds.

"Listen," said Silda, holding tightly within herself the screaming impatience she felt at these oafish villains. "The man I love is held here. In return for the treasure you promised to help me—"

"We promised nothing, my lady. I give you thanks; but we take the gems and depart."

"You, Kando," said Lon, hearing what Lyss the Lone said and knowing that had been there all the time, and knowing, too, it made no difference to him. "You, Kando, are a faithless cramph, and no friend of mine!"

"You'll think differently when we are safe away with the treasure."

Fraipur held the heavy knife in his right hand and the wisp of straw in his left. He felt, he distinctly felt, the straw twitch.

The knife was a lethal enough weapon, something like a single-edged kalider. Yet the wizard knew that the straw was immeasurably the more powerful weapon. He lifted it, turning to the gang who were prizing open the next chests.

"You will do as the lady commands. We must hurry. Follow me."

Without waiting to see their reactions or if they followed, Fraipur marched toward a blue-swathed door in the far wall. Instantly, Lon the Knees was up with him. Silda cast a look at the thieves. Kando dropped his sack of loot. He drew his knife. The others whipped out their weapons and crowded up. With Silda leading they hurried after Fraipur and Lon. The blue-covered door swung open. The little husk of straw in Fraipur's hand appeared to burn into his fingers. He saw. Understanding of what was going on sleeted over him like a lightning bolt.

"Lon!" he said in a firm hard voice that made the animal-handler jump. "On the bed. Throw your knife."

Silda barged in. She saw. She felt the bile in her, the scarlet rage, the horror—and the pain and agony and love. Lon threw. At the last, Arachna must have realized, her powers shrieking a warning. But Fraipur knew that he wielded occult magics superior, frighteningly superior. Lon's knife flew.

Alloran switched around, startled, and his hand reached for his sword hilt. The Mantissae remained fast. Their normal expectation of being told what to do checked them for those few vital heartbeats—those heartbeats that measured out the time in which the heart of Arachna ceased to beat.

Everyone was held and gripped. They stared at the bed. The knife hilt protruded from the rib cage. The body shriveled into a grayish-black leathery carapace. The gorgeous glowing face of unutterable apim beauty flowed and melted and sloughed into the low-browed, tangled-lock face of a female Kataki with the snaggle-teeth and wide-spaced eyes, narrow, cold and hostile. And yet—and yet about that face and body clung tantalizing hints of another strain. The grayish skin glinted as it were with a golden pigment imperfectly matched, the face in its bone structure might have elements of a nobility entirely foreign to a Kataki, male or female.

The long flexible whiptail tremored, rippling its entire length down the bed. The hand, the left hand at the top of the tail, flexed, opening and closing, and flopped back, cupped and still.

Thinking of Korero the Shield, the emperor's shield bearer, a golden Kildoi with just such a powerful tail hand, Silda guessed at the truth. Arachna was the fruit of a miscegenation of Kataki and Kildoi. The quick and immediate stab of sympathy for her passed Silda and left her with the hollow feeling that the fates are unjust to all seeming, and unfitted to rule the destinies of frail humankind.

Still, Arachna need not have turned her arts into the evil ways she had. Sympathy existed. That was all. More sympathy, Silda felt, was owed Arachna's mother...

With wild shrieks of abandonment and despair the Mantissae leaped into action. Their bladed whiptails sliced up. Daggers glittered. Kando's gang recoiled and then, under the thrall of sorcery or because they saw there was no other way for it, they fought.

Silda ran to Drak. He turned, dazed, shaking, the sweat starting out all over his body. Alloran looked on from his chair, the sword in his fist, and he did nothing.

"Silda...?"

"Drak. Here—" With efficient hands, Silda ripped the blue silk cloak away from the shriveled body of Arachna, swathed it about Drak. She made him sit on the edge of the bed. He stopped shaking. He looked up.

"I suppose you'll tell me. But first there must be things to be done urgently..."

"Plenty. Alloran, for a start."

"Alloran?"

Drak didn't know what the hell had been going on; but it didn't take a genius to guess at most of it. Damned sorcery! He swiveled himself about and so looked on King Vodun Alloran.

The man still sat, gripping his sword. The sweat on his forehead glistened thickly, more profuse than the sweat upon Drak. He shook. The sword splintered lights into the overheated air of the chamber where Kando's gang fought the Mantissae. Silda felt perfectly content to leave all that physical exertion to them. After all, that was what she'd taken all this trouble to bring them here for, wasn't it?

Drak stood up. His left hand clasped the silk cloak. He stretched out his right hand.

"Silda. Lend me your sword."

Silda gave him the drexer.

Drak, sword in hand, advanced and planted himself before Alloran.

"Before you die, Alloran, you must know—"

Alloran interrupted.

"Majister! I *do* know. I *know*. Kill me and have done. I deserve only a contemptible death." He threw his sword onto the carpets.

Suddenly and bewilderingly unsure, Drak stared at this man, this traitor, who had caused so many deaths. There were meanings here that, on the surface were plain enough, and yet whose hidden truths might be twisted in ways that would make a mockery of justice.

Fraipur moved forward, avoiding a Mantissa who fell down choking her lifeblood out. Long Nath turned for the next one, gripped by a hatred so profound he could not resist it. Fraipur, in his turn, studied Alloran.

"Yes, San Fraipur," said Alloran in a voice hoarse and low. "I owe you the deepest apologies. I wronged you. I feel the shame, for you have been loyal to my father and to me, and I treated you..." He shuddered. "Slay me, San, and rid the world of baseness."

The straw twitched like a grasshopper.

"How can you be blamed for actions forced on you by another? Arachna bewitched you. Now she is dead, you are your own man again."

"I know. I am in torment for what I have done—"

"What Arachna has done."

Fascinated—and repelled—Silda kept silent. She could see what Fraipur was talking about and appreciated the justice of it. Just that, after all the bloodshed...

Drak drew a breath. What had happened had happened. He'd digest the details in time. Right now he had the winning of this damn war and the clearing of the whole of Southwest Vallia in his hands. He was not going to let an opportunity like that slip by, no, by Vox!

Seventeen

What chanced at the Villa of Poppies

That time in Southwest Vallia became known as the Hyr Kataki Jikai.

The ordinary folk just did not like Katakis. The Whiptails made their living through all the activities of slaving. For a person unfortunate enough to be taken up as a slave the world might just as well have ended. Slaves called slavemasters and slavers greeshes, a contraction in the Kregish of kleesh and grak. Kleesh, a word of so insulting a connotation it could drive a man into a frenzy of rage, and grak, that evil word meaning work, run, slave until you die beaten by the lash, added together gave vent to much of the feeling ordinary folk liable to be taken up as slave could express only in words.

The Great Kataki Hunt swept through the countryside.

There was little the Prince Majister could have done to prevent the outburst even had he wished to do anything to halt the execution of justice.

San Fraipur, restored to his green hooded robe and golden belt with rapier and main gauche, saw a little more. He spoke seriously to Drak as they took wine in an inner room of the villa given over to Drak's use.

"The people detest Katakis; but many of them do not object to owning slaves."

"My views on that are known."

"It will not be easy."

Drak sipped and said moodily, "What is?"

Silda had taken herself off the very day after the fraught happenings in Vodun Alloran's villa. She had been called away by the Sisters of the Rose, of course. How could a fellow who would one day be emperor have an empress continually going gallivanting off like this? He thought of his mother, and sighed, knowing that she had had to put up with his father's continuous absences. Queen Lush, on the other hand... Well, she had arrived in great state and with enormous pomp and circumstance.

His brother, Jaidur, had changed considerably since Drak had danced at his wedding away down south in the island kingdom of Hyrklana. His wife, the queen, had gone home because of the expected happy event. Lildra didn't go chasing off over the world, did she?

Like a stage demon, Jaidur came in at that moment demanding wine. Yes, he had changed from the harum-scarum reckless rascal who'd hated the whole world and not really known why. Since his reconciliation with their father, and his gaining the crown of Hyrklana, he had settled down to responsible government. Now he was due for a family, and more than likely it would be twins. The puncture ladies were confident.

There was going to be a whole new generation festering about under Drak's feet soon. Didi, the daughter of his sister Velia and Rog Gafard, was a grown woman now, of an age with his youngest sister, Velia. What, wondered Drak, did young Didi make of having an aunt with the same name as her dead mother?

"I saw Queen Lush in her palanquin as I rode over," announced Jaidur.

"Yes?"

"Very grand. Had to shade my eyes against her jewelry. She was heading this way, brother."

"Oh."

"Queen Lushfymi," said Fraipur in a surprisingly prim way, "is a most remarkable woman. She does have some powers of thaumaturgy, I believe, or so I have heard, though they have not been vouchsafed me."

Drak stood up and emptied his goblet.

"Think I'll take a stroll to see Alloran. I'm not absolutely decided yet. Hang him, banish him, let him take up an appointment in the army, or restore his kovnate of Kaldi to him."

Fraipur's hot feelings of anger against the kov had passed. He did say: "When the kov was under the spell of that vile woman, he had a way of deciding knotty problems."

"An old Kataki custom," said Jaidur when Fraipur explained about the fighting men apportioned a decision each, the winner deciding. "Saw it in the Eye of the World."

"Ah!" said Drak, memories boiling up.

"Mind you," went on Jaidur, "there was a Kataki lord, feller called Rukker, when I was Vax Neemusjid, well, he, I think, had the faintest spark of humanity about him. Faint, mind, and I'd not like to meet him when he discovered he'd stolen rocks instead of our gold. Ha!"*

Drak started for the door. He thrust thoughts of the inner sea of Turis-

---

* see *Krozair of Kregen*, Dray Prescot #14. *A.B.A.*

mond, the Eye of the World, from him. That was where he and his brothers had received a great deal of their education. The Krozairs of Zy disciplined lads well and fairly and made men of repute out of them. As a man of repute he was scuttling off with a feeble excuse instead of waiting to greet Queen Lushfymi. What a coil!

"I'm with you, Drak," said Jaidur, finishing his wine.

Fraipur stood up, and at once, as a prince, Drak said: "You are welcome, San."

"Thank you, majister—I beg your pardon, jis."

Majis was the correct familiar diminutive for emperors, kings and princes. The little word jis, which meant "sir" was coming into general use.

They went out by a side door and the sentry slammed himself up to attention. Under the lights of the Twins, the two second moons of Kregen eternally orbiting each other as they orbited the planet, they walked across to the outer gate in the wall where the sentry here slammed herself up to attention as rigid as her comrade at the door. Drak acknowledged and the three men walked along the street toward the villa where Alloran was now quartered. It was not the same one. That still had not been named, and now never would be, by Alloran. He was quartered now in the Villa of Poppies, with a reasonable staff to attend him.

The sentries here, all Drak's people, were pleased to see him. A few moments conversation with them ended as Drak, answering the question on all their lips, said: "I give thanks to the Invisible Twins made manifest in Opaz that Endru and Carlotta are out of danger and mend well. The news has just reached me."

"Hai, jis!" they said, pleased that their comrade Jiktar and the Jikai Vuvushi were alive.

Going into the Villa of Poppies, Drak reflected that his father often used to say that while he despaired of these folk who would thrust their bodies between him and danger, making a man feel small in the sight of Zair, it remained still a marvel and a warming wonder.

A great deal had occurred since the bandy little fellow—Lon the Knees—had given Arachna her quietus. His brother had flown in with a tremendous force of skyships, thirsting to smash the enemies of Vallia. Alloran, shaken to his foundations, had given orders to his own forces to cooperate to the full with the Prince Majister. The mercenaries were continued on the payroll until they could be repatriated. Silda's father, Kov Seg Segutorio, had left the aerial armada to fly direct to Vondium. He had a new bride with him. Perhaps, considered Drak, going into the hallway leading to the apartments Alloran used as his withdrawing room, Silda had gone to Vondium. Tricky business, that, meeting a new stepmother. Silda's mother, Thelda, had been lost in the Time of Troubles, a sad story.

Alloran rested in a limbo at the moment, for his future was undecided, and he was now addressed as koter, the simple way of addressing a Vallian gentleman. Drak was well aware that the final decision would rest with the emperor, together with the Lord Farris and the Presidio. Paktuns could be repatriated; but the position of those native Vallians who had sided with Alloran in his treacherous revolt was different. Drak fancied that the fate of Alloran would decide the fate of his adherents. Many, of course, had already run off, sensible people.

Well, not necessarily so sensible. That was a shaming thought if carried through to its conclusion. He halted as a Khibil guard first snapped to attention and then, putting his fist onto the door handle, opened the door for the prince.

The apartments were comfortably furnished and Drak had given orders that Alloran was to be treated correctly and his necessary wants attended to politely. A little Fristle fifi, her fur of that silvery dove gray that enchanted in a fashion quite different from the golden Fristles, sat sprawled in a gilt-legged chair sobbing her heart out. The maroon and gray ribbon shook as she shuddered with each agonized wail.

Three strides took Drak to her. He bent.

Through her despair, she heard him and looked up. She had not been crying long; very soon her pretty face would be a raw wreck.

"What ails you, fifi?"

"The kov—" she managed to choke out. She pointed to the inner door.

At once, Drak understood.

"Jaidur! Fraipur! Smash that door down!"

Drak didn't even bother to check to see if it was locked. It would be. He started in on the panels with his drexer, his brother joined him, and Fraipur began to work his dagger into the crevices around the lock. If they understood or not, Drak didn't know or care; but at the urgency of his manner they set to. The door splintered and burst in.

Drak sprang into the room.

From a hook a rope drew down, taut and spinning, and in the loop the neck of Vodun Alloran was clenched fast. The chair lay tumbled on its side.

With the rush of a maniac Drak hurtled across the carpet, knocked a table over, sending a vase of flowers flying, slashed the rope asunder with his sword.

Jaidur, leaping like a leem, caught the falling body in his arms and lowered Alloran to the carpet. Fraipur bent and cut the rope free.

Alloran's eyes were closed, his face drawn, haggard with agony. The weal on his neck still glowed red.

"Pump his arms!" commanded Drak. He bellowed outside, "Send for the needlemen! *Bratch!*"

Not content, he ran across to the door. The girl was just standing up, unsteadily. Drak eyed her. "Run for the needleman, fifi! Run!"

Jaidur called out: "He's breathing."

"Thank Opaz!"

Still not content, for the little Fristle fifi had clearly been in a terrible state, Drak ran out after her to the doorway. He caught a glimpse of her silvery-gray fur as she raced toward the gateway. She was screaming. A guard rushed in, halberd up, looking ugly.

"The needleman!" bellowed Drak. "Bring him in here instantly! Run!"

"Quidang!"

After that all Drak could do was let Fraipur get on with doing what he could to revive Alloran, and then wait as the needleman, apprised of the urgency of the situation and yet unknowing what the exact emergency might be, rushed in and, seeing what his duty was, set to.

Alloran had not dangled there overlong. He would survive.

"The gray ones smiled on him, jis. I will just stick him a trifle..." Here the needleman deftly inserted half a dozen acupuncture needles to take away any pain. "He'll live."

Drak sighed with relief. Close. That had been closer than he liked. Had Vodun Alloran died before any decision had been reached, the news would have sounded most ugly in the ears of the world. Damned ugly. The Prince Majister, folk would say, had had the kov put out of the way...

"Place a guard on him," Drak told the cadade, and the guard commander nodded, understanding.

"He won't get a chance to do it again, jis."

"Make it so."

A few days later when Alloran had completely recovered, he sent word that he craved an audience with the Prince Majister. Drak happened to be taking a bur or two off from the pressing business of organizing the multifarious items necessary, and was playing a game of Jikaida with his brother. The board was filled with the ranks and columns of marching figures, all exquisitely carved and painted.

"H'm," said Jaidur, capturing a Jiktar, and cupping the piece in his fist. "I'll warrant Alloran is sweating blood right now."

"Your Eleventh Fleet—"

"Not mine. It is the Eleventh Fleet of the Vallian Air Service. I am merely the King of Hyrklana. Kapt Thando runs the Eleventh." He reached for the silver dish of greeps, slender, bright green shoots that must be cooked expertly and with precision as to temperature and duration to bring out the flavor. "What of them?"

"We sent a fast flier to Vondium with the news and have had no reply."

"That does not worry me. There has been a delay. That is all."

"Until I know what Farris and the Presidio decide, I do not particularly wish to see Alloran."

"Then," said Jaidur with a flash of his old reckless ways, "make him wait. Let him sweat some more blood."

"I suppose so. It is cruel—"

"Life is."

As though at random, although to Jaidur it was no non sequitur, he added, "I was sorry to miss Silda."

"She would joy to see you."

"Aye. I'll tell you, big brother, there was a time when if you had not been around I would have—well, Silda is Silda. When I met my Lildra it happened, as they say, as though we were shafted by the same bolt of lightning."

"I am happy for you."

"Of course! I am married and a king. Brother Zeg is married and a king out in Zandikar. Now Uncle Seg is married again—and a king. You limp along, brother, you limp along like a leem with but five legs."

Drak shifted uncomfortably in his chair.

"If I married Queen Lushfymi, then I might be King of Lome—"

"If!"

Drak felt surprise at the scornful, scoffing tone.

"She is a most remarkable woman, and I feel a very real attachment to her."

Like his twin sister, Dayra, Jaidur had no hesitation in rushing recklessly on, not caring for his brother's finer feelings, knowing them to be misguided in this instance.

"You marry that one, Drak, and you'll regret it. There is only one girl for you—"

"Who is never here. Who has no idea of what being a queen or empress entails!"

"You benighted onker!" quoth Jaidur, disgustedly.

Drak switched about and changed the subject in a marked way. "We have not fought since we were children in Esser Rarioch. Now, as to Alloran. My vote in the Presidio is for clemency. The poor devil was engulfed in sorcery. If I do not hear soon I shall make the decision—"

"Pardon him?"

"More than that. Give him back his estates and his title. His treachery was not of his volition."

"That is sooth. And we have fought—in Zy, when the Krozairs tested us—"

"That was without malice."

"Ah!"

Swinging away from the Jikaida board upon the table and standing up with a jerky, irritable gesture of his fist, Drak burst out, "By Zair! I wish I knew where Silda was now!"

Eighteen

Queen Lush—heroine

Not all the mercenaries hired by Vodun Alloran quietly accepted the needle and agreed to repatriation.

Leone Starhammer reined in and looked down on the village cupped in its little valley. It still burned. The black smoke hung greasily above collapsed roofs and fallen walls. Corpses lay about in grotesque contortions.

"The bastards have been through here, and recently," said Leone. She turned to Queen Lushfymi who rode at her stirrup.

"Then they cannot be far off," said the queen.

"May the Gross Armipand rot 'em." Leone lifted her gloved hand. "I'll get the girls moving. We'll have these Pandrite-forsaken cramphs—"

"You will use the rest of the brigade, Leone?"

A regiment of zorcabows and a regiment of zorca lancers had been placed at Leone's disposal. But they were male regiments. She sniffed.

"Only if we have to—"

"I think it would be wise."

"Yes, majestrix."

They were near enough to Rashumsmot, in all conscience. The paktuns were pillaging their way to the next port of call where they'd no doubt burn and slay and loot before seizing the ships there. That Queen Lushfymi, who had chosen to ride out with her bodyguard regiment, chanced to be the one to stumble on this band of paktuns, meant in her eyes that she had been chosen by Pandrite to effect their destruction. There was no hope of taking them into her employ—not now, not with Drak and his views hovering. If only... Well, that was all gone, smoke blown with the wind...

As the brigade moved forward with scouts out ahead she reflected despondently and with a panic threatening to erupt, a panic she kept firmly battened down, that she just had to get Drak to speak soon. She was not growing any younger. Oh, yes, her arts kept her beauty intact and she'd not age for many and many a season yet. But she felt the passing of time, felt it cruelly.

Her spies reported that the common folk adored her. Most of them would welcome a marriage that would join the powerful Empire of Vallia with a wealthy country of Pandahem. Old enmities could be forgotten. The future looked bright.

And she, Lushfymi, would be Empress of Vallia!

She would have to have at least one child. Well, that was a sacrifice she was willing to make.

She'd pay that price and as soon as the brat was born, or the twins—for they were regarded as bringing good luck on Kregen—he or she could be taken off by the wet-nurses and she need never see it again except at formal functions. She wasn't prepared to risk losing her figure, no, by Pandrite!

Of course, she would love her child. She did not get on with children; but her own would surely be different. Just look at the deplorable family life of the emperor!

She'd make sure Drak toed the line, that was for certain.

The scouts had spotted the mercenaries now and Leone's trumpeters pealed out orders. The brigade shook out. They were by a fraction just under a thousand strong, for they'd taken losses in the campaign and the crossing to Rahartdrin had not been easy. The paktuns, Leone estimated, numbered four or five hundred.

"Smash them," said the queen. "No prisoners."

Leone began to give orders concerning the girls to stick by the queen as the charge went in, when Lushfymi interrupted. She spoke tartly.

"No, Leone! I shall ride with you and the regiment this day."

"But—majestrix!"

"Don't argue, Leone. The paktuns do not stand a chance against us. There is no danger."

Privately, Leone told a couple of hefty Deldars to stay one each side of the queen and not to leave her, no matter what.

"And drag her zorca off out of it if it turns nasty."

"Quidang!"

Leone Starhammer knew what she was about. The paktuns had only about a hundred mounted with them, and she guessed the queen dismissed the footsoldiers as a mere trifle. People got killed making foolish mistakes like that. Leone organized the attack properly, and did not take any more chances than any commander must take. The zorcabows moved forward, shooting, followed by the lancers. The bodyguard regiment, QLJV, struck in from the flank.

The result was not in doubt.

The smells were, as usual, offensive, the screams distressing. No one liked to see a zorca writhing with a dart through that supple flank. The paktuns fought for their lives, and then broke. As a wave surges up the shingle the brigade roared in and completed the rout.

A last despairing shot from a line of crossbowmen before they threw down their weapons and ran soared from the routing mass. One bolt struck Queen Lushfymi in the side. She did not fall from the saddle because the Deldars grabbed her.

Horrified, Leone shrieked for the puncture ladies.

Red blood oozed only a little, a very little, around the cruel iron barb embedded in Queen Lushfymi's soft side.

368

*   *   *   *

"Look, Milsi my dear," said Delia, Empress of Vallia. "When you bring your knee up you must bring it up with force sufficient to drive a man's insides up past his breastbone. Nothing else will do."

"Yes, Delia," said Milsi.

"And," said Silda, "it is wise to kick him as he falls down."

"I understand the rapier well enough," said Milsi, Queen Mab of Croxdrin. "But this throwing people about and twisting their arms and legs, and hitting them so that—"

"So that they do not give you any further trouble."

"Yes, Delia."

A tremendous crash shook the rafters on the opposite side of the salle, and the three women turned to watch, smiling, as the pile of girls there sorted themselves out. They'd been indulging in a free-for-all, and the tangle of arms and legs looked like knitting after a chavnik had played with it. Here in Lancival, no courtesies and privileges of rank existed in the structure of the Sisters of the Rose, so that Milsi, as a novice initiate, could forget she was a queen.

"You're coming along splendidly, stepmother," said Silda, and her light laugh told Milsi that the understanding between them was ripening in its own good time into affection. Neither woman wished to rush this totally important relationship.

"I am glad to hear it, stepdaughter. This Hikvar is an art I may learn. But the Grakvar!" Milsi gave a slight shudder. "Slashing a thick black whip about! That is bad enough, Opaz knows. But when I consider the Jikvar— well, I am lost for words to explain my feelings. They—"

"Not all Sisters of the Rose go through Lancival, Milsi," interrupted Delia. "Your feelings do you credit. If I do not sound too stupidly pompous, we in the SoR bear a heavy responsibility with the burden of the Jikvar upon our Order. There—am I babbling, Silda dear?"

"In no way, Delia. I did not have to snatch my claw from the knapsack, a makeshift jikvarpam, down in Rashumsmot. But—" here she turned to look hard at Milsi "—but had the necessity arisen, there would have been a number of evil folk without faces down there."

"Evil doers were sent swimming in the Kazzchun River in Croxdrin," said Milsi. "I suppose the swiftness and degree of justice may vary; the intention remains the same."

A girl clad in white leathers entered the salle. She moved with a brisk grace, her color up, her head high. Rapier and main gauche swung at her side, the jikvarpam with its red stitching neatly nestling by her hip. Straight to Delia she marched, then halted and gave the slightest tilt of her head in respectful greeting.

"FarilSheon, Delia. News."

"SheonFaril, Yzobel. Tell us."

"Queen Lush has been sorely wounded. A crossbow bolt in the side. The puncture ladies give her a fifty-fifty chance. The Prince Majister is distraught—"

"By the hairy black warts and suppurating nose of my husband's famous Makki Grodno!" Delia saw it all, saw it all in a flash, and was appalled and angry, venomously angry.

"I'll go—" said Silda.

"Of course, my dear. Opaz alone knows what mischief will chance now." But Delia knew that Silda, too, had grasped the implications and possible consequences of this disastrous news.

Milsi said, "Seg is up in Balkan now and wants me to join him. Silda, if you want me, I'll come with you."

Impulsively, Silda stretched out her hand.

"Please—Milsi—"

"That's settled, then," broke in Delia. "Yzobel—organize a fast flier, the swiftest voller we have."

"Quidang!"

"I know that stubborn, upright, sober son of mine." Delia started off for the changing rooms. "If we women cannot fashion a scheme of honor in this, then he'll deserve to be lumbered with Queen Lush, by Vox, he will!"

With which tangled sentiment, Delia led them in their headlong flight down to Rahartdrin.

Yolande the Gregarian looked in the pottery dish upon the side shelf so many times a day she lost count. The water in the dish, of an odd silvery metallic hue, just sat there, doing nothing, just plain damned water.

"You're wasting your time," Crafty Kando told her. He had accepted the needle, as they say on Kregen, and went on with his life in the old ruffianly way.

"What went—somewhere—Kando, can come back."

"Not in this life, Yolande, no by Diproo the Nimble-fingered. The witch is dead. Her gems vanished with her. That is just plain water."

"All the same, I'll keep the water. You never know..."

"How I wish I'd pocketed some of the gold! That might have remained gold instead of sorcerously vanishing—"

"You can't blame the lady Lyss the Lone. She did warn us—"

"Oh, aye! And we were used, Yolande, used. The only good thing to come out of this affair is the death of Ortyg the Kaktu and his cronies."

"They'll set the Ice Floes a-rocking."

"Aye, by Beng Brorgal!"

When Lon the Knees came in, Yolande had put on a clean dress, fluffed up her hair, and wore a nice scent.

Lon flinched back as he entered. For a moment he thought a powcy had perfumed the room before he'd died and rotted instantly.

"Lahal, all," he said, and made play with a vivid green and yellow kerchief.

"Lon!" beamed Yolande, almost squirming with pleasure, desire and female intentions. "Come in. Wine?"

He sat down and accepted the wine. Yolande was about to open the proceedings on her own account, when Kando said: "Is there any more news on the queen's condition? You ought to hear all the gossip at the prince's stables."

"She still lives." Lon sipped. "They say she is so stuck with acupuncture needles a hedgehog would look bald."

Yolande stood up and went across to look in the pottery dish. The water remained water. On the way back she took the opportunity to pass by Lon's chair and put a hand on his shoulder. Lon felt the hand of doom. He remained very still. The perfume overwhelmed him and he flapped his kerchief as though driving away a fly.

"Lon, my dear," cooed Yolande. "Such a nice position you have now. Why, the Prince Majister of Vallia takes you on, gives you a smart livery, lets you take care of his zorcas! You need a fine strong woman to look out for you now you are doing so well."

"One day, one day, I expect, Yolande..."

"You oughtn't to leave it too long, you know. There are lots of conniving women who'd be only too anxious to take you on. Then they'd run you ragged, nag all day, fleece you of your cash—why, Lon, my dear, you need a proper woman to look after you."

Crafty Kando, thoroughly enjoying all this, hid his face in his tankard. It was ale for him. Lon, as the potential next husband, drank the wine.

Making a manful attempt to change the subject, Lon said: "They've been plagued dreadful over in the main island. They've had frogs fall from the sky, a plague of insects, and I did hear the dead rose—"

"I'm sure I don't wish to hear about that!" burst out Yolande. She smiled. "More wine, Lon my dear?"

Kando decided he'd better speak up now and leave poor old Lon to fight a rearguard action when he'd gone.

"Look, Lon. I've a little scheme on tomorrow night. I could do with a couple of fast zorcas to—"

"You're not stealing my zorcas, Kando!"

"No, no, you fambly. Just borrowing."

"Well, I dunno. The prince has a fellow up there, Nath the Strict, who's his orderly. He has an eye like a gimlet."

"Well, Lon," said Kando, expansively. "He can be outwitted by an old leem-hunter like you!"

"Probably. I'll think about it. But I'm not going to act like an onker and lose my position. The prince trusts me."

"Of course! He likes you. He won't mind if you borrow a couple of blood zorcas. And, Lon, I need 'em for the scheme to work. Speed, d'you see?"

"Oh, I see all right."

"Good! Then that's settled. Tomorrow night."

He stood up, said his thank yous to Yolande the Gregarian, and started for the door. Hastily, Lon stood up.

"I'll come with you, Kando. Work to do, you know."

"Oh, Lon!" exclaimed Yolande. "Surely you will stay for another cup of wine? And there is something I want to show you—"

"Thank you, Yolande; but I must get on about the prince's business. It's all go."

Almost killing himself laughing, Kando went out and Lon the Knees, a fixed smile on his face, his kerchief at the ready, fairly bolted after him. They called the remberees and fled into the night. Yolande sighed, pursed up her lips, and then—just in case—trotted over to have another look in the pottery dish.

Nineteen

Queen Lush gives an order

Thandor the Rock bashed his right fist numbingly against his breastplate—he adhered to the old ways, did Brumbytevax Thandor Veltan ti Therfuing in saluting as other trifles—and bellowed out: "Well, jis, I've looked at 'em. They were coming along, coming along. But we'd have chewed 'em up and trompled 'em down, aye, by a Brumbyte's Elbow!"

"Come in, come in, Thandor, and sit yourself down and take a glass of wine." Drak indicated the chair across from his own, and the table between loaded with rather good wines.

The two Kapts sitting on the elongated chair, after the fashion of a sofa, left as much space as possible between them. Kapt Logan Lakelmi was well aware that he was an extremely fortunate man to be sitting here being treated politely as the commanding general of an army instead of being in a ditch somewhere with his head parted from his shoulders, or swinging in an iron cage with the birds disposing of him piece by bloody piece.

The Prince Majister had merely said, "You obeyed the orders of your lord, Kapt Logan. If there was sorcery influencing you, we cannot say. You were a traitor to Vallia. But you may keep your life. I think you will serve the empire and the Emperor of Vallia faithfully from now on."

Lakelmi had replied, "I believe, majister, that I, too, along with many other people, was ensorcelled. I regret what has passed. I shall hew to your person and pledge my loyalty to the emperor."

Even so, Kapt Enwood nal Venticar, with scarlet memories of battles and death, would take a time to get over what had passed. He was, as he was at pains to repeat whenever possible, an old Freedom Fighter from Valka. Valka, in his and other people's opinions, because of the struggles they had endured, bred the best soldiers, tacticians and strategists in all Vallia.

The third Kapt in this comfortable withdrawing room where Drak chose to be at ease while he sorted out the problems confronting him wore an ornate uniform in which the amount of blue cloth contrasted strikingly with the clothes of the others. Kapt Nath Molim, the Trylon of Polnehm, had brought no army with him from his native land. He'd voyaged aboard an argenter from Lome. He came to request the queen for assistance in her country, where turmoil had raged rife for many seasons. Like Vallia, the island of Pandahem was struggling to resume normal life after the Times of Troubles.

Nath Molim had been shattered to discover the queen sorely wounded and near death.

The people still loyal to her even after her long absence overseas were growing disheartened. They understood why she had fled away from them; now the evil people who battened on the unhappy land threatened to overwhelm the last bastions of resistance. Nath Molim hoped that the queen's great friendship with the imperial house of Vallia would produce men, arms and money for a great jikai to sweep their enemies out of Lome.

"I swear to you, majister," he'd said to Drak, "as the Glorious Pandrite may judge me, that not one loyal soldier of Lome joined those armies from North Pandahem who attacked you here in Vallia. They came from Menaham, Tomboram and Iyam. Also, we have been much ravaged by the pirates from the Hoboling Islands who grow more daring every season."

"I believe you, Trylon Molim," said Drak, not yet on friendly enough terms to call the fellow Trylon* Nath.

Now, in this comfortable room, when Brytevax Thandor the Rock entered, Nath Molim fidgeted with impatience and the hope and desire he could persuade these Vallians to help him with men and treasure.

The detailed inspection carried out convinced Thandor the Rock that Alloran would in the near future have created a halfway decent Phalanx; he had not reached that stage yet. All the same, it was thankful that Thandor's three Kerchuris had not had to fight the two of Alloran's. The Rock valued his brumbytes...

---

* Trylon: rank of nobility below Vad and above Strom. *A.B.A.*

Comments were made about the various armies and the conversation remained exquisitely polite. Drak was worried sick about Queen Lush; but he could still find a lurking amusement in the way in which these men waltzed around each other. This was a kind of watershed. Anything could happen. This Molim fellow, now. He was quite young, smart, with a sharpness to him, a cutting edge, a fellow out for Number One all the time. There was one elegant solution that Drak fancied his father might even enjoy.

"Trylon Molim," he said, waiting for a pause in the conversation. "There are many paktuns awaiting repatriation. Many of them are from Pandahem. I think it possible I could convince the emperor and the Presidio to find the gold to pay them. They would fight for the queen in Lome and free the country for her. I do not promise, mind. But I believe this to be equitable." He was about to add that he owed the queen a great deal; he did not.

"Majister! This is just the news I was hoping for."

Kapt Logan Lakelmi, anxious to please, said: "Give me the word, jis, and I will take my army to Lome."

"That must await the decision from Vondium."

"Yes, jis."

Drak wasn't at all sure he relished the idea. It held murky possibilities for the future.

Through the sensible arrangement of the two armies for forage and supplies, the men were now spread out over a considerable area. Here in Rashumsmot lay only the bodyguard regiments with a few ancillaries for support. At least, Lakelmi's plan would take care of his army... Alloran's forces on the mainland, commanded by the Kataki Twins, had collapsed. They would provide strength for Kapt Lakelmi. As for the two Katakis, they had disappeared with their Whiptail followers.

Drak glanced over at the wall by the door where his great Krozair longsword hung. Why didn't he just take all these decisions himself? His father had once told him in that gruff way: "You do not walk in my shadow, my lad, or ever will if I have any say in the matter."

But it was damned hard not to feel that he did so walk in his father's shadow all the time. His father was just so bloody good at everything—well, except being civil—and he had the yrium, that magical charismatic power that bound men and women to him, made them loyal and everready to follow him to death and beyond. Drak did not feel he shared that power; Silda was in no doubt that he possessed the yrium.

Faintly through that door he heard a commotion with a lot of shouting and yelling. Almost immediately Nath the Strict hurried in.

"There is a Jikai Vuvushi who says she must see you, jis, at once. Most urgent. The lads hold her—"

"Send her in!"

When Nath the Strict ran out he saw the girl had in some miraculous way freed herself from the grips of the guards and was running fleetly toward the door. At her back the bows lifted, arrows nocked and the cruel iron barbs ready to rip into her flesh.

"Hold!" bellowed Nath. "The prince will see her!"

Mandi Volanta fairly hurled herself through the open door. She took in the room of high-ranking officers, spotted the Prince Majister, skidded to a halt before him.

"Majister!" she fairly screamed out. "They are killing Leone! Leone Starhammer! Queen Lush has given orders to have her killed! Please, majister—do something!"

"Quite right and proper, too," spoke out Trylon Nath Molim into the abrupt hush. "The woman failed in her duty to protect the queen. Therefore she must die."

"Out of my way!" snarled Drak, and leaped for the door. He raked down the longsword as he ran.

Shouted orders, the stamp of booted feet, all a rush and a scurry, and at the head of a parcel of his lads he was out in the roseate glow of the Maiden with the Many Smiles. Mandi Volanta was up with him, directing him, shrieking for the men to run, you hulus, run!

Incongruously in Drak's brain, as he pelted on, the knowledge that the queen lived flamed. She had regained consciousness. And her first order had been to take vengeance on Leone, whom she blamed for her misfortune.

That, of course, was the way of the great ones of the world, of queens and empresses. It was not the way of the new Vallia.

His mother, the divine Empress Delia, would not countenance such an atrocity for an instant. But—that was the way of the world in which Queen Lush had been born and grown up and learned to understand and bend to her will...

Drak could not find it in his heart to blame the queen.

Sprawled in the entrance gate and across the courtyard and up the stairs, the bodies of Jikai Vuvushis scattered. There were men amongst them, too, corpses wearing predominantly blue clothes. These were people in the retinue of Trylon Nath Molim, clearly, ever ready to obey their queen. This handiwork was perfectly normal for a queen, everyone knew that.

Leone Starhammer and her girls had barricaded themselves in the top floor of the villa and they resisted stubbornly. The fight was a bloody business. Drak roared into action at the head of a mingled mob of his bodyguards, yelling out for the Lomians to lay down their weapons or be chopped without mercy.

The business was touch and go. A few cunning strokes from the Krozair longsword, a couple of lopped heads, and the Lomians understood. They heard what the prince shouted at them, and knew they must believe. If they did not—they were dead men.

As for Drak, he was perfectly prepared to slay all these Pandaheem. He valued Leone's girls. The Lomians were from Pandahem and had been implacable enemies of Vallia from long before Drak had been born. There was no contest of loyalties.

The odd fact did not occur to him until they were clearing up that many of Leone's Jikai Vuvushis were from Lome in Pandahem, too...

The smell of blood and the stink of fear were merely part of normal life after a fight. Leaving everything to be sorted out by his people, accompanied by a strong guard, Drak took himself off to see Queen Lushfymi.

He found her in the wide silken bed very much in command of herself, most of the acupuncture needles withdrawn, her face immaculately made-up, her hair a shining marvel. Those violet eyes were heavy with remembered pain. She sat up against silken pillows, and she smiled dazzlingly as he entered.

"Drak! How nice. I knew you would come to see me as soon as—but you are very quick! I have only just sent my tiring women away."

Instantly, she had him at a disadvantage, as it were bent across her knee, his backbone about to sunder.

He swallowed.

"Queen—Lushfymi. About Leone—"

"Oh, her, the stupid woman. I reposed great confidence in her, Drak. I felt affection for her. But she failed me abysmally. Forget her. Tell me all the news—"

He did not, he told himself savagely, he did not feel like a small boy being chastised.

This woman understood power and the management of that inscrutable and overwhelming commodity. She would make such an empress. The fabled Queens of Pain of ancient Loh might tremble with envy.

When he told her that he had saved Leone Starhammer she became outraged. Her face took on a menacing look that would have struck terror into the purest of her subjects.

"You had no right to interfere with my justice!"

"Lushfymi, look, that was scarcely justice—"

"Of course it was! Does the workman keep a broken tool? Does a warrior retain a worthless sword?"

"It wasn't Leone's fault—"

"Oh! So it was my fault, was it?"

"No, of course not—"

"Perhaps we had best forget this, Drak. After all, I think we must come to a conclusion soon in our relationship and you do know in what fond regard I hold you." She smoothed the silken sheet. "I am sure you thought you were acting for the best."

"Yes—"

"So let us brush aside the silly woman. If Leone lives, then she is lucky for now. Nath Molim is most anxious for us to go to Lome and drive out all these awful villains preying on my country. Between us, we can do it."

Feeling despicable, Drak took refuge in saying, "The decision must rest with the Presidio and the emperor."

"Ever since he fell through the covering of my palanquin, Drak, I have felt an affection for your father."

That wasn't quite as Drak had heard the story from his mother; he let it pass without comment. Lushfymi was a formidable woman, a queen acting perfectly within her rights, and a force of personality and character able to deal with any and every aspect of running Vallia as empress.

Lushfymi, conscious of the power she held over Drak and yet frustratingly aware that the conclusion for which she hungered appeared as far away as ever, lay back on her pillows. She smiled, a wan yet brave little smile. She knew she was beautiful, not just because everyone told her so but because she could see the evidence in her mirror day by day.

"Drak, dear, I am very tired. I am so pleased to see you, but—"

"Of course."

"Drak—kiss me before you go—please..."

He kissed her on the cheek and she turned her head so that her full soft lips met his. She knew all there was to know about kissing. Drak drew back, feeling the passion there. He managed a smile, and then turned and contrived to keep from stumbling as he made for the door.

By Zair! What an empress she would make! And what a wife! He could not mistake the naked passion blazing in her, and no matter how much of that was for the position of empress and how little for himself as a man, whatever she spared him would be more than enough for any man. No other woman had ever aroused so deep emotions within him, except for Silda, of course; but Silda was different.

The next day his mother, Silda, and her new stepmother, Queen Mab, flew in. They were closely followed by a second voller bringing Senator Naghan Strandar, a senior and highly valued member of the Presidio, from Vondium.

The welcomes were genuine and warm, the rejoicings great. Drak found Milsi to be delightful. She, for her part, saw at once that Silda had better marry Drak quickly. The man was a splendid person; but he needed a great deal of female instruction. With Lushfymi acting as the wounded heroine of a battle, for all that the fight had been but a skirmish, Silda's light was being eclipsed.

Naghan Strandar brought the decision. Alloran was to be pardoned on account of sorcery, and to be restored as Kov of Kaldi. Drak was pleased.

During the next days the mercenaries, willing to go fight for Queen Lush if they were paid, prepared to embark for Lome. The town hummed with activity. During this time there were opportunities for enjoyment, dances, routs, balls and festive occasions. Lushfymi mended apace. Silda and Milsi got on famously. And the women scrupulously made no mention of the reason for their visit, were exquisitely polite to Queen Lush, oohing and aahing at her version of the battle in which she had been wounded.

Delia, sizing up Leone Starhammer, agreed to take the Jikai Vuvushi into her personal regiment. There was no chance that Leone could serve Queen Lush again, and every chance she'd die of the attempt if she made it.

The mercenaries sailed in the fleet gathered by Alloran in his attempt to conquer the islands. Naghan Strandar informed the Lomians that the Presidio had vetoed Kapt Lakelmi's plan to take his remaining forces to Lome. He would go with Alloran back to Kaldi. The large island of Womox, off the west coast, had been recaptured by Delia's Blue Mountain Boys. Vallia was being reunited. North Vallia remained to be brought back into the fold. But the Vallians were aware that they were being held in reserve against the horrendous invasions of the Shanks, fishmen from over the curve of the world, who would destroy all of Paz if they were not stopped.

News came in when the town lay quiet after all the excitements that Kovneva Katrin Rashumin had been in hiding with the wizards in their island of Fruningen. She was returning to her kovnate of Rahartdrin. Delia was overjoyed at the news, for Katrin was a trusted friend of standing. San Fraipur smiled, nodding, and said words to the effect that wizards of his home were not onkers.

One day Milsi said to her stepdaughter, "Silda, my dear, I really do think I must join your father in Balkan. He needs me up there."

"Very well, Milsi." Silda wasn't going in for the mother style of address. "I understand. Give him my love."

Delia said, "I think my son is nerving himself for a decision. It is useless to prod him. I think, Silda, Milsi and I are doing more harm than good here."

"Delia!" burst out Silda. "That can't be true!"

"I think it is. We are clearly supporting you. We are a pressure group. Poor Queen Lush, wounded, alone, with no one to urge her suit!"

So Silda had to stand and wave them good-bye and call the remberees. What they said was true; it hurt to see them go.

To stifle off that feeling she made up her mind to go and see the person she had promised herself to go see for longer than she cared for. She tried not to be ungrateful. There was, also, the question of gold to be accounted for...

At this time Drak made up his mind that as soon as Queen Lush was fit to travel they'd be off back to Vondium. With Katrin Rashumin returning, and Kapt Enwood and the army here, this corner of Vallia was safe.

Naghan Strandar told him that the Presidio had been divided over the fate of the traitor Alloran. The emperor had pointed out that the Prince Majister, as the man on the spot, was in the best position to judge. "They all acknowledged the truth of that, Drak. I can say I am mightily pleased at the respect they all hold you in."

So to return to Vondium should not create problems.

He could not deny that he would be pleased to see his father again. He might be an old devil; but he represented to Drak a very great deal of what life was about. His father had always been honest with him, except for these mysterious disappearances, unexplained, and he had only once ever thought with any certitude that his father had lied to him.

One day in Esser Rarioch, seasons and seasons ago, Drak had spotted a wonderful golden and scarlet hunting bird and had called out in surprise at the gorgeous raptor. His father had denied that the bird existed. Yet Drak had seen it. Of course, he'd been very young at the time, and much smoke had blown with the wind since then and he'd grown up. Maybe that had something to do with it?

He pulled on light russet hunting leathers over a shirt of linked mesh and, dressing without thinking about it, strapped on rapier and left-hand dagger. Calling for Nath the Strict, he raked down the Krozair longsword, bellowing: "Nath!"

A footman, scarlet of face, hight Brindle, popped in hurriedly. "Nath has a demon in his guts, jis. Lon the Knees—"

"Send Nath my condolences. Lon the Knees will handle the zorcas." He went out quickly, feeling stifled indoors, needing a breath of fresh air. He told the sentry to alert the Hikdar in command of this day's duty squadron.

At the stables Lon was competence itself. A fine blood zorca was brought out, Stiffears, and Lon handled himself and the zorca splendidly. He assisted the prince to mount. No one could guess from his rubicund face that if the prince had turned up a glass later, disaster would have befallen Lon the Knees.

Silda walked into the courtyard, over the cobbles with the wisps of straw scattered about, and saw Drak astride the zorca.

Lon faded into the shadows of the nearest box. He hadn't seen Lyss the Lone since all the excitement, and was enraptured to see her come visiting him now. He thought the prince wouldn't mind; but you had to be careful when you held a responsible position in the Prince Majister's Stables!

Silda was in a mood that sizzled like water dropped into hot fat.

"Off to see Queen Lush, I suppose?"

"I was going for a ride." The stiffness of Drak's tones made a pikeshaft look crooked. "Now you mention it, I think I will. Thank you for the suggestion."

"Oh, you are most welcome."

"The queen is wounded, you know, and—"

"Rubbish! There's nothing wrong with the fat old madam now!"

"You forget yourself!"

"I don't! But I wish I did!"

Drak, face like the base end of a marble statue, touched his spurless heels into the zorca's flanks and Stiffears bounded away. Drak and Silda, both their heads seething with half-understood anger and anguish, parted.

Lon closed his mouth.

He made a slight movement and caused just a tiny chink of sound. Instantly the sharp point of a rapier pressed against his stomach. Silda stared into the shadows.

"Lon?"

"Aye, aye, Lyss, it's me. What I can't understand is why you're still here and not lying with your body there and your head here! You spoke to the prince—"

"Forget him, the great onker! I came to see you."

Lon felt convinced that the brightness in Lyss's eyes was far greater than could be explained in any except one certain way. He swung about as the gang crept quietly into the stables. They had waited until the prince left. Now Crafty Kando, looking at Lyss, said, "We're here. And so is the lady."

At once Silda was herself again. She fixed Lon with a look. So he felt obliged to explain. Kando had borrowed the two zorcas he'd requested, and the job had been completed. Now far greater game was afoot. The whole gang required zorcas.

"He is a fat slaver, Lyss! He still has slaves out there, hidden. He has gold! Rafak is a chicken ripe for the plucking! Ride with us!"

"If this Rafak continues as a slavemaster," said Silda, "he breaks the law."

"Exactly!" crowed Lon.

"Then he should be reported to the Watch, or the Prince—"

"We don't have much truck with the Watch. And we value his gold, believing it should come to us—"

"What am I to do with you?" said Silda, thoroughly cheered up after that dismal encounter with Drak. "This sounds promising. A spot of mischief thrashing a slaver is just what I need."

Swathed in dark hooded cloaks, riding a string of the Prince Majister's blood zorcas, the gang rode out. Silda rode with them. Drak had needed to go for a ride to rid his head of cobwebs; Silda craved more than a simple ride to rid her brain of the festering agony and anguish there...

Lon the Knees gave up trying to puzzle out what he'd overheard. Perhaps he hadn't heard all that at all. Perhaps he'd dreamed it, hiding in the zorca stall... He, too, felt that a spot of action would clear his head.

The petal shape of an airboat skimmed over the riders and swooped ahead to vanish beyond trees cloaking a rise.

Moving at a brisk pace, for there was a lot to be got through, Crafty Kando's gang with Lon the Knees and Silda Segutoria, very much Lyss the Lone, rode for the criminal hideout of the slavemaster, the Rapa Rafak the Lash.

Some time later with a great deal—but not all, by the Furnace Fires of Inshurfraz, not all!—of his ill humor jolted out of him by the ride, Drak cantered back. The duty half-squadron rode in rear, looking forward to a wet and the opportunity to relax in their various raucous, nefarious or slumbrous ways. A jurukker of the guard detailed to Queen Lush galloped frenziedly toward Drak.

"Prince! The queen! She is beset by Katakis!" The rider skidded his zorca around, spraying dust, still bellowing.

"The queen! Assassination! Hurry, jis, hurry!" Without hesitation Drak slammed his heels into Stiffears' flanks. The zorca leaped ahead, responding at once, and in the same instant Drak hauled up on the reins, as a figure darted from the side to stand directly before him, one hand flung aloft.

"What the hell! Out of the way—or..." Drak was going to say he'd run the figure over; but he saw the long plain robe, the turban toppling over one ear, and so he guessed at once, with a distinct sensation of his heart turning over and lodging in his throat. He knew, did Drak, he knew.

"Drak! Silda! The Katakis attack her and her companions believing you to be there. She is sore beset... There is little time left for her..."

Twenty

In which Lon the Knees witnesses the true joy

On the day Queen Lushfymi gave orders to have the captain of her bodyguard killed the girls had resisted the murderers in defense of Leone Starhammer. Since then nearly all of them had signed up with the Empress Delia. So it was that when the Katakis landed from their airboat to assassinate the queen they were met by the guard detailed by the Prince Majister to watch over the queen.

The guards sent a messenger and then barricaded themselves in the villa. No thought crossed Queen Lush's mind that this was divine retribution. She saw no connection between her perfectly logical and legal order and this inspired assassination attempt.

One of the guards said that the leader of this cut-throat bunch of Katakis was Stromich Ranjal Yasi, twin brother to Strom Rosil Yasi. Accurate archery pinned the Katakis in the grounds, and two rushes were fronted and bested. The queen was perfectly composed. Hikdar Nervil remarked that they could hold out for some time yet, but that numbers were against them.

Queen Lush said, simply: "The Prince Majister will soon be here. He would melt the Ice Floes of Sicce to be at my side."

"Assuredly, majestrix," said Nervil, seconded to Drak's PMSW from 3EYJ, and took himself off to the dangerous corner where the shrubbery grew altogether too close to the walls of the villa.

For Silda, the ride to Cottmer's Hollow knocked some of the bad humor out of her. The ride alone began to affect her. She shouldn't really have spoken to poor Drak like that; after all, he was completely deceived by Queen Lush. She'd have to make it up to him, as soon as possible. All the same, he was so stubborn! If only she could knock some sense into him as the zorca between her knees was jolting the bad temper out of her!

Crafty Kando organized the onslaught brilliantly. Silda could quite see why the gang needed zorcas; they could hit Rafak the Lash, free his slaves and steal his gold, and be back in town before anyone knew anything about it.

Rafak, his vulturine features convulsed, feathers bristling, his arrogant beak bent to one side, was not slain. The slaver with his assistants was bundled into one of the tumble-down shanties at the center of the hollow. Massy trees surrounded the place, which was gloomy and dank, and well named for Cottmer's Caverns of horrific legend.

Silda realized she would have to fend for the slaves herself. She went around freeing them, and they set up a caterwauling, running about, wringing their hands in joy, overwhelmed by the tragedy and then the release. Lon the Knees, after a single thought, joined Silda in her work.

Crafty Kando and his cronies sought the gold chests.

So it was that when the flier landed and the Kataki Strom led his people into this vengeful attack upon the man who had authored his downfall, he was not aware that the Prince Majister was not in Cottmer's Hollow. Yasi was convinced that the string of zorca riders from the prince's stables escorted the Prince Majister. Now he would exact his revenge.

Shrieking shrill Kataki war cries, the Whiptails rushed in, weapons glittering.

Silda grasped the situation in a single all-encompassing glance and dragged Lon into the shanty where Kando and his people were ripping everything to pieces in their search for gold. Crossbow bolts thudded into the walls and ripped through the mean little windows. The consternation and uproar in the hut could not be allowed in any way to influence her.

Lon saw her switch the plain knapsack forward. She dived her left hand in, and he remembered what had happened to the spinlikl when he had done just that. Then he gasped.

Silda raised her left hand high and shouted at the rabble in the shanty.

Clothing that left hand, glittering, evil and magnificent, a Claw, a thing of oiled sliding steel, of cruel razor-sharp talons, turned Silda into a true Jikai Vuvushi of the Sisters of the Rose.

"Listen to me, you famblys! Those Katakis out there—all they're after is slaves and gold—your gold! And you as slaves! They will not take me."

Her Claw struck sparks of fire from the honed talons, turning, opening and closing, evil and beautiful...

She'd taken up the jikvar in the emergency quick-action grip and now as Kando's people yelled and swirled around like a disturbed ant's nest, Silda strapped up the Claw properly onto her left hand.

The opening moves from the Kataki side consisted in driving Kando's people into the shanty, of rounding up the newly released and bewildered slaves, and then of sorting out the rest. Silda reasoned out this probable course of action and then gave vent to her feelings on certain subjects.

"You refused my offer of swords. How many of you retain the spears I provided? And not a bow among us! By Vox! It's enough to make an honest Jikai Vuvushi take up knitting!"

"It's enough to make an honest thief know when to keep his station," pronounced Yolande the Gregarian, with a meaningful look at Kando. Some of the others started in slanging Kando, each other, themselves for their own stupidity, and Lon the Knees for providing the zorcas that got them into the mess. To Silda it seemed a bubble burst in her head. They made her laugh, these people and their thieving antics. Her ill-humor now had but one direction, one target. Katakis!

"If we just stay here and wait for them to attack when they are ready—" she spoke in a hard, clipped fashion Lon had heard her use once before "—they'll chop us for sure. We must break for the zorcas, and ride. All of us, together."

"These walls may not be much," rapped out Kando. "But they stop the crossbow bolts. If we stay here they can't shoot us, and if they try to break in, we will chop them."

"Aye," said Lop-eared Tobi, waving his knife about. "But I'll go with Lyss the Lone. I trust her."

"I'll stay with Kando," said Ob-eye Mantig, and he showed the spear he had kept.

The others started up for and against the plans.

Keeping watch out of a crack, Lon yelped: "You'll have to make up your minds sharpish. Here they come."

Silda recognized that these folk had little hope of escaping this imbroglio.

If they were not killed out of hand they'd wind up as slaves. And that fate might include her...

Hissing shrieks of battle spitting from the Katakis heralded their attack that would finish off the people sheltering in the shanty. Silda swung to face the ramshackle door, Claw poised, drexer snouting, ready.

The phantom form of Deb-Lu-Quienyin, glowing with a ghostly light, faded. He had used his kharrna to project his image mile after mile across Vallia to warn Drak. What effect this sorcery might have on his men did not concern Drak now.

Queen Lush!

Silda!

Drak did not have to make a decision.

There was no agonized despair over what he must do. He wrenched the reins about and Stiffears, unused to such summary treatment, gave a little snort of reproval. The queen must be cared for and protected, nothing less would satisfy a prince of so upright a character, so he yelled savagely at her messenger.

"Ride for the Villa of Poppies! Rouse out Kov Vodun and his men! Bring all the people you can from anywhere you can—and ride like the Agate-Winged Warriors of Hodan-Set!"

"Majister...?"

But Drak was gone, heels clapped into Stiffears, slapping the zorca's rump, hurtling him on. His duty half-squadron followed, picking up speed. Hikdar Nath the Meticulous yelled across at the youngest jurukker of the squadron.

"Jurukker Vaon! Ride for the barracks, get anyone you can, dig 'em all out! Ride for Cottmer's Hollow—and Vaon—*Bratch!*"

"Quidang, hik!"

Vaon's zorca leaped away heading for the barracks.

Drak, Prince Majister of Vallia, rode like a crazy man.

If anything happened to her! If she was killed, wounded... Those Zair-benighted Whiptails were expert at man management, and women in their nets could hope only for a cruel fate to be curtailed by death. He was under no illusions. He remembered what his mother had told him, speaking in soft unhappy tones, repeating what his father had said. Once his father had sought to save Velia, the first Velia. Oh, no, real life was not like the romances of the theaters, of the puppet shows, where the valiant prince always rode to the rescue in time.*

Stiffears was now under no illusions either; he recognized the urgency in the rider on his back, and true to the pride and prowess of a blood-zorca, he responded. He stretched out into a long headlong gallop that

---

* see *Renegade of Kregen*, Dray Prescot #13. A.B.A.

384

swept him over the ground like a bird. Low in the saddle, glaring ahead, Drak forced the zorca on, and he could feel the blood in his body thumping in time to the staccato clatter of the hooves.

Very quickly they left the road and went roaring across open country, soaring up wooded slopes and pressing on across shallow streams, racing over the open heathland.

If anything happened to her, Drak promised himself in rage and useless vengeance, he would hang every Kataki sky-high, every one, no matter what, from this day on until he was sent down to the Ice Floes of Sicce to meet the Gray Ones and perhaps make his way to the sunny uplands beyond. Every last damned one...

The door was smashed and hung from one hinge. They'd piled up benches and the table and fought the intruders back; but Long Nath lay coughing blood from a Whiptail's bladed steel in his guts, and Nath the Swarthy sprawled dead, his throat ripped out. Crafty Kando lunged his spear into a Kataki who screeched and fell back beside a fellow who lacked a face.

Lon the Knees had seen Lyss at work, and he shuddered even as he thrust his spear through a crack in the walls, and heard an answering yell. The Katakis attacked from all sides of the shanty, trying to break in, so the occupants had no chance to follow Lyss's plan and force their way out and away astride the prince's zorcas.

No one now questioned Silda's right to give orders and to take control of the defense of the hut. These folk recognized a professional at work. The first Kataki through with his bladed tail high ready for that twinkling downward slashing blow or that treacherous and devastatingly quick upward lunge, leaped forward, sword flashing, to seize his prey, and Silda's Claw raked and the Kataki did not scream as he fell away. Difficult to scream without a mouth, let alone a face.

The acrid stinks in the hut, the sweat and blood, all meshed to make a miasma of horror. The thieves, seeing there was nothing else for it, fought wickedly. Well led, they fronted and hurled back the first Kataki attacks. But time was against them. If the Whiptails gave up trying to take the merchandise they might fire the hut and burn them out...

The table and benches groaned and slid away from the pitiful door. Three Whiptails sprang through. Kando ducked and put his spear into the last one's ribs. Of the first two, one looked—for a single heartbeat only—most stupidly at his stump of tail, the steel blade tinkling across the floor. Then the drexer investigated his inward parts and before he had time to fall, in that cunning swirling movement of the Claw, his comrade gushed blood and brains and stumbled emptily back.

"They keep coming," snarled Kando, swiping sweat from his forehead. "I think, my lady Lyss, we are done for."

"Dee Sheon will aid us, Kando. We fight until we can fight no longer."

Lon stuck a Whiptail trying to bash the crack wider with an axe. He peered out. Then he swung back to shout at Silda: "They're pulling back at the rear, Lyss. I think—"

"Yes, you are right. It's one last charge into the door. After that, if we live, they'll burn us out."

The parcel of thieves prepared themselves. They would resist, they would fight back this one last time. They would not be taken up as slaves by Katakis. Silda allowed one regretful thought that she had not seen her father for far too long, and she mourned her mother. As for Drak, well, the stars had remained icily aloof...

"Here come the greeshes!"

Smashing their way over the tumbled table and benches the Katakis forced their way in. They slashed and hacked and the spears darted and stabbed in return. Silda's sword cut and thrust, and her Claw flamed brilliantly. The cunning steel talons sprayed blood. She cut down two Whiptails, and a third ripped his tail-blade across her thigh. She did not notice the sting. She brought the Claw around and rearranged his features. His blood hit Lon, who blinked, and drove on with his spear. From the back of the hut knives flew expertly.

A looped rope entangled a Kataki and as he stumbled Yolande stuck her knife into him.

As Diproo the Nimble-fingered was their witness, the thieves fought.

The force the Katakis put in was just too much. In the next few moments the thieves would be overwhelmed. Silda took a fresh grip on herself, snouted the sword up, a single glistening bar of red, slashed her Claw before her eyes. If this was the way of it, why, then, this was the way of it...

The Krozair longsword, among the most formidable weapons of all Kregen, simply cut through the Katakis as a reaper cuts corn. Drak ploughed through, scattering arms and legs, tumbling heads, berserk. He cut a pathway through to the smashed door, striking down without a vestige of mercy at the backs of the Whiptails trying to break in. He was a devoted instrument of destruction.

His duty half-squadron, very professional, took care of those Katakis who were rash enough to stay to contest the outcome. Drak burst his way into the hut.

He saw Silda, smeared in blood, her Claw a glistening horror, slide her sword into a Kataki and swirl the Claw around to destroy another. He chopped the remaining Katakis with swift, economical blows, coming back to his senses, using all the skill inherent in the Disciplines of the Krozairs of Zy. The last slaver fell. Drak halted, sword uplifted, staring at Silda.

"You are safe," he said, stupidly, feeling the shakes beginning. He lowered the sword and bowed his head.

Silda could say nothing. She needed to breathe.

Lon the Knees saw it all.

He had given himself up for lost, and now the prince had rescued him and the others. There would have to be some nimble explanations about those zorcas. He saw the prince drop that terrible sword. He saw Lyss the Lone drop her sword. That awful Claw-thing on her hand fell to her side. Lon saw. He saw the prince step forward and take Lyss into his arms. He heard him speak.

"Silda! Silda—a fool, I've been—"

"Hush, Drak. You are here. I am here—"

"Oh, yes!"

Lon's mouth tried to close and would not.

"And, Silda, we shall be married at once. If you will have me—?"

"There is never anyone else, ever, Drak—"

"When I heard—Deb-Lu warned me—I knew I would not want to live without you—"

"Nor I you—"

"And, Silda, my heart, we are going to be so happy the whole world of Kregen will marvel!"

"Oh, yes, Drak, my heart. Oh, very yes!"

OMENS OF KREGEN

To Larry and the Secret Seven

A Note on Dray Prescot

Lit by the red and green fires of Antares, the planet Kregen, four hundred light-years from Earth, is a world harsh yet beautiful, terrible yet alluring. There any man or woman may achieve what the heart desires, if they plan and struggle in keeping with the innate purpose within themselves. Kregen has its share of weaklings and the faint of heart; but their names are not writ large in the footnotes to the Sagas to be found under the Suns of Scorpio.

Dray Prescot, as described by one who has seen him, is a man a little above middle height with brown hair and level brown eyes, brooding and dominating, with enormously broad shoulders and powerful physique. There is about him an abrasive honesty and an indomitable courage. He moves like a savage hunting cat, quiet and deadly. Reared in the harsh conditions of Nelson's navy, he is a man driven by forces he barely understands and at which we can guess only through what he tells us of his story.

Called to be the Emperor of Vallia, he is putting the finishing touches to the reunification of the islands after the Time of Troubles. The famed and feared Witch of Loh, Csitra, has Pronounced the Nine Unspeakable Curses Against Vallia. Drawing constant strength from his consort, the Empress Delia, Prescot, together with his blade comrades, knows he must deal with the witch and her child, Phunik.

This confrontation, which the Vallians cannot guarantee to be final, they are all somberly aware will not take place under the streaming mingled opaline radiance of the Suns of Scorpio.

Alan Burt Akers

One

Concerning the crime of old Hack 'n' Slay

Old Hack 'n' Slay, caught with his fingers in the regimental funds, went on the rampage.

He hurled the first three fellows out through the windows of the tavern. The clientele huddled away into corners, including even soldiers from various regiments who knew old Hack 'n' Slay and like the ordinary citizens wanted nothing to do with this fracas.

In a furious melee six of his fellows poured all over poor old Hack 'n' Slay. They heaved up and down like men clinging to a boat in a gale.

Scarlet of face, ferocious of eye, old Hack 'n' Slay roared his refusal to be taken into custody.

"Calm down, Jik!" yelped the Deldar who hung onto one arm and was flapped up and down like a bird's wing. "You're nabbed."

Flagons of wine went every which way, strewing the floor with their pungent brews. The fumes coiled into the nostrils of the combatants. Yet no one drew a pointed or edged weapon. This was a strictly regimental matter. The lads of the 11th Churgurs would settle this among themselves. Old Hack 'n' Slay might have dipped his sticky finger into the regimental funds, he remained Jiktar Nath Javed, the regimental commander, commanding also the 32nd Brigade, of which the 11th Churgurs formed a part, and he was well known and liked.

"I'll have the Opaz-forsaken money tomorrow!" bellowed Jiktar Nath Javed, throwing a bulky soldier over his shoulder. "Lemme up!"

"No good, Jik! Grab that foot, Ompey. His arm, Cwonley, his left arm, you great onker!"

Crash went a table, and jugs and bottles smashed into vinous ruin.

"Get his feet from under him."

"I'll twist all your ears off, you horrible—"

Up and down the length of the tavern, The Cockerell Winged, the struggle blistered on. Hack 'n' Slay was no man to be dragged down even by six of his own hefty lads.

"Listen to me, you pack of famblys. I'll—"

"Yowp!" gobbled a churgur as an elbow nudged his ribs. The rest piled on. In the end they coiled a cunning loop of rope around his ankles and he crashed over to hit his nose on the edge of the upturned table. He let rip a rafter-shattering roar. Then they were on him like ants on a honey pot, holding him down, lapping him in rope, trussing him up like a chicken for the pot.

He kept on roaring his head off so they stuffed a kerchief into his horrendous maw and then wrapped that up in a scarf. Seeing there was nothing else for it, old Hack 'n' Slay quieted down and they lifted him up like a rolled carpet and took him off.

Through the pleasant evening they went, with three of Kregen's moons high in the sky casting down their refulgent pinkish light and the scent of Moonblooms filling the air with fragrance.

People out to enjoy themselves turned to stare. The soldiers just marched grimly on, their commander slung over their shoulders, conscious of the indignity of these proceedings yet not giving a damn what the passersby might think.

This was serious. Jiktar Nath Javed, old Hack 'n' Slay, just given the command of the 32nd Brigade, had pilfered the funds of his own regiment. Only because the division inspectorate had called and found the discrepancy—hell, they'd dumped the empty cash box out onto the parade ground for all to see—had Jiktar Javed been caught out.

Dumped down in the cells he gave up all resistance. They removed his gag and bonds, they took away all his belts and harness, all his weaponry. Sitting slumped into a corner, head on hands on knees, he gave no more trouble that night.

In the morning, after he'd washed and dressed punctiliously, they gave him slursh with red honey stirred in, three fried eggs with a huge hunk of bread, and a pottery dish of palines, whereat he swore they were trying to starve him.

Initially he was run up before the divisional commander, Chuktar Enar Thandon, a neat and dapper man, a Strom, with a clipped moustache, a mouth like a wound and eyes that could, so the swods in the ranks said, bore straight through the toughest armor around. Chuktar Thandon was flanked, in a matter of this seriousness, by the other two brigade commanders. They stared narrowly at Jiktar Nath Javed. For his part, Nath had little time for Lords.

The hearing was fully recorded by an almost silent Xaffer, who scribbled down his notes in his own particular method from which later he would write up a full report. Guards stood at the doors and windows of the commander's room, a place half office, half duty room, fully armed and armored after the churgur way.

The proceedings began with various witnesses establishing that the strongbox had been full of gold and silver coins, and was now empty.

Other witnesses swore they'd seen old Hack 'n' Slay in such and such a place at such and such a time. The evidence bore in remorselessly.

Eventually, Nath Javed bellowed out: "I don't deny I borrowed the cash—"

"Borrowed?"

"Aye, borrowed—"

Old Hack 'n' Slay had risen through the full ten grades within the Jiktar rank. A Jiktar normally commanded a regiment. As a Zan-Jiktar, his next step was to become the first grade within the Chuktar rank, an Ob-Chuktar. Normally, Chuktars commanded brigades and various higher formations as required. Just why old Hack 'n' Slay had not received the promotion he must have counted on was not apparent then. It must have been a sore point with him, though.

"You are a Jiktar, Nath," said Enar Thandon. "A Zan-Jiktar. Are you telling us you have amassed debts your pay cannot honor?"

"Not debts—well, not just debts."

"But," put in one of the brigade Chuktars, Ongarr Fardew, commanding the bowmen, "you admit you stole the money?"

"No, you great fambly! I merely borrowed it—"

"Moderate your tone, Nath. We are all friends here."

"Friends?" Hack 'n' Slay spat it out. "I wonder. Friends would listen to what I say, by Vox, and not sit in judgment overhastily."

"We do not sit in judgment." Enar Thandon rapped that out sharply enough. Then, with even more sharpness, he added: "Yet."

"This is merely an inquiry to establish your guilt," said Chuktar Ongarr Fardew. He spoke in a neutral way; Nath Javed scowled and, about to roar out the obvious reply to that, was interrupted as Enar Thandon in his acidulated way cut in.

"You admit you took the money from the cash box. You admit you have debts you cannot pay. I feel it would be inadmissible in officers of honor to find you anything less than guilty."

"I didn't steal the rotten money—"

"There is no other construction we can put upon your actions."

"Agreed." The Court of Inquiry was unanimous.

After a few further formalities, very necessary in matters of this kind to ensure that the legality of the proceedings could not be challenged at a later date, the court gave instructions for old Hack 'n' Slay to be wheeled out and back to his cell.

As Enar Thandon said to the others, as they stood up and prepared to go about the more mundane business of the day: "Our new emperor is such a stickler for justice under the law, one dare not put a foot wrong."

"Aye," said Chuktar Bonn, commanding the 31st Brigade. "One gains the impression that after we smashed Hamal into the ground we have taken up their disease of laws and lawyers."

"Hamal," said Enar Thandon, in an off-hand, sneering way. "Them. They have been our enemies for many seasons, and now our new emperor welcomes them as allies and friends."

"Some friends." Ongarr Fardew expressed supreme contempt.

Talking amicably among themselves, the three Chuktars of the 30th Division of infantry went out into the streaming mingled radiance of the Suns of Scorpio. That glorious ruby and jade illumination lay athwart the land, drenching the world in color and light. These three were wrapped up in their own concerns, barely noticing the brilliance of the day.

All these events were witnessed by Deldar Naghan the Abstemious. A long, mournful-looking fellow with a suspicious cast to his features, he was a superb soldier and a man who served loyally. As a churgur, a man heavily armored, and armed with javelin, shield and sword, he possessed the powerful physique and bodily strength to serve in the ranks of the shock infantry.

He did not spit as the three Chuktars strutted off. But he did say to one of his swods: "They're all jumped-up, young Dolan. Mark me, when we get up north where the action is they'll sing a different tune."

Dolan, young, freckle-faced and green, couldn't help but say: "If they hear you, Deldar, they'll fritter your hide."

"They can try. I wonder what'll happen to old Hack 'n' Slay."

That the 30th Division of infantry was a raw outfit was manifest. They had been stiffened by a cadre of experienced swods and Deldars. Too many of their Hikdars, men who commanded the company-sized pastangs, had come in to that rank direct instead of being promoted up through the grades of Deldar. There were very many young lads in the ranks, eager youngsters, maybe, but callow and not yet hardened into the requisite toughness required of swods who went into battle and put their lives on the line.

Deldar Naghan the Abstemious wiped his mouth and went about his duties with punctiliousness. He could feel sorry for old Hack 'n' Slay, with whom he had served before; but then, Jiktar Nath Javed, old Hack 'n' Slay, had been caught with his fingers in the regimental chest. That was not like the old fellow; but it was not a clever thing to have happened in a well-regulated regiment.

What did happen to the Jiktar whose fingers had been so careless as to scoop up gold and silver belonging to the regiment was educational. With the summary findings of the court of inquiry, written out fair in the flowing hand of the Xaffer, to guide it, the court-martial could only bring in a verdict of guilty.

Nath Javed said, in mitigation, that he had expected to receive his promotion to ob-Chuktar from the moment he took over command of his new 32nd Brigade. This had not happened and he had not therefore received the increase in his pay.

"I needed the money for a personal matter and merely borrowed it to be repaid when I received my pay."

"But you were not promoted ob-Chuktar and therefore—"

"And therefore I was left stranded!" roared Javed. "No cash in the strong-box and no pay to replace the gold!"

With the verdict of guilty, the next burning question was the punishment.

In the end the Divisional commander commuted a harsh prison sentence and corporal punishment to a mere Reduced To The Ranks.

Zan-Jiktar Nath Javed, in sight of promotion to Chuktar, commander of a brigade of churgurs, now became plain Nath Javed, a swod in the ranks.

The only real expressions of regret were heard in the ranks of the 11th Regiment.

The parlous situation of the Empire of Vallia, even as late as this with most of the islands brought back under the control of the emperor, could not condone a man being discharged. He'd serve out his time in the ranks.

The 30th Division was due to march north soon to reinforce the armies up there tackling the upstart and fraudulent King of North Vallia. Enar Thandon expressed himself of the opinion that he did not really wish to see old Hack 'n' Slay serving, even in the ranks, in any of the regiments under his command.

He was, therefore, packed off—as a mere swod—to a depot where he spent his time training raw recruits.

The money was not recovered. Javed would not say what had happened to it, apart from the statement that he had used it to pay an unjust debt.

Under these blows of fate he withdrew into himself, becoming harder and more harsh with all those about him. As a first-class fighting man he knew how to train up youngsters, and was invaluable in the depot. He said he would repay the entire amount of money to the 11th Regiment, and every pay day he deposited what he could of his pay to that end.

He continually badgered his new superiors for a transfer to an active regiment in the field. They regarded him as far too valuable for their purposes in training up fresh troops to part with him.

So Nath Javed, old Hack 'n' Slay, soldiered on.

And the days passed.

Deldar Naghan the Abstemious took it upon himself to find an excuse to visit the depot where Javed labored.

The place was situated a few miles outside the capital, Vondium, and consisted mainly of huts, cooking lines, and mud. Also, the assault courses were fiendish in their difficulty.

After Naghan had watched a few coys being driven through their paces, he managed to have a few private words with Javed.

"Nath Javed!"

"Here, Deldar," said Javed, standing at attention, hardly looking at the Deldar, who wore medals upon his chest as rewards for valor in battle. Naghan the Abstemious, long and hard and much experienced in the ways of swods, rapped out in exasperation what he felt deeply.

"Nath Javed! When you were a Deldar I was a swod, and then you were a Hikdar and then a Jiktar, and I became a Deldar. And now—"

"So it is you, Naghan. Well—and now it is as it is."

"But it needn't be!"

"You would have me appeal?"

"By Vox, I would. There must be an explanation for what you did—"

"There is; but I cannot give it. Let it be for now, Naghan. Come. For the sake of our old friendship, let us go for a wet."

Naghan the Abstemious did not acquire his sobriquet because he did not drink. Like any soldier in the new armies of the emperor, he drank in quantities sufficient to make him happy and merry and never to make him drunk. Idiots got drunk. They did not last long in the new armies raised by the Emperor of Vallia.

Settled comfortably with their tankards on the scrubbed sturmwood table between them, Naghan persisted.

"If you appeal, Nath, you must be heard. That is the law. You can appeal direct to the emperor himself and he will—"

"He is up north fighting this King of North Vallia, who is an unhanged rogue if ever there was one."

"Yes, my friend, like others closer to home I could name."

"Oh, they have had it in for me, I know that. Why did I not receive the promotion that was my due? But for that, all would have been as happy as a sennight of the Lady Soothe herself."

"You could explain to the emperor."

"What? D'you think he knows about the tribulations of ordinary folk like us? He is far away and busy and far too high and mighty to concern himself over matters like this."

"I have heard differently."

"Oh, aye! There are stories put around. Have you ever seen the emperor?"

"Well, I was on a parade once where he—"

"You see! On a parade where he was merely a glittering figure seen through a haze. I mean close up, like you and me, to talk to. He has no time for unlucky folk like me."

Naghan the Abstemious expressed himself as entirely dissatisfied with the whole affair. He tried and failed to persuade Nath Javed, old Hack 'n' Slay, to lodge an appeal.

"I'll soldier out my time trying to teach these youngsters the tricks of the trade. By Vox! They try my patience at times."

"Well, my friend, I will not insult you by expressing my concern and my regret. Just that—well, by the cropped ears of Vikatu the Dodger, I shall miss you when we march north."

Javed glanced up over the rim of his tankard.

"Aye, Naghan, and I you. I may have been a Jiktar; I hope I did not forget my friends."

"Would I be here, else?"

They drank companionably for a space, then a few kreutzin, training up to be light infantry, skirmishers, started a fight, and Nath Javed and Naghan the Abstemious, as befitted old campaigners, kampeons both, quaffed their draughts and took themselves off out of a common tavern brawl.

Javed escorted Naghan the Abstemious back to where his hired preysany stood with drooping head awaiting the ride back to Vondium.

As Naghan swung up into the saddle, among good wishes and remembrances, he said: "And your sister, Nath, the lady Francine. She is well, I trust?"

A spasm crossed Javed's fierce face.

"I pray you do not speak of her, Naghan, nor her husband, Fortro."

"As you wish. They had a daughter, did they not—?"

"Please, Naghan. By Vox! I do not wish to talk about little Sassy. No, Never!"

The Abstemious was not entirely blind.

"If I have offended you, Nath Javed, then I apologize. I bear you only well. And—you stubborn onker—if you will not appeal to the emperor, what more can I do?"

"Remember, you are a Deldar and command ten men or more, and I am a swod in the ranks."

"May the light of Opaz shine upon you, Nath Javed, and the keenness of sword and the cunning hand of Vox ever defend you from your foes."

"Opaz go with you, Naghan. You have my gratitude."

Riding his hired preysany under the light of the Moons of Kregen, Naghan the Abstemious, as he said afterward, felt strongly the mystery surrounding old Hack 'n' Slay's fall from grace. Whatever had caused him to steal the money, or borrow it, wrought significantly upon him.

Still, there seemed nothing to be done. The world would roll around and the twin suns, Zim and Genodras, would rise in the eastern sky on the morrow, and life would continue.

Perhaps there was no great mystery after all.

Poor old Hack 'n' Slay, there did not seem much of life left to him. So Deldar Naghan the Abstemious rode soberly back to Vondium pondering the vicissitudes of fate and the wayward turns a fellow's life took before they shipped him off to the Ice Floes of Sicce.

Two

The Empress and Emperor of Vallia Dance

The marriage between Marion and Nango was celebrated with great pomp and magnificence in Falkerium, the capital city of the kovnate province of Falkerdrin. As promised, the emperor danced at Marion's wedding.

Marion Frastel, the Stromni of Huvadu, found herself in a delicate situation. Huvadu was a province right up in the northeast corner of Vallia, and was currently in the hands of the usurping and self-titled King of North Vallia.

Because of this she was low on funds. Her brand new husband, Strom Nango ham Hofnar, owned estates in the Black Hills of Hamal. He was, it was generally believed, a wealthy man. Hamal, the most powerful empire in the southern continent of Havilfar, had for very many seasons been in bitter conflict not just with the Empire of Vallia but with just about every country the Hamalese airfleets could reach.

The two had met out there in adventurous circumstances by the Mountains of the West, and had fallen in love.

Strom Nango, it was also generally believed, was financing Marion. Certainly, the splendor of the wedding brought a sparkle to life, made folk realize there was more to living than fighting and wars and sudden death.

That thought must have been in Marion's mind as she looked up at her husband. She was a short lady, and Nango overtopped her by a head and he was not one of your tall fellows.

"We do not have long, my heart. The army marches for the north so soon—" he began.

They stood by a silken-draped pillar in the dancing hall of the palace where the wedding guests laughed and chattered, danced and drank, indulging in themselves the joy they knew the happy couple were experiencing.

Marion stared up fiercely.

"And you do not think I will let you go off by yourself, Nango?"

"Your regiment of Jikai Vuvushis is committed to the emperor."

"He will release me, I feel sure, in order to go up and reclaim my lands. Think of it, Nango! To have Huvadu back again!"

"Splendid, of course. You have never visited the Black Hills? No. They can be very lovely at certain seasons."

"And we will visit them. After all, if we can find a good reliable airboat we can visit where we like when we like."

"I shall buy the best voller in all Hamal, Marion."

She stood on tiptoe in her golden high-heeled shoes to kiss him. Laughing, flushed, they kissed and then—after a pleasant period—parted. Nango picked up a crystal goblet from the side table and handed it to his bride.

She half-turned to take it, smiling, lifting it to her lips. Her gaze passed beyond her new husband's shoulder.

"Oh!" she said. And, then: "Here is the emperor now, Nango, dear. I shall ask him directly."

She and Nango stepped aside as they turned to face. She inclined her head just a trifle, as was proper in these surroundings, and Nango, who had the nonsense of slavish inclining and scraping knocked out of him in Vallia, gave a polite nod.

"Majister. Isn't it all wonderful?"

"It is all wonderful, Marion. You and Strom Nango have put on a splendid affair. And now you are skulking in corners, kissing. I claim the dance you promised me." At that moment Strom Nango bowed again.

A charming voice, by Vox! the most charming and delicious voice in two worlds, said: "And I, my dear Strom Nango, claim my dance with you."

"Majestrix."

The Empress of Vallia looked radiant. Well, of course, by Zair, whenever did the Empress Delia not look radiant? Superbly dressed in a sheer gown of a color tending to lavender, with just two small pieces of jewelry, her hair a shining marvel, she was simply gorgeous—aye, and cunningly devious with it, too. With very little exaggeration it is true to say that there are regiments and whole armies ready to fight and die for the empress Delia. And, because she is Delia, this distresses her.

Nango was dressed in a slight variation on his usual Hamalese kit, which here in Vallia looked exotically strange. He wore gray trousers and a white shirt, over which the green cape on its golden cords did not strike a jarring note. He wore nothing of blue.

He and Delia swung off onto the floor. The music soared up, a pleasant rhythmic tune, and Marion held out her arms.

Marion was an accomplished dancer, and glided smoothly along. But, being Marion, she could not refrain from saying: "I am glad that no unfortunate occurrences have taken place at my wedding. I did feel for poor Ling-Li."

Two points were of note here: one, that that confounded and double-damned Witch of Loh, Csitra, and her ripe-for-hanging hermaphrodite child, Phunik, had indeed not sent through their sorcerous arts some vile plague upon us. They'd deluged thousands of rats upon the wedding of Khe-Hi-Bjanching and Ling-Li-Lwingling.

The second point of note was that those two were puissant Sorcerers themselves, a Wizard and a Witch of Loh, and ordinary folk always spoke very warily about *them*. They were good comrades and welcome in Vallia and Marion had grown a little used to them.

400

She went on in her way to make the casual and unthinking remarks that struck in cruelly. Csitra visited these plagues upon Vallia, and her Pronouncement of the Nine Unspeakable Curses against Vallia was directed against just one person's willpower and resolve.

"We have seen some remarkable sorceries," chattered on Marion, dancing along with the music. "I do hope that awful Csitra witch falls down and breaks her neck."

"There is the King of North Vallia first—"

"The armies of Vallia gather against that one. He is doomed. Everyone knows that."

"Oh yes, everyone knows that. They also know there will be hard fighting before he is finished. And, after that, there is Drak and Silda to be married and proclaimed Emperor and Empress of Vallia."

She did not quite stop dancing; but her rhythm faltered.

"And you would really and truly, majister, do that?"

"Of course. I have sworn it."

"It will be a marvel in the world. And I wonder what the dear empress has to say?"

This was impertinence on the grand scale. It didn't matter. In the old days these remarks of Marion's might well have caused the removal of her head from her shoulders. Still, she was a likable soul, and, much like another grand lady I had known, always meant well.

"The moment my lad Drak and his bride Silda are married and on the throne, I shall be off. I can promise you, Marion, that if the witch Csitra's neck is not broken in a fall, then I shall most probably break it myself."

"Yes," she said, following around in a neat double-step of rhythmic grace, "yes, you will need all the armies to go up against Csitra."

"Oh, yes," I told her most solemnly. "All the armies."

"And my regiment of Jikai Vuvushis, who serve you most loyally, majister, will go too."

"As to that," I said, whirling her around and depositing her safely on her feet and into the arms of Nango, "we shall see."

Delia said: "A splendid wedding, Marion. And Nango dances almost as well as a Vallian." She laughed as she spoke; but there was truth in the remark. Vallians are a happy lot, singing and dancing far more than the Hamalese.

Nango held his new bride, and laughed at the sally. I glanced at him and felt he was not affecting amusement. We'd make a good Vallian of him yet!

"All the same, Delia," I said. "I am a Vallian by adoption, so that—"

She took my arm and whispered in my ear.

"Only one little yellow sun. Only one silver moon. And no diffs, only people like us!"

Without a word I seized her and whirled off into the next dance. What Marion and Nango thought I didn't care. If they were a tenth as happy as Delia and I—when the damned Star Lords allowed us that freedom—they'd be more lucky than any ordinary humans beings could expect in two worlds.

As followed in any respectable function in Vallia, it was not long before the singing began.

As this was a wedding, we tended to sing more of the sentimental ballads; but as there were many soldiers and fliers here some of the old rip-roarers were bellowed out as well.

We sent the newly weds off in fine style, and managed to make Marion break down into a fit of the giggles, which was a good augury for the future.

After that a little group of us got into a corner around a table loaded with flagons and glasses and plates of palines and other fruits, and we sat, drinking and talking amicably long into the night.

These times of comradeship remain always warm and heartening memories. Zair knew, I welcomed and relished these moments among friends. They are, as anyone with an ounce of wisdom knows, precious in lives filled with the bustle and clamor of the day.

Nath Famphreon, the new kov of Falkerdrin, had given us the run of his palace. Now he sat drinking with us, a young man and still learning; but, by Krun, he had learned a very great deal in the very recent past.

Nath na Kochwold, the commander of the entire Phalanx Force, an upright man and a good comrade, wanted to straighten out the arrangements of locations for the various Phalanxes and Kerchuris.

Kapt Erndor was there, grim and yet far more at ease than heretofore. He would be taking the bulk of Turko's Ninth Army north. Turko, of course, the Kov of Falinur, would have to return to his kovnate and carry on sorting out affairs there.*

There were others around that table and sprawled on the sofas, some you have met before in my narrative and others who so far still have not found a mention.

Together in friendship we were good comrades all.

Despite my long seasons on Kregen, four hundred light-years from Earth, I still found myself blinking at the amazing contortions folk like Korero the Shield could perform. Mind you, he did have four arms and a tail equipped with a powerful grasping hand. He rode ever at my back in battle. Now he used any of his five hands. In this I knew I was in error; he was a Kildoi, and they, like Pachaks and Djangs, who have more than an apim's miserable allocation of only two arms, are mighty strict about which particular hand is used for which particular purpose.

---

* Kov: duke. Kovneva: duchess. Strom: count. Stromni: countess. Kapt: general of an army. A.B.A.

Now Marion and Nango had gone, Turko could say outright what was in more than one of our minds without offending the happy pair.

"Y'know, Dray, it's a great pity good old Seg was not with us today. He's a fellow for a good wedding."

"Aye, Turko. And Inch, also."

"The truth of the matter is," said Nath Famphreon, "and I speak as a newcomer to your circle—Marion was really only concerned that the emperor was here, with the empress."

Sharp, the new Kov of Falkerdrin. He was right, though, no doubt of it. Seg with his wife Milsi had gone across to Balkan where Seg was the new High Kov. In this he had my blessing, for Balkan was a rich province that traditionally kept out of politics. The place would give him immense wealth and a secure base. I so much valued my true blade comrade Seg Segutorio that I joyed for him in this turn of good fortune.

"I trust Seg will take the reins into his own hands without trouble," said Delia.

"Sink me!" I burst out. "If anyone gives Seg Segutorio any trouble I feel sorry for the poor benighted idiots."

"True, my love, true."

We talked then in general terms about the condition of Vallia and in detail of the problems we faced. The island empire was now all but reunited. Once that was successfully accomplished Drak and Silda could take over, leaving Delia and me free to follow our own wishes for a change.

Kapt Erndor leaned forward and said: "The troops are in good heart, praise Opaz. The 30th Division is due in tomorrow from Vondium. They flew up."

"What," said Turko in mock surprise. "You mean to say Lord Farris actually spared some of his precious aerial fleet? Marvels and wonders will never cease."

"With this last campaign, kov," said Erndor, "we are much better off for air than we've ever been."

"We'll need all the fliers we can get over those damned mountains."

"What is the mettle of the 30th?" Nath Famphreon wanted to know.

"Raw," said Erndor. "They are commanded by Strom Chuktar Enar Thandon. A cold fish. Still, they have one good regiment, the 11th Churgurs commanded by old Hack 'n' Slay."

At that moment my attention was distracted by what appeared to be a column of heated air rising from the opposite corner where the marble floor, of tiles in brilliant yellows and greens, supported an enormous jar of Pandahem ware. The flowers growing there perfumed the air most pleasantly.

Delia said, sharply: "There!"

Before any of us could react, the column of air thickened and coalesced and turned into the figure of a man.

For a tense moment we all stared. Then we relaxed.

That figure with its long plain robe, its massive turban about to topple in confusion over one ear, the wise, commanding and yet endearing face, told us this was an old comrade.

"Deb-Lu," said Delia. "So you came to the wedding at last. Welcome."

"I have already spoken to Marion and Strom Nango. That is not the purpose of my visit to you."

At once my nerves quivered alert. When Deb-Lu-Quienyin, a most powerful and puissant Wizard of Loh, used his kharrna to pay calls through the occult other dimensions, things tended to happen.

He moved forward and, as was often the case, the lighting where he was—and that could be anywhere at all, by Krun—illuminated and shadowed his face and figure differently from the way the lights and shades fell in Nath Famphreon's palace.

"Lem the Silver Leem," he began.

I surged upright, all the blood rushing to my head. My rapier was half drawn before I was aware.

"Dray," Deb-Lu said, commandingly. "Rest easy. There is nothing for you to do—"

"Nothing to do! There will only be nothing left to do when all the stinking adherents of Lem the Silver Abomination are destroyed and forgotten!"

"Quite so," cut in Delia. "And suppose, Dray, we allow Deb-Lu to tell us the news? Before you burst a blood vessel."

"Very well, my love," said I, most meekly.

"The news is soon told." Deb-Lu made an ineffective gesture to push his turban straight. "A temple was reported in Vondium—"

"By the Black Chunkrah!" I was incensed. "The foul blight tries to fester in Vondium the Proud itself!"

Delia put a hand on my arm. I put my fingers on hers, and, as ever, felt—well, never mind that. The Wizard of Loh went on speaking, taking my outburst in his stride. But we all knew the vileness of the creed of Lem the Silver Leem. Its devotees practiced the torture, mutilation and murder of young girl children. They carried out their grisly rites in order to gain preferment within their horrendous cult and glory in the sight of Lem.

"Joldo Nat-Su, the city prefect, was informed. He did what was necessary—"

"Burned the obscene lot to the ground," rumbled Turko.

"Aye, Turko. Joldo did that. There were very few survivors from the temple. The business was done and was seen to be done and is now over with."

"But," I said in a voice of granite.

"Indeed, Dray, but. We believe there are other temples. The blight was brought in with the mercenaries and has kept well underground."

"Damned mercenaries. I shall return to Vondium at once—"

Delia squeezed my arm; she did not speak.

It was left to Deb-Lu to say: "Hardly wise, Dray. You are about to finalize the reunification of all Vallia. No further temples have been discovered so far, and when they are they will be dealt with. I merely informed you to keep you abreast of a situation I know to be of great concern to you."

"Too damn right it's of great concern."

Delia put her finger on the nub of the problem. She said crisply: "What news of the witch, Csitra, Deb-Lu?"

"Ah," said old Deb-Lu in his most infuriatingly wise way. "At least someone has a head upon their shoulders up there in Falkerdrin."

Turko laughed at this, and the company appreciated the justice of the remark. Quite clearly, if I went roaring back to Vondium, the capital city, to sort out the Lemmites, I would be seen and Csitra would by this time have inserted another of her agents, duped tools, to spy on me.

Then she would send another of her plagues within the ghastly scheme of the Nine Curses against Vallia.

Csitra only used a sending of horror to places where I was and where I was known to be. She suffered from the serious delusion that I could be persuaded to care for her, as she lusted after me, through cajoling force.

The most serious aspect of the situation was that folk tended to blame me for all the horrors that descended upon their heads. Well, by Krun, and they were perfectly right. If I succumbed to the witch, the plagues would go away.

As I had no intention whatsoever of succumbing to her wishes, and I did not want my people to suffer from the Nine Curses, then I had to live in places where we were sure Csitra could not spy on me.

"Very well," I said, in a right old grumbling way. "You are right: I'll go up north and bash this King of North Vallia. But I want continuous and timely reports on the Lem blight."

Then the obvious—a horrible—thought occurred to me.

"Deb-Lu—you do not think Csitra has a hand in this latest outbreak of the Lem abomination?"

His wise old face with those crinkly lines showed a moment's hesitation. Then he spoke out fairly.

"My best intelligence suggests she has nothing to do with it, Dray. I keep up an Observation upon her and her uhu, Phunik, down there in the Coup Blag. But—and I stress the shadowy nature of all this, Dray—but I cannot guarantee this one hundred times out of one hundred."

I sat back. What a moil all this was! There was so much to be done, in Vallia, in the grouping of continents and islands called Paz, so much effort to be put into our struggle against the Shanks, that interruptions like Lem the Silver Leem and this fool witch Csitra acted like stinging insects festering around an animal's eyes.

Deb-Lu was quite right. I had to deal with the most important factors first. Csitra, by her actions, had thrust herself into the limelight as the next objective. Still—

"Deb-Lu, have you anything further on the far eastern question?"

This referred to the Shanks, those implacably hostile Fishheads, and their attack upon the large island of Mehzta over on the remotest eastern fringe of the grouping of Paz. I did not want our own people to learn of this yet, for purely selfish reasons. We had to clear up our own problems, and those of the lands near to us, before we could expend our limited strength in remotely distant operations.

And this distressed me, for my good comrade Gloag was from Mehzta. His homeland was being ravaged and despoiled so that the rest of us could use the breathing space in the Shanks' attack to good purpose.

"Nothing, Dray."

I nodded. I noticed that here, Deb-Lu was calling me Dray instead of Jak, as was very often his custom.

With that apparently bumbling and yet active enough movement of his, Deb-Lu turned to look across to the side. We all knew he was not looking at what we could see in our comfortable corner of Nath Famphreon's palace.

What he was looking at had existed where he was.

He nodded his head with such vigor the turban toppled dangerously close to falling. He spoke. We could not hear what he said.

He swung about to face us.

"Khe-Hi has just paid me a swift visit instead of cutting into our conversation."

If anyone not a sorcerer told you he understood the protocol and the way of polite manners between Wizards of Loh—never believe him. Wizards were a law unto themselves. I could see no reason on Kregen why Khe-Hi-Bjanching should not use his kharrna to pay us a visit while Deb-Lu-Quienyin was here.

Deb-Lu went on: "You will hear the news soon enough, for a swift messenger is on the way. Advance knowledge could prove useful." He made a dab at his turban. "The upstart King of North Vallia has pre-empted your attack. He has struck down in force stronger than would suggest a mere raid, has routed your frontier force, and is marching south looting and burning."

Three

An aerial skirmish

From the air, the vadvarate province of Kavinstock looked peaceful enough.

The ruler of this province, holding the noble rank of vad, had been Nalgre Sultant. He and his son Ornol, members both of the once-powerful political party of the Racters, had vanished after their defeat and the reunification of Kavinstock with the rest of Vallia.

As the small armada sailed on through the level air, I studied the land below. It looked in good heart, although occasionally we flew over areas of decay and destruction resulting from the late war.

Far ahead over the horizon the ugly smear of black smoke rising into the air told us that death and destruction still prevailed here.

"The black-hearted cramphs," said Targon the Tapster at my side.

"Aye, Targon," I said, heavily. "We have come a long way since first we met. And it seems to me all that time there has been fighting and war."

Targon the Tapster, with other redoubtable fellows, had helped form the bodyguard that had turned into the First Emperor's Sword Watch. They took it in turn to command the regiments. They detested going anywhere without me, or of letting me off the hook to go adventuring on my own without them along. The same fractious desires animated as well the lads of the Emperor's Yellow Jackets. And, as I well knew, the two new regiments in my guard corps, the Emperor's Foot Bows, and the Emperor's Life Churgurs, shared that dedicated devotion to my person.

All of which, as I have said, made me feel very small, and gave me considerable qualms for the safety of the kampeons in the regiments.

We'd grabbed every flier we could lay our hands on and had flown up as fast as we could drive the vollers. With a foul wind, the vorlcas, the massive aerial ships that depended on sails and their ethero-magnetic keels to move them along, were severely restricted. They'd fly up eventually, though, Opaz willing.

Kapt Erndor, Nath na Kochwold and the other commanders would move heaven and earth to get up and into action just as fast as they could.

Targon said: "And you are confident the city of Tali will be able to hold out?"

"Tali is a sizable place, with many towers and walls sixty paces thick, for I paced them myself. Still, there is no certitude in a town holding out against a siege."

"We will distract them long enough."

"I don't want a lot of casualties," I said.

"We are all your juruk jikai. The guard corps will not hang back in a fight."

"That's what I'm worried about."

Over the deck to where we stood in the prow, Delia walked up with that smooth grace that always catches the breath in my throat. She heard the last words of our conversation.

"I feel exactly the same about my guards," she said. "Nath Karidge is such a bold reckless fellow."

Nath Karidge commanded the elite regiment called the Empress's Devoted Life Guard. Also, Delia had a second regiment of jurukkers, a composite regiment of bows and churgurs, a powerful force designed to operate in conjunction with Nath Karidge's First EDLG.

Even then, we hadn't been able to cram everyone aboard who wanted to fly north with us.

We did have with us a force very essential to the type of warfare carried on in these latter days in Vallia.

Although the fliers had been able to accommodate only two squadrons of aerial cavalry, we had taken those in preference to three squadrons of ground cavalry. The saddle birds were flutduins from my kingdom of Djanduin, magnificent chargers of the air. Flown by highly trained flyers from Valka, they were worth their weight in gold.

Marion's regiment of Jikai Vuvushis also flew with us; they were still without an official name and I'd managed to reduce their numbers to half. The balance would come on with the advance forces of the main body. I guessed Marion herself, off honeymooning with Nango, would have a few words to say when she found out. She would bring them up very smartly, I did not doubt.

What looked like a dark cloud over the land ahead drew out attention.

This blot of darkness covered a white road below and straggled out into the fields on either side. It did not take an old campaigner long to know exactly what we were looking at.

Before anyone could say anything, I spoke in my old hateful, harsh, intemperate way.

"The best service we can render those poor devils is to fly on and smash up the hostiles. When pursuit ends and the enemy are driven back, these people can return home."

"You are right," said Delia. "But I feel for them—feel terribly."

The refugees trudged along. Some of them looked up and a few waved.

Our bright scarves trailing over the bulwarks, the splendor of our paintwork, the glitter of weapons and the ugly snouts of our ballistae and catapults might appear grand and lordly sailing along in mid-air. I wondered how much they would reassure those people below. It is hard to see any good in the world when your farm has been burned and your family slain.

The smoke cloud ahead thickened and grew closer.

The King of North Vallia had been clever. The fortress town of Tali had been sited on the approach road from the Mountains of the North. The stout walls and strong garrison were there to prevent incursions. This clever king had struck far to the west, almost to the coast, and bypassed Tali.

He would know that a force would march out to dispute his passage. They had done so, and had been routed.

Now he had a clear run south for as far as he wanted to go, pillaging and burning. Only when we had gathered sufficient forces to meet him in pitched battle, he would be thinking, might he expect more opposition. And, the scheming devil, he was in great strength himself. This, it seemed clear, came from new hordes of mercenaries he had recruited from overseas.

The lead voller in which we flew, dubbed *Heart of Imrien*, was not over-large and I intended to use her as the headquarters ship. Aboard flew men and women close to Delia and me.

Our intelligence from the northern provinces over the Mountains of the North in what was now the kingdom of the usurping and self-styled king of those regions was sparse. The general assessment was that he did not have considerable strength in the air. Our plan therefore was to use our air and avoid a direct land battle until the rest of the army came up. That was the plan.

How many times in the past have I said: "That was the plan." And how very very many times has that plan gone awry!

We sailed on, searching the ground ahead for signs of our opponents.

Heart of Imrien, as I have said, was not an overlarge specimen of voller. She possessed a structure corresponding to a raised forecastle of a terrestrial galleon, with a slightly higher poop. She had but the one fighting top, and this square battlemented fortress was supported by four stout masts, cross-braced and served by ladders.

There was no reason at all why, in the air, the first sightings should be made from this fighting top; the fact remains, they were.

"Fliers!" screeched down the lookouts.

Up ahead of us, whirling like autumn leaves, the forerunners of our enemy's aerial armada swept down full upon us. They came on with demonic speed, swirled along by the breeze which blew in our faces. There looked to be a lot of them. A deuced lot of them.

Our trumpets pealed out and the drums beat to quarters.

Our aerial sailors ran to their stations. The soldiers carried aboard, tough kampeons all, formed up. They were experienced enough to know when to leave one aspect of the approaching fighting to the experts.

My bowmen could shaft as well as any, and when it came to handstrokes then my lads yielded to no one in Vallia.

There was practically no time between the first sightings and the onslaught.

"Fluttrells, mostly," said Captain Voromin.

"Aye."

The wide-winged birds bore on, a flutter of color and brightness through the air.

I said to Targon: "Make sure the lads are armored. There will be time for that."

"Aye, and time for slaying thereafter."

"Yes, And tell the proud-necked fellows to keep their fool heads down."

With a clanking groaning the first ballista loosed. These weapons were the superior gros-varters of Vallia, throwing rocks or darts, as suited the occasion and the target. I didn't bother to see what shooting was made. It seemed to me there were enough birds out there to soak up all the fire we could hammer out and still have enough aerial-borne warriors left to break through and make the attempt to land on our decks.

Delia said in her rasping voice: "And, you hairy graint, where is your armor?"

I cursed. By Makki Grodno's diseased intestines and dripping eyeballs! If I didn't trot off and don armor, Delia never would. She would stand at my side, shoulder to shoulder, and trade handstrokes with these reivers of the air.

"Very well. Come on—and for the sweet sake of Zair, let us hurry!"

For I had seen enough to know these fluttrells were flown by flutsmen, bandits of the air, mercenaries of bloodthirsty nature and heart-stopping habits.

Strapping up a breast and back I struggled with the buckles. The breast fastened up and the back refused to go easily. I nearly left the confounded thing off, but Delia rapped out: "Put it on!"

She was right. In these nasty affrays some protection for your back is more important at times than a breastplate. You don't see the blow from the rear that knocks you over. After that your head is off or your inward parts are displayed for the world to see.

Rushing back onto deck from the arched opening to the cabin we shared, I was in time to see the first of the flutsmen make their attempts to land on *Heart of Imrien*. Korero the Shield sprang out before us, hefting two enormous shields and a sword distributed between his five hands.

"Hai, Korero!" I said.

"This won't last long," he said, and circled his shields to loosen up his muscles.

I confess I felt that "Hai!" a trifle overdone. I felt dull and wooden, not so much apathetic as resigned to frustration. I had no interest whatsoever in fighting bloody-minded flutsmen. They would be men and women from many nations come flying into Vallia to feast, as they imagined, on the bleeding corpse of the old empire. Some news of the new empire had traveled overseas together with startling information on the new emperor and the new armies of Vallia. This new lot of mercenaries could have come from anywhere; I had the idea they came from a long way away.

"You look," said Korero, "as though you've lost a zorca and found a calsany."

"Aye, and I must use up good shafts on these rasts."

The great Lohvian longbow gripped in my left hand, the cunning draw as perfected by Seg Segutorio imparting immense energy into the bow, I drew and let fly. The rose-fletched shaft took a rider from the air and I didn't bother to see where he went, but drew and loosed against the next.

That first attempt by the flutsmen to land on our decks proved a dismal and costly failure to them.

Quite apart from the varters that simply blew the riders from the air, the massed ranks of bowmen picked them off with precision and finicky accuracy. As I say, it does not do to meddle with the kampeons of ESW or EYJ.

Still, as I had sourly predicted, there were enough flutsmen for some to break through and touch down on the decks of *Heart of Imrien*.

The Lohvian longbow went down on the deck and the great Krozair longsword went smack into my fists. Well, now...

"Dray—" called Delia.

"Yes, my heart," I said, without turning.

The leading bunch of flutsmen tumbling from their birds leaped into action with the remarkable poise and agility of true fighting men of the air. A pity they were such a pack of desperadoes of the unholy kind fit only to be sent down to the Ice Floes of Sicce. Given a better chance in life—well who knew what they might have become?

As it was we had to chop them, and chop them fast.

Now I refer to the Lohvian longbow and the Krozair longsword as "great" more often than not. This is because they are great. There are longbows and longswords on Kregen that are not great.

The Krozair brand snicked this way and that, thrust and withdrew, and as I belted into the lead elements of the fliers on our deck I left a wake of slaughter abaft. There were others with me. In a fighting frenzy of action we belted the flutsmen across the deck and those that were not cut down just fell overside.

The vollers were not flying all that high in the air, but the fall was enough to pancake anyone foolish or unfortunate enough to try the drop.

"There are still plenty of them left," observed Targon the Tapster. He was smeared with blood not his own.

"Flutsmen like easy pickings."

We stared out into the brightness of the day where the black dots of

411

saddle flyers curved and pirouetted as their riders summoned the nerve for a second onslaught. The other vollers in our little squadron had all fared as well as we had done. There was a little pause in the proceedings.

Then the lookouts perched aloft bellowed down.

"Airboats!"

"So this unpleasant King of North Vallia has a proper fleet now, has he?" remarked Delia, with an endearing tilt to her chin.

"How many?"

A pause for counting, and then: "More than twenty."

"H'mm," I said.

Once contemptuous of the silly remark, I now saw its value in covering up the absence of thought.

The lookouts shouted down again.

"More than thirty."

"Ah," I said.

Delia threw me a suspicious look. Casually and with what I hoped was an insouciant air, I strolled over to the bulwarks and leaning out peered ahead. Well, yes, I could see the fliers out there, bearing on, chips of rust against the light.

More than thirty? We had in this squadron sixteen vessels, a mixture of fighting vollers and larger ships designated transports for this operation. This op was, as I have explained, intended to harass the enemy from the air and hold him until our main forces could come up.

Now the devils had provided their own air, a completely new force of which we had no intelligence. Therefore, the situation had changed, the odds had altered and the stakes had been raised.

There was no question of sending our own aerial cavalry aloft. Our two squadrons, hardly more than a hundred and twenty flyers, would be hopelessly outnumbered. I did not relish the idea of a single Valkan astride his flutduin being attacked by ten or a dozen flutsmen.

"They fly on apace," said Targon.

"So I observe," I said.

"It will be—interesting."

The lookouts screeched down for the third time.

"More than forty!"

Now was no time for vacuous expressions like: "H'mm." Now was no time for shilly-shallying, and most certainly now was no time for me to act like some proud intemperate and bloody stupid emperor.

"That's it," I said. I made my voice into that rasping and unpleasant gravel-shifting voice of old, and even good old Targon the Tapster jumped.

"All out." I fairly hurled the words at the helmsman, using the old foretop-hailing lungpower that had carried commands through many a gale in the Bay of Biscay. "Reverse Course! Speed lever hard over—full speed ahead!"

Carrying on with the bullroarer of a voice, I shouted commands to the signal Deldars to run up the flags to spell the message out to the rest of the squadron.

"You, Dray Prescot, are running away!" said Delia.

"Too right," I told her, still wrought up. "By Zair! I'm not having all these people of ours chopped uselessly."

The small almost secret smile that touched her lips heartened me. Delia knew me well enough. She'd seen me change from a hot-headed and damned stupid fighting man into an emperor who was somewhat more cautious of other peoples' skins. As for myself, well, I suppose had there been no one else to concern myself about, I'd have gone raging into that hopeless fight and you would not now be listening to my words as I relate my story of my life on Kregen.

The fliers of our squadron curved in the air, swinging about in graceful arcs, all their brave flags flying.

"Cap'n," I said in a more moderate voice to Captain Lorgad Voromin, in command of *Heart of Imrien*, who stood like a bluff barrel girt with leather armor and with feathers in his helmet, face like a beetroot. "Cap'n, I crave your pardon. Would you kindly allow your command to fly last in the squadron?"

"With all my heart, majis."

In the violence of those moments before I'd shouted the orders to reverse course, I had been so wrought up I'd thrown overboard altogether the etiquette of ship command.

Of course, I should have requested Captain Voromin to give the actual sailing orders for his own ship. I had trodden on his toes with a vengeance. He was a bluff old sea dog, transferred to aerial duty, and I thought he would understand. We had not served together before; I had a shrewd idea he knew my mettle.

If he decided to cut up rough or to try to indicate his perfectly understandable resentment, I'd have to think on, as they say.

The clouds of flutsmen were for only a few moments thrown by our maneuver. They sensed victory and came flying in with renewed vigor.

This was to be expected.

Heart of Imrien dropped back through the squadron to take up station in the rear.

We did not sail in this position alone. On our starboard flew *Pride of Falkerium* and to our larboard *Azure Strigicaw* paced us carefully. Both ships were crammed with men, fighting vollers, and were mighty comforting, by Krun, I can tell you.

A youngster, Ortyg Thingol, all rosy cheeks and brown curls, smart in his cadet's uniform, rushed up with a signal slate. I'd seen the colors breaking from the signal yards of both *Storm Rising* and *Nath's Hammer*, the ships carrying our aerial cavalry squadrons.

Before the signal cadet had time to gasp out anything at all I snarled at him: "No, Cadet Thingol. Signal back Request Refused."

He went scarlet clear up past those fetching brown curls.

"Quidang, majister!"

Galloping off back to the signal halyards, he fairly broke the speed records. I sighed. If my precious aerial cavalry lads had their wish and took off, the squadrons would just simply be ripped apart. They would be wasted for nothing. They might buy us a few moments of time. That kind of exchange might be regarded by your puissant high and mighty emperor as a fair deal; it did not suit me.

"Here they come," said Targon the Tapster in a matter-of-fact way.

"Shaft the cramphs good."

Bows bending, gleaming in the light of the twin suns, slender shafts flashing outwards, feathers all aglitter in the radiance. Crossbows clanging and twanging, and the cruel bolts hurtling. Varters coughing their ugly chunks of rock, or driving their long barbed darts deeply into enemy flesh. Oh, yes, by Krun, we shafted them.

Because of our hurtling onward speed the windrush drove our flags stiffly to the rear, making the reading of signals difficult for ships ahead and astern. Partially to overcome this problem, the aerial sailors of Kregen fitted up guy lines on the outside of the flags, by which means they could draw the outer edges around to make the flags more easily identifiable. This could be done for short moments only. Even then, more than one set of flags was ripped to shreds.

"Signal to the lead voller," I rapped out. "Change course to south southeast." We were rushing along almost due southerly.

I wanted to avoid drawing this ravening pack on our heels over the heads of those refugees.

By this time we were really shifting along. After two more abortive attempts at us, the flutsmen were left to our rear, for no fluttrell can fly as fast as a voller at top speed.

The pursuing airboats kept on after us, and I wondered if they were picking up their aerial cavalry, or if they had not yet mastered that tricky technique. We kept up a watch for what went on back there; but the distance and the haze of afternoon rendered accurate observation difficult. There were far fewer fluttrells in the sky; that could simply be because they had called it a day and flown back to their base.

The haze thickened into the outskirts of real clouds.

Captain Voromin rubbed his hands.

"If we are to run away, majis, then a few handy clouds will not come amiss; no, by Corg."

"Right you are, Cap'n."

Lorgad Voromin had been the master of one of the superb sailing galleons of Vallia. Now he had transferred to the Vallian Air Service he took, as I had instituted recently, the rank of Jiktar as the commander of a largish vessel. Still, we all called the old sea dog Cap'n still, which pleased him.

Weirdly enough, this business of running away did not distress half as much as I anticipated. Those folk who had known me in the long ago when I'd first arrived on Kregen would snort with derision at what I was now doing. Dray Prescot, they'd say, laughing, Dray Prescot run away? Never!

In these latter days, concerns over wider issues than merely my own skin motivated me.

The clouds whisked by, thickening and then thinning and then churning into a white froth that rolled back over our forecastle and along the deck like spilled milk.

Before the opportunity was altogether lost, I managed to get off further signals to the squadron. Their instructions were to bear straight on until we broke out of the clouds. We were making slightly under nine db's.*

With the flutsmen left straggling to the rear we had the sky to play in.

There had to be a plan to fetch success out of apparent failure.

Captain Voromin, in a quiet conversational voice, said: "The clouds will thin soon, I can feel that in my bones." Then he went on: "As the bitter blast blows the leaves away, so the wide-winged bird breasts the wind and soars."

"San Dweloin, I think, Captain. But I could not put my finger on the exact stanza," said Delia.

Voromin let rip a pleased wheezing snort.

"Aye, majestrix, San Dweloin, who, being dead these three thousand seasons or more, is a great comfort to me."

There was no need for me to marvel at Voromin's love of poetry. I'd been thinking of him as a "bluff old sea dog." Well, he was, to be sure; but the cliché rang hollow set against the pretty discussion of verse that ensued upon the deck of *Heart of Imrien*. And, as we thus discussed the niceties of poetry, so the clouds thinned and I knew the time for decision grew near.

By quoting those two particular lines, Voromin clearly indicated what he wanted to do. I gathered the quotation came from San Dweloin's poem "The Force of Human Nature," written in his old age and extolling light and life over darkness and death.

Well, that light came very often after a damned long dark tunnel.

"Yes, Cap'n," I said, breaking into a point of the over-use of alliteration. "If you'll kindly signal out for the flutduins to be loosed on my signal, I shall be obliged."

"Quidang!"

---

* db's: dwaburs per bur. A dwabur is five miles and a bur is forty minutes. *A.B.A.*

"Let us gain more height. Certainly I want to clear the tops of the clouds before we leave them."

There was no great ensuing bustle as the voller lifted, for the simple reason that the Deldar at the controls merely pushed over his levers and the vessel rose smoothly through the clouds. Aboard the other vessels of the squadron as we flew from cloud to cloud and passed alongside the flanks of the monstrous masses of whiteness our signals were picked up. There was no guarantee that all the vollers would read the signals; we might lose a few carrying straight on below us.

Of the various classes and types of airboats manufactured on Kregen, we had since our alliance with Hamal had the opportunity of acquiring new types. Still troubled by the destruction caused to her shipyards during the wars, Hamal was not yet back to full-scale voller production. Therefore, we had very few vollers in which the onward force contains also the air within the envelope. We had to keep our heads down behind the windscreens. The clouds when we lanced through them went past like boiling milk all streaming in long lightning flashes of vapor.

I said to Larghos Hemlok, the first lieutenant: "Fires nice and hot, Hik Hemlok?"

He smiled with a peculiarly bloodthirsty look.

"Bright and hot, majister. Bright and hot."

If I mention that the first luff's name of Hemlok had no connotative meaning with the word hemlock in terrestrial usage, that is true; he remained a fellow who could hemlock an opponent's drink in the middle of a passage of arms.

"By Corg!" quoth Captain Voromin. "We're going to have ourselves a lovely lot of bonfires!"

Well, that was the plan. Simpleminded enough; but something better than tamely running away.

Soaring and leaping through the air, *Heart of Imrien* sailed up between two vast expanses of white forming a chasm in which a fleet might be lost.

So mixed up and out of formation had the squadron become by this time that I was positively gratified to spy six other vollers fleeting along with us. The other ten would be haring along between the masses of cloud. Well, what had to be done would have to be done with the ships available to me now.

Higher and higher we climbed until, with the exception of a few towering cumulus pinnacles like Mount Everests piling away left and right, we broke through into the light of the twin suns. That streaming mingled radiance of Zim and Genodras bathed all the clouds in a rosy jade glory. The view was breathtaking. Still, we were not sightseers, we were warriors of the air, and we were after our prey.

Tradition means a great deal on Kregen.

Even though we flew in a Vallian Air Service flier, and for Kregen all the modern appurtenances surrounded us, still the lookouts used the time-honored words.

The lookouts screeched down the sightings in the hallowed way.

"*Sail ho!*"

Out from those mazy masses of clouds below and to the rear of us the first of the pursuing vollers rocketed out like avenging demons.

Four

Ambush in the clouds

Captain Voromin handled *Heart of Imrien* beautifully. His orders to his helmsman were crisp and not to be misunderstood. Lookouts positioned along the lower fighting galleries kept up a constant stream of information regarding the movements and courses of the hostile vessels. Our ship cut tightly around in a sweet one-eighty-degree turn and pounced.

The signal to release the flutduin squadron was passed. Unfortunately, I could see only one cavalry-carrying vessel, *Nath's Hammer,* still in company with us. When the flyers took off the thought occurred to me they looked far more like the blown leaves in San Dweloin's poem than the "wide-winged birds breasting the wind."

They didn't bother to form up. They simply flew headlong for the enemy ships. I tore my gaze away. They had their orders and they knew their business. They would get on with what they had to do just as we were getting on with what the situation required here.

Inevitably, when fire is maneuvered and manhandled aboard ship, particularly a painted wooden ship, extreme caution and care must be taken, and some language is used.

The Ship-Deldar, purple and engorged, bashed his stick about and actually put a steadying hand to the carrying pole. The fire went below in good order contained in its pottery and metal canister. I decided against going below myself to the lower gallery. I'd done my share of setting ships alight.

Voromin's reversal of course and immediate swoop into combat left the lead ships of the enemy force no chance whatsoever. As they debouched from the clouds so we sailed above them. One, two, three, the flaming pots of combustibles went over the side. One, two, three, and then one, two, three again.

"They've caught the leader!" screeched up the last in the chain of message relayers. This was young Cadet Ortyg Thingol. His higher voice near cracked with excitement.

And, a heartbeat later: "And number two's burning!"

We circled like a hawk above fluttering prey. Alongside Delia I could look down from a perch in the bulwarks. Captain Voromin occupied a similar niche on the other side, reserved for him. I might be the emperor, but when Captain Voromin wanted to look over this side of his ship, I'd have to shift out of the way sharpish.

The view below stretched away and away, dizzy with perspective. Out from the massed and bulbous shapes of the clouds flew the pursuing vollers, popping out like fish leaping from the seabreakers. As they appeared so our flutduins whirled above them, their riders hurling down firepots. Some missed. Some fizzled out. Some were extinguished by alert fire parties on the decks of the ships beneath. But many did not miss, did not fizzle out, were not extinguished.

The pursuing ships burned.

Through the warm sharpness of the afternoon air I could smell the stink of burning below. Black clouds roiled away, smearing all that white brightness with their foulness. I do not like to see ships burn. The act is indecent in the sight of a sailorman.

For the sake of the unity of Vallia, and subsequently for the unification of all Paz and the defeat of the Shanks, these abominable acts must be committed.

Like minnows darting this way and that with the light of the suns glinting along their flanks, the ships twisted and turned in midair.

As I have indicated, *Heart of Imrien* was not an overlarge flier. She could not maneuver with the same agility as a sleek, fast voller of the smaller types. She could swerve well enough about in the air to perform the duty now called for. Captain Voromin handled her smartly. We had coursed clean over the three lead ships and set them ablaze before the enemy reacted.

After that it would be a matter of clawing for height and speed and outmaneuvering our opponents.

Pride of Falkerium and *Azure Strigicaw* swirled into action, flaming the following ships. I tried to count the numbers of the enemy, and amid all the headlong rushing of ships through the air, of smoke and cloud and of the saddle birds gyrating like autumn leaves in a gale, the task was difficult. I fancied something like eighteen ships had pursued us on this course. The others could be anywhere. So, for that matter, could the rest of our squadron.

"They do not," commented Targon the Tapster in my ear, "they most certainly do not care for this."

"Nobody would."

Targon referred to some of the other members of the choice band who had followed me when, as Jak the Drang, I'd aspired to be Emperor of Vallia, folk like Naghan ti Lodkwara, Cleitar the Standard, Dorgo the Clis and Uthnior Chavonthjid. "They're scattered about the squadron," he said with great satisfaction, "and those who aren't here will kick themselves when I tell 'em, by Vox!"

"I believe Mazdo Voordun is aboard *Strelviz Lancer*," I said. "And, see, there she goes plummeting down on that fellow with the green and yellow hull—ah!"

"Yes!" said Delia. "The poor ship is burning."

"Poor ship, my lady," said Targon. "She'd have burned us if she had the chance."

"Yes, I know and, of course, you are right. All the same, when a ship burns the world is a poorer place."

Targon held his peace. I agreed with Delia; but I perfectly saw the common-sense position of my ferocious jurukker commander.

These fellows of mine in the guard corps, well, they didn't go in much for high-flown and imposing-sounding ranks. They were of the emperor's bodyguard. When they told a chuktar to jump, he jumped.

And, I hasten to add, I kept a close eye out to see that this was not abused. The last thing I wanted was to create an elite, hated throughout the army. That was not my way, and was strictly counterproductive. Targon gave a hitch to his safety belt. Since a certain disastrous accident, I'd intemperately ordered that belts be manufactured, each with its own pair of small silver boxes that gave lift, and further instructed that they be worn by aerial sailors.

Delia and I both wore these safety aerial belts, and as far as I was concerned in the hurly burly of warfare among the clouds, they were as useful as armor. By Krun, yes!

The ambush we had sprung on those hostile ships pursuing us had worked perfectly. Our six ships had disposed of the majority of the enemy forces, and our splendid flutduin squadron saw off the balance.

Now, of course, I started to fret over the fate of the rest of our squadron of vollers.

We might have been successful; the others might not have fared so well.

By Vox! What it is to be an emperor and shoulder such vast responsibilities! The quicker my lad Drak took over the better. That was the sober truth, and all the secrets of Imrien would vouch for it.

The encompassing white cliffs of cloud closing in on us in billowing massifs, the narrow alleyways of clearer air between, the swirling, darting forms of the airboats, all worked upon my sensibilities. The picture was beautiful, all a wonder of blues and whites and flowing brilliant radiance; I could still smell the stink of those burning ships, and did not like that smell, did not like it at all, by Krun.

Captain Voromin said: "Where away now, d'you think, majis?"

I had to bring my confused senses back to the issue at hand. Men's lives were at stake. Good men, my men, and the lives of loyal women, too. I straightened up, and I kept my hand gripping onto Delia's hand. The firm reassurance there was mightily comforting, I assure you, mighty comforting.

"I think," I said with a deliberately contrived drawl, "I really do think, Cap'n, you may draw a course of sou' sou'west."

"Quidang!"

Onward we hurtled with the air rushing past over the windshields. Visibility remained inconstant, with patches of misty cloud trailing streamers between the main masses. Below us the ground fleeted past, patched with light and shadow. We saw little sign of occupancy down there for the folk had no wish to be taken up as slaves by the soldiers of the King of North Vallia.

The outlying arm of cloud before us billowed majestically into the afternoon sky. The twin suns smote the edges into cusps of palest apple green and orange—red fire, darkening into jade and crimson. Against the floods of light and the massy heart of the clouds, were those fleeting specks the shapes of airboats twisting and turning in combat?

Bright speckles of flame fell tumbling down. Captain Voromin had no doubts.

"They've caught 'em," he said, lowering his telescope.

Targon, eager and looking mighty hungry, voiced the thought in our minds.

"Yes, Cap'n. But who has caught whom?"

"*Storm Rising* has loosed her birds." Voromin rattled off the names of three other ships of ours he had identified. "I think the catching was mutual."

"If all ships are present," I said, "we will even up the fight when we arrive. Pray Opaz we are in time."

With all the speed with which our silver boxes could power us we ramped on and hurled our vollers into action.

Because *Nath's Hammer* had to retrieve her flutduin squadron she was late in coming up; by the time she arrived we were in the thick of it.

Two of the ships from North Vallia closed in on us. After the initial clashes, few firepots were thrown; the action became far too close for dangerous antics of that nature.

Grappling hooks flew and their cruel iron barbs fastened like talons on bulwarks and galleries. The roaring yelling of men in combat crescendoed. With howls of rage, the enemy tried to board.

"I suppose they shout like that to keep up their spirits," observed Targon, loftily. The ranks of ESW remained silent. The archers poured in a lethal sleet of shafts that swept away the oncoming line of enemy.

Korero's upturned shields deflected a few arrows. They had been loosed from the fighting top of the ship opposing us, for the sturdy bulwarks protected us from shots from the enemy deck. Before I could rip out the obvious command, Deldar Phanton Vimura, in command of our lads in the fighting top of *Heart of Imrien*, directed his bowmen onto the enemy fighting top. The contest might have been interesting—archers versus archers—but the aerial ratings handling one of the stern gros-varters angled their weapon up and let fly with an enormous chunk of rock.

Their first shot clipped a slice out of the side of the top; the next pulverized the entire wooden side facing us.

Bodies spilled out.

Targon said: "I believe they did not expect to find us so crammed with soldiers. Time now, d'you think, to go and blatter 'em?"

"I'll—" I began.

Delia said: "I'll go with you."

I said: "Righto, Targon. Off you go."

Without waiting to listen in to the domestic row he was well aware was about to break out in the imperial household, Targon shot off to the lads. They still didn't put up a cheer as they reformed from shooters to blatterers and went charging over the bulwarks. That deadly silent and irresistible rush promised far more menace to the foe than a lot of caterwauling. When our lads did yell in the moments before they hit the enemy ranks on his own decks, they shouted. Aye, by Vox, then they shouted loud enough to blow the blasted enemy away!

"You continue to amaze me, husband."

"Why? Because I do not relish having you spiked through or fall overside?"

"I am wearing a safety belt—"

I grumped up, feeling a fatuous fool. "Aye, aye, so you are. But on the first count—"

"I am coming around to the belief, as I may have pointed out to you before, that you, Dray Prescot, are growing soft."

A tremendous racket broke out aboard the ship to our starboard with a seething commotion upon her deck. The vessel to larboard appeared to be ours already. The lads had simply gone headlong in and hurled away all opposition.

"Anyway," I said in my best growly hairy-bear way: "It's too late now."

"Targon was right, I judge. They are an aerial fighting force and had no idea we had so many troops aboard."

We watched as the officers charged with the various duties saw to what had to be done. Some of the North Vallian fliers escaped and plunged like fleeing rabbits into the clouds. There was little chance we would catch them in those masses of vapor before nightfall, so pursuit was not carried out. Prize crews went aboard the captured vollers.

Hundreds of flags flew bravely against the twilight as we retraced our course to alight at the forward base camp established at the Well of Parting. Everybody felt elated at the unexpected successful outcome of our expedition.

"Soon the main body will join us," said Korero. "Then I wonder if you'll give me such a peaceful battle."

"We've won a small aerial skirmish," I said, and I own my tones were somber. "The big fight is yet to come. In all honesty, Korero, I cannot answer your question."

"As San Blarnoi says," observed Delia, "hope alone does not sickle corn."

"Nor does it cause a change in the breeze." I was watching the leaves of the trees growing around the well. "But, as I'm an old sailorman, the breeze is shifting. It won't be long before the Fleet is up with us. Then, my friends, we shall see what we shall see."

Five

I inspect the zorca lines

My lad Drak flew up to see me at the camp of the Well of Parting. Delia and I shared a simple tent—oh, yes, true, it was a trifle more grand than any of the others; but as Deft-Fingered Minch pointed out, I was, after all, the fellow the people had chosen to be emperor and so I ought to make a bit of a show for their sakes.

Deft-Fingered Minch, a trusted comrade and a kampeon of great renown, was the man in command of the folk who cared for me on campaign. Delia's own arrangements were equally Spartan. She was aglow with happiness at seeing her son again and as they embraced I own I felt that silly but wonderfully understandable family pride in love and affection.

Drak looked tremendous. He was a big and powerful man, solidly built yet lithe and quick on his feet. I thought he was handsome, although he'd bristled up at any suggestions I made of that kind. He had that damn-you-Prescot look about him with the arrogant Prescot beak-head of a nose. Yet Delia was in him, too, giving him far more grace and poise and downright aristocratic manners than any I could aspire to.

"And, Drak, my dear," said Delia as she released him, "where is Silda?"

Drak swirled off his cape and I put a jar of ale into his hand.

"She has gone up to Balkan to see her father. I sent a couple of regiments with her—"

"Ah!" I said.

"And what does that mean, father?"

"Just that you'll be those two regiments short when you march off against this King of North Vallia."

"Me!"

"Aye, my lad. You."

He drank and then he did not wipe his hand across his mouth; but he did say: "By Mother Zinzu the Blessed! I need that!"

I said: "The Mountains of the North stretch across Vallia from Zaphoret in the east to Kavinstock in the west, where we are now." I gave Drak a hard stare. "There are the two traditional routes north and south, one to the east and one to the west. Two."

He drank again, looking at me, and then he put down the jar. I made no move to refill it. He put a hand to the outer buckles over his shoulder to release his armor.

"I see." The tang of the buckle came free. "You go north from here and I take the Army of Northeast Vallia and we strike inward together."

"Precisely," I said. "So why are you taking off your armor?"

"Dray!" said Delia. She swung to face me. "Are you such a monster?"

I humphed up at this. "Time," I said. "It will take time for Drak to get across and organize and march."

"One night?" She gave me that old look that curled the toes in my boots. "Since I saw Drak and Silda a great deal has happened."

I went over and ripped open the other buckles on Drak's armor, snatched off the breast and back, and tossed them down on the rugs. "Of course. Absolutely."

"Now you are in a bad temper."

"Yes, and I'll tell you why. I want to go to the wedding of Drak and Silda, the soon-to-be Emperor and Empress of Vallia. That wedding must be held in Vondium the Proud, the capital city of the Empire of Vallia. Yet if I go to Vondium that she-leem Csitra will spoil the wedding."

For a moment, silence closed in on us in the tent.

"And if I go chasing off to deal with Csitra first, as I wanted to do, that could take months. I wouldn't ask Drak and Silda to wait. So the difficulty remains."

Delia, as I may have remarked before, is not only the most beautiful woman in two worlds, she is also the most clever and devious, not to say downright cunning.

"I shall," she said, and her words and little gesture effectively dealt with the subject, "I shall have a few words with dear Deb-Lu."

"Excellent, mother," exclaimed Drak. "And now I would like another stoup and I am ravenous. Did I tell you that Silda sends her love and respects...?"

I slouched off to a totally unnecessary inspection of the zorca lines where the swods might find me a stoup and where we could have a yarn or two before I returned for the evening meal.

If I sound like an old graint with a thorn in his foot, then, well, by Vox, I suppose I was.

The lines of the various regiments were well spread out. Sometimes too close proximity creates frictions that besides being totally unnecessary lead to internecine strife. The swods were most welcoming and a jar was produced instanter. In the nature of things I could not know all the faces around the campfires; I knew most of them, though.

They wanted to know what the future held and some of them, the newer lads, wanted to know when we'd be going home. I have expressed my views on those great commanders and captains of history who led faithful armies all around the world on gyrations of conquest. Eventually, the soldiers become tired and soured. No sane man wants a continual career of conflict.

A policy of rotation was strongly in force. So I was able to reassure them and, perfectly truthfully, say that home was distinctly on the agenda. As to the old argument about home-leave sapping a soldier's willpower and determination, if a fellow—or a girl—is fighting for their home and loved ones, that spur should surely sustain their spirits.

When affairs go well, that is, of course. When the course of the war drags and the outcome is uncertain, why then all manner of mischiefs may darken the imagination. Walking slowly between the lines of tents back to that splendid tent where the flags flew and the guards stood to, glittering and imposing figures, I tried to sort out what I really wanted for the future.

Csitra had to be dealt with. The continents and islands of Paz had to understand that they must cling together in alliance against the Fishheads, the Leem Lovers, the Shanks who raided from over the curve of the world. There were many matters outstanding between me and the Star Lords. It seemed to me the Kroveres of Iztar would find busy occupation dealing with the evil cult of Lem the Silver Leem.

Delia stepped out of the tent and said in that delightful way: "And have you found the calsany yet?"

I said: "While you are with me I could lose a million zorcas and never notice."

At once she moved forward and slipped her arm through mine. The guards stood lance-stiff—for, of course, on Kregen there are no ramrods—but I knew they were taking all this in with alert enjoyment.

In the tiny space between the outer and inner flaps of the tent she stopped and kissed me. I kissed her; by Zair! This was what mattered in life, and all the rest could go hang.

We went on through and a little party had gathered to meet Drak, as was proper. During the meal and after, we talked and many of my thoughts found expression. Drak brought up the point of what forces he would be allotted.

"You commanded the First Army down in the southwest. The Second is over in the northeast. I suggest you retain command of the First, taking up what forces you require and can be spared from the southwest. Vodun Alloran will move the Ice Floes of Sicce to make amends, so that corner of the island is now safe."

"Very well. And the Second Army?"

"You assume command of both. You're going to have a hell of a task breaking through and hooking left."

He nodded and sat back in his seat. A very tough and very hard man, this son of mine, a man destined to be an emperor, as I surely was not. Well, perhaps that is wrong. Perhaps the destiny that was forced on Dray Prescot through being a sailorman and soldier, a slave, a mercenary, a kaidur, has brought him to the ranks of various nobilities, and does also include the sentence being passed on him of being a king and emperor.

"Turko sent a lot of his Ninth Army up to help Seg," Delia pointed out.

I'd retained the name of the Eighth Army for sentimental reasons, connected with thorn-ivy, and was using it again for this campaign into North Vallia.

"Of course," went on Delia, "knowing Seg as we do we must not be surprised if he inspires the people of Balkan and becomes their High Kov very quickly and then marches over the mountains to help us. Yes?"

Drak said: "I hope Silda..." Then he stopped himself.

Delia and I knew what was in his mind. Well, I'd suffered enough for Delia's sake, and now Drak suffered for Silda.

Now it is not my intention to give a blow-by-blow account of the North Vallian Campaign. The broad outlines of our plan were followed through with accuracy enough to ensure that the plan worked.

Drak took elements of the First and Second Armies around the east of the mountains and I took my Eighth around the western end of the mountains after we routed the hostile advance force at the Battle of the Blue Lizdun.

Now that the end was in sight we were joined by many folk who, even in the troublous times through which we had gone, had contrived to remain neutral. Neutral, one should add, in stance, for any neutral may have to suffer armed men marching through his lands and eating his produce and doing the unwholesome things badly led armies do even if the sufferers are not openly enemies.

Maybe it is churlish of me to say that; but we could have done with the help of these people earlier on. One such, of course, was the lord of Balkan; but he had reached the end of his journey upon Kregen and had shuffled off to meet the Gray Ones beckoning on the Ice Floes of Sicce. He died without living issue. Seg's campaign up in Balkan came, in after years, to be talked about as a marvel of diplomacy, tact, firmness and plain good commonsense. He had the Balkans solidly for him in a miraculously short space of time.

The pronunciation of Balkan is not like the terrestrial "ball" but like "bat." I mention this because Seg's Hyr Kovnate of Balkan was nothing like the Balkans here on Earth. Also the stress falls on the second syllable: Bal*kan*.

He sent me regular letters by merker, those spry young folk who skim through the air aboard their birds carrying important messages. We had instituted the merker system in Vallia on a small scale, importing from Djanduin a useful colony of the small fast birds used there, the fluttcleppers.

I was seriously considering asking some of my winged friends who lived down south in Havilfar if they might not care to emigrate and come to live with us in Vallia. It seemed to me a flying man or woman was even more suitable as a merker.

Still, that must be for the future.

Right now we had the North Vallian campaign to fight and to bring to a successful conclusion.

The days went by in marching and flying forward until we bumped the hostiles again and then we would fight. Battles were fought of intense ferocity. Others were over after our first charge.

Drak's fortunes prospered on the east. And Seg, that astounding blade comrade of mine, Seg Segutorio, did just as Delia said he would.

The merker flew in with Seg's latest. He had gathered a goodly force and was headed through the Kazzchun Pass to create mayhem in the center of North Vallia, in the province of Durheim. As he wrote: "I have experience of a River called the Kazzchun, so it is suitable, my old dom, I learn about a pass with the same name."

I smiled as I read this. The kovnate province of Durheim lay to the east and was separated by the River of Golden Sliptingers from the hyr-kovnate of Erstveheim to the west. My Eighth had sent a corps to the south west into the finger of land containing the vadvarate of Thothveheim, and the main body of the army was now pushing hard to the northeast through Erstveheim. Drak had to negotiate the trylonate of Tremi before bursting through into Durheim.

So, like the three flukes of a trident, and those three prongs would cooperate fully, we were poised to rip the fraudulent kingdom of North Vallia to shreds—and then to repair and reunite with the homeland.

Marion said to me one day as the wind blew over our shoulders, fluttering scarves and swelling the sails of the vorlcas: "Prince Drak will surely detach a force to march north?"

At her shoulder stood her husband, Strom Nango. I could not detect avarice in either of their faces; rather Marion looked sad, and Nango concerned.

"Cheer up, Marion. I expect Drak will do so; but I will send him a direct order to that effect. After all, I am still the emperor, am I not?"

She did not rally to my feeble humor.

"Thank you, majister. To think that at last I shall return to Huvadu. I never believed it, not in my heart."

Nango said nothing.

I was a trifle perplexed. "By Vox, Marion! I'd think you'd be overjoyed."

"Oh, I am happy that Huvadu is to be mine again. Yes, that is true. But when I go there to take command of the force Prince Drak sends, I shall leave you. And I shall leave my splendid regiment of Jikai Vuvushis." She put the nail of her middle finger under her eye. "And I shall leave the Empress Delia."

There was nothing much I could say to that.

I did say: "You have our best wishes, Marion."

Then, with a flash of inspiration that came, I suppose, from cowardly cunning, I added: "Oh, and, of course, Marion, you must take your girls with you. I won't hear of anything else."

Before she could react—and I'd no idea how she would take this stroke—Delia turned up and I was able to slope off and see about a gros-varter that had been shooting crookedly.

Six

A dagger in the night

The Battle of Gwalherm turned out to be a desperate affair.

This upstart King of North Vallia cleverly drew us onto a strongly fortified position which, in the normal way, we would have bypassed and possibly masked. As it was he'd sited the line of entrenchments across a convenient line of march. We were into the battle almost before we were aware.

In the end we managed to tumble him off, and a magnificent charge by a division of heavy cavalry finally threw him out.

I call this king an upstart. Well, by Krun, and so was I.

All the same, my upstartedness was the result of the people of Vallia calling me to be their emperor. We had heard stories of the cruelty of this North Vallian king, who apparently went by a number of names. The latest name he was using we gathered was Nath the Greatest Ever. Previously, he had been known as Naghan the Mighty, and Larghos the Magnificent. What his real name might be, no one knew. That, then, is the reason I have not given his name before in this narrative. But now we were closing in, and the time for names was either approaching or was past.

Northwest of Erstveheim in a kind of slice of the coast lies the vadvarate of Venga.

Well, now. Venga. The Vadnicha of the place, Ashti Melekhi, had long since taken her way to the Ice Floes of Sicce. I wondered how she fared there, and if the fates that draw their harp strings into the long moaning sounds of destiny had yet passed her through to the sunny uplands beyond.

We had to send a force into Venga, that was clear.

I had negated the idea of splitting the Eighth Army into a drive northward into Evir as well as our eastward push to link with Seg and Drak.

Still, Venga would lie at our backs as we pressed on east. In the end a Corps was formed and sent off under the command of Chuktar Modo Na-Du, a Pachak of immense competence from Zamra. We were by those divisions weaker; but now that Vallia had, all but these northern provinces, been re-united, we had reinforcements coming in gratifyingly often.

Later on as we sat around the campfire after we'd visited the wounded and sung a few songs with the swods, Delia said to me, "You were hard on poor Marion."

"You think so? I am not sure. She was mighty proud of her girls."

"Yes. She gloried that they were part of the emperor's jurukker jikai."

"You know how itchy I get when I see girls in battle—"

"I do know." She put her hand on my hand, and I curled my fingers and held hers. "You're a funny old stick, particularly one who is an emperor. Y'know, Dray, we ought to have had Jilian form the guard Jikai Vuvushis."

"I would have liked that. Jilian Sweet Tooth. I wonder where she is now and what deviltry she's up to."

"She has her mission in life."

"Aye."

Jilian was an old comrade. You may spell her name Sweet Tooth or Sweetooth, I gathered, either being correct. I believe I preferred the former.

Over our heads the glittering majesty of the stars of Kregen flashed and twinkled in their massed glory. Up here in the north of Vallia the nights grew frosty. The fourth Moon of Kregen, She of the Veils, cast down her golden-roseate light. All about us rose the sounds of an army encampment at night. The sentries patrolled. I lay back.

"The quicker we meet up with Seg and Drak the better."

"We will, my heart, we will. And then?"

"So much to do—"

"There always is. Drak and Silda's wedding, for a start."

"Don't remind me."

For a space we were silent, relishing the night.

Then Delia said, "This Nath the Greatest Ever may form up to challenge us again on Losobrin's Edge, or he may throw himself into the town of Erdensmot and defy us there."

I made a face. "Neither prospect charms me. I have no desire to charge up against the entrenchments he can arrange on Losobrin's Edge. I'm told the place is formidable. But then, a siege of Erdensmot will not be pretty."

"If we march around him—"

I know I sounded fretful. "If only Farris could scrape up some more fliers for us!"

"One would have thought," said Delia with some acerbity, "that now Hamal is safe they would be able to build as many vollers as were required."

"There is continual trouble over by the Mountains of the West, as we know. I suppose that's it. Anyway, we continue to build vorlcas; but wood is getting to be a problem now."

"The Singing Forests grow wood enough, for the sake of Opaz!"

"Aye. We will have to establish vorlca yards there. And, my heart, you will notice how cleverly I am leaving all the appointments of new nobility to Drak? There are many provinces at present ruled by our justicars. Once the wars are over, we must find good faithful folk to be made up to nobles."

Delia gave me a calculating look. "Old Nath Ulverswan was the Kov of the Singing Forests," she said.

"Yes, he was a Racter, too, I suppose. He never said much, did he?"

"Old Clamped Jaws. The point is, the Singing Forests lie due south of the Mountains of the North, immediately to the west of Seg's Bakan."

I saw what she meant at once. Also I noticed she said "Bakan," the old name, instead of the newer "Balkan."

"You think the Presidio will agree?"

"If you tell them, they will."

"I'm not so sure. I don't want to carry on ruling by fiat. The Presidio must be seen to rule fairly. I'm thinking of starting up elections—"

"Elections? But we are an empire, Dray!"

"I was elected to be emperor."

"Oh, yes, of course; but that was different."

"Well, I'm thinking of it. I'll speak to Drak about Seg and the Singing Forests. Mind you, Seg might refuse."

"He might. But there is Milsi. She is level-headed."

Because we were who we were and clearly wished to sit by the campfire and talk, we had been left alone. If anyone wished to speak to us they knew they had only to make themselves apparent. We were accessible in a way previous rulers had not been.

A slim figure approached the fire, and stopped, and stood waiting. Delia called out: "Yes, my dear? Step forward."

The girl walked into the light of the fire. She wore half armor and carried a rapier and main gauche and looked just such a Battle Maiden as existed in their thousands in most of the armies of Kregen. Her face, rosy from the reflected fireglow, did not smile. She looked indrawn and serious. I did not recognize her.

Neither did Delia. She was not, I judged, a member of the Sisters of the Rose.

"What is it?" said Delia, and her voice was not quite as gentle as before.

"A message," said the Jikai Vuvushi.

Now I'm no stickler for protocol or for stupid and slavish kow-towing, as you know, by Krun. Yet this girl ought to speak with more civility to Delia on more than one count.

I started to stand up.

With a shriek chillingly demoniacal, a scream of utter madness, the girl hurled herself forward, and the long slender Vallian dagger in her fist glittered in the light of the moon.

That lethal blade struck viciously down at Delia.

Without drawing a weapon, so filled with terror for Delia and hate and loathing for this murdering girl, I hurled myself forward.

Now Delia of Delphond, Delia of the Blue Mountains, is expert with very many of the varied weapons of Kregen, but if there is just one weapon of which she is the consummate mistress, that is the long slender Vallian dagger.

My desperate lunge forward, highly dramatic and mock-heroic, was completely unnecessary.

The silly would-be murderess had no chance.

Delia twisted lithely aside, took the girl's wrist, twisted, pulled, there was a sharp cry of pain and a glitter of starlight on steel, and the girl stood laxly staring at the blade pressed against her throat.

"Well, now," said Delia. She spoke evenly and her breast rose and fell smoothly with her breathing. What a wonderful girl is Delia; calm, compassionate, tempestuous and passionate, she is all things in all, and then I looked at the slender sliver of steel and I shuddered all the way down to my boots.

A girl in the russet leathers of the Sisters of the Rose ran up, her bow lifted and arrow nocked and half-drawn. Following her appeared a gang of my lads, and Delia's girls. They all looked extraordinarily fierce and yet apprehensive in the firelight.

"It is all right," called Delia.

"Had the emperor not got in the way," said the Sister of the Rose. "I'd have shafted the assassin, clean, the instant she whipped out her dagger."

"I'm sure you would, Zandi, and I thank you. Now perhaps you'd ask the girl a few questions."

Mind you, I was still shaking; but at the same time I knew I had an enormous smile wrapped all around inside my skull. This slip of a girl, this Zandi, a Sister of the Rose and a Hikdar in Delia's personal bodyguard, knew how to cut a fellow down to size—even if that fellow happened to be the husband of the woman she served with devoted loyalty and the emperor to boot. Maybe because I was Delia's husband, this Zandi didn't think much of me, didn't think I was good enough for her mistress.

Well, by Zair, and didn't I know I wasn't!

The would-be assassin was held firmly. She lifted her head and stared at Delia. Her eyes had a blank fey look, a glaze of uncaring madness that repelled.

"You need ask no questions, tikshim."

At this the guards holding her gasped at the insolence and the insult. They shook her and one rasped out: "Speak to the empress with civility."

"Empress!" The tones jeered. "Empress of nothing! Your Vallia is doomed and you with it."

I stepped forward. Now my anger had to be controlled or I could lose all I wanted on Kregen.

"Csitra," I said. "If you harm Delia, the Empress of Vallia, you will earn my undying hatred and enmity."

"The woman can mean nothing to you, Dray Prescot! I am your chosen mate!"

"As to that, Csitra, fate may decide some things. But not all."

"You said you would visit me in the Coup Blag."

In the drugged voice of this poor duped girl before me, was there a hint of petulance? Could the demoniacal Witch of Loh far away in South Pandahem share weak human emotions to the extent of feeling sorry for herself?

Delia said in a metallic voice: "So that's it."

"Listen, Csitra. I shall visit you, believe me, as I promised. Maybe you will not enjoy that visit. But I repeat, and you will do well to heed my words."

"Yes, Dray Prescot?"

I ground the words out as though I were spitting granite chips.

"If you harm one hair of Delia the Empress of Vallia's head, I shall surely slay you."

As I finished speaking in that stupid puffed up way, but with absolute sincerity, I caught a movement in the corner of my eye. The girl's head snapped up and she turned to glare over my shoulder.

"Who is that standing there beside you?"

I half turned to look.

Drill the Eye, one of the commanders of the Yellow Jackets, stood there looking vacant, his mouth hanging half open.

I said, "A soldier. Now, Csitra, do you hear me?"

As I spoke I wondered what on Kregen Drill the Eye, a mighty kampeon, commanding the archers, was doing standing like a loon with the hay in his hair. Odd.

"I hear you. If I do not harm this woman, then you will come?"

"As I said before, Csitra, you have my word."

The girl slumped. The guards held her up. I turned around to speak to Drill the Eye, for I thought I had it, and he spoke up in a wheezy voice.

"She has a most powerful kharrna, Dray, most. She was not sure; but she suspected."

"Deb-Lu?"

"Aye, Dray, aye. And I must apologize to Drill the Eye for using his eyes to see through."

"He'll understand. He won't mind."

"I sincerely trust so. I have been Keeping an Observation upon Csitra and am coming to learn something of her ways. But this latest attack—"

"Has failed."

"Praise under the Seven Arcades is due."

Delia put out her hand to me and said: "I think I will go in now."

At once I put an arm about her waist and we turned for the tent. I spoke over my shoulder.

"Fanshos, the incident is closed. Deb-Lu, continue with your work, for little else stands between us and disaster."

So we went into the tent and took a little wine. Nothing can shake me like any threat to Delia. I would not care to account for my actions if ill befalls her.

Just before we went to sleep, I said softly: I shall have to make that trip very soon, my heart."

"There is still much to be done—"

"Oh, yes, there always is. But, right now, nothing is more important in all the world."

Seven

The Battle of Bengarl's Blight

I said, "It's pointless to call for volunteers."

"Naturally," agreed Delia.

"So I shall just have to choose a few likely lads."

"And lasses, of course."

"Oh, of course."

She eyed me. We were taking the first breakfast, of bosk rashers and fried eggs and enormous quantities of the superb Kregan tea, and dishes of palines to follow. Her look quite clearly summed me up.

"You need not try to slip away by yourself. And I shall bring my best girls. As Dee Sheon is my witness, Dray Prescot, I'm not having you run your fool head into that she-leem's lair without—"

"I know, I know," I groaned.

"Well, I'm going," said Targon the Tapster, "and that's settled."

The other commanders of ESW and EYJ all chimed in saying that of course they would go.

Nath na Kochwold, Kapt of the Phalanx, just held up a paline in his fingers, stared at me, said, "I'm ready for the off right now," and put the paline into his mouth with great enjoyment.

No one dreamed of not going to the horrendous terrors of the Coup Blag.

This situation was not quite the same as that confronting me when I'd shot off to Hyrklana to dig out Naghan the Gnat, Tilly and Oby from the Jikhorkdun. It was similar but not the same.

Korero the Shield simply said: "It's about time I went on an adventure with you again."

By this time in the campaign I had all the regiments of my guards corps with me in the Eighth Army, so there were so many kampeons about the glitter of gold and the glint of medals fairly blinded a fellow.

I said to Nath Karidge, a *beau sabreur* commanding Delia's EDLG: "It'll be on your feet, Nath, if you're lucky. There's no riding zorcas down there in the Coup Blag or through the Snarly Hills."

"One must make sacrifices from time to time."

I marveled.

Mazingle is the name the swods give to discipline. This crowd of people around me now were most mazarna. That is the absence of discipline, unruly, rowdy. They were that, right enough.

That afternoon, in absolute character, Nath Karidge was observed with an enormous pack stuffed with sand on his back, smothered in weapons, carrying a giant water bottle, and wearing stout marching boots, striding out across the bleak moorlands. As a rider he was getting into trim for a spot of walking. How like him!

When he came back he said to me: "By Lasal the Vakka! My legs are like putty."

I said, "You will be with the empress."

He stared at me as though I were bereft of my senses.

He managed to blurt out: "Where else?"

I shook my head. These fellows! Nath Karidge was happily married, and with new additions to his family. Yet he would cheerfully give his life for Delia. Of such mettle are the men of Vallia, who do not serve blindly.

Covell of the Golden Tongue had recently been fashioning a superior new poem cycle devoted to the heroes of Vallia. He thirsted for all the news of them available, going to extraordinary lengths to learn their stories. When he wrote, his verses carried the lilt and rhythms exactly suited to the personality and deeds of his subject. An invaluable master poet, San Covell of the Golden Tongue.

The most serious aspect of the whole affair of Csitra's attempt to assassinate Delia was simply the fact of the deed itself. The poor girl whose mind had been taken over by the witch, of course knew nothing of what had passed. She was a new arrival from Vondium, come up to join her regiment.

Delia said: "And how many more people are there from Vondium possessed by this she-vampire? She will have sent them all over Vallia looking for you!"

"Yes."

"She knows where you are now. Are we then to expect another of her horrible curses?"

"She would have done so already, if she could. I suspect Deb-Lu has managed to achieve some mastery over her powers."

"I sincerely trust so, by Vox!"

Shortly after that Khe-Hi-Bjanching and Ling-Li-Lwingling turned up, adamantly determined to go with the expedition to the Coup Blag. They were two people I really welcomed along.

With them actually with Delia, I felt a little easier in my mind about the witch.

With this—admittedly fragile—new development in affairs, I could make the decision I had trembled to make before.

To the assembled officers of the army I said: "News has just reached me that Prince Drak and Kov Seg have linked up and are approaching the River of Golden Sliptingers. Their opposition has suddenly materially weakened and they have made unexpectedly good progress."

Kapt Erndor grumped up and said: "So we know what that portends."

"Aye," I said. I didn't like the note of grimness in my voice. "We have recently been blessed with a considerable flow of reinforcements. You'd best reform your Ninth Army, Erndor and make sure you take some of the better regiments."

"Thank you, jis, I will that. What are your orders for me?"

"Why, Erndor! To march shoulder to shoulder and bash this Nath the Greatest Ever."

"If my guess is right, and I think it is, and he has denuded his front against Prince Drak and Kov Seg, he is likely to leave his entrenchments on Losobrin's Edge and his billets in Erdensmot, and mount an attack."

"Which is precisely what we want him to do, is it not?"

"Absolutely," said Nath Famphreon. "Although he will now inevitably be in great strength. The reports of fresh mercenaries arriving daily are explicit."

"So there's no question of us flying off to the Coup Blag until we've blattered the fellow. When his paktuns have all run back home again and the land is peaceful—then."

Well, I have said I am not intending to give a blow by blow account of the North Vallian Campaign. There were many battles, a few sieges, and a lot of marching, a damned lot of marching. But now we could brace ourselves for what we all hoped would be the last big encounter. The self-styled King of North Vallia had concentrated almost all his forces against us in the west hoping to knock us out before turning back to finish off Drak and Seg.

When I calculated out the odds I was fully and painfully aware that I was dealing in the lives of men and women. Still, for this last time—until the unholy Shanks arrived on our shores.

The two armies were in good heart. Some of the units were raw; many were hardened by this and previous campaigns into veterans, and there were the kampeons, the heroes of Vallia, men and women to be cherished.*

One odd fact emerged from all this, to Kapt Erndor's puzzlement. He had the 30th Infantry Division under command. As he said to me as we met for the last time before going out to our respective armies: "Odd, by Vox. The 11th Churgurs have Jiktar Nogad ti Vendleheim commanding. I was sure old Hack 'n' Slay had them."

Across the moorland we could see the opposing array. I nodded as Kapt Erndor said: "Well, may Opaz ride with you this day. I'm off."

"Opaz go with you, Erndor." Then I concentrated on what was to come, all preparations over and what was not done would never be done.

The place was simply a portion of the vast sweep of moorland up there

---

* Here Prescot gives the composition of the Eighth and Ninth Armies together with long lists of names. A.B.A.

in Erstveheim. A tiny village, of no more than a dozen or so tumbledown houses, a tavern and a posting house, and a temple to their obscure local god, stood out forlornly between the lines. The village's name was Bengarl. Most unkindly, the swods dubbed the area Bengarl's Blight, and so that was how the battle acquired its name.

The aerial duels were fought out savagely. Birds wheeled and fluttered against the radiance of the suns. Many fell. Ships burned. This phase of the proceedings lasted longer than usual, and our vaward was running into contact before the air was fully cleared.

There was no doubt in any of our minds that our Vallian Air Service, and our flutduin squadrons, would do the job. Against ferocious opposition it just took longer.

The skirmishers, called on Kregen 'kreutzin', darted in and flung their javelins, shot in their bows, then skipped away, evading with lithe skill. All the same, they did not escape entirely unscathed.

Our dustrectium* lashed out. The superbly trained Bowmen of Vallia, using the Lohvian longbow, ripped enemy formations to shreds. But they had Bowmen of Loh over there, too, paktuns earning their hire. The archery duel became bitter.

Not wishing to stand my lads still under this punishment, I gave ready assent to the vociferous requests for a general advance. The air smelled damp with that mingled aroma of wet grasses and gorses, of tiny purple flowers, of wet earth. The radiance of the suns strove to pierce through layers of mist. The lines advanced.

Our Phalanxes, battle-winning weapons, sent up their paeans. Their long pikes all slanted up as one, and on the command the front five ranks' pikes went down, pointing those small deadly heads at the enemy. The banners fluttered. The bugles sounded. With their crimson shields raised, their bronze-fitted armor glinting and their helmets all bent grimly down, the brumbytes charged.

Nothing stood before them. They swept away ranks and lines of cavalry and infantry alike. Surrounded by their Hakkodin, the double-handed sworders, the axemen, the halberdiers, they looked like the Wrath of God made manifest.

Our job was just to hold the enemy. We had to grip him and grapple him, to hold him steady. We were the anvil.

Kapt Erndor's Ninth Army was the hammer.

The onrush of the Phalanxes halted as the bugles pealed. The brumbytes remained in solid masses, file by file, Relianch by Relianch, Jodhri by Jodhri. Their chodkus of archers ran forward in the intervals to lay down barrages of shafts onto the reeling foe. And the flags! Those flags flying over the Phalanx warmed my heart, I can tell you. On what was my own

---

* Dustrectium: firepower as delivered by bows, slings and engines.

436

personal battle standard, a simple color consisting of a yellow cross upon a scarlet field, the insignie of the brumbytes were embroidered in golden and silver thread. Each Relianch flew its own color, brilliant with the special devices which told the world just who stood ranked beneath that standard. Those colors were no longer my own personal flag, the tresh fighting men called Old Superb.

Old Superb was carried by Cleitar the Standard. Ortyg the Tresh carried the Union Flag of Vallia. Volodu the Lungs was there, his massive and battered trumpet ready to peal the calls over the battlefield. Korero the Shield, as ever, lifted his shields at my back. Yes, the little group around Delia and myself formed a party most precious to me.

Ranked away to left and right waited the solid and silent lines of the guard corps. They were all there. Delia's guard corps, also, stood awaiting the call for action.

Our heavy infantry trampled forward like a herd of elephants in full cry. The bowmen kept up their sleeting discharges. Our artillery, varters and catapults, drenched the enemy lines with rocks and darts.

Once again, and this time shoulder to shoulder with the churgurs, the Phalanxes advanced. The cruel pikeheads went down, the shields lifted, every helmet slanted forward. In crimson and bronze, as they say in Vallia, the brumbytes charged.

The mercenary forces serving this Nath the Greatest Ever recoiled. Like good quality Paktuns of Kregen they fought well and earned their hire. I did not fault them on that this day of the Battle of Bengarl's Blight.

Nath na Kochwold cantered up astride his zorca, flushed, inspired, waving his arm.

"They are magnificent! Magnificent!"

"Yes, Nath. The whole army of Vallia is magnificent."

He laughed, elated. "Oh, yes. But of them all—my Phalanx! There is the true glory!"

He rode on, passing from one wing to the other and taking the time to call on me en route.

Nath Famphreon, as the Kov of Falkerdrin, would normally expect to command a sizable force. But he had been under the shadow of his formidable mother for a long long time. He had requested that he ride as my aide, and to this I had agreed. Now he came racing up forcing his zorca on. He took off his hat and waved it wildly.

When he was fairly up with us he burst out: "The cunning cramph! He has sent a flank force of cavalry. They strike at our left flank."

"Then our left flank cavalry will see them off." I spoke with deliberate calm. I wasn't sure, for I had not inquired, if Nath Famphreon had ever witnessed a great battle before, let alone fought in one.

The outcome of Nath the Greatest Ever's surprise flank cavalry attack was not in doubt once our Chuktars moved our own cavalry across. The mounted action was interesting as I was afterward told. Our totrixes and nikvoves backed up by a goodly force of swarths, tumbled the enemy cavalry into ruin.

We did not use our zorca cavalry in this action.

Many of them, still trained as Filbarrka had specified, shot and lanced and created merry hell with the enemy.

A flyer spiraled down above us. The girl rode a flutduin, so no one shot her out of the air.

"Majister!" she shrieked as she volplaned over our heads. "The Ninth come on! In two burs they will hit!"

"Excellent."

"Things do seem to be going rather well," observed Delia, "although my people tell me our casualties are mounting."

There was no need for me to say anything to that last remark. Delia, I knew, shared my abhorrence for warfare. We had to fight, and when we did we fought as hard and as well as we could. Casualties—even the word has an ugly sound.

The noise from the field blew about us as the breeze shifted flukily. Our sailing ships of the air had tacked up and taken a goodly part in the fighting; now they were struggling to remain on station. One or two had been brought down by enemy shots from upturned varters.

Targon the Tapster, clearly sent by his comrades, edged his zorca over. I saw him.

"Targon?"

I knew what he wanted, right enough.

He spoke formally, in earshot of the rest.

"Jis. I have been entrusted with the mission of requesting you to let us—" Then he broke down, and burst out: "Let us get at them, for the sake of Vox and all his mailed host!"

"There is time yet."

He looked savage, but he knew my ways.

"Then let the ripe time come quickly. The Phalanx will be above itself after this day—"

The old rivalry! "They do well. So will you. Just keep the lads on a tight leash until they are loosed."

"Quidang!"

He cantered off back to where his comrades waited in a clump of palpitating expectation. They stood on foot, and their orderlies held their zorcas a little way off. I felt for the lads, felt for them deeply. If I committed them to the battle at the wrong time, they'd be the ones to suffer.

I should ride with them myself; I would not do so, for I knew damn well that Delia would be knee to knee with me.

438

"I rather think—" said Delia to cover over the hollowness that fell between us after Targon took himself off. "I rather do think that girl who screeched down from the flutduin was Trudi ti Valkanium. She's related to Vangar, as you probably do not know, seeing that they are from Valka and you are the strom there."

"I knew," I said, most equably.

"She opted to join the flyers rather than the fliers. Vangar couldn't understand that."

"He will be taking over from Farris, soon, to command the Vallian Air Service. Farris, though—"

"I know. But there is nothing he will allow us to do, although I have suggested it to him."

What a bloody miserable kind of life this is when we all have to grow old and die!

And, you will perceive, we spoke thus to cover our deeply distressed feelings at the sights and sounds that so affronted us on the field of battle.

The rolling charge of the Phalanxes, for there were two full Phalanxes with us on this day, drove like battering waves against yielding rocks. Along the whole front the opposing armies clashed. Our heavy infantry, the churgurs, ran in disciplined formation forward, hurling their javelins. These bulky stuxes drove the shields in splinters from the hands of the enemy. Then the foot soldiers slapped their shields front and forward, whipped out their drexers and so, swords in fists, smashed into their foes.

Drak had brought up from the southwest the First Phalanx and the Fifth Kerchuri of the Third Phalanx. Each Phalanx was divided into two wings, called Kerchuris. Each Kerchuri consisted of six Jodhris, each of the six Relianches. The Sixth Kerchuri of the Third Phalanx had joined with their other half, coming from Turko's Ninth Army. Up in the northeast and now commanded by Drak, the Second Phalanx was driving on to meet us. Seg had with him the Fourth Phalanx. As for the Fifth, its Ninth Kerchuri still remained in Vondium, a very necessary precaution, while its Tenth was with Drak.

So, as you will perceive, Kapt Erndor, smashing down to form the hammer to our anvil, had no Phalanx with him.

Our First and Third Phalanxes were—as many said and as many vehemently denied—the two premier pike formations of the Vallian army. On this day of Bengarl's Blight they performed magnificently.

The fleeting thought crossed my mind to wonder how the new 30th Infantry Division fared, and what Erndor had meant when he'd been surprised that the Jiktar he dubbed old Hack 'n' Slay did not command the 11th Regiment of Churgurs. This 30th Div had been given to Erndor to allow him some substance to his rear and as cover for his forward advance. Erndor had all our mounted infantry with him. The old days when we'd mounted men on any kind of saddle animal we could find had not alto-gether gone. There were still regiments mounted on preysanys—and they bore the crude jokes and witticisms leveled at them with stoic bluntness.

As you may well imagine I looked forward to the day when my kregoinye comrade Pompino returned from Pandahem with lavish consignments of hersanys from the island. Despite all, I missed my Khibil comrade.

And I refrain from comment on the Divine Lady of Belschutz.

Delia lifted in her stirrups to peer across to the right. Instantly, her shield bearer, a massive and lethally dangerous Djang called Tandu Khyn-lin Jondermair, shifted himself astride his joat to keep his twin shields at the right angle. His movements caused his steed to trample all over the dainty hooves of a zorca ridden by a flying aide. Tandu did not notice.

Tandu's son, Dalki, held Delia's personal standard proudly aloft.

Delia said: "There is movement on the right flank."

Now anyone who describes a battle to you in graphic details concerning every portion of the field and what transpired there has received infor-mation from many people involved. No one can see it all, not even the C-in-C.

What was going on was relayed to us quickly enough by a flushed girl astride a flutduin. She landed and hared across to our command group. What she said indicated that the King of North Vallia, besides trying to be clever, fancied he had worked out a system to beat our Phalanx.

The early left flank attack of cavalry had been designed to draw off our mounted forces. We had commented that the North Vallian mercenaries did not appear to be in the strength we anticipated. Nath the Greatest Ever had held a sizable force back, and now he flung a mass of cavalry at our right flank with the clear intention of striking the right-hand Phalanx in the side.

"We are the anvil," I said. "So we hold."

As was proper, the First Phalanx took the right of the formation. I had no doubts that they would hold.

With a division of churgurs flanking them, with their own Hakkodin and archers, and supported by our own right flank cavalry, they could grapple and grasp these paktun cavalrymen, hold them, pin them, and by that time Kapt Erndor should be up.

Well, that was easy theory, easy for me astride a nikvove at the back. For the swods in the ranks the story, although finishing in the same way, was somewhat different in the telling, as I knew, I knew full well, by Vox.

One of our casualties, a simple swod, was out of Delia's regiment of the Sisters of the Rose. She fought bravely and skillfully, and died heroically. Her name was Fruli Venarden. She had recently joined us from Vondium. In between joining us and her death, she had tried to assassinate the Empress of Vallia with a long slender dagger.

I spoke generally, so that all in earshot might hear.

"I believe this is the moment of crisis. This is the time, then." I turned to Nath Famphreon. "Nath, would you be good enough to ride over to Targon and the rest of the rascals and inquire if they would care to ride across and blatter the flank that they can see attacking our right flank?"

"With all my heart, majister. And I shall ride with them."

"You may do so, an' you will, and may Opaz go with you. But, Kov Nath, you ride on your own time. I am not paying you wages to get yourself killed."

He laughed at that, young, fresh, freed by the death of his mother into a world of liberty he had never dreamed existed. "*I* would pay *you*, majister, for the privilege!"

Then he was off, fleeting across to the commanders of my guard corps. They wasted no time. Old campaigners, kampeons, hardened by civil war and struggles against slavers and aragorn and reivers from across the sea, they were men habituated to victory. They were in motion at once.

Well, the noise and confusion, the horrid screams of wounded men and animals, the raw stink of blood, the taste of dust on the tongue even in the damp gorse of the moorland, the lowering mist over all turning the radiance of the twin suns in a ghostly twilight of red and green to a corpse-pallor on every face. Well, as I say, the Battle of Bengarl's Blight took place, and men and women died, and Kapt Erndor came up and between him and us we squashed the King of North Vallia's mercenary forces as a fruit is squashed in the press.

I will not dwell on it.

We won.

The battle was costly to us. There were far more casualties than I cared for, far far more, by Zair.

Our ambulance service had been strengthened over the seasons, and the somber hooded carts moved carefully among the piles of corpses seeking those with life still left. The needlemen and puncture ladies were hard at work.

Our light cavalry and aerial cavalry took up the pursuit. Now was not the time to be squeamish over making sure the victory was secured.

The prisoners—and there were very many of them—were told they would be repatriated. Even at this late date some of them were unaware that Vallia had ceased to employ mercenaries. They were astonished when they offered their services to us that they should be refused. They had fought well and earned their hire. They had honored their contracts. Why, then, should we refuse their employment?

I knew I had to think again about this policy of mine. What if, instead of Vallian citizens lying dead on the battlefield, they had been paktuns from foreign lands, paid their hire for fighting for us? Well, would not that be a better arrangement for Vallia's sons and daughters?

Delia said to me as we dismounted from our nikvoves: "Come on, you great hairy graint. Everything is being attended to. Bengarl's Blight is a great victory. Now come into the tent and have a good wash and something to eat and drink."

"Aye," I said. "And now Vallia is whole again."

Eight

Drak and Silda

Deb-Lu-Quienyin said: "Khe-Hi and Ling-Li and I have managed to fabricate what one might call a Hood of Misalignment."

We were sitting comfortably in our tent, and wine had been served. Delia looked marvelous in a robe of lavender, and her feet were bare. She did not wear toe rings. I wore a plain lounging robe of yellow, girded by a scarlet sash. As for Deb-Lu, well, he wore what was clearly a brand new robe, plain, yet contriving to look as though he'd slept in a haystack all night. His turban toppled, as ever, dangerously over one ear. Khe-Hi and his bride, Ling-Li, looked perfectly turned out in correct and expensive and yet not sumptuous robes.

"The task was interesting, if difficult," said Khe-Hi-Bjanching. He looked at his wife. "Ling-Li was fantastic."

Deb-Lu let rip a dry wheeze of a chuckle. "By Hlo-Hli! These two lovebirds make me wonder why I never married!"

With all the sedateness of a Witch of Loh, Ling-Li said: "Dear Deb-Lu. Who'd have you?"

Delia turned her laugh into a sound that frizzled me right down to the backbone. We all knew Ling-Li, after that start that could have been so awkward, was fitting into the group easily. She and Khe-Hi shared a special relationship in sorcery that made them far more powerful as a team than they were individually.

"And this Hood of Misalignment?"

"It means, in layman's terms, that if Csitra uses her kharrna for a sending, tries to inflict another plague, it will strike dwaburs away from its intended target."

I said: "I don't want innocent folk suddenly embroiled in sorceries—frogs and insects and suchlike falling out of the sky on their heads."

"We can deflect the plague accurately enough to drop it into the sea, for example."

"Pity the poor sailors on a plague night like this."

"We can," said Deb-Lu, "ensure that Vondium is kept clear of interference for the period of the wedding."

"That," pointed out Delia with great satisfaction, "is splendid for us. But we cannot harm innocent people."

"We will ensure the plagues drop into an empty ocean."

One of the jurukkers on guard duty, Nath the Point, put his head into the tent opening to bellow: "Prince Drak, jis, the Prince Majister of Vallia!"

Instantly, Drak walked in, flinging his cloak off. He looked dusty and only a little tired if travel-stained. Once again, I remarked to myself his commanding figure, his air of habitual authority.

The lahals were exchanged and wine was poured and Drak slumped down into a chair and stuck his booted feet out.

"So we've done it," he said. "At last, thanks be to Opaz."

"Where," Delia wanted to know, "is Seg?"

"He's gone up to Evir, mother. He took a little army with him, too."

"Ah," she said. And then: "Milsi is a splendid wife for him. But—Thelda..."

"He's all right," I said in a gruff way that displeased me. I felt for my blade comrade, Seg Segutorio, in the matter of believing his wife Thelda was dead only to discover she was alive and married to a fine man and with children by him.

"I believe so."

"It's in my mind to offer Lol Polisto the kovnate of Evir. That would please Thelda."

"Oh, it would!"

Then we both laughed. Oh, yes, we were cruel to poor Thelda. She always meant well and disaster trailed her. Still, good friends in the northernmost province of Vallia was a seemly prospect, Zair knows.

It was left to Ling-Li to ask the next obvious question.

"She went with her father. I offered to go, too, but—well, family business."

"Very much our family, soon, Drak," pointed out Delia. "You will have Thelda as a mother-in-law."

At this point in my narrative, pursued by the ghosts of a million music hall jokes, I will move onto the time we spent in Vondium for the wedding and what followed.

The most delicious item of gossip going the rounds, and the subject of considerable investment in the way of gambling and betting on the chances, was the simple question: "Would Queen Lush attend the wedding?"

There were at least two schools of thought, and the odds varied with each. One said: "Queen Lush turned down by Prince Drak will never go to his wedding to another woman." The other said: "Queen Lushfymi of

Lome is a great and marvelous woman of considerable powers who would never dream of insulting her hosts in Vallia by refusing to attend the wedding of the Prince Majister."

So, you took your pick and you laid down your golden talens, and you awaited the outcome. I didn't tell Delia; but I placed a small sum on Queen Lush coming to the wedding. Petulant, with a high opinion of herself, overly imperious, she still remained a fine woman through all the flattery and flummery that had gone to her head. Her tragedy was that she hadn't married a good man like Drak long since.

If fate had not thrown the ivory cubes the way they'd fallen, Delia's father would still be emperor, and Queen Lush would be empress. Had he not been killed, would Vallia have been spared the Troubles? No, decidedly not. Vallia had been marked for plunder while her citizens squabbled.

Now—the period of Drak and Silda's wedding turned into a fairy-tale time. The brilliant days moved along like acts in a play, limelit, larger than life, gorgeous with color and action and poetry. Everybody bore a smile. Old enmities were laid aside. Children received presents when it was not their birthday or a Day of Meaning, and they understood that when a Prince Majister of Vallia marries, then the days of the ceremonies are sacred and vitally important to the welfare of the country.

The guest lists filled a thick volume of beautiful Kregish script written out fair for all to see.

Who came? Far better, by Vox, to ask who didn't come!

By lavish use of our best and fastest airboats, with Delia handling a great amount of the detailed planning, folk were brought in from all over those parts of Kregen that had featured in our lives.

For the first time in many many seasons, the whole family was united and under one roof. Incredible!

Drak's twin sister, Lela, flew in with Tyfar. They could not stay long for they were embroiled in a nasty business out on the western borders of Hamal; but I joyed to see my blade comrades again. Delia was radiant with happiness. The nudges and winks, the sly comments; and still, as far as I could see, Prince Tyfar of Hamal, and Lela, Princess Majestrix of Vallia, were still circling each other like strange dogs without an idea in their heads how to resolve their love and follow Drak and Silda in the obvious course.

A particular joy to us was to see King Zeg of Zandikar and his family. They flew in from the Eye of the World, the inner sea of Turismond, and we had long talks into the night about the Krozairs of Zy, and how the Zairians fared against the green Grodnims, all of which I will relate in its proper place. Queen Miam looked more lovely than ever and the children were a joy.

Zeg's twin could not be with us. We thought of her, though, the first Velia. When the second Velia, released for the occasion by the Sisters of the Rose, walked into the private room where we talked, Zeg's face lost all its color. He did not quite sway. But he put a hand to the back of his chair, and I noticed the yellow skulls made by his knuckles.

"It is uncanny," he said.

"No," I said, and damned sharply, too. "Velia was lost to us, and her husband, Gafard, the King's Striker, the Sea Zhantil. And in love Velia was given to us. But this is Velia, and she is her own person and owes no debt to the dead."

This was a highly important point and one I would not have misunderstood.

Didi also was there, daughter to Velia and Gafard. From what I gathered, these two youngsters, Velia and Didi, were right hellions with the Sisters of the Rose, and we could expect mischief and adventures from them in the future.

Jaidur, King of Hyrklana, and Lildra his queen, turned up with their new arrivals. Delia said to me one evening: "I think there may be a rift in the lute there, Dray."

"They fell in love with the speed of a bird through the air. They seemed idyllically happy. If you are right I am most upset—damn it all, by Krun! It can't be true!"

"I hope I am wrong. But be prepared."

It is not all sweetness and light in romance on Kregen, oh no, not by a long chalk.

Then Ros the Claw arrived, clad in black leathers, swinging her whip, rapier and main gauche strapped around her slender waist, her fearsome Claw in its bag. As Delia kissed her and said: "Dayra! Lahal and Lahal, my dear," I itched to find out how Dayra, alias Ros the Claw, had fared and if Jilian was with her, and then Jilian Sweet Tooth walked in, another edition although subtly different from Dayra of those splendid Jikai Vuvushis of the Sisters of the Rose.

There was much news to be learned.*

Finally, I wonder if you can understand my pleasure as I welcomed in

---

* Prescot goes on with the guest list. The only sensible thing for me to do is merely to list the names without disrespect to their importance in Prescot and Delia's lives. Nedfar, Emperor of Hamal. Kytun Kholin Dorn. Ortyg Fellin Coper and his wife Sinkie. Prince Vardon Wanek and his wife Natema and family. Gloag. Hap Loder and an uproarious ferocious band of Clansmen. Pompino the Iarvin— without his wife—and the rascally crew of Cap'n Murkizon, who, I am happy to say, called frequently on his Divine Lady of Belschutz. King Filbarrka and Queen Zenobya, a splendid pair of comrades. Pando and Tilda were invited, and arrived to wonder—but that is another story. There were many friends Drak had made in his own adventures. And the same went for Silda, notably Lon the Knees. Unmok the Nets. Duhrra of the Days. Just about all the nobility of Vallia attended, as was proper. All the people of the household and those close to us. The list was apparently endless. *A.B.A.*

two rascals, who pretended to be quite unimpressed by the glories of Vallia, since they'd seen them all before, and shook their hands in a mutual explosion of glee.

"Stylor!" they crowed, and engulfed me whole.

Yes, my two favorite rascals from the Eye of the World, Nath and Zolta. Ah! What times we had seen together!

Among the greatest joys for Silda in those tumultuous days was to throw her arms about her twin, Valin, and her elder brother, Drayseg. These two had much to relate, all of which I will tell in due course.

Then Lol Polisto turned up with his wife, Thelda, and their family.

Delia was superb.

The confrontation could have been embarrassing and disastrous. Seg had had a few adventures, and, again, what transpired there is grist for another story. Suffice it to say that Seg and Milsi, and Lol and Thelda, acted with natural courtesy and politeness and, indeed, they were four fine people able to come to terms in a civilized manner with what had happened to them.

It is my experience that going through an adventure with another person, risking your life and fighting free of perils, does not automatically make you life-long comrades. It very often does. It is not mandatory.

Now—to the wedding of Silda and Drak.

Well, as you may imagine, my mind flew back to those days in Vondium when Delia and I had been married. The Proud City was vastly changed; many great buildings had been destroyed and not rebuilt. Yet we had continued with our building program, concentrating on structures of use rather than ornament. The circuit of the walls was immensely stronger now. So as Drak and Silda took the prescribed and formal routes through the city on the different days devoted to the various ceremonies, they passed through a city in the process of rebirth.

Just as I had done on that long-ago day, Drak wanted the procession to pass by that certain inn and posting house by the Great Northern Cut called The Rose of Valka. When I had been banished by the Star Lords to Earth for twenty-one miserable years, Drak had grown into manhood and had taken over the reins of the island stromnate of Valka. He had been called the Young Strom. For all my love for him, I couldn't see myself parting with Valka until they shipped me off to the Ice Floes of Sicce.

Since the Times of Troubles there were many vacant estates in Vallia. Drak would be well served in lands and wealth.

The Suns of Scorpio poured down their opaline radiance upon the face of Kregen, and the canals and avenues of Vondium glistened brilliantly in the light. Flags and banners, ribbons and scarves, massive banks of flowers, decorated all the ways. Fountains played. And the people gathered in their thousands to yell their heads off as Drak and Silda passed.

Much treasure had been spent in providing wine and food and palines for the folk. Everyone was happy. As for the presents showered on the bridal couple, they filled room after room in the palace.

What a week that was, when my lad Drak married his sweetheart!*

And not a single sign of the baleful influence of Csitra disturbed the joyous occasion.

What particularly pleased me was to note that among all the throng of friends and comrades, no one jostled for a better position. No one tried to pretend they were more important than anyone else. Among all the people well aware of the pecking order of Kregan nobility, the ranks fell naturally into order. I suppose, being human, among them there were rivalries. But, on this day, everything went off smoothly and without a single hitch.

Toward evening of the last day, after a procession that had wended its gorgeously barbaric way about the canals, everyone of the guests and high nobility, and as many of the citizens of Vondium as could be squeezed in, crowded into the vast Kyro of Opaz Omnipotent, Best and Greatest.

The square in its immensity could hold thousands of people, and its extent had been considerably increased by the destruction of buildings all along one side. The people perched on the rubble looked like flies.

Bands played music and the people sang. Sweet scents invigorated the evening air, and the Moon Blooms drenched everything with their perfume. The whole mass of people were intoxicated on emotion and the splendors of the occasion.

With care I had selected a Stentor Corps, men with expansive lungs and carrying voices, and these were stationed about the Kyro to carry on the words spoken from the dais to the furthest corners.

The priests performed their final rites. Various notables spoke in praise of Drak and Silda. Drak and Silda, themselves, each said a few heartfelt words.

Man and wife, they turned as I called: "Now."

Drak said: "If it is your wish, father."

"It is your mother's wish, also, my son."

Delia said: "Yes, oh, yes! And I shall say so!"

My arm about Delia's waist, my right hand at my side gripping the old Savanti sword, I stepped forward and Delia stepped forward with me.

The radiance of the Suns of Scorpio fell full upon us. We stood looking out across the Kyro of Opaz Omnipotent, and over that immense multitude fell a deep hush.

I raised that superb sword high and the light flashed upon the blade.

I made it short and brutal.

"People of Vallia! Friends! Opaz has willed this joy upon us in the happiness of Prince Drak and Princess Silda." I twisted the sword and the opaline

---

* For a description of Prescot's marriage to Delia, see Dray Prescot #6, *Manhounds of Antares*. A.B.A.

radiance gleamed. "The Empress Delia and I have decided. I have to tell you now that the Empress and I take our farewells of you. We abdicate." Absolute silence in that enormous congregation. I repeated myself. "The Empress Delia and I abdicate and renounce the crown and throne of Vallia."

Delia called across: "I, the Empress Delia of Vallia, abdicate and renounce the crown and throne of Vallia."

The stentors bellowed repetitions of our words over the heads of the throne. The crowd began to stir.

I half turned, still holding Delia, to stare at Drak and Silda.

"On this happy wedding day here stand before you the emperor and empress."

The sword above my head glittered a shaft of light.

"Hai Jikai, Drak, Emperor of Vallia. Hai Jikai, Silda, Empress of Vallia! Hai Jikai!"

Then the tumultuous roars burst full-throated from the crowds.

"Hai Jikai! Drak and Silda, Emperor and Empress of Vallia!"

Nine

Armada against Csitra

I, Dray Prescot, the Lord of Strombor, and Krozair of Zy, was no longer the Emperor of Vallia.

"By Zim-Zair!" I said. "And about time, too!"

"Well, my old dom, you always said you would, yet precious few people believed you."

Thelda chattered on, fussing away: "I can't believe it, Dray, my dear. Why, if I were empress I'd *never* abdicate." Then she put her head on one side and in her funny way added: "But it does mean I am now the mother of the empress. That is *very* nice."

Lol Polisto gave her a look and I noticed Milsi put a hand to her mouth to hide her smile.

After we'd seen the married couple safely off, a few of us had gathered to talk over the events of the day and, inevitably, given the situation, to gape at Delia's and my decision.

The lads of my guard corps were in a quandary.

I said to Targon and Dorgo and Cleitar and the other chiefs: "You are the emperor's bodyguards. You formed yourselves at a time when the emperor's life was in danger. Your duties remain. There is the emperor to serve."

"Yes, but he's not you!"

"He is my son and the emperor."

Just before they took themselves off to sort it out among themselves in the democratic way they'd set up in the guard corps, Targon said very suspiciously: "This doesn't mean we're not going with you to the Coup Blag. Oh, no, we're not having that, by Vox!"

"No, by the Blade of Kurin!" and: "Not likely, as Jorgo of the Snicker-snee is my witness!" and: "We're all going, by Bongolin!" And other similar vehement affirmations.

Balass the Hawk said, "A good sword and shield man, that's what you want down there, Dray."

Oby snapped out: "You're not leaving me behind!"

Hap Loder, who ran the fearsome Clansmen for me out on the Great Plains of Segesthes, wanted to know about this Coup Blag, and expressed his interest in tagging along. Others made inquiries; all seemed to feel a little holiday up there in the Snarly Hills would do wonders for their circulation.

K. Kholin Dora was perfectly convinced that a four-armed Djang would be perfectly at home in the mazes of the hill. Vomanus, Delia's half-brother, having recovered from his illness, said in his lazy reckless way that he was going too. And the feckless fellow *still* had rust spots on his sword.

"By Krun!" I said to Delia. "The wedding has made it worse. Now we're inundated with folk all clamoring to go."

"Aye," she said in her practical, devious way: "And that might be a good thing, too."

Seeing what she meant, I agreed. All the same...!

Farris said: "I have been having a quiet word with Emperor Nedfar. There are genuine troubles which cause this lamentable lapse in the supply of airboats."

I made a face. After only a short stay, Tyfar and Lela had returned to western Hamal. They'd spoken a little of what they were up to out there. Nedfar expressed concern for their safety, and added: "But you cannot muzzle these young people for ever."

"They see their duty as bringing the production of fliers back to normal," said Delia. She spoke bravely; but I could see her concern and suffered with her.

Just because Drak and Silda were safely married and off enjoying themselves did not mean that the rest of us gave up celebrating. No chance of that yet, by Krun!

During this time of a continuous whirl of pleasure, of dances and routs and balls, all in the best traditions of Kregen, we began to assemble forces for the expedition to visit Csitra.

Farris intimated that he could put what was a considerable force of airboats at our disposal. The armed forces of Vallia were being reduced. We had won the wars and re-united all the islands of the empire; now was a time for consolidation on all the other fronts of civilization crying out for attention; agriculture, building, canals, education, trade and commerce of every description. So, with the soldiers and airmen returning home, we could take our pick of fliers, flyers and swods.

In the end I made the sensible decision of taking just about everyone who clamored to go along. Drak had said that he would release from his service in Vallia anyone we asked for.

So I told the lads of the guard corps to work out a system by which half of them went to the Coup Blag and the other half stayed with their duty to the emperor.

Nath Karidge, commanding EDLG, in a pitiable state, came up to me and poured out his woes.

I said, "The fact is, Nath, you command the Empress's Devoted Life Guard. The empress is now Silda."

"I have no desire to affront her, or Seg, or you or Delia. But I feel I must resign."

I nodded. "And you will form a regiment? Devoted to Delia?"

"Aye."

"There is no need to tell you of my feelings, Nath. I thank you. This thing can be arranged with tact and discretion. Just make sure EDLG remains the elite and splendid regiment it has always been."

"There will be no problem with that."

There were many details involved in the handing over of power. Naghan Vanki, the emperor's chief spymaster, waxed surprisingly effusive when I thanked him for his work. He had always been cold and distant. He was devoted to Delia, and he swore to carry on his work for Drak and Silda.

The fleet prepared and the names were chosen. I will not list them all; as they appear in this my narrative so shall you meet them.

The two Wizards and one Witch of Loh—whom I hesitate to call "ours" seeing these sorcerers are their own magical people—worked hard and cunningly on fashioning defenses against Csitra's sorcerous spite. One day they told me that they had perfected devices of power sufficient to deflect a considerable amount of her thaumaturgical wrath.

"Ling-Li and I will be flying with you," said Khe-Hi with a smile at his new wife. "Deb-Lu will cooperate at a distance."

"If we can nullify Csitra's power," confirmed Deb-Lu, "the result will lie in the hands of the folk with you."

"I have every confidence," I said, meaning it.

A great many events took place and numbers of important decisions were taken at this time with which I will not burden you; suffice it to say that life rattled along with not a moment to waste or to spare. And, then, finally, we were off.

The Armada against Csitra took off.

The ships were there, many of whose names you are acquainted with. We had no vorlcas, all were vollers, whose two silver boxes controlled speed and height by maneuvering them in their bronze and balass orbits. Toward the end of life the silver boxes would dull and turn black. Sometimes there was no period of grace whatsoever. Generally speaking, though, the silver boxes lasted through many a season of flying.

Great the cheering when we took off, great the uproar, and great the moaning and lamentations of those left behind. Deb-Lu waved us off, assuring us that Csitra and her uhu child, Phunik, could not observe our departure.

"Remberee!" we called down, and the answering remberees floated up, dwindling and fading as we gained height and set course for Pandahem.

"Well, my old dom, we've done it."

"Aye," I said. "I hope the return is as happy as the departure."

"Cheer up, you hairy old graint," said Delia.

"Yes, Dray," added Milsi. "When this is all over you and Delia are to visit us in Croxdrin."

"I look forward to that," I said. I was thinking of what lay between; had I known—well, I suppose I would still have gone on; but I'd have been in an even worse mood than I was.

Due south from Vondium we flew, across the coast and out over the Sea of Opaz, glinting and glistening in the light of the twin suns. Presently we angled our course south southeastward so as to cross the Pandahem coast on the Bay of Panderk. Straight across Tomboram we flew, cutting sharply east out to sea again to fly around the Central Mountains of Pandahem via the Koroles.

Looking down on those twisted alleys of water between the islands, seeing those lush green mountains rising from the sea, brought back the memories, I can tell you!

Out to our left stretched the Southern Ocean, and as we followed the curve of the coast around through south to southwest we could spy ahead of us the Sea of Chem.

Along that coast I had sailed aboard Pompino's *Tuscurs Maiden*. That splendid argenter had been burned by me. I could not regret the act for it had helped to gain a victory; I looked back without relish. Below us the coastline wended its way as we flew on. Soon we would reach far enough for us to turn north. We'd vetoed the idea of flying up the River of Bloody Jaws. On that river lay Milsi's realms. We did not want to attract attention and alert the bush telegraph, although all below was jungle by now.

The voller in which we sailed, *Pride of Vondium*, was large, splendid, immensely powerful, a skyship of Hamal. Delia said: "Milsi and I have to fly across to *Rose of Valka*. There is a meeting we must attend."

There was plenty of time before nightfall and our change of course. I grumped up, though, and said: "And you need not tell me what your precious meeting is about, wife. You will be back before the suns set?"

"Long before, you aptly named Jak the Sturr!"

When they'd flown off in a small voller, I said to Seg: "You know what that's all about?"

"Aye. Sisters of the Rose. But I own I am glad Milsi has joined. She is changed, yes; but I think for the better. She is lucky Delia—"

"And Delia is fortunate that you found a girl like Milsi." I did not speak of Thelda.

"We'll show you a time in Croxdrin, my old dom." Seg waxed enthusiastic. "Only—don't fall in the river again."

"I can still hear those jaws snapping at my heels."

Seg laughed, throwing that handsome head of his back, his wild black hair rippling in the breeze. His fey blue eyes regarded me with enjoyment. "We had a few wagers, though."

"Aye."

"I'm for a wet."

Down in the cabin with the ale before us, for it was too early for wine, we sat talking of this and that. The lookout's hail reached us, screeching like a broken violin string.

"Sail ho!"

We went up on deck; we did not hurry.

Sweeping in from the sea swarmed a fleet of fliers.

Jiktar Nogad ti Thorndax, the captain of *Pride of Vondium*, a stout experienced Air Service officer, rubbed his chin.

"Don't recognize 'em, jis."

Nobody did. As the approaching airboats swept in toward us we counted them to find they were fifty to our thirty-eight.

The odd thing that struck us was that they appeared all exactly alike. They could all have been stamped from the same pattern.

"Deuced odd," said Vangar ti Valkanium, who had flown with us despite the fact he was slated to take over the Vallian Air Service. "Never seen a fleet with every ship identical before."

And still no quiver of alarm crossed my idiot mind.

Those ships out there were garishly painted and all were of the small-to-middle size of voller, with but two decks. Their upperworks were square, chopped-off, brutal constructions. They didn't go in for fighting tops as did we; but they had fighting galleries below. They came on at a fair speed.

"What of their flags?"

Telescopes were training on those fifty ships. No one volunteered to recognize the flags.

Garishly though those awkward-looking upperworks were painted, the lower hulls were all a uniform black.

Ortyg Thingol, brown curls and bright eyes dancing with excitement, handed me a telescope. Into the circle I centered the lead ship.

So I saw and I knew.

How in the name of Opaz this monstrous thing had occurred I did not know. But I knew what I was looking at, and I knew what must follow.

In a calm, firm voice, I said: "Comrades, we have a fight on our hands. Those devils are Shanks."

Ten

Nath the Impenitent

When I recall that aerial battle I am filled with horror and revulsion, and scathing self-contempt, and also a foolish fatuous pride.

Our thirty-eight had the beating of their fifty, there was no doubt of that.

Supreme though they might be on the seas, the Fish Heads had nothing like our experience in the air. Their ships were very good; most—not all—of ours were better.

We could see the Shanks crowding their upper decks, helmets and tridents arrayed in ranks. Their catapults hurled. They were far more reckless with fire than they were at sea. I saw one black-bottomed ship in the midst of the melee sling a blazing firepot at one of our vessels, and miss, and the missile smashed full into one of their own. She burned.

We lost ships. But for every one of ours lost they lost four. And, it was clear, they did not like the outcome. They were used arrogantly to winning all their sea battles. So now they fought as only Shanks can fight, vicious and deadly and without mercy. Well, and Opaz forgive us, we fought back in the same way.

To interpolate now what I afterwards discovered, as is not my wont in this narrative, I will say that the silver boxes powering the Shank vollers contained a different mix of minerals from those supplied by Hamal and Hyrklana and other nations of Paz. The Shanks used up the power of some of the minerals, and they therefore had to carry spare silver boxes to replace those exhausted. They had, in fact, to operate their power source with a fuel supply backup.

So, as I say, we were doing all right. Seg and I kept shooting anxious glances at *Rose of Valka*. Delia and Milsi were aboard her. She lashed out all around her and saw off her four Shanks. Then, just as we were congratulating ourselves on a smashing victory, one of the Shank vessels, ablaze from stem to stern, flew full tilt into *Pride of Vondium*.

I saw that awful flame-spitting mass hurtling down on us. There was absolutely no time to drag our ship out of the way.

Wearing their aerial safety belts, men and women threw themselves overboard.

Seg hitched his bow up his back and yelled to me: "Overboard with you!"

Pride of Vondium, enveloped in flame, was falling headlong through the air. The flames had burned through some control ropes, and the silver boxes must have been jolted apart. We were dropping at a frightful speed, and the flames and heat blew blisteringly about us.

I saw Ortyg Thingol sprawled on the deck in the line of the advancing flames. Blood smeared his brown curls. Seg yelled again, leaping forward: "I'll grab young Ortyg! Over with you, Dray!"

Flames spouted up from the deck around our feet.

"And leave you!" I jumped forward to assist Seg with our young cadet.

A wall of fire burgeoned directly before me. Beyond that hellish heat Seg and the lad must be trying to fight their way back to the bulwarks. I put my head down and an arm over my face and, thus looking down through slitted eyes, half-blinded, I saw a shiny scorpion clicking his feelers on that flame-reeking deck.

Through the infernal racket of the fire, his voice reached me thinly and clearly.

"We always said you were an onker, Dray Prescot. You must jump and save yourself. The Star Lords wish it."

"To hell with the Star Lords! I'm not leaving Seg—"

"Jump, Dray Prescot, or risk the wrath of the Everoinye!"

Cunning entered my soul.

"You need me, Star Lords. You have said as much. I will not leave without Seg and the boy. If you can—save us all!"

The blueness whirled up so smartly I had no time to gasp. The Everoinye could strike with appalling swiftness when they had to.

I was hanging upside down in the branches of a spiny tree and all about me squeaked and chirruped and screamed the noises of the jungle.

I shook my head and it stayed on my shoulders. With a convulsive twist I was right side up and ready to confront whatever grisly predator of the jungle might regard me as an afternoon snack.

Seg's voice called: "Ortyg's safe, Dray. What happened?"

He might well ask!

Looking carefully around, I spotted Seg on a lower branch of the tree with Ortyg in his arms.

"We must have fallen through the burned deck," I said with some caution.

"Yes. I suppose. It was hot, my old dom, deuced hot. There was a flash of blue—curious."

"Well, we made it safely down. We'll have to try to signal the fleet. They must have won the victory by now."

"Sure to."

"So it's up rather than down?"

"You recall this jungle? Up, I'd say."

"What about the boy?"

Ortyg's high voice rang out. "I'm no boy, majister. I am a full-grown man. I can manage to climb a tree!"

"By the Veiled Froyvil, my old dom, we have a leemcub here!"

So we started to climb up. The trees were stout enough to afford us ample support until we could reach along one of the lower laterals of the crown and so gaze up through a gap at the brilliance of the sky above.

There was not a single airboat in sight.

"This," said Seg, digesting this new information, "alters things somewhat."

"Aye."

A black dot floated into view over the trees.

"Hai!" roared Seg. "Down here!"

The man suspended in air on his belt looked down and then he slowly pulled the control levers apart so that the silver boxes lowered him gently. He would, we saw, land in the next tree along. There was no way he could gain forward motion from the belt.

"So," I said. "It's down, now."

"Aye, my old dom. Down it is."

"Meet us at the tree here!" I bellowed.

The man hollered back: "Quidang!"

"A swod, is my guess," offered Seg. "Anyway, you have a damned intemperate way with you. He recognized—"

"The voice of command? And thank you!"

"Well, it's true, as Erthyr the Bow is my witness."

Clinging to the branch, I said: "Let's have a look at that cut in your head, Ortyg."

"Yes, majister."

I gave him a hard look, and his brown eyes widened. "Not majister, Ortyg. Not majis; not even jis. You call me Jak. Is that clear? Jak!"

"Yes, majis—Jak. Clear."

"And if you forget, Ortyg," said Seg with deep menace, "you will be left here in this jungle alone to fend for yourself."

"Your head's all right," I said. "We'll dress it when we reach the ground."

The climb down was arduous enough, Krun knew; but we touched the mould of the jungle floor at last.

Then we saw to Ortyg's head with the medicaments in our belt pouches. I gave Seg an inquiring look.

"You're known around these parts, King of Croxdrin. Might Seg not be a little, well—"

"I'm not that well known. But I won't be Seg the Horkandur. And—" here he fixed me with a baleful stare. "And not the Fearless, either, or any other of your so-called funny names."

"All right. We'll think of Seg the Something."

"Tell me, please," put in Ortyg, a hand to his head. "Why are you not to be called majister, Jak?"

"Because there are plenty of evil folk around only too ready to take advantage of ransom."

Seg bore down on the lad. "That's why. We are simple koters, us."

"Very well, Seg, Jak."

A man's hoarse voice reached us. "That you, doms?"

"Hai, dom. Over here."

He joined us as we stepped away from the twined bole of our tree. His uniform was a shredded black mess, his hair was singed, his face was a scarlet blot. But that hair was good Vallian brown, and those ferocious eyes were level and Vallian brown. He looked to be an old kampeon, tough as old boots, in service for seasons.

Smoothly, Seg said, "Lahal. I am Seg, this is Jak and this is Ortyg. We are lucky to be alive."

"Lahal. I am Nath."

There are very many Naths on Kregen, seeing that the legendary Nath equates with the terrestrial Hercules, more or less. I sighed, and this Nath, seeing that reaction, managed a ferocious grimace and said, "Nath, called the Impenitent."

"Nobody else?" inquired Seg.

"Not that I saw. A chunk of rock from one of those fishy devils knocked me off *Shango Lady*. They were all going off to the west like stink when I fell."

"Did you see the flagship burn?"

"Aye, a grisly sight. Some ships dropped down for survivors. But that happened a long time ago."

"Do what?"

He was not taken aback. "Aye. We drove to the west in pursuit of the devils, west and north. *Pride of Vondium* burned a long ways back."

Seg would not understand how we'd contrived to get here, that seemed certain. The Everoinye, for their own inscrutable purposes, had dropped us down a long way from where we'd begun, and this Nath the Intemperate had been knocked off by chance to join our little band.

All about us lay the jungle of South Pandahem.

The rank stink of rotting vegetation, throat-choking, filled the miasmic air. The light was poor. Blotched whitenesses disfigured the tree boles. Vines looped everywhere. And through this labyrinth prowled the predators.

Nath the Intemperate retained his sword, a drexer. Ortyg had a Vallian dagger. Seg's longbow was not in his hand, although a quiver half-filled with rose-fletched arrows remained strapped across his back. Well, he'd built a bow before in these parts.

Seg also had a drexer. I—stupidly, stupidly—did not have my superb Savanti sword. I had no bow, no drexer, no rapier or main gauche. I had my old sailor knife scabbarded over my right hip. And I did have a Krozair longsword strapped to my back, and that was not stupid at all. Not stupid at all, by Zair!

The drexer is a superior weapon, a straight cut and thruster developed from the Hamalian thraxter and Vallian clanxer and with our attempt at the Savanti sword. I wished I had the sword I'd worn at Drak and Silda's wedding.

"We'd best make tracks," said Seg. "Find a clearing or some civilization."

"I hear it's all jungle for hundreds of ulms," said Nath the Impenitent. "Little villages, though, I suppose?"

"Some not so little. We'll have to go tsleetha-tsleethi for some time."

"And," said Seg with sincere seriousness, "beware traps."

Now I have made it sound as though we'd all tumbled down out of a battle into a jungle and were all taking it as a mere matter of course. This is not so. But there was no good making a song and dance over the dangers. Our main concern, Seg and mine, was what had happened to Milsi and Delia.

We had to deal with the current situation, get clear of that, and then we'd find out.

Walking along softly and cautiously we heard from up ahead the sound of people talking, and then the cheerful clink of bottles and glasses. Ortyg started forward.

"We are saved, praise be to Opaz!"

"Hold it, young 'un," and Seg's broad hand fastened on Ortyg's shoulder. "I told you. Beware traps."

We parted the leaves carefully and looked out into a clearing at the center of which stood a plant with a bulbous stem and waving tendrils.

"A Cabaret Plant," said Seg. "That'll spine you and gulp you down like a jelly."

We bypassed the plant with great respect.

After that, Ortyg stuck close to Seg. I was glad. I'd seen the way Seg had welcomed his two sons, Drayseg and Valin. He had not seen them for season upon season. Emotions aroused anew in him then must be working to make Ortyg recognize the affection Seg was bursting to display.

The Cabaret Plant with its deadly orange flower on that lashing stalk was not the only danger. There were man-made traps to catch some of the more tasty animals living here. We struck a trail. Well, now...

"Thank Opaz," said Ortyg. "At least we can walk a little easier now."

"You, my lad," Seg told him, "will not be walking along that trail—unless you want to wind up down a pit with stakes stuck through you, or hanging upside down in the air, or—"

"Quite," I said, and Seg laughed and punched Ortyg lightly on the shoulder. Nath the Impenitent said nothing, but his ruby-red face squeezed into a smile.

Later on he told us that he'd been in the army but, being bored out of his skull and the wars more or less finishing, he'd transferred to the Air Service. He was an ordinary voswod, an aerial soldier; but he was training to become a more proficient crewman. He saw a future in the air he had never expected, had given up as lost.

"Wonderful things, the airboats. Never thought I'd live to see the day I served in one."

Seg said sharply: "You were unconscious in the back of a cart. But I've a funny feeling we've been this way before."

"If you say so," I said equably.

"By the Veiled Froyvil, my old dom! I do say so. And I'll wager a month's pay that just ahead of us lies the town of Selsmot. And, therein, the tavern of jungle delights, The Dragon's Roost!"

Eleven

Of two kovs at The Dragon's Roost

"So you did come back," said Mistress Tlima, wiping her floury hands on her blue-striped apron. "I always said you would return, Dray the Bogandur—although you call yourself Jak now."

"If it please you, Mistress Tlima. It was Jak Dray, anyway."

"Oh, it is no concern of mine."

"Named for that pig of an emperor, I suppose," said Nath the Impenitent. I turned sharply. He spoke quite mildly; yet there was no mistaking the heartfelt anger in his words.

"Pantor Seg," called Tlima, taking no notice of Nath's outburst. "Help yourself to some of our local ale. We have palines just collected."

Seg smiled that winning smile of his. "As ever, you are kind to wandering travelers, Mistress Tlima. And here is this imp Ortyg to plague us further."

"You will not, I trust, pantor, take him when you go along to The Dragon's Roost."

"He is no callow coy; he is a man with a man's spirit."

Ortyg, very sensibly, remained silent, although I admit this was partially caused by a mouthful of palines.

While all this pleasant byplay went on, I found myself brooding savagely on the greatest fresh problem presented to us in Paz. We had airboats. We had always believed we held this advantage, a kind of ace in the hole. And now—the Shanks—or Shtarkins or Shants or any one of a hundred different names for the evil Fish Heads who came reiving from over the curve of the world—also flew airboats to our mighty discomfort.

I thought to myself, stranded there in an insignificant little town lost in the jungles of South Pandahem, I thought most violently that I needed a word with the Star Lords.

That they would send for me in their own sweet time I did not doubt. By Vox! They had a deal of explaining to do.

Once again the question of priorities forced itself on me. Csitra must be dealt with. There was no question about that. The Shanks must also be dealt with, and, equally, there was no doubt about that. What the blue blazing hell were Shanks doing flying over Pandahem when all my intelligence said they were miles and miles away over in Mehzta?

The only obvious explanation was that this was a new and different bunch of the Fish Heads.

Mistress Tlima said, "We saw a boat that flew through the air yesterday. It came down just outside the town. The people in it—just ordinary diffs, mind—went to The Dragon's Roost."

"Ah!"

"Why, Pantor Seg! And do you really mean to go again?"

"I do, Mistress Tlima."

"Well, may the good Pandrite watch over you, that is all I can say."

From The Dragon's Roost inn, expeditions had been formed to go up into the Snarly Hills to the Coup Blag in search of the rumored hoards of treasure buried there. Seg and I had traveled with just such an exploration party. Now it seemed another was forming, and this bunch had their own voller. Capital!

"If they take us," said Seg, as we walked through the dusty main street just before the rain fell.

"Oh," I said, sounding mighty cheerful, almost cocky in my stupid arrogance. "Oh, yes, they will. We've been there before."

"True, my old dom, true."

"I'm coming, too," said Ortyg.

"Oh?"

"Certainly, Jak. Without a doubt."

"If I'd had you to train up," said Nath the Impenitent, "you'd have been a Hikdar in no time, and a kampeon to boot."

Once again Mistress Tlima had furnished us with the simple clothes of these people to replace our own burned and ruined garments. We had paid her, and this time in Vallian gold. She had made no comment. We approached that famous stoop leading up to The Dragon's Roost.

"Leave," I told the other two, "the talking to Seg."

"Aye, Jak," and: "Aye, Jak."

"Remember, we are not from Vallia. Oh, we hail from North Pandahem. They don't much care for those folk down here; but they don't hate them as much as they do Vallians or Hamalese."

"It's all Pandrite here, remember. And Armipand if you want to throw a curse at someone." Seg sniffed and said: "Squish pie."

"Excellent. Now if—"

"But he isn't, and we are, and here is the inn."

So into The Dragon's Roost we trooped.

At the far end of the wooden stoop, bowered in greenery against the heat of the suns and the hiss of the rains, loud voices raised in argument. Two men, big and burly, stood there slanging each other rotten.

"By Krun!" in a high nasal whine. "You call yourself a lord! You're nothing better than a clodhopper with his nose forever in the mud."

"You are a kov," came the answer in thick and impassioned tones that cut through like whetted steel. "And I, too, am a kov. That you are from Hamal causes me wonder."

"Wonder, clod-hopper? Wonder that a noble of so great a nation should set foot upon this stinking island?"

"No, Kov Hurngal ham Hortang. Wonder that my rapier has not already sought your backbone through your guts."

"You presume too much." The nasal whine thickened. "I shall have to teach you a lesson, you Pandaheem yetch."

We stood quietly, waiting and watching. If these two idiots slew each other, what did that matter to us?

I'd be interested to see how this Hamalese kov, named Hurngal ham Hortang, acquitted himself against Kov Loriman the Hunter.

For, that was who it was, standing bulky and impassioned, wrangling with a hated noble from Hamal.

Their right hands crossed their bodies, swathed only in light clothing for the weather, and fastened on rapier hilts. Their left hands gripped the hilts of their main gauches. If Kov Loriman was killed, should I bother? He had been one of the leading lights of our trip down into the horrors of the Moder in the Humped Land where we had found monsters and magic, and some fabulous treasures that evaporated in the clear light of day. His passion was hunting. He sought out locations where he might test himself and his swordarm against monsters. That, I thought then, was why he was here about to go up against the terrors of the Coup Blag. I was wrong.

I wondered with little interest if he would recognize me, let alone remember me. What did I care? He was here, so therefore why should not I be also? I could brazen out a story.

A rich, silken-smooth golden voice called: "Why, notors! I do declare you quarrel just to spite me."

The woman stepped lithely and with a voluptuous swing of her hips out onto the stoop. She was clad in a sheer gown of sliding green silk, clinging to her body, and her form was amply rewarding to anyone with an eye for plastic female beauty. Her face remained in shadow. Her hair sheened, caught up in a net of pearls.

She addressed these two nobles as notor, the term for noble in Hamal and Havilfar. Here in Pandahem the word was pantor, as in Vallia it is jen. I watched fascinated as she set her arts of coquetry to chasten these two blowhards.

Kov Loriman did not put her down as I had seen him insultingly dismiss another fine lady. He turned and bowed.

"My Lady Hebe. I maintain my honor—"

"Of course, and I admire you so much for it, notor. But, then, so does Kov Hurngal, does he not?"

"What does he know of—"

She stepped to Loriman's side and put her hand, surprisingly brown in so fine a lady, upon his arm.

"Now, now, kov! This quarrel is over a nothing, and does credit to— well—" and here she laughed that throaty delicious laugh. "Credit to what, I ask you?"

Simmering like a volcano about to blow, Loriman glared upon the Hamalese. For his part, Hurngal glared malevolently upon Loriman. I admired the way this Lady Hebe handled the situation, for very soon she had both of them eating out of her hand. Whatever the cause of this quarrel, though, I fancied the animosity in these two ran so deep that it would not be slaked until they fought the duel they both so manifestly craved.

Well, it was no business of mine. Seg stepped up.

"Llahal, pantors!" he cried in his open cheery way. "Llahal, my lady."

They swung about as though one of Csitra's plagues had stung them up their rears.

"Who the hell are you?" demanded Kov Hurngal. "We have a private party here."

"I am glad to hear it," said Seg in that soft way which could send shivers down the backs of those who knew him. "We have come to guide you to the Coup Blag."

Well, after that it was a matter of the Llahals and then the Lahals, and we were invited in and so we sat down in that corner alcove window seat with the polished sturmwood tables loaded with jugs and flagons. We ignored all the insults. Loriman did not recognize me. We explained that we had been to the Coup Blag and wished to return to bring away more treasure.

"Gambling, you see," said Seg, "is a vice."

They guffawed at this and relaxed and were agog to hear all we could tell them. We attenuated the true story. I fancied if they knew it all they'd think on about going and then turn tail and run as far and as fast from this place as they could.

The voller, inevitably, belonged to Kov Hurngal.

He had ridden roughshod over the locals' detestation of Hamalese, and had distributed much gold, so that he was tolerated.

That toleration might end with a knife between his ribs if the balance of the party did not soon arrive so that we might depart.

He and Loriman treated us with the casual, unthinking near-contempt of one kind of noble. We were pantors, and vouched for by the people of the town; we were not in their class and therefore were of value only as tools.

That we had been accepted as nobles was perfectly understandable to young Ortyg Thingol. Nath the Impenitent merely assumed we were a couple of young lords with the Vallian expedition. He appeared completely adjusted to his position in the situation. I summed him up as a doughty fighting man, one of Vallia's finest. More than once I had to nudge him to halt the habitual: "By Vox!"

"By Pandrite," I said. And then, out of deviltry, I added: "Or 'By Chusto!' or, even, 'By Chozputz.' Brave oaths, both."

These were oaths I had invented when Dayra, Ros the Claw, and I had adventured together with Pompino in North Pandahem.

"Very well, Jak. Outlandish place, this."

"Aye. It'll get more outlandish."

Trying how the new oaths rolled on his tongue, Nath the Impenitent burped out: "By Chusto, Jak! I look forward to it to enliven the tedium of the days."

Any expedition of delvers exploring ancient ruins where they suspect treasure is buried, any expedition with plain common sense, come to that, must include in its company some form of wizard or witch. That goes without saying.

Seg and I decided that we four should stay at Mistress Tlima's rather than The Dragon's Roost. This we felt would ease friction. Mistress Tlima's husband, a quiet, obliging man, was far better company than the bunch at the grander inn.

Seg was creating merry hell that there was not a decent longbow in the town. He bought a short bow and looked at it with his mobile lips twisted up, so that I had to smile.

"The thing is, Seg, we know that Csitra took over Spikatur Hunting

Sword." SHS had been a mysterious organization dedicated to the destruction of Hamal. Well, all that was over; but now the adherents of Spikatur simply assassinated anybody who took their fancy, or so it seemed, and burned property that did not please them. Csitra had assumed control of the SHS and was using it for her own dark ends.

"My guess," said Seg, "is that Spikatur has served its purpose for the witch."

"I tend to agree."

Now I'd regaled my comrades with tales of the Moder when we'd spend roistering evenings in that wonderful fortress palace I called home, Esser Rarioch in Valka. They'd listened fascinated to Deb-Lu and my scary adventures down the Moder of the Moder-lord Ungovich. The Humped Land, Moderdrin, the Land of the Fifth Note, lay far away in the center of Havilfar.

"So," I said. "Is Loriman here solely for that hunting? He was of Spikatur. There is no doubt of that."

Seg gave me a look as he went on carefully polishing up that little bow.

"You mean, is Loriman a tool of the witch's?"

"Aye."

"Instead of coming here as a member of Spikatur Hunting Sword?"

"Aye."

"Either way a shaft in his guts might solve the problem."

"He's a useful man in a tight corner. I think I'll test him out and gauge his reaction."

Soon after that, having brought in supplies and prepared ourselves as best we could, and with the rest of the expedition joining, we all observed the fantamyrrh as we stepped into Kov Hurngal's voller. Up from that small speck of civilization in the wilderness of the jungle we flew, slanting up into the mingled streaming lights of the Suns of Scorpio.

With the speed lever hard over we pelted full speed ahead for the Coup Blag.

Twelve

Over the Snarly Hills

Over the Snarly Hills we flew swift and straight as a lance stroke.

Below us the rain forest and the jungle reeled past. Those frightful hills up which we had toiled and then struggled down only to clamber up again, passed like models in a child's playroom. High above those clearings we soared where the pools of water, oily with poison, reflected light in a queasy way. The last pool in its clearing also carried that betraying sheen of evil. The Slaptra, the plant that struck lethally at sound, flattening the ground around the pool and gouging deep spadelike depressions in the mud—the Slaptra was gone.

"Someone's been doing a spot of gardening," observed Seg.

Before I could reply, San Aramplo said in his haughty Khibil way: "There is evil in the water. I sense it most clearly."

"The poison killed the plants growing in the water. They were Slaptras."

"Of course. A sensible arrangement."

When Seg and I had discovered that the sorcerer going with us was a Khibil, Seg had given me such a comical look of despair I'd almost burst out laughing. A sorcerer is always high and mighty. Any Khibil regards him—or her—self as a member of the most superior race in all of Kregen, noses in the air, all hoity-toity, Khibils. Their fox-featured faces, with those arrogant reddish whiskers, their sharp eyes, their cutting ways, were very familiar to me.

This wizard, San Aramplo, was a member of the Thaumaturges of Thagramond. They were a small cult, widely spread, and reputed, as so many of Kregen's varied assortment of sorcerers are, to wield real and supernatural powers. They were not, of course, in the same class as any Wizard of Loh.

This foxy-faced Khibil mage had sensed the poison in the water, and the evil of it, as Fregeff, the Fristle wizard, had done before him. So San Aramplo had some genuine powers.

We all just hoped he would be able to handle the magics of the maze we were about to penetrate.

When he went into the purple-curtained opening to his private cabin, Nath the Impenitent gave a rolling wriggle to his heavy shoulders, and said, "Sorcerers. Never could abide 'em."

"Ah, but," piped up Ortyg Thingol, "they are not all the same. San Bjanching was very helpful when I couldn't understand my mathematics lessons."

This was news to me, and I listened with lively interest. It seemed Khe-Hi was helping out in the education of the youngsters training up. Very good!

"They're all too big for their boots," said Nath. "Sorcerers, nobles, lords and ladies. They don't have time for us common folk."

Ortyg yelped: "Oh, come on, Nath! It's not as bad as that!"

"I've seen life, my lad."

There was little Ortyg could say to that, except a lame reply that, well, and, by Vox, he was going to see life too!

"By the Veiled Froyvil, Nath! You may not like the fellow; but he is going to be invaluable to us, believe you me."

No one commented that, if Seg and I were pantors down here in Pandahem, and as we were Vallians, then we were jens in Vallia. That put us in the bad graces of Nath the Impenitent; yet he treated us with unfailing courtesy, and we imagined he recognized in Seg and me fellow kampeons, fellow adventurers in the face of this life he so detested.

We flew at a moderate height and despite the wind of our passage we could smell the raw rank stink of the jungle below.

This voller of Kov Hurngal's flew well enough, and we suspected she'd been fitted with brand new silver boxes for the expedition. Her name was *Hanitcha Triumph*. She was capacious enough to take upward of a hundred souls as passengers, and was reasonably well-provided with varters and catapults. She had but the one fighting top and her lower fighting galleries were on the narrow side. Still, painted bright blue and green, with a quantity of gimcrack work and gilding, she looked pretty enough. She was, without the shadow of a doubt, far far better than marching through the Snarly Hills, by Krun!

Vainly, as we bore on, I kept a lookout for other fliers in the air, hoping to see some of our Vallian comrades continuing our interrupted expedition.

The idea of actually flying right up to the Coup Blag and landing before that fantastically sculptured cliff face and then marching in, somehow did not seem smart to me.

"We ought," I said to Seg, "to land a little way off and march the rest."

"Aye. You're right."

From the cabin opening hung with golden drapes stepped the Lady Hebe. She appeared to affect a net of pearls for her hair at all times. Her gown was of blue, shorter, and girded with a broad golden belt. Her sandals were marvels of nothingness. As for her face, well, she had widely spaced eyes, dark under level brows. Her forehead was broad and tinged with that darker tone I had noticed in her hands. Her nose was short and her mouth full. She was a lady who knew her own mind, strong-willed, and quite able, as we had observed, to stoop to coquetry to gain her ends. She was a vadni, so in the pecking order of nobility she was one rung below a kovneva. And she was proud, no doubt of that. Also, I thought she was sad.

A man stepped up to greet her, smiling, smirking rather, bowing fulsomely. Some folk on Kregen will tell you a Rapa cannot smile. Well, they have predatory beaked faces, vulturine features, and their feathers come in a bewildering variety of colors—although beware those of the darker hues!—and so one has to read the expressions from experience and this fellow's beak clearly smirked.

"Tyr Rogarsh," said the Lady Hebe.

They walked off together. The Rapa, this Tyr Rogarsh the Rattler, wore solid leather harness such as would be worn by a flutswod, with a brace of swords and brilliant feathers matching his own whiffling in his helmet. At his throat the wink of gold gleamed and scintillated and told the whole damn world who and what he was.

"He's useful," said Seg. "I gather as a mercenary he was employed by Hamal, rose to be Chuktar, did well in a number of scraps—until he ran into our lads from Vallia."

Ortyg laughed with delight. Nath remained mute.

"So now he's tazll, unemployed, and so seeks to continue his expensive habits by plundering tombs."

"That's what they appear to believe the Coup Blag is. Just a burial mound with lashings of treasure within."

"And the bandits who used to infest the place?"

"Long gone and it's the ancient tombs story now."

"Something doesn't add up here." I cocked an eye over Seg's shoulder. "And here's the last member of the expedition, Strom Tothor ham Hemfar. He, I judge, looks even more useful."

The numim roared out a rollicking "Lahal!" and strode up, a glorious golden lion-man, big, lithe, rolling with muscle. His ferocious face beamed upon us. He wore plain leather harness, and the weapons he carried were strictly no-nonsense practical man-slayers, none of your fancy jeweled pinkers here, by Krun!

We returned the Lahal, and Strom Tothor bellowed out his good humor.

"Have you seen that rascal Rogarsh, notors?"

"He has just gone for a tour around the deck with the Lady Hebe, notor."

"Ha! Well, I owe him a beating at Jikaida. His Pallan destroyed mine, and I want the return, and this time I shall surely crush him into the board, by Numi-Hyrjiv the Golden Splendor!"

You couldn't help warming to the lion-man. A splendid race of diffs, numims, and I counted at least one as a blade comrade. I dearly wanted to ask this Tothor if he knew Rees ham Harshur, the Trylon of the Golden Wind, lands that had now, alas, almost all blown away. Well, I'd try to elicit the information when the moment seemed opportune.

"You play at Jikaida, notors?"

"Occasionally," said Seg, for Jikaida as the premier board game of Paz in Kregen is universal. Unless the game was completely beyond your mental capacities, you played Jikaida. For those who did not, Vajikry, the Game of the Moons, were small beer as compensation.

"The Lady Hebe is a cunning player," went on Tothor. "You have to watch her left flank Chuktar."

I knew the ploy; but I didn't want to give anything away at this stage. We were simple block-headed lords out for adventure and fun. I said, "It would be best if we did not land too close to the Coup Blag. We must march the last dwabur or two."

"You think so? I will be guided by you in this. I'll speak to Kov Hurngal. He is, after all, in command of the expedition."

From what we had been able to make out, Kov Hurngal had been fired up by the Lady Hebe to go to the Coup Blag. She thirsted after adventure, and, with it, gold. Now the wars were over, apart from the disturbances over on the Mountains of the West, which few people seemed to take seriously, to hear them talk, there were thousands of soldiers and mercenaries out of a job. The Rapa Rogarsh and the numim Tothor had been recruited as stout companions in the venture, for they had served aforetime with Hurngal.

All these principals had with them, very naturally, a cloud of retainers, of servants and slaves. A little army was due to venture into the maze.

Kov Loriman had with him his group of tough Chuliks. I wanted to know how he had become involved with Hurngal and Hebe.

There was no love lost between the two kovs. Maybe the lady was the cause?

Where she hailed from had not been vouchsafed us yet. But if Hurngal, Rogarsh, and Tothor were Hamalese, then she might well also be. Loriman now said he came from western Pandahem, from the land of Yumapan, directly south over the mountains from Queen Lush's Lome.

One item we picked up displeased me. For all the new understanding and alliance between Vallia and Hamal, the Hamalese aboard *Hanitcha Triumph* still retained their enmity toward Vallians. Loriman usually evaded the subject. As for the sorcerer, he remained aloof from us all.

Seg and I had passed on a warning to Hurngal anent the saddle flyers we had encountered hereabouts. They were brunnelleys, with four scarlet clawed feet, their feathers in blue and brown and mauve. They were a good solid reliable saddle bird, and fetched their due price in the flutmarkets.

"Saddle birds?" Hurngal said dismissively. "In Pandahem?"

"Aye," Seg told him, keeping his temper.

"Well, we know how to deal with them in Hamal."

So, as well as scouring the sky for traces of our comrades, we also kept a smart lookout for hostile flyers.

Shortly after that I began to think it would behoove us to descend. Ahead over the eternal tops of the trees rose a rounded hill. Below that would be the carved rock face, and the pool, and the entrance.

I spotted Kov Loriman leaning against the bulwark entirely alone. Some of the crew were keeping themselves busy fussing over a varter, others were scrubbing out, so I said to Seg, "Hold on. I'll test him with the oath of Spikatur. See how he reacts."

"Aye, my old dom. I'll keep an eye on you."

Moving casually I walked up the deck toward Loriman. Now the Hunting Kov might allow slaves to wash him and dress him and even feed him; in the matter of weapons he was a different personality. He had a whetstone out and was methodically sharpening up his left-hand dagger.

"Lahal, notor," I said pleasantly. I may add that I found speaking pleasantly easy enough at the moment. "We will have to land soon. By Sasco, I'll—"

With blurring speed the dagger switched up and a single spark of fire blinded from the blade before the point pressed against my throat.

"You yetch! A nulsh of Spikatur Hunting Sword! I'll slit your throat across from ear to ear!"

Thirteen

Loriman the Hunter listens to me

In that fraught moment I knew there'd be no hesitation in my blade comrade, Seg Segutorio. Not a single whisker of hesitation, by the Veiled Froyvil, no!

With a desperate twist and jerk and a cunning arm lock, I managed to swivel Loriman around sideways.

The cruelly barbed arrow from Seg's bow went *thwunk!* most evilly into the wooden bulwark.

"Hold on, Seg!" I yelled. "The idiot has it all wrong!"

By this time, I may say, Loriman's dagger was in my fist and he was inspecting the point with apoplectic eyes that wanted to cross.

"You rast!" he managed to choke out. "I'll have you jikaidered and then your tripes drawn and your—"

"Quiet down, Loriman." I held him in a Krozair grip on his neck so that he could barely move and speaking cost him an effort. "Are you telling me you no longer belong to or support Spikatur Hunting Sword?"

"You are a dead man—"

"Oh, for the sweet sake of the Lady Dulshini's leprous knees! Listen, you fambly. I fought SHS for many seasons. If you are truly against them now, then we are allies."

He tried to shake his head and that was a mistake, for his face twisted in the stab of pain. "I gave my life to Spikatur. And I was betrayed—"

"So," I rapped out, casting a shaft not entirely at random, "you go to the Coup Blag, which was infested with the rasts of Spikatur, to exact revenge."

"Aye, by the smoking blood of San and Pandiflur himself!"

"I am heartily glad to hear it. You have my admiration for seeing the light and attempting to expiate your guilt."

He gobbled at this, whereat I gave him a smile so that he flinched back. "I shall release you now. Remember, far from my being a dead man, you are if you do not stand quietly and talk in a civilized way."

When I let him go he stumbled and rubbed his neck. But he recovered with leem-speed. His right hand hovered over his rapier hilt. Then his eyes swiveled to the arrow in the bulwark.

"Look, kov," I said with ostentatious patience. "If you stand against Spikatur, then you are my ally."

Abruptly, his look became hard to fathom.

"All right," I rattled on in my old harsh way. "You want to kill me now. Well, you won't. I may slay you if you annoy me."

Just then a voice hailed down from the deck above the cabin roof.

"Notor? Is all well?"

The Rapa Rogarsh leaned over, feathers bristling.

"Tell him all is well, kov. For I assure you, it is. Otherwise, of course—"

The Hunting Kov shouted up in somewhat of a croak: "All is well, you great fambly!"

"Quidang, notor."

I shouted up: "Tell Hurngal it is time we landed."

By this time it was quite clear my face held that old hateful expression people call the Dray Prescot Look of the Devil. Loriman was sweating. About then he started to realize I was not someone he might trifle with.

I spoke up to take advantage of the moment.

"Look, Loriman, I bear you no ill will." Well, that was not entirely true; but since his change of allegiance from Spikatur Hunting Sword I fancied something might be made of him. "I must tell you this fast. I've no idea what these other famblys think they're getting into in the Coup Blag. I've been in there, and so has my comrade. We got out more dead than alive, and we were lucky to get out at all." He tried to say something, and I carried on natheless. "Shut up and listen! There's a damned Witch in there I'll hazard is a sight more powerful than our Khibil mage. It's going to be tough." I'd summed up this Hunting Kov down the Moder. He was a man consumed with self-estimation, true; he was also damned useful in a fight against just the sort of monsters and powers we were going up against. If he were presented with a challenge, he'd accept it. I was, in street parlance, handing him a dare.

I finished up. "You'll be putting your life on the line, Loriman."

He sucked in air and his chest swelled; but I did not think there was conscious braggadocio in that, he wanted to get some fresh air into his lungs.

"You do not," he said in a voice as grating as crocodiles on gravel, "address me as you should. You call me notor."

"I'll call you an onker if you shilly-shally about now, you great—great onker of a kov! Don't you understand what I'm telling you?"

He shook his head and it occurred to me he was suddenly out of his depth and—perhaps for the first time for a long time—unsure of himself...

He had to get it through his thick vosk skull of a head. I tried a different tack. "I'm a reasonable sort of fellow, Kov Loriman. I detest violence. I do not go in for hunting anything that moves. But if that pleases you, then so be it. You'll find targets in the maze."

He said in a dulled kind of voice, like leaden balls falling on a leaded slate roof: "I think I have seen you before."

I betrayed not a flicker of interest. After all, it didn't really matter if he did recall that I'd been along when we were down the Moder; but, as you know, I find a juvenile kind of amusement in disguises, and false names, and hiding my light under a bushel.

So, not recking what else might come of my words, I said: "Perhaps in the Sacred Quarter of Ruathytu? It is of no consequence. To defeat Spikatur we have to stick together. I am willing. Are you?"

He knew what I meant, right enough.

"I should have you killed on the spot. It is odd that I do not call at once for my guards."

"Your Chulik bully boys?" I smiled. "Your guards can try. Hanitcha the Harrower is like to carry them off."

"I believe—" he started to say and then Rogarsh yelled: "Kov Hurngal intends to land right outside the rock!"

"The stupid, stiff-necked cramph!" I burst out. Then I hauled myself up. I pondered. I felt quite certain Csitra would know we were coming, although, from what Deb-Lu had told me, she would not know I was along. So we just landed and got out and went into the entrance. That would make little difference.

Loriman must have realized I had thought the matter over when I said, in a different voice: "Very well. It is all one." For he did not make a scathing remark about my weathercock decisions.

So, as we flew on to land outside the front door to Csitra's maze, Loriman, rubbing neck, and I, exchanged a few more pleasantries. I was not fool enough to think he would not seek revenge for the slight to his honor. So I was able to feel pleasure when he spoke out forcibly.

"You are the man known as Jak the Horkandur. Very well, Jak the Horkandur. I warn you. We may be allies in what lies ahead; but when it is over, you shall answer to me in the matter of honor."

470

"Done," I said.

Then he said, "You are a fool of so reckless a rashness, I wonder..."

What he wondered I did not inquire. I spoke pleasantly, again, quoting from the bard Larghos the Lame, dead these five hundred seasons. Loriman scowled and then, amazingly, his heavy, bristly features broke into what I assumed was a smile.

"I shall enjoy venturing with you. And even more what will follow."

"If you get out alive." I nodded at the Khibil sorcerer who came out onto the deck and stood poised by the rail staring down and forward. "He will have to earn his hire."

In what the Hunting Kov said then, I heaved up a sigh of relief. He had accepted me, and with me Seg and Ortyg and Nath, as allies in the ordeals ahead. He spoke without condescension, seriously, discussing our prospects and our resources.

Of the Khibil, he said, "He came to me highly recommended. He has worked miracles in Hamal. His power is great. Also he has a ring which protects him."

"Two items, kov. One, I put no store by rings of protection, or anything else, come to that. Two, I suspect you are the real leader of this expedition and not that blowhard Hurngal."

"Oh, I believe in rings of power. But, yes, this expedition occurred as a result of my work."

The voller slanted down. The suns were declining and their light mingled in a sheening opaline haze. Below us the lake stretched, brown and placid, with the waterfowl quarrelling on the sand spit.

"There are Spiny Ribcrushers growing there. You'll smell 'em. Steer well clear of *them*."

"Tell me of this maze."

We leveled out and alighted soft as a feather. I told Loriman something of Csitra's evil handiwork, and felt amusement when he said, "It sounds like a commonplace copy of a Moder. Now, there, Jak, is a maze to destroy the stoutest hearts."

"It's bad enough. The witch is called Csitra. She has a child, a hermaphrodite called Phunik."

"Phunik? I have heard whispers that the Hyr Notor who commanded in Pandahem and was beaten in Vallia and destroyed in Ruathytu was named Phu-Si-Yantong."

I confess, when I heard that name I felt a ticklish old thump of the heart.

"The father of the uhu Phunik."

"Then I owe him death, swift and merciless."

"Excellent!"

Then Loriman said something that revealed more of his character.

"When we are with the Lady Hebe, you will speak to me properly, with propriety. If you do not, our compact is broken and I shall kill you instantly."

I said, "I am never rude to ladies unless they deserve it."

Loriman put a hand to his mouth. "I must say, despite all, I am beginning to feel regret that when this is all over, you must die."

"Oh, we'll see, we'll see."

Seg called across: "We're landing, Jak."

"Aye. The Hunting Kov here and we are allies."

"You say sooth? Well, one must sleep in whatever bed one can find. I'm kitting up."

Loriman stared as Seg strolled off.

"Another one like you, is he?"

"Oh, no." I felt pleasure as I spoke. "Seg is far worse than I am, believe you me!"

His mouth opened and then shut with a clack. After a space, he said: "I have things to do before we venture inside."

"And I, too. I will see you there, then."

He had a mass of heavily armored guards, and slaves, and retainers, and porters, to organize. I had only to strap on my harness, sling a sack of supplies over my shoulder, and I was ready, weapons to hand.

I said to Ortyg Thingol: "You're not coming into that damned place, young Ortyg."

"Why ever not?" Since he'd been calling me Jak, the rascal had fallen away in his language. I didn't mind.

"Because I say so. And you, Nath the Impenitent, are excused the duty if you wish it."

"Oh," said Nath in his abrupt and not quite surly way: "I'm going. There's gold. I need gold."

He would be valuable. I explained a little of what we might expect, enlarging on what Seg and I had already related to him, and he did not change his mind.

So, in a great straggling mob, we all walked up to the square and hard-cut opening in the rock. The whole face of the cliff above us, entangled with lianas, was sculptured into grotesque and obscene figures. The Lady Hebe took one look, and turned her head away. Loriman was on one side and Hurngal on the other. They vied with each other for her favors in a most pathetic way. But that convoluted rock, the tangled strings of lianas, the screams of the waterfowl, the heat and stink of the mud, the stinging attacks of the pinheads which had to be continually brushed away, all conduced to a somberness of mood no ludicrous shuffling for position by two grown men about a girl could obliterate or alleviate.

There was no sign of an inscription inviting me to enter. There were the usual ritual curses of doom upon anyone venturing in. We took no notice of them.

"That, at the least," said Seg, "is something." Shouldering our packs, weapons in fists, torches flaring, we entered the maze of the Coup Blag.

Fourteen

Into the Coup Blag

Five minutes later I was on my way out of the maze of the Coup Blag.

Under my arm a kicking, wrestling, screaming bundle of trouble tried to trip me up, to bite me, to do anything to stop me from carrying it outside.

Brown curls writhing as though they were Medusa's snakes, Ortyg Thingol jackknifed up and down under my arm. Stolidly, I marched out into the last of the suns light.

"Why can't I go? Why? Why?"

Drak, willful as he always had been, had never reacted in quite this way. I remembered him climbing the trees in the walled garden of Esser Rarioch.

I said, "When I say a thing, I mean it. But, Ortyg, there is another reason. A most important reason, and a secret."

He gasped as I dumped him down on his feet. "What reason, Jak? What secret?"

I looked around with a highly conspiratorial glance for the voller. "Why, I need someone reliable, someone I can trust, to keep an eye on the airboat. If there's any trouble, you'll have to fly the voller and make sure you come back to rescue us."

"Me? Fly the airboat? Rescue you!" Watching him I saw the visions of glory exploding in his head. It was all there, Ortyg Thingol, air cadet, rescuing the emperor... No. How stupid. Well, it was taking time to adjust. But Ortyg was hooked.

I consigned him into the care of a gentle Relt, with ink stains on his feathers, secretary to Kov Hurngal.

Then I turned and started back for the entrance and Deb-Lu stepped out from bushes that might have eaten a flesh-and-blood man, and said: "Hai, Dray. Delia and Milsi are safe, praise be to Opaz the Unknown."

"Thank you, Deb-Lu, thank you. I shall tell Seg. But you are very faint—"

"I do not wish to alert the witch. But I thought you should know. The fleet had repairs to carry out and all that kind of aerial business to attend to. They will sail for the maze as soon as they can."

Without a remberee, his phantom figure vanished.

Those of you who have followed my story since those first days of mine on Kregan will understand something of my feelings. Liberation, thanksgiving, a sudden seeing of the world in different colors, the stinks turned to scents, the cacophonies to melodies—all this and more. I fairly ran back into the damned Coup Blag to tell Seg the good news.

The darkness stretched up, down, and sideways past the entrance, with a lonely spark from a torch waiting to guide me. In the first stone-cut chamber Nath the Impenitent stood leaning up against the wall, the torch in his left fist. The light revealed the two doors at the far end.

"Hai, Jak," he said in his gruff way. "Seg is leading on the rabble. I waited to tell you the way they went."

"The last time," I said, "Strom Ornol chose the right-hand door, and that leads to passages we know. Also, Nath, my friend, in places like these it is not wise to lean up against the wall."

He pushed himself erect with some alacrity.

Then he said, "It is odd, by Vox—by Chusto. In the normal way I would have stood to attention the moment you showed up. But you and Seg are not like the real lords I have had the misfortune to know in the past."

I could still smell the betraying scent of the Spiny Ribcrushers from outside. This Nath the Impenitent had a real down on the aristocracy, and who was to say he had no right? I'd be interested to hear his story, but he remained reticent on that score. He did say he needed gold. Well, most folk do.

"Oh," I said, moving toward the right-hand door, "there are lords and there are lords."

"Aye. And one of 'em is this Kov Hurngal. Seg said he'd been down the right-hand door, so—"

"So the oaf chose the left?"

"Yes."

"That is the kind of lord, Nath, we really do not need."

"I've known some in my time who had a remedy for them."

"Like the Fegters, or—"

"We'll have to hurry if we wanta catch 'em up."

Without another word on that subject we approached the left-hand door. Although I do not pretend to any vast knowledge on the proper construction of Moders and Mazes of the Coup Blag quality, I felt that I would not be surprised if the routes through the two doors joined up in the near future.

The corridor beyond the door showed gray walls flecked with striated veins of glitter. The torch cast its orange glow ahead and the walls seemed to jump in and out of focus. I spoke seriously.

"We do not have a ten-foot pole. We must assume that the party ahead tested the floor for traps. That does not mean there won't be any newly laid for us."

Nath said, "Hold on, Jak! That must mean that—"

"Precisely. Also keep a wary eye aloft for the green slime. Or the newer gray gunge. That is not pretty."

From the way I spoke with an intensity of feeling that was out in the open before I realized, anyone would be forgiven for turning a little gray-green themselves. Nath just cocked a suspicious eye around, rolled his shoulders, and started out along the corridor. I brisked up. He was like to prove a good companion.

We caught up with the rest of the party as they were indulging in the usual, and tiresome, arguments on which way to go. They stood in a large circular chamber.

Seg was saying, "I really think it doesn't make much difference which way we go."

"You onker," rapped out Hurngal. "Of course it matters, otherwise we won't know where we've been or are, will we, voskskull."

Loriman, face scarlet, wanted to argue with Hurngal, as a matter of principal, yet he couldn't understand what Seg meant, either.

There was no spiral staircase in the center of this room to lead us down into the depths. There were three doors, all looking exactly the same. The slaves were already sitting on their bundles, or stretched out on the floor—which was free of dust—and the guards were standing about looking ready to earn their hire.

Eventually, and at pretty short order, too, Kov Loriman blew up.

"By Hito the Hunter! This place is a maze, is it not? We must keep track." The look he gave Seg indicated with absolute clarity that he'd lost a lot of faith in my comrade.

I said nothing.

Seg spoke in his disconcerting neutral voice.

"I have given you my opinion." He spotted me. "You must make the decision between you, if you choose to disregard my advice." He sauntered across to me, stepping carefully between the resting slaves.

With a quick word to Nath, I drew Seg aside.

"I've just had a visit from Deb-Lu. Milsi is safe—"

"Praise Erthyr the Bow! And Delia?"

"Also. Now, my master bowman, we may bend all our energies to this blasted place. I look forward to some enjoyment from Kovs Hurngal and Loriman."

"Aye. And what of the fleet?"

"Knocked about, refitting, due as soon as they can make it. No idea when that will be."

A burst of profanity made us turn, to see Hurngal stride to the center door and give it a thumping kick.

Instinctively, we braced ourselves for whatever horror might leap from that portal.

The door opened onto a corridor which the torchlights showed to be wide, high, and covered with inscriptions. No one, I ventured to think, would be able to read whatever was inscribed there.

"There! A capital way in." Hurngal looked pleased with himself.

Quietly, Seg said: "These people are taking the whole business far too lightly. By the Veiled Froyvil! Anyone'd think they were out for a gentle stroll and a nice picnic in the light of the suns!"

"Aye. It's all a trifle unreal at the moment."

"When they get a few Lurking Terrors gnawing at their throats, they'll find out."

We all trooped along the corridor. At least they had men up front prodding the floor with ten foot poles. Even the most confident idiot could see the sense of that. A strong yellow light shone from the doorway ahead.

We debouched into a smallish semi-circular room. At the center the head of a spiral staircase cut a dark and ominous hole in the smooth floor. Just above that poised a slate slab. The shape would exactly fit the hole. The lid was upheld by bronze chains extending to the far wall. Above the chains a little balcony, something like a minstrels' gallery, projected from the stone wall.

"Now I don't like the look of *that!*" exclaimed Loriman. Well, he'd been down the Moder and therefore should be expected to take this place a sight more seriously than did the others.

"It would be best," said the Khibil sorcerer in his haughty, distant, way, "if you removed the lid."

"Exactly what I was about to say," said Hurngal. He swung on his slaves. "Get on with it! *Bratch!*"

The slaves duly bratched, jumping into the work as though their master stood at their backs with his cane.

The slate lid was manhandled clear of the opening and the slaves jumped aside and allowed it to fall. Instead of shattering into pieces, as would have been expected, it remained intact. It rolled around flatly on its rim, exactly as a coin will squat shuddering onto a table. We all stared and then our attention was riveted by a cackling laugh from the balcony.

Up there a grotesque figure, all dripping greeny-black robes and tassels, waved its arms at us. Skeletal fingers beckoned mockingly. It cackled. Its hood concealed its face except for its mouth, which leered.

San Aramplo brushed up his whiskers and said, "I do not know the name of that. But I shall call it a Cackling Leer."

Loriman's reactions were predictable.

He snatched his bow from the Brokelsh who carried it, slapped an arrow against the string, drew and let fly. The shot was good. The arrow passed clean through the Cackling Leer and bounced harmlessly off the wall.

A gasp of astonishment composed of many individual expressions of fear, surprise, disbelief, rippled around the crowd in the chamber. Hurngal held up his hand ready to quell the disturbance, and the Cackling Leer glided from the balcony, passing, apparently, through the solid wall.

"Ah," said Seg, "now maybe they'll understand a little more."

"Unhealthy, that thing," said Nath the Impenitent.

Torches revealed the spiral stairs to circumnavigate the opening twice before reaching the floor below. Each tread could accommodate two men abreast. Strom Tothor in his bold lionman way roared out that he would go first. Sword in fist, he started down the stairs.

Seg and I exchanged glances. In places like the Coup Blag, stairs are notorious.

Seg shoved up to the head of the stairwell, grabbed a ten-foot pole from a guard, and started down to join Tothor. I own I felt jumpy, nervous, and highly wrought up. If a stair tread opened up and swallowed Seg; if one spewed a thicket of darts through his body; if a scimitar-like blade swept up between the joins to slice him—I pushed my way through the throng clustered, hesitating, around the hole. They let me through readily enough. I skipped down after Seg as he stolidly thumped each tread before trusting it.

"The damned riser, Seg. They can spit nasties."

"Aye. I'm giving them a thwack as well."

We reached the foot of the stairs and Tothor, with his numim roar bellowed: "All clear!"

The torch showed a dressed-stone passage extending in both directions. We stood aside as the people came down, two by two, and together left us to go marching up the right hand passageway flaring his torch.

At the center of the last group of guards came the Lady Hebe. She was dressed appropriately enough for the expedition, with moccasins upon her feet, the robes discarded and replaced by a chamois-skin tunic.

She reached the bottom step and went to walk past us. I was sure she intended to say nothing. She did not even look at us.

The fellow at her back loomed large even for a Chulik, and his shaven head had been coated with gold leaf. His pigtail, likewise, was sheathed in gold leaf. His armor was complete, his weapons many, and his bearing such as to convey to everybody that here was a man not to be contumed. We knew that the Lady Hebe reposed trust in him.

A laugh drifted down the stairwell.

We all looked up.

Up there the hooded form of the Cackling Leer showed, peering over and down at us. The horrid cackle scratched at our nerve-endings. The echoes bounced like a swarm of insects around the spiral stairway.

We all heard the creaking, groaning, heavy sound, and I suspect most of us guessed what it was instantly.

A round black shape appeared at one side of the hole. Like an eclipse, the lid slid over the light, making that inhuman groaning sound. The cackling faded and was gone. Gone like the light. Stygian darkness enveloped us and our sparks of torches.

"I believe," said Seg, "that no matter how many slaves they try, they won't budge that stopper."

Fifteen

Of the cost of discovery

The Chulik took his helmet off his belt and put it on, covering up the golden-covered skull of which he was so proud. Pride is one emotion Chuliks know. Trained from birth to be fighting men and mercenaries, they know little of the gentler human emotions. His three-inch tusks stuck up from the corners of his mouth and, of course, they were banded in gold.

"We will get out when we have to, my lady."

"Yes, Scancho, I do not doubt it for a moment."

At least somebody was trying to keep their spirits up, then.

The Lady Hebe went on: "It were better if the others do not hear of this at the front. Tell your men the same, Scancho. If they disobey me they know it will go badly for them."

"Quidang, my lady."

Giving Seg, Nath, and me a searching stare, she said: "You had best keep your black-fanged winespouts shut, too. *Dernun?*"

I was enchanted. She'd used a common flowery description more often found among the low-life of Kregen than among the nobs. Then, the way she'd cut that dernun out, capiche, savvy, gottit, marked her as well-habituated to command. I formed a pretty little theory regarding the Lady Hebe.

"I shall inform Kov Loriman and Strom Tothor," I said equably.

Again that damn-you-to-hell stare. Then: "Yes."

The Chulik, who wore Jiktar markings, started to bristle up, but I started off down the passageway and Seg and Nath shouldered after. Still, the woman provided another interesting if unimportant enigma down in the mazes of the Coup Blag where the enigmas, besides hurtling at a fellow thick and fast, were important, frighteningly important, by Vox.

The others had marched past a series of doors which now stood open and I suspected they'd had a look inside each one. All were uniformly empty, some clean, some dusty, and some stinking with putrefaction still hanging on the air.

Hurngal had left a slave at the intersection of a cross corridor. The poor fellow shook on his naked feet, his bald head—alas unbuttered—shining with sweat. He directed us straight ahead and, with Hebe's party trotting along, we followed the slave to the next chamber. This was quite unremarkable save for the corpse of a man newly slain in the corner. He was apim, and, I thought, not one of our party. We hurried on through the center door of five and so, traversing a twisting passageway that turned generally left rather than right, we came to a brilliantly lit hexagonal room of considerable size. Here the expedition once again was involved in discussions on the best route.

Looking at the room, I said to Seg, "It is not the same, clearly, but it presumably serves the same function as the one we visited."

"Aye."

"In that case—"

"In that case, my old dom, I am going to broach some of this wine we are carrying outside instead of inside."

Nath the Impenitent stared at us; but he took his cup of wine readily enough. The rest joined up and the Lady Hebe stood closer to Hurngal than she did to Loriman.

Now this hexagonal room contained twelve doors set equally in the sides. Each door was of a different color.

The corpses of two chavonths lay toward the center, and just beyond them a pile of bones spilled in such disorder it would need a paleontologist to decipher to which species of diffs they had belonged. There were, also, and these I marked well, over by the black door, half a dozen hellhounds. They had been hacked to pieces. The slaves would not go near them, and the guards prodded them experimentally.

Eventually Hurngal led off through the green door and the rest traipsed along after. When the chamber was nearly emptied of our people, Nath said: "We'd best get on."

"Sit easily, Nath. They'll be back."

"Oh?"

"Unless the green door is the right one."

"I see."

I wondered if he did, but I let that pass. He'd find out quickly enough when the expedition marched back in through another door, tired and frustrated.

This they did quite quickly, to see that we three sat at our ease, drinking sociably.

"How in a Herrelldrin Hell did you arrive here before me?" demanded Loriman. "I did not see you pass."

I said, "We did not, pantor. If the leaders of the expedition had listened, we could have told you that you stood ten chances out of twelve of returning here."

"Well, you rast," cried Hurngal. "Which damned door is it, then?"

"That, we cannot say for certain. Last time and not from this chamber although from one very like it, the turquoise door led to a banqueting hall."

"Then I shall go through the turquoise door," declared Hurngal, as though he'd chosen it himself.

"I would really like to rest for a while," said the Lady Hebe. Her Chulik cadade, her guard captain, glowered at her shoulder.

Loriman opened his mouth, and Hurngal snapped out, "Very well, my lady. For a short rest only, mind, for by Hanitcha the Harrower, I mean to take away the gold from this place."

After we had rested, we trooped through the turquoise door and the lead fellow with his pole, a Rapa, had time only to let out a single screech before he vanished into the hole his prodding opened up.

We looked down the hole; but the torches showed merely blank walls as far as we could see.

We edged around the trap and went on, and now the prodders prodded with divine devoutness.

All the same, a tough-bodied and heavily armored ranstak, with those hooded eyes and compressed features, staggered drunkenly. A shaft from a slit in the wall had spat out and transfixed his neck. He fell over sideways, thrashing with his tail very much as a Kataki would do in similar circumstances. The prodders now regarded every slight shadow in the walls with the gravest suspicion.

Well, they were learning, and it was taking the lives of men to teach them.

I bent down to the ranstak. From his thick waist I unstrapped one of his leather belts. This one swung the scabbard for a short sword. The blade was neat, trim, not too broad, admirably suited to the close-in work one must expect in tunnels and caverns.

Giving the ranstak a salute with the blade, I committed him to the care of his god, whose name I did not then know, and went on.

"You did not," observed Nath, "take his armor."

"Wouldn't fit."

With the short sword at my side to add to the longsword partially hidden down my back under the brown cloak, corded back, from Mistress Tlima, I was well on the way to equipping myself. Seg and Nath would do the same, in time, for it was quite clear the expedition was going to suffer more casualties.

I knew Seg had his eye on a tall red-headed fellow who strode along lithely, his bow in his fist.

480

What shifts we come to when needs we must!

All the same, I did say to Seg: "Maybe in confined quarters, Seg, a compound reflex may be handier than a long. Same as swords."

"Such beliefs may fester in the minds of the feeble, my old dom. I know what I know about bows."

Well, you couldn't say fairer than that, for in my view there is no finer bowman on two worlds than Seg Segutorio, known hereabouts as Seg the Horkandur.

At the next opportunity when we were traversing a bridge over a chasm boiling with fires, smoldering with fumes that sickened us, I eased my way close to Loriman. From the vast cesspit in the floor rose a cloud of black winged figures. Their eyes gleamed red, their fangs were serrations of yellow needles, their clawed wings flapped black against the glow. With screeches wrung from hell they flew upon us in a swarm of biting, tearing, clawing terror.

At once everyone was smiting away, slashing and swirling their weapons, desperate to keep these furry little horrors off. Each was not much larger than a fairly grown crow, but their rows of needle teeth ripped flesh away; their claws fastened like grappling hooks. I had a brief glimpse of a Rapa covered with the things as though they nested on him. His feathers erupted among gouts of his blood.

The short sword proved handy, able to swat the flying horrors away as though I played at some macabre game of tennis. Loriman's blade dazzled alongside. How many of the things there might be there was no way of knowing. We all started to run across the bridge, swiping away over our heads. The slaves, as is usual, suffered badly.

Without stopping to reck that Seg stayed with me, I hung back, trying to give some protection to the half-naked slaves as they ran, using their burdens to give themselves some protection. The flying beasts stank of the cesspit below. The fires and fumes, the smoke, the dizzying swarms of furry devils, created a scene direct from an authentic portrait of hell.

San Aramplo, the Khibil mage, crawled on his hands and knees and slaves were tripping over him. I got my left hand under his armpit and hoisted him. There was not a mark on him and I just missed a swipe at a little flyer who nipped in to rip down San Aramplo's face. The needle teeth rebounded.

"No time, no time," the Khibil stuttered. He held out his right hand and tried to make a sign, and at once he almost fell, twisting himself out of the way of a fresh attack. That one I did not miss and smashed back into the inferno whence he came.

"If they cannot harm you, stand up and magic them away!"

"It is not as easy as that, you hulu—let me go!"

I gave him a hefty shove in the direction of the tunnel mouth at the end of the bridge. "And keep out of the way of the slaves!" I bellowed after him.

Seg's sword flicked a black-winged horror from my shoulder. "We appear to have an apology for a sorcerer with us this time, my old dom."

"Aye." And slash, swipe, blow after blow, driving the things away.

We gained the shelter of the tunnel entrance, and turned to look back at the bridge. Bodies lay there, and scattered bundles, and much had fallen into the pit.

We were penetrating deeper into the heart of this evil maze of the Coup Blag; but at a fearful cost.

Sixteen

"I never was fond of skelebones!"

Among the many half-obliterated marks cut into the walls at corners and turnings, the heart, lobed, slashed through with a sword, passed as just another sign among many. That mark was the sign of Spikatur Hunting Sword.

Hurngal had one of his people busily cutting a fresh mark at points where we changed direction. He used the Kregish block script initials H.h.H. I had to smile. I wondered just how many folk there were in Hamal with those self-same initials.

Loriman cast me a quizzical look. We'd paced each other since leaving that bridge of midget flying horrors and I had lost that opportunity of talking to him.

With floor, walls, and ceiling well tested before us, we marched on through a succession of chambers wherein the magnificence of the furnishings, the grandeur of column and pediments, of frieze and gallery, might have overawed but for the decay and mildew, the damp and worms that infested everywhere. This was like walking through a palace lost for centuries.

We ran across two Bearded Phantoms, fought and slew a scaled risslaca with horned head, managed to avoid some whining Mind Leeches, and were nearly done by a pack of skeletons. These last clanked and clattered out of wall-high slots of stone. Well, I'd handled skeletons before and, Zair willing, had the knack of it and would do it again.

I unlimbered the Krozair longsword and set to work.

With Seg at my side and Nath slashing and cursing away next to him, we went at it hammer and tongs. Yellow bones flew through the air. Grinning skulls toppled. People were screaming and running, the puffing dust stank in our nostrils, we sweated and hacked and hewed and slashed the skeletons into fragments about us.

Twice I hewed down a gangling but lethal bundle of bones from before Kov Loriman. He grunted and swore and swung his sword in massive blows that sundered the sere bones like kindling.

When it was all over, we waved our open hands to sweep the clinging dust away and to gain a little fresh air. The light remained level and constant, not as brightly yellow as in some of the rooms but amply sufficient for our needs.

Seg shook his wild black hair back.

"By the Veiled Froyvil! I never was fond of skelebones!"

"They'll do for you," ground out Loriman. "I have hunted them before. If they fasten their jaws in you—you're done for."

"I," put in Nath the Impenitent, "have not fought these skelebones of yours before this, having always lived a rational life. By Chozputz! One does see life down here!"

"And death, if you don't jump sharp enough." Loriman abruptly turned from being a normal decent comrade into the domineering Hunting Kov as he bellowed at his retainers: "Collect up your bundles, you lazy cramphs!"

Then he swung back to glare haughtily at me.

"I said I had seen you before, Jak, the Bogandur, although you were not dubbed the Bogandur then. I thought you dead."

"You got out past the statue of Kranlil the Reaper," I said. "Yes."

He sucked in a breath. He stared at me as though I'd risen from the grave before his eyes just like those poor damned skelebones.

Then he said, "We did well, did we not, in the Chamber of the Flame in that Armipand-begotten Moder?"

We talked for a space about that fraught time. Loriman told me he considered this maze vastly inferior to that one at Moder.*

I said, "I have often thought of you and wondered how you fared." Then, because I could not stop my prattling tongue from waggling, I added, "You are somewhat different now from what you were then."

"I have seen what happened to Spikatur. That would turn a saint."

I'd told Seg many and many a time a great deal of what had chanced down the Moder, so he was able to keep abreast of the conversation.

Loriman said, "That great damned bar of iron you call a sword convinced me. I did not really believe, not until you spoke."

The Krozair longsword had carefully gone back into the scabbard so cunningly hitched over my back. We walked on out of that chamber of

---

* See: *A Fortune for Kregen,* Dray Prescot #21. A.B.A.

desiccated skelebones and into another where we had a brief set to with a pack of Crippling Crabs. The next room offered the chance to get to grips with a herd of mummies, all duly linen-wrapped after one of the fashions of Balintol. Some of these we burned.

The Lady Hebe, sheathing her sword, walked over to say, "I would like a rest now, and Hurngal wants to press on."

Before Loriman could stop himself, so wrought up was he on this sore point, he burst out: "I see! When you want me to do something for you about that damned man then you ask. I see!"

"If that is the way you wish to speak to me, after all that has passed—"

"Aye, Hebe! Passed seems right. I'll tell Hurngal, d'you understand that? I'll *tell* him!"

On that instant a hullabaloo broke out from those in front who had just passed out of this chamber, exclamations of astonishment and cries of wonder and delight.

I believe I knew what this meant. Seg said: "Y'know what that means, Jak?"

Everybody ran off to see the new wonders for themselves. I put a hand to my chin.

"Aye. There's a big room up there beautifully furnished, with tables groaning under food and drink, and comfortable beds and curtains and everything weary delvers could require. And, Seg, y'know what that means?"

"I do."

Neither of us wanted to say the confounded name aloud. But both of us knew that Csitra had provided the repast and rest, and that was clear evidence that she had us under observation, was spying on us.

We were drawing closer to her. Slowly we were finding our way through her maze of tricks and traps, of monsters and magic. What we both recognized was that she was in control. She would allow us to reach her only when she wished, after she and her uhu Phunik had had their fun with us.

Had Khe-Hi and Ling-Li been with us, as had been planned, would there have been a difference? Perhaps this Khibil sorcerer might yet live up to his high reputation. I was confident enough to take a wager on it that had Khe-Hi been on the bridge when the little flying furry horrors attacked he would have banished them back to their cesspit before they could stick a single needle-tooth into anyone's flesh. Still, maybe the apparent lack of competence of our Khibil San Aramplo had not drawn Csitra's attention, for it was certain she'd have known if Khe-Hi and Ling-Li ventured in—unless, well, if Deb-Lu could sneak in here without her knowing, then so could his colleagues, surely...?

So with these muddled thoughts in my noggin I trailed along with Seg after the mob into the splendors we anticipated.

484

Seg and I sat down at one of the laden tables and began to eat and drink.

Loriman said, "Is that wise?"

Seg swallowed down and reached for a fresh bottle.

"The last time the food had no ill effects."

"By Numi-Hyrjiv the Golden Splendor!" bellowed Strom Tothor. "Save some for a thirsty fellow who's walked a wearisome way!"

Seg laughed and handed over the bottle and the lion-man upended it over his mouth.

Everywhere people descended on the food like famished warvols. The slaves ate themselves into stupors, and Hurngal had to order the guards to keep the slaves away from the drink. I wondered if these guards would stay away from it themselves for long enough to remain compos mentis. The notion of a pack of drunken slaves and guards rollicking about these treacherous passageways might seem attractive; it would be self-defeating in the end.

The pathetic way in which the Lady Hebe and Kov Loriman circled around each other, allowing far more than the usual required amount of body space, might have been amusing in other circumstances. Kov Hurngal looked to be in the driver's seat here, winning all the way down the line.

Loriman stormed over to us and threw himself down on one of the marvelously upholstered and decorated chairs, all twining vine-leaves picked out with gold leaf and pearls. His eyebrows made a black bar of baffled fury.

"That man!" Having, as it were, broken the ice with us and put his foot in it, he accepted the consequences of confidences. At that, I suspected he, being the choleric, outspoken damn-you-to-hell person he was, welcomed the opportunity he found so rarely of being able to talk to someone instead of shouting orders or insults at them.

I leaned forward on the smooth linen napery. "When I said I believed you to be the leader, I see I was wrong. But that man—"

"I am the instigator. The Lady Hebe was *my* friend, and she very willingly agreed to get to know Hurngal and persuade him to finance the expedition."

"Ah," said Seg, wisely. "These things always cost money."

"And you, kov—" and here I gave Loriman a look he must recognize as shrewd "—spent all yours either for or against Spikatur."

"Aye. Both."

"We all have our own purposes for venturing here. You just picked Hurngal out of a hat?"

"More or less. He has money, connections, and he is Hamalese."

Loriman, like the fabled Spatzentarl Volcano on the lost island of

Naripur, boiled and bubbled within himself and refused to allow himself to blow up. He simmered dangerously close to an explosion, though, and he wanted to talk to someone; that was perfectly plain.

"Why Hamalese?"

"Oh, I trusted he would be killed down here."

"Yet the Lady Hebe—"

"I did not intend to bring her. That was her and that cramph Hurngal's idea."

Seg said, "I had the honor and the wonderful good fortune down here to meet the lady who is now my wife, praise be to—" A tiny hesitation, then: "Pandrite All-Glorious."

Loriman was too wrought up in his own problems to take much notice of what anyone else told him. He brooded, brows drawn down, face fierce, gripping a golden chalice slopping with red wine.

"When Spikatur fought against the Hamalese, those were the days. Now, Spikatur is criminal."

I said, "You know that this witch runs SHS for her own dark ends?"

"I didn't. She will die with all the others, never fear."

"At the moment she merely toys with us. This is a kind of refined torture in which she specializes. Her uhu is less subtle. They will amuse themselves with us for a space yet, and, in Armipand's vile truth, we have seen very little of the horrors yet."

Well, Csitra did toy with us. A full record of our travels and travails on this occasion in the Coup Blag would run to many cassettes, I feel, but if you can taste the flavor of the place, the darkness and the unexpected illumination, the sense of constant pressure, of eyes watching, of ears listening and the sudden devastating onslaught of nightmare creatures, beasts of claw and fang, and insubstantial wraiths of mind-numbing power, if, I say, then perhaps you may also gather a little of the expedition's growing distress.

One item of information I did not pass on to Loriman was my belief that Csitra had no further use for Spikatur Hunting Sword, and that therefore the organization was already finished. Loriman, in the mood he was in, might not have relished that. Also, he might have decided to quit the search and attempt to march his people out.

By this time, as we wended our way deeper and deeper into the maze, Seg, Nath, and I were fully armed and accoutered. Seg had his long bow; the poor red-headed fellow from Loh had vanished head first into a giant stone flower that came alive and sucked him in. His boots and his bow were all that were left of a stalwart Bowman of Loh.

This continual drain of lives was wearing the expedition down.

Everyone wondered who would be next.

The principals of the party originally made the decision to enter the

Coup Blag. Their reasons might vary; still they were responsible for themselves.

"By the agate-winged jutmen of Hodan-Set!" rasped Kov Loriman. "We must be drawing near by now!"

We slid cautiously down a slanting ramp of pure white marble, shiny and slippery under a pervasive yellow glow from the fire-crystal ceiling. I hitched the longsword and the torch I carried stuck through my belt—unlit, of course—more comfortably, and slid down with Seg and Nath. The ramp debouched into a chamber of somber magnificence.

Thirty or forty heavy iron-bound boxes stood stacked against one wall, half-draped by a green curtain with golden tassels.

"Treasure chests!" shouted Kov Hurngal, and strode across exultantly.

He touched the chests and nothing happened. We dragged them down and nothing happened. We opened the first and threw the lid back—and still nothing happened.

The chest was crammed to the top with golden coins.

Loriman's lip curled as Hurngal directed his people to transfer the gold from chests to sacks.

"At last!" cried the Rapa zhanpaktun, Tyr Rogarsh the Rattler. "By Rhapaporgolam the Reiver of Souls! It has taken long enough, but we have found the treasure."

Seg said to Loriman, "Two things, kov. One, gold is too heavy for delvers to carry out. Two, I understand the witch is capable of causing it to turn molten and burn and flow away to nothing."

"Aye," I said, nodding. "The gold will melt, although it may not have been this witch who caused that when I witnessed it."

Loriman's heavy face showed a grimace of pleasure. "Is Hurngal then on a fool's errand?"

"Oh, there is probably genuine treasure about," said Seg, airily.

In their manic delving the slaves were simply scooping handfuls of gold from the chests and filling their sacks, not bothering to empty one chest before passing on to the next. Nath hitched forward a wallet he'd picked up.

"Gold is something I need. If it melts, it melts. That I will risk, by Chusto!"

He reached into the first chest which had been pretty well emptied before the slaves simply scooped up the easier gold from chest to chest. I looked at him with sympathetic understanding.

A corpse-white tentacle as thick through as a man's arm whipped out of the box, lapped Nath, dragged him in.

"Nath!"

I leaped. I reached the chest and was dragging out my sword when a second tentacle slapped its corpse-white length about me. Headfirst I went into the box after Nath. The bottom of the box did not halt that hurtling descent. Neither did the floor of the chamber.

Helplessly, wrapped in tentacles, Nath and I plummeted down, clean out of the chamber into pitchy blackness.

Seventeen

Concerning a toad's supper

We hit the water with an almighty splash.

Deep, we were dragged, deep beneath the surface. The tentacle constricted about me like a steel band, trapping my left arm. The short sword remained in its scabbard. There was no time now to wonder how Nath fared. In that automatic gasp as the tentacle caught me and hauled me down, my lungs had not exactly equipped me for a dive underwater.

Accounted a merman as a swimmer and a fish as a diver though I may be, I am only apim. Air! If I didn't get a breath of fresh air pretty damn quick I was done for.

The old sailor knife scabbarded over my right hip came out with oiled sweetness.

I knew where the tentacle was, all right, I could feel it pressing in on my chest. I put the knife against it and then with a burst of savage anger sawed the blade across, and across again, and then lifted it, dug the point in, and so sawed again like a manic witch stirring a magic brew.

The tentacle unwrapped and nearly took my knife with it. The blackness surrounding me was shot through with little flecks of fire. They were in my eyes, not in the water.

Something big and soft bumped against my side. There was just time enough for me to stay the automatic knife thrust. This bulky lolling object was Nath the Impenitent and I felt the thick tentacle about him. I severed that one as I had severed the one pinioning me.

Grasping Nath and queasily conscious that whatever monstrous thing had seized us with his tentacles might have more than two, I shot for the surface.

I knew that here in Csitra's maze, created for her enjoyment, at least one lake swarmed with fish and monsters all teeth and jaws. They'd chew up a school of piranha before breakfast.

Nath in my left arm, my legs kicking, I retained the knife in my right fist. Something cold hit my thigh and I struck down without thought.

Fish or another tentacle, I did not know. Whatever it was, it went away.

Just when I knew I couldn't last another heartbeat, my head popped out of the water into air that, musty and stinking of fish though it was, tasted like the best Kregen air on a headland of Valka.

I hoisted Nath up, used the back of my hand on his cheek, and looked about into that unremitting darkness.

No! Not quite! A leaching sickly green light, low on the water, just ahead. It could not be far. Using my legs easily, trying not to make a commotion in the water, and towing Nath along at my side, I persevered, and felt the shock of relief as my feet hit soft mud.

By the time I'd crawled out and pulled Nath clear, we were both covered in the evil-smelling gunk.

Nath still breathed and after I'd pumped some water out of him he spluttered and spat and choked out: "By Vox, Jak! You saved me. I thought I was on the one-way journey to the Ice Floes of Sicce then."

"We're not out of it yet, dom."

"No. But I give you thanks for my life. Now where?"

"Look there."

The green light emanated from a swarm of tiny creatures like glowworms contained in a transparent shell dangling on a line. I noticed the creatures were not trapped, for some crawled to an opening and flew off, extinguishing their light as they did so. The line depended from a spiral extension from the forehead of a monster like a giant toad, horse size, that sat crouched and waiting with open mouth. The green light dangled before that open gaper.

As we watched, a bat-shape, all glints of orange and silver, swooped with jaws agape at the cluster of fireflies. With a single convulsive gulp, the giant frog took him, took him in whole. The wide horny mouth snapped shut, the flaccid skin of the throat bulged and swallowed, and the mouth opened again ready for the next.

We did not approach the green light bait, and the monster toad ignored us.

"Looks as though we are stuck," commented Nath.

"I'm not prepared to peg out on a filthy bit of mud watching a toad catch his supper."

"So?"

"I've no idea."

With an enormous splashing and a sucking sound the water boiled and a tentacular shape reared upward. Green light glinted from its glistening hide. Corpse-white tentacles snaked aloft, striking unerringly for a hole in the unseen roof—a hole that appeared where it had not been before, that disgorged a shrieking man, and that closed up again the moment its evil work had been accomplished.

The massive body with one of its two tentacles fastened about the man, fell back into the water. We saw no more of that poor devil.

"Magic and monsters," said Nath. "I see."

"We can't stay here forever," I said, somewhat peevishly. "Let us go and explore."

The torch I carried thrust through my belt would need to be dried out before it could be used; the spare in my pack was roused out, tinder and steel were struck, and we had a light.

"When delving," I said, "it is wise to wrap everything in waterproof oiled silk or membrane."

"I'll remember."

I quite liked this Nath the Impenitent. Laconic, he had a nice caustic way with him.

Our torch had no attractions for the orange-and-silver batlike creatures. They lusted after tender green fireflies, and were consigned to the inward parts of the monstrous toad. We left him to get on with his supper, and I wondered how long he had been there, and how long he would have to remain there in the future.

The spit of mud ahead broadened in the light of our torch into a graveled way that led into a wide shelf of rock above the water.

The going was treacherous. We were still dripping from our harness, and the leather would need some attention in the not-too-distant future. The temperature, on the cold side, was not too inconveniencing, and we made out a flight of steps leading upward into the darkness above the reach of our torch.

"Yes, Jak, I know," said Nath before I needed to speak. "Stairways are treacherous here."

"We must go up."

"Assuredly."

Prodding with our swords, checking everything twice over, we made our way up.

Nath's sword point went clean through the apparently solid rock of a tread.

"Painted parchment. There'll be stakes under there, sharp."

"Aye."

A loose stone lay dead in the center of the top step.

I stretched out, and this time I used the longsword. A quick twist sent the stone skittering off. In the same instant a damned great set of spears slammed across the head of the stairway. They ripped across with points glittering. Those points, still glittering and unstained with our blood, tucked neatly into slots cut to receive them. The five spears formed a gate to our egress.

"Um," said the Impenitent. "Awkward."

"If they're on springs we may be able to force them back."

"Then, by Chozputz! Let us try!"

"Stand by the points. When I have them drawn enough, slip through."

He didn't argue. I laid hands on the second and third spear haft, drew in a breath, and hauled back.

The springs were powerful. I could feel the resisting pressure; but I put my back into it and hauled with a will and slowly, slowly, with a creaking groan of protest, the spears eased back. The points came free of the slots. Keeping the movement smooth I forced the spears back and back and then Nath with his guts drawn in, slipped through.

With a smashing ripping sound the spears socked back into their slots as I released them.

"Now you, Jak."

Nath hauled. He hauled with a will and the sweat started out on his forehead. His biceps bulged. He swore and struggled and got the spear-heads out of the slots and then he could force them back no farther.

"They're slipping!"

I put my fists on the hafts just beyond the shaped heads. I arched my back. I thrust. I pushed the spears back, and Nath laid on again with a surge of power, and with a final burst of frenzied energy, the spears were free and I could slide through.

"By Vox!" he said, panting. "You have the strength of a dozen nikvoves!"

I made no answer but turned around to survey what new perils we must encounter in this ghastly place.

At this point Csitra and Phunik put on a splendid show for us. At least, for the poor wights who were trapped down here.

First, a procession of mewling goblins fell on us. After we had chopped them, a crazed herd of Shrinking Phantoms gibbered and clawed to their own destruction. Three Lurking Fears nearly had us; but we rallied and drove them off with contemptuous words as well as cold steel. A handful of unnamables were hewed to pieces, and coiling vapors which stank like a fish souk in a drought sent us, green-faced, charging full on them. Then, after a few more passes with objectionable creatures both material and immaterial, we were confronted by a clacking collection of skeletons.

"Skelebones," declared the Impenitent, highly disgusted. "We know how to deal with *them!*"

So, deal with them we duly did, and left bits and pieces of sundered bones strewn upon the rocky floor.

"Somebody is failing to impress, dom," said Nath. "That I truly declare."

"You are right. But we are not out of it yet."

The passageways we cautiously traversed were still jagged; but we progressed up two more floors and the architecture of the corridors became more refined.

One room into which we peered with due precautions, for the door stood open, revealed a hideous idol of a demon god upon a throne. "No," I said, rapping it out, sharp and hard. "We will not go in there."

Shortly thereafter we ran across a chamber sumptuously decked and spread with a banquet for two. So, down we sat and ate and drank.

"They like to keep their victims nice and fresh," said Nath. "That suits me."

He drank, I noticed, without his habitual and automatic rationing of himself, for he was a swod of Vallia. He also did not realize the potency of some of the wines. In any event he caught himself, and threw the last flagon onto the floor. But his tongue was loosened.

In no regular order I learned he'd been apprenticed to a silversmith but had preferred to go off and learn the trade of armorer. He was the first son of parents who, having bred four fine sons and three beautiful daughters, went and got themselves drowned in one of Vondium's canals. Then the troublous times hit Vallia, and Nath had gone off to be a soldier, something hardly available to anyone of Vallia unless they went abroad to be a paktun.

He had never been a mercenary. He had fought Vallia's enemies. He had a chestful of bobs; but he'd lost the medals when he'd been knocked off *Shango Lady*.

"Then it all went wrong," he said, and the mournfulness that would have been amusing at another time rang painfully true. "Those Opaz-forsaken Leem-Lovers!"

I sat quiveringly alert. Now what?

"Took her, they did, took my sister's little Sassy. Gave her sweets and a new white dress, and a bangle. My own sister, Francine, and that husband of hers, Fortro. It was their fault. If I'd found 'em, I'd have killed 'em stone dead on the spot, by Vox!"

I waited. He rambled on, a broad palm against his forehead, his elbow on the table.

"Bought her back, I did. Gave those stinking rasts broad red gold for little Sassy."

I ventured, "But you have paid them. Do you still need the gold to repay the debt?"

"Debt? Aye, it's a debt. They said I stole the money. Stole it from my own regiment. Well, I borrowed it and then I was disappointed of my promotion and there was no gold. I could have managed it, I could."

Now, when I used to be the Emperor of Vallia, I could not obviously know everything that went on all over the entire empire. When Nath rambled on about his court-martial and the way the nobs had it in for him, I knew I had no knowledge of that particular court-martial, although as a matter of principal I'd tried to have the records of everyone sent to me for perusal. You can't be everywhere at once. All the same, I felt guilt. I *ought* to have known.

"They sent me off to train up coys. And reduced me to the ranks. So I joined the Vallian Air Service when the wars at last ended. And here I am."

I took some comfort from the fact that had Nath done something for which he had received the death sentence, then I would most certainly have known fully everything there was to know about his case. I had the case of Renko the Murais as a guidelight, there.

Stating the obvious, I said, "I suppose you refused to plead guilty and so acquired your sobriquet of the Impenitent."

"Assuredly so, Jak, assuredly so."

Then his head went down plonk upon the table and he started to snore. He blew a neat little circle of bread crumbs away from his head on the table.

Such, then, it seemed, was the tragedy of this man's life. What he had said of Lem the Silver Leem remained ominous. I just hoped the temple of his sister and her husband was the same as the one the prefect had burned down.

If the evil cult ever got a grip in Vallia, bad times would follow. Then the odd and unsettling notion occurred to me that I had to think of these problems not as the emperor, but as merely another citizen. Oh, yes, I still had broad lands and many estates in Vallia; Delia and I would not starve. Drak and Silda had the imperial provinces now.

I had not asked Nath why he had not demanded the right to have his case referred to the emperor, for I had heard the way Nath contumed the said emperor.

This hairy, hard, barrel-bodied fellow snoring away with his head on the table just did not like the aristocracy. Well, I'd had a few run-ins with them in the past myself.

After a good rest and another meal we set off again. We passed through a series of uninteresting corridors where discarded flang husks crunched underfoot to reach a tall and most imposing archway. The doors were shut.

"I'm not going back," I said, and pushed the right-hand door. It moved smoothly open.

The hall within was vast. Opulent encrustations festooned ceiling and columns. The drapes were velvet thick and wine red. The marble floor shimmered in its whiteness. The sweet scent of flowers on the air reached us pleasantly. Ranged tier on tier around three sides stretched upholstered benches. They were uniformly empty. At the center of the hall and the focus of the tiered seating lay a pool of water. Thick marble walled the water. The liquid sent gentle drifts of steam upward.

"Capital!" declared Nath. "A bath is just what we need."

I agreed. We poked all around and found nothing untoward. The water, when we tested it, was warm and aromatically scented and most inviting. We stripped off and plunged in.

Well, and—of course—we should not have done that foolish thing.

When our heads broke the surface after the dive all the tiered seating was crowded to capacity with gawking crowds—not apims, men and women, but ghouls, creepie-crawly horrors, skelebones, vampires, all creatures of horror, leering and gibbering upon us.

The croaking hissing noise they made filled us with revulsion. They were enjoying the entertainment.

And the water grew hot.

It heated up with incredible speed. In only moments it would reach boiling point.

The night's entertainment here was plain. We were to be boiled alive for these horrific creatures' pleasure.

Eighteen

Deb-Lu's boiling water trick

We both started swimming like madmen for the marble lip of the basin, and the water swirled and boiled and forced us back as though we sought to swim up a waterfall.

I was making progress; but the water grew hotter and hotter, and I did not wish to leave Nath.

Through the steam, something—and it was not a random something—made me glance toward the doors we had entered. Seg stood there, with Loriman and the Khibil sorcerer. Seg was shaking San Aramplo like a rag doll. Other members of the expedition could vaguely be glimpsed crowding up.

The sorcerer shook his head, and there was in the unhappy gesture his hand-tendered resignation, denial and despair.

My head went down, steam boiled up and I could see nothing further.

The bloody water was hot. Like the Tormenting Baths of a Herrelldrin Hell, the water scalded and ripped at us, breathing became an agony, and all the time I thrashed and splashed on and Nath spluttered away at my side.

Then, with a sudden awfulness breathtaking in its authority, the water rose from the boiling pool.

I landed with a thump on my feet on the marble floor of the bath. Nath sprawled out, gasping like a stranded fish. The water lifted, swirled, formed, became a single shining ball. Lights glinted from the glistening surface. The ball spun and rivulets of silver and red and ocher and green reflected in dazzling runnels from the surface. A single enormous globe, it hung over our heads.

I could still smell the hot steamy atmosphere of the boiling pool. The water did not drip from me. Like Nath, I was bone dry. All the water coalesced into that supernal globe above our heads.

With stunning speed the globe flattened, became a disc.

Faster and faster that disc whirled like a circular saw laid on its side to slice logs. Faster and faster. And then the flat disc spat itself in a Catherine wheel of watery destruction, spewed out to drench the tiered seating and all those macabre watchers there!

Gibbering and shrieking, those ghastly travesties fled.

The hall emptied of that blasphemous life and left only the people of the expedition crowding in, shouting to us.

Nath and I climbed out and started to put our clothes on and buckle up our harnesses.

"Jak! By the Veiled Froyvil, my old dom, I thought you boiled and served up tasty then!"

Amid a babble of greetings, I told Seg that he was the greatest, grandest, most splendid fellow in all of Kregen. Then I relented, for I had been more than a trifle over the top in emotional terms, and added that I was mightily surprised to see he'd still survived some of the traps all the wagers in gold under the suns would never spot.

He responded in kind, and we started off happily slanging each other's prowess, until I said that I was glad the Khibil sorcerer had done his stuff at last.

San Aramplo shook his head. For a Khibil, and a Khibil sorcerer at that, he looked highly cast down.

"I could do nothing. Pantor Seg here tried to make me, but I knew I could not."

"But you did!" rasped out Loriman.

"Oh, aye, I did. But I felt a force through me, a force I have never experienced before in all my seasons as acolyte and master mage of the Thaumaturges of Thagramond."

I gave Seg a look. He knew. So one of our Wizards of Loh, or our comrade Witch of Loh, had reached in with their superior kharrna and, using San Aramplo as a tool, had turned the boiling water trick against those ghastly gawkers.

"You did exceedingly well, San," boomed Kov Hurngal with all the confidence in Kregen. "My trust in your reputation was well-founded. Well, I am not surprised. I am not easily deceived in these matters. We can go forward now in better heart for the power in our midst."

Ignoring all the irony in that pompous declaration, for that was what one expected of Hurngal's character, I recognized the kernel of truth. The party should feel a little more secure now.

My guess was that Deb-Lu had been the mage to perform that trick through Aramplo. Despite the fact that the Khibil had no real idea of what had gone forward, I went up to him and warmly thanked him, expressing my conviction that his powers were awesome in their magnitude.

He merely nodded an acknowledgment, rapt in thought, obviously trying to discover what the hell he'd done to bring this result.

Nath gave him a rollicking round of thanks, also, and so, much heartened we looked around the chamber for what there might be to be found, as, for example, loot.

"What happened to you?" I said to Seg.

"Passages, rooms, traps and monsters," he said. "There are more avenues in this maze, I swear it, than in the defiles of Mount Hlabro herself."

"It is my belief we draw near to the heart of the maze."

"You think so? Well, I believe it. But I wouldn't let Hurngal hear you. He is firmly of the conviction that we are marching along the way out."

"Yes. That is in character, too."

And we both laughed.

The ranks of the slaves had been considerably reduced; those that were left trudged along with their sacks of gold slung over their shoulders. I just hoped they had the savvy to chuck the sacks down when the gold started to melt.

These proceedings bore in on me strongly that we were an expedition without—apart from Seg and Loriman—experienced delvers in our company.

We could have done with a few of those stalwart Pachaks who made a living bringing out treasure from ancient tombs.

We wandered on through a series of well-prodded passages where we lost a fellow who so assiduously stuck his ten foot pole into the flagstones ahead of him, he failed to look up. We heard the screams and uproar. By the time we reached the place, the poor fellow had been engulfed and deliquesced by green slime. Everybody passed the spot with great respect.

I'd very much soft-pedaled my account of Nath's and my doings when I told Seg, as I knew he had his, but I couldn't refrain from telling him about the monstrous toad thing that caught his supper with the aid of a lantern of fireflies on the end of a fishing rod. Seg was enchanted.

We skirted past the green gunge, engaged in a philosophic discussion over the meaning of such an entity in the scheme of things Kregan. While we thus talked openly about arcane abstract matters, we interpolated the odd thought directly concerned with our task here in the maze. No doubt remained in my mind that Deb-Lu, Khe-Hi and Ling-Li had successfully arranged a Cloak of Concealment about Seg and me, and Nath, too, given the thoroughness of the Wizards of Loh.

There could be no doubt, either, that in a confrontation with a super-naturally powerful Witch of Loh, a simple fighting man with his sword was of little account unless he had the active assistance of friendly Wizards of Loh.

Through us, then, would the sorcery be channeled at the last. I hardly relished the thought; but it was merely a thing that had to be done.

"By the diseased and dripping pustular excretions of the Lady Dulshini's armpits!" I burst out, for the dear Lady Dulshini had perforce to stand in for Makki Grodno in these here parts. "We've just got to get to the confounded woman and her brat!"

"We will, my old dom, we will, all in her own good time." Seg spoke in his infuriatingly cheerful way, knowing exactly how to stir me up. By Zair! But Seg Segutorio is the best comrade a man could hope to find on two planets!

Every man is a duality. He is dark and light. I detested Csitra and both feared and loathed her uhu, Phunik. Yet could I coldly slay the woman? She was possessed of the delusion that, because she harbored a passion for me, I must return her affections. Because of that she had caused great grief in Vallia, attempting by the sending of her Nine Unspeakable Curses to break me off from the people of the island empire.

Yet one could see her view of affairs, could, if not sympathize with the poor deluded soul, at least make a civilized guess at understanding her motives. How deeply was she still under the baleful influence of her mad husband, Phu-Si-Yantong, thankfully dead and gone to the hell he deserved?

Could I calmly march in, protected by comrade Wizards of Loh, and lop off her head in cold blood?

I began to think I would shirk the task. Seg would have no hesitation, but then, Seg was a blade comrade, the finest archer in two worlds, and he'd slay anybody for my sake. I wanted desperately to keep Seg out of this messy business.

In the end, of course and damned naturally, it was all down to me, plain Dray Prescot who was no longer the Emperor of Vallia, thank Zair.

Ranging up alongside me, for we were taking turns to lead, Nath said that Hurngal was confident we were nearly out of the maze.

I looked ahead down the passageway over the heads of the guards and the slaves with their sacks of gold, seeing the torches flaring in the shadowed spots. Up front Hurngal would be driving his people on, half mad with excitement over the treasure. Csitra's wiles lured the poor fellow on to a destruction that I doubted, despite Loriman's accusations, he deserved.

Nath said: "I believe, Jak, I told you somewhat of my history?"

"Aye."

"This remains in confidence between ourselves?"

"Of course!"

Then, because I fully intended to find out the truth behind his court-martial, and I wished to give him an inkling of light, I added: "Perhaps I could assist—"

"I thank you, dom; but it's highly unlikely. I know how these high and mighty ones of the world operate."

Somebody screamed up front; but we could not delay. After a time we passed a poor Rapa who had been caught in a blast of acid-breath from a marble statue.

"Yes, I know," continued the Impenitent. "My eldest sister, Lelia, a fine handsome girl who might have made any match she chose, joined the Jikai Vuvushis. Internal politics—that's how they attempt to dignify the quarrels among the nobs—split the Sisters of the Sword, so Lelia joined the Sisters of Voxyra, who were formed from the splinter group who couldn't stomach the underhand wiles of the haughty ladies of the Sword sorority."

"A smallish sisterhood," I said, "but they put powerful regiments into the field."

"My sister became a zan-Deldar and then an ob-Hikdar and I sincerely trust in the light of Opaz she is alive and thrives and will make it to Jiktar."

"A lofty ambition."

"The Javed family fight for Vallia!"

So that was his name. Nath Javed.

"All," he said with genuine bitterness, "except for poor sweet innocent Francine who was so badly led astray by that worthless Leem-loving husband of hers."

One interesting fact here was that Nath's violent antipathy for the emperor and the aristocracy did not prevent him from fighting for Vallia. I wanted to probe deeper; but Loriman stalked up and we had, perforce, to stop talking about Vallian affairs.

"I swear I will do that man an injury before long!" stormed the Hunting Kov. "I can bear only so much!"

"Now what, kov?"

"They're all certain up there that we are nearly out of the maze. I am not so sure. But if that cramph speaks to me like that again, I shall forget my vow not to harm him. The Lady Hebe does nothing to help me keep my word. By Hito the Hunter! I swear she goads us both!"

Now I understood why this choleric, fleshy, full-blooded Hunting Kov had not already driven six inches of steel into Kov Hurngal's guts.

I was making a few bland placating remarks when we debouched into a colossal chamber, of tall columns, a cool green light, of a roof lost amid a myriad rustling batwings and of walls draped dramatically in alternate widths of blue and gold. The place was crammed with furniture. There was like to be treasure here!

Halfway up the wall to our left a railed balcony extended around the angle to cross the door in the wall through which we had entered. There were no doors in the side walls I could see. At the far end of this place a different floor level about a third of the way across, offered an attractive seating area. Seg, Nath and I, very carefully, made our way there and sprawled out on comfortable settees that remained chairs and did not wrap their spiked arms about us. There was on the low tables an ample supply of wine, miscils, and palines, pleasant light fare which we munched as we watched the guards and slaves rummaging and ransacking the chamber for treasure.

I relented.

"Jewels, Nath, that's what you want in preference to gold. I hope you find a chestful."

"So do I." He sounded suspicious. "But will they melt away too, like the gold?"

"Chances, Nath, chances!" roared Seg, amused.

The Impenitent took himself off and we lost him among the glass cabinets and chests and tables covering the floor. Although markedly different, this place bore some similarity to a room down the Moder, and I wondered if perhaps Csitra had employed a Moder lord to design fresh attractions in her Coup Blag maze.

Seg swallowed his wine and said: "Interesting to see how Hurngal explains his theory of marching out. This place, big as it is, has only the one door. He'll have to retrace his steps."

"He'll bluff and bluster through. The Impenitent has a few shrewd observations to make about nobles."

"Some nobles."

"Seems Nath's only run across the wrong 'uns."

Strom Tothor walked up the shallow flight of steps to our higher railed area roaring in his lionman way that he was parched and famished. He launched himself at the bottles. Some of his people dumped their loads on the floor below and took seats a little removed from their master. They fell to with gusto.

Kov Loriman's Chulik guards, paktuns all, were not slow to fill their bellies as well as their wallets. They joined Tothor's retainers and a kind of relaxed club atmosphere dropped over us, all sitting up in our railed area, eating and drinking and watching what went on as best we could. The whole situation, eerie though it was, held a heightened fascination in our very normalcy in these weird surroundings.

Loriman joined us from the opposite end of the area and he was chewing on a chicken leg.

Seg said, "I'll forage."

The bat-creatures remained clustered upside down from the ceiling. The chamber with its forest of pillars stretched a long long way to the far end. We saw Nath and the Rapa zhanpaktun come striding up to us, both with sacks bulging over their backs. I smiled.

Carrying a silver tray between both hands, Seg came back to our table. The tray was loaded with goodies.

"Masses of stuff back there. Enough for an army."

So, there we sat, gorging away.

Few slaves or guards were to be seen among all the furniture and treasures down there. I couldn't see the sorcerer or the Lady Hebe; but there was just a glimpse of Hurngal between two glass cases looking toward us. He turned around and went off to the far end of the chamber.

Shortly thereafter, the Lady Hebe's guard captain approached. The cadade marched smartly up the flight of steps and saluted Loriman with punctiliousness and then stood waiting to be noticed.

"Yes, Scancho?" said Loriman taking the wine glass from his lips.

"Pantor! The Kov Hurngal requests you attend him at the door."

"Oh, he does, does he?"

The way the request was phrased was bound to inflame the Hunting Kov.

And then one of Rogarsh's Rapas, feathers bristling, beak gaping, waving his arms about like a maniac, ran full tilt out from the furniture and bolted up the steps. He made no attempt at protocol or waiting to be noticed.

"We have been betrayed!" he shrieked. "Kov Hurngal has taken his people out and shut the door and bolted it fast! It is unbreakable. We are locked in. We are trapped in the maze!"

Nineteen

Kov Hurngal's treachery is repaid

When the shouting and raging and futile hammering at the door at last finished, I thought Kov Loriman was in fair case to blow up completely. The choleric face was a single scarlet blot, the eyebrows marvels of bristling anger, and he kept opening and closing his fists like claws, as though he had Hurngal's neck fast clenched there.

"The treacherous traitorous bastard!" he choked out, stuttering with the rage that possessed him.

I caught Seg's eye and nodded so we took ourselves off out of it for a space. Nath followed us. He looked downcast.

I said: "Did any of you see the outside of that damned door when we marched in?"

"No. Both leaves were folded right back against the wall." Seg spoke quite calmly. "The Rapa says there was a bar as big as a treetrunk, and bolts of iron."

"There are ways of breaking down doors. That does not cause me concern. The effect on Loriman is unpredictable. And Hebe has been deprived of her cadade and has gone off with Hurngal."

"Scancho works for Loriman," said Nath. "He was given the cadade's job to keep an eye on her for the Hunting Kov." The way Nath said that indicated clearly his view of kovs, whether of the hunting variety or not.

"When Loriman intrigued to get Hurngal's cash and influence," said Seg, "he didn't bargain that the lady in the middle would go over to the other side."

"Well," I said, and I brisked up, "we'll burn the dratted door down and then we'll get after the witch."

Amid shouts and counter shouts, Loriman sent all his and the others' people off to knock on the walls and uncover the secret doors that had to be here somewhere.

There were very few slaves trapped with us. They had not ventured up onto the railed area to eat and drink and they'd clustered among themselves. Now we could see that Hurngal had swept up everybody's slaves he could lay his hands on to carry his treasure. A bold confident planning kind of rogue, this, then.

I picked up a slender wooden chair and smashed it against the floor. It splintered into pieces.

Loriman ripped out: "By Armipand's black belly, Bogandur, that may do your bad temper good. It won't help us find a way out of this trap."

"On the contrary, kov."

Seg broke a wooden table up very smartly.

I said as I reached for another chair, "We'll burn the damned door down."

"Oh!" said Kov Loriman, the Hunting Kov.

The listlessness of this stranded party of adventurers, as though they labored under a doomdark fate, materially lightened when they set to work to pile inflammables by the doors. During our travels through the maze we had slept on and off, and it now seemed fitting before we set fire to the door and escaped that we should rest. Loriman would have none of that.

"After the rast! Top speed. I'll cut him down where he stands, the yetch!"

A few moments' reflection convinced me that it was not worth tangling with Loriman over this. He was right, from his point of view, in pursuing the treacherous kov as quickly as possible.

That we had other fish to fry appeared to have been forgotten by him. Now, he lusted for revenge.

Although the sacred and magical number on Kregen is nine, there are many stories and legends current of the Secret Seven. These fabled champions, skilled, tough, quick of foot and eye, never downcast no matter how their losses mount, striving always to climb the ladder of success, provide a clarion call of honor and striving to the children of the lands of Paz on that monstrous and beautiful, terrible and lovely world of Kregen four hundred light-years from the world of my birth.

Revenge, the Secret Seven had proved in many a lusty tale of adventure, paid no dividends.

I said, "Very well, kov. We have yet to reach into the heart of Spikatur."

"We will, we will. Pandrite the All-Glorious will guide our footsteps after I have struck down that cowardly Kov Hurngal ham Hortang."

So we fired the huge jumbled pile of lumber heaped up high against the doors and retired to the railed area to await results.

The smoke wafted in flat oily streamers and the flames spat merrily. The clustered bat-creatures on the ceiling began to stir, to flutter wings, and to drop down erratically. San Aramplo had happened to mention that he believed these creatures to be Wargovols. They swooped down in droves, uncertain, disturbed, and circled and so sought to regain their perches in the ceiling. And the smoke wafted up among them and their shrill squeaking pierced through with a menace we could not avoid.

The lumber stacked up burned through in gouts of flame and the doors still burned when Kov Loriman seized an axe from one of his Chulik guards and hurled himself forward. Like a crazy man, he hacked and hewed at the door amid the smother of ashes and dust, the clouds of smoke and the spurts of flame. He burst the charred wood through and the leaves of the door creaked open.

Blackened, bloated, bold, the Hunting Kov smashed his way through the ruined doors to freedom.

"Hai!" I roared, giving him some of the accolade he deserved, for he was a spritely fellow, and yet withholding the "jikai" which was totally inappropriate at this juncture.

Seg said: "He may be a right bastard; but you have to give the old sod credit, by Vox!"

The brown breechclout I had had from Mistress Tlima was now soiled and in a distressing condition. I went across to the nearest red velvet drape and slashed a length free with the short sword. I fashioned this into a breechclout and drew the ends around my waist and up and so fastened all securely with the broad lesten hide belt with the dulled silver buckle. I own, the thought of the brave old red, even though it was more crimson than scarlet, heartened me.

Seg did the same.

We had to make a run for it at the end when the Wargovols, smoke-maddened, whirled down in a fluttering storm of wings.

They did not follow us from that chamber.

No difficulty at all presented itself to hinder us in our pursuit. The way Hurngal had taken was obvious and easy to follow. That route was marked. We simply followed along the trail of corpses.

As we pressed on so we saw that the character of the dead changed; at first they were all slaves, half-naked, weaponless and without burdens, then we saw the sacks flung down among the corpses and soon there were more guards than slaves and then no slaves at all and only fighting men lying there in their own blood.

"The witch is enjoying herself," I said to Loriman. I'd bustled up through our people in order to get near him—just in case. His purple-veined nose had simmered down a trifle and his anger was now of that icy contained variety so frightening in a choleric fleshy fellow. "She is torturing these poor devils."

"I care nothing for them. I hope Hurngal is suffering. And if he lets any harm come to the Lady Hebe..."

Strom Tothor spoke in a most shrunken lion-roar. "They take all attention, for we are unattacked."

"Quite."

Loriman forced the pace on. "We must be close to the way out now. That is why the witch is so ferocious."

I did not disabuse him, for in his rage he was contradicting his earlier belief and agreeing with Hurngal. Among the dead littering the passageway lay many a fine hyrpaktun with the golden pakzhan at his throat, and many a mercenary with the silver pakmort. Csitra, I felt, had played with us enough and was now finishing it.

If she had indulged in another quarrel with her hermaphrodite child Phunik, both their attentions would be absorbed. Csitra had her limitations. It was possible to escape whole from the Coup Blag. There was, also, the overly handsome young man called Pamantisho the Beauty to slake Csitra's lust and keep her occupied.

We entered another of the enormous rooms in this labyrinth, of similar proportions to the chamber in which Hurngal had trapped us. By that treachery he had materially assisted his own doom, for we were a powerful fighting force.

So thinking, I strode into the chamber, and stopped, stock still, and everyone stopped with me, and so we gazed upon the hecatomb. We saw the end

503

of it, there, in those wildly distorted bodies, in the agony and terror on those tortured faces, in the drippings and drenchings of blood splattered everywhere. They were all dead, all of them. San Aramplo the Khibil sorcerer was there in the shambles, and, as we could see, his arts had failed him.

Kov Hurngal was there. We recognized him by his armor and clothes, for his face was ripped off. A broken sword gripped in his fist told he had fought valiantly.

Near him lay the Lady Hebe.

Nobody went near Kov Loriman. We all gave him a wide berth. He knelt by the dead woman, head bowed, and knuckles on the floor, almost like a whipped and beaten curdog. He remained like that until the next phase in this ghastly maze, and no doubt might have stayed like that until he died of hunger and thirst.

Nobody said anything. We looked about like men drunk on terror.

Now the whole oppressive atmosphere of the Coup Blag descended on us. We were conscious of the weight of rock pressing down all about us. We found it difficult to breathe. Sweat started up all over our bodies. We all felt that amidst the horror and the terror we, also, must have reached the end of our adventure.

At the far end of the chamber a balcony extended the full width of the wall. How deep it might be I could only conjecture, for it was covered by green curtains and the hall under the balcony lay in deep shadow. Along the left-hand wall the balcony extended as a small gallery at a lower level. On the right-hand wall the balcony reached much farther and this extension, too, was covered by green curtains. That it projected only a couple of feet could mean that it was that narrow, or that its extent lay farther into the depths of the maze.

Green and red lights shone in the shadows under the balcony. They were not all in pairs. Some there were grouped in fours. The scuffling sound of furtive movement scraped on the marble pavement. The eyes brightened and grew nearer. Lambent green, smoky red, they leered upon us in their hundreds.

Slowly, out from the shadows of the balcony into the brilliantly chandelier-lit chamber, the horrors advanced. They wriggled and squirmed along; clawed feet rang sharply against the marble, soft and slimy pads made sucking sounds, some of the monsters flew hovering. So the host of nauseating monstrosities came fully into the light to reveal all their murderous hideousness.

"So that's what happened to these poor devils," said Seg. He reached up for a rose-red-fletched arrow.

Nath the Impenitent drew his sword. His face was set. "We're done for, doms. But we'll give 'em a fight."

"The last great fight," said the Rapa, Tyr Rogarsh the Rattler. His feathers had never looked more colorful.

"Aye," said the numim, Strom Tothor ham Hemfar. "The last battle. And, this will be a High Jikai."

Scancho the Chulik guard captain just set himself ready to honor his dark Chulik code.

So these people with me prepared for the last great fight, a struggle that would in Zair's own truth be a High Jikai.

There was no doubt that we were doomed, as the folk with Kov Hurngal had been doomed.

"What in the name of Numi-Hyrjiv the All Glorious are they waiting for?" demanded Tothor.

For the horde of unspeakable creatures shuffled and clicked and clacked and squirmed—and waited.

The green velvet curtains covering the balcony parted down the center. Slowly they pulled apart.

"I see," said Seg. "The bitch."

On the balcony and bathed in an uncertain light reared a golden throne. Its edges were hard and defined where they were not smothered in chavonth pelts and ling furs and trailing multi-colored silks. High above the throne the monstrous head of a scaled risslaca gaped down, wedge-shaped jaws extended, forming a mantling canopy. The eyes were hooded ruby lights. To stand before the throne and gape up gave any onlooker a creepy feeling of ominous and malefic power ready to strike.

Half-naked Chail Sheom lay chained about the steps of the throne and weird men and women gripped the leashes of weirder beasts. The coiling miasmic stink of a multitude of overpowering scents wafted down.

Yet throne, scaled dinosaur canopy, the pearl-strung slave girls, the half-tamed throne beasts, and all the glitter of gold and gems paled beside the woman who sat in the chair of the throne.

Her face, as pale as the snows of the north, held no tinge of color. Severe, erect, dressed in black and green with much gold, she surveyed us with those eyes like sliding luminous slits of jade. Her dark hair swept down over her forehead into a widow's peak and was combed into long tresses over her shoulders. A small replica of the wedge-shaped dinosaur head studded the center of the jeweled band around her hair.

So she sat, her pointed chin propped on a beringed hand, arm girt with the glitter of bracelets. She brooded on us and on what would follow when she gave the word to her creatures to begin the slaughter.

We would fight. We would put up a brave show. We'd go down bellowing our defiance, shrieking the "Hai Jikai!" as our guts spilled, our faces were ripped off, or our heads rolled bouncing across her marble floor.

Seg stood calmly, bow half-drawn, ready for the end. The others waited in the same grim silence. This, then, was the end?

I threw off my leather war-harness. Clad only in the red breechclout, with the Krozair brand glittering before me, I stepped out alone.

"Csitra!" I bellowed in that old foretop-hailing roar and the echoes rang around that stupendous hall. "Csitra! I gave you my promise to visit you. Well, lady, here I am!"

Twenty

The Scorpion of the Star Lords

The echoes of that shout rang and rustled and so died in the chamber.

Csitra did not move. I fancied those slit eyes of jade slid to regard me. Well, by Zim-Zair! She could hardly miss me, could she, stuck out as I was like a sore thumb before the remnants of the expedition.

What my comrades at my back were doing I didn't know; I just hoped they'd let me get on with it. Now I had to concentrate every ounce of my willpower to confront this stupendously powerful woman. If she willed, she could whiff me and all of us away in a single casual gesture of those slender white fingers, ring bedecked. At least, I supposed so.

At last she spoke, breathily, on a gasp. "I do not think I really believed you, my love."

Those last two words made me cringe.

"But you are here." Her voice grew in strength. "You did come to see me as you promised."

"Certainly," I said.

"But why like this? You might have been killed, for I did not know. Oh, my heart, if one of my clever traps had... I cannot speak it. You must come up here at once, I will send..." She was fluttering like a teenager going to her first real grown-up dance. "You are here! You have come to visit me in the Coup Blag! That surely must mean—"

"Mother." The whispering fragile voice penetrated with utter clarity into the hall and with utter horror. "It means he is here to be slain, surely?"

The green curtains over the side balcony parted. The first thing I heard sent a shudder of remembered revulsion through me. The tiny golden bells, tinkling and tintinnabulating around the palanquin, heralded the arrival of Phu-Si-Yantong, as now it heralded the presence of his brat, the uhu Phunik. The Wizard of Loh's procession came into view on the balcony.

All sliding cloth of gold curtains, massive bull-horned Womoxes to carry the chair, chained and beaten Chail Sheom half-naked yet draped with pearls, obscene beasts hardly of Kregen, a retinue of damned Kata-kis as evil a bunch of slavers and slavemasters as you'd hope not to meet, guards of fantastic and eerie appearance—yes, the child of Phu-Si-Yantong and Csitra could put on a show. As for the uhu, only a glimpse of a dark shadow against the red-gold and purple-black, the tilt of a small imperious head, furtive, furtive...

"That's a pity," came Seg's cheerful voice over my shoulder. "And, my old dom, you were getting on so well with your light o' love."

"You wait," I said, without turning. "I think we must try a few falls for a remark like that."

"Absolutely. I'll wait. Shall I shaft the little horror?"

"You can try. I doubt—"

"Aye, you're right. Damned magic."

This pleasant byplay took heartbeats only, and Phunik's hateful voice whispered on. "You cannot be serious, mother, surely? For this man is dangerous and must die."

"No!" Csitra's gasp slapped like an open palm against a fleshy cheek. "He belongs to me!"

Now Phunik proved him, her or itself a true child to Phu-Si-Yantong. The voice scratched now like a nail against glass.

"Very well, mother, as the Seven Arcades witness the compact. You are no longer to be trusted to carry on my father's work. I shall dispose of this offal here and then you, too, must join the man, if that is your desire."

Phunik gave Csitra no time to reply. A shaft of pure white light sprang from the palanquin.

The light splashed against the floor ten feet from us, and the floor boiled and burned and melted. The sound of the uhu's laugh of pleasure was unmitigated evil. The next blast would do for us.

The corpse of San Aramplo stirred. He sat up. The Khibil's whiskers were as red as ever; but his face was the color of lead and green cheese, glistening, blank, shrunken. The eyes opened. His hand lifted, pointed.

"Die!" screeched Phunik and unleashed his power and between the uhu and the dead Khibil grew a shining disc of radiance, spinning, spitting off sparks of power, hissing with malefic energy.

Phunik strove. The uhu must have realized what went forward here. The Khibil was dead, yet he stood up and opened his eyes and raised his hand and poured forth occult power!

Between the two sorcerers, one in his palanquin and the other dead, grew the famed and feared Quern of Gramarye. Fed by the combined forces in opposition, the radiant disc of raw energy moved. Slowly at first, and then with more assured power, it surged through the air toward the balcony and the palanquin and Phunik.

How many, I wondered, how many of my three comrades were using their kharrna thus to afford us protection? Deb-Lu with his funny toppling turban, Khe-Hi with his smart alec manner, and Ling-Li with all the secrets of a Witch of Loh—yes, the three of them should have no problem in dealing with the uhu Phunik even if he was the son of Phu-Si-Yantong and possessed of great Kharrna.

The whispering fragile voice screeched.

"Mother! Help me!"

Khe-Hi and Deb-Lu between them had struggled with and overcome Phu-Si-Yantong away in the arena of the Jikhorkdun in Ruathytu, capital of Hamal. He'd had Csitra to help him at a distance; he had failed and the Quern of Gramarye had smashed his evil genius into some other and occult realm of death.

Phunik knew only too well how his father had died.

"Mother!" The screech was frantic. "*Help me!*"

"Remember Phunik's promise to you, Csitra!" I bellowed up.

"Phunik is my child—"

"The child of Phu-Si-Yantong and sworn now to slay you, woman!"

"*Mother!*"

San Aramplo's corpse jaws clacked open.

The voice was that of Deb-Lu-Quienyin.

"Your assistance would be useless, Csitra. The child should never have been born, as you well know. The Seven Arcades are not to be insulted or deceived."

The rampaging circle of liquid light roared on and over the balcony and, just at the end, it constricted and contracted and lanced like a single battering ram shaft of pure radiance, whisked the palanquin away to nothingness.

San Aramplo said: "We knew you would help the uhu, Csitra; misbegotten child or not, Phunik was yours. Do not mourn him or feel your help might have made any difference. The child was doomed from the moment of its conception."

The Khibil sorcerer collapsed, returning whence he had come, gone again to join his predecessors in the Thaumaturges of Thagramond.

"Do I believe all this?" demanded Nath the Impenitent. He glared balefully at the gibbering horde of malformed creatures under the balcony.

A shrilling vibrated the air. My eardrums pained. With the disappearance of Phunik many of the more obscene and grotesque creatures in his retinue also vanished. The Katakis glared about stupidly, their bladed tails circling dangerously above their heads. The Chail Sheom were wailing and carrying on. The Womoxes just ran away, bellowing.

The roof of that stupendous chamber split.

The floor cracked across, the flames and foul-smelling fumes boiled up. Smoke black and choking began to fill the hall.

Nath the Impenitent turned to me, his face a sweating mask, and said, "Dray! Phunik's handiwork is collapsing. You must all get out at once! Run!"

Seg rapped out: "Deb-Lu knows what he's talking about. Come on, my old dom! Sprint!"

"Aye! Up there—see through the crack in the roof—the Suns!"

A whole section of wall smashed down, bringing the adjacent roof with it. Columns were toppling and spilling their drums across the floor. Like madmen we all started to clamber up the rubble to freedom. A Chulik was struck by a dislodged capital and fell, blood streaming from that shaven head. I grabbed his arm and hauled him on, and Nath seized his other arm and together we scrabbled somehow up the slope of detritus.

The gratitude with which I saw that emerald and ruby radiance pouring through the ruined roof shook me with its violence. To breathe fresh air! To walk in the light of the Suns of Scorpio! To get out of this vile place!

I cast a look back. The hall continued to disintegrate although the thrilling vibration slackened and died. My ears still sang with the reverberations. Yet the balcony whereon Csitra sat enthroned in so much sumptuous glory remained intact. Some parts of the Coup Blag had been fashioned by her. The maze still existed and only those portions designed by Phunik would be destroyed.

The Impenitent had my harness slung over his shoulder and now he said: "You'd best put this on, Jak. Scabbard that damned great bar of iron."

"Yes," I said. "My thanks, Nath."

I took my gear without looking at Nath. She continued to stare up at me, those slits of jade startling in the pallor of her face. Around her existed the faintest haze, and I guessed she had encased herself and her throne and retainers in a Caul of Protection.

What was she thinking?

Her power had been seriously weakened. No longer could she call on the kharrna of her child to reinforce her own.

Was she still suffering under the passion for me that had so deluded her crazed mind? Or would she now hate and loathe me because her child was gone?

Balancing on the broken shards of the hall, I swung the wounded Chulik around into the path of another.

"Take care of your comrade, Chulik!" I snarled at him, and he grasped the wounded man and went scrabbling on up the slope of rubble toward the light of the suns.

"Go on! Go on!" I yelled. I motioned to Nath and Seg, savage, intemperate, not to be disobeyed. Seg wanted to come down. I said, "This I must do, Seg."

"Don't be long. That's all. Or I'll be back."

Good old Seg! So, in the end, I was left alone on that smoking pile of rubble staring down on Csitra as the Witch of Loh gazed somberly up at me.

And, in that fraught moment, as I truly believe, I did feel sorry for her.

She had been led into paths of wickedness by Phu-Si-Yantong and, no doubt, by her own willful passions. The devil had tempted her and she had succumbed. Yet, now, her husband was dead and her child was dead. I did not know if she had other children. Her dreams had vanished. She was alone.

A slithering slide of rubble smashed into the marble pavement off to the side. I ignored the disturbance. Still she stared up, and I swear the brilliance flamed from those slits of luminous emerald eyes. If she put forth her kharrna now and blasted me on the spot... But she must have recognized the futility of that. She must have known that she could not hope to defeat three mages who would instantly hurl their kharrna through me to smash the coruscating Quern of Gramarye upon her.

With a grating metallic sound the green curtains began to close over the throne and its sumptuousness and upon Csitra, the Witch of Loh.

Just before the curtains closed to blot her from view, I heard her through all the uproar of a collapsing palace hall call out to me.

"Despite all, Dray Prescot, I do not yield my claim on you. That, I will never give up!"

She was gone, the green curtains shivering together.

A prodigious crash from the hall as though the bottom of the world had caved in at last drew my attention to what was going on out there. Smoke and dust obscured the air. Columns fell like ninepins. Kov Loriman still knelt by the body of the Lady Hebe and as I caught a distorted glimpse of him through the smoke the floor in front of him parted as though sliced by a knife. A fault line, sharp and distinct, opened and the marble floor dropped away. The Lady Hebe vanished into the depths and Loriman was left kneeling on the lip of the chasm.

He extended both arms as though in prayer.

Although the deed would not be in the character of the man, had he leaped into the gulf after the lady, I would not have been surprised.

Leaping fallen heaps of masonry, I reached him. He stood up with the stiff motions of old age. Now was no time to take chances. I had plans for this man, vast plans, and if he balked me by killing himself off, I would be mightily displeased.

So I hit him flush on the jaw and seized him and so slung him over my shoulder.

Noxious fumes boiled from the chasm that had swallowed the Lady Hebe. The balcony where Csitra sat enthroned might be the only portion of this hall created by her; all the rest, being Phunik's, was disintegrating. Hefting Loriman like a sack of potatoes, I scrambled over the rubble, feeling the floor lurching, started for the slope which led to freedom and the light of the suns.

Chunks of masonry and brick from the collapsing ceiling still rained down. Tiles skated like bats. Statues did not come to life—nothing unusual for Kregen if they had—but tottered and fell. Seg appeared at the top of the rubble slope, saw me, and started down.

Like a squall of sleeting hailstones a curtain of stones slashed down between us.

Seg's yell just reached me. "Leave him!"

"Stand fast! I can make it!"

The rubble began to slide away from under my feet. My legs pumped, and stones, bricks, broken tiles and flat chunks of plaster seethed away, sending up choking clouds of dust.

A scorpion appeared and stood on a smashed capital and waved his feelers at me. His arrogant sting curved up over his back. He spoke to me, words that drilled through the bedlam of a collapsing palace.

"You must put him down, Dray Prescot, Prince of Onkers. You must save yourself for the work the Star Lords demand."

"And this man is a part of that work, scorpion, onker yourself!"

"You must do as you are commanded."

A damned great chunk of brick came from somewhere and hit me glancingly on the shoulder. Could Csitra be hurling these brickbats at me in an occult temper?

I started off, clutching Loriman, scrabbling and heaving up the rubble.

The agile figure of Seg showed ahead as I glanced up, scrambling down to me.

Another bulky shape sprang into view abaft Seg and started down. Nath the Impenitent might hate and detest the lords he'd known in life; he found Seg and me of different mettle.

Even if a magical palace fell down about my ears, I, Dray Prescot, the Lord of Strombor and Krozair of Zy, wasn't going to be beaten by a damned heap of rubble.

The blue radiance swept in fast and sharp, bloating into the phantom form of the giant Scorpion. Coldness washed me, I was swept up and away, head over heels into a limbo of nothingness.

Well, one thing I knew. I intended to have a few hard words with the Star Lords this time when they thumped me down before them. Super-human entities or no damned superhuman entities—very hard words, by Zair!

WARLORD OF ANTARES

Warlord of Antares

Dray Prescot has been described by someone who has seen him on this Earth as a man above middle height with brown hair and level brown eyes, brooding and dominating, with enormously broad shoulders and powerful physique. He moves like a savage hunting cat, silent and deadly. There is about him an abrasive honesty and an indomitable courage.

Reared in the harsh conditions of Nelson's Navy, he failed to find success on Earth. When the Savanti nal Aphrasöe selected and then rejected him for their purposes, he was taken up by the Everoinye, the Star Lords. They have flung him through four hundred light-years of empty space to the planet Kregen, orbiting the binary Antares, many times. On Kregen, beautiful and terrible, exotic and mysterious, Prescot's innate talents flowered and he secured success beyond his wildest dreams.

Now the grouping of continents and islands called Paz are threatened by the Shanks, fish-headed reivers from over the curve of the world. Prescot's task now is to unite all of Paz in alliance against the aggressors. Not all the people of Paz are willing to forget their old enmities. And there is Csitra, the Witch of Loh, who lusts after Prescot and would drag down all of Vallia to ruin for his sake. In the passionate, shrewd, charismatic figure of Delia of Delphond, and his family and blade comrades, Prescot possesses riches past the mundane dreams of empire.

Alan Burt Akers

One

Metal

I, Dray Prescot, the Lord of Strombor and Krozair of Zy, whirled head over heels helplessly through a tempestuous void into the black boiling belly of hell.

"What the hell's going on?" I bellowed. It felt as though I yelled with a mouth full of feathers.

Around and around I went, up and down, and I sincerely believed I was being pulled apart, as those unpleasant Echenegs pull people apart with a variety of wild animals. I tried to curl up into a fetal ball.

This experience was entirely new. The Star Lords had sent their giant blue Scorpion down to snatch me up from Kregen. I expected to be taken through various chambers and possibly be transported in a marvelous chair that hissed, and so be able to speak to those distant, immortal and superhuman entities the Everoinye.

Instead I was being torn to pieces in a black whirling madhouse.

Just what, by the putrescent eyeballs and pustular nose of Makki Grodno, was going on?

I know I am a fallible clown. The years spent on Earth trying to make a career in Nelson's Navy had been blank for me. I'd had a few successes since being hauled up by the ears and dumped down into trouble on Kregen. Yes, I supposed I was some way on to the grand scheme of uniting the peoples of the lands of Paz.

This time, when I saw the Star Lords, I'd said to myself, this time I'll have a few very hard words for them.

So they dragged me up in the midst of a whirlwind, battered my ears with blasts of wind and horrendous noise, tumbled me upside down and inside out for all I knew.

My heels hit hard and jarred clear up the spine into my skull.

I staggered forward. The blackness like the ear cavity of a Lepecranch bat folded about me. I blinked.

Well, I still wore the brave old scarlet breechclout. I still had the Krozair longsword. Apart from those two items and the sailor knife scabbarded from its belt over my right hip, there was only me.

With a convulsive heave I stumbled up. I shook my fist at the impenetrable blackness.

"All right, you high and mighty Everoinye! Come on! Let's be having you!"

If anything, the wind screeched louder and more fiercely, and a cold cutting edge of ice crept into its teeth.

"Damn you, you indifferent—" I roared on, verbiage of almost meaningless bravado when set against the awful forces colliding about my insignificant form. The words were stoppered in my throat.

A single slashing streak of viridian green swiped all across that blackness and drove sparkles and spots of brilliance into my eyes.

That searing shaft of green lasted only a couple of heartbeats and was gone; I knew who—or what—it was.

That was the impetuous and icily contemptuous Star Lord the others called Ahrinye. I thought he would be no friend to me.

The whole world shifted and swung and I fell to my knees. I didn't know if I was on a world, any world, or drifted on a shard of rock between the stars, or was buried deep within some unguessable hell.

I knew the Star Lords to be fallible, as was I. I could not believe those superhuman entities of vast intellect and distant purposes to be fools. Again, as was I. Their powers were so great that the limited imagination of a mortal man might never encompass a fraction of a jot or tittle. As the universe swept up and down and around and around I tried with barbaric savagery to hold on to the central idea that the Star Lords needed me.

With my own puny willpower I had fought them in the old days when I imagined them indifferent and opposed to all my own wishes. In our more recent alliance I had glimpsed reasons why they had chosen me to do what I had to do for them. I had not fought them recently. But, now...

When all this nonsense settled down and the world became right way up again, I'd have a few words to say, by Zair, a few words!

A looseness in the air about me and a lightness in my limbs heralded another change. The universe steadied. I could smell nothing. The darkness shifted about me and I felt harsh rock beneath my feet; but I could smell nothing and that is always very strange, very strange.

When the pale yellow streak appeared horizontally and glimmered with spectral fires, for a few treacherous moments I imagined this to be Zena Iztar. But this yellow was not her glorious golden yellow, refulgent, bringing a reassurance and a promise. Zena Iztar and I had not met for too long a time and I guessed she was about some supernatural task in realms and dimensions unknowable to mere mortal humanity.

Against the yellow streak, which widened steadily, sharp black peaks stood out like saw edges. I confess it took me a little time to realize I was watching the dawn.

That lemon yellow runneled between the mountain peaks. Shadows lay long and sharp-edged. Each of the scattering of boulders and pebbles all about me on that circular plain cast its own individual shadow. The peaks ringed the plain, and ringed me, too, as though I stood in prison.

Desolation is the only word to describe that place.

I didn't give a damn about the desolation. Only one thing mattered now—and the horror of it made me put my fist onto the hilt of the Krozair longsword, gripping not in bravado but reaching out for reassurance and put a pulse throbbing evilly in my temples.

For if this was the dawn, as indeed it was, and that yellow glow was the sun, as it probably was, why, then I was no longer on Kregen.

The twin suns of Antares, Zim and Genodras, stream down their mingled opaline radiance upon the world of Kregen, red and green, ruby and emerald. Not yellow.

The only other world of which I had any experience was Earth, and Earth has a little yellow sun.

I did not break down in despair, as I had every right to do. I did not think I was on Earth, for the feel to my body recalled a fever dream of the African coast. In the next instant the blackness returned and the madness of whirling about upside down swooped upon me.

When, after what seemed if not an eternity then a damn long time, I was once more plunked down on my feet, I felt convinced that the Star Lords were in deep trouble. Those awesome beings had the power to hurl me about the world of Kregen willy-nilly. They could fling me four hundred light-years back to Earth, and reach out and bring me back—when they chose.

Now, it seemed, they were fumbling what ought to be the simple task of dragging me up into their presence.

I stood upon one of what looked like a worldwide series of metal boxes. Each box was of the size of a decent three-bedroom suburban house. That homely image did nothing to reassure me in the face of this alienness. I felt the oddness, the strangeness. Just metal boxes for as far as I could see, and the alleyways between them slots of shadow, menacing and unfriendly.

Nothing moved in all that metal expanse.

The sky was just a silvery white distance, an even flow of light that illuminated the hard metal and thrust blackness into the slots between.

Because there seemed nothing else to do, I thought I'd take a look at what might exist in the alleyways, seeing that the tops of the boxes were uniformly flat, empty of anything, and dismally uninteresting.

At the corner of the box a metal ladder ran down the side. The rungs were spaced for a normal-sized person. In the context of the inhabitants of Earth, normal-sized can be understood. In those of Kregen it has to be understood to refer, as I use it, to apims, Homo sapiens sapiens like me and the rest of us terrestrials.

518

The rungs of the ladder struck cold. I went down hand under hand and, oddly enough, I recalled the days when I'd had to descend from the rigging via the shrouds instead of as a youngster I'd been in the habit of sliding down the backstay.

The damned ground was all metal, too.

Extending about five feet up from the ground, the wall of the box was discolored. Instead of that steely-silvery sheen, the metal looked rusty, pitted and corroded, as though steel and alloy were breaking down.

The alleyway here was about twenty feet across and the box on the opposite side was also decayed.

Down here the perspective both loomed and towered.

The vanishing point was just that from the extended lines of the edges of the boxes, and I fancied they dwindled out of sight far more sharply than logic would suggest. I did not understand what I was looking at. That goes without saying; but I say it nevertheless in the light of much information that came my way later, information I am sure many of you listening to my narrative on these tapes have been born into.

The dizzying perspective extended to the right and to the left.

Either way, therefore—it didn't matter as far as I could see—would do. So I set off to the left and at the first intersection I took a single step out and immediately whipped back, flat against the metal wall, and the Krozair longsword snouted up.

The man out there wore a complete harness of armor and he carried a nasty-looking sword in his fist.

I waited.

Nothing happened.

Catching a breath and dropping low, I let an eyeball peer around the corner.

The man just stood there.

I watched him.

He stood, silent and motionless. His armor appeared to be fashioned from the same silvery-steely metal as that of the boxes. And from his ankles to his chest, the corroding rust of decay struck pitmarks that caught the light and turned the metal into a granular web.

After a time I straightened up and walked out.

"Llahal, dom," I called in the formal Kregish greeting.

He made no reply. I studied him a trifle more closely, the longsword now hanging at my side. The blade was ready for action, I can tell you, ready for action in a jiffy!

His sword puzzled me, for it was cylindrical as to blade, without guard or quillons, and from its hilt a corrugated tube ran to the pack on the fellow's back.

His face was entirely covered, save for grillwork which I fancied was located in an odd place for either breaths or sights.

519

"Llahal!" I called again.

No reply.

I walked across to him.

Now many folk account me a fellow who walks softly. Some say I move stealthily, and others with less humor say I move sneakily. Either way, on a metal floor, I made no sound.

One of this armored man's legs fell away from his body. He keeled over. His leg crumbled to powder as it hit the ground, and his body tumbled down, to sprawl out in a tangle of metal arms and one metal leg.

I stopped moving.

All I could think was that the vibration through the metal ground had been the final straw in his destruction.

The metal rang with ironic sweetness as it struck the metal ground, a sound incongruous in these arid surroundings.

There was nothing I could do for the poor fellow, so with a word or two to Zair and Djan and Opaz to light him on his way down to the Ice Floes of Sicce, I marched on.

The furtive scuffling sound from ahead came as a positive relief.

Flat against a metal side of a box, I stared down the alleyway.

A thing like a horse-sized caterpillar came into view. He clumped along on a multitude of little legs all going up and down in a rippling rhythm. His four eyes protruded on stalks. His feeding proboscis uncurled as he reached a corroded wall on the next box and I swore he put the end against the decayed metal and started to suck it in. I could have sworn, yes; but it did not seem rational. But, then, what the hell was rational around here just lately?

His body was colored in much the same steely-silvery sheen as the metal all around, and black hairs sprouted here and there. His eyes were red. He slurped the rotten metal in, and soon he'd cut himself a semicircle and was starting on the next sweep.

From locations just beneath and either side of his feeding tube a pair of grasping claws were folded limply. He did not use them to rip the metal away. By their size and ruggedness I fancied he'd have no trouble doing that if he came to a section of metal not quite decayed enough for him to suck up.

There is no pleasure in killing animals. There are really only two reasons or excuses for slaying animals, one that they are dangerous pests, and two you need to eat. I was sharp-set by this time; but this metal-eating caterpillar struck me as being a not particularly tasty dish. So I turned around and went the other way.

Judging by the increasingly desperate state of my stomach, I must have marched on for a good long time. In all that journey the boxes and the alleyways did not vary. I ran across a dozen or so more armored men in the alleyway and a couple more on roofs; not a one of them spoke and none moved. Their armor was in the process of decaying, so I judged the poor devils had been a long time dead.

Also I saw a couple of dozen of the metal-eating caterpillars. I gave them all a wide berth and went on.

What I hoped to achieve by this senseless wandering escaped me. I couldn't just stand in one spot and wait to die. Surely, if I persevered and went on long enough I must come across someone, or something other than these mindless ranks of boxes? I might, if I was not dead of hunger and thirst beforehand.

Just as I'd reached this conclusion in my miserable thoughts I heard a sharp hissing from ahead.

That hissing sounded familiar. It sounded remarkably like the hissing the magical chair of the Star Lords made as it whistled you along from chamber to chamber.

A dark object appeared from an intersection about a hundred yards ahead, flashed across from right to left, vanished.

The shape in the fleeting instant I'd glimpsed it could have been the shape of a Star Lord's chair.

I ran up to the cross alleyway and stared down; there was no sign of the chair and the habitual silence of this place clamped down again.

After that a number of chairs hissed past and always, infuriatingly, across alleyways too far off, so that there was no way I could hail. Always assuming, that was, that anybody sat in the chairs.

The metal boxes possessed doors, as I discovered, of many different sizes. There was no way I could gain ingress. The gap between door and jamb was hairfine thin, and there were no doorknobs, handles or any other system of opening. That there must be a system to open the doors was obvious, otherwise they wouldn't be there; I could not fathom it out.

Soon I was progressing through an area where the decay of the metal walls was far advanced and where large numbers of the caterpillars fed contentedly. I took considerable detours to avoid them.

At one corner I spotted a caterpillar who had been at full stretch, retract his body and go rhythmically off in search of fresh decay. Where he had chopped away left a jagged-edged gap.

Very cautiously I looked inside.

All was in darkness.

The silvery light spilling in from outside revealed what seemed to me to be more ranks of boxes, one after the other, receding into the dimness. There appeared no point in going in there to find a lot of small boxes when I had a lot of big boxes out here to play with.

Yes, I was growing more and more hungry and more and more annoyed.

What I imagined to be the final annoyance, although in that I was wrong, hissed past close at hand. A chair shot out of the alleyway opposite and pelted on and vanished past me. It went by close. And the damned thing was empty.

So, I lifted up my head and voice and I roared out: "Star Lords! What in blazes is going on! Are you all asleep, or are you all senile?"

Echoes rolled around eerily.

"Sink me!" I burst out. "I wish those doddering old fools would get both oars in the water."

Nothing responded so there was nothing I could do but march on in hope.

I didn't go near any of the dead men in their decaying armor. They hadn't been struck down in a fight, so it was a good guess that they'd died of disease. I did not wish to have anything to do with that.

Only one of them was not wearing full harness. He was a numim, and his ferocious lionman's face lay lax and crumpled in death. He carried a water bottle at his belt. I licked my lips. But that water could be the death of me. The numim's chest was crushed in, a most unappetizing sight, and a curved sword lay on the metal near his right hand.

I went on.

Now I really was hungry, and no doubt about it.

Pretty soon I'd join the caterpillars and rip off a chunk of decaying metal and find out what their diet tasted like. They looked big and chunky and well fed. Perhaps the corroded metal was really tasty. I pushed aside vivid mental pictures of pies and puddings, of steaks and gammons, of fruit and vegetables and endless cups of tea, and stalked on. And more and more my gaze was drawn to that rotten and tempting decaying metal.

"By the Black Chunkrah!" Head up, feeling a fool as though I was under observation, I marched over to the nearest wall and ripped off a handful of scrunchy metal.

It felt like biscuits just holding together; crumbs fell away. I molded the handful in my palm. I looked at it. I sniffed it. No smell. Cautiously I tasted a tiny portion with the tip of my tongue. The hardness at once melted into paste. And the taste—deuced odd. Like vinegar, and yet not sharp and unpleasant, with a touch of gherkin in there, and spice, and a generous portion of piccalilli and tomatoes, and, under all this bizarre mixture, the feeling that, yes, by Krun, this was metal I was eating.

I ate some more. After a couple of handfuls it became more than palatable. I could guess that a fellow could get addicted to this stuff. This, therefore, would not do. I did not know of any metal-eating caterpillars on Kregen.

Munching the paste, well, teeth were unnecessary for, as the caterpillars did, I could simply slurp it down once it had been moistened, I trotted on.

I confess I felt in a more reasonable frame of mind. That state of mind was still bloody in the extreme, mind, and I stored up the fruitiest epithets in my skull for use against the Everoinye—when and if they ever put in an appearance.

Now I know about the Mysterious Universe and all that, and of the mystifying nature of humankind's choice, of destiny and all that, and of the inevitability of death; but I hadn't chosen to come here, I was not at this moment concerned with the mystery of the universe, and I most certainly did not intend to die here.

I was interested in the mystery of this place, for understanding that might hoick me out of it.

There appeared to me in all sober reality little chance that I *could* understand this crazy gaggle of metal boxes.

The miserable nagging doubt began to creep in that I had chosen the wrong way, that I should have gone right instead of left.

I can tell you, the bonhomie brought on by an unexpectedly good meal in a place not at once apparent for gastronomic delights, wore off sharpish, very sharpish, by Vox.

In this churlish frame of mind the fact that the metal was not corroded on the boxes I was passing took time to sink in. What made me realize this were the antics of a caterpillar I'd automatically switched alleyways to avoid.

He was lifting his head and aiming that feeding proboscis and shooting a jet of liquid in neat patterned swipes over the wall. The liquid glistered with the sheen of the rainbow before vanishing.

"So that's it," I said. "These hairy horrors squirt some gunk on the metal, that starts to rot away, then they trundle along and slurp it up."

That made no difference to my taste for the stuff. I've eaten far worse than that on Kregen.

Farther on, with pristine boxes all about me, I ran across an object that—at last!—signaled a change.

A slender, near-gossamer tower rose up into that indeterminate silvery sky. The lacework of the weblike struts and girders, delicate and fairy-like, formed a contrast of overwhelming power.

Approaching that enchanted spire with great caution I stared up its height. I couldn't see the top against that all-encompassing whiteness; but it was remote and far distant, for the latticework blended and formed a line no thicker than a hair before it was lost to my vision.

Now why I did what I did might have remained a mystery to me, had not a memory of Zena Iztar occurred to me. When, as Madam Ivanovna, she had visited me on Earth, she had said: "When the need to strike arises, you must strike with a gong-note of power."

What the blazes she'd meant then I'd no idea.

But the memory recurred to me now, and as Zena Iztar might move in mysterious ways but always to a purpose, I whipped up the great Krozair longsword and struck the flat against the latticework of that fairy tower.

The structure gonged pure and mellow.

In the next instant I was upside down, buffeted by a mad whirlpool of blackness, hurtling head over heels out of the blackness and into a refulgent blueness. I gasped as I landed with a thump.

Noise burst about my head, men shouting and arguing, women laughing and screaming, and in my nostrils stank the stenches of a tavern, of rancid fat, of burned meat, of wetted sawdust, the smells of spilled wine and ale and the cheap scents of women.

Two

Of Emperors in a Thieves Tavern

Apart from the too-obvious fact I was in a tavern, I had absolutely no idea where on Kregen I was. Well, that was the usual engaging way of the Star Lords. The Everoinye would drag me off from whatever I happened to be doing and chuck me down somewhere to do their dirty work for them. It was beginning to look as though they were genuinely incapable of doing that work themselves.

Instead of their habitual practice of tossing me in at the deep end to face horrendous perils stark naked, this time I still possessed the scarlet breechclout and the longsword, the belted loincloth and the sailor knife.

Everyone in the tavern must have thought I'd fallen from the balcony along this side of the taproom.

I regained my balance and, rather naturally, the longsword remained in my fist. The blade snouted up and the samphron oil lamps caught and runneled in a golden silver glitter.

An absolute—a deathly—hush fell over the tavern.

No one spoke. No one moved. All that raucous laughter, the screaming of insults, the savage words that must inevitably lead to a fight, all the hullabaloo died as though a giant door had slammed.

They were a rough old lot. Most of them would cross the road to avoid the Watch. There was probably more stolen property about their persons, and no doubt in the landlord's cellars, than would comfortably fit into a six-krahnik wain. Their faces showed the marks of hard experience, of cunning and skullduggery, of thievery and mayhem. Also, they were not too clean and many were scarred and more than a few one-eyed.

In this company the sudden arrival of a stranger was like to see that foolhardy wight with a second mouth to laugh with, a mouth stretching across his throat.

The immediate action into which I had dropped was pitifully obvious. A young lad was being bullied by a hulking brute and in the next few moments would have had his head knocked in and the purse removed from his belt. If this was the state to which the Star Lords had reduced me, then I was very deep down indeed.

Then I contumed myself for a proud idiot. Any injustice must be fought, and if the injustice close to hand appears pitifully insignificant, it is not, and must be fought as hard as the greatest of injustices. For of the small the great are fashioned.

And still that cutthroat crew stood silent and still, glaring on me as though I was a ghost, an ib broken from the flesh and blood body.

Suddenly, as though flung from a catapult, the lad pushed himself up from where the bully had bent him back over the table. He leaped up and instantly dropped down and went into the full incline, nose in the filthy sawdust and brown breechclouted rump high in the air.

A yellow-haired woman, very blowsy, whose bodice strings were unlatched in a slatternly way, screeched in a shriek that pierced eardrums.

"It is! It is the emperor! It is Dray Prescot!"

Then—and I swear it as Zair is my witness!—that whole ruffianly crew from bully to pot boy, thumped down onto their knees, stuck their noses into the sawdust and elevated their bottoms in a sea of rotundity.

In a voice that cracked out more like a whip than a roar, I shouted: "If you know who I am, then you know I do not like the full incline. It is not seemly in a man or woman. By Vox! Stand up!"

The rustlings and surgings and gaspings as they struggled up really were funny; I could see the humorous side of this; but I was all at sea here and in too much of a hurry to laugh. Which is always a mistake.

There was no surprise to be felt when the lad and the bully and the yellow-haired woman all started in shouting at one another and at me, accusing, counter-accusing. The row was over the woman's affections, a perfectly ordinary squabble. Harm might have come to the lad. So the Emperor of Vallia had dropped in to sort out the problem and see justice was done.

They were not surprised, once they'd overcome the initial shock. Everyone in Vallia had read the books, read or heard the poems, seen the plays and puppet shows, telling of the deeds of Dray Prescot. No one bothered to wonder how the emperor could be in so many places at one and the same time. He was Dray Prescot, and so he could be expected to turn up in times of trouble.

An old buffer with lank hair, three front teeth and a look of a dyspeptic owl sitting on a stool to the side, and saying nothing, ought to be the one.

I said: "Dom, tell me the rights of this."

He led off at once, cacklingly, relating how young Larghos thought he was beloved of Buxom Trodi, who was enamored of Nath the Biceps.

"They but gulled the lad, majister, and no harm done. But young Larghos pulled a knife—"

I glared at the youngster.

"Did you draw steel in this quarrel?"

He flushed scarlet and stammered. "Yes, majister."

Probably he had intended to scare Nath the Biceps off before his head was bashed in. I suggested that.

"No, majister. That is, yes, majister; but I did not want to kill Nath. If the knife had stuck him a little, I would not have sorrowed."

Nath the Biceps, boiling up, broke out with: "I was only going to clip you side o' the ear, you great fambly!"

"So the matter is settled." I spoke like granite. "You must find another light o' love, Larghos."

"Indeed, yes, majister. Thank you, majister."

"Thank you, majister," chorused the other two.

I stared around the taproom by the light of the samphron oil lamps. A place like this would normally be lit by cheap mineral oil lamps. A thieves' den, then.

I spoke forcefully.

"You have evidently not heard. I have renounced the crown of Vallia. I am no longer the emperor, nor is the divine Delia the empress. Our son and his bride now rule. Hai, Jikai, Drak and Silda, Emperor and Empress of Vallia!"

One or two of them called out a "Hai, Jikai."

Others shuffled their feet. A lot had reason to turn their heads. I felt the puzzlement.

"What ails you, doms? Why do you not give the Hai, Jikai to our new emperor and empress?"

The lank-haired, three-toothed buffer piped up, speaking for all.

"We heard, majister, as my name is Orol the Wise. We scarcely credited that you would turn your back on Vallia and leave us, thieves though we be. For our sons and daughters have served you well. We have nothing against Prince Drak and Princess Silda. But you and the divine Delia are emperor and empress. Opaz knows that."

I couldn't very well ask them where I was. Well, I could, and they'd answer and most of them would think this merely another whim. But I fancied I didn't need to ask. I thought I was in Vondium, the capital of Vallia. I thought I was in the old city, in Drak's City, a place apart, a city within a city, the haunt of thieves and runaways, of disaffected folk and of assassins.

"Yes," I said. "Your young men have served as kreutzin and have done prodigies. But all our loyalties go now to the new emperor and empress."

"It's not right," spoke out a fellow with one eye and a scar to match.

I shook my head. Well, of course, this whole scene was farcical. Here was I arguing the rights and wrongs of empire with a bunch of cutthroats in an evil-smelling tavern. Yet the situation was serious. Was this the attitude of many of the citizenry of Vallia? If so, it portended ill for my lad Drak and his gorgeous bride Silda, the daughter of my blade-comrade Seg Segutorio.

So, in that lugubrious and squalid tavern I spoke up and told them somewhat of the dangers of the Shanks from over the curve of the world, how they raided us.

"These devilish Fish-heads burn and pillage and seize all. Now they will attack inland as well as our coasts, for they have fliers."

At this there was a murmur of alarm and horror.

"Yes, doms, we in Vallia are in for it. All the lands of Paz must unite together to resist these Leem Lovers. If we fail to act together now, we will not have another chance."

A fellow with a glint of silver at his throat, wearing a leather jack and with a scar across his jaw that gave his whole countenance a leering and lopsided look, shouldered up. He carried, I noticed, a drexer for a sword. In his left fist he held a tankard which slopped suds; but he was not intoxicated. His right fist rested on his broad lestenhide belt whose buckle looked to be gold. I say looked, the ways of these folk in Drak's City are cunning in forgery and artifice.

"Emperor," he cried. "Majister. We have fought for Vallia against the Hamalese, and against the Clansmen from Segesthes. We have fought the damned Pandaheem. Now you ask us to make friends with them, perhaps to kiss them on the cheek."

"If necessary," said I, speaking up. "If you care for a mouthful of whiskers, that is."

That raised a few titters.

He was not to be deterred. He had darkish hair which grew low on his forehead, and darkish eyebrows which knit furiously together as he scowled.

"You say, majister, you are not the emperor any more. You are *our* emperor, and we have fought for you. I have never fought in any of Prince Drak's armies."

I had him to rights now. I didn't know his name—well, even with the memory conferred upon me by the Savanti nal Aphrasöe, I couldn't know the name of every swod in the army.

But he'd be one of the mercenaries who'd returned home from service overseas and would have been used as a drill-master for the young lads from Drak's City who had been volunteered into the new Vallian army by the Aleygyn, the chief of the assassins of Drak's City. He wore no rank markings; he'd be a Deldar at the least. I had not missed the silver glitter at his throat marking him for a mortpaktun, a renowned mercenary.

"What regiment?" I said.

"Fourth Emperor's Yellow Jackets, majister."

"A right hairy bunch. I know of your deeds. Your name?"

"Ord-Deldar Yomin the Clis, majister."

"Very well, Deldar. I tell you in Opaz's twinned truth, I have renounced the crown and throne of Vallia, I have abdicated, and the divine Delia, also. The Emperor Drak and the Empress Silda are now your lawful lords and lady. It is to them we all owe our duty."

Those ferocious eyebrows of his twisted about at this. Then a sudden and cunning expression turned his face into a veritable mask of shrewdness.

He flung up his right hand, excited with his own discovery.

"Listen, doms!" he bellowed. "I have riddled it! I see it all! All the lands of Paz must unite and we all know there is only one person who can perform that prodigious task."

"Aye!" they cackled it out, laughing at their own access of understanding. "Aye! Only one man!"

"Of course Dray Prescot and the divine Delia must have someone else on the throne of Vallia, for they are to lead all Paz! It is sooth. Hai, Dray Prescot! Hai, Delia! *Emperor of Emperors and Empress of Empresses*! Hai, Jikai! Hai, Jikai!"

So they all took it up, caterwauling it out, over and over, and a fine show they made of flashing wicked-looking knives and cudgels and coshes in the air. What a rapscallion bunch!

And I stood there, like a loon, like the fallible fool I was. I, Dray Prescot, the Lord of Strombor and Krozair of Zy—and various other bodies besides—was now to add to my burden of titles a fresh load of responsibility hung on me by a pack of rogues in a dissolute tavern!

It was enough to make a plain old sailorman snatch off his hat and throw it on the ground and jump on it, by Zair!

The pandemonium hullabalooed on and it might have gone on until the Ice Floes of Sicce went up in steam for all I knew. But a blueness swept in and I felt the cold and the wind and I began that long fall upward into the giant blue form of the Scorpion, huge and ghostly and radiantly blue above me.

What that plug ugly bunch in the tavern thought I didn't know. They'd just put this flashy vanishment down to another of those fabulous Dray Prescot tricks, to be repeated in story and song and regaled to one and all around the hearth, around the campfires, in hall and hovel alike all over Vallia.

528

Around me the blueness swelled and bloated with that phantom form of the Scorpion. The red flush spread across my vision and there was not a single spark of golden yellow or, thankfully, of acrid green.

As I whirled up through the void so I realized all my anger against the Star Lords had evaporated. I couldn't sustain that juvenile emotion under the stress of sheer continued existence. Emperor of Emperors? I didn't want to be an Emperor of bloody Emperors!

So, out of the blueness I somersaulted and so crashed down thump into a room into which I had never been before. I knew I was about to speak with the Star Lords, and anyone who spoke to *them* needed to think long and deeply on what he said. Long and deeply, by Zair.

Three

I treat with the Star Lords

Mind you, I *ought* still to be angry with the Star Lords.

Their information had told me the damned Shanks were attacking Mehzta, hundreds of dwaburs away to the east. The conquest of the island would take them some time. We could not send our own troops because of the troubles through which we were going. You have time, the Everoinye had told me, you have time to settle affairs in Vallia and to prepare Paz for the Shank invasion.

And the fishy-headed devils had turned up to attack us in Pandahem, just south of here.

Not only that, the Shanks used airboats, fliers that sailed through the air and fought us with fire. Yes, the Star Lords should have warned of that.

That was the bone of contention I had with them.

The room, oval in shape and with curved cornices, held a cool mild light which came from a source I could not identify. It simply permeated all the space. There was a single chair, with arms, a back and with deep upholstery in an ivory color. There was a table with a single central leg. On the table—a flagon and a glass.

This time I did not hesitate. I crossed to the table, poured a full glass of the wine, a light yellow, and then sat down in the chair.

All this, mark you, without so much as a by your leave.

The walls had been done out in intricate curlicues of flowers and leaves, of grasses and ferns, all in natural colors, and the effect was soothing. A white rectangle against the wall facing the chair rather spoiled the effect.

A voice from thin air spoke and I couldn't understand half the words, even with the genetic language pill the Savanti had given me. I sat still, sipped the wine, and said nothing.

I was, if the truth be told, rather husbanding a growing resentment. Those damned Shanks in their airboats! The Star Lords should have warned me.

The voice spoke again, and this time testily.

"Look at the picture and think of what you wish to see."

"What picture?"

A sigh. "The white rectangle, onker."

So I looked and I thought.

Far below there was jungle. It smoked hot and harshly green into the glare of the Suns of Scorpio. The fliers streamed on in perfect formation. My viewpoint moved in dazzlingly to the lead ship, that superb voller called *Pride of Vondium*.

She stood quite alone right up in the prow, magnificent, glorious, the suns catching those outrageous auburn tints in her hair and burnishing them to bronze. She was clad for war, girt with swords, and with a bow in her fist. She stood peering ahead and down, searching, searching.

My heart called out to her, called despairingly and forlornly, for she could not hear me, could not know I gazed upon her with such longing.

"Delia," I cried. "My Delia of the Blue Mountains, my Delia of Delphond."

Was it just coincidence?

As I thus cried out in that mystic chamber among the Star Lords, so Delia started, and looked up and then about her. Her face—glorious, glorious!—turned so that she looked, as it were, full upon me.

Like any fool I held out my arms.

She smiled, suddenly, dazzlingly, so that I felt the shock of it.

My Delia smiled, and I felt the comfort of that, sundered from her by unimaginable gulfs.

The picture misted and died.

Wild and chaotic thoughts clashed and jumbled in my skull. What a foolish useless lump of a husband I was! How my Delia seemed always condemned to search for me. And yet—I shivered at the thought that if that splendid armada from Vallia found what they looked for, if they discovered the Coup Blag they would find also the Witch of Loh, Csitra, secreted inside like a spider at the center of her web.

She had lost her child, certainly, and her power was much reduced. But her malignancy continued unabated. She would do all she could to harm Vallia in her insane pursuit of me.

There was comfort to be found in the presence with Delia of the Witch and Wizard of Loh who were our loyal companions. Their combined powers should be enough to counter the kharrna of Csitra.

There was no time for more thought as the thin voice from empty air spoke again.

"Think again, Dray Prescot."

This time Seg Segutorio jumped into the picture, almost as though he was there in the room with me. Good old Seg! His wild black hair and fey blue eyes, his bowman's shoulders, all filled the screen with his presence. His handsome face was wrought into a scowl and he was telling someone I could not see to jump. There was no mistaking that.

He looked still to be in the bewildering mazes of the Coup Blag, and yet I'd thought he'd scrambled free through the hole in the roof. Well, I'd find that out soon enough, I did not doubt.

If Seg really still wandered about in the maze, then no doubt Nath the Impenitent remained with him. Perhaps also Loriman the Hunter was there. Maybe they hadn't made it through that split in the roof of the chamber as it collapsed and fell about our ears. They remained therefore in deadly danger.

The fleet from Vallia led on by Delia had clearly been searching. Yet the Mages from Loh knew where the maze was, for they had succored me there and fought and destroyed the uhu Phunik, Csitra's child.

Therefore—and the revelation struck me once again with the power of the Everoinye—therefore my friends searched for me.

The Star Lords manipulated authority in so terrible a fashion that the Wizards of Loh were as puny mewling mortals in their grip. For all their mystical mastery, the Lohvian sorcerers could not scry my whereabouts when the Everoinye had me in their grasp.

The next item at which I chose to look would have raised the blood pressure of any honest seaman of Paz.

The ocean sparkled in a ruffle of blue-green and white. I could not smell that tangy sea breeze there in that secret room; but in my imagination I could snuff up the ozone and the seaweed and the fresh riot of air as the breeze blustered past.

Three ships burned upon the bright face of the sea.

From the little that remained I took them to be argenters, broad-beamed merchant craft. Above them circled the hateful black-hulled fliers of the Shanks. The airboats with their brightly-painted squared-off upperworks had given the three ships of Paz no chance. Fire pots had rained down. It was now all over, and had I been there instead of watching that terrible scene from an unknown distance I could have achieved little more.

Little more than nothing would still be nothing.

"Yes," sighed that nasal voice. "There is your task, Dray Prescot, and yet—"

"Hold it, hold it," I interrupted, not recking of the damned power of the Star Lords. "I know all about that lot. Why didn't you warn me of them?

You said the Shanks were over in Mehzta. Yet they are here off the coast of Pandahem and likely to—"

Instead of cutting me off peremptorily with cutting sarcasm, as they would probably have done in the old days, they interrupted with: "The Shanks are in Mehzta. The fight sways back and forth. These are Shtarkins, along with Shkanes. Their use of vollers is recent."

"That doesn't alter the fact you should have told me."

A spark of their old arrogance spurted.

"We are not answerable to you, Dray Prescot. You answer to us!"

"Yes and no," I said, and heard myself speaking, and I was in a fair old state, I can tell you. This was quite unlike normal dealings with the Star Lords, unknown arbiters of life and death. I realized I was holding the glass of light yellow with a grip that would fracture the globe if I didn't manage to control myself.

The Star Lords went on to apprise me of the details of the vollers run by the Shanks, details that I shall pass along when they become relevant, and something of what they said calmed me down. All the same, I felt that the bargain I fancied we had patched up between us had been seriously endangered, and I had been betrayed.

"Not so, onker. You have had time to deal with your problems, there is time yet to go. We shall tell you when that time comes, never fear."

I did not slang them. I wanted to know why what had happened to me since being snatched up from the collapsing palace, leaving Seg, and arriving here, had occurred. The details seemed to me so bizarre as to warrant an explanation that, in all probability, I would not understand.

The voice gained an edge as it answered.

"You need not know why. We have many responsibilities and in Kregen we—" and here when I interrupted, not understanding, the voice snapped: "The easiest concept for you to grasp is melting pot. Yes. We are almost sure your brains can understand that."

I wasn't sure: I didn't say so.

"A dead numim, did you say?"

"As a doornail, poor devil."

This was followed by a long silence.

After a space I said: "I did see, earlier, the green presence of Ahrinye—"

"Silence, onker!"

Well, if the young and arrogantly energetic Ahrinye was trying a scheme on against the other Star Lords, he might well be successful if their powers really were fading. And young? Maybe he was a million or so years less in age.

Presently the voice—and I thought it was by a shade different from the first—said: "Our responsibilities sometimes demand assistance."

Almost, almost I blurted out: "Call on me, any time." But I managed to keep the black bile down.

The Star Lord went on: "If we so will it, you will be called on to serve in the bacra area—"

"Bacra area?"

"Where you were, fambly."

That did not mean anything to me.

"But we deem you to be more useful following the course we have set out—"

"A course I initiated before you suggested it, Star Lords! I don't forget that."

A silence.

Typical of the Everoinye, they loftily ignored that point. It was, in truth, a petty point, and indicating my own stupid self-esteem. They indicated they were unhappy at the way I risked my neck for purposes other than theirs. They'd twice now hoicked me up out of it when I'd tried to pull first Seg and young Ortyg, then Loriman, out of danger. But, and I felt a sudden coolness down my spine at this, they told me a thing I should have realized.

"We understand you to be reckless and a daredevil and an onker of onkers, Dray Prescot. We suppose you to continue thus. Maybe, one day, we shall not require you, and your usefulness to us will be at an end."

"Come the day!" I bellowed up. "Come the day!"

"You forget—"

"I don't forget! Those two times are the only times you've lifted a finger to help me. You've never worried yourselves over my skin. I'd have been dead a thousand times by now for all you care."

The silence this time seemed to be charged with that insufferable pressure that clamps down just before a thunderstorm.

"We are sending you back now, Dray Prescot, to rejoin your comrades."

"I see. Tell me. All this trudging about mazes and underground corridors. Can you give me something to help me see a trifle better in the dark? Is that beyond your powers?"

"Not at all. A trifle."

"Well?"

"You were ever ungracious in your ways."

"I'm gracious to those who are polite to me."

Let them suck on that one, the high and mighty bunch of onkers!

From the white rectangle hanging blankly on the wall a shaft of pure white light hit me in the face so that I blinked, and cursed, and flung up a hand. If this was their idea of a joke it hurt.

This might not be a joke. This might be a new form of punishment for insubordination.

"Remember your tasks, Dray Prescot. You have reunited Vallia. Now your task is to unite Paz—"

"That's easier said than done, despite all our grand talk. The task is greater than I imagined."

"Of course."

I fumed away and saw I'd get no farther. At least, I'd given the Star Lords a piece of my mind, not that they needed much in the way of extra brains. Maybe their powers were fading; they were still so immeasurably stronger than any other force I knew of on Kregen, they remained superhuman and all-powerful.

The transition rustled in on wings of blueness and I was up and away again, like a scarecrow blown headlong in a gale. Just as I went I reflected bitterly that they'd not given me a magic torch or something to light up the darkness, the stingy taskmasters.

Whirling around I went thump down on my feet. Rock scraped underfoot and the orange flare of torches burned into my eyes. The passage was rough hewn and the light shone in brilliantly from the corner. A man stepped around the edge of stone into view.

"Hai, my old dom. I knew you'd be around here somewhere."

Four

Horrors in the Coup Blag

Our greetings were necessarily brief, for, as Seg said: "There's an unfriendly monster fellow with a horrendous set of gnashers chasing us. I've shafted two of his eyes; but we need to find a little space to tackle him properly."

Nath the Impenitent, bulking hugely in the passage, roared on half-dragging the suddenly unimposing form of Kov Loriman the Hunter.

The Hunting Kov was a husk of his former self. Gone were the bluster and arrogance. Gone was his imperious look. He appeared shrunken. Since his lady had been slain and swallowed up in the earth, he had scarcely moved under his own volition.

"Hai, Jak," rasped out Nath the Impenitent, fiery-faced, spiky with contained anger. "We must get on. The beast is snapping at my heels."

There was no time or need for me to argue.

If these two said run, then I'd run. If Seg, who is the finest bowman in two worlds, had shafted the beast twice, and the thing still lived, then running was clearly and eminently the most sensible course of action.

Nath held up a torch in his left hand. His right dragged on Loriman. Seg held a torch in his left hand, and his right grasped his bow with the arrow nocked in that old and cunning bowman's fashion.

I wondered why Seg was doing it cack-handed; there was no time to ask now as we ran on along the corridor. The floor caught at our feet, rough-hewn as it was. The light glanced weirdly from the jagged walls and roof. The place held a musty stink as of last week's socks left and forgotten in the laundry basket.

Before we'd reached the next corner the beast rounded his corner and rumbled along the corridor after us.

I cast a look back.

Nasty. No doubt of that. And the loss of two of his four eyes made his temper even worse. He looked to be all spine and scale, with grasping fore-limbs, claws and, as Seg had said, a jawful of gnashers. Nasty, right enough. We ran on.

The chamber into which we pelted around the next bend lofted high and vasty into purple mistiness where the flare of our torches merely touched the edges of mystery with orange. There appeared little comfort for wan-dering adventurers here.

"This'll do," said Seg, full of confidence.

Most unkindly, I said: "P'raps a flat-trajectory compound reflex might—"

"Oho!" burst out Seg. "You're a backstabber too, are you?"

He thrust the torch at me, transferred the great Lohvian longbow into his left fist and took up the nocked arrow into those supremely capable archer's fingers of his. We could hear the beast roar from the tunnel. Our torches threw a little light and I blinked, for their radiance held an odd glow to me now, as I paused in the chamber. The light glinted on scale and spine and on two fiery eyes.

Seg loosed.

A watcher would say he blurred into action; the loosing of the two shafts was so swift, the second following the first so rapidly, that the whole trans-action was over in a twinkling, the two arrows flying almost before Seg moved.

"Well," said Nath the Impenitent. "I shan't have to run dragging this damned lord about, now. I thank you for that, Seg the Horkandur."

Seg smiled and then looked at me.

"Little flat bows," he said. Then he shoved that superb Lohvian longbow up on his shoulder and whipped out his knife.

As I went over with him to help dig out his four arrows, Seg said over his shoulder: "Not until we meet the next horror, Nath."

The first two arrows had merely destroyed the eyes. The second pair had penetrated deeply into the brain. I left those two to Seg.

Truth to tell, as I believe I have struggled to explain, the death of wild animals, even monsters intent on devouring me, is always a saddening and chastening experience.

Nath the Impenitent let rip with his grunting snort of a laugh when we rejoined him.

"The next horror is likely to be seriously conulted by you mad pair."

Conulted, as I may have mentioned, means to receive a nasty shock, a body blow, and I found its usage, and particularly by a rough tough customer like Nath, in these surroundings, decidedly charming.

Also, and this pleased me immensely, Nath with his ingrown hatred and contempt for lords and nobles, had quite grown to accept Seg and me as companions.

"Oh, aye," said Seg in his raffish offhand way. "We'll conult a few more of the confounded creepy crawlies down here yet. But with half the maze vanished away I fancy it won't be long before we're out of it altogether."

The way Seg easily accepted the heights—or depths—of sorcery involved here did not amaze me. His own fey nature told him things that more lumpen mortals could never understand. With the death of the Witch of Loh's hermaphrodite child, the uhu Phunik, its ethereal constructions had vanished. Opulent underground chambers, palaces of wonder, had not simply whiffed away with Phunik's death. Oh, no. There had been a gargantuan upheaval as the fabric of the normal universe resumed its shape and the distortions of magical art withdrew.

In other words, the whole lot fell down in a hell of a smother.

Most of the people in the party who had ventured down into the maze of the Coup Blag had got away, scrambling up the slippery slope of detritus to emerge into the lights of the Suns of Scorpio.

Kov Loriman, shattered by the death of his lady Hebe, existing now like a man drugged or in a trance, had been the cause of Seg's, Nath's and my enforced further entrapment in the maze of the Coup Blag.

By this time, as was clearly apparent, old Nath the Impenitent recognized he was lumbered with Kov Loriman. Nath was conscious of his insular Vallian blood, and of the fact that the lords of the land cared nothing for him, and this famous Hunting Kov was not even Vallian, he was from Yumapan in the west of the island of Pandahem. Well, Nath would be saying to himself, they might be stumbling about in a damned hole in the ground in Pandahem, he'd drag this haughty noble out of it by the scruff of the neck and then pitch him over onto his nose. This, I fancied, would also be the reading Seg would give to the situation.

The rocky corridor turned twice upon itself and then led into a room where some light seeped in from a webwork of cracks in the ceiling.

"If that lot's due to fall down—" began Nath, ominously.

"—we'll depart with the utmost urgency," finished Seg, cheerfully.

Loriman slumped to the stone floor with a thump. His head hung down so that his armored shoulders peaked. He'd lost his helmet. Looking at this once blustery, damn-you-to-hell fellow, I experienced a sudden, quick, quite surprising stab of pity.

Mind you, if Delia was—well, never mind that.

"Two exits," sang out Seg. "D'you have a fancy?"

"They both look the same," observed Nath.

"Toss a blade," I said.

Now the meaning of a couple of odd looks Nath had given me when he'd met up with me again revealed themselves.

"Need to stand from under if you toss up that great bar of iron, Jak."

He'd seen me use the Krozair longsword in action; now I realized he'd seen me step out with the old scarlet breechclout and with the longsword cocked up and, of course, all the legends and tales of Dray Prescot would have come into his mind. That was how Dray Prescot, the Emperor of Vallia, whirled about the world, righting wrongs, rescuing both princesses and tavern girls from danger, slaying dire monsters and putting Vallia back together again and recreating the empire as a place where folk could live happily in safety.

There would be absolutely no connection in his head. I was Jak the Bogandur, admittedly a lesser noble of some kind; but a decent enough fellow for a lord, as was our comrade Seg the Horkandur. The Emperor of Vallia was altogether another fellow, a rogue and cramph Nath detested wholeheartedly.

He'd already said he disbelieved the tales about Dray Prescot. Well, that made two of us.

Once we were out of this maze I'd have to make the attempt to put the record straight. Nath had been court-martialed, and I had promised myself that I'd have that lot sorted, too. The main priorities now were getting out of the Coup Blag, of finding our Vallian aerial fleet, and of going and bashing the fliers of those Opaz-forsaken Shanks.

We went through the left-hand door and found only another of these baffling corridors.

Loriman shambled along like a drugged wild animal chained and leashed by callous performing-animal handlers.

"He won't be much good if we get into another fight." Seg paced along like a savage wild animal himself, chained and leashed by this damned maze.

"Maybe that would bring him back to his senses."

"If that were so, then bring on the fight sharpish."

None of us recognized any of the passageways and chambers through which we made our way. These subterranean burrowings would be either natural formations or sorcerous constructs fashioned by Csitra. All Phunik's magical architecture had vanished along with him, and good riddance too, by Krun.

We spoke little, going cautiously.

Nath the Impenitent did say, with that grumbly growl: "There's been no food lately and my insides are like the purse of a pickpocket at an orgy."

I thought of my scrunchy meal of caterpillar-rotted metal, and said nothing.

Noise from up ahead halted us. After a long time of listening, we moved carefully forward along a tunnel hung with tapestries.

Any damn tapestry can hide a fellow with a bow or a knife, ready to degut you. We inspected everything with enormous thoroughness, and even then one of the tapestries detached itself from its hangings and like a monstrous bat swooped down on us.

We flailed about with our swords, and Seg put a torch to the flapping horror and scorched it away. It flip-flopped off, burning, crackling to shredded blackness.

We caught our breaths.

"Strangle your eyes out and your head off, that," remarked Nath. Any amusement I might feel at his by now complete adaptation to the requirements of survival in the Coup Blag had to be indulged in when we were out of it.

We went on toward the source of the noises ahead, and we gave a pretty hefty tug at each tapestry as we passed. There were only three more we had to torch.

The noises increased in volume and sorted themselves out into two varieties. Both varieties were exceedingly ugly. One was the screams of women. The other was the sound of nuzzling and grunting as of beasts feeding.

Seg's face, which I have often described as handsome, as, indeed, it is, shocked suddenly with blood. He took the appearance of an eagle about to swoop. When my blade comrade appears like that, it is best for evildoers to run and hide and pray they are not discovered by Seg Segutorio.

Nath ripped out: "That sounds like—" and then he started off after Seg.

Kov Loriman flopped sacklike onto the floor.

If what was going on in the chamber up ahead was as my comrades and I suspected, then this would be the opportunity—evil and heart-breaking though it be—to revive the Hunting Kov. If I had read his character aright, then despite all his arrogance and haughty treatment of others, his slavish indulgence in hunting, this situation would appeal to those traits of character I knew him to possess which had not been deadened by his lofty station in life. I seized him under his left shoulder and fairly dragged him along the passageway.

The women were of many races, diffs and apims. Not all were young and beautiful, though they mostly were younger rather than older, and their condition suggested they were kept hard at arduous tasks when they were not employed as they were now. Some retained remnants of clothing. None wore ornaments or jewelry. And they screamed.

The bestial sounds came from the gorilla-faced malkos who were, after all, men, even if they were not apim. They were employed as guards by Csitra in her maze of the Coup Blag. They were unpleasant, brutish customers, and Seg had dealt firmly with a bloodthirsty pack of them when he'd met the lady Milsi, who was now his wife.

I hauled Kov Loriman up straight. I had not drawn my own sword, and so was able to draw his and thrust it into his hand. I wrapped his fingers about the expensive hilt.

Loriman was a Pandahem noble, widely-traveled, as I guessed, who'd been to many countries and down to the southern continent of Havilfar. He'd seen a lot of the world in his travels, during his hunting forays. He would have heard of the legends and stories clustered about the name of the Emperor of Vallia, Dray Prescot, and like any sophisticated man, would have considered them palpable falsehoods. Still and all, he'd have heard of Dray Prescot in his scarlet breechclout with the great Krozair longsword flaming.

Now it is quite clear that in this my narrative I tell you of the surface of things openly, thus allowing you the pleasure of teasing out the inner meanings. I do not mean hidden meanings. They are plainly there for those who see beneath the tapestry of the language. Language itself, whether of Earth or of Kregen, is at once a communication and a barrier.

Kov Loriman had to be made to see what his eyes told him was going on. And this meant I delayed my own entry into the fight and assistance to Seg and Nath.

So, and without any hidden meanings in this case, you can see that I thus risked the lives and sanity of these poor half-demented and savagely brutalized women.

Seg shot. There is little that can be added to those evocative words. Seg Segutorio shot.

Nath the Impenitent, sword a brand of flame, leaped down into the chamber and started to lay about him. Malkos screeched, spouted blood, and died.

Most of the gorilla-faced diffs were without armor. Their weapons were piled against one wall. They had been chasing the women, joying in the licence allowed them by the Witch of Loh. Bestial though they were, they died like any mortal man.

I saw Nath swing his sword in a cunning drawing stroke. The malko's head flew off to roll bouncing on the filthy straw-matted floor. Crimson blood from the severed neck spouted across the white bosom and neck of the girl still clasped in the malko's arms. The crimson splash seared into white skin. The woman drew a breath to scream, and the headless body fell away, tumbling onto the straw. She put her hands to herself, looking down, and she could not find the breath to scream any more.

Nath surged on, his brand a bar of crimson. Seg's shafts spitted malkos as they ran for their weapons.

I shook Kov Loriman as a teacher shakes a recalcitrant child.

"Look, Loriman. Look on what goes forward here. If that lady there were the Lady Hebe—"

The girl to whom I pointed, slim and shrieking and naked and distraught almost beyond reason, struggled in the grip of a malko so passionately involved he had failed to grasp the significance of the other uproar going on about him.

"Suppose that were the Lady Hebe, Loriman! She might be dead; there are many other ladies demanding your service. You are called the Hunting Kov, Loriman. Is your prideful selfishness so profound and your arrogant self-esteem so great, that you have forgotten you are a hunting kov and—"

There was more I was wound up to spout into his ear. But he let rip with a groaning, snorting howl of anguish. He snatched up the sword in his fist. His face tautened, lost its slack look of imbecility, hardened into a semblance of the Hunting Kov I knew.

"By all the gods of Panachreem!" he screeched.

He whirled the sword once about his head and tore free of my grasp, hurled himself down into the melee.

"And about bloody time too, by Krun!" I said as I unlimbered the Krozair brand and roared into the fray.

Some of the malkos, naked as they were, had reached their stacked weapons. They took up their swords, thraxters mostly, and turned to face us. There was no doubt in their minds that even after this surprise which had brought down a number of them, they would quickly dispose of us four foolish souls.

By this time Seg had knocked off most of the isolated targets. Those remaining were masked by the caterwauling women or by the tables they used as barricades or even by Nath and Loriman. Seg stashed his longbow and drew his drexer and with sword in fist joined me as we hurtled into combat.

Five

How Loriman the Hunter returned to life

Dour, stocky, withdrawn people, malkos, prone to savagery beyond the bounds of reason. They have much body hair. Their gorilla-like faces are capable of expressions, emotions clearly discernable to any apim. Now, as they battled back at us, after lust came rage.

Seg's quiver was empty. So that was the real reason he had stopped shooting. His sword flamed alongside mine.

No fighting is a pretty affair, no matter how the romanticists attempt to dress it up in fine language. Oh, yes, there is a panache, a surge of blood and a feeling that what you are about, being worthwhile, uplifts the spirits. But it is a dreadful business. When a heavy steel blade swishes through the air powered by the muscles and energy of a full-grown man, and strikes flesh and blood, the results may be grotesque, outrageous, gory and, inevitably, horrible.

The malkos, being paid guards, fought well.

The Impenitent appeared to be in his element, striking shrewd, economical blows after that initial strike of decapitating fury. In the past I had worried over Seg's prowess as a bladesman; I worried no longer, for he was superb. Kov Loriman now demonstrated that he had recovered from that black pit of despair. I was not sure he had fully recovered; for this business his sword work proved more than adequate.

So we smashed and hacked and thrust and destroyed.

There was no surprise to a Kregan in seeing some of the naked women snatch up fallen weapons, daggers, knives, swords, and spring like furies upon the malkos. They had many indignities to avenge, and while vengeance is a child's game, here one could understand and in part sympathize.

We did not slay them all, for at the end a handful ran off through a secret door that opened in the blank stone wall. It clashed shut and Seg just had time to drag a frenzied girl away before she was crushed between the closing stones.

"Kill them!" she screeched, twisting and writhing in Seg's grip. "Slay them all in the name of Pandrite the All-Glorious!"

"Armipand will surely take them all up into his special terror," said Seg, easily. "Now you just rest quietly, young lady, and get your breath."

She panted, hair swirling, chest heaving, her body all a glisten of sweat. The long dagger with the blood smeared upon the blade and splashed up her arm formed a fitting accessory for such a spitfire girl.

Already Nath was cleaning his sword.

The Hunting Kov looked about as a man looks upon the dawn after he has freshly risen from his bed.

He stared at Seg and he stared at me, and he said: "I remember."

I nodded in acknowledgment. It was left to Seg to say: "Good. I am glad to see you recovered, kov. Now perhaps you'd take out your knife and help."

With that Seg started in on the task of recovering his arrows.

When we'd cut them all out and cleaned them up, Seg was disgusted to find that two of the shafts had broken through.

"You must expect shafts to break, Horkandur," said Nath.

Seg began stripping the arrows down, removing heads and flights and nocks.

"That is true, my old Impenitent; but in our situation not to be relished."

Loriman spat out: "In our situation that damned witch will be watching us and know where we are and will—"

"Just for the moment," I broke in, "I think she has other problems on her mind."

"And, anyway," said Seg, stowing the salvaged arrow parts in his pouch, "In this present situation we have all these women to concern us."

Most of the screaming and crying had stopped and the women were trying to find bits and pieces of clothing from the malkos. Many of them also took up weapons to add to those they had already used. The display of naked female bodies was covered up. One or two of the girls began to mutilate the malkos and I, in a state of indecision, wondered if that should be stopped when Loriman bellowed.

"Stop that, you creatures! Hunting and killing are one thing; what you are about is another."

One of the girls, very pale of skin, with frizzy dark hair, her teeth filed to points, stared back, the knife in her fist dripping blood onto the legs of the malko flat on the floor.

"What do you know of—?"

"I know enough of your dark Rumay customs, harpy!"

The Impenitent growled out: "I don't like it; but you can see it from their point of view."

"If it's their custom," said Seg. "Anyway, it doesn't hurt the malkos, seeing they're dead."

"I will not tolerate Rumay rituals," ground out Loriman. "And that is final. *Queyd-arn-tung!*"

The woman glared back, her eyes like rinds. She hadn't bothered to collect any clothes, being too intent on her task of ritual revenge and absolution, and dark blood splotched her pale shapely body.

"One last cut, then, master."

Loriman opened his mouth and I cracked out: "Do it!"

She cut and held her trophy aloft and Loriman, face congested, swung toward me.

"What do you know of this, Jak the Bogandur! This is women's evil work against men—"

"Alive yes; dead, is it of consequence to an unbeliever?" I gave him a hard stare and he, while not exactly flinching back, braced himself. "Or, Kov Loriman the Hunter, are you, too, a believer?"

"Were I not under a vow to desist from chastising you, Jak, I would challenge and strike you down where you stand!"

Seg laughed.

The Impenitent, enormously pleased at that moment, sang out: "Here, doms! There is food and wine!"

Loriman gave me a look that might have drilled through the best armor steel. He breathed in so that his harness creaked. Then he hunched up his left shoulder, swung his sword around in a gesture of complete contempt, and went off to where Nath had found the victuals.

Seg said: "He'll do himself a mischief one of these days."

"I am glad to see he is getting back to his old self. And, I tell you this, Seg. He won't want to leave the Coup Blag when we do."

"Quite."

The truth was obvious to both of us. Loriman would now insist on finding Csitra and dealing with her. She, or rather her hermaphrodite child Phunik, had slain the Lady Hebe. Loriman would never forget or forgive that. His desire for revenge was a cancer that burrowed far too deeply for rationality to alter.

We went off to the table where Nath and Loriman were stuffing their faces.

The women gathered around to eat and drink, and a weird-looking crew they were.

We elicited their stories, which were sad and cruel and painfully familiar.

Kidnapped, they'd been brought to the maze and employed on menial tasks, abused and ill-treated, seeing their only escape in death.

"So we shall have to take them all along with us." Seg braced himself up. "Well, if we have to, we have to. By the Veiled Froyvil, we can do it!"

Nath nodded in agreement.

Now people speak of your complete soldier very often as a man or woman who thinks, lives and talks only of soldiering. There are such unhappy wights about, on Earth as on Kregen. They are not complete human beings, that seems clear. They have their uses. A fellow takes up soldiering because he has to, there being no alternative at the time. As soon as he can, he finishes with it.

My misfortune on Kregen had been that circumstances dictated that my life and soldiering had been intimately intertwined for a long time, a damn long time, too long a damned time, by Krun.

So Nath, a Vallian, was in my eyes a complete soldier who understood far more than simple soldiering.

Loriman chewed and swallowed and said: "I agree the women must be saved, if that is possible. But they will be an encumbrance when we face Csitra."

"Ah," said Seg.

"What, Horkandur, does that 'ah' mean?"

A noble very much used to having his own way, this Kov Loriman. As a kov, the Kregan rank approximating an earthly Duke, he did not have to be too careful in considering other people's finer feelings. He'd arrived at the conclusion that Seg and I were not to be treated in quite the offhand and unthinking way he handled other people. This understanding, being new to him, clashed with his natural instincts. He intended to go and find Csitra the Witch of Loh and exact revenge. He couldn't quite comprehend that we did not share that desire.

"It means," said Seg, "there are other shafts in the air."

"Explain yourself!"

I caught Seg's eye, and he smiled that damned mocking smile of his, and nodded, as much as to say: "Righto, my old dom, you have a go at this onker."

I faced up to the Hunting Kov.

"Listen, Loriman, and listen good. You need to exact revenge upon Csitra. I, also, have suffered at her hands, as has Seg, as have many of our friends."

Loriman tried to interrupt, as much in anger at my tone as what I was saying. I brushed him aside and went on in that hard, intemperate bash-on way of Dray Prescot.

"Csitra can be contained. Her evil was mostly the result of her forced alliance with Phu-Si-Yantong, a most unsavory character whom you might have known as the Hyr Notor. Well, he is dead and well stuffed down on the Ice Floes of Sicce. Yantong and Csitra's child, Phunik, attempted to carry on the evil work of his father, and now he, too, is dead, blown away in the Quern of Gramarye. The witch has been severely punished already."

"But not enough—"

"Any revenge in the matter of the Lady Hebe is strictly up to you, Loriman. I tell you now in all seriousness that Csitra's power is insufficient to create further mischief. Her occult meddling can be countered by superior kharrna. This is true, Loriman, believe me as you believe in the Great and Glorious Pandrite."

His left fist was gripping and ungripping upon the hilt of his scabbarded sword. His lips twisted. He could see in my face that old demonic look, and he didn't like it at all. But he listened.

"From the grouping of continents and islands over on the other side of the world of Kregen come the Shanks. Fish-heads. They burn and slay and spare none, apart from a few wights they keep as slaves who'd be better off dead. These are the foes we here in Paz must confront."

"I know of the Shkanes, the Shtarkins. They are all evil, as the Shanks are evil. We will fight them, yes. But before that I will cut down this Csitra, Witch of Loh or no damned Witch of Loh. And that is also true, believe me!"

His words hung on the close air of that chamber, echoing and ringing. I just hoped our Wizards of Loh were able to continue their occult caul of protection over us.

Nath the Impenitent broke the spell.

In his gruff way he rasped out: "At least I shall be spared the task of dragging the Hunting Kov about by the collar."

Seg laughed, as amused as I by the contrast.

As though the casual use of the names of powerful sorcerers summoned up their opposites, the phantasmal form of Deb-Lu shimmered against the wall. His newish turban toppled dangerously over one ear, his kindly face was marked by intense concentration. His robes, as always, looked as though he'd been pulled through a hedge backward. But his power was undeniable.

He beckoned.

"That," said Seg, "is the way out."

"Aye."

Kov Loriman the Hunter wanted to continue the argument; but with the Wizard of Loh to act as our guide out of the Coup Blag, we had no wish to hang about further. With the women straggling along before and aft, we set off to follow Deb-Lu. Loriman's face resembled black thunder.

"Very well, then, run! As for me—there is a task set to my hands within this evil place."

Six

Concerns a Star of Death

The Hunting Kov acted on his own words without a heartbeat's hesitation.

His bulk shouldered the women aside. One tumbled to her knees, hair falling forward, her cry lost in the general hubbub. Loriman charged back, returning the way we had traversed.

The women cowered out of his way, distressed, not understanding as he barged past like a runaway chunkrah.

At the last he turned to look back.

His face, always hard and arrogant, held now a flushed look of triumph. There was in that fanatical expression an expressive wealth of dedication. Slave to his ideals of hunting, Kov Loriman had now been consumed utterly by them.

He visualized in Csitra the Witch the ultimate quarry.

The dust of the corridors, the rank smell of the women, the feeling of pressure of millions of tons of rock pressing in all about us, added as it were a tonal palette to the emotions flooding Kov Loriman.

He shook his sword aloft.

"By Hito the Hunter! She shall not survive me, that I swear by Pandrite the All-Glorious!" He slashed his sword down. "*Hai, Jikai!*"

He swung about, the light glanced once upon the metal of his harness, and he was gone.

Seg laughed. "By the Veiled Froyvil, my old dom! I'm swamped to know if I'm sorry or glad to see the back of the fellow!"

"Oh," I said with a nonchalance I did not feel. "We'll see old Loriman again, never fret."

Nath the Impenitent sniffed. He had an arm about the waist of one of the more comely of the ladies. "I give him the chance of a hot cinder in the Ice Floes of Sicce if he goes up against the Witch. By Vox, she'll devour him whole!"

"Let us press on, doms," I said. I did not say to Nath that with the occult caul of protection afforded by our friendly Wizards of Loh, Loriman shouldn't come to too much harm. That is, if the caul had been extended to encompass him in its magical embrace.

I trusted Deb-Lu had done that. I needed Loriman for a key part in my schemes.

The decision had been long in coming, and hard in the taking. But, come it had and taken it I had—now all that remained was to implement it.

"Come along," I said in a tone of voice that made Seg favor me with a quizzical look. I knew I sounded far too casually light-hearted for this grim situation; but the decision, once taken, set that part of my worries free. And good old Seg would buckle down to his part in the scheme, that I knew, after he'd had a good old moan.

The girls set up a screaming just then and surged back on us in a frightened mob. There was a splendid display of thrashing arms and legs, of half-naked bodies tumbling one over the other, of faces screaming in fresh fear. The smells became near overpowering.

The fellow who caused all this stood like a gnarled tree, legs wide apart, black and golden armor—all shiny leather and dull metal and golden studs and rivets—relieved by a dramatically flung-back scarlet cape. His helmet held a skull-crest and surmounted a face of compressed ferocity, of down-drooping mustaches, of serrated sharpened teeth, of veinous-crimson eyes, of nostril slits pulsating like the underbelly of a fish.

Harsh and compelling without a morsel of humanity remaining in him after a lifetime of bloodshed, this Kanzai Warrior Brother was no figment of sorcerous imagination.

The Kanzai take in recruits from any suitable race although it is said they favor Chuliks and Khibils and Laceroti, and train these acolytes into adepts and Warrior Brothers. After that the world of Kregen is their oyster.

We were not overly bothered with them in Vallia, for the old emperor's grandfather had cleared them out in a wholesale rubbish-clearance that was now the subject of many songs and stories. Pandahem had its share of Kanzai Brothers.

This fellow carried a thraxter and a shortsword scabbarded at his waist above the skirts of the laminated armor. He appeared to have no missile weapons, and this appearance was deceptive. He carried no bow; he had other nasty objects he could hurl with neck-slicing speed.

The Kanzai despised shields.

Now, from its scabbard he drew a chunkscreetz and this swordbreaker was more like a Japanese Sai than a European swordbreaker. Of strong iron, with two curved quillons designed to trap and snap an opponent's blade, the swordbreaker was a weapon that had to be taken into account.

He moved with precise control, each movement taking a segment of time between periods of absolute stillness.

The length of chain he swung from a pouch made Seg draw in a quick breath. At one end of the chain swung a three-bladed knife, and the other a three-tined grappling hook. The thing was a Kregen adaptation of the Japanese Kyotetsu-shoge. The Kawa-naga, as an improvised weapon, varied subtly. I shared Seg's distrust of these cripplers.

The links of chain spun about his head. His thin lips widened in a smile of invitation. He did not boast, for that is not the way of the Kanzai.

Nath blurted out: "I'll settle his hash—"

"Stay, Nath. Maybe we can talk to this Kanzai Brother rather than fight him."

"As soon hold back the River of Golden Smiles with your bare hands."

The dulled metal chain links went whirr-whirr-whirr in a circle before the adept. He swung the chain in a bewildering series of patterns, of figures of eight and loops and cunning underhand passes. He went through what was clearly a training discipline. It was impressive, I'll say that, by Krun.

That Seg stood with his bow ready for instant action was a situation so normal as not to warrant comment.

I called across: "I do not wish to slay you, Kanzai. There has been too much blood shed here already. I would ask you to allow us and these poor women to pass."

The girls had quieted down to a low moan here and there and a muffled sob. They were resigning themselves to what was about to happen and not much caring for that.

You can't take your eyes off a woman of Kregen when her blood is up and she smarts for revenge.

A swooping streaking line of silver struck from an outflung arm and hand straight for the heart of the Kanzai.

Before the girl had time to drop down, her knife slashed in to meet the slanted swordbreaker and bounce and chingle into a harmless arc and clang against the stone of the floor.

"Very pretty," said Nath, on a breath.

The girl's hair moved like a pit of snakes as she flung herself forward. Her flung knife had failed; now she would try her other weapons on this Kanzai adept.

The iron swordbreaker had flicked a bare hand's breadth to deflect the girl's knife. As the girl screeched and hurled herself at the Kanzai, I found myself wondering if he could thus easily deflect one of Seg's Lohvian arrows.

I shouted in an evil voice: "Do not slay her, Kanzai, or you are a dead man."

Whether or not he took notice of my braggart words I couldn't be sure; in any event he merely tapped the girl on the head and stretched her in slumber on the floor of the chamber.

The chain resumed its whirring menace around his head.

"He is challenging us, that is certain sure." Nath the Impenitent puffed his cheeks. "Insolent cramph."

If we hadn't had these confounded caterwauling women along, the situation would have been amusingly comical. As it was, our first duty now was to see the women safe.

Some of them were perfectly capable of looking after themselves in most situations they'd encounter on Kregen. This particular fate had just proved too much for them.

"We must push on," I said. "We don't have time to shilly-shally about down here now. There is a lot to do."

"I suppose I shall have to shaft him, then."

Seg didn't sound happy at the prospect. Like me, he is a fellow well past the time when blood-shedding held any attractions.

Nath said: "He's mighty clever with that chunkscreetz."

For reply Seg merely flexed those marvelous archer's shoulders of his and lifted the bow.

The Kanzai erupted like a tent in a gale.

The swordbreaker vanished into its scabbard. The whirling iron links clattered to stillness. His right hand raked into a cunningly-opened pocket and whipped out with a silver glint of metal between the brown fingers.

The Star of Death whirring like a woodchuck drew a line of destruction from the Kanzai's hand to—my actions were controlled by a force outside of myself. I stepped up and the Krozair brand twitched before Seg. The glittering Star of Death and the superb longsword met and rang like a carillon of best silver bells from Vandayha.

The little star-shaped horror spun away, spinning, hit the ground and then, oddly, ran along like a child's toy.

The Kanzai remained perfectly still. Seg did not loose.

For those few heartbeats we remained still, like a posed group in a museum. The chains remained silent and unstirring. Another Star of Death showed in the fingers of the Kanzai. This time he held it aloft, twirling it.

That movement broke the uncanny rigidity that held us all, and yet the Kanzai did not hurl his Star of Death, Seg did not loose his deadly Lohvian shaft.

The Kanzai Warrior Brother called across to us.

His voice was gruff, throaty, harsh, clanging with the resonances of a lifetime's application to the demanding rigors of combat.

"Jikais! A stand-off."

"Impudent devil!" exclaimed Seg, under his breath. "I can shaft him where he stands, one, two, three, and Havil take his damned swordbreaker."

This Seg could do. No doubt of it. And, mark me, there was not an iota of boasting in his instinctive remark.

A tinkle of metal did not distract us. The Star of Death toppled onto its side. It had rolled along in a strange lopsided way, rhythmically bouncing in its progress. Something like a Japanese Shuriken, it was asymmetrical, its Kregan creators imparting a swooping deflection to its flight. Even so, the Krozair disciplines had enabled the Krozair longsword to deflect it from its intended target.

"Jikais!" called the Kanzai again.

"He," observed Seg with some relish, "sounds suddenly apprehensive."

"Didn't expect his Star of Death to miss."

"Quite."

"Shaft him, Seg," counseled Nath in his unruly bellow.

The Kanzai heard that.

The metal links stirred ripplingly across the cavern floor. The upflung throwing star glittered.

"Do you adhere to the decadent Rumay customs, doms?" he called across.

"No!" yelled Seg in a virulent voice.

I said nothing. Truth to tell, it might have been interesting to discover the adept's reaction had we acknowledged the Rumay customs to him.

"That is as well." He lowered the Star of Death.

"Look," I said once more. "We can't hang around here." I shouted then, and I admit I put a little testiness into the bellow. "Kanzai! Stand aside and let us pass or you will suffer the consequences of your own foolishness."

I started forward, the Krozair brand in my two fists, ready to swipe away a Star of Death or two or remove his head if he didn't shift.

For a moment he hesitated. Clearly, he didn't like what he saw of us. Just what he was doing down here in the Coup Blag was his affair and of no real interest to us.

The Star of Death vanished into its pouch. The links of chain coiled miraculously into loops and were stowed. As he stepped aside his right hand fastened on the hilt of his thraxter.

I stood next to him. I stared at him balefully.

"The ladies will now pass, Kanzai. *Dernun?*"*

He nodded and that gruesome skull atop his helmet, flounced with feathers, bobbed. He used his left hand in a gesture to indicate we were to pass.

"Get the shemales moving, Nath!"

With a scurry and bustle, and with many a white-eyed sideways glance at the adept, the girls scuttled past. Some did not scuttle. Some walked arrogantly past, heads high, swinging in their gait and bold. These were women who had not first sought for clothes to cover their nakedness but had first snatched up weapons. The Kanzai eyed them as they strutted past as he would have scrutinized any potential foe.

When all had gone by I said: "I give you thanks, dom." I went to move off and then halted and turned to say: "And you? Down here?"

"I have my mission."

That's all we would get out of him. As a Kanzai Warrior Brother, an adept, he was answerable only to his master.

It takes all sorts to make a world and Kregen is a world of many wonders, many marvelous oddities, by Zair!

Turning to march off after the others, I heard him draw a breath and in the same instant I'd ducked, swerved and sprung about to come up with the longsword pressing against his ribs. I halted the thrust.

He took a step back, a very smart step back, and his face expressed stupefaction.

"I was just—" he began. And then he swallowed and burst out: "By the Names! I do not know your Disciplines, dom; but you are sudden, most sudden."

I glared at him, eyeball to eyeball.

Some cheap remark could have come so easily to my lips then.

I contented myself with a simple: "That is so, dom. Remberee."

"Remberee, dom. I shall not forget you."

---

* dernun?: Savvy, understood, capiche? Not very polite. *A.B.A.*

Seven

In the cavern of beauty

The shimmering manifestation of the Wizard of Loh Deb-Lu-Quienyin beckoned us on toward a gargoyle-crowned opening, black and ominous, jagged in the wall of the cavern.

We'd traversed a considerable quantity of corridor since our meeting with the Kanzai Warrior Brother. The women complained—very naturally—yet it was as obvious to them as to us that we had to keep moving and find a way to escape from the Coup Blag.

Old Deb-Lu's turban was straight upon his head and he did not need to lift a hand to prevent the absurd headgear from toppling. His face looked grave.

Faintly, no louder than a distant whisper of wind, the sound of rushing water filtered through that gap of dark and evil aspect.

"The women need to rest up again, Jak," called Nath. He marched at the back, shepherding the females along much as a ponsho-trag shepherds along his flock of woolly ponshos. He carried two of them, more or less comfortably, and it was clear to Seg and me that he was forming an attachment.

Just how wise or foolish that was down here in this magical maze remained to be seen.

"I don't like the look of old Deb-Lu," said Seg, in a quiet voice.

"There's trouble up ahead, that's for sure."

"Better to have everyone rest up first, then."

"Aye." I called back to Nath. "We'll take a breather, then, you Impenitent."

"Quidang!"

The women flopped down and stretched out on the bare stone of the floor, grateful for the rest. Nath deposited his two with care and then stalked up to join Seg and me.

The girl with the pale shapely body and dark frizzy hair who'd hurled the knife at the Kanzai also walked up. She made a grimace of distaste that revealed the cruel sharpened teeth.

"Well, men, if we must go forward let us get on, for the sake of Mayruna the Perforater!"

"You would leave your friends here?" demanded Seg.

"Not my friends, man, of whom there are few left. These other frail fools, yes, of course."

Rashly Nath the Impenitent burst out: "Your Perforater is not to my liking, woman!"

She gave him a look, an upward, slanting, calculating look that seemed to strip away skin and flesh.

"That is very true, man. Mayruna the Perforater is not to your liking in this world or the other."

With what I hoped was a nicely judged amount of acerbity, I said: "We cannot push on yet, young lady. When the women are rested, we will see what that water ahead brings us. Is that clear?"

She opened her mouth and I haven't the faintest idea what she might have said. I cut in sharply.

"So it would be less foolish of you to go and rest now, like the others."

She had retrieved that flung knife so contemptuously disposed of by the Kanzai adept. Her brown fingers twitched once in the direction of the knife's hilt, and then she puffed her cheeks, turned away with the frizzy hair glinting with the crystal overhead lights. Dust and dirt matted the hair. She said nothing and went back to drop down and find what comfort she could from the hard stone floor.

"Keep an eye on that one, Nath," said Seg in his serious way.

"Aye, Horkandur, aye. I don't fancy her knife tickling between my ribs."

"She has friends here," I pointed out.

"If, Bogandur," said Nath, "they are all like her it will be exceedingly interesting."

Seg pursed up his lips. I could sense something had been worrying away at my blade comrade, and now, without showing the slightest impoliteness to Nath by not taking up his comment and introducing a fresh, he said: "We have been spared the visitation of monsters and unwholesome beasties lately. Yet I fancy the Witch will not let us go without taking a last crack at us. Yes?"

"Indubitably," said Nath, who was fond of the word.

"Aye," I said. "And with all these women along—"

"My point, precisely." Seg's fey blue eyes showed a bright merriment. "Our ferocious lady friends of the Rumay persuasion may then earn their keep."

Nath rumbled a huge guffaw from his stomach, highly impressed by the indubitableness of the proposition.

Not for the first time—and assuredly, by Vox, not for the last—I found myself rejoicing in the company and companionship of good comrades. Yes, yes, I love to go off adventuring alone, wearing the brave old scarlet and swinging a great Krozair longsword; but equally I joy in adventures shared with boon comrades.

And here I pulled myself up sharply and with a most unpleasant jolt of guilt.

What the hell was I doing contemplating going off adventuring when all of Paz demanded my utmost exertions? We had to escape from this damnable Coup Blag, Witch of Loh or no damn Witch of Loh, and then I had to see about organizing the countries to fight shoulder to shoulder. And by countries one always means the people of the nations. There would be no easy ride trying to convince some of the rulers in the lands of Paz to work together. The task which, in the early days, I had considered to be just another problem set to my hands, was altogether far greater and fraught with bristling difficulties I had not foreseen.

The simple answer and the one I had at first thought to be the one the Star Lords intended was just to go around to these various lands and gain control.

That meant conquest, naked war and conquest.

Or, it would mean that if there were no subtler way I could take over the running of a nation.

Now I saw that for one man to go around making himself king of this and prince of that was paranoia of a sublime madness. It was megalomania on a grand scale.

No. There had to be other ways, and just at the moment I had no idea what those ways might be.

Oh, yes, assuredly, I had a scheme dreamed up for Pandahem which I intended to put into operation the moment we were out of here and running free. But that was but a small chunk of the main problem.

"You look, Bogandur," said Nath, "as though you have lost a zorca and found a calsany."

"Rather, Nath," I said with feeling, "found a woflo."

"That you cannot ride."

"Unless the one shrinks or the other grows."

"Most profound," put in Seg. "And I'm starving."

Nath rumbled up a grunting cough.

"I wish you hadn't said that, Seg. Now I am reminded that my guts are like the last flagon at dawn."

"And," shot back Seg, "I wish you hadn't mentioned anything to do with flagons."

The little sally-affray gave us some tithe of amusement. I stood up and stretched and looked around.

Seg stood up as well and said: "Yes. Time to go."

Nath rolled off to get the ladies moving.

Again Deb-Lu appeared, shimmering and ghostlike.

The jagged opening into which he beckoned us did not look inviting. But trusting the Wizard of Loh absolutely as I did, I had no hesitation in heading directly into that Stygian blackness.

The sound of rushing water rustled and echoed about us, bouncing from the walls and drumming in our ears.

Feeling cautiously ahead, probing with the longsword, I made slow progress. Here, safety was far more important than speed.

Just rushing blindly ahead would get you killed stone bonkers dead, no doubt of that, by Krun!

The eeriness of this alien underground maze must not be allowed to affect our nerves. Yes, we were deep underground, walled by millions of tons of rock, creeping along in total darkness, prey to all the imagined fears the human mind can invent. Yet we had to hold onto our courage and press on and front the dangers and terrors as they leaped upon us.

The faintest iridescent shifting of mingled colors from a rockface far far ahead indicated the presence of distant light. With that faint and far off glow ahead the whole feeling to this cautious crawl through darkness altered. As we went on so the light strengthened. Our angle to the rockface shifted and gradually the predominant color emerged as an eye-searing viridian.

"Shades of Genodras," I said to myself, and prowled on. The twin Suns of Scorpio, Zim and Genodras, might be shining away in the Kregan sky outside, or, for all I knew, it could be pitch dark and some of Kregen's seven moons float refulgently among the stars. The diurnal rhythms of the world had, for the moment, been abandoned.

The noise now boomed and reverberated everywhere so that I was convinced a waterfall of some size lay in store for us.

Dampness in the air lay on the lips and tongue. The stone floor slicked with moisture. Along the walls as the green light intensified grew algaes and lichens, and the skipping figures of tiklos appeared and vanished among the crevices.

"I suppose," said Seg in a resigned and injured tone of voice, "we won't be able to drink the dratted water."

"Dunno, Seg. Maybe now Csitra's had her wings clipped natural things are back to being natural."

"At least the she-witch did feed us from time to time."

"Aye."

Directly ahead the green light poured through a wide opening set at an angle so that the radiance bounced from the rock face opposite. The noise now reached a painful intensity. The women stumbled along with their hands clapped over their ears.

Deb-Lu's figure showed to the side of the passage. A crevice in the rock, a mere jagged crack stretching from the floor up to a peak something like ten feet overhead, slashed a streak of blackness against the shining stone.

"Through there!" exclaimed Nath. "When there's a large opening ahead?"

"The Wizard of Loh has not failed us yet." I looked back over the mob. "Keep together." With that I plunged into the crack of blackness.

Cobwebs slurred furrily across my face. Irritably I brushed them away and pressed on, sword extended. The floor was rough and littered with detritus fallen from the apex of the fault. The noise lessened at once.

The experience was spine-tingling and unpleasant. The crack broke to the left and then to the right, and more clinging cobwebs festooned around my head. A distant wash of green light glimmered in a vague triangular shape before me. I took a breath and smelled dampness and green growing creepers and the oily and unidentifiable smell of alien life. I forced myself on and stepped past the broken end of the fault onto brown and golden gravel.

"All clear!" I bellowed back and then moved on a few paces to inspect this new and enormously vast cavern.

Light diffused green and gentle from the unseen roof—only a radiance seeped down from overhead. Winged creatures flew and darted, streaks of blue and white, among the stalagmite-like spires clustered around the left-hand wall. The golden brown gravel gradually merged with golden sand leading to the edge of a river. The roaring of the waterfall reached through a drift of spray spilling from the tunnel mouth where the river entered the cavern. The green growing smells, wet vegetation, trailing waterweeds, and the unmistakable smell of lavender coulory blended to form a not unpleasant cocktail of scents.

"Well," said Seg stepping out, "what have we here? Fish for supper?"

Then his fey blue eyes, surveying the scene, softened. He looked around and said: "Y'know, my old dom, this is a remarkably pretty place to find so deep underground."

"There are even trees growing with their roots in the water. And those birds—if they are birds—look quite unthreatening and cheerful."

The women trailed out of the crack in the cavern wall and incontinently flopped down on the gravel.

Nath deposited his pretty burdens and came over to join Seg and me.

"A forest under the ground!" he exclaimed.

"Could be an enchanted forest, my old Impenitent."

"Very probably, Horkandur. If so, we can surely avoid it by going around it."

"In," said Seg waspishly, "dubitably."

"Let the women rest for a time," I said. "We'd better search for the way out."

Nath heaved up a grunting sigh. "I don't much care, Bogandur, to leave the women unguarded down here."

"You are right, of course, Nath. And you will do the honors?"

"I will."

"If anything occurs," said Seg in his light and casual way. "You start yelling and then defend them all and hack and slay until we get back, right?"

I looked at Nath and saw him give a sudden start, as though thoroughly surprised and taken unawares. I'd no idea what could have caused that.

"I will," he said again, and this time in a much harsher and much shorter snap.

The pale shapely girl with the frizzy hair walked across. With her were her companions, and their hair, too, spiked out, and I guessed that in times of stress it, too, could resemble the snake tresses of a Medusa.

"We will search one way, man, if you search the other."

Most of them were half-clad. All had knives, spears or swords, and they looked a nasty bunch to argue with. Their Fuzzy-Wuzzy appearance reminded me I had no Martini-Henrys or Gardner guns to deal with them.

"Very well." Then I added: "I do not wish to continue to call you woman, woman. Would you favor me with your name?"

Now names are matters of great and imperative importance upon that miraculous and marvelous world of Kregen. Many peoples employ only use names, for their own name if known to an enemy confers power to the foe. She gave me a look, a hard appraising look. Dust glinted in her hair.

"You may call me Shalane, man."

"Very well, Shalane."

The group of Rumay fanatics went off to the right and as we trailed off in the other direction, Nath said: "They are not Battle Maidens; but many Jikai Vuvushis I have known who glory only in the uniform and the pomp and the show of being a War Woman would run screaming at the sight of them, aye, by Vox, many of them."

"Oh, aye," said Seg. "A most scrapworthy bunch."

So we set off to explore this new world we had discovered deep underground and to encounter what new perils it might hold.

Eight

"Save your breath for breathing!"

With our usual wary step, Seg and I walked along following the course of the river downstream. Nath remained with the women and the Rumay fanatics went upriver. We would then circle the cavern seeking egress.

"Y'know, Seg, there has to be a reason for a place like this."

"You mean a place of beauty among all the horrors of the Coup Blag?"

"Right. This is not quite the sort of cavern we're accustomed to finding deep in the heart of a mountain."

"We're well down underground here, all right. But I rather fancy this cavern is still in the mountain above the outside ground level."

"And that causes an idea to form, perhaps?"

"Aye, by Vox, an idea of some fraughtness."

"I agree."

"Well, my old dom, if it is the way, it is the way. By the Veiled Froyvil! We've come through thinner scrapes before this!"

So, not much caring for the idea in our heads, we went on along the river bank. Vegetation with the abundant water and never-ending light grew profusely and we saw many varieties of plants that I'd never seen before.

The blue and white flying creatures were joined by others of multicolored feathers, and they swooped and cavorted above our heads.

"Ah!" exclaimed Seg, and darted forward. "*Palines!*"

I lost no time in joining him and picking the bright yellow berries and stuffing them into my mouth. Palines—ah, they are a boon Kregen confers almost anywhere you travel and they'll keep you healthy and clear hangovers and generally make life worth living.

The scents of this delightful place sharpened about us. We breathed in refreshingly. The nonsensical notion flitted across my mind that one could live here in perfect tranquility for the rest of one's natural span.

The river ran smoothly and shining under the radiance. Fish leaped. We saw no sign of aquatic predators.

The colors and sounds and perfumes of this place delighted us. The trilling of the birds complemented the scents of the flowers in a sensory palette soothing and yet exhilarating. Here, the weary could rest.

We saw the place where the river entered the cliff face from some way off. Trees clothed the lower portions; the rocks frowned gaunt and bare above. We walked on, alert for danger even as our senses were soothed by the beauty and serenity of the cavern. Soon we stood before the river's exit.

"Ugly," commented Seg. "Dratted ugly, by Sasco!"

The river plunged into its carven hole, fashioned into the likeness of a snarling mouth. The sculpted face surrounding that unwholesome oriflee bore the likeness of a devil, a Kregen devil, which puts those of Earth to shame.

The rock here glistened dully with a green patina. The river rustled between the banks and plunged over smoothly and evenly with little spume or fuss. The blackness of the hole into which the river entered was of a blackness highly disturbing to those of nervous dispositions. I owned to myself that I tried to lighten the effect by a lightness in thinking of that damned hole; if you didn't feel amused by it you'd run screaming. Some of those poor women with us were most definitely of a nervous disposition, unfortunately.

"Come on, Seg, let's find the way out of this place."

"I'm with you. Unfocuses your eyes, does that blasted hole swallowing the river."

We gave the demonic face lowering down above us a last look, then we set off along the base of the cavern wall.

I suppose, to be honest, we both knew what it would come to, that there would be no escape from the deed. Still, we searched diligently all the way around for the way out, until we reached the gap in the rock through which the river entered the cavern. Then we went downstream to the camp.

Shalane spat and said: "There is no way out but the way we entered."

"D'you want to retrace your steps in there?"

A great hullabaloo started at this, and Seg and I went off to eat some of the fish Nath had caught and cooked. Some of the women had brightened appreciably in these pleasant surroundings, and were busy about our camp. I do not much care for fish; I recall that meal with pleasure.

In the end, of course, there was nothing else for it.

I felt no surprise when, staring up at the demonic face swallowing the river, some of the women turned around. They went back to the camp, calling that they would stay here.

"We can't leave them!" Nath looked outraged.

"We cannot in all conscience force them to go against their wishes, can we? They will be safe here—"

"But—forever?"

Seg said: "We'll talk to 'em again. It won't be all that bad, by the Veiled Froyvil!"

Eventually six of the women remained adamant that they would stay. They could do without men gladly.

"So be it."

"Havila have you in her keeping," said one of the women who was not staying, bold of face and grasping a spear.

From the slain malkos the Rumay women had taken axes as well as swords and spears, and we set to work to chop enough branches and trees to make sufficient rafts. They were bound together with lianas, and everyone pitched in to help.

While everyone was busy I glanced up to see the ghostly form of Deb-Lu standing beside me. He nodded and tried to make his serious look revert to his usual kindly expression. This time he whispered: "It is the only way."

"Yes, for we will not go back."

"May the Lords of the Seven Arcades go with you, Dray." He rustled up the hint of a smile. "And Vox and Djan and Zair, of course, also."

He vanished.

Seg came across and said: "He has no more news?"

"Only that this *is* the way out."

"That's all right then!"

And Seg swung off to shout at a girl fumble-fingering a botch of a knot.

"You'll ride on that raft, shishi, and if it falls to bits, you'll only have yourself to blame."

"Men!" she flared up at him, swirling red-brown hair about her naked shoulders. "You should be tying this."

"I'll show you—then you finish the rest."

This was quite unlike the Seg Segutorio I knew who was always punctiliously polite and gallant to women. He did not much care for the bunch we'd saved from the malkos, that was clear. Apart from the Rumay fanatics, whose beliefs and actions were self-explanatory, others of these women held secrets that made me wonder just how much trouble we were storing up for ourselves. It could be the women had been imprisoned after a process of justice, even in the Coup Blag. I doubted it; but it was possible.

Nath the Impenitent's whole attitude was quite different. He had already sorted out the women in his own mind. He had the leems and the ponshos marked.

The two girls he had been caring for were, I had to admit, in a different class from the others. Nath had chosen well, and yet these two, pretty though they were, shared all the toughness and spirit of the Rumay fanatics.

No one questioned Nath's right to share a raft with these two girls: Seg and I sorted out who would sail with whom, and suggested to Nath he take more of the ladies with him.

"The three of us will have to take different rafts, that is obvious. I don't like it; it is a duty laid on us."

"It is, my old dom, a duty only if we choose to accept it."

"By Chozputz, Seg! You are right, and yet I'd far rather we did not have to accept the mission, take on this heavy burden."

Nath rumbled out: "The Rumay women can handle themselves, doms. It is the others we must care for."

In the end we had it sorted out and the little armada of rafts lay on the bank of the river, waiting.

We ate of the cooked fish and of handfuls of palines. Among the trailing vines and plentiful leaves of the trees against the cliff, small agile figures clambered to gibber at us. The women left here would not need to exist on an exclusively fish diet.

I didn't fully trust to the lianas to lash the rafts and so had insisted on using other materials as well: split bark twisted and plaited, proved excellent. The rafts were serviceable. I hadn't served as a Powder Monkey and as a First Lieutenant in Nelson's Navy for nothing. Well, by Krun, I *had* got nothing for it, that was true, and I suspected my lack of success on Earth had a great deal to do with what others considered my considerable success on Kregen.

We ripped up blankets of moss and heaping mounds of leaves to form pliable cushions and we lashed everyone down with many strands of our plaited ropes. When all was ready Seg, Nath and I launched the other rafts, then Seg and I lashed Nath down and launched him, and I lashed Seg down and launched him amid an icy silence of reprobation that he was not the last.

As the current swirled him off he yelled back: "One of these days you'll take a risk too many, you stiff-necked hulu! I can be spared from Kregen; you—"

"Close the black-fanged winespout, my old dom!" I hollered back. "Save your breath for breathing!"

In the next instant Seg aboard his raft whirled into the black demon-guarded opening.

Lashing myself down as securely as I could, I felt my priorities of safety had been correct. Going first was not the peril that going unsecured would be.

Using forearms only, I thrust the long branch at the bank and eased the raft the last few inches off the mud. The current caught us at once, and we spun about, caught and sucked along with instant force. The smell of the mud, of the algae, of the water, struck up with physical force as we hurtled along.

The girls aboard my raft squealed; but they were very good and tried to keep silent. I think three of them fainted as we burst from the soft green radiance into the unholy darkness of the tunnel.

Phocis, a dark-haired girl with a full fresh face who clutched a spear at her side, stared up at me in the stern. At the moment, the raft had swirled around and I was going first. The branch with which I had equipped myself as a pole and rudder was completely useless for the moment.

Then Phocis and all the others vanished in the gloom.

As I saw it the main problem would come if the roof descended low enough for us to strike our heads. A makeshift arrangement of branches lashed upright and with cross-members would never protect us from the jags at this speed; it might give us a little warning.

Well, I will not dwell on that horrendous ride along an underground river in almost total darkness. Phosphorescence glimmered along the walls from time to time, enough to show us the long sliding gleam of the water. I managed to twirl the craft so that I was at the stern and able to steer. The girls lay low at my feet. Phocis still clung onto her spear. We hurtled along, a chip in a millrace, and all our fates were in the hands of whoever controlled them; certainly they were not in ours.

No, I will not dwell on that experience.

A thought occurred to me and, oddly, it comforted me in that ghastly situation. No one had volunteered to return through the mazes of the Coup Blag. All had chosen the perils of the underground river in preference to the horrors of Csitra's domains.

More than once the roof descended so that I, the highest of the crew, had to duck fiercely. The rock looked highly unfriendly, ready to slice like razors.

And—all the time and with deadly meaning—the river increased the speed of the current flow.

To dwell on that spirit-shrinking experience? No. I may be Dray Prescot, called by those whose paths I have crossed the Bravest of the Brave; I do not wish to repeat, even in remembrance, the journey down that subterranean river.

Twice we saw strange mingled lights falling upon us from rifts in the roof. I judged that we were approaching the edge of the mountain where faults in the structure allowed the streaming radiance of Zim and Genodras to filter down to this underground world. We were close to the outside now and in moments we shot out into the resplendent brilliance of daylight.

Here was the moment of truth.

Here we could win or lose all.

The river spewed out of its worn hole in the side of the mountain and fountained down in a waterfall. The noise boomed enormously. Spray engulfed us. I held on and counted and as each figure followed the next as we went helter-skelter down that slope of water I felt the rise of a bubble of nausea into my throat.

We hit.

The raft splintered into fragments.

Everything went up and down and around and around.

There was only noise and sickness and water and confusion.

Deep under the surface we plunged. Instinctively I thrashed with arms and legs. The lungful of air would not last long. The surface held life, and I fought fiercely, feeling the bruising battering of that headlong smashing impact.

My head broke through and I gulped in glorious Kregen air. Tossing the hair back and staring around, I saw heads in the water, and, also, saw the danger in which we still remained.

Phocis spluttered up at my side, still clutching her spear.

We began to grasp the wretched girls and swim with them away from the impact area of the fall. The noise engulfed us. Spray sleeted into a white mist. Slowly we managed to drag ourselves farther off and strike out for the bank.

Ghostly memories of my original arrival on this marvelous planet of Kregen occurred. Then I'd sailed down the River Aph aboard a leaf boat and had dared the might of a waterfall by many many times higher and more spectacular than this exit of the underground river from the mountain of the Coup Blag. Those days did not seem dim and distant, rather, they formed a portion of the living tapestry of my career on Kregen. Just as this very day as we reached the bank and hauled ourselves out, dripping wet and panting, formed another of the links in the living tapestry.

"By the Veiled Froyvil, my old dom! That was a tidy little to-do!"

561

"Aye. I see we have lost some of the women."

"An unavoidable tragedy, Bogandur," said Nath. "We have saved the majority, and for that we must rejoice and give thanks to Opaz the All-Glorious."

"That is so," said Seg, "and to Erthyr the Bow. One of the Rumay women's rafts vanished completely."

"If they are caught in the eye of the fall, then by this time all hope must be abandoned for them."

Gradually we dried ourselves off and sorted ourselves out. Phocis, who had kept herself very much to herself previously, proved a tower of strength in soothing and helping the weaker women. The Rumay fanatics were fit and ready, it seemed, to take on a crack regiment of Chuliks.

"We," said Shalane, making a direct statement, "will move off at once. We cannot stay here."

Her dark hair was already drying and frizzing out, and now it had had a wash it gleamed far more splendidly than ever it had done in the maze. Her fierce downdrawn face showed she was in no mood to argue.

Around us the banks stretched to low cliffs crowned with bushes cutting off further vision. The sky beamed gloriously above and the twin Suns of Scorpio cast down their mingled streaming radiance to light the world in an opaline haze of splendor.

Sniffing with enormous appreciation at the wine-rich Kregan air, looking upward and expanding my chest, I saw an airboat fly into view above the bushes.

Her hull was a dense black. Her upperworks, painted in a bewildering variety of clashing colors, were squared off and hard, pierced for throwing engines, frowning ominously above us.

"By all the imps in a Herrelldrin Hell!" burst out Seg in fury. "Dratted Shanks. That's all we need right now!"

"Keep absolutely still!" I bellowed, yet not so loud as to reach up through the air to that silent flier up there. "Do not move as you value your lives!"

Nine

Of bushes, beliefs and airboats

The deadly Shank voller up there flew with ponderous purpose across the river. We crouched low and still, deathly still.

This vessel must be from the fleet we had fought on our way over

Pandahem. If our own fleet had managed to regain contact—and anything could have happened during the time Seg and I had been stumbling about in the Coup Blag—then I had to hope a Vallian voller would fly over soon.

No one moved a hairsbreadth until the Shank vanished over the farther bushes.

"Of course," said Seg, helpfully, "he could have spotted us and given no indication, and be landing troops right now out of our sight."

"He could," said the Impenitent in that grunting gruff way of his. "And there could be one of our own fliers about right now, ready to pounce on him."

"I'll go for a scout around." Seg didn't waste time arguing but started off at once to the bush-lined crest.

Shalane, spiky and venomous, spat out: "Our fliers, man?"

Nath opened his mouth and I said: "There are many other islands and continents in Paz, Shalane, besides Pandahem. All of us, together, fight the Shanks."

"If they are men like other men then I will fight them," she said, in an offhand, dismissive way.

"Oh," I said. "You'll find them somewhat different, if you haven't fought them before. But I don't doubt you'll be able to cut a few trophies."

"Sanka," she said to one of her girls. "Get up there and scout. I don't trust a man to do a proper job."

Sanka scurried off, all frizzy hair and naked flesh, with a nasty-looking sword swinging at her side.

Shalane swung back to Nath. "You said 'our fliers', man. What nation in Pandahem are you from that has airboats?"

Nath cast a glance at me that summed up fury and annoyance at his lapse, and, also, I sensed, a great deal of damn-you-to-hell with respect to this ferocious woman.

"We have come through quite a deal together, Shalane." I returned the scorching stare she gave me, with interest. "But we are not yet comrades in arms. There is much you do not know that you will discover later."

"Now."

"Perhaps."

"You said there are other islands besides Pandahem."

"And continents."

"Other islands. I thought you three men strange. I have heard of Vallia."

"Have you heard, Shalane, that Vallia and the nations of Pandahem are now allies against the Shanks?"

She showed the chiseled teeth in a grimace of malicious amusement. "Even the Bloody Menahem?"

"Well—" I started, whereat she laughed aloud.

"Man, man! Your words fall upon you and crush you."

With what I considered exemplary patience I went on: "By Chusto, woman, listen! With the exception of those idiots of Menaham all of Pandahem stands with Vallia."

"I shall believe that when I see it. I have heard, also, of this Emperor of Vallia, Dray Prescot. The stories in the souks are marvelous but quite unbelievable."

"Those stories are trifles to amuse children." Then, because even here I couldn't malign the good-heartedness of the Vallian and Valkan storytellers, I added: "There is a kernel of truth to them. It is enlarged upon."

Nath rumbled out: "Dray Prescot! Emperor of Vallia! I'd as lief crush him beneath my heel as give him a Lahal."

"So you, Impenitent," snapped out Shalane waspishly, "are not Vallian also?"

Nath—who, remember, was ferociously proud of being Vallian—puffed up his cheeks into scarlet globs and his scowl would have cracked a window at fifty paces. "As to that, woman—" he started, rumbling like a volcano.

I cut in.

"No more time for shilly-shallying, Nath. Tell this poor woman Shalane the truth."

Her fist clenched convulsively on her sword hilt.

"Poor woman, man! I'll—"

Sanka came into view fleeting down the slope waving her arms. Seg ran astern of her and, I suppose, some deviltry got into him so that in all this petty wrangling he didn't intend to be beaten into second place.

Seg speeded up and slid past Sanka so that she seemed to be running backward. I cast a quick glance at Shalane and tried not to take any glee from her black look of anger at this fresh indignity.

"The rast is returning," said Seg, breathing evenly, completely unruffled. "And there's another following him."

I'd not been entirely consumed by the arguments with Shalane and had selected a likely site where bushes grew thickly to the margin of the river. I pointed.

"All in there and still as woflos when chavniks prowl!"

We all ran across and huddled in the bushes.

This vegetation wasn't thorn ivy; I did not believe any Thorn Ivy Trap would be sprung here.

Our joy at escaping from the grim confines of the maze had been swiftly transformed into sick apprehension at sight of the dreaded Shanks.

Some of the women had been bruised, all had been battered, and I wanted to get them into the care of a puncture lady as soon as might be. I most certainly did not want to get into a fight with them on our hands. Yes, the Rumay fanatics would fight, of that I had no doubt; just how well they would do against the incredible ferocity of a fish-headed, trident-armed Shank remained conjectural.

564

As far as I could see, they had not done at all well where the malkos were concerned. Again the idea crossed my mind that all these women were criminals imprisoned in the maze. That might, for all the oddity of it, square with Csitra's character.

As we waited and trembled crouched over in our bushes I tried to put that thought together with the notion that the vast and beautiful cavern from which we had taken passage down the river was outside the witch's jurisdiction. If not that, then that Deb-Lu-Quienyin had curtailed her power in that direction.

That Deb-Lu had not put in a recent appearance I judged was caused by his attention to other duties. He had a vast realm in which to be constantly vigilant and, unlike those ordained as kregoinye by the Star Lords, could not be in two places at one and the same time.

With an eyeball screwed to a chink in the leaves, I watched the steady and catlike progression of the Shank flier.

I knew Seg was chafing to shaft the cramphs up there, and clamping down on his very natural desires to shoot.

In this situation all we could hope to do was wait for the Shank air-boat to fly away. A nasty problem troubling me was—why had the bastard flown back?

A slender but sinuously-muscled form at my side stirred and an elbow dug into my ribs.

"Keep still, Phocis. If not to prevent the Shanks seeing us, then for the sake of my bruised ribs."

"By the Wooldark Mitraeus, Jak! You are enough to make a girl forsake her vows."

Then, for she was looking out at an angle from me, she said in a sharper voice: "Something dark came flying out of the hole where the waterfall begins. I lost it in its descent. Like a log."

"I hope it wasn't one of our poor girls trapped on a rocky ledge in there and washed down after us."

Seg whispered: "There's the second voller."

Even as he spoke both ships of the air speeded up and rose. They circled and raced across the river and then I saw something that made me clench my teeth together until the jaws ached.

A Vallian flier swooped down trying to evade the pounce of the two Shanks. She was a scouter, trim and fast; but they hemmed her in and all the time they were shooting at her.

The outcome of that fight could not be in doubt.

Battered and smashed, her steering gone and her lift decaying rapidly, the Vallian dropped down.

A fast scouter, she was of a type I recognized only because we'd bought half a dozen from King Filbarrka and Queen Zenobya, whose realms in

Balintol were firmly allied with Vallia. She carried blue and yellow checkered flags, whereat I knew she was from my kovnate island of Zamra. Now this was odd, as I did not recall any similar vessels in the fleet that had sailed to Pandahem. Therefore, reinforcements must have been sent us. This was good news. The bad news was that this scouter was doomed and her crew just about done for.

She hit heavily and ripped into shreds. Agile figures dark against the suns' light leaped out and the silver wink of stars from their weapons held cold comfort.

The Shanks landed promptly but unhurriedly, and disgorged rank after rank of fish-headed fighting demons.

In a low-voiced monotone Nath Javed the Impenitent cursed everything, from fate, the Ice Floes of Sicce, the benighted of Opaz, the forsaken of Vox, the destroyed of Kurin, his own bad luck and, finally, himself.

Then he said: "Well, it all had to end one day. I cannot skulk here."

Seg said in his lightest and most flamboyant style: "Oh, aye, my old Impenitent. I agree. But I do not think we will walk away from this fight."

"Indubitably."

Shalane, from her bush, spat out: "You are not going to—no, you cannot? Surely—"

I said: "You may not believe now, Shalane, that this is your fight and the fight of the Rumay belief. But it is so."

With that I stood up, unlimbered the great Krozair longsword and with a lilting: "*Hai, Jikai!*" roared out of my bush and along the riverbank full tilt at the packed ranks of the fish-headed Shanks.

Ten

Wounds

This was not the first time and—if the cruel fates spare me—not the last when I thus roared into the charge with Seg Segutorio to shoot me in.

As I bounded on, roaring my fool head off, so Seg's shafts flowered overhead.

A master bowman, the finest archer on two worlds, Seg. His strings were dry from his pouch, safe from the watery passage of the river. The crimson-fletched shafts skewered into the packed ranks of the Shanks.

I did not count the number of times Seg shot, for I knew he did not have arrows enough to dispose of the foe; I did see two arrows at least pierce through two men each, and I judge I saw a third that penetrated through three Shanks before its force was expended.

Through the thunder of blood in my head I heard the heavy beat of footsteps alongside, and the lighter patter on the other side. Nath the Impenitent, enormous, scarlet, bursting with passionate intensity, hullabalooed along determined to keep up and swing into action at the same time. Phocis fleeted along, and a single swift glance showed me her spear held most professionally in the hands of a most determined young lady.

Well, like us all, she would take her chances in the coming conflict.

The lads from the downed Vallian flier had not been idle. They'd rigged a varter from the wreckage and now the bolt-thrower began to hurl its cruel iron darts into the massed Shanks.

Just before our pathetic little bunch from the riverbank hit I spotted the two left arms of the yellow-haired men wearing Vallian Air Service uniforms. This did not surprise me. I'd set up communities of Pachaks on Zamra. They were citizens of Zamra and of Vallia. They were, also, fighting men of absolute integrity and of deadly skill and cunning.

"Hai, Jikai!" I bellowed.

Well, by Vox, if this was to be the last great fight, as I believed, then I'd use that great war cry properly and for the final time.

We hit the Shanks and in an instant were involved in a melee of striking and dodging, of ducking and of bashing as we sought to exploit the gap created by Seg's masterful shooting.

The Krozair brand swept and lopped, struck and thrust. It was essential to use economy, to strike with force just sufficient for the purpose. Try it in the red-blood-roaring madness of an affray! Nice theories fall apart under the manic goad of battle.

We exploited the gap and by thus concentrating our onslaught we could deal with those Shanks who could get at us. The others, for the moment, until they could rally themselves, were out of it.

Seg joined us for the melee. Then in the contorted actions of battle, where you smite to the front and dodge and trust no one is smashing down on your back, I saw the Rumay women.

They fought like slinking devils, low and upthrusting, fluid, bitter and without mercy.

All the same, they died, as the Shanks died. Phocis took a tine through her upper arm and I swept the fish-headed creature away in two halves. The tine was smooth and not barbed, for it was a melee-trident and not a throwing weapon, so it came out suckingly easily enough.

"Leave me and go on," she panted out.

"I can fight here as well as anywhere."

There was time to say no more as the Shanks, rallying, pelted at us again.

Seg and I fought them as we had in the old days. Nath fought them and learned, I did not doubt, many new tricks of nastiness.

From the flank the Pachaks screeched into a wild attack. I believe it is a part of their mystique that they cast off their helmets and let their long yellow hair stream free. They go berserk. This in people of the character I know them to be always has struck me as suspiciously unlikely. For instance, this bunch from the downed voller did not cast off their helmets. Their straw yellow hair streamed abaft them as they charged and they were wild and abandoned to the passions of battle; as to being genuinely berserk—I do not think so.

Even with all the Pachaks and all the Rumay women and the other women like Phocis who joined in the battle, we could never have gained the victory over this number of Shanks. We would have fought the last great battle. Someone, somewhere, might have spoken of the deed as a High Jikai. Probably not. We would have died and been forgotten.

Phocis had drawn a scrap of cloth from her shirt around the wound. She was using the Shank trident as a weapon. She forced herself up and fought alongside us, wielding the three-tined trident with consummate skill.

Soon her blood on the metal was joined by that of Shanks.

Shalane swirled like a demoness, appearing to shed sparks, striking in all directions at once. Her tigress girls struggled and struck, fought and died. I surmised they had not met the Shanks in battle before and were not in the same awe of the Fishheads as those who had had the misfortune and the glory to meet them.

A shadow passed over us.

I did not look up.

It was very necessary at that moment to despatch the fellow to the left side who was trying to stick his damned trident into Seg's side.

The Krozair brand sliced and the Shank screeched and fell away and then—again very necessarily—the Krozair brand was needed on the other side where Phocis, cleverly spitting her opponent, momentarily left herself open to a third thrust. Here I thrust past the incoming tines, bouncing them off with the blade and so going on to haul up without punching clean through backbone as well.

"Like a damned beetle on a pin!" Phocis retrieved her trident and instantly set to again, raging.

The raw stink of blood, red blood and green ichor, smoked into the air. The ground muddied with blood. And still Seg and I, Nath and Phocis and Shalane and the Rumay women battled on. This madness could not last.

Nath stood amidst a heap of Shank corpses, roaring defiance. Shalane appeared to be everywhere, cutting and cutting. Seg's cool skilled swordsmanship cleared the ring, and Phocis with her Shank trident stopped many a Shank dead in his tracks. But, still, it could not last.

In one of those uncanny little lulls that obtrude in almost any fight where muscles are the only motive power, Seg flicked drops from his blade and stared balefully at the Shanks just across from us. They were forming up for another of the charges that had proved unsuccessful.

I said: "Seg..." There was an unmistakable tone of warning there.

He scowled back at me. "All right, Dray, all right. Not yet, anyway."

He could fight with cool professionalism, could our Seg Segutorio; equally, if the mood took him he'd go roaring into the fray with all a Pachak's berserk fury and a whole shovelful more. This was a legacy of those strange mountains and valleys of the land of his birth, Erthyrdrin, the northernmost country of the continent of Loh. And Loh is as mysterious a place as you can want.

The Shanks started to fidget and move and shake their weapons again. Not all wielded tridents.

"Here they come again," called Nath. He was covered in blood and looked to be in an exalted mood. "Hack 'n' slay!" he bellowed, the words clear and distinct and forming a battlecry. "Hack 'n' slay, my lads, hack 'n' slay!"

"Aye!" ripped out Seg.

This next onslaught was ferocious and frightful. I saw Shalane go down with a spear through her, and in that microscopic section of time I could spare for a thought about her I surmised the wound would not be fatal.

I knocked two Shanks down who were trying to spear Seg, and Phocis stuck her trident through the eyes of another. The Krozair brand flamed around, and a fourth attacker's arm fell off. Seg sliced his man and we cleared the ring.

I saw Nath, bloated, scarlet, huge, smash over sideways with a trident sticking into him with an obscene wiggle of the shaft.

So this is how it goes, I said to myself, one by one they will go down and Seg and I will be left to the last.

The two girls cared for by Nath must have joined in the fracas after the initial charge. Whatever the truth of the matter, they appeared now and flung themselves wailing upon Nath. He lay like a fallen oak tree, arms wide, and I swear his expression was exactly that he must have worn when being thrown out of the tavern, after he'd spent all his soldier's pay.

"Hai, Jikai!" I vomited the words out and swung the Krozair brand over my head. I did not feel a fool doing this outrageous gesture and mouthing the great words. If it was to be all over, then get it all over with.

The Shanks did not appear to wish to continue the combat.

They were milling about. If those cold-hearted reivers from over the curve of the world could be said to be hesitant, uncertain, then they appeared at a loss now.

Then we saw the reason and set up such a caterwauling row as would have brought the Watch of any strict city out in a sweat rash.

A skyship had touched down beyond the two Shanks and her fighting men, her voswods, had alighted, formed their ranks as they had done a hundred times in practice drills, and, heads down and spears leveled, swept down on the Fish-heads.

The Shanks fought damned hard. Shtarkins, I believed them to be. Their fishy heads and fishy smells repelled me; but they were wonderful sailors and navigators. They fought with vicious intensity now that they were outnumbered and on the receiving end.

And so, now, it could not last. And, this time, it was the Shanks who would not last, praise be to Opaz.

In the end they tried to make a break for their airboats; but the Vallian skyship commander had spotted that possibility and had thrown a blocking force out. No Shanks reached sanctuary.

I looked around the field. We had made the Shanks suffer; they had caused us injury.

The dead were heaped up dolefully. Then I felt a jolt of surprise. Among a pile of Shtarkin dead lay the Kanzai Warrior Brother we had met in the maze of the Coup Blag.

We'd never known his name. The dark log Phocis had spotted leaping out of the waterfall tunnel was now explained. We'd been far too absorbed in our own combat to notice the Kanzai adept. Yet I recalled, there *had* been a moment in the fight when the pressure lessened unaccountably.

From the evidence before us, it was perfectly clear he had fought magnificently. I lifted my bloodstained sword in salute to him, and commended his warrior spirit on its way down to the Ice Floes of Sicce.

"I wonder if he realized he was fighting for Paz," said Seg. "He wouldn't believe it; but he was."

"A most judicious thought, Seg, and one we must make sure Shalane understands."

"Here comes the skyship landing force commander. He's a Jiktar. And I think—yes—" Seg shook his head, letting down from that sudden sharp scrutiny: "It's old Hodo Fra-Le. I had a right go at him over the state of his archers a few seasons ago."

"His lads seem to have done all right here."

"Oh, aye. I went up to Zamra and fairly ran 'em ragged until they were up to scratch."

I did not give a laugh that would have been the normal accompaniment to my next thought; laughter on this stricken field spoke of the manic laughter that referred only to itself and the battle. My thought was that Seg was such a stickler in anything connected with toxophily that no one would feel surprise if he went down to the enemy before a fight and tried to smarten up their shooting as well.

Hodo Fra-Le, a Pachak, clad in armor and with the integrity of his race strong upon him, marched up with a small group as bodyguard. He wore bobs and the medals had been well-earned. His Pachak face wore a pleased expression over the natural hardness and I guessed he was intrigued by the situation into which he had stumbled.

"Llahal! I am glad to see some of you survive."

Sharing a natural curiosity he checked our group first, already knowing he had saved the crew of the scouter.

Seg moved out very sharply up front. Big and extraordinarily powerful though he may be, Seg can move like greased lightning, as they say in Clishdrin, when necessary.

He towered over Hodo Fra-Le, for Pachaks are not among your taller diffs of Kregen, and he clapped a friendly arm over a shoulder and bent his head and spoke most amicably and forcibly. Anyone listening to Seg Segutorio talk under those circumstances would devoutly believe.

What Seg was doing was making sure he preserved my anonymity. It didn't matter that Seg thought I sometimes played at the mysterious a trifle over the top; if I wanted to conceal my identity under a nom-de-guerre, than he would do his damnedest to see the deceit worked.

When Hodo wheeled up he squeaked out: "Lahal, Jak."

"Lahal and Lahal, Hodo. You arrived opportunely."

"We have been searching for the fleet, majis—Jak. Since we arrived from Zamra we have not made contact."

"Deb-Lu must soon rectify that," pointed out Seg.

"I trust so, jen." Hodo addressed Seg correctly as Jen, Lord, and if anyone overheard they'd know he was not from Pandahem, where lords are Pantors.

As we walked along to try to sort out the mess, I realized the stupidity of that thought. Anyone could see Hodo Fra-Le was not of Pandahem, what with that enormous skyship in the background!

Nath the Impenitent was not dead.

I felt a tremendous lift of the heart at this news, and gave thanks to Opaz and Zair.

Nath was shifted off into the skyship's sickbay and the two girls—Perli and Sanchi—went with him. The skyship, a splendid vessel built in Hamal and given the name *Zamra Venturer* was the answer to our immediate problems.

Her captain, Jiktar Nalgre Voernswert ti Zanchenden, warned by his land force commander, welcomed me as Jak. The stories told in the souks had one benefit, at the least.

Our other wounded were cared for. Shalane was desperately injured and hovered on the slippery slope down to the Ice Floes. I would not care to see her die. Phocis, by contrast, with a medical poultice on her punctured arm would be as good as new tomorrow.

This was not the time for congratulation or for slackening of effort.

Yes, we had won free at last from the maze of the Coup Blag. We had the wonderful benefit of having airboats in which to fly over the inhospitable jungle. We all felt the enormous relief as a physical burden removed from our shoulders. But we could not relax. There remained far too much to do if we were to save Paz.

Although Jiktar Nalgre managed to remember to call me Jak instead of majister, he was all aquiver to put up a good front and do well. Seg told him to take *Zamra Venturer* around to the other side of the mountain so that we might find out what had befallen our youngest comrade, Cadet Ortyg Thingol.

He'd been left outside the mountain with Kov Hurngal's airboat and an ink stained Relt stylor, Hurngal's secretary. Ortyg had resisted being left and only a promise that he was in the most important position of having command of the airboat and having to rescue us had mollified him.

Now here we were flying in a mammoth skyship. I heaved up a sigh. Well, brown-curled handsome and romantic young air cadets have to learn the hard facts of life like anyone else, by Vox.

I decided to leave the voller in case Kov Loriman the Hunter did emerge into the suns' light. As for the Relt, now his employer, Kov Hurngal, was dead he was free to stay or fly with us.

As for the Rumay women—the downing of their leader affected them all in a way that, to me at least, came as a surprise. They were stunned and apathetic. Sanka, who assumed the command, made one attempt to rally them. After that they all sat in a huddle crooning ritual dirges. I did not say as I felt very much like bursting out: "Shalane ain't dead yet, you famblys!"

"They'll have to be kept sequestered from the crew," pointed out the ship's captain, Jiktar Nalgre Voernswert ti Zanchenden. He was often known as Nalgre the Blunt. "They're enough to frizzle the heart of a stone-monster."

"They'll be all right when Shalane gets better."

"By Corg! I devoutly trust so!"

So, in much better heart than we had been when last the twin suns Zim and Genodras set over the shadowy face of Kregen, we flew off to find the rest of the Vallian armada.

Eleven

How old Hack 'n' Slay stood up

The real world of Kregen, as my Kregish friends are fond of remarking in many proverbs and adages, is always changing, continually surprising, exotic even to those born under the streaming mingled lights of the Suns of Scorpio.

Yet there are places familiar and dear because of that.

Seg and Milsi were adamant that we could now spend the time with them we had promised. Delia—ah! My Delia smoothed all and so we flew off to Croxdrin where Milsi was Queen and Seg was King. Along the River of Bloody Jaws we had had adventures, with more to come, no doubt; for now we could just be ourselves and enjoy life. That, after all, as the wise men say, is the reason we are here at all.

Shalane mended slowly and so we had packed her and her Rumay fanatics off to Vallia to be cared for by the first sorority who volunteered.

"I rather hope it will be the Sisters of Samphron," said Delia, smiling as she took in the scent of the bunch of flowers just brought into the rooms in Milsi's palace where we were quartered. "Or the Little Sisters of—"

"What?" I teased her. "You're scared of what they might do to your girls of the Sisters of the Rose?"

When she let go of my hair and let me get up, I blew out my cheeks, and said: "One tumble deserves another."

"We are due for dinner and Milsi's view of etiquette coincides with mine, you great hairy graint."

"Quidang!"

At dinner we naturally discussed the points of contention still bothering us. Outside, the river shimmered under the radiance of Kregen's first moon, the Maiden with the Many Smiles. The service inside was just as smoothly brilliant. Kov Llipton, a handsome numim, and his wife, the lush Rahishta, attended. Llipton ran Croxdrin for Milsi during her absences. There was no sign of Princess Mishti, and while this saddened Milsi, she was aware that the girl still needed time to put the clamorous thoughts seething in her head into order.

There was absolutely no news of the whereabouts of Csitra.

The Witch of Loh had vanished. Our three mages, Deb-Lu-Quienyin, Khe-Hi-Bjanching and his wife, Ling-Li-Lwingling, reported that all trace of Csitra's sorceries had been removed.

"Do you believe this to be the end of the Witch War, then?" demanded Delia.

"Never, by the Veiled Froyvil! We've not heard the last of that black-hearted one!"

"Agreed, dear," said Milsi.

"I agree, also," I said. "And you, Delia?"

"Yes, except that..."

We waited and then, as Delia instead of going on with what had been in her mind lifted a crystal goblet of rich red, Milsi burst out: "Delia? What do you mean?"

Delia put the goblet down with precision. Everyone around the table looked politely at her. She wiped her lips with excruciatingly bright-yellow napery.

"Khe-Hi and Ling-Li said they could sense a distinct change in the witch's—oh, I do not know what arcane words they employ for their arts—in her kharrna, in her center of sorcerous emission. They were uncertain and dear old Deb-Lu was unable to confirm."

"Confirm what?"

"Would you care to explain what wizards mean when they talk their gobbledygook together?"

"No."

"It is just that we must expect the unexpected."

I was about to make the superfluous comment that, on Kregen, one has always to expect the unexpected to stay alive, when Kov Llipton leaned forward to speak.

The lionman spoke gravely. "Forgive me, but you talk, majisters and majestrixes, of Wizards of Loh with great familiarity."

I sat back.

Yes, what Llipton said was half-true. We tended these days to think of the three mages as our comrades, as friends, before Wizards and a Witch of Loh.

Milsi said on a breath: "We never forget their power, kov, never."

And that was true, by Krun!

"They are unaccountable folk," went on Llipton in that serious tone. "What they do they do. They follow their own mysterious purposes. They bow the head to no one."

I took up a small handful of palines from the silver dish. "What you say is right, kov. Yet I have known a Wizard of Loh much reduced and brought down who served a tyrant slavishly. That was in the Hostile Territories of Turismond."

"I have heard of them, of course. They are being settled by colonies from all over nowadays, I hear." Llipton brushed his numim whiskers. "By Numi Hyrjiv the Golden Splendor! majister, what sorcery could thus enslave a Wizard of Loh?"

"Oh," I said, thinking of Umgar Stro, "I do not believe sorcery was involved. But, as to our friends who also happen to be mages, they are a part of the empire now. And we are exceedingly fortunate for that."

"Exceedingly," said Seg, and I knew he was thinking of the times Deb-Lu had used his kharrna to our benefit.

"Well," said Delia in her brisk fashion, "Khe-Hi and Ling-Li have gone back to Loh. Their children must be born there. Otherwise, they could not become real Wizards and Witches of Loh."

"The patterns must be preserved."

So we talked as we sat on around the table which bore the ruins of the splendid meal we had demolished.

Later that evening as we prepared to retire in the sumptuous chambers put at our disposal, Delia said: "I am always a little fretful when Khe-Hi and Ling-Li and dear Deb-Lu are not close by."

"Yet Deb-Lu worked his miracles at a distance—"

"Oh, I know! But, all the same—"

"All the same you will stop fretting and come to bed like any empress— no, confound it! By Zair! Sometimes, glad though I am to be rid of the job, I forget."

"Drak and Silda make an exemplary pair as emperor and empress. I am content."

So, by Vox, was I!

After we had spent a short time in Milsi's and Seg's realms of Croxdrin, we took our farewells, called down the remberees, and took off for Vallia.

Flying north with the combined fleets we saw not a sign of Shank airboats. We had reconnaissance out everywhere searching for the base we were confident they must have established to support this forward thrust. So far no sightings had been reported.

We broke the journey halfway to call in on the country of Jholaix, in the extreme northeast corner of Pandahem. Here Milsi was able to visit with her relatives, and—I believe I have no need to tell you who have been following my story—we had a riotous time. Jholaix produces what are considered the best wines of this part of Paz.

We met with folk there who were dissatisfied with the way events were turning out, and we materially furthered our cause. I felt confident that Jholaix, with Milsi's relatives, friends and contacts, would prove a powerful ally.

There is little need, it seems to me, to relate the scenes of pandemonium and celebration that occurred when we returned to Vallia. The citizens had accepted Drak and Silda as the new rulers. Yet all felt that special allegiance to the divine Delia. Oh, yes, we had a tremendous shindig, I can tell you, and we made, as they say in Clishdrin, the welkin ring all the long night through.

Our first visit the next morning was to see how Nath the Impenitent fared.

He was sitting propped up in a vast bed in the villa we had made over to his use, with his friends Perli and Sanchi dancing delightful attendance. Phocis, too, had a wing to herself and a few of her friends remaining from their fraught ordeal down the Coup Blag.

The Little Sisters of Patience had taken Shalane and the Rumay fanatics under their wing. There, as Delia said with a half-smile, it was all bread and water, prayers and housekeeping. "They will soon," she said with a pert shake of her adorable head, "grow tired of *that*."

"I must admit, my heart, I am disquieted at our bringing the Rumay fanaticism back to Vallia."

"Agreed. Once Shalane and the other wounded are well, they must make their decisions for the future."

"Aye. If Jilian Sweet-Tooth were here she'd soon knock them into shape in her regiment of Jikai Vuvushis."

"She still pursues her own ends, as you know. If they wish to join a regiment, all well and good. I feel that they will choose not to do so. They are independent to a fault. It will probably be best for us to send them back to their homes."

"Aye."

As for Nath the Impenitent, he was genuinely glad to see us.

Seg and I went in first, bearing gifts, and he greeted us in the old happy way we had established during our comradeship down Csitra's damned magical maze.

I had made immediate enquiries of my chief stylor, Ob-eye Enevon, and he had rapidly ransacked the files and plunked down on my desk the details of Nath's misdeeds, punishment, and subsequent fate.

"Old Hack 'n' Slay!" I exclaimed. "So that's who he is. No wonder he jumped at the words, and he used them during the fight around the downed vollers. And he robbed his regiment's cash box. Well, I know why he did that. And he would have repaid but for the malignancy of his divisional commander."

"Chuktar Strom Enar Thandon," said Enevon, nodding. "His report is certainly damning."

I told Enevon that Nath the Impenitent had taken the money from the regimental strong box to save his sister's daughter from the abhorrent followers of Lem the Silver Leem.

"Then," said Enevon, "it was a worthy deed."

"Aye. Nath would have repaid had he been promoted. As we can see from the file, his promotion was blocked by this same Enar Thandon."

"He was commander of the 32nd Brigade of churgurs, yet he was not promoted from Jiktar to Chuktar."

I rapped my knuckles on the file.

"I suspected the Impenitent was a good soldier, and this proves it. See the list of his bobs. No, by Krun, this won't do in the Vallian Army. I'll have a word or three with Enar Thandon—" I shut up. Then I said: "This will have to go to the emperor, Enevon."

"Yes, jis, no doubt of it."

I gave him a leery look. "Jis, Enevon?" Jis, a contraction of majister, was now more and more used in the meaning of "sir."

"Reminds me of the old times, Dray."

"They had quite a fight getting Nath into the cells."

"I'll see the papers go to your son, then."

"Please, Enevon. Now I'll go and see the old Impenitent."

So, there were Seg and I, with our gifts, and Nath roaring at us from the bed, scarlet-faced with pleasure.

"Jak! Seg!" he bellowed. "Lahal and Lahal. Come in and have a stoup. I am being capitally provided for, and by whom I've not an idea in a Herrelldrin Hell."

We shook hands in the Vallian fashion, and Perli and Sanchi poured parclear, for it was too early for ale.

"We're glad to see you are feeling better, Nath," said Seg, lifting his glass.

"Oh, aye, fit, fit! But you're late! Young Ortyg has comforted me a great deal. Tell me where you've been and what fresh adventures you've had." He heaved up a sigh. "I confess I'm sorry to have missed 'em."

"Nothing of importance, Jik," I said.

He spilled his parclear.

"Jik?"

I looked at him. He put a finger to his lips and said:

"So you knew my name when I spoke in the Coup Blag. That life is passed and best forgotten."

"Nath Javed," I said. "Jiktar of the 32nd Brigade of Churgurs. Old Hack 'n' Slay. Caught with his fingers in the regimental funds."

"Yes, yes, I told you and you swore to hold your tongue. But not my rank or the brigade—so—"

Seg lowered his glass and spoke in his powerful way. "Nath, we detest the evil creed of Lem the Silver Leem. We are dedicated to its utter overthrow and destruction."

"I will give you amen to that, doms. Aye, by Vox!"

"Good." Seg was brisk. "When you are recovered, we will do somewhat regarding the vile people who took away your sister's daughter."

Nath moistened his lips. "I have hated all lords and nobles, and the emperor, and with good reason. Now there is a new emperor. Will he be any different?"

Seg started to say something and Nath went on in almost a ruminative way. "Yet, you two, the Horkandur and the Bogandur, are lords also, as I know. Yet I do not hate you. You are dear comrades. Are there, then, lords and lords?"

"There are. And, one of them, Enar Thandon, I believe, will rue the day he acted as he did."

Again Nath started. An uproar began at the door and young Ortyg Thingol burst in bearing a flagon of ale and shouting that the hour of mid had passed and Nath was due his wet. He saw Seg and me. His bright face flushed with color and the brown curls danced. He was mightily discomfited.

"Majister!" he croaked out. The flagon shook. "Your pardon, majister, I did not know you and Jen Seg were here."

"Evidently," growled Seg. He glanced at me in so comical a way that I broke out laughing.

Nath shot up in the bed.

"Majister!" he bellowed. "What is this about majister?"

I said: "I crave your pardon, Jik Nath, for deceiving you. But it was, as you can see, essential that I be known as Jak the Bogandur. You do see that?"

His eyes popped. He tried to speak and gobbled for air. At that moment Delia and Milsi entered, bringing their gifts, and bringing a radiance and warmth into the sickroom.

"Dray!" called Milsi. "So this is the fearsome Impenitent!"

For a moment the confusion that followed left me a trifle breathless. Now Nath had said he'd never seen the emperor close up and that was why he'd not known me. He must have seen the empress, even though he may have denied it.

He scrabbled up in the bed, shedding sheets, trying to claw his way out and stand on his feet. He stood up all right, swaying, bursting sweat all over that scarlet face.

"Majestrix!" he roared out, and fell full flat on his face.

Seg and I hauled him back into the bed and then we all stood around looking down on him.

So, as you see, even a dedicated noble- and emperor-hater like old Hack 'n' Slay cherished the divine Delia and would serve her past death.

The needleman was called. Nath was out to the world. We were shooed out and left, telling Perli and Sanchi, dumb with shock, that we would return.

"D'ye see the old Impenitent's face?" demanded Seg. "When he remembered how pally he'd been treating the Bogandur!"

"He will," said Delia in her most practical way, "get over it."

"If this means he'll be loyal to Drak—"

"I do not think, my heart, there will be any doubt of that."

What young Ortyg Thingol said was correct; it was past the hour of mid and therefore, acting the part of respectable citizens, we could legitimately make our way back for a long and thirst-quenching drink of ale. Wine would come later.

Now these days in Vondium the Proud City, capital of Vallia, where I was no longer the emperor, I had fancied I could have a deal of time to myself and generally laze about. Some hope! There always seemed something to do.

Drak and Silda and the Presidio were busily carrying on the work of putting the country back together again after the Times of Troubles. We conferred with many people you have met in this narrative of my adventures, and many others who worked nobly for Vallia. The army was in good heart. The great galleons of Vallia were being built again. The Air Service was painstakingly increasing the aerial fleets; but that work was dependent on the good news out of Hamal and Hyrklana where vollers were constructed. Supplies of airboats and saddle animals were being bought from Balintol.

All in all, we had precious little time to spend to ourselves.

The terror of the Witch of Loh's Nine Curses against Vallia had been removed, or so we believed. And, still, there was no news either of Csitra or the Shanks.

One evening we had gone through what I considered the tedious business of an enormous State Function. Drak and Silda looked the part of emperor and empress to perfection. When, at last, we could doff the ceremonial robes and remove the ornate mazillas, tall gem-encrusted collars that fair enclosed a person's head, we felt we had earned a small portion of time for relaxation.

Many of our friends and comrades gathered in the newly-furbished Corbitzey Chambers, hung with ruby-drapes and lit by many samphron oil lamps. The air was scented sweetly with Moon-blooms, and the tables groaned under food and drink. The assembled company would start singing soon, in the well-established and hallowed traditions of Vallia.

The Lord Farris and Nath na Kochwold were talking quietly in a corner with Seg and me when a gong-note sounded and a messenger walked into the brilliantly-lit chamber. Roben ti Vindlesheim standing with us glanced across and then went on talking in his dark-browed intensive way, concentrating on his beloved canals to the exclusion, it seemed to his amused and affectionate friends, of everything else.

Mantig Roben had been appointed by me when I'd been emperor to put Vallia's once-superb network of canals back into good condition. Many of the waterways had fallen into disuse. A bustling land full of commerce and travel needs canals, by Vox. Roben, quick-mannered, absorbed in his own work for Vallia, was just one more of the good comrades gathered about the throne during and after the Times of Troubles.

Seg said: "The messenger goes straight to Drak, Dray. They are learning."

"And about time, too, by Bongolin."

From the trim and clean appearance of the messenger we knew he had not flown here astride a saddle bird but had flown aboard a voller. Watching Drak's hard, competent face, so like my own and yet so unlike, I saw the flashing expression there reveal not indecision but a weighing of different courses of action. Indecision and Drak did not often lie together.

The major indecision of Drak's life so far had been his shilly-shallying about Silda.

Now he glanced across at my corner, saw me watching him among all the throngs of gaily-clothed folk between. He started across. As he approached I felt my old heart banging. Drak was every inch an emperor, by Zair, and I was proud of the lad.

I waited for him to speak. A hush fell about the group and more folk, curious as ever, formed a ring.

"It is Menaham." Drak's left fist rested on his rapier hilt. "The Bloody Menahem. We all wondered what would chance with this new king they have. Well, now we know." He glanced around, and only a fool would see indecision on that powerful, dominating and—yes—handsome face. "The imbecile has invaded Iyam and carries fire and the sword across the land toward Lome and Yumapan."

Halted in his passionate tirade about the canals, Mantig Roben ti Vindlesheim was the first to speak. It was, as it were, a continuation of his thoughts.

"Let them hack each other to pieces in Pandahem, jis. We have Vallia to heal and rebuild. It is no concern of ours."

From the growl of assent, quite a number of the folk there shared that sentiment.

Drak's head thrust forward obstinately. He stared full at me as he spoke, a lowering, brooding look of concentration. He knew my aims for Paz, all right, knew them damned well.

"This is evil news, yes. It destroys much we in Vallia have worked for. But it does concern us, for it concerns Paz."

Twelve

Of the Mystique of Paz

Mysticism forms a vital ingredient in the lives of some people who cannot exist without the thrills and terrors of supernatural experiences—or quasi-supernatural delusions—and the feeling they are communing with forces beyond those of nature. There are other folk who see no need for flummery of this kind to explain the disasters and successes of life. They are in touch with aspects of nature quite satisfactory to them.

When millions of people devote themselves to the service of an abstract ideal, surely, some will say, mysticism reaches an apex, no matter what the ideal. Others will say that practical self-interest and the well-being of their fellow humans motivate their actions.

The theory for the moment could be ignored; we needed the results. When my lad Drak spoke so intensely about Paz, I felt enormous relief. I had not been sure that he would put matters in the same order of priority that I had done. He had, I'd noticed, been furbishing up the palace at a faster rate than in my days as emperor. But in matters of importance he could see clearly enough that what we in Vallia were doing or trying to do—was really a matter of simple common sense.

Nowadays, when the word Paz was spoken, there clung around the sound an aura of mysticism, of grandeur, of yearning. Invisible trumpets pealed and carried the name Paz.

Most folk could feel that little shiver up the spine at the idea of Paz. The continents of Turismond to the west, Segesthes to the east, Loh between and Havilfar to the south, joined by the islands of Pandahem and Vallia formed the grouping of lands known as Paz.

"The news is certainly evil for the poor devils of Iyam," said Nath na Kochwold.

Seg said: "Are there no more details?"

Some, a little, of the tenseness drained from Drak as he turned at once to answer Seg.

"Precious little, Seg. Only that this insufferable new king of theirs doesn't understand mercy."

"In that case he may be king for a very short time."

One or two of the people smiled at this, and Naghan Strandar in his familiar way laughed, agreeing.

When I'd been putting smashed-up Vallia back together, and being lumbered with the job of being emperor along the way, people had gathered about to help. You know a few of them. It was diashum* to work and, if necessary, to die for Vallia.

When as emperor I'd run the Presidio and court, do not believe that the fighters, bankers, architects, artists, flyers, musicians—many and many splendid folk of diverse talents—were a chorus of approval. I was not surrounded by yes-men. Oh no, by Vox, very far from it.

We all shared the dream, we differed in the way of human nature in how that glittering dream might best be realized.

So, now, as the news of this maniacal King Posno's invasion of his western neighbor was discussed, there were voices lifted passionately to say that we needed no further entanglements abroad. Money and work were needed in Vallia. Mantig Roben spluttered as he said: "With the money and manpower you will waste fighting in Pandahem I can rebuild many dwaburs of canal. There is our country's wealth."

Somebody ripped out: "If you live to sail the waters of your precious canals, Mantig."

---

* diashum: magnificent. A.B.A.

"This cretinous cramph King Posno is not invading Vallia, is he?"

"The Pandaheem recall what happened to them the last time they tried."

"Well, then, my point is proved."

Somebody else wouldn't have that, and vehemently carried on the argument. I caught various eyes, and we sauntered away to find ourselves a quiet retiring room where the news might be discussed more fully and more logically.

I said: "If I were callous, as many emperors are callous, I would say this was not evil news, was good news, was most excellent news."

"How can that be, when the alliance falls into ruin?" demanded Nath na Kochwold.

"Why, Nath," I said, completely unable to refrain from teasing my splendid blade comrade. "I confess I am astonished. I thought you joyed in putting your Phalanxes in motion."

"As to that, you know I do—oh. I see." His face reflected a wry realization that, once again, he'd been taken for a gentle little ride. "Will you show any preference in your selection?"

"Now then, Nath," I said. And again, I confess, I spoke only half in jest. "You are forgetting."

"Your pardon. It is not easy." Nath na Kochwold, who had won his name in that great battle, considered that all his Phalanxes were perfect. He knew, also, that over the seasons I had out of experience formed certain attachments to certain Phalanxes.

What was true was that in the Phalanx Vallia had a battle-winning weapon. Nath had taken this gentle jesting in good part, and now he turned to Drak and said: "Well, then. And which Phalanxes will you require. All are ready."

"When we work out the forces to go, then you'll know."

"Quidang."

"It is good news, father, in that sense." Drak did not drink from his golden and jeweled goblet but nursed it between both hands, face intent. "We may impose our will upon Menaham after we have defeated them."

"There is no doubt about that," said the Lord Farris.

I opened my mouth, saw Seg glancing at me, and closed that fount of spouting babblement.

"The only fault in the logic is that the Bloody Menahem are so—so bloody." Drak spoke with feeling.

"They may be forced to bow the neck, they may be bribed, they may be—"

Nath cut in: "They could all be exterminated."

Farris, as tough now as ever despite his age, sucked in a breath. "Yes, Nath na Kochwold. If such a deed were required to be done, I would choose you for the task."

"I stand corrected, Farris. You are right." Nath spoke openly. Then his passionate and justice-demanding nature burst out. "But, all the same, that would settle the issue."

Cutting in and alleviating some of the tension, Larghos the Sko-handed pointed out: "The realm of Tomboram to the east of Menaham is firmly allied to us. They will help."

Mantig Roben said: "Yes, good, a sound point. Let Tomboram shoulder the task in its entirety."

"We would have to support them with cash, Mantig," said Drak in a mild voice. "So your canals would still not profit by that scheme. We must play our part."

Seg said: "This business of Tomboram could be more tricky than we suppose. Menaham and Tomboram, traditional enemies for hundreds of seasons, do not take their eyes off each other. We have fought there before. So..."

No one was louche enough to say out loud what Seg meant: "What has happened to allow Menaham to attack westward without fear of attack from the east?"

I said more sharply than I intended: "Drak. Have you heard from your mother recently?"

"Three days ago, explaining that she could not attend today."

"The same for me," I said. "Seg?"

"Milsi sent at the same time, same reason."

"That appears satisfactory, then. Seg?"

"Oh, I'm with you, my old dom. And I think Nath the Impenitent is well enough. He might enjoy a little exercise."

"Capital."

Both Seg and I knew well enough that our ladies would spit rivets when they discovered we'd gone off adventuring on our own. Still, they were tied up with the Sisters of the Rose, and they had adventures enough, by Vox!

Drak said in his serious voice: "Father. You will—"

"Oh, I will, all right. Don't fret."

Nath na Kochwold swelled up his chest and stared at me with great bitterness.

"Some people," he said, grinding out the words. "Some people have all the fun. Rest assured that—"

"Look, Nath," I said. "You have been offered an imperial province as Justicar from me, and I believe the Emperor Drak will honor that pledge. Yet you insist on remaining with your Phalanxes. If you want to come adventuring with Seg and me, you have to renounce certain things."

"So that is why you renounced the throne and crown of Vallia? To go adventuring? Well, many may believe that."

"It has a ring."

"Aye. After this next fight of my Phalanx. Then I will decide."

Nath na Kochwold could be the emperor's Justicar of any imperial province he chose; he could not tear himself away from that terrible war instrument, the Phalanx. I do not think many in that small private room would take a wager on Nath's final decision.

Drak sounded more resigned than irritated when he said: "I suppose you won't take a proper army with you, father? Just you and Seg and a few choice spirits?"

"D'you take an army when you go adventuring?"

"*When!*"

Seg laughed. "I think, Drak my bonny emperor, I really do think that your father hasn't stopped laughing since he dumped that job on you."

"That, Uncle Seg, I am all too ready to believe."

I didn't miss that little word "uncle" in there, the old affectionate if inaccurate way our children called my blade comrade Seg. There would not be, I knew, much chance they'd address Milsi, Queen Mab of Croxdrin, as Auntie Milsi, because now they were grown up.

Farris then started on the practicalities of the venture, which I could leave to him with certitude. Besides being retained by Drak as the Justicar Crebent who ran Vallia with the Presidio when the emperor was absent, Farris was still the Commander of the Vallian Air Service.

"Just keep this whole thing secret," I said. "You know what happens when folk get wind of an adventure."

A mellow, jovial, not quite wheezing voice chimed in then, to say: "Lahal, all. I would be the first to jump at the chance of adventuring with you, Dray. But I have other shafts in the air."

"San Quienyin!"

We all stood up as a mark of respect as Deb-Lu-Quienyin entered and found himself a comfortable chair. His atrocious turban, new though it might be, was already beginning to loosen and slip over one ear. He beamed on us.

He was real and not a projection through occult space. He took wine and drank and said: "The developments may be turned to our advantage, if we strike surely."

Drak said: "I will lead the army and—"

"Majister." Deb-Lu's word brought instant attention. "With respect, better for you to attend to Vallia's needs."

Drak was not fool enough to argue with a Wizard of Loh when said Wizard of Loh spoke so positively.

"We are needed here, Drak."

"In that case..." And here Nath na Kochwold jumped in with both feet. Drak laughed.

"Very well, Nath, you ferocious brumbyte!"

There were other preparations to be made. When all was ready and we boarded the voller a few days later, I had to admit to myself that I missed Delia's firm and delicate hand on the helm of my destiny. I always felt much better flying off to harebrained escapades when she organized our logistics. So, with that thought in the hollow space between my ears and with a few choice spirits, I shouted down the remberees and the voller soared up into the mingled streaming radiance of the Suns of Scorpio.

Thirteen

Of mud, blood and a zorca horn

Rotting garbage piled head-high along the street scraped at nostrils and back of throat with rancid stenches. Smoking torches threw scraps of erratic illumination upon the macabre scenes, gleaming upon frenzied half-naked bodies, glinting upon pools of stinking water slimed in the ruts and runnels of the mud-choked street. The air crackled with high, empty screams of laughter, with shrieks of pain and the spitting conflagrations of the fires burning at every corner.

"By Vox!" breathed Seg. "Is every town of Menaham like this inferno?"

Beggars, thieves, prostitutes, pickpockets, the jetsam of society, existed in the poor quarter of the town of Gorlki in Menaham. License held absolute sway. Brutality, the dictate of the strong and ruthless, controlled all. Shrieking women ran like maenads, and lust-crazed men screamed after them like satyrs. If one wanted a medieval hell as a scene for a painting, then there would be no need to go further than this stinking Hades in Menaham's Gorlki.

"This does not sit well with me," said Orso, neatly guiding his zorca around two drunken men collapsed in each other's arms, the knives falling laxly from their fists, their fight for the money-purse overtaken by the wine they had drunk. A wild-haired crone whose rags flapped like the rusty-black wings of a magbird darted in, cackling insanely, to snatch up the purse. Even as she scuttled off, so others descended on her like warvols, shrieking.

The stinks overpowered with the effluents of hell.

"I have seen much evil and sadness in Vallia," said Nath the Impenitent. "But nothing like this."

"Praise be to Opaz."

"Oh, aye. A life here is not worth a Hamalese toc."

Orso drew his sword. The drexer glittered cleanly in that midden of filth.

"Best, then, to be prepared."

Nath's fist, resting on his hilt, did not tighten. I knew he'd draw and be in action before Orso, even so, even good as Orso was. He'd finagled his way into joining us because Drak had asked me as a favor to take him. Drak owed a favor to Orso's father, a wealthy financier, and as Drak was not going himself, then Orso might go with me. I had accepted because I did not want my son, the new emperor, loaded down with favors that might be called in on less favorable occasions.

Orso Frentar held his back upright, and gazed about keenly and kept a firm grip upon his blade. Balass the Hawk had tried him out in swordsmanship and professed himself as satisfied as Balass ever would be in matters of the sword.

We all wore long dark cloaks that fell over the hindquarters of our zorcas. We wore flat leather caps. We did not look imposing or wealthy; but we rode zorcas through this human quagmire and it would only be a matter of time before we were jumped.

A zorca with the single twisted spiral horn, close-coupled and mettlesome, is, after all, the finest four-legged saddle animal of Paz. So we rode alertly.

Not knowing this town of Gorlki, and the night drawing on, we'd entered through the nearest gate on the road we'd followed since leaving the voller. That gate, the Gate of Penitence, led directly into this disgusting portion of the town. The sights were bad enough, the stinks worse, and the iniquity the worst of all.

Our plans were simple and straightforward enough.

A diplomatic mission had been dispatched from Vondium to Tomboram. Also, spies had been sent in parallel to flesh out the picture of what was happening there.

The Vallian Expeditionary Force, to be led by Nath na Kochwold, to assist Iyam against the Menaham invasion, would go in over to the west, probably near the border with Lome. Queen Lushfymi of Lome was fully involved.

So, that left us to follow along in the wake of the triumphant Bloody Menahem and discover what we could and suss out the most appropriate places to strike.

As Orso said: "The first place is this stinking hell. Torch it all!"

"And then," pointed out Seg, "where would the poor devils who live here now go?"

The Impenitent had rapidly adjusted to the new situation vis-à-vis himself and Seg and me. He continued to call me Jak as others had done in the same situation.

Now he said sharply: "Keep an eye on your calsany, Orso!"

The two pack calsanys trotted along on their leading reins. The panniers and pouches draping them must prove well-nigh irresistible temptations to the thieving fraternity.

Orso gave an impatient tug at his leading rein and his calsany lumbered up alongside Nath's. I hadn't wanted to take Orso along. His father, Lango Frentar, rotund and shining with perspiration, much decorated with gold, pressed. Drak had stated his request in a matter-of-fact way. I'd said, I recalled: "Well, Orso, if they bring your head back in a bucket, I will not be held responsible."

In his scornful, high-tempered way, Orso rapped back: "If they bring my head back in a bucket, majister, it will deserve to rattle around in there."

"So be it." So, Orso Frentar rode with us.

The filth of the street splashed and slimed under the dainty hooves of the zorcas. They didn't much care for the stench of this noisome place. I well knew that many a street of my own Earth, and not so long ago at that, presented the appearance of an open sewer, running green from wall to wall. Here and there barricades had been set up to direct the sewerage, and beyond on raised stoops shops and tatty bazaars sold wares of dubious value. Every other building seemed to be a pothouse, and most of those were dopa dens.

I settled the flowing cloak more comfortably upon my shoulders. A leather bandolier of terchicks nestled over my right shoulder and I felt the need to draw and throw with the utmost rapidity to be essential at the moment.

The Krozair longsword was scabbarded to the saddle. At my belt I wore a thraxter and a rapier and main gauche on their separate belts. As always, my old sailor knife nestled over my right hip.

We must have looked a formidable enough quartet for the more casual of the cutthroats to eye us malevolently and then to sneak away. Women importuned us, screeching creatures of contorted features and wild hair, eyes white blots in faces grimed and stained. Everyone dressed in rags; at least, we saw no one who wore what would be dubbed decent clothes.

Up ahead must lie the more respectable parts of this frontier town of Gorlki. Certain of the denizens of this human jungle decided we would not live to reach that haven.

We were without doubt foolish to ride through these slums; but, then, we were strangers and had not known.

Seg cocked an eye forward to where a wood and plaster balcony, called a jetty, overhung the street.

"Up there."

"Aye."

Ragged scarecrow-like objects up on the balcony flapped tattered clothes about themselves. They looked like rusty bats, wings abristle, ready to swoop down upon us as we rode past below.

On the opposite side of the street an open bonfire constricted the width. Weird caricatures of people danced about the fire and to the side tumblers and fire-eaters cavorted to tease a few copper obs from a small and gawping crowd.

The confusion and noise racketed all about and the hiss and splutter of the flames added an ominous accompaniment.

I said: "Nath, Orso. Heads down and ride like the Agate-winged jutmen of Hodan-Set."

Seg and I dropped back. Our comrades jollied their zorcas into a run and the calsanys lumbered along aft. Pretty soon those calsanys would do what all calsanys do when they are startled and upset. That would make no difference at all in this stinking cesspool of a street.

Nath and Orso rode hard. They did not put their heads down but brandished their weapons, glittering in the crimson violence of the fire.

Four blackened raggedy shapes dropped from the balcony.

They misjudged the fall by a hand's-breadth only, fooled by that sudden onrush. Seg's blade slashed twice and so did mine. Four bundles spun away from the zorca hooves. Their blood splashed into the mud, unnoticed and immediately forgotten.

"Here come their fanshos!" screeched Orso.

Instantly he was at work slashing ferociously at the pack of starveling human wolves trying to drag him from the saddle. Their grimed faces shone with sweat and the fat dribbled from their last meal. Their eyes curdled white and glaring and their black-fanged winespouts shrieked threats and curses. There were enough of them to keep us busy for a mur or two and then we'd ridden them down, cut them down or—a zorca when annoyed becomes spiritedly ferocious. Orso's zorca was clearly his personal animal and trained by him.

Orso's zorca lifted his head, neighing, it seemed to me, in delight. A ragged bundle stuck through by the twisted spiral horn wriggled and flopped and a pair of filthy blood-smeared hands tried to force the spitted body off that cruel horn.

Orso shouted: "Quey-arn."

At once the zorca lowered his head, shook, and the dying man slipped off into mud puddled by his own blood.

"They do not like that," called Orso. "These scum do not like it up 'em, believe me."

"Oh, aye," said Seg as we cleared the last of the shattered band of robbers. "Oh, aye, Orso. I believe you."

Orso, it was clear, heard nothing of the undertones in Seg's reply.

Some way ahead a fresh altercation took our attention.

Directly before us torchlights splashed luridly from the Gate of Dolors set in the inner wall of the city. We were nearly out of the slums. A party of Moltingurs, fighting amongst themselves, failed to notice the two gauffrers stealing the prize over which the Moltingurs fought.

Orso laughed. "The fools have stolen the girl and now they will lose her through greed."

The scene, distasteful as it was, was thus correctly read. The Moltingurs had taken the girl, a Lamnian maiden of considerable beauty, to sell to the highest bidder and before that transaction could be completed, the quarrel over the spoils had given the sneaky gauffrers the chance to steal the Lamnian girl to sell themselves.

Nath said: "They have only just brought her into this hellhole, for the gate is no distance away."

"Aye."

"It is clear she does not live here."

"Aye, for she is still clean."

I gentled my zorca and edged him over to the two gauffrers. Sharp rodent faces alight with greed, they carted the struggling girl like a sack, her golden fur glorious in the torchlights. I hit them over the head with the flat, one after the other, and they tumbled to the mud.

In the same instant Seg was off his zorca and taking up the girl's bound form. Her eyes, wide and frightened, glared above the gag. Seg slung her over the zorca before him and vaulted into the saddle. The close-coupled zorca provided just room enough with none to spare. Seg led us in our last rush for the Gate of Dolors and we were through before the Moltingurs woke up to the facts of life.

"That was—sudden," said Orso as we reined in. "You were very quick."

Nath the Impenitent was comfortably getting back to the old companionship we had enjoyed down the Coup Blag, and now he said in his rich, juicy voice: "Oh, I've seen 'em faster, believe me."

And Seg laughed.

"We'd better find a decent tavern and then see about getting this poor girl home." He bent and removed her gag and then helped her to the ground. The cobbles here were dry and reasonably clean. Nath whipped out his nasty-looking knife, and before the girl had time to flinch he'd snicked her bonds free.

In a superb attempt to hold onto her breeding and courage, she said: "I thank you jikais for—" and then she keeled over and would have toppled headlong if Seg's strong bowman's arm had not lapped her slender waist.

"Well, now," I said, most helpfully.

"She must be got into a bed and a puncture lady sent for quicker than a cisfly spits," said Seg. He lifted her and started for The Leather Bottle a few doors along. We followed. The Leather Bottle obviously was not the best of taverns; but this was an emergency.

The landlord, an Och hight Niswan the Lop, was only too anxious to help when Nath showed him gold, and Orso slid a bloodied cleaning cloth over his sword blade.

The puncture lady, of three chins, ample bosom, starched petticoats and smelling of peppermint, tut-tutted and threw us out of the upper bedchamber and, later, pronounced the oracle that the Lamnian maiden would live, allowed us in, took her gold and departed swinging her bag of mystery.

"Well," said Seg, smiling with that handsome face of his most reassuring to a defenseless lady in these horrendous happenings. "I'm glad you are feeling better."

"They kidnapped me," she whispered, her face still drawn with remembered terror and sick apprehension. "They were going to sell me—it was horrible!"

I confess I sounded most priggish when I couldn't stop myself from saying: "You must expect this sort of thing to happen in a slave-owning society."

"I'm not—quite sure—how do you mean?"

I felt annoyed I'd been such a boor, but good old Seg smoothed it over and she said her name was Yamsin Weymlo and her father was a merchant. Being Lamnian, this was usual.

Orso said: "You were lucky, Yamsin. Now had Katakis taken you, the gauffrers would have been chopped and you'd be—"

"Quite," snapped Seg, chopping Orso's indelicacies.

"We'll get word to your father right away," I said. "Now you rest easy. We'll be on hand and if you need anything, just shout."

Her golden fur gleamed against the pillow and her beautiful face, beautiful to anyone of any race with eyes to see, relaxed a tiny amount, enough to reassure me.

"Yes," she whispered. "I give thanks to Mother Heymamlo. And, I give thanks to you, my four jikais."

Fourteen

I take up a collection

The mingled lights of Antares streamed into the upper chamber of The Scepter and Wand, a luxurious inn and posting house of Gorlki adjacent to the Wayfarer's Drinnik beyond the walls.

Yamsin Weymlo lay asleep in an adjoining bedchamber with her own nurse and handmaidens to care for her.

Sitting in a deep brocaded armchair, her father, Dolan Weymlo, munched palines and kept ratatatting his fingers on his knee. He looked worried.

He'd thanked us effusively for the rescue of his daughter, the light of his life, and only female relative now his wife, the gentle Pilsi, and passed—as he confidently believed—through the Ice Floes of Sicce to the sunny uplands beyond. He had discovered his daughter's loss only a short time before we'd reported her safe, and that short time had aged him.

But the worry nagging at him was not connected with his daughter's peril. That had passed. His misfortunes persisted. Frankly, he told us what plagued him.

"I am a merchant, well, almost all us Lamnians are merchants, and agents of the king pestered me for supplies for this pestiferous war." He lifted a paline; but he did not put the luscious berry into his mouth. "Wars may bring profit for those unscrupulous enough to batten on other folks' misery. I prefer the profits of peace."

"You are, then, Horter Weymlo, exceeding wise."

"A wisdom bought by hard experience."

"So," I said. "A shot at random. You brought these supplies for the king and his army was most grateful. But you have not been paid, nor are likely to be paid."

His shrewd old eyes looked up. "You are a merchant, too, then?"

"No. But it is not difficult to know the ways of the great ones of the world. They do not often vary."

"True, by Beng Feylam the Bonder of Warehouses."

Nath had really no need for the little grunt of agreement, and then the checked intake of a breath, and then a scuffle of his booted foot. Nath the Impenitent, old Hack 'n' Slay, had had his views of at least some of the great ones of the world changed lately.

"This king," said Seg, who since his winning of a kingdom had become a trifle more tolerant of monarchs—a trifle only, mind. "He is new to the throne I hear."

"Aye. His uncle died as inconvenient uncles in the way of ambitious nephews do die from time to time."

Lamilo, the Lamnian with only one arm, clad in sober but sumptuous clothes next to Weymlo, leaned closer and whispered. What he said was easy to guess.

"Yes, yes, good Lamilo," said the merchant. "That is sooth. But I judge these jikais to be men of honor. Besides, they are not of Menaham."

"All the same, horter, some care—"

"I tell you, I am past caring in this."

Orso shuffled and spoke up. "We thank you for your hospitality, Horter Weymlo. We are glad to have saved your daughter from a hideous fate. But, now, I think we must take our leave."

Seg threw a swift amused glance. I judged Orso was trying to extricate me from what he considered a sticky and uninteresting situation. Little, I feared, did the gallant Koter Orso Frentar know of Dray Prescot!

Immediately the Lamnian rose and gathered his gold-embroidered robes about him. They are shrewd, are Lamnians, and yet so often their countenances express perpetual surprise at the world's follies. This is, of course, a potent source of strength in their merchanting deals.

"If you must leave so soon... I give you my thanks and may Havil the Green speed your ways."

I cut in. "Horter Orso is concerned for the welfare of our zorcas." I gave Orso a stare. "Thank you for thinking of them. When you have finished no doubt we will meet in the taproom."

He was hooked on his own hook and so could do no more than nod stiffly and leave. I breathed in and out when he'd left the room and said to Weymlo: "Pray, be seated, horter. I fancy there are matters we may discuss."

He glanced at me, shrewd and sharp, and then resumed his seat. He took up a crystal goblet of parclear and looked at me over the rim. "You are paktuns seeking employment?"

"We are tazll at the moment, yes. But we are in no hurry. If you deign, I'd like to hear more of this king."

"King Morbihom of the Iron Hand." He smiled. "Yes, I know the sobriquet is ridiculous. He chose it himself."

"He is leaving a wake of destruction through Iyam."

"Destruction, terror and the loss of all hope. If he is not stopped soon— rather, if he does not stop soon—he will be on the borders of Lome."

Lamilo, Weymlo's stylor, said: "We must follow in the path of the king to speak with him personally."

Weymlo waved a beringed hand. "Easy to say, Lamilo."

They told us that they'd asked for payment through the usual channels and had been fobbed off. They'd approached officials of various authorities within the army and the persons in charge of supply, to no avail. Now, they had determined to go to the commanding Kapts in the field to bring pressure on the responsible officials to pay up.

"Why not," said Seg, "go straight to the king?"

"Exactly!" cracked out Stylor Lamilo.

"Tsleetha-tsleethi," counseled Weymlo. "The Kapts first. Through them the king will be swayed."

"The king is swayed only by the queen and by his Wizard of Loh, this Al-Ar-Mergondon whose name be..." Here Lamilo stopped speaking with a snap of his Lamnian jaws. Only fools speak ill of wizards, even when the wizards are dwaburs away.

"What is known of this wizard?" said Seg into the awkward little silence.

"He is powerful, abrupt, terrible in his wrath."

A chill seeped around our bones there in that upper chamber of The Scepter and Wand.

The relationships between king, queen and wizard might follow well-established patterns, or this instance might throw up an entirely new stratification and power-arrangement. Familiar or unfamiliar, the situation had to be turned to our advantage.

Weymlo insisted we stay for the first meal of mid, traditionally a light snack, followed by the more substantial lunch of the second meal of mid. Here the superb Kregan tea could be drunk as well as parclear and sazz. We tucked in and over the meal learned more of the local situation and what we might expect to encounter as we progressed toward the battle front.

Suddenly and out of the blue, a complete non-sequitur, Seg said: "May Havil the Green look down!" He sounded serious. "Orso! We have completely forgotten him and he is down in the stables or the taproom waiting."

"Ha!" and Nath the Impenitent downed his cup.

"I," I said, standing up, "with your leave, Horter Weymlo, will go down."

Seg was having enormous difficulty in not bursting out laughing, and Nath was stuffing his face. Weymlo nodded and said: "By all means," and I trotted off.

The blackwood stairs from the upper floors led into the taproom; Orso was not there. In the other direction a narrow brick-walled passage led to the inner courtyard.

A few freymuls and preysanys were tethered up and quietly drinking from the trough. A soughwood tree overhung a corner of the yard. A few blooms wilted on a windowsill. Dust tasted on the air.

"Orso!" I called. No answer.

Two sides were lined with stables. Most of the split doors were closed. A flutter of movement just inside an open door drew my attention and I walked across and went into the dimness beyond. My mouth opened to call Orso again.

A very sharp blade caressed my neck from ear to chin. I stood absolutely still.

"Stand still," rasped the unmistakable tones of a Rapa. "Or you are a dead man."

The redundancy of the remark escaped the Rapa, who moved around, the knife still pressed against my neck.

His dingy feathers smelled unpleasantly. His clothes were a collection of castoffs from half a dozen different sources. He was well-practiced with a knife, that was patently obvious, and his ferocious vulturine face, beaked and menacing, indicated that he knew exactly what he was doing.

"Back into the shadows."

We moved farther into the dimness. He was smart, no doubt of it; but I'd been lax, no doubt of that, either.

"Drop your weapon belts."

I did so.

"Now move away."

I moved farther into the straw-smelling stall.

He stepped back. His beak tilted. "Now hand over your money." The knife gestured eloquently.

The small lesten-hide bag of gold, silver and copper tucked into my broad waist belt held enough to satisfy this small-time holdup Rapa. He weighed it and fondled it. When Seg and I went off adventuring, we mostly carried our gold in pockets inside our belts. And elsewhere. The Rapa did not ask. He pulled the string of the money bag with his beak and then made a mistake.

He cocked his head on one side and looked down at the bag. The dimness made him look longer than he should have done.

The intervening distance passed in no time at all and I was on him. A stunning blow to his wrist, a grasping turn and the knife was in my possession. I gave him a backhander across the beak and he stumbled back, spitting feathers.

One hand to his face he glared at me with that lopsided look of Rapas. Absolute baffled fury engorged him

He said: "I think I made a mistake."

"Quite possibly. Hand back my money."

He threw the purse onto the straw at my feet.

"So we are quits, then."

I said nothing but continued to stare at him.

"You have your weapons and your money. Give me back my knife and I'll be off."

"I'll keep your knife, dom."

"By Rhapaporgolam the Reiver of Souls!"

But he turned and went toward the open door. As he reached the jamb, I threw his knife. It struck through a flapping rag of his clothes and pinned the filthy cloth to the wood. He swung about at once, beak quivering.

He half-raised a hand and I shook my head.

"Now hand over all your money."

He couldn't believe this. The hand lifted farther so I whipped out the old sailor knife and poised.

"Your money, dom. Or this one is through your eye."

Hissing with that gobbling, guttural hiss of enraged Rapas, he fished out his money bag and threw it down.

"And the rest."

He found some more coins tied into the corners of his clothes.

"Take the knife from the wood, very carefully, and throw it down."

By this time he realized he wouldn't outthrow me.

At the last he looked back, his feathers most bedraggled, to say: "I shall remember you, dom."

There was nothing I wished to say to that, and he mooched despondently off into the mingled lights of Antares. I picked up his knife, and it was a cheap blade of Krasny work; still, it threw accurately. His money amounted to little enough, by Krun, and most of it wasn't his to start with, anyway, I didn't doubt. There was still no sign of Orso so I took myself off to the upper room.

"No Orso?" said Seg.

"No." I put the Rapa's money on the table and said to Stylor Lamilo: "Would you see this goes to a deserving charity, stylor, as a favor?"

"Of course. But—?"

"Oh," I said, sitting down and picking a juicy paline from the dish. "I just took up a collection for a good cause."

Fifteen

Murlock the Spry

Dolan Weymlo proved an interesting traveling companion, for his merchanting business had carried him into many parts of Kregen. He had transacted profitable deals in lands I'd never visited, and had met folk of whom I had no knowledge.

The old stories of people with an eye in their chests and legs growing from their foreheads were trotted out.

Weymlo, I fancied, used these as a test. Nath believed in these caricatures, and hung on Weymlo's every word, eyes wide open and ears flapping.

Orso, upright and scornful in the saddle, rode on by himself. We were content that our traveling arrangements should thus be settled, but as I said to Seg: "There are four of us, and we should be united. I approve of Orso riding solo; I do not much care for the division it may cause in our ranks."

"He's young and the blood's fair bursting around his body," said Seg. "He'll measure up when the shaft nocks the string."

As we rode westward through devastated Iyam, the twin suns shone splendidly and the weather was brilliantly perfect even for Northern Pandahem. This island is blessed in many ways. The east-west central spine of mountains cuts the island into two distinctly different parts, their characters at variance. Down south lie the festering jungles. Up here in the northern parts the weather was noticeably warmer than in Vallia; but nowhere near unpleasant.

So, under dappled skies and with nature smiling all about we rode past blackened ruins, obscene in their gutted shells, past gibbets festooned with their dreadful freight, past fields where the loosely thrown soil failed to cover the decomposing and stinking corpses. Oh, yes, the triumphant path of this great King Posno, who called himself King Morbihom of the Iron Hand, was most easy to follow.

We were attacked only three times.

The miserable and desperate creatures hiding in ruins or among crevices of the hillsides, could be shooed off with a show of force. The flash of blades indicated to them that they had not picked on a merchant's defenseless caravan. On both occasions Weymlo ordered his people to leave parcels of food as we rode off.

The third attack was of a different nature.

Being a Lamnian with merchanting skills in his blood, Dolan Weymlo had been unable to resist concluding a few deals in Gorlki. We had a string of calsanys and plains asses with us, loaded with merchandise that—at least in theory—should fetch good prices when we came up with the army. He and Lamilo rode preysanys. The lady Yamsin rode a freymul, often called the poor man's zorca. Also there were the bodyguard mercenaries already hired.

They were a motley crew. There was not a real paktun among the mercenaries. Most paktuns would be off in the king's army, naturally, and these were low-quality soldiers or youngsters just starting out on the mercenary life. They were not, I judged, to be classed as masichieri who, while calling themselves paktuns, are little better than mere drikingers, bandits.

We four had politely refused Weymlo's offer of employment. We rode with him from mutual advantage, we gaining the cover of a sizable force, and he gaining the added protection of four professional blades.

So, the third attack came in with a whoop and a holler, and with deadly meaning.

These were deserters, riffraff from the army, drikingers, men desperate in ways far deeper and darker than the desperations of the miserable wights whose homes had been destroyed. This is not a paradox. These gentry were bound for Cottmer's Caverns no matter who caught them. And they knew it.

Orso slashed into action at once, kneeing his fighting zorca into a frenzy.

Our mercenaries faced this first serious challenge. When Seg, Nath and I roared out ahead, sweeping away the first ragged charge, the mercenaries took heart and pitched in. They fought as well as they could, and I do not doubt that more than one raw youngster discovered something there of what being a mercenary entailed. We lost only three of them, two dead and one wounded who would recover.

Just before the fight Seg and I had slipped the silken cords of our pakzhans out so that the golden wink of the zhantil-head device glittered at our throats. Only paktuns who have earned great renown are given the accolade of the pakzhan from their peers. They are known as zhanpaktuns. Those with the silver mortil-head device, the pakmort, are known as mortpaktuns.

I have known brigands to simply run off immediately they spot a wink of gold at the throat of the fellow they thought they would attack and rob.

Nath the Impenitent, of course, having served only in the Vallian Army, was not a mercenary. Orso Frentar had not served as a mercenary, either. Here we had further opportunity to observe his swordsmanship, which had been learned at the best academies of Vondium.

"Very neat and precise," was Seg's verdict.

"I will not pass judgment until we have been in a real hack 'n' slay situation."

"Balass the Hawk's very words."

"Aye," growled out Nath. "In the bash of a melee, fine theories are blown away like bubbles."

Seg started to say: "Indu—"

And Nath roared out, joyfully: "—bitably, Horkandur!"

We rode back to join the caravan and the servants climbed up from under the plains asses. No one in his right mind would shelter under a calsany in those circumstances.

Stylor Lamilo walked carefully down the line of pack animals, counting.

"Not one lost," he reported.

The captain of the mercenaries, a Fristle hight Foison the Stroke, preened his whiskers and took the credit for this successful execution of the duties for which he and his men had been hired. As a cadade, Foison the Stroke should go far in his chosen profession.

A hoarse shout attracted our attention.

The bushes where the deserters and brigands had secreted themselves hemmed the area in a trifle, although the broad lands stretched beyond, and among the dark bundles of dead bodies an arm lifted.

"Soho," exclaimed the cadade, Foison the Stroke. "One still lives. Well, by Odifor, he will not live long."

He hefted his thraxter and strutted out, his cat-face venomous.

I turned at once to the Lamnian merchant.

"Horter Weymlo." I spoke urgently. "Do you not think it wise to question this fellow? He could prove useful, if you can order your cadade to stop in time."

"Foison!" called Weymlo at once, without quibbling. "Hold! We will ask the fellow a question or three before you spit him."

Foison swung about, the sword high. Then he spat back in his catman fashion: "Quidang!"

The brigand was dragged up. He had been wounded in the foot and had lost blood. A fearsome scar, still red and recent, bifurcated his left cheek. He was an apim, thin and scrawny, with a disreputable mop of brown hair, two front teeth missing and with a ferret-like look of desperate cunning about him. Yet he faced up to us openly enough, hopping on one foot, held by guards.

"Here he is, horter," said Foison. "And a nasty rast he is. The quicker the sliver slides between his ribs the better."

Weymlo licked his lips. Gentle as a rule though they are, Lamnians by reason of their vocation inevitably brush up against violence. He put on a stern expression.

"You deserve death. Have you anything to say?"

When the brigand spoke, he tended to whistle by reason of those two missing teeth. He made himself stand up on his one good foot and he squared his shoulders.

"I am Murlock known as the Spry." Well, that cognomen fitted, I judged. He went on: "I was condemned unjustly for a crime I did not commit. I escaped. Around here the only way to stay alive is to join a band. Otherwise you are dead, either by the bands, by soldiers, or by hunger."

"That I believe," said Weymlo.

"When I escaped, I was wounded—" Here he motioned to the scar. "I was forced to stay with the drikingers. I did not fight you. That I swear by Pymanomar the All-Seeing!"

"A likely story!" cut in Foison, spitting derision.

"It is true! I hid in a bush and Gartang the Kazzur, as bloody-minded a devil as ever breathed, cut my foot because I did not attack with the others. Him, I slew."

"Ah!" said Seg. "Then show us."

So off we all trooped into the bushes, and there lay a hulking great Brokelsh with a knife still in his throat. His clothes and harness betokened a drikinger with pretensions to grandeur. Murlock the Spry stirred the body with his wounded foot and gave a yelp of agony.

"Look at the knife and I will tell you what is engraved on the handle."

Foison gestured and one of his men bent and, after a struggle, dragged the bloodied knife free. Weymlo held out his hand, distastefully, and then looked at the handle.

"Well?"

"In the Mercy of Gashnid."

"That is what is engraved on the handle," said Weymlo, looking up.

After that there was some discussion; but we all felt we could believe this Murlock the Spry's story. After all, he was not the first unfortunate to be forced temporarily into a bandit gang. Nor, I fancied—at least on Kregen—would he be the last.

"Bind up his foot and put him on the back of a calsany," ordered Weymlo. "And then let us depart from this benighted spot."

That, then, was the sum total of our adventures during this first leg of our journey to find this King Morbihom of the Iron Hand.

For, as is obvious, the best plans of Vallia would be served if we could reach this maniac king and talk to him.

During the ride, among other items of information I had from Weymlo, the fact that he hailed originally from Tomboram offered me the opportunity to inquire after my friends, Tilda and Pando. After the wedding in Vondium they had returned home. Weymlo had nothing more than my secret agents had already reported to me. He did add that the King of Tomboram had taken a sickness.

Seg cocked an eye at me and said: "If old Inch hears this, well, he might—well, who knows?"

"That tall streak might do anything."

I let the matter rest there for it is, after all, as you must realize, another story altogether.

Seeking this insufferable King Morbihom of the Iron Hand we rode across Iyam and so approached the border of Lome.

Looking around at the ruins of yet another burned town, Seg shook his head and said: "Poor old Queen Lush!"

I agreed. I trembled for Queen Lush's realm.

Yet there were issues at stake here far greater than the well-being of a queen and her realm and its people. King Posno, the idiot King Morbihom of the Iron Hand, had to be stopped, and stopped damn quickly, for the sake of all Paz.

Sixteen

Concerns a meal by the king's camp

The great, all-conquering King Morbihom suffered a set-back and his forces, bested in the field by Queen Lush's army of Lome, recoiled upon the town of Molophom.

There, at last, we caught up with the king.

Or, to be truthful, we caught up with the Kapts, the court, the hangers-on and camp followers, all the tumult of an army on campaign temporarily defeated and thirsting for revenge. The immediate result of Weymlo's request to meet with the Kapts of the army was a brusque refusal.

No one said: "I told you so."

Rings of campfires burned into the night on the ground outside the town. Inside all was uproar. Drunkenness was a mere everyday occurrence. Pillage, rapine, burnings and hangings went on all the time. The place was picked over like the skeleton of a kipper.

All the rumors spoke of fresh troops with Queen Lush. Powerful regiments from that hell hole over the sea—Vallia, Vallia the Vile—had raced to her rescue and the defence of Lome.

"Still," we were told, over and over. "The king is not defeated. We have more soldiers. Next time the land will run red with the blood of Lomian and Vallian alike!"

While the Bloody Menahem were bloody in the extreme, as anyone who had dealings with them could tell you, there still remained Menahem and Menahem, men and women different in outlook and degrees of bloodthirstiness.

Weymlo and Lamilo went in search of those who might listen to reason and further the just cause of an honest merchant being paid for the wares he had sold.

Morbihom himself, for I suppose it easier to call the idiot by the grandiose name he had dubbed himself instead of his own name of Posno, had no truck with the town of Molophom, blackened and half-ruined as it was. His guarded enclosure, bright with flags and striped marquees, was set up on a level stretch of pleasant sward beside the River of Rippling Reeds. Here no one would imagine his army had just suffered a reverse.

As in most armies of this nature when many of the soldiers were mercenaries, it was possible to ride around without too much hassle. Seg and I were challenged only when we tried to enter the king's enclosure, and here we were able, simply enough, to allay any feeble suspicion by our status as hyrpaktuns. We would be welcomed with open arms by the recruiting officers of the king's army.

Using a familiar ploy, I said to the Deldar at the gate: "We will be happy to join the king, Del. Give us a few days to—well, dom, you know."

"Aye, dom. Well enough. One day, and soon, I trust, I will wear the gold." And he touched the silver mortil-head at his throat.

"My felicitations," said Seg as we rode off.

"A cutthroat bunch," I observed.

"A blade at their throats rather than the gold would seem equitable, by the Veiled Froyvil!"

Among our comrades, Seg and I were known as a comical duo, and when Inch was around as a jestful trio; at times like these our thoughts were far enough from the comical to reach right around in the vaol-paol and start us laughing from the other direction. Once you could no longer laugh, even at such horrendous creatures as the Menahem Kazzurs, then you were done for.

Trotting off, we spied on the other bank of the river a stockade forming a long line of palings. Sentries patrolled. A casual question to an Och carrying water from the river elicited the information that this was the prisoner stockade.

The same thought occurred to both of us.

"There is no doubt at all." Seg was positive. "Erthyr would approve of no other course."

"You are right."

"Oh, indubitably."

We arrived back at the little camp set up away from the army encampments to find stupendous news.

Lamilo and Weymlo beamed their furry Lamnian smiles at us. Bundles and bales were being opened and Yamsin was busy superintending the arrangement of the wardrobe and the presents.

An appointment had been made with Kapt Rorman the Indestructible, general of the Second Menaham Army. The Lamnians were due at the general's tent just as the suns went down.

We congratulated them and wished them well and then went off, leaving them to their excited preparations.

Murlock the Spry, most unspry-like with his foot bandaged and propped on a log, called across. His thin face with the raw, healing scar looked as apprehensive as ever. He'd been employed as best he could around the camp, and Weymlo had dropped a few silver dhems into his hand. Now he wanted to know what his fate would be. As he said: "If the king's men find out—"

"No fear of that, at least yet," Seg told him.

"I suppose you'll be off and running the moment your foot heals." I stared at the offending appendage.

He looked even more guilty.

"As to that, doms, I do not think so. If you would take me, I would serve you well. And cheaply."

"Doing what?"

"My father, may his bones never be disturbed, was a Third Under Chamberlain at the Second Court of the Palace of Exotic Delights. I trained up to follow in his illustrious footsteps." He shook his head. "Alas, the Mensaguals, the cruel Arbiters of Fate, dictated otherwise."

Seg snorted in amusement. "We are in no need of those kind of entertainments, Murlock."

"Ah, but, horter, I am well-trained in the management of a household. You would be served in the field as you have never before been served. I know."

He didn't know, of course. Seeing our faces, he went on: "My punishment was over a mere peccadillo—why, the girl was more eager than I! I swear it by Pymanomar the Ever-Just! I must try to make my way in the world again."

Seg and I held ourselves in check and did not burst out laughing. In the end we said: "Very well, Murlock the Spry. And see you are as good as your word."

At that his cares fell from him. He bounded up on his wounded foot and danced across to us, shouting: "My thanks, horters! Thrice blessed in the name of Havil!"

"Your foot," pointed out Seg.

"A miraculous cure, horters!"

"Murlock the Spry," I said. "More likely Murlock the Cunning."

"Cunning in providing all your wants. You will eat tonight as you have not done on this journey!"

Nath and Orso, strolling over, listened to this fresh news with fascination. Nath licked his lips.

"I trust the rascal is as good a cook as a liar."

"I shall see to it that he tastes every morsel before I eat it," quoth Orso.

That evening we saw the Lamnians off, and splendidly sumptuous they looked for their meeting with Kapt Rorman.

Then we settled to taste and test the meal prepared by Murlock the Spry. He had shrugged off caustic comments about his foot's improvement, and had disappeared during the early part of the afternoon. Under the first fuzzy pink rays of the Maiden with the Many Smiles, we sat down to dine.

No doubt about it. Murlock was a blue-ribbon chef. He was not as good as Emder, or even as Deft-Fingered Minch; but he was top class. We sat back after the repast, not bloated but comfortably full.

"So that is how they eat in a place like the Palace of Exotic Delights," remarked Nath, picking his teeth. "The prices must be ruinous."

Murlock, just carrying away four plates all together, plus four smaller plates and four used glasses, plus sundry other items, halted and swung about. For a thin ferrety fellow he looked wrought up.

"Horter! Were you not a renowned hyrpaktun wearing the gold pakzhan I would challenge you for the insult!"

"Do what?"

"D'you think my illustrious father worked in a mere tavern? The Palace of Exotic Delights is one of the king's palaces beside the Azure Lake in Pelasmohnia!"

"Oh," said Nath, quite unrepentant.

We managed to soothe Murlock's ruffled feathers and he produced what was a superior wine, a vintage with which I was unfamiliar. We sat around the fire drinking companionably, and when Murlock had finished the washing up, he was called to join us.

"How," demanded Orso, "did you steal this food?"

"We do not much fancy the late food's owners cutting up rough," put in Nath.

"The food was come by honestly, horters, that I swear by Pyman—"

"Yes, yes," Orso crackled, wiping his lips. "Enough of that. We believe you even if a million wouldn't."

As Seg said: "There are Menahem and Menahem." He meant, of course, that Murlock as a palace servant, not slave, was not quite the same as your normal Bloody Menahem. I reflected that he had, at least, stuck his knife into the neck of Gartang the Kazzur neatly enough. He might not be as soft and flabby as so many palace servants become.

The night flowed on about us with the scents of night-blooming flowers mingled with the woodsmoke from the camp fires.

Presently Seg said: "Well, my old dom. And where are our Lamnian friends, then?"

"There is little need to worry our heads over them," said Orso. "They are skilled negotiators."

"The negotiating was done when the deal was struck. They went to collect payment due to them."

Nath rumbled out: "I like 'em, them Lamnians."

"Job for us tonight," Seg told him. "So banish all thoughts of your sack."

Murlock looked disappointed. He heaved up a sigh and said: "If you demand my services later, horters, then naturally I am at your command. I was hoping—there is a sweet little shishi in the—well—"

"It seems to me," said Seg and he was bottling up his enjoyment, "that you chase anything female you see."

"Not anything, horter. There is taste."

"Ah, of course!" And Seg laid a wise finger alongside his nose.

"All the same," I said, rather heavily. "That does not tell us where the Lamnians are."

Murlock stood up. "Before I go off duty, with your permission, horters, naturally, I will make enquiries."

"Yes, yes, very well," said Orso.

Seg and I, together, said: "Thank you, Murlock."

Orso looked at us after Murlock had gone into the moon-shadows. His face was intense.

"I am forced to call you Jak, majister, and you, jen, as Seg. I am not a noble; but my father is incredibly wealthy and may buy a dozen lords. He may yet buy a title, if he chooses. Yet you treat these scum as though they are koters and brothers in arms."

Seg and I waited for each other to speak, and so Nath in his rough way rumbled out: "Doesn't hurt to treat a fellow decent, Orso. Never know when he might have a knife in your throat."

"Come the day when he ever gets a knife near my throat!"

Seg changed the conversation then and we talked desultorily of this and that until Murlock returned.

He did not sit down as he was gestured to do. He said: "I have a second cousin in Kapt Rorman the Indestructible's camp kitchen staff. I can come and go freely. My appearance is much changed." Here he touched the scar.

"Well? Get on with it!" That was Orso.

"The Lamnians have been arrested and detained at the king's pleasure."

Orso just sneered at the news, clearly persuading himself that he'd expected duplicity all along. Nath rumbled out a curse and started to talk. Seg cut in and I said: "The plans remain. But it will be just you three, now."

I stood up and put a hand on Murlock's shoulder.

"You have, I think, a cousin in the king's camp kitchen staff."

At his abruptly scared nod, I went on confidently to say: "Exactly so. Then we will stroll up there and see what may be done about our Lamnian friends."

Seventeen

Al-Ar-Mergondon

The glow of a more golden light impinging on the fuzzy pink radiance of the Maiden with the Many Smiles heralded the breaking of She of the Veils from cloud wrack. Mingled moons' light fell across the camp and the river and the wrecked town and one could be forgiven for believing that in that luminescence the countryside slept peacefully.

I did not have to take Murlock the Spry by one ear and run him over to the king's enclosure. He trotted along willingly enough; I knew he'd take himself off the moment he had a chance.

In the streaming mingled golden and rosy radiance of the two moons, we approached the guarded gate. Over most of Paz the first and third Moons of Kregen are generally known as The Maiden with the Many Smiles and She of the Veils. The two second moons, the Twins, have many and various names all over, and as for the three hurtling lesser moons, so often are they referred to in the terms of endearment one uses to pets their names are legion.

"No!" whispered Murlock, grabbing my arm and trying to haul me away. "Not there!"

He dragged me off the beaten path leading to the gate.

What he intended made absolute sense. He led us around to the other side of the enclosure where a small gate gave admittance to the slaves and servants. Small though it might be, this gate, too, was guarded.

"Let me do the talking, horter."

"Am I slave or servant?" I had taken the trouble to collect a parcel of sticks as firewood and bound the bundle with string. Down the center snugged the Krozair blade, so the thing took after the guise of a fasces.

"Servant." Here Murlock shifted my swords he wore strapped to his waist as though they stung him. He was strictly a knife-man. He might learn, given time and life. He carried the bottle of Risslaca Ichor wrapped in straw and slung from his left shoulder.

"Llanitch!" called the sentry in due form.

Obediently we halted.

"Second chef Apgarl the Sauce's cousin come to see him, jurukker, on a matter of high culinary policy."

Murlock rapped that out in the same hard formal tones the guard had used ordering us to halt. Now Murlock relaxed and went on in a different tone of voice: "It's the Havil-retarded clingberry and mustard sauce, dom. Won't go right nohow. My cousin's the expert in that field and I have to get it right for the morning, without fail."

"You cooks have it soft as it is," growled the sentry; but he, too, relaxed, and after another gibe or two waved us into the king's enclosure.

"You're in, horter," squeaked Murlock. "So I'll be off." The enormity of what he had done must have caught up with him about then, for he did look a strange color.

"Not yet, dom, not yet. Stick close."

"You could have brought your friends as well. I'd have got them through easy." Now the deed was accomplished he dwelt with pride on how he had fooled the guard; he did not want anything further to go wrong. "And the Lamnians won't be caged up here, surely? Not in my experience."

"They're not ordinary prisoners taken in a fight."

We were approaching the cooking area and the scents really were quite delicious. The cooks never slept in King Morbihom's camp, for he would call for food, anything from a light snack to a twenty-course banquet, at any hour of day or night. Torches lit the scene. There was no secret now where Murlock had acquired the high-class ingredients for the meal he had cooked us. The Kapt's cook was a cousin. I guessed the catering families were intertwined through the whole structure of Menaham society.

"Maybe they aren't ordinary prisoners. They're not here!"

"We will see."

Now the problem of secreting a weapon in a pile of firewood is that, sooner or later, you have to dump the wood near the fire.

I began to regret my stubbornness in lugging the Krozair brand along with me. This was work for daggers and knives, perhaps a rapier or thraxter. Still, stubborn I, Dray Prescot, am... My friends call it obstinacy and others dub it pig-headedness. I was stuck with a decision and must, therefore, in the best traditions of Kregen, make the most of it.

When I captured the first passing soldier, treating him summarily and dragging him somewhat forcibly into the rose and golden shadows of a tent, Murlock's alarm increased.

"All right, Murlock. I won't treat any of your array of cousins like this. Satisfied?"

He licked his lips. "Only that Garhand the Pickler, who deserves to be pickled. You won't pass as a guard."

"Rather tart, is he? Don't intend to—not yet."

The guard rolled his head around and mumbled: "Luli! Don't go away, Luli! Luli, c'mere—"

I took his chin between my fist and hefted him up and glared at him. I made him see the devil look. He flinched.

"Where are the Lamnian prisoners, dom?"

"Can't say—"

"It's your life."

Very little persuasion was needed for him to blurt out the location of the tent in which the three Lamnians were being held. No decision, as far as he was aware, had been reached on their fate.

"The king will prize more contracts from them in return for their lives," said Murlock with the air of one who understands the business of affairs of corrupt courts. "Now can I go?"

"Just don't get caught, you Spry, you hear?"

"Once I depart from your company, I have every right to be here visiting my cousin."

"Well, if you take him Risslaca Ichor, he's a bigger fool than his cousin."

"Remberee, horter. I hope I see you again."

"I shall want a slap up first breakfast!"

"Ha!" And off he went to see his cousin.

No matter how many times you creep into a tent to rescue somebody, no two times are alike.

Each and every time can see your fool head off and bouncing. I hadn't missed Murlock's way of taking his leave. That: "Once I depart from your company" when he would normally have said a far more colloquial way of taking off.

And, as I am sure you will have realized, all this time I was wrestling with my conscience over my usage of the Lamnians in quite this way. My conscience is sometimes an elastic beast, and at others a constricting dungeon of the deepest depths and finest steel bars. Of course I'd do what I could to help the Lamnians escape. That is obvious, by Vox! As to squeezing their money out of the king—well, that was a splendid idea and one I subscribed to. Just how it was to be done remained a mystery, to me, at least.

The guard wore a broad green and blue sash over his armor, which was of a common kind, and the sash across my jack gave the same impression. Often where armor is not all that easily come by and no two sets of harness are alike, regiments and formations are denoted by sashes, favors, feathers. In his helmet tufted blue and green feathers. I put the helmet on and then strapped up the longsword over my back. I'd taken a drexer from the calsany pack in place of the thraxter I'd worn when first venturing into Gorlki.

So, with the sash and the feathers, I looked just another hired guard. I pushed the pakzhan down out of sight.

The idea that I was on a desperate mission occurred to me, to be pushed aside.

Murlock had served his part. He'd gotten me in, he'd brought in my weaponry and armor, and now it was all down to me.

Going carefully in the fuzzy moonlight I managed to avoid tripping over any guylines and so fetched up before the tent indicated. At that precise moment, as the gods smiled upon man's foolish endeavors, an uproarious hullabaloo started up on the opposite bank of the River of Rippling Reeds.

Good old Seg!

He'd judged it to a nicety even he couldn't have anticipated. He, Nath and Orso were now hard at it over there, creating mayhem and busily liberating the Lomian and Vallian prisoners. The reaction on this side of the river came commendably quickly and soldiers ran yelling from their quarters. There was a clumsy rope-propelled pontoon arrangement provided to cross the river and the soldiers ran down to the bank to line up at the gate to board. I strolled across to the two sentries on the prison tent.

I used a well-worn device.

The burden was this: "Hai, doms! You have all the luck. The Jik wants you over there, and I'm stuck here on sentry go. May Havil take it!"

Eagerly, they ran off, guessing they would have some skull-bashing in prospect. I took up a properly soldierlike stance until they vanished into the moons-drenched shadows, and then I went into the tent.

Just in time I managed to avoid Yamsin's pottery cup. The thing flew up and shattered on the ground. I held her in my arms, as she writhed and twisted, calling me all the vile beasts she could lay her tongue to.

"Calm down, Mistress Yamsin. We must be quiet—"

"Horter Jak!"

"Aye." I stared hard at the Lamnians. "Swiftly and quietly and we are out of here and safe."

With all his merchant's nerves aquiver, Weymlo got out: "You are welcome, Jak, right welcome. We will never be paid by the king now. He would have our heads first."

"The cramph," put in Lamilo, in a most un-like Lamnian snarl.

"Fling your cloaks about you and follow me."

I wasn't at all sure it was going to be particularly easy; in any event in all the confusion we were able to slip out through the gate, leaving two unconscious sentries sprawled on the ground. We hared off into the pink shadows.

The opportunity was too good to miss.

"The best thing for you is to pack your camp right away and get well clear before dawn. With a good start you should not be troubled." I did not add that what I intended would materially assist their chances of complete escape.

"But you, Jak!"

"A trifle of unfinished business. Shall we meet in, say Linansmot? Perhaps in four days' time?"

"If we are not taken up, we will be there."

"Good. Off you go, and may Pandrite go with you."

"And may Pandrite the All-Powerful go with you, too."

I waited just long enough to see them well away and then turned back for the encampment gate.

The two sentries were just waking up as I entered. Helping them to further slumber I ran rapidly on before the swirls of confusion rip-roaring about swirled my way.

The king's pavilion, the largest and most grand structure, could not be missed. Even with the turmoil going on there was no chance of entrance through the front and I circled around to the back. My judgment suggested King Morbihom would merely go to the flap of his pavilion and give orders. He would not concern himself personally over a matter as simple as that of rounding up escaped prisoners. He'd send troops across the river and then return to the delights within his personal silken enclosure.

My old sailor knife slit down and the cloth parted and I was through.

Naturally, this sumptuous portable palace being on Kregen, it was not a single erection but a bewildering maze of cloth-hung passageways and rooms. Various marquee-sized tents joined together formed a lavish field headquarters. I turned to the right as I came to the first tent's junction with the next, and gave no thought to why I went that way.

One or two people were about, mostly slave; and these I ignored, only having to tap on the skulls of a couple of the king's personal bodyguard who proved inquisitive. I stepped out into a small enclosure, intending to cut right through the cloth into the next.

Two stout poles thrust into the ground to form a cross supported the body of a man. I stopped.

He wore sumptuous robes, and by the runic inscriptions and the fellow's flaming red hair, I took him to be from Loh, a Wizard of Loh. His face bore black marks; but it bore also the marks of passion and habitual authority. His turban lay to one side, dented in. His robes were ripped open and his shirt also, baring his chest. Streaky red marks like strawberry jam disfigured the skin.

He lifted his head as I entered.

"Drugged," he said in a slurred furry voice. "Memphees. The king requites me most unjustly."

"Al-Ar-Mergondon, I presume?"

"You are right. And now you are here you may assist me to escape."

"As to that—"

"Oh, I think you will. I have been expecting you, Dray Prescot."

Eighteen

I pay for our foe's supplies

Well, if it came to it, I could always pay the Lamnians myself. Out of friendship. However odd it might sound for me to pay good red Vallian gold to the purveyors of supplies to Vallia's enemies, it made solid common sense to me. I fancied that Weymlo, in order to make a living, and the king of Tomboram being sick and not going to war, had been decoyed into selling to Morbihom. Also, the illness of Tomboram's monarch probably explained Menaham's freedom of action.

I was in sufficient control of myself to betray no great start of surprise when this Wizard of Loh used my name.

Instead I looked around, saw the boxes and bales ripped open and vandalized, the overset tables and chairs, the spilled wine. I went up to Al-Ar-Mergondon, whipped out my knife, cut him free and caught him as he fell.

"Easy, san, easy."

"Yes. I am still weak. The devilish Memphees drains a man, wizard or no wizard."

"I know."

As, indeed, I did. That rascally villain, Vad Garnath, long gone down to the Ice Floes of Sicce, had had me drugged just before a Bladesman's duel. Memphees, concocted from the bark of the poison tree memph and the cactus trechinolc, seeps through the body and takes away the senses. Once Mergondon, helpless, had been trussed up, even his arcane arts had been unable to free him.

The thought occurred to me to wonder if Deb-Lu or Khe-Hi or Ling-Li could not have loosened their bonds.

"Such a task is not within my powers," said Mergondon.

"Come on, Mergondon," I said, determined that we should start our relationship on the right lines from the very beginning. "If we are to escape this hell hole, then you must brace yourself up. *Brassud!*"

"Of course. And all because the army suffered a reverse. I was blamed, the ingrate!"

"Step lively," I said, and began to retrace my steps. We were not disturbed going out as I had not been bothered coming in. A swathing great cloak around the wizard sufficed to conceal him and his hair vanished under my helmet. Outside in the moons' light I dragged him off in the direction of the river. He hauled up.

"This way, Prescot? I cannot swim."

"Don't fret over that problem. Come on!"

Approaching the river gate I saw the sentries clustered there and the torch lights flaring. Well, to have expected anything else would have been foolish.

"You will never—"

"Just shut the black-fanged winespout, there's a good wizard, san."

He said in the hardest tones he'd employed yet: "I had heard you were an unusual man, Prescot. I am beginning to see the stories are not exaggerated."

I unlimbered the great Krozair longsword.

"Stick closely to me. Make sure you duck when necessary. Apart from the guards, I don't want to cut your head off."

He gave an odd little shiver and then we headed for the gate and the guards.

They came at us to interrogate at first, and then, unfortunately for them and to my eternal sorrow, to die.

The blade swished and cut, hacked and slew, and every now and then did a little thrusting. Mergondon stuck to my back like a leech.

The guards pressed, shouting and creating a hellish din, and the work became warm. Mergondon mumbled something like: "I did not think it would be like this!" Then he shouted: "Jurukkers! It is me—"

A shriek burst from the guard trying to get at me from the side, drowning Mergondon's panicky call. The guard reeled drunkenly away. A long rose-fletched shaft had fair split his backbone in two.

In the next heartbeat Nath and Orso, dripping wet, shocked into action, laying about themselves. Seg's bellow rose above the din.

"This way, fanshos!"

A raggedy mob of wet fighters rose up from the bank and tore into the remaining guards. In mere moments it was all over. We caught our breaths.

Seg, beaming, hollered: "Righto, my old dom. All aboard!"

We piled into the pontoon which swayed alarmingly. The released prisoners were crowing with delight. Seg slashed the rope and the pontoon began to drift down the river.

By the time reinforcements ran up through the king's encampment we were in midstream and poling along splendidly.

I took hold of Al-Ar-Mergondon, bent down and put my whiskery face close to his ear. "Listen, san. Do not call me Prescot. Just Jak. It is, you understand, a matter of your life."

"I don't—"

"Jak. *Remember!*"

"This is no way to treat a Wizard of Loh!"

"Better, you will agree, than the way Morbihom treated you?"

He crouched down, then, and I fancied he was sulking.

While most of the released prisoners were from the Lomian army, some hailed from Vallia. Of them I knew only Nath the Iartus, a Hikdar, and he was able to outline for me what had been happening. He was, I may add, absolutely spitting rivets that he had been caught and not at all surprised that the Emperor of Vallia—or the ex-emperor—had turned up to rescue him.

Seg came over to say: "We've lost our zorcas, though."

"Yes. Probably not a clever move to go back."

"Orso is furious. He'd trained that zorca of his."

"So we observed."

Nath the Impenitent remarked: "Well, Murlock the Spry will do well out of it."

"He's busy cooking a breakfast we shall not eat."

"For that I mourn our loss," said Nath, and rubbed his stomach ruefully.

We managed to sleep fitfully as the pontoon drifted downriver and long before dawn poled in to the opposite bank and abandoned our craft. We set off due west, watchfully, and when we ran across a Lomian cavalry patrol we realized we had been traversing the no-man's-land between the two fronts.

After that it was a matter of everybody going off to rejoin their units and of our little group plus the wizard finding Headquarters. Nath na Kochwold welcomed us with enormous glee, and we ate and drank and told him what we had learned of the Menaham Order of Battle. Our spying mission was, for the moment at least, at an end.

Queen Lushfymi of Lome, nominally in personal command of her gallant army, had sense enough to put her trust with Kapts of proven skill. I was pleased to see the high commands of Vallia and Lome cooperating well. Personally, I refused to interfere and simply let Nath na Kochwold carry on in his own effective fashion, and extremely effective that was too, by Krun, in the running of the smart and powerful contingent from Vallia.

The Presidio had, as was their wont in these matters, given these forces the grandiloquent name of The Fourth Army. The lads were in good heart. They'd won the first contest in which they'd indulged after landing, and were ready for what was to come.

I paid my respects to Queen Lush and fabricated an excuse which would keep me out of her way. Orso decided to take up the offer of joining Nath's staff. He'd performed well in those aspects of our admittedly low-key adventure that demanded courage and resolution and skill. But there are other factors needed in the character of an adventurer upon Kregen who wishes to do more than merely carve a bloody path through human flesh, as they say in Clishdrin.

When that was settled, I said to Nath the Impenitent: "The papers have come through, and it's all settled. No stain attaches to your reputation. You are once again a Jiktar and as of now you are promoted at least to Ley-Chuktar."

"That is munificent, Jak. I would be churlish to refuse. But—what of the missing cash?"

"All paid back. Now—"

"By you, of course!"

I looked him in the eye, seeing his scarlet pride in that rugged face and the lifting of the weights on his mind, and I said in a harsh and damn-you-to-hell fashion: "Now, see here, Chuktar Nath Javed, sometime known as Hack 'n' Slay and sometime known as the Impenitent! You will earn that money! We have unfinished business with the devils of Lem the Silver Leem. When Seg and I next tangle with them, you will be up there battling with us. Is that clear?"

He gave a brusque nod. "Thank you, majister."

I did not misunderstand his use of majister here.

I went on: "There's a little job for you here, and then you're free to follow your own inclinations. You can go to Vallia and see about your sister, for instance."

"If Opaz wills."

"Of course. I arranged to meet our Lamnian friends in Linansmot. Take them the money owed by King Morbihom—"

"But, Jak! You're not paying for our enemy's supplies!"

Very little explanation was needed to show him what was in my mind and I finished with: "So they can supply us. They will be most useful."

"I'll get over to Linansmot straight away."

"Take a cavalry squadron with you, Nath."

"Quidang."

With that out of the way I went over to the tavern where we put up and found Seg and Al-Ar-Mergondon. I wasn't quite sure what to do with the Wizard of Loh. He kept fulminating against King Morbihom, with reason.

With Khe-Hi-Bjanching and Ling-Li-Lwingling away in Loh discovering what being parents was all about, and Deb-Lu-Quienyin as always busily occupied on a number of different schemes, it might be convenient, to say the least, to have another Wizard of Loh to help us.

He jumped at the offer.

With Seg using those marvelous fingers of his in creating a new bowstave at the table, and Al-Ar sitting across from me, the wine between us, I said: "Have you heard of a Witch of Loh called Csitra?"

"Csitra." He rolled the name around his tongue. "Csitra what?"

"That I have not discovered. She was mated with Phu-Si-Yantong."

"He is dead."

"Aye."

"I had heard of a Witch of Loh in connection with Yantong. That is all. The name means nothing to me."

"Perhaps, at a time convenient to yourself, you could go into lupu and discover her whereabouts."

"I will try."

All this, as you may hear, was conducted on a most formal basis. We were like two dogs sniffing around each other, ready for mere acquaintanceship and alliance or for real friendship, as the Mensaguals decreed.

Mergondon took his wine and before he drank, he spoke and, I judged, with something of an effort.

"The Wizard of Loh, Phu-Si-Yantong is better off dead, the yukpam,* by the Seven Arcades yes."

"Never was truer word spoken," said Seg, in his most cheerful fashion, working on his bow.

I felt a little surprise that a person like a Wizard of Loh should use so coarse a word as yukpam, particularly after the nature of the preceding conversation. Still, it takes all kinds to make a world.

He had expressed his gratitude without effusiveness and in a dignified way. Now he went on to say: "When the Yantong calling himself the Hyr Notor ran Pandahem, they were remarkable days."

"All Pandahem must work together now against the Shanks," I told him. "And that means Menaham, as well."

"King Morbihom has not had the privilege of my arts for very long. The man is a bloodthirsty simpleton."

---

* yukpam: A receptacle for containing muck. The nearest terrestrial equivalent would be scumbag; but that expression was not used at the time. A.B.A.

The gambit was accepted by Seg who said in his lazy way: "And you'd be the one to knock him down, right?"

"If the opportunity was vouchsafed me."

So, as I say, I was not absolutely sure what to do with Al-Ar-Mergondon. There was, and understandably enough, a tenseness about him, a feeling of uncertainty and unease, despite our efforts to reassure him.

The political situation inside Lome had been a constant source of concern—well, by Krun, that applies to most countries, I suppose—and those forces sent across by my lad Drak acting with decision as the Prince Majister had performed well. They'd assisted the folk loyal to Queen Lush and the land was coming back to normalcy when this treacherous attack from Menaham set everything boiling again.

Kapt Nath Molim, the Trylon of Polnehm, very smart, still quite young, and devoted to Queen Lush, had stood up under the test well. He remained, as Drak had told me, still very much out for Number One. His experience with our armies in Vallia had convinced him that the future for both our countries lay in mutual help and alliance.

Drak had shifted the mercenaries out of Vallia to help Lome. They had put up as resolute a resistance to mad King Morbihom as they could contrive, but they'd have been done for if the fresh army with Nath na Kochwold had not arrived.

The Fifth Phalanx was with Nath consisting of the Ninth Kerchuri Dayra and the Tenth Kerchuri Jaidur. Brytevax* Orlon Sangar commanded. He had commanded the old Tenth Kerchuri in that traumatic Battle of Ovalia, where we had set the Thorn Ivy Trap. Now, a seasoned warrior and commander, he was well aware that in the Phalanx we had the battle-winning instrument to give us the final victory.

Seg and I had chosen to set up our quarters in the upper room of The Throstle and Swill which stood on the opposite side of the square from The Rokveil Crown'd where Nath na Kochwold and the other ranking officers lodged. There were ample taverns and inns in this town of Mompass to care for us.

A messenger brought a note from Milsi saying she was let off the hook and wanted Seg to go meet her in Vondium.

"So the Sisters of the Rose do grant leave, then!"

"Sometimes," I said, remembering.

"Still, it is dratted inconvenient. I can't leave you and the army with this campaign on our hands—"

"You," I told my blade comrade with ferocity, "will take your voller and hightail it to Vondium right now. And give my love to Milsi. Dernun?"

"Quidang! And, my old dom—well, no matter, no matter..."

---

* brytevax: Short form of Brumbytevax, Commander of a Phalanx. From brumbyte, pikeman. *A.B.A.*

No need whatsoever for more words between Seg and me.

As a matter of policy, although both Seg and I detested all the flummery, I insisted that he be sent off with due ceremony. Guards turned out, bands played, banners flew. Seg Segutorio, King of Croxdrin and High Kov of Balkan, soared aloft on course for Vallia and Vondium. We called the remberees and the twin suns shone and the flags fluttered and trumpets pealed their high notes of departure. After that I took myself off to The Throstle and Swill to sink a flagon or two and shake off the black dog that descended, unwanted but not entirely unexpected.

Al-Ar-Mergondon came up and we settled to a game of Jikaida. He was good and the contest was close.

Nath the Impenitent had not returned from Linansmot, although the four days were past. I did not think for a single mur that he had taken the Lamnians' money and run. There were great strokes and adventures in store for old Hack 'n' Slay.

With a strange sigh and a flutter of all his features, Mergondon pushed back from the table. His eyes rolled up. The Chuktar he had been about to move slipped from his fingers and rolled across the table. A distinct sense of chill brushed across my skin. Mergondon went rigid.

"Dray," he said. He spoke in his own normal voice, with an added breathlessness that echoed oddly in the upper chamber. "Dray. Forgive my speaking to you like this through San Mergondon. Pay him my respects. He will understand the urgency."

"Deb-Lu!"

"It is Yumapan. The emperor has received intelligence that Morbihom intends to march onward after he has crushed Lome. An alliance is essential. He asks that you visit him."

"Reply," I said, standing up, "that I am on my way."

Nineteen

At the Eye of Imladiel

To hurtle on through the clean crisp air of Kregen! To stand in the prow of the voller and feel the wind in your hair and all the urgent vibrancy beneath your feet urging you on! Yes, to have flown headlong through the sweet air of Kregen is to have tasted life, my friends!

Below us the mountains whirled past, their peaks rising ahead of us, wreathed in snow, cloud mantled, superb. Mergondon knew the way through those granite masses, and we skimmed low over high passes where wild animals, shaggy and pelted, tossed their horns at us in defiance.

On through thin air we rushed. And yet on this journey I did not chase frantically onward to rescue a loved one, to snatch a sacrifice from evil priests of a vile cult or to plunge at once into scarlet action. Oh, no. Now I simply flew with this Wizard of Loh to talk alliances with Pelleham, the Emperor of Yumapan.

All the world could see that once King Morbihom had eaten up Iyam and Lome, he would attack Yumapan. The mountains had proved a barrier in the past. I had a shrewd suspicion that riding on his tide of success, Morbihom would have little difficulty in buying or hiring airboats for the coming campaign. There would be much booty.

Hitherto Pelleham's greatest concerns had been the renders from the Hoboling Islands. These pirates festered in the chains of islands and raided coasts at will, in between taking up fat argosies and their treasures.

Yumapan had extended into the south of the island of Pandahem, conquering the small kingdoms in the south and west and eventually establishing a natural frontier line. The country could with reasonable justification, then, call itself an empire.

That particular specimen of conquest had taken place a good few seasons ago and the situation was now stabilized. Morbihom was out to stir the cesspit again.

So it was natural that Pelleham should seek allies and his first thought must have been Vallia. It was natural, too, that he would wish to discuss the situation with me in the first instance on a semiofficial level. When he and I had agreed the agenda, as it were, the fanfares could sound and the official deputations meet and consult. Speed, clearly, was of the essence. That had been eloquently evidenced by the occult means used to bring us together.

Mergondon had simply said: "I accept San Quienyin's apologies to me. He must find using his kharrna debilitating and to speak through a fellow Wizard of Loh saved him much."

I didn't comment on that. I did feel a breeze of alarm. Good old Deb-Lu—surely he was not once again losing his powers?

The warmth of this area enfolded us once more as we descended from those high passes. The land spread below, lush and green and well-watered and filled with game. This was tremendous hunting country—for those who cared for it—and I recollected that Kov Loriman the Hunter hailed from Yumapan.

We were to meet Emperor Pelleham not at his capital city but privately at a noble's hunting lodge. Here we could escape prying eyes and ears, owned by damned spies sent in by King Morbihom.

"I came through here on my way from Loh," Mergondon told me. "Quite a few seasons ago, now. Not a very interesting place. The people seem able only to encompass one *idée fixe* in their lives."

"Yes, so I believe."

As though it was all a part of the same conversation, he added: "Just so I can see Morbihom squirm. By Hlo-Hli! The fellow is a worm!"

I did not reply. The distant glint of metal, high in the sky, caught my intrigued attention. Airboats are very few and far between in Pandahem. I stared closely, and Mergondon joined me at the rail to search between the clouds.

"There!"

"Aye."

Instantly, I recognized what I was staring at.

The shapely black hulls showed up hard and etched against cloud banks. The brilliantly colored, squared-off upper works lost much of their color at this distance but remained unmistakable. Shanks. The Shank armada flew steadily on course toward the south. We skipped between cloud masses for a time, tracking them; but their course would take them out over the coast of the island, and if they continued long enough without changing direction they'd hit Loh at Chem.

Mergondon said: "They look—purposeful."

"Extremely."

We saw no other fliers as we finished our journey and dropped down to land at the hunting lodge known as The Eye of Imladiel. Forests and open country surrounded the buildings and a considerable amount of agriculture was in evidence. We were expected.

Seen from the air the main buildings were arranged in the form of a letter W. Off to the north side rambling stables and outbuildings no doubt housed the functional parts of the establishment. To the east a cleared area of gravel had, resting in grand isolation on the golden brown, a single voller. She was a smallish ten-place craft and by her lines had been built in Hamal. She flew no flags. I brought our flier in neatly to land alongside.

At the far end of the landing zone a large collection of carriages rested, poles up, and lines of zorcas, krahniks and other animals were being exercised. The smell of lavender hung pleasantly on the air.

We were met by a fussy rotund chamberlain, all in blue and gold, with an honor guard of Chuliks. Every Chulik tusk was banded in red gold and their pigtails hanging from their shaven yellow heads were all plaited with blue and gold threads. No carriage or conveyance was provided for us; but the distance was not far and we walked along proudly enough.

I noticed an odd puzzling little shimmer about the parked carriages and the animals and put it down to heat haze rising from the gravel. The surface had been well-cared for and recently raked for not a single wheel-rut showed and only a few small tenacious weeds grew here and there.

"This way, excellencies!" chirruped the chamberlain, waving his ivory wand like a bandmaster, and obediently we followed him along a tapestry-hung corridor to the black balass doors with golden risslaca handles at the far end.

A trumpet pealed and the doors swung open.

Now at this point I ought to mention that, as I deemed the occasion ceremonial and important, if only of a semi-official nature, I had outfitted myself with some thought as to the proper appearance of an ex-emperor on a delicate mission. It goes without saying that I wore the old scarlet breechclout. But, over that I had donned a fashionable white half-robe, and over that a glittering golden cape. The thing was remarkable, really, I suppose, with a tall Vallian mazilla, and this collar, too, was all of cloth of gold. The cape was the genuine article and was reputed to be at least two hundred seasons old. It was still in reasonably good repair, and although I knew I looked a jackanapes in my own eyes, in the eyes of foreign princes I would look a proper prince.

Al-Ar-Mergondon, of course, dressed as a Wizard of Loh dresses, so that all the world may tremble.

In its own architectural fashion this long arched chamber was as remark-able as my foolish cape. Both held magnificence integrally within themselves; both suggested oldness gone to seed and carefully repaired. An odd shim-mer along the walls and pillars frazzled at the eyesight.

Down the right-hand side, ceiling-high windows were draped in deep-est purple. Each window was closed by a heavy horizontal bar of balass wood. Before each window stood a man dressed in green and black livery, with a steel chain in his fists. At the end of each chain hunkered a werst-ing. The vicious black and white striped hunting dogs, each with only four legs, opened jaws to reveal fangs they'd be only too happy to sink deeply into your flesh. I guessed they came from the islands of Nycresand off the east coast of Loh.

The other side of the room contained a series of enormous mirrors of polished silver, and that strange little shimmer clung about their surfaces, distorting the images within.

At the far end beneath a golden canopy, a reception committee awaited us.

The Chulik guards' iron-studded war boots did not ring upon the marble underfoot. They made dull thudding noises. My own ankle-high moccasins, soft and supple, made no sound at all.

As we approached the waiting group, I tried to throw off this stupid sense of oppressive stuffiness ailing me.

Here we were about to enter into important talks with the Emperor of Yumapan concerning the future well-being of Pandahem and of Paz. I stuck my chin in the air and stalked on. I could not stop my left fist from straying to the rapier hilt and I forced the constricting fingers to relax.

Curtains of that same deep purple hung against the end wall. Torches threw orange streamers into the mingled radiance of the Suns of Scorpio falling across the marble floor.

There were no flowers I could see blooming in this vaulted chamber, yet the air smelled of that raw rank pungency of damp vegetation, muddy stems rotting gently into a vegetable decay.

A further double rank of Chulik guards stood at attention in rear of the hosts. We drew closer over that shining marble floor. To the right stood a figure cloaked in blue with silver and golden moons and suns and comets emblazoned about his person, carrying a skin-bound tome chained to his waist. His bearded face peered gauntly from under the peaked hood of the robe. His eyes appeared mere white crescents.

To the left stood a woman, shapely in a deep purple gown that brushed the floor and left her shoulders bare. Hair of a blue-black coiffed high and threaded with pearls gave her an imperial air, yet her face, painted and kohled, denied that suggestion. Her lips were wide and thin and too red.

In the center stood a man in harness of war, metal and bronze, girded with swords, decked with feathers, hard, domineering, implacable. His powerful face looked shrunken to me, robbed of much of its inner strength and his eyes were far more pouched than I remembered and cloudy as though he had yet to recover from some grievous wound.

I did not think that Kov Loriman the Hunter was really Emperor Pelleham of Yumapan.

Perhaps he would think that Jak the Bogandur was not really Dray Prescot, ex-Emperor of Vallia.

We halted and the thudding of feet echoed to silence.

"Lahal, Dray Prescot, Emperor of Vallia," said Loriman. His voice slurred as though weary beyond bearing.

"Lahal, Kov Loriman."

The woman started at this, and the magician turned those uncanny crescents of whiteness toward me.

"You are—" he paused, and then, swallowing, went on: "You are most welcome, majister."

"I give you thanks. Where is the Emperor Pelleham?"

Perhaps he just did not recognize me. He had failed to do so before. The eye sees what the brain expects. He expected to see Dray Prescot, and not Jak the Bogandur.

Mind you, I was glad to see he had escaped from the Coup Blag. He might be a mighty hunter in most of the wrong ways; but he had been useful and I wanted him alive to further my schemes. The loss of his lady, which we had considered him over, must have treacherously struck again at him, in reflex, as it were, and reduced him. He was not as mindlessly numb as he had been; but it was clear he was not himself.

"The emperor?" He gazed about blankly, as though Pelleham might abruptly appear through a trapdoor in the floor. Then: "Oh, she will be here at once now you have arrived."

So, I suppose, thinking back, it was then that I was sure, and realized, and didn't even bother to begin cursing myself for the most credulous fool in two worlds.

I said, instead: "She?"

"Of course." He half turned that massive head: "Blow!"

The six Chulik trumpeters in the front rank blew the peals.

Their comrades leveled crossbows. Even all the Disciplines of the Krozairs of Zy would not give me the skill, speed or luck to swat away those dozens of bolts.

The purple curtains lifted on golden cords.

She walked in as herself. There were no tintinnabulations from golden bells, no pacing ferocious creatures from nightmare, no chained chail sheom, no hulking armed guards. Just a single woman in a dress of sheer white.

"Lahal, Dray."

"Lahal, Csitra."

Twenty

Csitra

Now that Csitra the Witch of Loh considered she had at last won outright, she was prepared to be all condescending graciousness.

She glowed with health and vitality. Her appearance was probably what she really looked like. Her hair, for example, was no longer jetty black, but the flaming red of the true Lohvian. Her face, hawkish, resolute, possessed that fragile off-center lack of perfect beauty that is the hallmark of pure beauty. She wore not a single gem, not a single adornment. The slippers that showed the tips of toes beneath the white dress glinted gold. That was the sum total of show.

Her arms were bare. The white dress was cut deeply to her navel. No diamond glittered there and I did not expect to see one.

She lifted those bare white arms and said simply:

"You are most welcome, my dearest Dray."

"Oh, I dare say. Why all the flummery to trick me here?"

"Please."

"We have really nothing left to say to each other. Except that—"

"Yes?" She put both hands to her breasts.

"Except that while I do not regret his passing, I feel sorrow for you as a mother that your uhu is dead."

"It were better we did not speak of Phunik—now."

"Yes. I suppose so. Well, and what do you propose, Csitra?"

The situation was perfectly clear, of course. She had probably experienced not the slightest difficulty in putting poor old Kov Loriman the Hunter under her spell. He was like a zombie now, obeying without question. I'd have to see what could be done about him. She'd tricked Mergondon into believing it was Deb-Lu who spoke through him. A clever ruse that, so that true voices were not heard.

I just hoped Mergondon had had the sense to shoot off an occult message for help to Deb-Lu. The truth is, I counted on that elementary scream for succor.

Then Al-Ar-Mergondon, Wizard of Loh, said: "What are your orders for me now, sana?"

Thus easily was my stupid bubble of hope burst.

I gave him a look.

He flinched back.

"Yes," he said, and he fairly spat the words. "You have been finely caught, you onker, and by Hlo-Hli, I am glad I had a hand in it."

"What," I said. "What harm have I ever done you?"

"None that I can think of, save that the sana dotes on you..." Here he hauled himself up sharply. If he'd been about to criticize Csitra, he sensibly thought better of it.

And, too, another strand of the plot came clear. This idiot Mergondon was enamored of Csitra; ensorcelled by her or not, he lusted after her and would do her bidding just as readily as poor old Kov Loriman.

The whole situation looked a damned sight blacker than it had at first, by Krun, damned blacker!

Those ranks of crossbows all leveled at my guts represented an argument I couldn't counter.

I squinted casually at the purple drapes concealing the rear wall. A door there? Not necessarily. Csitra might have any sorcerous methods of effecting an entrance.

Hell's bells and buckets of blood!

There just *had* to be a way out of this mess!

And Csitra put that way to me, cooing sweetly as any turtledove, and twice as venomous as the deadliest snake in two worlds.

"Why are we standing here like this, so stiff and formal? Come along, my dearest, and we will share a bottle and talk together."

I had to say: "I take it you'll bring all the guards and their crossbows, too?" and the moment the stupid words were out of my mouth I wished I hadn't uttered them.

"Why, of course, my love! For our protection."

She was wise enough to know how to keep a fellow down.

Instead of leaving that somber purple-draped chamber with the werstings and the Chulik guards, we were waited on by scantily-clad slave girls who brought in table and chairs, flagons and glasses, bowls of fruits and palines. I sat down. There wasn't much dratted else I could do.

Loriman and his magician and the black-haired blue-gowned woman retreated a few paces and stood with Mergondon in a group looking surreptitiously at us.

"Kov," said Csitra in a voice like brass bristles brushing down steel. "Tell Ban Urfenger and the Lady Lara to look away."

"At once, sana."

"And move further off." And she waved an elegant ringless hand, shooing the four away.

Mergondon shot me a nasty look.

"He will not harm you, my dearest. For one thing, he does not have the kharrna. And for another he knows what will happen to him if he made any attempt."

"You have them well-trained."

"Anyone who serves me, yes. And—anyone who stands in my way." She put her hand on mine upon the table.

The shock struck through with repugnance and yet—and yet... Like the shocks played with at Electric Parties at the turn of the century, it thrilled through me, there was no doubt of that. The thrill of repugnance? Certainly there was nothing of the lure of the forbidden here. I'd see her dead and consigned down to the Ice Floes of Sicce, and probably spare her one salt tear. On reflection, no, I'd waste even a single tear on the witch.

"You are not drinking, my sweet."

These endearments grated on me. I detested them. Poor, stupid, foolish, evil woman... Well, she wasn't all evil, I truly believed. As you know, I strive ever to find the good in people. Very few people, if any, are totally evil. Perhaps Phu-Si-Yantong had been the nearest to total evil I'd known, and his unwholesome influence had created the monster Csitra the Witch out of whatever kind of girl she had been aforetime.

"I find I am not thirsty, and my appetite has deserted me."

"Oh, come now." And she started to wheedle me with a paline, like any doting mother trying to get her baby to eat.

All this told me in the most eloquent terms that she considered she had won, had really and truly won. Only a little time and effort, she obviously believed, were needed to conquer me completely.

And—what the hell could I do?

Her own personal protection must give her confidence that a brainless blow of a sword would not hurt her.

In a different situation her confidence would have amused me. She worked busily at maintaining this cozy teatime atmosphere. The crudity of a sword blow in this situation, quite apart from its uselessness, would inject a coarseness very far from what she was attempting to achieve.

Very well, then. A sword blow? A slashing stroke of the great Krozair longsword?

I am not sure if something of the Hamlet syndrome affected me. Poor, silly, confused woman, she might well be better off dead. Yet I did not relish that task despite all that had passed. Her powers were real: that I did know.

She made no attempt to influence me as she had once before and I believe she understood that that failure would be repeated here. She went about her task with other weapons and using other means.

The little chamberlain joined the four onlookers. The Chulik guards remained impassively alert. And the rank smell of damp vegetation hung perplexingly in the air of that splendid chamber.

I shifted around on the chair so that I might easily whip the Krozair brand free of the scabbard.

Just how long I would have before the sleeting storm of crossbow bolts tore me into fragments I did not know. If they were to destroy me, then destroy me they would. The idea persisted that the steel would bounce from Csitra. She was her own best protection and the crossbows represented mere gloss within her occult realm.

I said: "You tell me that you love me and want me for yourself. How long, do you think, that would last?"

Her startlement, I judge, was genuine.

"I do not understand you, my love."

"A plaything? For you? Is that all you want?"

She flared up.

"You do not comprehend the depth of my passion for you, Dray! There are no words, there is not room enough in all the world to squeeze in half of my feelings."

"Maybe in two worlds?"

"What—? Do you mock me?"

"No."

"What do you mean, in two worlds?"

"I don't think you would understand, Csitra. And, if you did, you would recoil." I went on in a hard and most unpleasant tone. "At least, that has been my experience with other Wizards and Witches of Loh."

She favored me with a look that was like the blinds being drawn up on the glory of the Suns. She licked her lips. "So you know of the Sunset People? Is that why—?"

"I know of the Savanti, yes. That is not why."

"Then am I truly blessed! I am proved! There is between us an unbreakable bond, Dray, and you cannot deny it!"

I was about to burst out with: "By the Black Chunkrah, woman! Of course I can!" But I held my tongue. This deluded witch lusted after me, and that, besides being her misfortune, was highly inconvenient for me. There was a name, a person, not mentioned yet. All my own sorrows were nothing beside the terror tearing me apart that Csitra would harm *her*.

I thrust those ghastly thoughts aside in panic lest Csitra, or Mergondon, could truly read another person's mind.

Khe-Hi and Ling-Li were away in Loh. I found myself tensing up in anticipation that good old Deb-Lu must put in an appearance soon. He had the power to thwart this witch. Working together, with Deb-Lu handling Csitra and I taking care of the Chulik archers, we could escape this moil and I might come out alive and whole.

And, still, the idea persisted that perhaps, just perhaps, I overrated Csitra's powers and a steel blade could finish her.

This farce had to be played along further. If I made the stroke and it failed, she must finally understand that she could never win me. After that, well...

That risk could not be taken until all else failed.

"I have labored long and successfully for this outcome," she prattled on. She was amazing. She was acting like a blushing maiden with a strapping lad at the farmyard gate. "I find I am a little weary. We must rest and then we will have a lovely banquet and talk and you will see."

"Very well."

She had deluded herself into believing what she wanted was true and had occurred. Like any trapped animal I must wait my chance. We made a macabre pair, to be sure.

She stood up and out of simple politeness I rose also. She smiled that calculating witching smile and walked off, swaying, and the purple drapes fell into place and she was gone.

Kov Loriman came over and said: "You are a most fortunate man, majister."

Following the kov, Mergondon spat out: "Undeservedly. If I had my way there would be short shrift for you, Prescot."

I ignored the mage and said to Loriman: "You do not recognize me, Kov Loriman?"

"We have never met to my certain knowledge."

His speech was still slurred, his eyes clouded. There was nothing I could do to bring him out of his tranced state. In matters that did not touch upon Csitra, he appeared to be himself. He announced his intention of going hunting on the morrow. First thing. The woman, Lady Lara, and the blue-gowned mage, San Urfenger, joined in the conversation. The sheer matter-of-factness of these people's conduct might have amazed me but for the malignancy now plain in Mergondon. During the talk of this evening's banquet and the hunt tomorrow his caustic interjections obtruded the reality of what passed here.

A silver gong note sounded muffled. The chamberlain skipped off toward the wall of silver mirrors and one swiveled open. He went through the opening and a moment or so later returned in a hurry bearing a sheet of paper.

"Yes, Hursey?" said Loriman, extending his hand.

"Bad news, pantor, very bad news."

Loriman took the paper, read and then looked up with a deal of his old bash-on regardless temper flaring.

"It is from the Emperor Pelleham. The capital is attacked by a swarm of airboats. He commands our instant assistance. This changes all."

"Those devils the Bloody Menahem are attacking us already?" exclaimed the Lady Lara.

Loriman crackled the paper in his fist.

"The emperor does not mention the Bloody Menahem."

They started up a babble of talk amongst themselves.

I said: "It is not the Bloody Menahem. These vollers are Shanks."

Mergondon ground out: "It is of no concern to us."

"But yes, san," said Urfenger, turning those white crescents of eyes upon the Lohvian sorcerer. "It touches us deeply. We must assist the emperor."

"If they are Shanks or devils from Menaham, we must hunt them all down!" roared Loriman.

I said: "A Vallian air fleet has been hunting these Shanks. If a message can be got to them..."

"That is beyond my powers," said Urfenger.

Loriman, Lady Lara and I looked at Mergondon.

He said: "I do nothing without the authority of the sana."

"But—" I began.

"*Queyd-arn-tung!*"*

"Hursey," rapped out Loriman. "Carry this news to the Sana Csitra. Hurry!"

"At once, pantor."

So, there we all waited like patients outside a dentist's door until the great sorceress made her entrance.

She had changed into a gown of crimson and gold, all glitter and sliding ruby gleams. Her hair was coiffed up and smothered with gems. She did, indeed, look magnificent with her golden eyelids and golden fingernails; I did not care for her at all but had I done so I would have preferred her as she'd looked earlier.

---

* Queyd-arn-tung: No more need be said. *A.B.A.*

The situation was plain enough and she nodded her head and pursed up her lips. She gave an excellent portrayal of a great princess deciding upon the destinies of nations, and well aware that an audience studied her every move.

"This is, sana, after all," spluttered Mergondon into the argument, "no concern of ours."

"But, sana," protested Loriman, almost as vitally alive as he used to be. "These villains of the air will destroy our city and—"

"I agree it is no concern of ours." Her voice like cut glass chiming, silenced the babble. She turned that queenly head to regard me. Her eyes—they were green at the moment—veiled as the golden eyelids descended. She knew exactly what she was doing.

"And you, dearest Dray. What do you say?"

I said: "If a message may be sent to the Vallian air fleet they will put down these dratted Shanks."

"A message?"

"Mergondon can do it. So, too, can you. You have proved it often enough in the past."

"Yes, I did, did I not? I once spoke to you, I recall, through the lips of a corpse."

"Yes."

"Should I do it? Why should I do it?"

"The Shanks are enemies to us all."

"They have not harmed me."

"Yet."

"You are then so sure?"

"Yes."

She pursed up her lips again, very coquettish, very undecided, a maiden unable to choose between two pretty hats.

"I can easily send a message to your aerial fleet, my love. I can do so at once."

"Then I give you my thanks—"

"Oh, dear heart! I want much more than that!"

So, then, I saw it all and the pit and the way I had fallen headlong down upon the stakes.

Slowly, she nodded, and her little finger touched the corner of her mouth, and dragged down the lower lip.

"That is right, Dray. I will do what you ask when you promise me you will do what I want."

I closed my eyes.

The capital city of Yumapan, wonderful and splendid as it no doubt was, the safety of Emperor Pelleham's domains, were not the issue at stake here. If we could smash or disperse that Shank fleet that had been plaguing Pandahem we would have struck a powerful blow and given ourselves another valuable breathing space for the greater battles ahead. Politics and love, well, they mix at times like oil and water and at others are inseparably intertwined.

I could deny this woman what she wanted and allow the Leem Lovers to devastate a city, a country. I could. I did not think the latter action was that of a man.

The obvious thought occurred to me. Any promise made under duress is not binding. Poor Harold of England was hooked on that one by William the Bastard. I could promise this woman anything and then repudiate my word. I could.

I most certainly would not—could not—repudiate Delia.

"Very well," I said, speaking as evenly as I could. Her head went up. Her hands half-lifted. Her nostrils flared. She must have heard that constricting choke in my voice.

"You swear?"

If my hands shook now I was done for.

I answered very smartly. Any shilly-shallying now, any words like: "Is swearing necessary between us?" and prevarication, and this woman would know I lied.

"I swear."

It meant nothing.

She smiled now and it was as though honey dripped from her mouth. "I will send the message myself. I know how to find your grand fleet well enough, and to direct them to Yumakrell. This fellow Pelleham should be relieved."

San Urfenger fairly jumped forward. "Thank you, sana, thank you. And we must all ride to join the fight."

She looked at him with the vacant air of one who discovers an itch on the back of the neck during an important affair. "Ride? Ah, yes. And you, kov, will wish to ride to the rescue, also?"

"Yes, sana."

"I shall retire to the private rooms you have placed at my disposal. When I have done as the emperor of emperors, Dray Prescot, requires of me, we shall take the voller and fly away to mutual happiness. Dernun?"

"Understood, sana. And I thank you."

The whole thing, this whole business, from the moment she'd made her entrance to now, had been conducted on a passionless plane of logic, of bowing to the inevitable. I sensed that any display of emotion would smudge the effect as of mud upon a bright canvas. There were other ways of chicanery, I'd discovered, to deal with this pitiless progress.

Her departure was as grand as her entrance. We all stood to watch her go, and I did not doubt that she would contact the Vallian air fleet and direct them to their quarry.

After that we two were to fly off in the voller to everlasting happiness. Ha!

I said: "Kov, I gather this Eye of Imladiel is your hunting lodge?"

"It is."

I walked to the table and sat down. "Then perhaps you would be good enough to order food. I think we must all be starving."

"At once, majister, at once." He was properly subservient as a kov to a great and puissant emperor of emperors. Anyway, how the hell had Csitra got hold of that?

The serving wenches brought in food, and splendid though it was I rammed it down and quaffed without taking notice of the viands at all. Mergondon remained sullen. Csitra had said he did not possess the power to harm her; I assumed she was right but was not prepared to risk much on it.

I'd thrown off the grand golden cape and was in the act of raising a goblet to my lips when Loriman stood up. His face bore all the old look of intemperate authority, scarlet and glowing, and the scales had fallen from his eyes. I knew then that Csitra had done as she had promised.

"Jak the Bogandur!" ground out Loriman. "What the hell are you doing here?"

"I am glad to see you still alive, kov."

"Of course I'm alive, you rast! And now we may settle the differences between us."

My first reaction was one of amusement. Then I felt annoyance. Loriman had vowed not to fight me until we were both safe out of the Coup Blag. He suffered from feelings of loss of dignity, he fancied I had slighted him, and he thirsted after redress. Well, now we were both safely out of the Coup Blag. He drew his rapier and glared at me.

"On guard, you cramph, and by Hito the Hunter, I shall spit you through."

"Lord!" croaked out Urfenger. "Please—"

"Silence, san! This is a matter of honor."

"Look, Loriman," I said, and I still sat and I did not draw my sword. "You have to go fight the Shanks—"

"They will still be there when I have taught you the lesson you so richly—"

"—deserve," I said, thoroughly fed-up. "All right, you onker, so be it. And don't say I didn't warn you."

I drew my rapier and main gauche and we set to. He was a fine swordsman, as I knew; but I'd already seen him in action and knew his mettle and standard. His tricks were cunning and used with power; my counters were just that sufficient fraction more diabolical and more powerful. We circled and the blades clashed and rang and I cut the leather straps holding his armor and then the tunic and so, carefully, ribboned his clothes. He sweated and roared and grew sweatily more and more scarlet and then I disarmed him with a turn and a flick and placed the point of the rapier at his breast.

"Do you bare the throat, Loriman?"

His idea of honor was perfectly sufficient for him to bellow defiance and allow me to slay him. I knew that.

I said: "I told you, Loriman, that our mutual enemies are the Shanks. I shall not kill you, for you have much fighting ahead against the Fishheads."

"You shame, me, you—you—"

"Not so."

San Urfenger appeared, a blue-robed shadow in the corners of our eyes.

"Majister, your pardon." He moved closer to Loriman. "Pantor, you do ill to cross the will of the emperor of emperors, the emperor of all Paz."

Loriman's eyes rolled whitely. He licked ineffectively at spittle drooling from his lip. "The emperor...?"

It was clear to me, although not to Urfenger, that the lifting of the spell on Loriman had canceled out his recent memories of me. He started to shake. He began to stand up and pull away from my rapier point.

"At this moment," said Urfenger, "the Shanks attack Yumakrell and the life of the Emperor Pelleham is in danger. It is there our duty lies, kov."

"Emperor of Paz?" said Loriman. He looked wild, enraged, as though monstrously cheated. "Jak the Bogandur—*Dray Prescot*?"

"Aye," I said, and flicked the rapier away and held out my hand. "And a friend."

We were held by this pretty drama, locked into a circle of desires and dying hatreds and burgeoning new horizons. A crimson and golden movement heralded Csitra's entrance. She glowed with vitality and beauty and the inner ecstasy of ultimate victory. Sweet the triumph in her breast!

The Lady Lara gave a squeal of alarm.

My gaze switched around. Mergondon stood with legs braced wide, a look of demoniac hatred upon his face and a crossbow leveled full on me. His finger tightened upon the latch.

"*No!*"

The scream of a tormented soul burst from Csitra.

She flung herself forward, arms wide, red hair flowing, flung herself full before me.

The crossbow bolt entered her breast, pierced her through.

Loriman's voice smashed out above the screams.

"Guards! Feather him, and feather the Chulik whose bow he took! *Bratch!*"

Instantly a score of bolts ripped Mergondon and the poor stupefied Chulik guard to shreds.

Loriman swung back to face me, face engorged, brilliant with anger and resolve.

"You see, Dray Prescot, how I dealt with you in all honor?"

"Aye."

"For the future—give me time."

"Until the Shanks arrive in full force. Until then only. Dernun?"

"Quidang!"

So, then, I bent to Csitra, the Witch of Loh, who had given her life for me out of misguided love.

Blood dribbled from her mouth. She moved a hand, the fingers curling like petals. I took her hand, and pressed, and so stared down upon her.

"You see, Dray my dearest, how it was? All my arts could not prevent it. The Seven Arcades call."

"Csitra," I said, and could not go on.

"Oh, yes. You will live. You are the Emperor of Emperors, the Emperor of Paz—"

"That is nothing."

"It is. And there is—the empress..."

"Yes."

Her eyes dulled over. She gripped my hand and the strength passed from her fingers. Her head lolled lower.

"You did love me, Dray, didn't you?"

I looked down on her and I knew, even then, even in that charged moment, that I could not lie where the lie touched my Delia, my Delia of Delphond, my Delia of the Blue Mountains.

I opened my mouth and saw that there was no need for an answer.

She was gone, gone down to the Ice Floes of Sicce to be met by the Gray Ones and to make her way through the mists and so seek the pathway to the sunny uplands beyond. I hoped her journey through the Seven Arcades would be accomplished without pain. She had suffered pain in her mortal life and now she was gone I wished her well.

So died Csitra, the Witch of Loh.

Thus ended the Witch War.

Epilogue

"Thus ended the Witch War."

With these words the tape from Dray Prescot whispered to silence.

I just sat, half slumped forward in the wing armchair, and stared at the cassette player; but I saw—oh, I saw the rolling plains of Segesthes, the treacherous jungles of Pandahem, the glitter and rush of swifters upon the Eye of the World in Turismond, the riotous confusion of the Sacred Quarter in Ruathytu, the glisten along the canals and boulevards of Vondium, the Bravo Fighters swaggering in the enclave city of Zenicce.

And, too, I saw Aphrasöe the Swinging City and a simple leaf boat with a Scorpion for crew sailing down the River Aph where Dray Prescot's adventures on the fascinating world of Kregen began.

From that beginning until now there have been over two and a half million words in Dray Prescot's narrative.

Many people have passed before us limned in the magic fire of imagination, men and women of forms unknown to this Earth, people of heroic stature and trembling cowards, rogues and fools, ordinary folk trying to live ordinary decent lives, adventurers and swashbucklers, men and women of a diversity to make up a whole planet.

We have tried to discover the mysteries of the Savanti and the Star Lords and with Prescot have abused their spy and messenger the Gdoinye knowing that the blue fire of the Scorpion hovers, close and menacing...

For the moment I have received no more tapes from Dray Prescot.

There is not a shadow of doubt in my mind that he is upon Kregen now deeply involved with the many projects under his hand, still defying the Shanks, still attempting to reach an understanding with the Star Lords, still trying to complete all the manifold tasks besetting him.

Oh, no; Dray Prescot with Delia—Delia of Delphond, Delia of the Blue Mountains—and his family and friends still battles on, undefeated and defiant under the streaming mingled lights of the Suns of Scorpio.

Alan Burt Akers

A Glossary to the Witch War Cycle

Compiled by Els Withers

References to the five books of the cycle are given as:

WWK: *Werewolves of Kregen*
WOK: *Witches of Kregen*
SOV: *Storm over Vallia*
OOK: *Omens of Kregen*
WOA: *Warlord of Antares*

NB: Previous glossaries covering items not included here can be found in Volume 5: *Prince of Scorpio*, Volume 7: *Arena of Antares*, Volume 11: *Armada of Antares*, Volume 14: *Krozair of Kregen*, Volume 18: *Golden Scorpio*, Volume 22: *A Victory for Kregen*, Volume 26: *Allies of Antares*, and Volume 32: *Seg the Bowman.*

A

agio: a custom practiced by mercenaries of putting their wealth into a common pot before a battle, those sharing it out being fewer than those contributing.

Alexeyim's trakir: a hefty sliver of iron sharpened at both ends and hurled in battle by the Alexeyim to deadly effect.

Alloran, Kov Vodun of Kaldi: Sent by Prescot to liberate southwest Vallia. Became a traitor and tried to usurp the throne of Vallia under the influence of Arachna, but upon her death became once again loyal. *SOV*

Applica the Bounteous, Temple of: a temple in Rashumsmot. *WWK*

Arachna: a sorceress of mixed Kataki and Kildoi ancestry who suborned Vodun Alloran; was killed by Lon the Knees. Prescot says that this is not her real name, which is too long and complex to be used conveniently. *SOV*

Aramplo, San: a wizard, an adept of the Thaumaturges of Thagramond; a member of the second expedition to the Coup Blag; died on that expedition. *OOK*

Ava: an island off the northwest coast of Vallia.

Azure Strigicaw: a voller in the fleet meeting the invasion of the King of North Vallia. *OOK*

B

bacra area: a strange region of house-sized metal boxes and giant metal-eating caterpillars visited by Prescot; it holds some unknown significance for the Star Lords. *WOA*

Bakan: an old name for the province of Balkan.

Barange Fairshum: a palace in Falkerium.

Battle of Bengarl's Blight: the final battle in the reunification of Vallia. *OOK*

Battle of Blue Lizdun: in which Prescot's army defeated the advance force of the King of North Vallia. *OOK*

Battle of Corvamsmot: in which the forces of Prince Drak defeated those of Vodun Alloran. *SOV*

Battle of Cowdenholm: which ended in a draw between the forces of Prince Drak and those of Vodun Alloran. *SOV*

Battle of Farnrien's Edge: in which the Vallian Freedom Army soundly defeated the forces of Layco Jhansi. *WWK*

Battle of Gwalherm: in which the Vallian Freedom Army conclusively defeated the King of North Vallia. *OOK*

Battle of Marndor: in which the Vallian army defeated the forces of Layco Jhansi in Falinur. *WWK*

Battle of Swanton's Bay: took place in the Southwest Vallian campaign; ended in a defeat for the imperial forces. *SOV*

Belzur the Aphorist: a playwright renowned in all Vallia.

Beng Brorgal: the patron saint of tavern brawlers.

Beng Debrant: the patron saint of animal husbandry.

Beng Feylam the Bonder of Warehouses: a patron saint of merchants.

Bengarl: a tiny village in the province of Erstveheim; site of the Battle of Bengarl's Blight.

"Black was the River and Black was her Hair": a maudlin song of Hamal.

Bolto the Knot: the ship-Deldar of *Logan's Fancy*. *WWK*

Branka: a thief of Rashumsmot. *SOV*

Broken Vaol-Paol, The: a dance for a large group of people.

brunnelley: a four-legged saddle bird, colored in mauves, blues, and browns, with a yellow beak and red claws.

brytevax: short form of brumbytevax; the commander of a Phalanx.

C

Cabaret Plant: a carnivorous plant of South Pandahem which lures its victims with sounds resembling conversation and the clink of glasses.

Cackling leer: a grotesque denizen of the Coup Blag, all dripping greeny-black robes and tassels, with a leering mouth.

Caul of Protection: a sorcerous spell of protection.

Cedro: the nephew of Kov Vodun Alloran. *WWK*

chark: a gray, shaggy wild beast. Normally hunts in packs, although the rogues are most dangerous. Said to possess a rudimentary language of their own.

Chem, Sea of: the sea south of Pandahem.

Chemsi the Fair: a mistress of Vodun Alloran. *WWK*

chunkscreetz: a type of sword used by a Kanzai Warrior Brother.

conult: to give someone a tremendous buffet about the heart, either physically or psychically.

Coup Blag: a maze of horrors in South Pandahem, which was used as a trap for Prescot by Csitra and Phunik. *OOK, WOA*

crottle: a word describing the effects of burning or charring food so that it becomes tasteless and generally inedible.

Csitra: a witch of Loh, the widow of Phu-Si-Yantong. Lured Prescot to the Coup Blag to destroy him, but became enamored of him, allowing him to escape. Pronounced the Nine Unspeakable Curses against Vallia. Ultimately gave her life to save Prescot. *OOK, WOA*

D

The Dancing Flea: a low-class tavern in Rashumsmot. *SOV*

Dolours, Gate of: in the inner wall of Gorlki.

The Dragon's Roost: a tavern in Selsmot. *OOK*

Drak Exalted, Hall of: a large chamber in the Imperial Palace in Vondium.

Drill the Eye: a commander of the Emperor's Yellow Jackets. *OOK*

Durheim: a kovnate province in the center of North Vallia.

Dweloin, San: a poet who lived 3000 years ago.

E

Emiltur, Fangar: the Jiktar of a Valkan archer regiment. *WWK*

Endru, Vintang ti Vandayha: the Jiktar of one of Prince Drak's personal bodyguard regiments. *SOV*

Enwood nal Venticar, Kapt: Drak's right-hand man and chief of staff as Prince Majister of Vallia. *SOV*

Ephanion, Nalgre: the Jiktar of a Valkan archer regiment. *WWK*

Erclan: a Jurukker in 2ESW. *WWK*

Erstveheim: a hyr-kovnate province to the west of Durheim in North Vallia.

F

Failsham, Gilda: the Chuktar of Vodun Alloran's Jikai Vuvushis; a member of the Sisters of the Sword. *SOV*

Fakransmot: a village in Falkerdrin.

Famphreon, Kov Nath: the son of Natyzha Famphreon, Kovneva of Falkerdrin. Became Kov upon her death and his rescue by Prescot from Ered Imlien. *WOK*

Fardew, Ongarr: a brigade-Chuktar in the Vallian Army; one of the judges at the hearing of Nath Javed. *OOK*

The Feathered Ponsho: a tavern in Tali. *WOK*

Fintle: the family name of triplets, Oby, Dwaby, and Sosie, all working as secret agents of Vallia. *WOK*

Flick-Flock: a gambling game played with multicolored rods.

Foison the Stroke: the cadade in the caravan of Dolan Weymlo. *WOA*

Fortro: the brother-in-law of Nath Javed, who sold his daughter to the adherents of Lem. *OOK*

Fraipur: a wizard of Fruningen, in the service of Vodun Alloran, who helped rescue Prince Drak from Alloran. *SOV*

Fra-Le, Hodo: a leader of Zamran archers sent with the reinforcements to the armada against Csitra. *WOA*

Francine: the sister of Nath Javed, who sold her daughter to the adherents of Lem. *OOK*

Frant: a middle-sized island off the northwest coast of Vallia.

Frastel, Stromni Marion of Huvadu: a member of the Sisters of the Sword; her band of Jikai Vuvushis was used by Csitra to spread the plague of werewolves in Vallia. *WWK*

Frentar, Lango: a wealthy Vallian financier. *WOA*

Frentar, Orso: the son of Lango Frentar; went with Prescot's expedition to Menaham. *WOA*

The Frog and Jut: a tavern in Vondium. *WWK*

Fruningen: an island which serves as the home for a school of wizardry.

G

Gah: a continent of Schan.

ganchark: a human being cursed with the propensity to transform into a chark; similar to a werewolf. *WWK*

ganjid: a potion used in conjunction with dudinter to kill a ganchark. *WWK*

Gartang the Kazzur: the leader of a band of brigands in Menaham. *WOA*

Gliderholme: a small market town of Falinur.

Golden Sliptingers, River of: separating the provinces of Durheim and Erstveheim in North Vallia.

Goordor the Murvish: a legendary sorcerer of Murcroinim who killed the ganchark of Therminsax. *WWK*

Gordoholme: a village in Vennar.

Gorlki: a town in Menaham.

Grace, Avenue of: a street in Falkerium.

Greatheart: a zorca purchased in Falkerium by Prescot. *WOK*

greeps: slender, bright green shoots that must be cooked expertly and with precision as to temperature and duration to bring out the flavor.

H

Hack 'n' Slay: the nickname given to Jiktar Nath Javed.

Hallandlas: a town in Hamal north of Ruathytu.

Hanitcha Triumph: a voller used on Prescot's second foray into the Coup Blag. *OOK*

Hardolf, Nath: the captain of *Logan's Fancy. WWK*

Harveng: an apprentice of Deb-Lu-Quienyin. *WWK*

Heart of Imrien: the lead voller in the armada sent to meet the invasion of the King of North Vallia. *OOK*

Hebe, Lady: a member of the second expedition to the Coup Blag; was fought over by Kov Loriman and Kov Hurngal ham Hortang. Was killed inside the Coup Blag. *OOK*

Hemfar, Strom Tothor ham: a member of the second expedition to the Coup Blag. *OOK*

Hemlok, Larghos: the first lieutenant of *Heart of Imrien. OOK*

He of the Bright Face: the river separating the kovnates of Bormark and Malpettar; also known as She of the Mellifluous Breath.

Hern-vilar: a race of diffs with green skins.

Heymamlo, Mother: a Lamnia deity.

Hofnar, Strom Nango ham: a Jiktar in the Hamalian aerial cavalry; engaged to Marion Frastel. *WWK*

Hortang, Kov Hurngal ham: the leader of the second expedition to the Coup Blag. *OOK*

Hursey: the chamberlain at the Eye of Imladiel. *WOA*

Huvadu: a stromnate province located barely south of Evir in Vallia.

Hygonsax: a fort in the Mountains of the West in Hamal.

I

Imladiel, Eye of: Kov Loriman's hunting lodge in Yumapan where Prescot and Csitra met for the last time. *WOA*

Imlien, Ered: the Trylon who held Nath Famphreon captive. *WOK*

J

Javed, Lelia: the eldest sister of Nath Javed; a Sister of Voxyra. *OOK*

Javed, Nath: a Jiktar commanding the 32nd brigade of the Vallian Freedom Army; accused of stealing regimental funds, he was reduced in rank to swod as punishment and called Nath the Impenitent; ventured into the Coup Blag with Prescot and was later vindicated. *OOK, WOA*

jes: short form of address for a female superior.

Jikvar: a razor-sharp clawlike weapon used by the Sisters of the Rose.

jikvarpam: the bag used by a Sister of the Rose to carry her Jikvar.

Jinia ti Follendorf: one of the Jikai Vuvushis of Marion Frastel's regiment, bewitched by Csitra. *WWK*

jis: short form of address for a male superior.

K

Kadar the Silent: an alias used by Prescot in Falkerdrin. *WOK*

Kalden: the capital city of the province of Kaldi.

Kando, Crafty: one of a band of ruffians who helped rescue Prince Drak from Vodun Alloran. *SOV*

Kanzai: a martial brotherhood of Kregen, which takes as recruits mainly Chuliks, Khibils, and Laceroti; highly skilled and dangerous fighters.

Kawa-naga: weapon used by Kanzai Warrior Brothers consisting of a length of chain with a three-bladed knife at one end and a three-tined grappling hook at the other.

Kazzchun Pass: a pass in the center of the Mountains of the North in Vallia.

Kensha: a rosé wine drunk with a sprinkling of herbs.

khiganer: a tunic which fastens by a wide flap along the left side of the body and along the left shoulder.

K'koza: a country in Whonban in Loh, home of Nalgre the Point.

Krokan the Glorious, Street of: located in Rashumsmot.

krell: chief.

L

Laceroti: a race of diffs.

Lakelmi, Kapt Logan: a Lohvian mercenary in the service of Vodun Alloran. *SOV*

Lamilo: the stylor of Dolan Weymlo. *WOA*

Lara: a lady attending Kov Loriman the Hunter at the Eye of Imladiel. *WOA*

Larghos the lame: a bard dead five hundred years.

The Leather Bottle: a tavern in Rashumsmot. *SOV*

The Leather Bottle: a tavern in Gorlki. *WOA*

Lingloh, by: a Lohvian oath.

Little Sisters of Patience: a sorority of Vallia which took charge of the group of Rumay fanatics brought back by Prescot from the Coup Blag.

Llipton, Kov: the regent of Croxdrin in the absence of King Crox and Queen Mab. *WOA*

Logan's Fancy: a vorlca in the aerial armada of Vallia.

Lomon the Jaws: the cadade at the palace of Tali's Crown in Tali. *WOK*

Lon the Knees: a beast handler of southwest Vallia who became involved in the campaign against Vodun Alloran. *SOV*

Lop-eared Tobi: one of a band of ruffians who helped rescue Prince Drak from Vodun Alloran. *SOV*

Loptyg, Logan: a silversmith of Vondium. *WWK*

Lyss the Lone: an alias used by Silda Segutorio in southwest Vallia. *SOV*

M

Maisie: a young girl rescued by Prescot from the adherents of Lem. *WOK*

Makanriel: the capital city of the kovnate province of the Black Mountains.

Makolo: Inch's palace in Makanriel.

Mangarl the Mangler: the leader of a band of cutthroats in Falkerium. *WOK*

Mantig ti Fillan: a Kerchurivax fighting with Prince Drak in southwest Vallia. *SOV*

Mantig, Ob-eye: one of a band of ruffians who helped rescue Prince Drak from Vodun Alloran. *SOV*

Mantissae: the servants of Arachna. *SOV*

Mayruna the Perforator: sworn by and called upon by Rumay fanatics.

mazarna: lack of discipline.

Mecrilli, Floring: one of Marion Frastel's regiment of Jikai Vuvushis; used as a tool by Csitra. *WWK*

Mergondon, Al-Ar-: a wizard of Loh, advisor to King Morbihom. Controlled by Csitra until her death at his hands. *WOA*

m'Mondifer, Larghos: a kampeon of 1ESW who became a werewolf and was killed by Prescot. *WWK*

mobiumim: an official in a city, similar to a mayor.

Molim, Nath: the Trylon of the province of Polnehm in Lome. *SOV*, *WOA*

Molophom: a town in Lome.

Mompass: a town in Lome.

Morbihom of the Iron Hand: the name taken by King Posno of Menaham. *WOA*

Movang the Splitter: a Hamalese mercenary in the hire of Layco Jhansi. *WOK*

Murlock the Spry: a Menahem household servant and chef who assisted Prescot and his friends in Iyam. *WOA*

Myer, Pallan: responsible for education in the Empire of Vallia. *WWK*

N

Na-Du, Modo: a Chuktar in charge in the liberation of Venga. *OOK*

Naformo, Nath: a messenger of Natyzha Famphreon. *WWK*

Nafto the Hair: a guardsman who became a werewolf. *WWK*

Naghan the Abstemious: a Deldar in the Vallian Freedom Army; tried to convince Nath Javed to appeal his conviction of theft. *OOK*

Naghan the Chains: the chamberlain of Vodun Alloran. *SOV*

Naghan Deslayer the Fifth: a Kregan philosopher.

Naghan's Reply: a skyship of the Vallian aerial armada; destroyed in a storm. *WWK*

Nalgre the Point: a paktun who helped Prescot rescue Kov Nath Famphreon. *WOK*

Nath's Hammer: a voller in the fleet sent north to meet the invasion of the King of North Vallia. *OOK*

Nath the Greatest Ever: one name used by the King of North Vallia. *OOK*

Nath the Strict: Prince Drak's orderly. *SOV*

Nat-Su, Joldo: the city prefect of Vondium in charge of the Watch. *WWK*

Nevanter, Larghos, the Lace Merchant: the mobiumim of Vendalume. *WOK*

Ngrozyan the Axe, by: an oath of Ng'groga.

Nine Unspeakable Curses: pronounced by the witch Csitra against Vallia; they include werewolves, zombies, and vermin. *WWK*

Niswan the Lop: the landlord of The Leather Bottle in Gorlki. *WOA*

Nogad ti Therminsax: the Jiktar in command of *Pride of Vondium*. *OOK*

Nogad ti Vendleheim: a Jiktar succeeding Nath Javed as commander of the 11th Churgurs. *OOK*

Nojas the Shriven: a deity worshipped in parts of North Vallia.

Nol: Lon the Knees's twin brother. *SOV*

O

Olaseph the Nik: a Kregan philosopher.

olumai: a race of diffs resembling pandas.

Opaz Omnipotent, Best and Greatest, Kyro of: a square in Vondium, where Drak and Silda were married.

Opaz Unknown, Temple of: located in Vondium; site of the wedding of Khe-Hi-Blanching and Ling-Li-Lwingling.

Opnar the Silk: the tailor to Vodun Alloran. *SOV*

Ortyghan, Ortyg: a goldsmith of Vondium. *WWK*

Ortygno, Param: a dudinter-smith of Vondium. *WWK*

otlora: no-nonsense.

P

pam: receptacle, container.

Pelleham: the Emperor of Yumapan. *WOA*

Penitence, Gate of: in the walls of Gorlki.

Phindan: an apprentice of Deb-Lu-Quienyin. *WWK*

Phocis: one of several Rumay fanatics rescued in the Coup Blag by Prescot, Seg Segutorio, and Nath Javed. *WOA*

Phunik: the hermaphrodite child of Phu-Si-Yantong and Csitra. Together with Csitra tried to destroy Prescot in the Coup Blag. Killed by Deb-Lu-Quienyin and Khe-Hi-Bjanching. *OOK*

The Piebald Zorca: an inn in Vondium. *WWK*

Polnehm: a trylonate province in Lome.

Posno: the King of Menaham, who dubbed himself Morbihom of the Iron Hand and invaded Iyam, Lome, and Yumapan. *WOA*

Pride of Falkerium: a voller in the fleet meeting the invasion of the King of North Vallia. *OOK*

Pride of Vondium: the flagship of the armada against Csitra. *OOK*

Prishilla the Otlora: a physician of Vondium. *WWK*

Q

The Queng and Scriver: a modest inn in Falkerium. *WOK*

Quern of Gramarye: a radiant disc of sorcerous power which appears in battles between wizards.

The Quork Nightly: a tavern in Snarkter. *WOK*

R

Rahartium: the capital city of the province of Rahartdrin, largely destroyed by war.

ranstak: a race of diffs with tails, hooded eyes, and compressed features.

Rashumsmot: a town in the province of Rahartdrin, grown in importance since the devastation of Rahartium.

Repentance, Walls of: part of the city walls of Ruathytu.

Rippasch: vulture.

The Risslaca Transfix'd: a tavern in Vondium. *WOK*

Roben, Mantig ti Vindlesheim: an engineer appointed by Prescot to rebuild Vallia's system of canals. *WOA*

Rogarsh the Rattler, Tyr: a mercenary on Prescot's second expedition to the Coup Blag. *OOK*

The Rokveil Crown'd: a tavern in Mompass. *WOA*

Roombidge: a port on the north coast of Falkerdrin.

Rorman the Indestructible: Kapt of the Second Menaham Army. *WOA*

Rose of Valka: an airboat in the armada against Csitra. *OOK*

Rumay: a fanatical group of women, fierce fighters, with customs such as mutilation of dead enemies.

Rundle the Flatch: one of a band of ruffians who helped rescue Prince Drak from Vodun Alloran. *SOV*

S

Salvation: a fluttrell ridden by Prescot from Falinur to the Black Mountains. *WOK*

Sanka: one of several Rumay fanatics rescued in the Coup Blag by Prescot, Seg Segutorio, and Nath Javed. *WOA*

Sassy: the daughter of Fortro and Francine; sold by them to the adherents of Lem but redeemed by Nath Javed. *OOK*

Scancho: the cadade of lady Hebe's guard. *OOK*

Scauron the Gaunt: a man working in the service of Vodun Alloran; kidnapped Prince Drak. *SOV*

The Sceptre and Wand: a luxurious inn of Gorlki. *WOA*

The Secret Seven: fabled champions of many stories and legends of Paz.

Segutorio, Silda: the daughter of Seg Segutorio and Thelda; infiltrated the forces of Vodun Alloran and helped liberate southwest Vallia. Sister of the Rose. Married Prescot's son Drak. Became Empress of Vallia upon the abdication of Delia. *SOV, OOK*

Selsmot: a town in the jungles of South Pandahem; starting point for expeditions to the Coup Blag.

Shalane: leader of a band of Rumay fanatics rescued in the Coup Blag by Prescot, Seg Segutorio, and Nath Javed. *WOA*

shal-cadade: vice-captain of the guard.

Shango Lady: a skyship in the armada against Csitra. *OOK*

shbilliding: a riotous assembly of devotees of liquid refreshment.

She of the Mellifluous Breath: a river separating Bormark and Malpettar; also known as He of the Bright Face.

"Shush-chiff of Pavishkeemi the Beloved, The": a song of Pandahem.

The Silver Lotus: an inn in Rashumsmot. *SOV*

Sisters of Renunciation: a fictitious sorority often used by Sisters of the Rose as a cover-name.

Sisters of Voxyra: a sorority of Vallia; a splinter group from the Sisters of the Sword. *OOK*

Snagglejaws: a zorca of misleading appearance ridden by Prescot in Falkerdrin. *WOK*

Snarkter: a town in Vennar.

Snarly Hills: hills in South Pandahem among which the Coup Blag is located.

Snowy Mountains: a name for the mountains in extreme northern Vallia.

Solars Gratitude, Chamber of: apartments on the south side of the palace of Tali's Crown.

Spurs of Lasal the Vakka, by the: a light cavalryman's oath.

Starhammer, Leone: the Chuktar of Queen Lushfymi's regiment of Jikai Vuvushis. *SOV*

Storm Rising: a voller in the fleet meeting the invasion of the King of North Vallia. *OOK*

Strandar, Naghan: chief Pallan and a senator in the Presidio of Vallia.

Strelviz Lancer: a voller in the fleet meeting the invasion of the King of North Vallia. *OOK*

Strugmin's Rot: a disease afflicting fluttrells; among the symptoms is a yellowish cast to the feathers.

Sultant, Fanti: the daughter of Ornol Sultant. *WOK*

Sultant, Ornol: the son of Nalgre Sultant, Vad of Kavinstok. *WOK*

T

Tali: a city at the northern border of the province of Falkerdrin.

Thandon, Enar: a Chuktar in the Vallian Freedom Army; a Strom; one of the judges at the trial of Nath Javed. *OOK*

Thangkar, Rodo: a legendary werewolf of Therminsax. *WWK*

Thantar: a harpist blinded as a result of an accident in childhood. *WWK*

Thaumaturges of Thagramond: a small and widely-spread cult of wizards.

Thelda the Voluptuous: a mistress of Vodun Alloran. *SOV*

Thingol, Ortyg: a cadet aboard *Heart of Imrien.* Waited outside the Coup Blag while Prescot, Seg Segutorio, and Nath Javed ventured within. *OOK*

Thostan, Noni: the Hikdar of Marion Frastel's Jikai Vuvushis. *WWK*

Thothveheim: a vadvarate province on a peninsula in the west of North Vallia.

The Thread of Life: a play written by Belzur the Aphorist.

The Throstle and Swill: a tavern in Mompass. *WOA*

Tom the Toes: a churgur in the Vallian Freedom Army. *WWK*

Tremi: a vadvarate province east of Durheim in North Vallia.

U

Unstabi: a Chuktar of Undurkor Archers, who joined the traitor Vodun Alloran. *SOV*

Upvil: the landlord of The Leather Bottle in Rashumsmot. *SOV*

Urban the Unguent: a veterinarian of Snarkter, who treated Prescot's fluttrell Salvation. *WOK*

Urfenger, San: a magician attending Kov Loriman the Hunter at the Eye of Imladiel. *WOA*

Urnhart Boulevard: a street in Rashumsmot. *SOV*

V

Vannerlan, Ortyg: a Vallian Jiktar, killed in battle.

Vannerlan, Sushi: the widow of Ortyg Vannerlan. *WWK*

Veltan, Thandor ti Therfuing: known as Thandor the Rock; commander of Prince Drak's phalangite force in southwest Vallia. *SOV*

Venarden, Fruli: a Sister of the Rose who was used by Csitra in an assassination attempt against Delia; killed at the Battle of Bengarl's Blight. *OOK*

Venavito: an imperial province in southwest Vallia.

Vendalume: a city in Vennar.

Venga: a vadvarate province northwest of Erstveheim.

vimshu: a kind of small tiara.

Vimura, Phanton: a Deldar commanding the fighting top of *Heart of Imrien.* *OOK*

Voernswert, Nalgre ti Zanchenden: the Jiktar in command of *Zamra Venturer.* *WOA*

Volanch, Emder: a Chuktar in the Vallian Freedom Army. *WOK*

Volanta, Mandi: a Sister of the Rose who joined the forces of Vodun Alloran. *SOV*

Volgo: a strom in the service of Natyzha Famphreon. *WWK*

Voman, Ortyg: a Hikdar in the Fifteenth Lancers of the Vallian Freedom Army. *WWK*

Voromin, Lorgad: the captain of *Heart of Imrien*. *OOK*

W

Wenerl the Lightfoot: a kampeon of 1ESW; one of the werewolves' victims. *WWK*

Weymlo, Dolan: a merchant of Menaham. *WOA*

Weymlo, Yamsin: the daughter of Dolan Weymlo, rescued from kidnappers in Menaham by Prescot and his friends. *WOA*

Whonban: a mysterious place in Loh.

Wooldark Mitraeus, by the: a Rumay oath.

Y

Yolanda the Gregarian: one of a band of ruffians who helped rescue Prince Drak from Vodun Alloran. *SOV*

Yomin the Clis: a drill-master for lads in the Vallian army from Drak's City. *WOA*

Yuhkvor: an island off the northwest coast of Vallia.

yukpam: a receptacle for containing muck.

Yumakrell: the capital city of the Empire of Yumapan.

Z

Zamra Venturer: a Vallian airboat sent as reinforcement to the armada against Csitra. *WOA*

Zandi: a Sister of the Rose and a member of Delia's personal bodyguard. *OOK*

Zaphoret: a province at the eastern end of the Mountains of the North in Vallia.

zazzer: a type of warrior of the Eye of the World who drinks until reaching a fighting frenzy before battle. *WWK*

CPSIA information can be obtained at www.ICGtesting.com
Printed in the USA
LVOW08s0658180514

386216LV00001B/75/P